Per Sempre Medici

Book Six in the Medici
Warrior Series

by Emily Bex

Foundations Publishing Company
Central, Mississippi
www.foundationsbooks.net

Per Sempre Medici
Book Six in the Medici Warrior Series
By: Emily Bex
ISBN: 978-1-64583-074-0

Cover by Dawne Dominique
Edited by Laura Ranger

Published in the United States of America
Worldwide Electronic & Digital Rights
Worldwide English Language Print Rights

This is a work of fiction. Names, characters, businesses, places, events, and incidents are either the products of the author's imagination or used in a fictitious manner. Any resemblance to actual persons, living or dead, or actual events is purely coincidental.

The Medici Warrior book series is dedicated to my loyal fans who fell in love with all the Medici Warriors, and who waited patiently for each book to be published.

To the dreamers, those who escape into a world of fantasy, and all the hopeless romantics, remember the Medici's live in your heart for all time...

Acknowledgements

To my collaborator, my muse, and my sounding board for all things vampire, Johanna Morisette. Thank you for introducing me to your strange world of vampires, and the inspiration for the main protagonist, Shade. Thank you for listening to me babble, while you transcribed my words on the other end of the phone when I was locked in writer's block. Thank you for reading and re-reading every version until you were probably able to recite the book from memory. Without your prodding, the Medici Warriors would never have come to life, and Kate Reese would still be leading a boring life in a condo in Alexandria, Virginia.

Thanks to Alfred Music for extending the license to use a lyric from "Into the Mystic" performed by Van Morrison. Kate and Shade will be eternally grateful.

Table of Reference

Italian to English Translation	13
French to English Translation	15
1	21
2	29
3	34
4	40
5	43
6	52
7	55
8	59
9	63
10	69
11	76
12	83
13	89
14	93
15	97
16	104
17	108
18	116
19	123
20	127
21	131
22	135
23	146
24	149

25	154
26	163
27	170
28	179
29	186
30	190
31	196
32	205
33	212
34	218
35	223
36	233
37	237
38	243
39	249
40	254
41	257
42	263
43	265
44	268
45	274
46	276
47	280
48	286
49	292
50	295
51	299
52	306

53 310
54 314
55 319
56 326
57 330
58 336
59 340
60 343
61 346
62 352
63 357
64 383
65 389
66 395
67 400
68 406
69 419
70 430
71 435
72 444
73 449
74 457
75 463
76 472
77 477
78 482
79 487
80 491

81	498
82	502
83	507
84	511
85	516
86	521
87	526
88	535
89	541
90	546
91	550
92	558
93	568
94	575
95	583
96	592
97	599
98	602
99	607
100	613
101	617
102	619
103	621
104	625
105	627
106	630
107	636
108	642

109 646

110 652

111 657

112 663

113 665

114 670

115 673

116 680

117 697

118 704

About the Author 713

Italian to English Translation

Addio	Good-bye
Alzati guerrieri	Stand-up warriors
Amica	Friend
Amore	Love
Bambino(s)	Baby/babies
Bastardo	Bastard
Bel	Beautiful
Beleeza	Beauty
Bellissimo	Very beautiful
Bravado	Brave
Buonasera	Good evening
Cazzo	Generic curse word typically interpreted as fuck
Ciao	Hi/Hello
Dipendenzo	Addiction
Dolce	Sweet
Dormire guerrieri	Sleeping warrior
Familia	Family
Figlia/Figlio	Daughter/Son
Fino ad allora	Until then
Fratello	Brother
Grazie	Thanks
Guerrieri	Warriors
Impavido	Fearless
Lei e il mio vero amore	She is my true love
Madre	Mother
Meile	Honey
Mi/Mio/Mia	My
Coraggioso	Courageous
Moltobella	Very beautiful
Nostra Figlia	Our Daughter
Padre	Father
Per Favore	Please
Per Sempre	Forever

Rosso	Red
Scusi	Excuse me
Si	Yes
Signorina	Young Lady
Sorella	Sister
Stupido	Stupid
Ti Amo	I Love You

French to English Translation

Ma belle immortelle	My beautiful immortal
Ma belle ami	My beautiful friend
Bon soir	Good evening
Bon jour	Good morning
Sante'	Health
Oui	Yes
Mon ami	My friend
Mon Cherie	My dear
Maman	Mother
Papa	Father
Ma jolie fille	My beautiful daughter
Ma petite fille	My little daughter
Je't aime	I love you
Non	No
Mon petite ange	My little angel
Grand-mere	Grandmother
Grand-pere	Grandfather
Mon ange	My angel
Menage a trois'	Threesome
Pardon	Excuse me
Merci	Thank you
Mademoiselle	Miss

Medici Family Tree

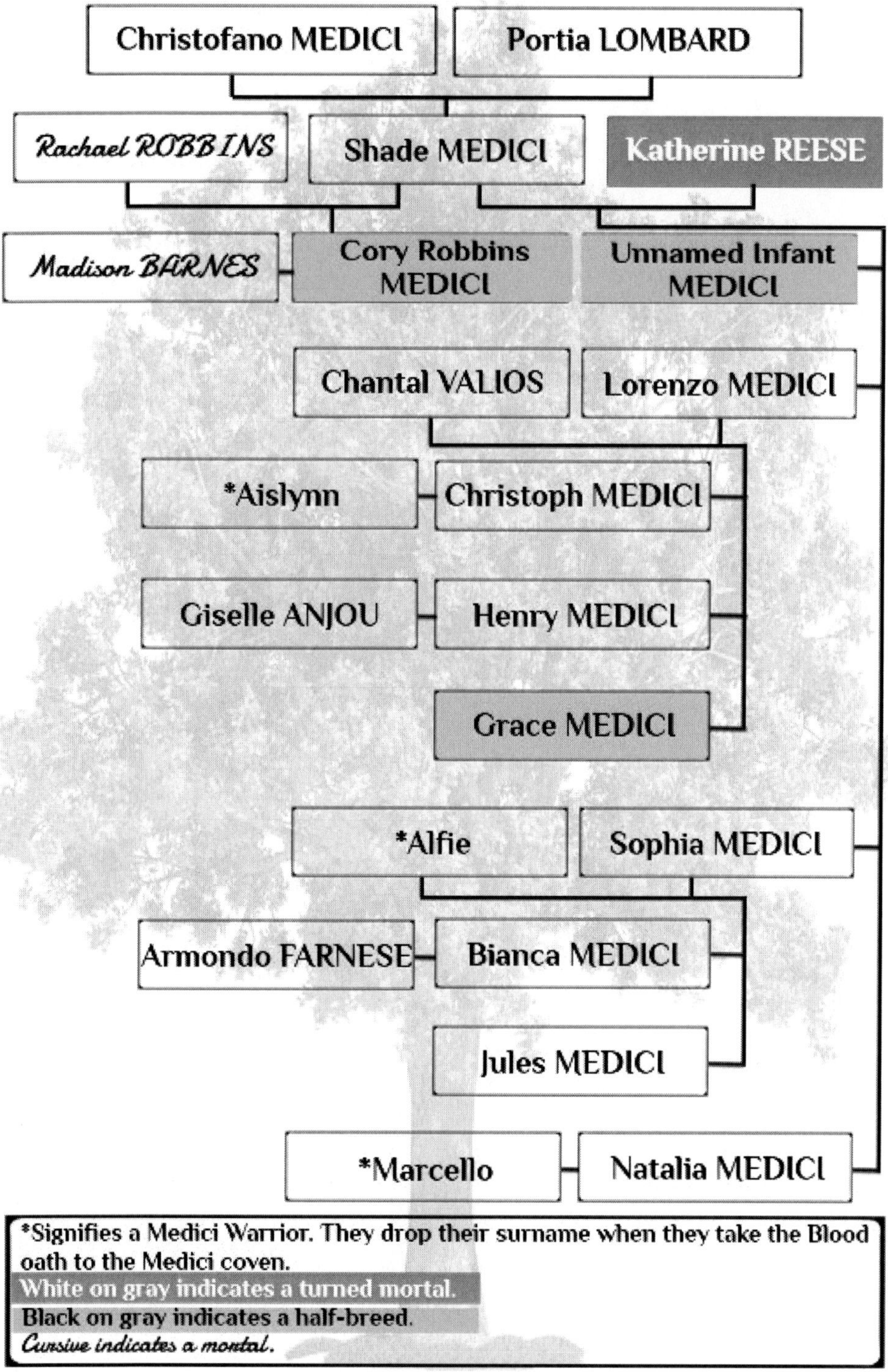

*Signifies a Medici Warrior. They drop their surname when they take the Blood oath to the Medici coven.
White on gray indicates a turned mortal.
Black on gray indicates a half-breed.
Cursive indicates a mortal.

Per Sempre
Medici

1

Kate examined her face in the mirror, and the changes were barely perceptible. She'd just realized it was Halloween in the mortal world. She was almost a hundred and fifty, and one-hundred-and-twenty-three years ago, on this night; she'd given herself up to him. She'd gone to that silly costume party Alec and Rissa had thrown every year and had finally given in to him. Her fingertips explored the skin around her eyes, and her skin seemed as taut and smooth as it did when she was twenty-eight, and he'd turned her. It seemed impossible to her that this much time had passed. The image in the mirror stared back, and she got lost in her own thoughts.

Her parents had died when she was in her fifties. She'd not been able to attend their funerals but visited their graves long after the other visitors had left. It was her only regret in choosing to become immortal. She'd maintained the lie of living abroad and finding excuses for why she could never visit them, and she knew it broke their hearts. Cory's mother had died in her late sixties. She had a heart attack in her sleep, and they'd all attended her service, and laid her to rest in a family cemetery in California. Cory had been devastated but also grateful they had mended their relationship. He knew his mother's last years were happy ones. Madison was gone now too. She had lived to be eighty, and still spent time at her potter's wheel, although her hands had not been as nimble as they had once been. Cory looked half her age when she died, and he loved her no less. Kate doubted he even noticed the physical changes in her. Kate noticed though and watched silently as the years took their toll on Madison's mortal body. It made her aware of the passing of time in a way nothing else in their life did.

After Madison's passing, she and Shade had told Cory he could move back into Bel Rosso, but he decided to stay in the home he and Madison had built together. He was a hundred and thirty-six now, and as a half-breed, he had aged more slowly. He looked like a very old man, though. His hair was grey and his walk a lot slower. It felt odd when he called Shade dad, and Cory looked like he should be the great-grandfather. None of them had any good data on how long half-breeds lived, so they had no way of knowing how much longer he'd be in their lives. But, for now, Cory still made his way to the camp every day, with assistance from Hyde, and sewed the leathers for the warriors. He remained a constant reminder to her, and to Shade, of the baby they'd lost, and what could have been.

She dropped her robe, and her nude body was reflected back at her, looking young and vital. Stepping into the shower, the water automatically came on to the designated pre-set temperature, and she closed her eyes, savoring the hot water and the steam that rose around her. Their children had all flourished, as she knew they would. Lorenzo had mated Chantal, and they remained together at Castello. Lorenzo, along with Alfie, maintained control of the camp in Florence, and Lorenzo had assumed the responsibility for the Medici covens in Europe. Lorenzo and Chantal had two sons who were grown men now, Christoph, named after Shade's father, Christofano, and Henry, named after Chantal's father. They had grown up in Castello, just as Shade had, and trained in the camp. Christoph lived here now, and was the SIC of the Bel Rosso camp, and Henry oversaw a new camp, and the expanded territories of the Valois family in France.

Marcello had been promoted to manage the warriors of the Council that had been established here in the States. The new Council had been established for almost a century. Shade had dedicated a large plot of land in northern Virginia, just outside of D.C. that had previously been a large horse farm, to the development of the Council. They'd built a large fortification that looked like a Victorian mansion to house the new Council. The mansion wasn't visible from the highway, and the private drive was gated, keeping mortals out. Kate felt better, somehow, knowing that Marcello was there with Natalia. Natalia had always had a strong affection for Marcello, and Kate often wondered if they would have mated had Natalia not been born to Council. They rarely got to see their youngest daughter, as Council rarely left the protection of the fortified mansion, but she would occasionally come home to visit.

Sophia and Alfie remained in Florence; their children grown now as well. Their first born was a daughter, Bianca, who remained at home with them as she wasn't yet mated. Bianca inherited Kate's and Sophia's stubbornness and red hair but had eyes of green. Sophia and Alfie had introduced her to every eligible male in Europe, but Bianca turned up her nose. She said she'd know him when she saw him, so they had finally let the matter lie. Their second child was a boy, named Giuliano, but everyone called him Jules. Jules had not been born a warrior, and like Natalia, had pursued a more academic path, obtaining a degree in law. He now lived in the States, often staying at Bel Rosso, assisting with the management of the many Medici business interests. It was a welcome change, to have the two grandsons here with them, even though they were both in their late thirties and well past childhood. They helped to fill some of the empty rooms inside Bel Rosso.

She stepped out of the shower, drying off with the towel, and drying her long, red hair. As she walked to the bedroom, the bathroom lights automatically turned off behind her, and the bedroom lights came on. Kate spoke softly, "Weather, please." The soft voice from the computer responded and gave her a full weather report for the next twelve hours, and then asked if she'd like an extended forecast. "No, thank you."

She looked at the bed where Shade remained in his death slumber, his dark curls stark against the white pillowcase. He was as strikingly handsome as the first night she'd seen him, and she smiled. The house looked much the same, and they liked it that way, but it had been modernized to accommodate the latest technology. She stepped into the walk-in closet as the light came on and walked to a computer flat screen mounted on the wall. The closet software held an inventory of everything in it, and she was able to search by category and select her outfit. As she tapped the screen with her fingertips, she heard a soft whir as the suspended rotating clothing rack slid into motion, bringing the chosen outfit to her. She removed the chosen sweater and jeans and grabbed a pair of boots before leaving the closet.

The temperature would drop tonight, as the weather was calling for a light frost. She stood at her vanity table and spritzed on her signature scent of roses. She'd changed it once a few years ago, but Shade had protested, and asked her not to change. She'd have thought, after all this time, he would welcome some variety, but he was soothed by the fragrance. She removed her lingerie from the drawer and slipped it on, before pulling on her jeans, and slipping the sweater over her head. She smiled to herself. In spite of the technology, Shade preferred to leave his clothes in the large armoire, and after all this time, he still couldn't find what he was looking for, or remember which drawer held his favorite shirts.

She'd intentionally woken before him, as she and Shannon had a call scheduled with their business partners in Italy to discuss the olive harvest currently underway. Their businesses were flourishing, but she never forgot the price they'd paid. They had an obligation now, to Marco's memory, to make sure the Medici enterprises were all successful. As the world had moved forward, their lives driven more and more by the technology that surrounded them, the mortals seemed even more drawn to their organic bath and beauty products, which allowed them an escape to luxury, and reminded them of a simpler time.

She sat on the side of the bed, and lightly ran her fingers through his hair, watching him as he slept. He'd secured his legacy with his children, and his grandchildren, and all the children that would follow. Their fortune was vast, and their coven covered two continents. Since the conflict with the *Mafioso*, they had not faced any significant challenges to their dynasty. Her gift of animalism, which Sophia and Bianca had also inherited, and Lorenzo's gift of fire-throwing, had so far held the other covens at bay. Shade never let his guard down, though. He was well aware that the very fact he held so much power, made his family a threat in itself. She drew the back of her fingers across the stubble on his cheek and touched her fingertips to his lips. How many times had she kissed those lips? She leaned over him, her hair brushing his cheek, and lightly touched her lips to his, and knew if the count was a million, it would never be enough. She whispered softly, "I love you, my savage warrior." She felt him stir slightly as she stood and left the room, the lights going out, plunging the sealed room back into darkness.

As she walked toward the stairs, she passed Theresa on her way to the laundry room. The house, once bustling with small children, was much quieter now. Kate made her way down the stairs and could hear Shannon's laughter coming from her and Luca's suite. She paused a moment before going into the office and headed instead to the back of the house. Opening the door onto the patio, Aegis jumped to her feet and immediately came to her. Kate dropped to her knees, and gave the wolf a hug, ruffling her fur and scratching behind her ears. The survival of the animals that had surrounded her after her turning, as well as their offspring, was a shock to them all. The Council monitored it closely, recording it for future generations. Of course, Sophia had her own brigade of animals that surrounded her in Florence, as did Bianca. None of them had any idea how long the animals would survive, but like the vampires they served, they remained strong and healthy over the years.

"Hey, girl," she whispered to the wolf, as Night Stalker emerged from the shadows, his eyes reflecting the light. She stood upright, and took a deep breath of the crisp, early autumn air in the hour before sunset. The leaves were starting to turn, and the sky reflected the same gold and orange colors of the foliage as the sun dipped behind the mountain range. She loved this land, and these people, and thought to herself that a thousand years here would never be enough.

***

Kate's scent lingered inside their bedroom, as Shade opened his eyes and breathed in the rose fragrance. He closed his eyes again, smiling to himself. She'd never lost her ability to arouse him, even when she wasn't in the room. He'd felt her when she left their bed, and could hear her showering and dressing, even in his death slumber. He tuned his senses, and could feel that she was outside, and happy. He laid quietly in their bed, as her feelings of contentment and happiness washed over him. Rolling over, he buried his face in her pillow, and wondered how he'd ever found her, or how he could have lived without her. He loved the home she'd made for them here. They had flourished; both as a family and a coven, and he never took for granted her contribution to both.

Groaning, he got up and made his way to the armoire. He rummaged through the drawers until he found what he needed, making a messy pile on the floor of the clothes he discarded. He knew she'd roll her eyes when she came back to their room and saw it, but she'd shake her head and say nothing. They'd been together so long, he knew the words she'd speak before they were out of her mouth, and yet he never tired of her.

The weather had changed, and it was a bit chillier than usual for this time of year. He selected a long sleeve tee shirt and pulled it over his head. His jeans had a hole in each knee. Kate kept reminding him he could afford new jeans, but he liked the feel of these. Lacing up his boots, he exited down the stairs and out the back door. He could see her looking over the remaining plants on the patio and smiled. Her ass was almost the most tantalizing thing about her, as she bent over the huge planters filled with flowers hanging on to the last fading blooms before the frost took them out. She loved working the earth and had turned their gardens into a paradise. Night Stalker stood up as he moved closer to *bel*, but their respect for one another remained mutual. They both kept a close eye on their mates. Shade knew she could feel him, but he moved quickly, grabbing her from behind. When she stood up, he snuggled into her neck, his tongue sliding along that vein that sustained his life. "You keep bending over like that, *mi amore*, and I cannot be held accountable for my actions."

She laughed, and Night Stalker started to romp in circles on the lawn, as Aegis lay calmly on the patio on the other side of the pool. They were never really alone, although, the house was calmer with the children grown. He spun her around. She squealed and struggled to get free. The landscape lighting came on, the dark settled over them, illuminating the pool and the surrounding gardens. "Don't get any ideas. Shannon and I have a conference call scheduled."

Grinning, he slapped her ass, she was all about the business. "Ideas? That wasn't an idea, that was a plan." Lifting her in his arms, she wrapped her legs around his waist, their laughter echoing in the night. "You know I hate having to schedule time for us, makes for a grumpy warrior. But I need to get to the camp. I don't know why. Christoph has everything under control." As he spun her around, her crimson mane was flying out like waves of autumn behind her. "Or maybe we could run away together."

She smiled back at him. "Run away? And where would you take me?"

The tip of his tongue slid along her lips, and he moaned softly as he squeezed her ass. "Paris, Greece, Rome, a secluded island, anywhere we can escape all the things we must attend to. Just you and me." Their eyes locked and their hearts beat in sync. He heard someone clear their throat and didn't need to look around. He knew it was Shannon.

Kate stared back at him, those impossibly blue eyes hadn't lost their ability to charm and hold her mesmerized. The idea of getting away for a few days had a lot of appeal. It was rare for them to be completely alone. She heard Shannon and knew the call had probably come through from Italy.

"Let me check my schedule. I rather like the idea of running away. Then you can surprise me." She kissed him again before he let her go, and she returned to the house with Shannon.

Shade watched her stroll back inside with Shannon, who flashed him one of those huge grins. He'd only been joking about running away, but truth be told, he'd love to have time alone with her. Some things, no matter how much time passed, never changed. They had obligations to their family, the businesses, and the coven. It was a never-ending demand for their time.

Making his way to camp, Christoph had things well in hand, and the warriors were working out, enjoying the cool night air. He'd lost count of how many springs had come and gone, or how many warriors had been trained here, far too many to count. Their training methods remained much the same, only the weapons had changed, and became more advanced with technology, although they still taught the warriors how to use the old school weapons as well. He walked easily around the groups of warriors in training, looking for the ones who stood out, but his mind was already thinking of where he could take Kate for a few days. He watched his grandson, Lorenzo's oldest, Christoph, and was reminded of himself. His black hair, height, and broad shoulders made him stand out among the other warriors. Christoph wore his hair shorter than Shade, otherwise, looking at him from the back, they were almost indistinguishable from each other. Like Lorenzo, Christoph rose quickly in the ranks as a warrior. He was a fine leader, and the warriors respected him. He observed his grandson in action, as he issued orders with confidence, and moved among the warriors, correcting them, instructing them, pushing them to each improve their skills, much as Shade had done when he trained warriors in Florence, and then here. He let his mind wander and remembered back to a time when he had Kate all to himself. He smiled now, to think of how hesitant she was. He'd never had to work so hard to get a female before, but she'd been worth the effort. He remembered following her when she was still mortal and watching her from the penthouse apartment, he'd rented across from hers. Then it struck him, a memory of an interrupted evening and he laughed out loud. He knew exactly where he'd take her. Suddenly, his night just became exciting. She'd love this destination.

2

Kate had checked her schedule and given him the nights she was available to leave, and he'd rearranged his calendar to accommodate her. There'd been a few things to coordinate in advance, and when the night finally arrived, she seemed intrigued to where they were going. He rather enjoyed keeping her in suspense. She had asked him several times where he was taking her, he shrugged it off, saying, "If I tell you, it isn't a surprise." He was hoping like hell she'd remember this spot when they got there. He wrapped up some last-minute details before hurrying upstairs. He'd teleport her, just like he had the first time. As he walked into their bedroom, she was brushing out her hair and he smiled.

"You ready to take off for a few nights, *mi amore*?"

She caught his eye in the mirror before turning to him. He had a smug grin on his face, and she knew he was up to something. She had finished her makeup and was about to get dressed. "Any hints? I need to know what to wear."

Taking her hand, he lifted her from her chair and slowly spun her around. "No, you are fine just as you are. No hints. Just take my hand, we are teleporting there. No more questions, *si*?"

She was still dressed in her silk robe and started to laugh. "You can't be serious." But before she could even turn to walk to the closet, he'd taken her hand, and lifted her away. She clung to him, as she felt the soft silk robe flutter in the wind, her feet still bare. "Shade! I need to get dressed."

She was laughing, still thinking he was playing a joke on her, but he didn't turn around. "Stop! Where are you taking me?"

He smiled but didn't answer. She was so beautiful. He'd never tire of looking at her. As they approached their destination, he gripped her hand tight. "Close your eyes, *mi amore*."

He heard her laughter and knew she had complied. He landed gently on the rooftop, Kate still in his arms. "Don't look!"

He set her down on her feet and turned her around, so her back was against his chest, as he stood with his arms around her. He snuggled into her ear, whispering, "Open your eyes, tell me what you see."

Kate felt the rough surface under her bare feet, and the air was crisp and chilly. She clenched her toes and placed one foot over the other, as he held her against his chest. Her hand automatically clutched at the robe, pulling it more tightly around her as she opened her eyes and gasped. They were standing on a rooftop in Paris. It was the same rooftop he'd brought her to more than a century ago, on the night he first fed from her and she was still mortal. The mattress was on the far side of the roof, covered in white satin sheets, and red rose petals strewn carelessly about. She remembered he'd brought her here on a whim, when he told her she could have anything she wanted, and she'd asked for Paris. They had started to make love when he'd been summoned back by his warriors. It was a memory she'd half forgotten, lying dormant in her brain, but came rushing back to her now after all this time. The Eiffel Tower still sparkled in the background. She turned and looked over her shoulder to see the white travertine stone edifice of La Sacre Couer, on the high point of Montmartre. She never tired of this city. She turned in his arms, looking up at him.

"As I recall, there was some unfinished business that involved strawberries, and champagne. But I was mortal then. You may have to make a substitute."

His heart skipped a beat. "I was hoping you would remember."

Taking her hand, he led her to the mattress covered in satin sheets. Without words, he untied her robe and let it fall effortlessly to the rooftop. He felt her shiver, but knew it was as much from his touch as it was the chill air. "Lay down for me, *mi amore*. Let me make love with you."

She lay down on the mattress, the sheets cool against her skin, and looked up at him as he towered over her. He pulled the black tee shirt over his head, and dropped it to the rooftop, his chest as broad and hard as when she'd first seen him. He placed one booted foot on the mattress, and she rolled to her side and unlaced it, tugging the boot from his foot, and then repeated the process for his other boot. He unsnapped his jeans and lowered the zipper before sliding them down his slender hips. She smiled back at him. "If anyone calls for help this time, just ignore them."

He chuckled. "If anyone calls, not only will I ignore them, but they are asking for their death. I have one thing on my mind, and I'm looking at her." He stripped off his jeans, as he laid down beside her. He asked her to lie on her back and close her eyes and watched as she complied.

"I'm cold," she whispered.

"Not for long, *mi amore*." He pulled a single long-stemmed red rose from the box by the mattress. Lying on his side, resting on one elbow, he lightly touched the rose to her forehead before drawing it down her nose. She wiggled her nose at the slight tickling sensation, and smelled the fragrant scent of the rose, as he dragged the velvet-soft petals over her lips. He watched as her lips formed a smile, and he reminded her, "No peeking." He drew the rose down her chest, between her breasts, and watched as the trailing rose created goosebumps on her skin. The rose skimmed lightly across her abdomen and brushed across the patch of tight red curls between her legs, and he saw her bite her lip. He sat upright, and gently parted her legs, so he could kneel between them. His advance was slow and methodical, as he lifted her foot in his hand and kissed the inside of her ankle before licking his way slowly up her leg, savoring that lily-white flesh that glowed in the moonlight. Her body was no longer unexplored territory but a map he knew by heart. He nipped gently at the tender flesh of her inner thigh and felt her tremble. "*Cazzo,* you are so damn beautiful, you make my blood rush, and my heart race."

His mouth and tongue felt hot against her bare skin, as he worked his way up her leg, and the soft nip of his teeth against her inner thigh caused a sharp intake of her breath. His touch was no less thrilling now. In many ways, it was better. He knew every inch of her, as she knew him, and knew where to touch with the lightness of a feather, and when to grip her hard and forcefully. They were like an orchestra that had played the same symphony, time after time, until it was perfection.

Sitting by their makeshift bed was a bottle of Midnight. When last they were here, he'd used champagne, but she was mortal then. He took a swig from the bottle before he gently poured it across her ample breasts and watched as rivulets streamed down her body, staining the white satin. He filled her belly button and let the rich liquid trail along her stomach and between her legs. Sitting the bottle aside, he licked the wine from her body, starting at her breasts. His tongue sucked at her nipple, rolling the bud inside his mouth, feeling them harden as his teeth nipped gently. He followed the trail of red wine down her abdomen, still tight and firm as he felt her hands tangle in his dark curls. Her body responded to his every touch, as her back arched and her breath came in sharp gasps. He burrowed his face between her legs, his tongue darting rapidly inside her, and lapping at her honey, until she writhed beneath him.

Sliding his hands under her, cupping her gorgeous ass, he lifted her hips slightly and began a long assault of her swollen sex, each lap of his tongue increasing his aching desire to be inside her. Sucking at her, she moaned and thrashed, and he continued to keep her on the edge of orgasm, backing off each time he felt her at the threshold. When he could wait no longer, he slid his body upward, letting his cock nestle against her wet curls and thighs. Crushing his mouth to hers, his tongue did its own dance inside her mouth. She suckled his tongue, tasting her own honey. His breathing became ragged as their tongues sparred.

Her breasts filled his hands as he fought to hold off his beast, when she took control, and rolled him on his back, crouching over him. Her hair hung forward, obscuring her face, and he felt its silky softness as her hair draped across his chest. Straddling him, she moved her hips in a seductive lap dance, sitting upright, and flipping her hair back over her shoulders. He wanted to be inside her, but her motions kept her just out of reach as she continued to tease. He gripped the side of the mattress, balling the soft satin sheets in his fists, as she teased and played, until he felt like he could move heaven and hell to be buried deep inside her. "*Bel*, please. I need you, now!"

"I seem to remember being teased with a strawberry." Her voice was breathy and labored, as her body screamed out for him. Teasing him caused as much sweet anticipation for her as it did for him. Still straddling him, she lowered her hips on his cock, sitting upright, her hands on his chest so she could see his face in the moonlight. She heard his deep moan, as his hands gripped her hips, and she settled into a rhythm of riding him. The noise from the street below filtered up to them, the sounds of the traffic and the voices of the people. They weren't visible to the people on the street, but knowing they were there and unaware of what was taking place above their heads added to the excitement.

He couldn't take his eyes off her. Her pale skin lit by the moon, her face an open book, displaying the passion and pleasure she felt. As his erection slid deep inside her, she leaned back, and he slid his hands up her thighs, gripping her hips. He sat upright, as she repositioned herself, wrapping her legs around his hips. His fangs scraped along her collar bone, leaving a soft trail of her blood. He licked at the shallow wound, feeling her blood snap and spark inside him.

She hissed when she felt his fangs drag across her skin, followed by his tongue as he licked at her blood. She bent to him and sank her fangs deep into his neck and heard his beast respond. Drinking deeply, the fire ignited them both, as his hold on her hips tightened and his thrusts become more forceful. She had him on the edge and waited to feel the sweet sting of his teeth in her own flesh.

Each time she fed from him, their bond became stronger, and he thought he couldn't possibly love her more. It was the feeling he craved more than anything else. He drove his cock deep inside her, feeling her muscles clench around his cock like a vice grip and his beast could stand no more. He bit into her neck and felt that spark and crackle in his veins as her blood hit him. It took them both to another plane, as they came together. He held her close as she rode out wave after wave of their ecstasy, until the sensations subsided, and he lay back on his back. She fell onto his chest, as they both lay quietly, panting, and their bodies covered in a light sheen of sweat.

"I know it took me a damn long time to make this up to you. I hope it was worth the wait."

She lay with her head on his chest, listening to the sound of his pounding heart. "You're always worth the wait."

3

Lorenzo woke early, before sunrise. He'd always been an early riser, waking before the sun. He attributed it to the discipline of being raised in the camp, and the high expectations that Marco had set for them all. Even after all this time, there was hardly a day that passed that he didn't think of Marco, and he knew, for his father, it was the same. He sat up in the bed, re-arranging his pillows against the headboard. He and Chantal had taken over the massive bedroom in Castello his mother and father had once occupied. His father had insisted, saying Castello was his now, and he was the master here.

Leaning comfortably against the headboard, he reached for the pack of cigarettes on the bedside table and lit up, exhaling the smoke into the room. Chantal slept soundly next to him. He knew she'd sleep for another hour at least. He looked at her with affection. They'd had a good life, and she'd been a loyal mate, and an excellent mother to their two sons. He reached down and lightly brushed the soft brown curls away from her face. She was easy going and good natured, but they'd had their struggles too. Theirs wasn't an arranged mating in the truest sense. Both were allowed to choose whom to mate, and he chose her freely. He loved her, and he knew she loved him. In the early years, she had a difficult time, as she'd been used to following her father's orders. Henri had raised his daughter in the traditional ways, where females were taught to defer to their master. She'd been much more shielded from the world than either Sophia or Natalia, and not given much leeway when it came to speaking her own mind. Lorenzo chuckled to himself, as he tried to imagine anyone putting a muzzle on Sophia. Natalia had made significant shifts in Council policy, granting females equal status to the males, but the older vampires were slow to change. When they were first mated, Chantal found it necessary to consult her father over every decision, instead of coming to him. If ever there was a difference of opinion between her mate and her father, she felt a strong conflict. It went against everything she felt she knew to defy her father's views, but then, she knew she shouldn't defy her mate either. It had created a divide between them and took a long time to work through. It was Amelie who finally saw her daughter's conflict and told Chantal that she wasn't dishonoring her father if she followed her mate.

Lorenzo was convinced that Henri, although concerned for his daughter's happiness, took some measure of pride in the fact his daughter still differed to him. The mating had been a good strategic move for the Medici, although that carried no weight in Lorenzo's decision to mate her. The Valois had a long history with the Medici, and Henri's territories covered much of France. Lorenzo's second son, Henry, ran the third warrior camp in Burgundy, near the Medici vineyards, and the Medici had been given chateaus and property as part of Chantal's dowry. Together, both families were stronger and more powerful.

Both of their sons had been born warrior, and both had inherited two gifts. Christoph had Lorenzo's gifts of fire-thrower and day-walker, while Henry had inherited the gifts of dream-walker and day-walker. They'd both trained as young boys in the camp at Florence and served rotations through their grandfather's property in the States, working at Bel Rosso and the California camps. The boys had made him proud, and both served the growing coven well. Christoph had remained in the States, assuming control of the camp at Bel Rosso, and Henry took on the new camp in France. He knew his children would mate soon, as would Sophia's children, and the Medici bloodline would be secured for future generations.

They had much to be grateful for, and Lorenzo never took that for granted. He took a deep drag on the cigarette, as the tip glowed in the dark room, and watched the smoke hang in the air as he exhaled. Still, he felt something was lacking.

Even as a small boy, he'd seen the passion between his parents and saw it still after all this time. There was an intensity in the love his parents shared that was absent in his own mating. He never doubted Chantal's love for him, but her love was reserved. She never refused him, and was a willing mate, but she never sought him out. He saw how his mother looked at his father, how she devoured him with her eyes. He'd watched their silent communication for years, the exchanged glances, the wink, the coy smiles, all communicating a desire that was being temporarily placed on the back burner until they could find a moment alone together. As children, he remembered the strict instructions delivered to the three of them, and obeyed by all except Sophia, to never enter their bedroom when the door was closed. Their desire for each other didn't grow less with time but burned as bright as when he was a young boy. He didn't have that with Chantal, and he knew he never would. It was simply not in her nature. There was no one else he'd prefer as his mate, and he didn't regret his choice, but he couldn't help but feel like he was missing something.

***

Chantal woke slowly, she could smell the cigarette smoke, and knew he was wide awake. He'd always wake before her and she rather liked waking to find him looking at her or touching her. He had a gentle way with her, as he had from their first meeting. She loved Lorenzo, he was faithful and caring and an excellent father. Their sons adored him. But he was also very busy. It wasn't unexpected. Her father had always been busy, managing their territories and their businesses. She understood her obligation to duty, especially since she'd been born a royal. Being mated to Lorenzo had exposed her to the world of warriors, an area from which she'd been shielded growing up. She knew Lorenzo was a great warrior, protecting his family, and their coven. When they were younger, she was always busy with the children, but now the boys were grown and out on their own. These days, she felt all she had was time, and nothing to fill the hours. Unlike her sister-in-law, Sophia, she'd not been trained in business. Her education focused on the arts. She felt she didn't have the skills to manage any of the vast holdings that belonged to the Medici. As a result, she'd taken to returning often to her parents' home in Paris. At least, there, she could help her mother with the charity balls, and the never-ending social engagements scheduled by them, or for them. She often wondered what Lorenzo saw in her, and what value she brought to the coven. She opened her eyes and greeted him in her soft voice, "*Bon jour*, Lorenzo."

The morning light was coming through the windows, and he could see her soft peaches and cream complexion, and the blue eyes, appearing almost too large for her face. He smiled at her as he put out the cigarette. "Good morning, *mon cherie*. I hope I didn't wake you." He leaned over to kiss her lightly, and she returned the kiss before rolling away from him to get dressed and begin her day.

She loved his pet name for her and smiled. She never got tired of hearing it. Climbing from their huge bed, she slipped on her robe and walked to the large closet, one of several that held her passion for fashion and shoes. "No, you didn't wake me. I was hoping to go see *Maman* for a few days. I have a need for a few new pieces of fall clothing. You don't mind, do you? I won't go if you don't wish for me to." She stopped and turned to look at him, still sitting naked in their bed, with the sheets covering his lap. His eyes were so blue, their intensity was visible from across the room, and he still wore his hair long. She scanned the tattoos on his shoulder and one arm. She remembered being shocked when she'd seen him nude for the first time. Tattoos weren't common in her circles, and she was startled to see them. She'd never cared for them, although she had to admit, they suited him.

He smiled to himself. He couldn't imagine why she'd need more clothes, but she'd been raised to wear only the latest designer fashions, discarding the previous year's wardrobe, as if it were somehow now contaminated. She'd always preferred the French designers to the Italian ones, and besides, it gave her an excuse to visit with her mother. "Of course. Rene must escort you, as always, but I see no reason why you shouldn't go." Rene had been the protector assigned to her since childhood, and after they mated, she wished to have him remain with her, as opposed to taking a new protector. Rene had been trained in the Medici camp in Florence, so Lorenzo had no hesitations about her keeping him.

Chantal scanned the vast closet, looking for an appropriate outfit. She dressed modestly, but fashionably, and wore only the top designers. "I'm grateful you allow me to go, Lorenzo. And Rene is always with me. I would never leave this house without him." She pulled out a suit and held it up to the mirror in front of her before turning to look at him. "There is a charity ball I'll attend with *Maman* and *Papa*. I'm hoping, perhaps Henry can join us. I miss him so much, and *Papa* asks about him often, so I thought, perhaps, it would be good to have him come and visit while I'm there. Is there anything you wish me to tell him?"

Lorenzo nodded his approval of the suit she held up for his review. "Henry would love that. Besides, I think he could use a break from the camp. They've had a busy year with the new warriors, a larger class than usual. No message, I speak to him almost every day."

He slid from beneath the covers and walked naked to his own closet and grabbed the first set of leathers he saw. Alfie was probably already in the camp, and he needed to get his ass moving. "You'll let me know you arrived safely, *si?*"

She shook her head, as he pulled on the familiar leathers. "*Oui*. Perhaps I will do some shopping for you as well." She chuckled, knowing he could care less about fashion.

He had a closet full of clothes she'd bought for him, some with the tags still on them. He did appreciate the soft feel of the cashmere sweaters she bought for him that he wore with his jeans. They both had social obligations to their covens, in both Italy and France, and there were occasions when he must give up his jeans or leathers and wear a suit. Still, he had more suits than he could possibly wear. "If it makes you happy, *cherie*."

She smiled, but the smile didn't reach her eyes. She should be happier. Lorenzo had always indulged her and would deny her nothing...but still. Her life felt robotic, and she needed something to fill the void. She was happy to be going home. She was an only child, and her father was overjoyed when she'd given birth to not one but two sons. She was hoping Henry would join them while she was there. She needed to see him, and her parents were always so pleased when they had his company. She stuck her head out of the closet and saw that Lorenzo was ready to go. "Seeing my son always makes me happy, and seeing you dressed like a civilized royal also makes me happy."

He stopped to slide his hand around her waist and pull her close, giving her a kiss. "Then perhaps you should shop for Henry. Maybe he has more room in his closet than I do. He doesn't yet have a mate to make sure he looks civilized."

"I have always kept our sons in the latest fashions. Henry, especially, relies on my taste in choosing for him what the ladies prefer." Standing on tip toe, she kissed his cheek. "Go to your post. I'll be off soon, and I'll see you when I return."

"Two days, *cherie*, then I'll need to feed." He kissed her forehead before leaving the room.

She watched him leave. Two days to visit her parents, and hopefully, her son, and some time to catch up with a few close female friends, then she'd come home and take care of her mate. She adjusted the collar of the suit nonchalantly. Her father had used feeders for many years, so as not to bother her mother. Chantal was well aware that wasn't a practice accepted in the Medici family. Her parents were in an arranged marriage, and they'd grown to love each other in their own way over time. She'd never witnessed any display of affection between her parents, and certainly not the open passion she saw between Lorenzo's parents, or his sister Sophia's mating. She'd observed them with a curiosity over the years, wondering what that kind of passion even felt like. She'd never be like Kate, or his sister, Sophia. Their lives were far different from hers. She was raised to never speak above her station, as the mate of a king. His decisions were final and not to be argued with. She couldn't count the times she'd sat with his family and said not one word, as they all loudly voiced their opinions. She cleared her mind of such nonsense and rushed to pack a few things and have Rene escort her home to Paris.

4

Alfie was wrapping up some last-minute details in his home office, as he poured another glass of Red Moon before he took off for camp. He was certain Lorenzo was already there. They still used Marco's old office, although it had been modernized into a technological war-room over the years. Aside from Marco's sword mounted over the door, there was no physical trace of their once great warrior there. They could feel him, though, and knew this was where his spirit lingered. Alfie and Lorenzo were as close as ever and ruled over the camp, as Shade and Marco once did. Their children had grown up together and remained close. Their first-born child and only daughter, Bianca, still resided with them, as she had yet to mate. Like Sophia, Bianca had also been born with the gift of animalism.

Sophia's spirit animal was a wolf that never wandered far from their villa and Bianca had attracted a jackal she called Buzz. Alfie had gotten used to the animals that always surrounded the villa, as well as all the animals Bianca adopted and brought into their home. He thought she'd attracted every stray cat and dog in all of Tuscany and welcomed them all inside. The house was full of dogs and cats, and he'd just gotten used to stepping over them.

Their youngest child, Jules, wasn't born a warrior, although his contributions to the Medici businesses were huge. Alfie struggled for a long time with that fact, as well as the fact he'd only been born with one gift, that of a day-walker. Nothing was said about this in the family, and certainly, Jules had been shown as much love as the other grandchildren Shade and Kate had, but it plagued Alfie's mind often. He wasn't born of royal blood and perhaps that was the reason his son didn't inherit the gene to be a warrior, or that he'd broken the cycle of grandchildren born with two gifts. He worried his blood wasn't strong enough and knew Shade had strong feelings about Sophia choosing to mate him in the first place.

He chuckled, remembering how they'd outwitted her father and mated without his permission, a night he'd never forget. She'd finally become his and his alone. With that thought, he looked up to see her standing in the doorway of his home office, hands on her hips, and a smirk on her lips. She'd loved him like no other, and her sassy mouth and stubborn attitude had never changed, and he was grateful, otherwise, she wouldn't be his Sophia.

"So, is there something you need, red? Or are you just looking for kisses and hugs before I head to the camp?"

"Kisses and hugs? And all this time I thought you mated me for my brilliant mind." She went to him and slid easily into his arms. "You can tell my brother not to keep you so long."

Grinning, he kissed her neck and pulled her close to him. "As for your brother, *you* can tell him not to *keep* me so long. He'll listen to you. There are times I get the feeling he prefers camp to home."

Sophia brushed his blonde hair across his forehead. "Hmm, I'm not sure it's his preference, but it does seem to work out that way. Does he talk to you? About that?"

"Not really. He loves her, but we all know Chantal had a very different upbringing. Something is bothering him, though, that's obvious. If Lorenzo wants to talk about it, he will. I learned a long time ago not to probe. If he's not ready to talk, there's no amount of pressure that will pry it out of him, so I keep my mouth shut. Does Chantal ever call you, or want to do things with you?"

She sighed and shook her head. "Not really. But I see it too. I don't think he'd ever say anything, because he's afraid it would sound like he doesn't love her, and I know he does. Lorenzo would never be critical of her. It's not his style. And she loves him...it's just, I don't know, a remoteness about her? I don't want to speak ill of her, Alfie. She's been nothing but kind to me, and she loves our children as much as she loves her own. She just has a problem expressing her emotions, I guess. She's more reserved than Natalia, and I thought no one could be more reserved than Natalia!"

Alfie laughed. "Hell, sometimes I wonder if all of you are truly related. You and Natalia are like night and day...and Lorenzo, he's totally Shade's son. But you're right. I know they love each other. Lorenzo mentioned the other night she'd gone to France again for a few nights. I can tell it's eating at him."

Sophia looked pensive, wondering if she could get her brother to open up to her. "Maybe I'll try to talk to him."

He gave her a squeeze before releasing her and heading off for the camp. “Yeah, well, good luck with that. I love you, red. And if I’m late getting home, it is your brother’s fault.” He turned and walked out the door, teleporting to camp. Another night of busting ass and knocking heads, as Marco used to say.

5

Natalia had overseen the modernization of the archives for the Council in the States and worked with Malachi to bring the same technology to the European Council. They had employed thousands to scan all the original documents into computer files, as well as provide typed transcripts of the old handwritten documents. Once that was done, she maintained a staff of a few hundred to keep the data current. She'd gone into Council at the age of twenty-five and had been there ever since.

Her private room was pleasant, and she'd been allowed to decorate it as she pleased. Her need for closet space was minimal, since she only wore the off-white hooded robes, and was known inside these walls as Ivory. Only her family and Marcello, still called her Natalia. She kept a few articles of clothing here for when she visited her family, and her mother maintained her bedroom for her at Bel Rosso, although her opportunities to visit were rare.

To distinguish the Council members from their European counterparts, their names were modified, although they wore the same color robes, and held the same roles. Here in the States, the green robe was worn by Emerald, and the orange robe by Amber, the blue robe was worn by Indigo, and the purple robe by Amethyst. Citron wore the yellow robe, and Ebony wore the black one.

Her father had allocated a large plot of land for the U.S. Council, and as each of the Council members were identified by Malachi and assigned their role, they too had moved into the Council, where they'd remain for the whole of their lives. She was the only female among the all-male Council, but her voice carried no less weight. She'd made sure of that. She knew her father was proud of her, but she also felt his sadness. It wasn't the life he'd dreamed for her. She found she was content here and felt fulfilled in her role and her contributions to the vampire community at large. She'd spent hours discussing her visions with Malachi about the changing roles of females in their culture and pushing for policy changes in both Europe and the States. The changes gave females equal power, and no longer required a mistress to mate, to hold onto her coven. Still, it was a lonely life, and she didn't know if she'd be as happy had her father not assigned Marcello to oversee the warriors assigned to Council. His assignment would also be a permanent one. Once a warrior was assigned to Council, just like the Council members, they'd never leave this post. Council members didn't mate, and they didn't hunt. The feeders who resided here were also permanent.

Natalia still used the feeders, so as to not raise suspicion, but it was Marcello's affection she sought. She fed from him when she could, but he could never be allowed to feed from her. She'd felt a bond with him, even when she was a child, and had watched him in the camp. Even then, before she ever understood her fate as Council, she knew her father would not have approved of her mating him. She often wondered if her father was aware of her attraction to Marcello, and made the decision to assign him here, knowing she'd seek him out. She'd never ask him, and she doubted he'd give her an answer, if she did. Whatever the reason, she was grateful to have him, although they must both be alert, and make sure their relationship remained hidden. Their love affair was one of stolen glances, and soft smiles, of accidental brushing of shoulders, and the intentional and lingering touch of hands when he gave her something for the archives. And when they were lucky, they'd steal away to the attic, under some pretext of retrieving old documents she needed him to carry for her. Occasionally, he found a way to enter her private rooms unseen and slept with her through the day. It was a rare treat to be held by him, as she was pulled into her death slumber. It wasn't perfect, but it would have to do.

***

Marcello had watched Shade's daughters grow up under the protection of his cousin, Luca. He'd always been intrigued with Natalia, but he was a warrior, and she was royal blood. He knew better than to overstep his bounds. He'd been as shocked as anyone when Sophia had broken the rules and mated with Alfie behind her father's back. He'd remained content to admire Natalia from afar and felt great sorrow when he'd learned that she'd been born to Council and would be leaving Bel Rosso, and he'd probably never see her again. Still, there was a part of him that celebrated the news, knowing she wouldn't be mated to another, and he knew even as he had those thoughts how selfish it was of him. He loved his life as a warrior and took pride in rising to the position of SIC of the camp, but it was a lonely life, and watching her leave was painful.

When Shade had asked him to take over the new post of Commander, overseeing the warriors assigned to the protection of the U.S. based Council, he didn't have to think twice about it. He had no illusions about their future together. If she was out of reach before, as royal blood, Natalia's position in the Council cemented the fact she'd never mate. But Marcello wasn't blind, either. He was well aware their attraction was mutual. Whenever she was outside at Bel Rosso, her eyes would find him. Whenever he was called to the house by Shade, she'd always find an excuse to appear. They had exchanged glances, and the occasional touch of hand, and somehow, they'd both made it enough.

Since living at Council, they had found reasons to interact, and without the watchful eyes of so many, it had become easier for them to find a private space, and what had started out as stolen kisses had evolved over the years. As much as they loved each other, they could never mate, he could never take her blood, but he cherished what they shared, allowing her to feed from him when they made love. It was a huge risk for them both. He had no idea what the punishment would be, but he was certain he'd be removed from the post, and Natalia would have to remain here. He never aspired to be mated and had been prepared to live his life in solitude, but now that he had her, even if in secret, he couldn't bear the thought of a life without her. He went to feeders, but she held his heart, and always would, and she knew it. He dropped everything whenever she called for him, her request a smokescreen for them to sneak away for private time together. For both of them, who'd been raised with no expectations of ever being able to mate or find love, their union was enough.

***

Natalia walked down the long hallway of the Gothic mansion, located on the Potomac in Northern Virginia. The land was prime real estate, worth millions for its location alone. She was one of two vampires on the Council that weren't day-walkers. She kept the records of all the births and knew most newborns today were born day-walkers. The Council would have frequent meetings about these patterns in shifting gifts and felt the evolution to day-walkers was a survival mechanism necessary in these modern times. She stopped at an open window high on the third floor where the Council had their private quarters, and looked out at the wide river, as the moon glinted off the water. She had often envied her brother and sister their ability to walk in the sun. She'd asked her father once when she was still a child, if he missed walking in the sun. He'd taken her on his lap, and held her chin, speaking softly to her, saying it was hard to miss what you never had, and to focus on the gifts she did have. She wasn't too sure about that now.

As she started down the stairs, lifting her long robe so as not to trip on the steps, she looked up to see Marcello on his way up. "Marcello!" It was impossible to disguise the joy in her voice.

Marcello was making rounds when he encountered her on the stairs. He knew her schedule and frequently managed his workflow to maximize their time together. The excitement and joy he heard in her voice when she saw him was well worth the planning to be there. He was a day-walker, which gave him the latitude to work around Natalia's schedule. She was so beautiful, even with no makeup, and wearing the simple robe, her eyes could take him to his knees. "Good evening, Natalia. Your mind seems preoccupied with something." He was careful not to touch her when they were in the corridors or stairways where they could encounter others. He lowered his voice, so only she could hear. "I'm hoping it's me." He winked and gave her a smile, his blue eyes twinkling behind the mop of brown hair.

Natalia pulled the hood further over her head, masking her face as she whispered, "You're always in my thoughts." She looked over her shoulder to insure none of the others were leaving their rooms yet. "I have work to do in the archives, and once the data is entered, the records will need to go to the attic. You can help me, yes?"

"Of course, just let me know when you're ready." His eyes darted around, as he listened for the sound of footsteps.

"It may take a few hours for them to finish entering the data." She lightly touched his bare forearm and felt the spark between them. "Come find me in the archives later."

Marcello saw Emerald enter the corridor, and he answered her, making sure his voice was loud enough to be heard. "I'm happy to help. I'll check back later." He nodded to Emerald. "Everything is under control. Have a good evening, both of you." Marcello quickly descended the stairs and continued on his way, his excitement to see her tonight held deep inside.

Natalia smiled to herself as she made her way to the archives. The large, well-lit room looked very different from the dusty tomb she'd visited in Florence. Her archives were a model of the latest technology. Records were stored by coven families in a large database and cross-referenced to include all mating's across covens. Most data was entered using a touchscreen keyboard, but documents could be retrieved by the sound of her voice. She was the only person who could retrieve the records once they were entered, and the computer system recognized her voice. Ivor had been slow to adopt the changes until her father had brought both he and Malachi here to see what she'd done. She could find any document within seconds. The originals were stored in temperature and humidity-controlled rooms and were cataloged in a way that would allow them to instantly locate the original paper document as well. She walked briskly behind the workstations of the data entry staff, who were housed on the campus in a separate building. Like the Council, their assignments here would be permanent. She directed them as needed, and answered questions, as busy fingers hammered away at the keys, and she counted down the minutes when she could steal away to be with Marcello.

Marcello kept one eye on the time as he worked through the night, checking in with each of the warriors at their assigned posts. He rotated their stations often, so every warrior was familiar with every inch of the mansion, as well as the grounds. As the night wore on, he made his way to the archives and watched as the workers filed out, one by one, as they returned to their private quarters. He waited until no one else exited and knew Natalia was alone. He rapped lightly on the door, and heard her soft voice call out, "Come in." He stepped into the room and was always impressed by the massive banks of complex technology. It looked complicated, but she moved around with ease, making a quick inspection at each workstation of the data that had been entered through the night. She was still in work mode, her attention focused on the records. He stepped up behind her and took her hand, squeezing it softly.

Her heart beat faster at his touch. She looked over his shoulder at the door. It was rare for one of the other Council members to enter the archives, but they did occasionally have business here. The storage room was always safe, as no one else went there, and she had the only key. Well, the only other key. She'd made a copy for Marcello years ago. "Meet me in the attic. I'll be there shortly."

Letting his hand slide along her cheek, he smiled at her. He lifted a file box filled with paper documents and turned quickly to leave the room. Walking briskly, he headed down the long corridors and up the stairs to the attic storage. Balancing the box on one hip, he slipped the key from his pocket and opened the door to the document's storage room. This space was reserved exclusively for storing the original documents and was rarely accessed by anyone other than Natalia. Closing the door behind him, he heard the lock automatically engage, and he set the box down on a worktable and waited for her.

Within minutes, he heard her key in the lock. When she entered, she made her way directly to him. He lifted the hood from her face, and exposed her rich, brown hair, and his hands quickly tangled in her thick locks as his mouth covered hers. He knew she wore nothing beneath the robe and loosened the ties at her neck. The robe dropped away, billowing in a pool at her feet, leaving her naked and exposed.

Marcello was the only male to have seen her this way, and her breath caught in her throat when his fingers traced her jawline and trailed down her neck, across her collar bone, to her breasts. His touch was light and patient. He'd always been gentle with her, like handling a rare crystal artifact that, once shattered, could never be replaced. He kissed her again, as his hand slid around her waist, and he pulled her to his chest.

Marcello knew what he held in his hands was a rare and precious jewel. She was his master's daughter, and one he'd never abuse or disrespect. His love for her had grown immensely over the years. They both knew it could never go any further, but for both of them, they'd come to accept it was enough. Marcello was no stranger to females. He'd hunted and used feeders all his life, and must continue to do so, as he'd never be allowed to feed from her. Still, he had no doubt about her love, or her loyalty to him. He was, without a doubt, her warrior. They needed no blood covenant to seal what was between them.

"It feels like forever since I've held you in my arms, kissed your lips. What is your pleasure tonight? Do you want to watch me undress, or do you want to undress me?"

She felt the texture of the leathers against her skin and was excited by the feel of his hard body. She smiled coyly. "I'll undress you. It's like opening a present, and I love presents."

She began with the leather jacket that fit him like a glove and bore the Council crest. She slowly unzipped the garment, exposing his smooth, hard chest. She brushed his skin with her fingertips and watched the goosebumps on his skin. She slid the jacket off his broad shoulders and shimmied it down his arms until it dropped to the floor. Marcello had always worn his hair long. It was light brown and kissed by the sun. His skin was a golden tan, and emphasized his bold, blue eyes. His lashes were as dark, and as long as hers.

She walked around him, her hand trailing along the waistband of the leather pants, until she stood behind him, and kissed his muscular back, right between his shoulder blades. "You're beautiful, Marcello."

Returning to stand in front of him, she slipped her hand inside his waistband and gave it a sharp tug, jerking him forward, before undoing the snap, and unbuttoning the fly. She sighed as she worked each button. "Someone needs to tell Cory this is the 22nd century, and it's okay to use zippers."

She heard his soft chuckle at her impatience to rid him of the leathers. She started to slip the leathers down his hips, when she heard him say, "Boots." She sighed again and knelt before him, unlacing the boots and helping him pull them off, before he kicked free of the leather pants.

"You sure make a girl work for her reward."

He laughed. "I thought you liked opening presents?"

She backed away slowly, drinking him in with her eyes. "So, show me what I get for all that hard work."

It was their foreplay, the undressing, and it stirred the fire in his belly, knowing what lie ahead. He smiled softly and growled. He lifted her in his arms and carried her to the soft blankets stacked in the corner. Laying her down, he began to kiss her softly, starting at her toes, and working his way slowly up her body, always stopping before he reached her throat. She drew him like a bee to honey. "You're so beautiful."

He tangled his hands in her hair, as his tongue slid along her collar bone. It was the only taste of her he'd ever have. His hand slid down her torso, between her breasts, and across her flat tummy, to rest between her legs. She was wet for him already, her anticipation as great as his own. He slid his hard body along hers, until they fit together perfectly. Kissing her passionately, he entered her and heard the soft moan from her lips. His blue eyes locked with her brown ones, and he moved slowly inside her, making every stroke count, for their encounters were few and far between.

She had to stifle her cries of ecstasy, and bit hard on her lip, as he mounted her. Their love making took place in soft spoken whispers, so as not to draw the attention of others. Maybe someday they could sneak away from here for a few hours, and she could allow herself to enjoy him with free abandon, but for now, they moved in silence. Their love affair had gone on for years, hidden from everyone. She savored his weight on her, and the power of his thrust, as he gripped her hips. She wrapped her legs around him, and slowly kissed his neck, before tasting his skin, preparing him for her bite, so he too would remain silent. She sank her fangs into his flesh and was hit with the power of his warrior's blood, so much more satisfying than that of the feeders. She couldn't stop the soft moan in the back of her throat, as she felt the heat surge between her legs, and she let herself fall into the orgasm that followed.

Marcello felt her fangs sink into his flesh. He knew his blood gave her strength, she was Medici, but he was still a warrior. He felt her reach her orgasm and he let go, exploding inside her. Closing his eyes, he turned his head away, ignoring the deep ache in his fangs, as he buried his face in the blankets, muffling the sound of his pleasure. How he wished he could be free with her, but they'd both accepted that was something that may never happen.

He rolled off her and pulled her to his chest, as his hands caressed her back and ran softly through her dark curls. He could lay here all night with her in his arms, but that too was a dream that was rarely fulfilled.

She lay quietly with her head on his chest, his arms draped around her, and felt safe and loved. She did love him, but she knew she'd never mate, never bear his children. And in the deepest part of her soul, she'd come to accept that. She loved her life at Council, and the freedom to make her own choices. She answered to no male, and there was a freedom in that that, few females in their culture would ever know. She felt her death slumber pull at her, and knew she had to hurry. She sat upright, leaving their makeshift bed and gathered up her robe, slipping it over her head, and replacing the soft leather slippers on her feet that allowed her to move about silently. She kissed him one last time before she left.

"I must go now. I can feel the sun rising." She stared into the deep sapphire blue of his eyes. "I love you, Marcello."

6

Chantal was having a wonderful day, escorted by her mother and her protector, Rene. Shopping was always a fun adventure, expanding her wardrobe, shopping for her sons, and enjoying her mother's company. Once back at the Valois estate, she found her father in his study, business as usual. Her mother excused herself to put away her purchases, as Chantal wandered into the study. She loved coming home to Paris, the chateau of her childhood felt more like home to her than Castello, and her *papa* always had time for her. She smiled as she saw him lift his head from the desk, his face lighting up as he saw her.

"I don't want to interrupt your work, *Papa*, but I wanted to see you while I was here. Henry will be arriving soon for drinks. *Maman* is putting away her purchases from today."

"Come in, *ma jolie fille*, I am always happy to see you. I see you and your *maman* have been out spending money. Come, join me. Once Henry is here, we can gather as a family, *oui*? You should visit more often. You know how much I love having you at home. Now, talk to your *papa*. How are things going for my favorite daughter?"

Chantal smiled. "Your only daughter is very happy today, *Papa*. I'm excited to see Henry too. He's as busy as Lorenzo. The warrior's business is never done, it seems." She looked down at her hands, fidgeting nervously in her lap. "It will be a short visit. I will have to leave after Henry's visit. Lorenzo expects me back at Castello."

Henri placed the cigarette into the long-stemmed holder and puffed away. He preferred the feel and flavor of the smoke through the cigarette holder. The deep purple satin brocade jacket made a soft whispering sound as he moved about, pouring himself another Midnight.

"May I interest you in a drink? I have tried the Red Moon your husband's family produces, but I admit it is too harsh for my taste buds. I much prefer the Midnight, and I'll leave the Red Moon for the unrefined masses and warriors." He took a tiny sip before realizing his gaff. "Not that your mate is unrefined. I did not mean to infer that. You know what I mean."

Chantal knew her *papa* spoke his mind, especially when it was just family. She always felt caught between her father and Lorenzo. She loved them both and tried to please them both as well.

"*Papa*, a Midnight would be perfect. Lorenzo is not unrefined. He was just raised in a different setting. It is his duty, and he does it with..." Hesitating, she wasn't sure what word was appropriate. Lorenzo was a dedicated and honorable warrior. The demands of the camp, the coven, and the vast business interest that covered Italy and Greece demanded much of his time and left her alone much too often. "He takes his duties very seriously, as do both your grandsons." Shrugging, she took the Midnight he offered. "I don't think I will ever understand it, *Papa*, even after all this time. You and *Maman* had an arranged marriage, and I know you both grew to admire and respect each other. But Shade and Kate, they seem to be, how do I say this? Open? They hide nothing of their affection. I sometimes feel very awkward when around his family."

He took a seat in the high-backed armchair by the fire, and held out his hand, indicating the seat across from him. "Sit, *ma fille*. You worry too much about these things. All mating's are different. And you forget, they are Italian, it is their custom to be more open in their display of affection. There is no shame in displaying your affection, it is just something I personally felt was best expressed in private. If your mate demands too much of you, or you feel uncomfortable, why not suggest a feeder? Your mother is quite pleased with our arrangement, and then you would have more time to visit here with us."

Chantal took the seat across from her father and sipped her Midnight. A feeder? Would she even want Lorenzo to go to a feeder? She knew none of the females in his family sent their mates to feeders. It wasn't something they preferred. Besides, she wanted to see more of him, not less of him. "I love him very much, *Papa*, I don't want Lorenzo to feed from another. I see so little of him now. I treasure the time he feeds and sleeps with me. I have always been a proper lady, never showing affection in public or amongst friends, as *Maman* instructed. Any display of affection is done behind closed doors and in private. But I promise to try to visit more often. I do enjoy you and *Maman's* company." Reaching out, she took his hand and squeezed it. "I will always follow the lessons you have taught me."

Henri smiled. "You are a good daughter, Chantal, and have made the Valois proud. You know you are welcome here anytime. Our coven has become stronger with your alliance with the Medici, so you have performed your duty to the coven as well. And your sons! Look at them. Both are strong warriors, protecting our lands. The Valois coven holds their newest queen in the highest regard. Do not forget these things. They are important to our survival. As for your mate, if you can find a path that is without conflict, that leaves you moderately happy, well then, I think that is well and good. He is good to you? Does not abuse you?"

Chantal shook her head quickly. "No, *Papa*, he treats me well. I have everything I could possibly want." Biting her lip softly, it was a lie, but she wouldn't tell him she didn't have his time, and she was lonely. "I do not think Lorenzo could abuse me if he wanted to. He is a warrior, but he has always been gentle and kind to me."

She could feel her son approaching and her heart bloomed. Her sons were her life, and she missed them both so much. At least she could see Henry fairly often. Christoph had been in the States with his grandparents for some time, and she wondered if he'd ever come back home to live. She missed the days when they were both small boys and depended on her. Those had been the happiest days of her life.

7

Lorenzo and Alfie wrapped up another night in camp with the warriors and were preparing to leave. Alfie slapped his best friend on the back. "Since Chantal is away, do you want to come home with me? Sophia would love to see you."

Lorenzo thought about the large, lonely castle with no mate to return to and didn't hesitate to take Alfie up on his offer. "Sure. I haven't seen Sophia in a while, and I'm sure she'd appreciate having someone different to nag for a few hours."

Alfie playfully grabbed the back of Lorenzo's neck and shook him. "I'll be sure to tell your sister you called her a nag."

Lorenzo laughed. "She's heard worse."

Alfie had felt for some time that there was something off between Lorenzo and Chantal. His mate seemed to be spending more and more time back home in France. Something wasn't right between them, but rules were rules, even in families. You kept your nose out of relationships. He'd never doubted Lorenzo's love for his mate, but something was sure the hell missing. As they joked and teleported out to the villa, Alfie knew Sophia would be glad to see her brother. They were a tight family.

The first thing Alfie saw when landing inside the villa was his beautiful green-eyed daughter, holding a kitten. She ran to hug him, and it made his heart burst with love. "Bianca! My beautiful girl, you've found another kitten? I've lost count. There are so many animals in this house. Where did you find this one?"

Bianca hugged her father with one arm, while holding the kitten in the other. "I don't find them. I think they find me." She turned to Lorenzo and gave him a hug. "Hi, Uncle."

Lorenzo was marveling at how much his niece and sister both looked like his mother. Their eye color had changed, and they were both taller than his mother, but the red hair and fair skin, as well as his mother's delicate facial features carried over with each generation.

Sophia heard the commotion in the front of the house, and came to greet Alfie, and was surprised when she saw her brother here again. He'd been visiting a lot lately. Sophia gave Alfie a kiss to welcome him home before turning to hug her brother, giving him a tight squeeze. "Brother, it's so good to see you. Everything okay?"

Lorenzo returned her affection. "Everything's fine. Chantal is visiting her parents, and Alfie took pity on me, bringing me home with him. I'm like one of Bianca's lost critters." He laughed easily, but the smile didn't reach his eyes.

Sophia could read him like a book, and flashed Alfie a look that he immediately understood. She wanted to be alone with her brother. Alfie slid his hand around his daughter's waist and led her away. "Come show me the whole litter. I know you didn't rescue just one."

Sophia grabbed Lorenzo's hand and took him into the living room in front of a roaring fireplace. "Have a seat."

Lorenzo took a seat by the fire, and leaned his head back against the chair, closing his eyes. He could hear the clink of glassware, as his sister poured them both a drink. "Here you go." He opened his eyes to see her handing him the full glass of Midnight, and he gratefully took it, swallowing down a big gulp. Sophia sat in the chair across from him, kicking off her shoes, and tucking her feet under her as she sipped at the wine.

"So, what's going on?"

He shook his head. "Nothing. Like I said, Chantal is away, and Alfie thought I might like to be with family."

Sophia watched him over the rim of her glass. She was silent a minute, to see if he'd add anything else before she leveled him with her stare. "Lorenzo, I know you better than you know yourself. Something's on your mind."

He sighed heavily. "Really, Sophia...don't read anything into this. I just came for a visit. I thought you'd be glad to see me." He laughed nervously.

She stared back at him. "I'm always glad to see you, and you're welcome here anytime. You know that. But I know when you have something on your mind. You hold your feelings inside, you always have. You and Daddy think you both have to be these perfect specimens of manhood, always protecting your females, and your children, never appearing vulnerable. But Mommy always knows when Daddy's hurting. She knows when to let him be the man, and when it's time to step in and take charge. You know what I'm talking about. You watched them both, as we all did. I try to be the same with Alfie." She laughed softly. "It's not easy being the mate to an alpha warrior. You guys don't make it easy. But I learned a lot from watching Mommy. And I know you, Lorenzo. I know you. I know when there's trouble in paradise. You think Alfie and I don't have our own issues? That we haven't had our own hurdles to overcome? I love Alfie with my whole heart, and I wouldn't change a thing, but that doesn't mean our world is perfect, so stop pretending you're okay, and you have nothing on your mind, because I know better."

Lorenzo emptied his glass and got up for a refill. He knew his sister wouldn't drop this until she had an answer. Even as children, she'd been able to read his moods. He refilled his glass and stood with his back to her. His voice was soft when he answered her, "I don't think Chantal is very happy. She goes back to Paris almost every week, always finding an excuse to be there. I'm afraid I'm losing her."

Sophia looked at his back, and the slumped shoulders, and felt the weight of the burden he was carrying. "Have you asked her? Have the two of you talked about this? Lorenzo, this is serious."

He turned around and looked at his sister. "Yeah, it's serious, and no, we haven't talked."

Sophia rolled her eyes at him. "Really, Lorenzo? Oh my god, sometimes you're just like Daddy! You can't pretend it's not there and hope it gets better. You have to talk to her. Figure out what's wrong. Wait...do you still love her?"

Lorenzo dropped back down in his chair. "Of course, I love her. I've never stopped loving her, but she's...I don't know..."

Sophia looked back at him and finished his sentence for him. "Distant? Remote?"

Lorenzo flashed her a look of annoyance, before silently nodding his head, acknowledging the truth of her words. Sophia sipped from her glass and wondered how much she should say. "Lorenzo, she's always been sort of, I don't know, reserved? It was that way even when you were courting her. I thought at first that was how she was taught to present herself to the public, and the private Chantal might be quite different. Over the years, as I've gotten to know her, I suspect that's just who she is. When we're together with her family, Henri treats Amelie with the utmost respect, and it's sincere, but I've never seen any display of affection between them. That's what she grew up with, and it's all she knows. But if she's going back to her parents' home this often, then something is bothering her, and it's your job as her mate to figure that out and fix it."

Lorenzo nodded. "And what if I can't fix it?"

Sophia gave him a look. "Seriously? Are you saying there's a Medici male that can't find a way to fix things with a female? Do you really want to be the first to win that title? Quit feeling sorry for yourself, brother, and figure out what your mate needs to be happy."

Lorenzo laughed softly. Sophia always did know how to throw a punch. "You're right."

Sophia scoffed. "Of course, I'm right. I'm my mother's daughter. Now get off your ass and do something."

8

Lorenzo spent most of the weekend with Sophia and Alfie but wanted to make sure he was home when Chantal returned. He'd come home early and paced the empty halls of Castello. The opulence of their home was something to see, but it was also a huge, empty space. It had come alive when their children were young, and you could hear Henry and Christoph running through the halls and up and down the stairs, staging mock battles with their swords. It made Lorenzo remember his own childhood at Bel Rosso, and how his mother had always kept him busy and entertained. There had always been people around, and something to do. As he stood inside these castle walls now, they were as silent as a tomb, and he could feel her loneliness. He knew he'd failed her, and it had never been his intention. He wanted to fix this, but he wasn't sure how, and he hoped it wasn't too late.

As Chantal and Rene teleported inside Castello, she thanked him and proceeded to walk through the hall of ancestors and up the stairs to the bedroom she'd shared with Lorenzo these many years. Her *papa's* words rang clearly in her head. She should be settled by now, content with what she had. She'd served her coven well, but it wasn't enough. She'd given the Medici bloodline two royal blooded sons to continue the legacy. She'd thought, with time, her sons would assume the responsibility for the coven, and her mate would have more time for her. But the coven had continued to expand, as had their businesses, and it kept all three of them occupied. She'd never give voice to her loneliness. He'd made sure she had everything she wanted or needed, except his time. She could feel Lorenzo in the great castle, and although she smiled, it was only halfhearted. He'd want to feed and make love to her, and he never left her wanting when it came to sex, but then he'd leave her to go to his duties. As she walked past the office, she noticed the light on inside. Quickly running her hand though her hair and brushing any speck of dirt from her designer suit, she tapped lightly on the door. "Lorenzo?"

He heard her come in and looked up. “My *cherie!* I’m glad to have you home. How was your trip?" He stood and walked to her, wrapping his arms around her, and felt her accept the hug, but she didn’t return it.

"It was fine, *Maman* and I went shopping and then Henry came to visit. We had a nice evening with family. Henry looks strong and fit, and he is happy being close to *Maman* and *Papa*. It was good to see him." She broke from the hug and began to turn away. "I will go to our room now. I need to prepare for bed. If you will give me about thirty minutes, I will be ready for you, Lorenzo."

He sighed. "Ready for me? Chantal, you speak of this as if it is a chore. I must feed, just as you must feed, but you’re the one I seek. Do you feel nothing?"

Chantal felt the sharp edge to his words. She looked down at the floor before looking back into those intense blue eyes. She feared her words had angered him. "No, I feel everything. I did not mean to displease you, Lorenzo. I only meant… I don’t wish to interrupt your work any further than necessary. I want to prepare myself for you." Shaking her head slightly, she struggled to find the words to convince him. "It is not a chore. I love you, It is our most intimate time together."

He stared at her, confused, her actions not matching her words. "Tell me how to love you, Chantal. Tell me what you need. I’m failing you somehow, and I don’t know how to fix it. You spend more time with your family than you do with me. Are you unhappy here? Are you unhappy with me? I love you, but I can see it’s not enough...we’re not enough. I feel you pulling away from me. Do you wish to be released? It would destroy me, but I wouldn’t keep you here if this isn’t where you want to be."

Chantal heard the frustration, the pleading, and the pain in his words. She could feel him struggling to understand her. Her biggest fear was to ask for more and be rejected. To make him feel that what he gave wasn’t enough. She felt her knees go weak and she gripped the large leather chair to steady herself. He wanted to release her? Her mouth felt dry and her heart constricted. She slid limply into the chair, her hand over her heart. She felt undone. "What are you saying? That you wish this? Why would you think I would want to be released? I love you. I just...I can’t..." She felt a tear run down her cheek, and she was embarrassed and quickly wiped it away.

Lorenzo was taken aback by her reaction and rushed to her side, kneeling at her feet. “No, *cherie!* I don't want to release you. I only want you to be happy, and I can see you're not happy." He wiped the tears from her cheeks, and gently kissed her. “Look at me, *cherie*. I love you. I have loved you from the moment I saw you. But I feel the void between us, and I don’t know how to fix it. Tell me what you need, and I will do it."

Chantal felt comforted by his actions and words. She had lived almost a hundred years with this man and if she wanted things to change, she needed to be brave. She needed to put her pride behind her and confess her true heart to him, here and now. His hands lay gently on her knees as his eyes pleaded with her.

"I miss our sons. I miss caring for them. I spent so much of my life raising them to be warriors, like you. Henry is always in France. Christoph is so far away, and I don’t know if he will ever come back. You have your warrior camp, your duty to the coven. I am left here to do what? I do not wish to complain, it is the female's job to raise the children, take care of the house and her mate. I hope you feel as though I accomplish those things. But there are times when I feel so lonely. I should let you get back to your duties. You have such responsibility. It wears on you greatly, and I only want to be a comfort, not a burden." She stood then and brushed past him quickly to stand next to the door. "Come to me whenever you’re ready, Lorenzo. It’s the only time I have you to myself, and I cherish that time."

Chantal turned to walk out the door but hesitated. "I don’t think you understand, Lorenzo. But your sisters, they have interests and obligations that occupy them. Your mother, she is the ultimate queen and has taken care of everyone. She has her businesses as well. I am simply Chantal Valois Medici, the mate of a Medici King. I am invisible, they see only you."

Her words crushed him. He felt he’d failed her completely. How could he have not noticed? But Chantal had never shown much passion, and rarely expressed her desire for him. He’d come to accept that was her nature. She never refused him, and accepted his advances in bed, and he had come to feel she was doing so out of some obligation as his mate. He'd go to her, and they'd feed, and make love, and he'd whisper that he loved her, but that wouldn't fix their problem. She felt adrift from him, and he didn't know how to reconnect. He couldn't bear the thought of losing her, of spending eternity in this castle without her to warm his bed. He followed her to their bedroom, but he already knew that tomorrow, he'd seek out the advice of his father.

9

Lorenzo woke early as usual and sat propped up in bed. He lit up a cigarette and smoked in the dimly lit room. He'd made love to her, and they had fed, but he still felt her distance. He looked at her as she slept next to him. He remembered the years when the boys were young, and they'd come running into the bedroom, and pounce on the bed, waking their mother. She'd pretend to be angry but would soon collapse in laughter with her children. He was trying hard to remember the last time he'd heard her laugh like that, and he was sad to realize he could think of nothing. He slipped from their bed and dressed quickly, sending a telepathic message to Alfie that he wouldn't be in camp today. He leaned over Chantal and kissed her softly and watched as she slowly woke.

"*Cherie*, I have some business in Virginia with my father. I may be gone over night since I can't meet with him during the day, but I'll be home as soon as I can. Will you be all right?"

Chantal felt her heart sink a bit. He was off once again, always running away from her. "*Oui*, I will be fine. Please give Christoph and your parents my love." She sat up in bed and looked at him already getting dressed in his leathers. "I do have some engagements in Paris, so if you will not be returning, I will just have Rene escort me to my parents and stay there the night."

"Of course, *cherie.* Whatever makes you happy."

He kissed her again and teleported out, feeling the weight of the world on his shoulders. He landed at Bel Rosso in the day light. He knew it would be hours yet before his father woke and he took the time to walk down to the camp, visit with his son Christoph, and catch up with some of the warriors he'd served with over the years. As the sun set, he made his way back to the house, and past the stables. He stopped and smiled as Angelo exited the stables and stepped up on the fence rail to greet him.

"Didn't know you were coming. Can I get a horse ready for you?"

Lorenzo shook his head. “I didn't know I was coming either. This trip wasn't planned. Some other time on the horse, I’m just waiting for the sun to set so I can see my dad."

Angelo bumped fists with him before returning to the stables, and Lorenzo resumed his walk to the house. Gi greeted him at the back door with a glass of Midnight. "Master is waking now."

"Thanks, Gi. I'm going to his office. Could you have him join me?"

Gi nodded silently as Lorenzo made his way to the familiar office. Not much had changed over all these years, and he found it comforting.

Shade was up and dressing and could feel his son. What the hell was this about? There was nothing stirring in Italy that he was aware of. Henry had things well in hand in France. Usually, Lorenzo gave him a heads up when he planned to visit. Kate walked from the shower looking like a vision, her hair still damp, and a sheer robe tied loosely around her waist. She still stirred his blood every time he saw her. "Our son is downstairs, any idea what that is about, *mi amore*?"

She ran a comb through her damp hair. "I feel his burden, lover, but no. I didn't know he was coming."

Just then, Gi tapped on the door and announced that Lorenzo was waiting in his office. "I will be down shortly Gi, *grazie!”*

He wrapped his arms around her, kissing the top of her head. "This has something to do with Chantal. I would bet money on it. I need to get to him. I feel his pain and confusion. Stick around in case I need some help." Kissing her neck, he growled. "Damn, how is it that our children are all grown, and they still can interrupt us?"

She was swallowed up in his embrace and laid her head against his chest. "Would you have it any other way? Our children will always need us, even when they're as old and gray as Gi."

Slapping her ass softly, he chuckled. "Let's hope like hell you still need me when I am that old and gray." Walking out, he was still smiling. *Cazzo*, he loved that woman. Walking into his office, he felt Lorenzo’s emotions even stronger. Oh yeah, this was about his mate. "Well, to what do I owe this visit? I am not complaining, just concerned. Damn good to see you, son."

Lorenzo looked up when his father entered. He’d followed his father’s example in all things and trusted his direction and guidance.

He only hoped his father could help direct him now. Lorenzo stood and gave his father a hug. "Dad, hope I'm not interrupting. I probably should have called."

Slapping him on the back, Shade walked to the bar and poured them both a Midnight before taking his seat behind his desk. "This will always be your home, Lorenzo. You are always welcome here." Shade sat back in his leather chair and sipped at his drink, closely watching his son's face. "Visited with Christoph yet?"

Lorenzo nodded as he took a seat. "Yeah, I spent the day in the camp. He looks good and seems very happy here. His mother will be pleased to hear that."

Shade noticed the tone of his voice when he mentioned Chantal. It was as he'd thought…trouble in paradise. "He is a great warrior, son. You gave me two grandsons that will keep this legacy alive and well. But why are you really here? You can tell me anything, you know that. We have kept no secrets from each other. Talk."

Lorenzo leaned forward in the chair, placing his head in his hands. "I don't even know where to start. I feel like I am losing Chantal. She says she still loves me, but she seems so unhappy. I even asked her if she wished to be released. She says no, but I'm afraid she's staying out of obligation or something. I don't know how to fix this. She's lonely, I know that. The kids are gone, and she doesn't have anything in her life. I can't be there all the time. How do I fix this?"

Shade wasn't surprised by his words. He knew his son deeply loved his mate, but he wasn't blind. Chantal had always been reserved and somewhat remote. Other than when her children were young, she rarely showed any outward display of affection. Lorenzo had been with her a long time now, and he wondered what had changed to leave his son questioning their future together. He was hurting and grasping at straws. "She does have something in her life, son. But that something has his priorities fucked up a bit."

Lorenzo looked up in surprise. "What do you mean? I love her! I've always loved her."

"But do you show her? Do you remind her daily that she is the most important thing in your life? I would say not since you are having this problem."

Shade sighed and set his drink down on the desk. Pulling open the desk drawer, he took out the pack of cigarettes and lit up, sliding the pack to Lorenzo. "Sometimes, you have to stop everything else in your life and make her your focal point. I struggle at times to keep all the balls in the air. Being a master, with responsibility for a camp and a coven, being mated, having children. Everyone wants a piece of you. It is easy to get pulled in too many directions and lose focus on what is most important. I'd occasionally lose my way, but your *madre* was good at reminding me. Your mate needs to know she comes first, and she is all you will ever need. Chantal wants your time and attention. She doesn't have your *madre's* temper, or Sophia's brashness. She will not speak up when she thinks she deserves more from you. That is not how she was raised. It is really simple. Make her blossom. You are going to have to work for it. She's not going to hand it to you."

Lorenzo stammered. "I tell her...I always tell her." He heard his father's words and knew he could do more. He hadn't made her his priority. He didn't bring her roses like his father had always done for his mother, he didn't will forth a song to make her smile, or dance with her spontaneously. Did they even have a song? He couldn't think of one, and yet he knew without hesitation that "Into the Mystic" was his parents' song. He'd done none of the things he'd seen his father do for his mother. He realized he knew more about his parents' relationship then he knew about his own. But then, Chantal never seemed like the romantic type. Her reserved nature led him to think she wouldn't respond to those things, and he'd never tried. It broke his heart to think he'd let her down, and not been the mate she needed. "I failed her then. I created this divide, not intentionally, but my lack of attention has caused her to drift away. That's what you're saying?"

Shade felt bad for him. "Lorenzo, you simply got caught up in your duties. Kids can make your life haywire. You forget romance used to live without boundaries. You still love her, and want her, and that is not failure. Telling her you love her is not showing her, son. Making love to her is not enough. She should be shown, told, held, and loved. Every spare moment you have and then some. The camp won't come to an end if you are not there every night. Do something unexpected, surprise her. Your *madre* was never sure what I was up to when it came to romancing her, and I bet if you asked her, she would tell you it was all part of the excitement." Shade locked eyes with him. "It is none of my business, but does she respond to you in bed? Because I swear you are not my son if you disappoint in that area. Does she prefer you use feeders? You do know Henri uses feeders a lot?"

Lorenzo nodded. "She never refuses me, and she does respond, but she holds back. Chantal has never been comfortable expressing emotion. The only time I ever saw her completely free from any restraint was when the children were young. I know her father uses feeders, and her mother seems grateful for it. She asked me once years ago if I'd prefer a feeder, and I told her she was the only one I wanted. Now I wonder if her offer was more for her benefit than mine."

Shade ran his fingers through his hair and shook his head. "No, son. You keep putting it back on her. Listen to me. Chantal didn't see anything of romance growing up. Perhaps she wants to please you, but she doesn't know how. She wasn't shown or taught. It is your job to show and teach her. It won't happen overnight. But Lorenzo, having a relationship is work. Don't ask her if she wants flowers, a new dress, a walk in Florence, just fucking do it. You might be surprised what lies inside her."

Lorenzo leaned back in his chair. "I always took my cues from her when I should have led her. I did this all wrong. Do you think it's too late?"

Shade smiled then. Shaking his head, he took a long sip of Midnight. "If you love her, and you want to keep her, it is never too late. Do you think I never struggled with your *madre*? Because there were a few times I thought I had royally screwed it up. But I refused to let her go, and that is the mind set you better have before you go back. Love will conquer all. If you want it, you need to earn it. Build your own love story. Every relationship is different and demands different things from you. Luca is quiet, and he loves Shannon's boldness and snarky mouth, and he shows her every day. Alfie is patient, and the perfect counterpart to your sister's stubbornness. He knows when to lead, and when to let go of the reins, so Sophia won't feel constrained. Your *madre,* she drew me like a moth to a flame, and she still does, but that flame would flicker and burn out if we both didn’t work to keep it glowing. There are times she is angry with me, but there is never a time she doubts the depth of my love, or understands that above all else, she comes first. You have lost sight of your priorities and you have some work to do, and you can’t fix it overnight. You straight now?"

Lorenzo smiled back at him. "Yeah, I'm good."

10

Lorenzo returned home to an empty castle. Chantal hadn't yet returned from visiting her parents. He remembered the years when he was single, and how empty the castle felt when he'd come back here after working all night with the warriors. How could he have not realized Chantal would feel the same? He stood in their bedroom, looking out the windows at the elaborate formal gardens. Chantal had nothing to occupy her time. His sister, Sophia, still had the company of Bianca, plus she was heavily involved in working with Luciano in marketing the wines from their vineyards to the mortal world. His mother had Shannon living under the same roof, and they were business partners in managing their companies that produced the products from the sunflowers, lavender, and olives. He knew he needed to spend more time with her, but he also needed to help her find a focus, something she was passionate about and could devote herself to as well. Still, he hated that he'd let himself become so absorbed in his work that he'd made her feel she was no longer a priority for him. He'd grown up watching his father shower his mother with attention, and yet he'd dropped the ball. The house at Bel Rosso was always filled with red roses for his mother. The vases were in every room and were automatically refilled as soon as the roses started to wilt. The petals were saved, to be sprinkled in his mother's bath, or on her sheets, or collected in mesh bags for sachets. Even now, if Lorenzo caught even the slightest whiff of a rose, he immediately thought of his mother.

Chantal had a signature fragrance too, it was light and delicate and suited her perfectly, but it wasn't something Lorenzo could identify. He turned and walked to her vanity table and picked up her perfume, sniffing it. It was the only fragrance she wore; Dior's Diorissimo. He had to look up the fragrance on the computer to see that it was lily of the valley. He was familiar with the tiny flower. He'd seen it in his mother's garden growing up. He summoned Antonio and asked him to find the gardener. Antonio rushed off, and had the gardener return to the house to wait in the office. Lorenzo joined him there. "Do we have lily of the valley growing in the gardens?"

The gardener looked confused. He'd never been summoned by his master before. "No, master."

Lorenzo was no gardener, but they were approaching the winter season now, so any planting would have to wait. "Can you make sure to add a lot of them to the garden please? My mother used to have it near the patio, and along the walkways through the garden."

The gardener nodded. "Of course, master. It is a small bulb plant. We can plant them in the spring. Anything else?"

Lorenzo paced. He was out of his league here. He knew very little about flowers. "Are there other kinds of lilies?"

The gardener nodded. "*Si*, there are many, Asiatic lilies, Calla lilies, Trumpet lilies, many species, many colors. Do you have a preference?"

Lorenzo waved his hand. "Plant them all. I want Chantal to see a sea of lilies when she looks out the windows."

The gardener nodded. "We can plant in the spring, and you will have them blooming within weeks. The lilies spread, so it will be easy to create a sea of lilies."

Lorenzo nodded his approval and dismissed the gardener. "Antonio!"

The butler reappeared. "Yes, master?"

"Call the florist in Florence. Call all the florists in Florence. I want Castello filled with lilies, always. As soon as the flowers start to wilt, replace them, understood?"

Antonio nodded and rushed to fulfill his master's command. Lorenzo paced, it was only a start, and he'd have to be more observant of her needs. He remembered his father willing forth music, and his parents dancing. They were always playing songs for each other. He and Chantal didn't have a song. She'd listen to music, and frequently, the songs would be in French, so he'd paid little mind to them. He went to the computer and asked to hear the most repeated song on her playlist. It was an old song. One he remembered hearing whenever his parents took him and his sisters for a stay in the Paris house. His mother would always close her eyes when this song came on and say, "This song is the essence of Paris." He looked at the song title, "La Vie en Rose."

He had the computer translate the French lyrics into English. It was a love song. A plaintive, heart achingly beautiful love song. His quiet, reserved mate had been hiding her romantic side. He knew it wouldn't be an overnight transformation, and he hoped he wasn't too late, but it was time for him to officially court his mate.

***

Chantal had spent another few days with her parents. She had attended an annual event for the Valois coven with her mother. Chantal had initially declined to go this year until Lorenzo had announced he'd be traveling to Virginia on business. She'd always enjoyed the social aspects of her duties, as princess to the Valois coven, and now she reined as queen over an even larger Medici coven. Most of her old friends had been in attendance. It took her mind off how much she missed her sons, and her *papa* was always pleased whenever she visited. As she teleported back to Castello accompanied by Rene, they landed together in the grand foyer. The smell of lilies hit her strong. She stopped in the middle of the foyer and slowly turned in a circle, her mouth slightly open in surprise and curiosity. There were vases everywhere, brimming with every kind of lily imaginable. Biting her lip, she looked at Rene with a questioning look. He shrugged, indicating he knew nothing.

She walked slowly through the ground floor of Castello and found every corner filled with the beautiful blooms. Her mind began to spin a bit, wondering what this meant. She hadn't ordered flowers and couldn't think of any occasion that would have called for them. She could feel Lorenzo, and knew he was in the castle, but continued to stroll through the rooms, looking at the glorious beauty the flowers brought, and how enchanting the scent was to her. She stopped just outside the ballroom and bent to smell the white calla lilies that filled the vase. She pulled a perfect specimen from the vase and continued to walk inside the ballroom, her designer heels making a small clicking sound against the marble floor that echoed inside the room.

She left the ballroom and headed upstairs to the bedroom she shared with her mate. He'd be getting ready to leave for camp soon. She'd purposely come home early, so he could feed if he needed to. She was a bit tired from the trip, and wanted nothing more than a long, luxurious bath and to change into a more comfortable outfit.

Entering the bedroom, she found Lorenzo sitting in one of the armchairs near the window, reading a book from the library. Printed books were a rarity in these days and times, and the massive collection of bound first editions that filled the library here were invaluable. Their bedroom was also overflowing with lilies. She smiled softly at him. "I see you are already prepared for camp tonight. Did you see Christoph when at Bel Rosso? Is he doing well? Did you give him my love?"

Lorenzo was disappointed that she made no mention of the lilies and was wondering if his efforts were too little too late. "Yes, of course. I spent the day with Christoph. He's running the camp and looks very happy. He said he'd plan a visit home soon. He misses you."

Slipping off her heels, she smiled, and her heart warmed. "I miss him too, and I'm glad to hear he will visit soon." She still held the calla lily in her hand and let it glide across her cheek, and she inhaled its delicate fragrance. "Lorenzo, is there a reason the castle is filled with lilies? Did I miss an event on my calendar? I am usually on top of such things. I did not order fresh flowers for the castle."

"You didn't miss anything on your calendar, *cherie*. The occasion is you. I ordered them for you. Tell me, did you have time to miss me while you were away?"

Chantal was taken aback. *For her?* There was no special occasion she could think of and she was slightly confused. She looked at him with a questioning look. "For me? I don't understand. It is such an elaborate gesture. The house is filled. I am fond of lilies, but I don't believe I have ever seen so many at once." She walked to where he sat in the chair and kissed him softly on the lips. "Of course, I missed you. I was very busy with the event with *Maman*, and the time flew by. But I did think about you, I always think about you." She walked to the vanity and sat down to brush out her hair and remove her jewelry.

He got up from the chair and stood behind her, unhooking her necklace for her, before kissing her neck. "Are you preparing for your bath, *cherie*?"

"*Oui*. Thank you for the lilies, they are beautiful. Unless you need to feed right away, I will have one of the maids draw my bath. I know you are busy and need to get to camp. I just wanted to relax a bit, take a long bath."

"Perhaps you wouldn't mind if I joined you?"

She turned in her chair, looking up at him. "Together? If it is what you wish, Lorenzo."

They hadn't bathed together since before the boys were born. How long ago that seemed now. They'd spent more time together then, and it was all new and exciting. Somehow, they'd lost that over the years.

"It is what I wish, *cherie*. I won't be going to the camp tonight. I have left you alone for far too long."

He took her hand and led her to the massive marble bathroom, and turned on the hot water, letting the tub fill. He willed the lights to dim and willed the candles to light as he stripped from his leathers, looking at the expression of shock on her face.

"Has it been that long, *cherie*? Tell me it's not too late to win back your affections."

The news he'd remain home told her he'd heard her words and understood she needed him to be with her more. She cast her eyes downward as he stripped from his clothes. "You are not home very often, Lorenzo, and it is not my place to complain."

When she looked up again, he was standing naked before her, her warrior. Everything about him was still hard and strong, muscled, and perfect. She'd never encountered anyone like him before. His hair was as black as night, still worn long, slightly past his shoulders. His body was incredible to look at, as hard and smooth as the statues of marble inside this castle. She stood before him, not shy, but not moving, still wearing her dress and in bare feet. "You never lost my affections. I think you just forgot they were still here."

He stared back at her. "Then how could you ever forgive my callous mistake. A woman as beautiful as you, should never be left unattended, or ever be made to feel she's been forgotten. I'll have to work hard to make it up to you, *cherie*."

He stepped in front of her and turned her around, so he could unzip the dress, letting it drop in a puddle to the floor. He lifted her hair and kissed her neck, planting soft kisses down her spine. He unhooked the expensive lace bra and slid it off her shoulders. His lips softly brushed the tops of her shoulders, his breath hot against her skin. His hands slid to her hips, and pushed the delicate lace thong free, until they too fell around her ankles and she stepped out of them. He took her hand and led her to the tub, now filled with hot water. He stepped in first, lowering himself into the water, and held his hand out for her.

She was confused by his sudden interest, and couldn't imagine what had sparked the change, but felt her heart lighten, eager to be with him. As he'd undressed her, his hands and lips traveling along her body, she felt a low burning fire stir in her belly. It was as if he were discovering her for the first time. She took his hand and stepped into the tub, sliding down softly with her back against his chest. It felt good to be skin to skin with him. Memories flooded her brain of a time when they were first together. How gentle and sweet he'd been with her. There was always a fire in his eyes, a glow of need and want for her. She turned to look at him over her shoulder, as the water lapped around them, and looked into his eyes to see that same look of fire burning there for her. She kissed him and felt him sigh, as though he were relieved.

She smiled coquettishly. "I rather like how you are working so far." She felt bold and didn't want to lose the moment. She laid her head back against his shoulder, as she lifted her hand to caress his face and wrap her fingers in his hair.

He took his time with her, using the sea sponge and the bottles of bath salts and scented soaps lined along the tub, to gently wash every inch of her, entwining his soapy fingers in hers, and relishing in the smoothness of her skin. She felt so good in his arms, how could he have ever let this slip away? He felt her relax, as she lay against his chest, and his arms encircled her, pulling her close, nibbling at her ear. She turned her head, giving him access to her neck, and he paused. *Is this how she thinks I see her? Just a source for feeding?* She wasn't his feeder, she was his mate, and he kissed her neck, and slid his hands beneath the surface of the water, and between her legs, listening to the soft gasp.

His skilled fingers ignited her need for him. Her voice was breathy, and she grasped his hard muscular thighs. "Lorenzo."

His lips were close to her ear as he whispered, "I haven't forgotten everything, *cherie*. I know what brings you pleasure." His fingers slid slowly and seductively in and out of her, as she gave in to him. He willed forth the song from her playlist, the song she must play when he wasn't home, and the room was filled with the sounds of "La Vie en Rose."

Relaxing against him, she let him pleasure her and got lost in the feel of him, the candles, and the hot water that lapped around them. Her head fell back onto his shoulder and her breathing was ragged as he made her body come alive. She was startled by the sound of her favorite song, and even more startled that he knew it was her favorite. She moaned loudly as her body craved more. Gripping the sides of the tub, she let go and felt the pleasure of her orgasm wash over her. It was a release of everything she'd been holding inside for so long. She curled into his chest as the song played on. "This is my favorite song. I love the lyrics."

He wrapped his arms around her and held her close, "*Si*, beautiful words, *cherie*. Somewhere along the way, I lost the words, but I promise you, I won't lose them again."

She felt safe in his arms, and she felt warmth from him that was different from anything she'd felt from him in years. It had been so long, since she'd felt as though he even saw her. "Please don't leave me tonight. I want to be held in your arms. Thank you for the flowers, for this night."

He stood and lifted her from the tub, placing her gently on her feet. He dried her with the towel and spritzed her with her favorite perfume. He brushed the damp tendrils of her soft brown hair away from her face. "Do not thank me. Never thank me. I have neglected you, *cherie*. You deserve this, and so much more." He led her back into their bedroom, where their bed had been turned down, and lying on her pillow was the most delicate sprig of lily of the valley.

She let go of his hand, and lifted the delicate flower to her nose, a smile lit up her face, her favorite. Turning to him, she blushed and smiled. "*Je t'aime, mon* king."

"*Ti amo, mon cherie*."

11

Lorenzo left for camp, feeling optimistic about things with Chantal. He knew they both had a long way to go to heal the divide between them, but they still loved each other deeply, and wanted their relationship to heal. He'd let her drift too far away, and hadn't made her his priority, and he had no one to blame for that but himself, as his father pointed out. Still, Lorenzo had concerns. He could spend more time with her, and be a more attentive mate, but the fact remained that Chantal spent much of her time alone. She'd expressed that she had no desire to learn the businesses that the other Medici females managed so effectively, and he had no ideas for how she might spend her time. He knew the solution to their problems wasn't going to be solved solely by his attentiveness and bringing her fresh flowers.

He entered the camp, and saw Alfie already at work, pushing the recruits through a standard drill. Alfie was a good teacher. He was firm but patient. He worked hard with those recruits who showed a true desire to improve but had little regard for any recruit who didn't pull his weight, and quickly weeded them out. One thing had remained, and that was the high standards for inclusion in the camp. The Medici still produced warriors that were unparalleled in their culture. He stepped up next to Alfie, who acknowledged him with a wink. "Did you get the message?"

Lorenzo looked at him quizzically. "What message?"

Alfie signaled to one of the lieutenants to take over, then threw his arm over Lorenzo's shoulder, leading him away from the training field. "Malachi sent a runner to the camp looking for you. I sent him to the office, told him you'd be here shortly. Is there a problem with Council, brother?"

Lorenzo shook his head. "Not that I'm aware of. Besides, I'm sure Natalia would have given me a heads up. Let me take care of this."

Alfie slapped him on the back. "Take your time, I got this."

Lorenzo headed in the direction of the old camp office where Marco had ruled for so long. He entered the office to find the runner sitting nervously. The runner jumped to his feet as soon as Lorenzo entered and bowed slightly. Council staff belonged to the Council, and weren't part of any coven, so Lorenzo wasn't his king. Still, they were expected to show respect to the coven masters.

"Master Medici. I am here on behalf of Malachi. He has requested your presence at Council. He said you may want to include your mate."

Lorenzo sat on the edge of the desk. "My mate? Did Malachi indicate what this was about?"

The runner shook his head. "No, master, I wasn't given any information in that regard. He said your father always included his mate when he came to Council. I assumed he was indicating he expected perhaps you'd do the same."

Lorenzo lit up a cigarette and offered the pack to the runner, who shook his head no. Lorenzo took a drag on the cigarette and released the smoke into the room. Chantal had never shown a lot of interest in the issues that impacted the coven and had never expressed a desire to attend Council. Like her mother, she'd been content to let her father take the lead on such matters. Still, Lorenzo found it odd that Malachi would mention it at all and thought perhaps it was Malachi's way of telling him the issue to be discussed, might impact his mate as well. He took the final drag on the cigarette before putting it out in the ashtray.

"Tell Malachi my queen and I will be there within the hour." The runner nodded and teleported out immediately. Walking back out on the training field, Lorenzo quickly spotted Alfie, and let him know he was leaving for Council, and for him to hold down the fort. Lorenzo headed back to Castello to find Chantal in their bedroom, reading. "My *cherie*, we have been summoned to Council. Do you think you can be ready to leave in an hour?"

Chantal looked up with a questioning look. "Council? Lorenzo, I have been to Council only a few times in the 100 years we have been together. Does this concern me? Of course, I can be ready if you need me. Give me a few minutes to change." She walked to her closet, and sorted through the designer wardrobe, organized by seasons, then by garment type, and color. She chose an elegant long-sleeved knee-length dress in a deep blue color and coordinating heels. She opened the sealed vault that held her massive jewelry collection, filled with sapphires and diamonds. Lorenzo loved her in blue because it enhanced the color of her eyes. She picked out a discreet pair of sapphire earrings and placed them in her ears before selecting the necklace and relocking the vault. Once changed, she reappeared but was still puzzled. "Lorenzo, seriously, why would they need me?"

He'd changed from his leathers into a suit. "I wasn't informed of the reason for the visit, *cherie*, only that Malachi wanted to see us. I'm sure it's nothing to worry about. You know Natalia would have called if she'd heard of any problems. Are you ready?"

She smiled at him dressed in a suit. It was rare to see him dressed in anything other than jeans or leathers. He looked so handsome. She quickly brushed off his lapel and helped him tie his hair back in a leather strip. Handing him the sapphire and diamond necklace, she turned her back to him and lifted her hair. "*Oui*, I will be ready once you help me with this necklace."

She felt his fingers as they deftly engaged the closure on the necklace and felt the light kiss on her bare skin.

"I love you in blue."

She cast him a glance over her shoulder. "I wear it for you."

He smiled at her. "The blue compliments the color of your eyes. I must remember to buy you more."

He caught her eye in the mirror as she looked at the necklace. "They were made for you, and from now on, you wear only sapphires and diamonds." He took her hand. "Ready?"

Her smile was soft, and she could feel the heat on her cheeks as she blushed. "I would be honored to wear them. I'm ready to go, but I admit I'm a bit nervous. The Council has always intimidated me. *Papa* always dealt with them." Chantal took his hand and they teleported to the Council.

Lorenzo laughed. "Nothing to be nervous about. I discovered, long ago, Malachi has more bark than bite."

He landed with her in the large entry hall where they were immediately greeted by the Medici warriors assigned to Council. The warriors nodded in respect to the king who no longer ruled them.

One of them stepped forward. “You are expected, master. Follow me, please."

Lorenzo slipped his arm around her, placing his hand at the small of her back, as they followed the warrior to the Council Court. Another warrior stepped forward and opened the massive wooden doors, announcing their arrival. They were led to a small table that faced the dais, where the seven Council members sat in their colored robes, their faces partially obscured by their hoods. Lorenzo pulled out the chair for Chantal, and made sure she was comfortable, before sitting next to her. Malachi stood, and waited for them to get settled.

“Thank you for coming on such short notice, Master Lorenzo. There is an issue we wish to discuss."

Lorenzo nodded. “No problems, I hope."

Malachi shook his head. "No, well, not exactly. This is not a matter that would normally involve you. The Council has an established protocol for such occurrences, but given your family’s history, we thought we should at least consult with you."

Lorenzo nodded back at him, feeling confused. "And what is this matter?"

Malachi sat down before proceeding with his explanation and sighed heavily. "This morning, one of the warriors found a half-breed left outside our gate. The infant appears to only be a few days old. As you are aware, most half-breeds end up abandoned at some point and left to live, or die, on the streets. They are not claimed by the mortal mother and rejected by the vampire who created it. We can't, of course, take in the infant for the long term. In the past, such infants left here were destroyed. However, given that your father not only acknowledged his half-breed son, but openly claimed him and adopted him into his family, the Council thought we would at least inquire as to whether you have any desire to adopt this...child."

Lorenzo was taken aback by the request. Was Malachi asking him to take on the responsibility of raising someone else’s half-breed child? He’d grown up with Cory, and knew him as his brother, not his half-brother, but this child had no blood bond to them. Besides, the burden for raising this child would fall more on Chantal. He turned to look at her, trying to read her reaction.

Chantal had been sitting quietly, looking straight ahead, her back straight in the chair, her hands held together in her lap. She listened to Malachi speak and at first wasn't attentive to his words, but then he spoke of a half-breed infant. She listened in horror as the words spilled from his mouth so casually, stating they would destroy the infant. She certainly knew about half-breeds, but until she'd met Cory, had never known one. She'd never had to consider their fate. She had no idea that half-breeds abandoned at birth were destroyed. Now, her heart hammered in her chest. She reached over and squeezed Lorenzo's knee under the table. Her eyes were large in her head when she turned to look at him. Her whispered voice was soft, and her breathing was rapid. "Please, Lorenzo, do not let them destroy this infant. I could not bear to live with the thought that we abandoned a helpless infant."

Lorenzo turned toward her, leaning in close, and speaking in a whisper. "*Cherie*, this is a big decision. This child is not of our blood. Cory was my father's son. You're not responsible for this life. If we take this child, he must be guarded and protected within our coven until such time as he dies, just as my mother and father still guard and look after Cory's welfare. Are you sure this is what you want? You are under no obligation."

Chantal had never felt so deeply about anything in her life. She locked eyes with him, her expression pleading with him. "*Oui*, I want this infant. Lorenzo, the child did not choose this life. It is an innocent. Surely, it does not deserve to be destroyed. We can take care of the infant. We have the means, and it will not be a burden but a precious gift. Our sons are grown. I miss them, holding them, raising them and having a purpose as a *maman*. Please, Lorenzo." She reached out and took his hands in hers.

He leaned forward until his forehead touched hers. "The child will be ours then, *cherie*. And I will love him as if I had planted him in your womb."

He looked up at Malachi. "My Queen wishes to raise this child as our own. I know he cannot be recorded in the Medici bloodline, but I ask that he be recorded as our half-breed son that we freely adopted. My father has shown us that the half-breeds can be an asset to the covens, and I would propose that, in the future, any half-breeds left at your doorstep be brought to us instead of being destroyed."

Malachi stood and waved his hand to the runner who stood at attention on the side of the dais, signaling him to go get the infant. "It will be done as you wish, Master Lorenzo. However, the half-breed that was left here is not a male child but a female. I hope that does not change your decision."

Chantal looked at Lorenzo, a flash of fear in her eyes. "A female? It does not change your decision, *non*?"

"Not for me, *cherie*. A life is a life. I will cherish a daughter as much as a son."

The runner returned with the infant, wrapped in a ragged blanket, and handed the child to Malachi. He stepped down from the dais and carried the infant to the waiting arms of Chantal. "My lady, we know nothing of this child, other than she can't be more than a few days old. As soon as you give her a name, she will be recorded in our records as an adopted half-breed to you and Lorenzo." He transferred the infant to Chantal.

Eagerly taking the infant into her arms, she cradled it to her chest. As she looked down, a soft glow lit inside her heart. The girl was tiny, extremely so, as were most half-breeds. Her skin had the pale transparency of a newborn, and her hair nothing but light fuzz on top of her head. She slept soundly, as tiny lashes fanned across her pink cheeks. As Chantal rocked her gently in her arms, the infant's eyes fluttered open and stared back at her, blinking several times. "Hello, *mon petite ange*."

Lorenzo watched her closely with the infant and could already feel the love in her heart. He knew already that this was a gift, and one that would heal her, filling the void he'd not been able to fill. He gently touched the silky fine locks on the infant's head. She looked healthy and alert, and had her eyes locked on Chantal's as if to say, "Are you my mother?"

Lorenzo looked back at Malachi. "Has she been feeding?"

Malachi nodded. "A wet feeder was brought in until we could decide this matter. She has been well cared for, and there are no problems with her health. She will thrive if given the proper care and protection." Malachi addressed Chantal. "I know this is sudden, but do you wish to name her? If not, you can let us know within the next few days."

Chantal looked up at Malachi. "She is so delicate and tiny. She will do well with us. I wish to name her Grace. I feel graced to have this chance again, to be her *maman*. She will bear the Medici name, *oui*?"

"*Si*, Grace Medici. It shall be recorded." Malachi turned and nodded to Ivor, who opened the ledger and picked up the quill pen. He was aware the young Natalia would have recorded this historic moment into their computer archives, but he'd never abandon the old ways. Malachi turned back to the couple. "I am sorry I don't know more about the infant. The half-breeds are rare, and most are not left at our doorstep. However, now that you have accepted this child, and word gets out, I cannot predict the outcome. You understand what I am saying, Medici?"

Lorenzo nodded. No one really knew how many half-breeds were out there. They were thought to be rare, but their numbers had never been tracked. By taking this child, and saying he'd take others, he understood there could be a steady flow of children through their home.

Chantal clutched Grace tighter in her arms, and the look on her face was one of determination. They would care for any children left abandoned, half- breed or not. She spoke before Lorenzo had a chance to. "It is our duty to care for this coven and this territory. I do believe we both understand your meaning, and we will gladly deal with each circumstance as it comes." She turned to Lorenzo. "As it should be, my king, *oui*."

Lorenzo smiled back at her. "I would never dare to argue with my queen. Come *cherie*, I think we have a lot to do when we get home. This little one needs your attention."

12

As they returned home, Chantal was still clinging to the infant in her arms and started issuing orders. They'd need a nursery, and she called Rosa, her Lady in Waiting, to get right on it. Rosa was surprised by the presence of the infant but didn't ask any questions. Chantal told her to set up the nursery in the bedroom next to theirs, so she'd be close. Rosa nodded, and answered, "Yes, my lady," as she scurried off.

Antonio appeared when he heard the commotion and tried not to look surprised to see his queen holding an infant. Lorenzo beamed back at him, as he gave him instructions. "The infant will remain in our room until the nursery is ready. Please fetch my father's old cradle from storage, Antonio."

The butler nodded and rushed to retrieve the old hand carved cradle. Lorenzo could already hear the buzz, as the news traveled through the castle that the master and his mate had returned with an infant. Lorenzo knew the news would travel fast, and he didn't want his parents to hear this through the grapevine.

"Do you need help, *cherie*? I can send someone to help you. I think I need to call my father before news gets out."

Chantal didn't want to relinquish the infant to anyone yet. "No, do what you need to do. I will send the staff into the city to buy some basics until I can shop for her properly. For now, I will take her upstairs and get her settled." She turned to go upstairs but stopped and returned to him. "You have made me so happy, Lorenzo. I love her already."

Lorenzo loved the look on her face. Unlike Cory, this half-breed wouldn't have to struggle on the streets. This infant would be raised as if she were born to them, and never know the shame of being a half-breed. He couldn't be more proud of her, than he was right now.

"I can see that *cherie*, and I have never loved you more. Go, take care of your daughter, and I will handle this."

She looked up at him. "Our daughter, Lorenzo, she is ours. We will love her together." She smiled and kissed him before heading up the stairs to set things into motion.

"*Si*, our daughter, *cherie*." Lorenzo checked the time as he headed for his office. It was getting close to sunset in the States and his father would be waking soon anyway. He touched the wide computer screen, and the automated voice inquired what he needed. “Call my father." The computer dialed up his father, and as he answered, he could see the image of his father, pulled from his slumber, and his mother sleeping next to him.

***

Shade heard the soft trill of the call coming through and knew that only his children would call at this hour. His death slumber was light, as it was getting near sunset, and he pulled himself awake to see Lorenzo’s image on the screen. He always felt a sense of foreboding when the children called during his death slumber. He felt Kate stir next to him. "Son, everything okay? Something happen?"

Lorenzo held up his hand. "I think it’s safe to say something has happened, but it’s nothing I wish to discuss on the phone. I know this is short notice, but if you could both come to Castello as soon as possible, I’d be most grateful."

Shade sat straight up in bed, as Kate tumbled from his chest, and shook the sleep from her eyes. "I do not like the sounds of this, Lorenzo. Is Chantal in any danger? *Cazzo*. We will be there as soon as the sun sets here. Just tell me everyone is safe?"

Lorenzo smiled at him. "Everyone is safe, I promise you. There’s no danger, so please don’t worry. This is just not something I want to discuss on the phone. Please come as soon as you can."

Shade sighed with relief but was still not comforted. "Fine, we will be there." The computer screen went blank, and he turned to look at Kate who was sitting up, staring at him with a worried look on her face. He reached over and turned on the light beside the bed. "You okay, *bel*? What the hell could this be about?"

Kate bit at her lip. "Do you think this has anything to do with his recent visit? Lover, you don't think he’d release Chantal, do you?"

Shade felt a wave of sadness wash over him. That would be disastrous for them all if Lorenzo had released her. He couldn’t fathom his son’s desperation. "When he left here, he seemed fine.

He understood without a doubt what he needed to do. He didn't sound like it was something he couldn't turn around. *Cazzo*. Do you think Sophia knows anything?"

"They're close, and I know she holds his confidences, but if something like that happened, she wouldn't keep it from us. Better to just go and find out what's going on than to try to guess. We'll just drive ourselves crazy."

The sound of the soft whir of the blinds opening filled the quiet room. "Well, isn't that perfect timing? Let's get dressed and teleport to Florence." As they both scurried to get ready, Shade sent a telepathic message to Luca, letting him know they were leaving. Kate was still pulling on her boots when he grabbed her hand and they teleported, uncertain of what they'd find at Castello.

Kate gripped his hand as they traveled at a rate of speed that was faster than usual and landed in the grand foyer at Castello. She finished zipping up her boot, hopping on one foot as the staff was running about helter-skelter in a flurry of activity. They were in such a rush they appeared not to notice the sudden appearance of Shade and Kate. *What's going on?* Kate called out to her son, "Lorenzo?"

Lorenzo appeared on the stairs with a smile on his face. "Come upstairs. I have something to show you."

Kate looked at him questioningly. He seemed genuinely happy, but she couldn't for the life of her figure out what would be so urgent that he'd summon them here. She tugged at Shade's arm, as they headed for the stairs and followed their son back to the suite he now shared with his mate. As they approached the closed door, Lorenzo looked over his shoulder and flashed a sly grin. Kate was getting annoyed.

"This better be good, Lorenzo."

Shade was more confused than ever. The entire house was like a zoo. What could be going on that had the whole household in an uproar. He scowled at his son. "Oh, this better be more than good!"

As Lorenzo opened the door, what Shade saw was even more confusing. Chantal was seated in a chair, cradling an infant in her arms. The newborn wore a long gown of the palest blush pink, with white satin rosettes sewn along the hem. There were tiny pink satin slippers, adorned with the same satin rosettes, on her feet, and a tiny pink ribbon attached to her wispy fine hair.

Kate saw Chantal holding a small infant in her arms and entered the room quietly, so as not to disturb the sleeping baby. She peered over the soft pink blanket lying loosely around the infant and looked at her angelic face. She touched the baby's chubby cheek with her fingertips. "What a beautiful baby." She was still confused and wondering why their son called them here, but figured he'd reveal his secret in good time. At least there didn't appear to be any problems between him and his mate. "Are you looking after the baby for someone?"

Chantal watched Kate softly touch Grace and she knew her response to this adoption would be a positive one. "No. May I present to you, your granddaughter, Grace Medici."

Just then, Grace opened her eyes and blinked, her small hands waving about in the air. "*Mon petite*, meet your *grand-mere*, this is Queen Bee, or as your brothers call her, Bebe." Chantal raised her eyes to Kate and waited for her response.

Kate looked startled. "My...grandchild? I don't understand. You were pregnant?"

Shade had no idea what the hell was going on, but he knew one thing for certain, this infant was a half-breed. He took a few steps closer, and then stopped. He looked at Lorenzo who had this stupid wicked grin on his face.

"*Mi amore*, the child is a half-breed. And son, you better explain immediately what this is all about."

Grace began to cry, startled by Shade's loud voice. Lorenzo chuckled. "Lower your voice, please. You're scaring your granddaughter. We were summoned to Council by Malachi. It seems the infant was left on their doorstep a few days ago. No vampire stepped forward to claim her, so they were prepared to destroy her."

Kate gasped and placed her hand at her throat. "Destroy her? I don't understand. Cory wasn't destroyed."

Lorenzo shook his head. "Cory was raised by his mortal mother, or at least, she tried to raise him. He wasn't abandoned to Council. I doubt Rachael even knew anything about the Council back then. We didn't have a U.S. Council, and she'd have had no way to get to Italy. But half-breeds who aren't claimed by either the mortal mother or vampire father are sometimes left at the gate of Council. It’s considered the humane thing to do."

Kate couldn’t believe what she was hearing. She’d been turned for more than a hundred years, and she’d never heard of this. “That’s not humane. That’s barbaric! Who would harm an infant?"

Lorenzo nodded. "And it’s why you have a new granddaughter. Chantal wouldn’t allow the infant to be destroyed either. She’s been adopted. Her name is Grace Medici." Lorenzo looked at his father, waiting for his response.

Shade answered in a soft voice, "May I hold my granddaughter?"

Chantal hesitated for a moment before relinquishing the infant. She placed Grace into his muscled arms. It was always such a sight to see a large warrior hold such a small bundle in his arms. Shade looked down at the wiggling infant and saw the most beautiful face. She was tiny and frail, as was common with half-breeds. He wondered if she knew her life had been spared today.

"Well, are you not beautiful, *si*? I am Papa Bear, or as my other grandchildren call me, P-bear. You are my little angel."

Grace stopped wiggling and cooed up at him.

"I haven’t heard that beautiful sound in a very long time. Welcome to Medici."

He turned to his son. "They would have destroyed her, without another thought. I am proud of you both for taking on this responsibility. She will be loved, *si*?" Walking to Kate, he kissed her softly. "I think you should hold your new granddaughter, Bebe."

As Shade slid the baby into Kate's arms, Lorenzo cleared his throat. “Well, uh, there's more to the story. We told Malachi we’d accept any half-breed abandoned to Council, so I hope you have love enough for those that may follow."

Shade spun around to look at Chantal and Lorenzo. "I would love them all, but I hope you know what you got yourselves into. You both agreed to this?"

It was Chantal who answered. "*Oui*. They did not ask to be born, and they cannot control what happens around them. No child should have to suffer because of our ridiculous rules. Castello is large, and we can certainly care for them, no matter how many. I hope Natalia can perhaps change how the Council sees these children. It is something I wish to see changed."

Shade smiled at her. "I am very proud to call you my daughter-in-law. Spoken like a true Medici Queen. I know Natalia is working on changing the minds and policies in the States, as it relates to our females having equal power. I see no reason why she would not advocate for this change as well. Cory is a perfect example of what the half-breeds can accomplish when loved and given the proper home."

Shade stood next to Kate, peering down at the small infant in her arms, as Lorenzo slid his arm around Chantal's waist, pulling her close. Lorenzo kissed the top of her head. "You made the right decision, *cherie*."

13

Chantal was nervous. It was going to be a difficult evening. She'd summoned her parents to Castello, just as Lorenzo had done with his parents, and they'd be arriving soon. She'd never given a thought to her parents' reaction to a half-breed when she'd agreed to adopt Grace, as well as any abandoned half-breed children that followed. Henri was old school in his thinking. He may not approve of such an act, and Chantal hated disappointing him. The deed was done now, and they'd have to get used to the idea of having a new granddaughter that wasn't of their blood.

She'd asked Lorenzo to be by her side, she wanted his support when she confronted her parents. Kate and Shade still remained at Castello to visit and be with Grace, but she wasn't sure whether having them present when she met with her parents would help or hinder. She'd finally decided her parents' first introduction to Grace should be a private one. She lifted Grace from the cradle she'd kept in their bedroom. She loved having the baby close by and didn't mind getting up and checking on her throughout the night. They had quickly found a wet feeder, and moved her into Castello, although Chantal would initially have the infant feed only from her to allow for the bonding. She loved this infant as much as she loved the two sons she'd given birth to, and she needed to make her parents understand this. As she was picking up Grace, Lorenzo entered their bedroom.

"Are they here yet? I am nervous. *Papa* will not like this, Lorenzo."

Lorenzo grabbed a leather jacket from the closet. "*Cherie*, this is your life, our life, yes? Our sons are grown, and they will mate soon, and start their own families. We will have grandchildren in our future, but that is not the same. If we choose to bring this infant into our life, then that is for us to decide and no one else."

He returned from the closet and stood behind her, as she rocked Grace in her arms. Looking over her shoulder, he peered down at the angelic face staring back at him, and it brought a smile to his face. "Look at her, *cherie*. She is beautiful. You know what her fate would have been. Even if her mortal mother had tried to raise her. That rarely ends well, and the children eventually take to the streets. She is ours now. Is she feeding well?"

Chantal was pleased with how Lorenzo beamed down at Grace, and totally accepted her as his child too. "*Oui*, she was sluggish at first, she fought me a bit. But she feeds easy now. I think she knows I am her new *maman*. Will your parents join us later?"

Lorenzo kissed the top of her head. "Yes, my father went to the camp to check things out and will be back any minute. My mother is still in their bedroom, I think, but they are both aware that your parents are expected momentarily. Dad said he'd give us a little time to meet with them privately, so they can enjoy their granddaughter. I already got a call from Sophia who wants to come over. I asked her to wait until after your parents had a chance to see her first."

Antonio appeared at the door in his starched white shirt and bow tie to announce that Chantal's parents had arrived and had been taken to the parlor. Lorenzo slid his arm around her waist. "Ready?"

Chantal closed her eyes and took a deep breath. "*Oui*."

Lorenzo led her down the grand stairs, but she stopped before entering the parlor. Looking down at Grace, it gave her courage to know she'd saved this infant. Looking at Lorenzo, she nodded that she was ready, and they entered the parlor together, to find her parents seated with glasses of Midnight in their hands.

"*Papa, Maman*, welcome back to Castello. Lorenzo and I have someone special we would like you to meet."

Chantal watched carefully as her *papa* stood, setting down his drink and giving her a stern glare. The sight of her holding a baby must be quite shocking.

"What is this, Chantal? I know I am not the most observant *papa*, but I am pretty sure you were not with child when you visited last week."

Chantal began to tremble slightly. He looked back at her with anger and confusion. "*Papa*, please listen and understand. Lorenzo and I were summoned to Council because this newborn was left at their doorstep. She is a half-breed. They asked us if we would take care of the child, or according to protocol, she would be destroyed.

You have raised me to do the right thing, to be loyal to our coven. I am the Queen of Medici. It is my duty to protect everyone in the coven. We have adopted this female child. Her name is Grace Medici. You have a granddaughter, *Papa*."

Henri backed away. "That is not my granddaughter, Chantal. I lay no claim to this half-breed. Valois blood does not run through her veins. She will lay no claim to the Valois fortune. These...offspring of the mortal and immortal unions are a blasphemy and should be left on the streets. You rescue her like a stray dog. I don't understand."

Chantal tensed up. She knew he'd resist the idea, but she didn't expect him to blatantly disclaim her. She felt the tears well in her eyes, but she refused to appear so weak before him. She felt Lorenzo's hand on her lower back and knew he would support her.

"How can you love *me* and not love my baby? How? I love her. I will continue to love her and raise her as my own." The emotion overwhelmed her, and she turned in Lorenzo's arms, clutching Grace to her chest.

Lorenzo embraced them both, as he soothed his mate. "This is our choice, Henri, and our path. She wasn't born to us, but we have adopted her, and she'll carry the Medici name. If you choose not to recognize her, that is your decision to make, however, my daughter won't know shame. She won't be shunned or looked down upon. If you can't find it in your heart to accept this child, then at least acknowledge her right to exist or you have no place here."

Chantal turned to face her father. She was going to stand up for her child. "I do not think like you, *Papa*. Generations have passed and we must strive to keep our race alive. She does have Valois blood in her veins, she has fed from me. I will not let you destroy a heart that will never know love and kindness. I certainly never thought you could be so cold to one who cannot defend themself. Lorenzo and I are in agreement about Grace. Shade and Kate support us as well." Chantal looked to her mother. "How can you call yourself Valois and watch an innocent infant be destroyed because of some arcane rule and ancient ways and thinking? I will love her."

Amelie wrung her hands. She'd like to go to her daughter and share in the joy of this new infant, but a half-breed? How could they ever present a half-breed in royal court?

“I'm sorry, Chantal. I will not go against my mate. Besides, the old ways have served us well. They are there for a reason."

Henri picked up his glass and emptied it of the Midnight, before setting it back down. "We will take our leave now. Please give our regards to the Medici and his queen. You are always welcome to come back home, Chantal, but the half-breed has no place in our chateau."

Chantal knew what she was about to say would be a defining moment in her life. She was being forced to choose sides now. Her voice was calm as she addressed her father. "If Grace is not allowed in your home, then neither am I. That is your choice, *Papa*, you have made your stand and I have made mine. If you leave now, you disown and lose your only daughter for eternity."

Amelie whimpered, as tears fell, and she held her fingertips to her lips. Henri puffed out his chest, as he bellowed loudly. "You would choose a half-breed over your own blood?" His eyes glared red. “I knew it was a mistake to allow you to mate with the Medici. They have corrupted your values and addled your brain with these ideas. Come, Amelie, say goodbye to your daughter." He didn’t give Amelie time to respond before he teleported them both out.

Chantal clutched Grace to her chest and felt her heart break. Falling to her knees, she shook, and Grace began to cry. Rocking back and forth on her knees, she wondered how this had happened. "What have I done? What have I done?"

For the first time in her life, she had spoken her convictions, and had gone against her father, but she wasn’t prepared for the pain she felt. She’d been taught to do as her mate commanded in all things. Lorenzo had given her the choice of taking Grace and she’d accepted, and in doing so, she had lost her family.

Lorenzo crouched down, soothing her and the infant who now felt her anguish. "Please, don't cry, *cherie*. He will come around with time. Your father is a stubborn man, but he won’t be able to go for long without his only daughter. Give them time."

Chantal looked back at him, her eyes reflecting her sadness. She appreciated his words of comfort, but Lorenzo didn’t know her father like she did.

14

Shade had returned from camp and rejoined Kate in their bedroom at Castello. He rather loved that Lorenzo and Chantal occupied their old room now, the same room that had been occupied by his parent's, centuries ago. As they left the room together and headed down the stairs, and the long hall to the parlor, Shade could feel Lorenzo's anxiety. He paused and could hear Henri's voice. He halted Kate in her tracks, knowing she could feel and hear the same things he did.

"Let Lorenzo and Chantal handle this. This was their choice, and I don't want to interfere unless Valois decides to get violent. But I will warn you, *mi amore*, all hell will break loose if he does!"

She nodded in agreement, and before they knew what had happened, they heard Chantal and the baby crying. As they entered the room, Shade saw Lorenzo crouching over his mate, as she held their new child. Chantal was falling apart, and Shade's temper started to boil over. Marching inside the room, he was livid. It was clear the old ways of thinking were still alive and well in Europe, and it would take time before the vampires moved to change their view.

"What in hell did he do? I have half a mind to leave and throttle his ass until he sees reason!"

Kate tugged at his arm. "Shade, no. Give them time. They love their daughter, she's their only child. I'm sure they'll come around in time."

Kate went to her son and daughter-in-law, and knelt next to them, as she laid her head on Lorenzo's shoulder. "Shh, please don't cry, Chantal. Your baby feels your anguish. Your parents have had a shock. As they see this child grow, and see the acceptance from the coven, they'll have a change of heart. We faced many in the beginning who didn't think we should bring Cory into our lives but look at him now. He lives freely among the warriors, and they treat him as one of their own. You have made the right choice. Your family has never been exposed to the half-breeds. Their reaction is to be expected."

Chantal raised her tear-stained face to the true Queen of Medici. Chantal knew better than most that her *papa* would stick to his beliefs, and her *maman* would never go against him.

"This is my fault. I have driven them away and now..." Hanging her head, she coddled Grace tightly. "She will never know the Valois love and honor. I have brought shame on my family." She stood as Lorenzo helped her and she felt embarrassed in front of Lorenzo's parents, and shame for going against her own father. She wanted to run from all the eyes that looked at her now.

Kate embraced her, the small infant between them. "There is never shame in doing what is right, or in standing up for what you believe in. Grace will know love, because you will show her, and she'll have honor and integrity because you'll teach her, just as you taught your sons. You aren't alone, Chantal."

Chantal looked at them, as their faces reflected pity and sadness. She backed away from Kate, still holding tightly to Grace who was restless and sobbing softly. "Lorenzo gave me a choice, and I chose Grace without a second thought. I promise you; I will love this child." She turned quickly and ran from the room and back up the stairs to the privacy of her bedroom. She needed to get away from them all and be with Grace and think.

Shade felt her anguish and pain. He knew Henri had destroyed a part of her, knocking down what little confidence she'd built. He'd broken her heart by making her choose. He looked to Lorenzo, who was hurting for Chantal, and he understood that pain as well.

"Henri has made a grave mistake. She stood up to him for once in her life, and he took her to task for it. I can't do a damn thing about this. I hope he will come to see things differently over time." He walked to the bar and poured himself a Midnight. "I know I have had some pretty serious arguments with my own daughters, but I don't know how any father could turn his back on his own flesh and blood." He downed the drink in one fluid swallow. "I know things have been difficult for you both lately. She needs you more than ever, Lorenzo. Don't let her push you away."

***

As Chantal entered their bedroom, she found Rosa waiting for her. The whole castle must know what had happened by now. She asked Rosa to take care of Grace while she showered and changed clothes.

Her whole body felt broken. Stripping, she removed the sapphire and diamond necklace and laid it on the vanity. She caught a glimpse of herself in the mirror, her eyes red, and her complexion splotchy. Quickly turning on the hot water, she got inside the shower and slid down into the corner, pulling her knees up to her chest. She tried to remember the words of advice Kate had given her. She wasn't sure of anything anymore. Could she just be a Medici? Could she turn her back on the Valois? Could she go the rest of her life without seeing her parents or the inside of the home where she grew up?

She didn't have answers to any of the questions. Pushing her wet hair back from her face, the pinkie ring glittered on her finger. Her *papa* had given her the solid gold ring, bearing the Valois crest, when she was 18. She'd never removed it since the day he slid it onto her pinkie. She removed the ring and threw it across the room. She'd never been happier than when she was raising their two sons, and now she had a chance to have that kind of joy back in her life. She had a daughter to raise and love. She'd show her parents loving this child made her fulfilled and happy, and maybe they'd come around or maybe not. All she had left was Lorenzo, Grace, and this huge castle. She loved them both and she'd do this, remain loving them. She quickly washed herself and got dressed, rushing to Grace. Dismissing Rosa, she pulled Grace into her arms and sat on their massive bed.

"I am so sorry, *mon petite ange*, your *maman* has had a bad evening. But I will always love you, no matter who says I cannot." Grace nuzzled into her neck and Chantal let her feed, and she felt calmness go through her. They'd be alright as long as they were together.

***

Lorenzo stood to follow her when Kate reached out and grabbed his arm. "Give her a moment, Lorenzo. Give her some space. She needs to make peace with this in her head, and her heart."

Lorenzo sighed, feeling helpless. "Why would he turn his back on his own daughter?"

Kate drew him to her. "Because he's hurting too, and he doesn't understand her choice. Chantal has never stood against him before. She's never dared to defy him, and when she finally did, he rejected her. She'll need you now more than ever, and I expect you to be there for her. Raising this child is a big responsibility, a lifelong commitment, and she can't do it alone."

Lorenzo nodded his head, as Kate continued, "Most half-breeds grow up feeling shame for something over which they had no control. Grace will have a head start in life. She'll never know that rejection and heartache, she'll never be cast out on the streets. You and Chantal have a chance to alter the course of how these children are managed in the future, and you make me proud. Now go to your mate, and your daughter, and let them both know they are loved."

Lorenzo made his way up the grand staircase to their master suite, to find Chantal lying in bed, and Grace feeding contentedly. "I can't remember ever seeing a more beautiful sight." He lay down next to her, and gently brushed the hair from her face. "We will be all right, *cherie*, you know that *si*? We will all be fine, you, me, and this baby. And any others who follow. This is our path to walk, and we walk it together."

Grace stopped feeding and struggled to look in his direction when she heard his voice. Chantal giggled softly. "That is your *papa*." Gently, she transferred the infant to his arms. "I am sorry for my outburst. I didn't mean to embarrass you in front of your family. I know that as long as Grace and I are together, with you at the head of this family, we will be fine. I would not change anything, Lorenzo."

He kissed her softly. "Nor would I, my *cherie*."

15

Donatella heard the rumors that spread across Italy and had created an uproar among the covens. Lorenzo and his mate had adopted a half-breed. Everyone well remembered when Shade had taken in his half-breed son, and although unprecedented, at least that child had been his own blood. This child that Lorenzo had taken had been abandoned at Council, and was in no way related to the Medici's, and yet they had decided to take the infant instead of letting it be destroyed, as was their tradition. She had heard Lorenzo had instructed the Council that they'd take any half-breeds abandoned in the future, although she had no way to verify that information. She relied solely on the gossip picked up by her two remaining house staff, as they were her only means of remaining in contact with what happened in the other covens. She was no longer included on anyone's social calendar. After the riff with the Medici's, she'd been even further isolated and shunned by the other covens. She'd learned to live meagerly, but the fortune that had been built up by her father, was dwindling. She had no additional means of income, and she was afraid she'd have to sell off the land and even her home before long.

After reviewing her finances, she knew she'd have to let the house maid go soon. She didn't know where she'd go if she was forced to sell her home, or how she'd make a living for herself. She'd been raised as a royal and expected to mate well. She could never have imagined her life would have turned out like this.

She'd heard that Shade and his mate were visiting Castello to see the new infant and felt like this may be her last chance. She'd swallowed her pride, and sent a messenger to Castello, requesting to see him. At this point, what did she have to lose?

***

Shade and Kate spent the evening with Lorenzo, Chantal, and Grace. Everyone was still recovering a bit from the blow that Henri had dealt to Chantal, but she had come around well to his response. She was tougher than she looked. Shade had heard her call her sons,

Christoph and Henry, telling them they had a new sister, and be sure to come home soon to see her. Both boys had already heard through the gossip channels that their mother had brought home a half-breed infant, and they had both reassured her they'd get there as soon as they could break away. Shade was relieved to see both his grandsons had been accepting of this new addition to their family. He'd watched Chantal and Lorenzo all evening, and felt the love emerge from both of them. He liked seeing them getting their lives back on track and renewing their commitment to each other. Sophia and Bianca had visited with them as well, eager to see the newest member of the family. He sat back and enjoyed watching the fuss the women made over the baby.

As Sophia and her daughter left, Lorenzo headed to camp and Chantal excused herself to put Grace down for the night, Shade found himself alone with Kate. He was refreshing their drinks when Antonio appeared in the room to announce there was a messenger for Shade. He scrunched his eyebrows and looked at Kate, shrugging.

"Send them in, Antonio. I will receive them here in the parlor."

The messenger stepped into the parlor and bowed his head in respect to the Medici. He'd seen him a few times from a distance, but this was the first time he'd been in his presence. "Master, I have been hired to deliver a message from the Alizzi."

He saw the scowl cross the Medici's face, and his queen rolled her eyes and looked away from him. The Medici nodded in his direction, indicating he was to proceed with delivering the message.

"She has respectfully requested an audience with you. She said she understands she isn't welcome in this home but hopes you will honor her request to speak with you, out of respect for the bond your two great families once shared."

Shade looked confused. *Dona wants to see me? What the fuck did that insane bitch want with me?* She hadn't contacted him in one hundred years, and now, out of the blue, she requested an audience. He was curious. Perhaps this could be something about her land.

"The Alizzi has paid you for your services?"

The messenger looked down at his feet. "I... uh, I owed her a favor, so I did not charge her for the service."

Shade huffed. "Sounds familiar." Calling for Antonio, Shade instructed him to pay the messenger before leaving. "You may return to the Alizzi and advise her that if I decide to honor her request, I will arrive before sunrise. *Grazie*. You are dismissed."

As the messenger scurried from the room, pocketing the coins, Shade downed the Midnight in his glass and poured another. He didn't say a word, but he could feel that fire boiling slowly inside his mate. "Go ahead. Tell me why I shouldn't go."

Kate stared back at him. "Really? I could make a list."

She stood from her chair and paced the room. "What could she possibly want from you after all this time? Whatever it is, I can't imagine any good coming from it. Lorenzo never speaks of her, never even mentions her name. Does Chantal even know? Lorenzo and Chantal are just getting back on track, it seems. Please don't let that woman back into our lives."

Shade watched her pace. He had to bite back his smile, because he was still amused by her anger, and that crimson hair flinging from side to side when she turned on her heels. Her face was flushed a beautiful pink. "Have I told you how much I love you today? Because when you get angry, you look fucking beautiful."

When she stopped and spun to stare at him, he held up his hand in apology. "I know, I know. I am just making you hot under the collar. Listen to me a moment. Dona has nothing. I've kept my scouts on her for a very long time. She is destitute. She has been shunned by every social circle. She never leaves her estate. Here is my guess. She wants to sell her territory and move on. Who better to buy her land than me?"

Kate closed her eyes and took a deep breath. "You think she wants to sell? I hadn't thought of that. It's possible, of course, but I still don't trust her. You're going to go, aren't you? I can see it in your face."

Shade gave her a sly grin. "You want her gone, do you not, *mi amore*? If I buy her land, she will be forced to move away. It is not just her estate; it is all of Umbria. The Medici controls everything north of Florence now. This would extend our coven further south. If this is her proposal, do you want another master taking it?"

She sighed as she listened to his argument. She was well aware that in the last century, the Borgia coven had slowly taken over all the covens in the south, and they weren't an ally of the Medici. If it was Dona's intention to sell her land, it would be foolish of them not to buy it from her.

"No, of course not. I'm sorry. I shouldn't let my emotions rule my decisions, especially after so much time, but I have no reason to trust her. Go. See what she wants. Just make sure she keeps her hands to herself."

He went to her and picked her up in his arms, spinning her around. "Woman, you worry too much. Now, I am going up to change into my leathers and go. I will not be long." He kissed her before setting her down on her feet. "*Ti amo, mi amore*."

After changing, he teleported out to the Alizzi. He flew over her estate, noticing the general decay of the gardens, and the lack of upkeep on the house. She was sorely in need of help with this place. He landed at the front door and slammed the door knocker hard several times, watching the rust fall from the once elegant entrance way.

The manservant rushed to open the door. They rarely received company. He was shocked to see the Medici standing on the other side. He bowed his head. "Master, please come in. I'll take you to the parlor and notify Mistress Alizzi of your presence." He led Shade into the sparsely furnished parlor and offered him a seat. The room was clean, but beyond that, there wasn't much to be said about it. Shade wasn't shocked, he knew she was in bad shape, and for just a second, he felt a pang of regret, but it quickly disappeared when he remembered what she'd done to his son. As he took a seat, he felt the antique chair creak and hoped it would hold his weight.

The manservant inquired, "May I bring you a Midnight?"

"Midnight will be fine, *grazie*." Shade took the drink, taking only a small sip before setting the glass on the small table beside him.

***

Dona received the news that Shade was here and was caught off-guard. She didn't expect him to respond so quickly. She had her maid help her into one of her finer dresses, and quickly touched up her hair and makeup. She hurried down the stairs and into the parlor. She entered the room with as much grace and elegance as she could muster, as he stood to greet her. She nodded slightly in his direction and extended her hand.

"I am grateful for the visit, Medici. I must say, I did not expect such a quick response."

Shade took her hand in his and bowed his head slightly. Waiting until she took a seat, he sat back down again and stared at her. The dress looked worn, and he wondered how long it had been since she'd had new clothing.

"I am only here in Florence for a short visit, and my time is valuable, so please let us skip the formalities and get down to business. What is it you wanted to see me about?"

Dona was flustered as she sat across from him. "Yes, of course, I appreciate you finding time for me. First, let me say congratulations on your new grandchild. As always, I am impressed with the generosity and openness of your heart. It is long overdue that we recognize the half-breeds and take responsibility. I commend you, and your son, for his actions."

He nodded. "*Grazie*. But I had nothing to do with it. Lorenzo and his mate, Chantal, decided on their own to raise the child." Shade leaned back in the chair, crossing one leg over the other knee. He stared back at her intensely.

Dona picked at her skirt, avoiding his eyes. "Shade...we have known each other a long time. We played together as children. I know our fathers had a plan for us, one that would have helped both covens, and provide protection to our mutual territories. I have accepted that you rejected this plan for our mating, but still, we remained friends well into our adult years. I don't think I have ever apologized for my reprehensible conduct with Lorenzo, but please know I have had a long time to think about it, and I truly regret the poor choices I made. I hope you understand I was desperate, I felt desperate, and my decision reflected that. I am not asking for forgiveness, because I don't think what I did is forgivable, but I am hoping that somewhere in your heart, you remember how things used to be and you can remember a time when you did not hold me in such low regard."

Shade just sat there, staring at her. She was sure taking her damn time getting to the point. Shade uncrossed his leg, and his boot hit the floor, creating an echo in the room. *How the mighty had fallen.*

"What happened is long past, but I will never forgive you, Dona. Let's make that very clear." He stood up then, and paced the room, staying close to her chair. He towered over her as she sat meek as a mouse, but he, more than most, was well aware of the sly fox inside her. "Why am I here?"

Dona stood. "Please, sit. I have swallowed the last of my pride asking you here. Do not make me get on my knees. Please."

Shade threw back his head and laughed "You have managed to be on your knees for most of your life. Spit it out, woman! Why am I here?"

She felt defeated before she even asked, but he was her last hope. "I wanted to ask you, beg you, for a loan. I am living on what little remains of my father's fortune. As you can see, the estate is in need of repair, and I can't afford the upkeep. My coven is gone. I have two house staff that have remained with me. I pay them very little, so they stay more out of loyalty, which I know I do not deserve. I am begging you, Medici. A few million is all I ask. For a man of your sizable wealth, it is nothing. Your properties would generate that much revenue in a single day. The money would allow me to stay here, and you have an ally on your border. Is that not worth something?"

Shade wasn't expecting this. She wanted a loan? And how the hell would she ever pay it back? She had some nerve crawling to him for money. He owed her nothing. He paced slowly around the room, making her suffer a bit more as she waited for his response. "Why don't you sell me your territory, then you will have enough to make a life for yourself?"

She followed him with her eyes. "And where would I go, Medici? I am part of no coven. My manservant brings me feeders. I don't ask where he finds them. I can't hunt. I was never trained to do so. At least I am known here, and the other covens have taken pity. At least I have their pity. If I were to sell the land, I would have to leave here, and the few people who still take pity. I fear I would not survive very long."

Shade thought about that for a moment. She made a good point. Even with money, she'd be vulnerable with no coven and no mate. Not his problem. She made this mess, not him. "No, Donatella. I will not give you money. You destroyed any chance of remaining in my good graces when you betrayed my son. That shame, you brought on yourself. When you are ready to sell, call me, otherwise, I will take my leave."

As he headed for the door, he turned to look at her one last time. She still disgusted him. What she had done he could never forgive.

Dona followed after him. "Please! You don't understand! There is no one else I can go to. I am begging you, Shade. If for no other reason, in memory of the friendship our fathers once shared. Please, reconsider, a smaller amount perhaps? One million?"

Shade stopped and stood with his back to her. It wasn't in his nature to leave a female this vulnerable. He closed his eyes, pondered her request, but couldn't bring himself to help her.

"Our *padres* are both long gone." He turned to look at her, and she looked broken and weak. "I will offer one thing."

She looked back at him, tears welling in her eyes. "Anything!"

As he saw her tears stream down her face, he knew they weren't fake. "I will pay your servants wages. If nothing else, they have been loyal to you and deserve a decent wage. I will have my accountant come by tomorrow and arrange payment. It will come directly from me to them. Your hands will not touch it. It is all I will offer." He turned his back to her and teleported out, straight back to Castello.

Dona collapsed in a heap onto the floor as he left her. She had nothing left, and no one else to go to. Her manservant responded, helping her to her feet. He'd overheard the Medici's offer. At least he'd be able to stay with her now. She'd slowly reduced his pay until he was no longer able to support his own family. He hadn't told the Alizzi that he was planning to leave. At least, now, he could afford to stay.

16

Shade teleported back to Castello and could see all the warriors training at camp. He spotted Lorenzo and Alfie with ease. He knew he should be down there with them, making an appearance with the newest class of warriors, but Kate would be waiting to hear the outcome of his meeting with Dona. Teleporting into the grand foyer, Antonio appeared quickly, asking if he could be of service. Shade shook his head, as he quickly made his way up the stairs. He could hear the women's voices coming from the bedroom he'd once shared with Kate. He opened the door slowly, and stood for a moment, watching his mate and his daughter-in-law fawning over the infant. Stepping into the room, they both looked up.

"I hope I am not interrupting. I just wanted to let you know I have returned, *mi amore*. I wish to speak with you whenever you are done." He leaned in to look at his newest grandchild, and softly touched her cheek. "You are such a beautiful angel."

Grace locked eyes with him, as if she understood his every word and gave him a smile and coos. Kate laughed as she slid her arm around his waist, leaning into him. "It would appear you haven't lost your touch, lover. Females of any age are not immune to your charms. Come, let's go talk." She tugged at his arm, as she led him back to the bedroom they now shared. "So, tell me about your visit."

"Well, at least you are in a good mood. Things did not go as I expected. Her summons to speak with me was not about selling her territory but to beg for money, a few million, in fact." He flopped down in a chair and laid his head back, closing his eyes as his hand automatically raked through his long-disheveled curls.

Kate looked at him, surprised by what she heard. "She wanted money? Are you kidding?"

As she spoke the words, it struck her how desperate Donatella must be to ask Shade for money or was it just that she thought she could still manipulate him, as she'd once manipulated Lorenzo. As she finished her thought, she heard her son's footsteps on the stairs. He was on his way to see Chantal and the baby, but he stopped in their open door. Kate looked quickly between her son and her mate. "Lorenzo! You're home early."

Lorenzo nodded in his father's direction. "My father reminded me I have obligations outside the camp. I'm trying hard to be a better mate. You guys okay? Looks like I interrupted something."

Shade lifted his head and looked in his son's direction. "We were having a conversation about my whereabouts this night. And I am sitting here contemplating if you should know about it. After all, you are master and king of this territory." He reached inside his leather jacket and pulled out a pack of cigarettes. "I need a damn smoke, that is one thing I am sure about."

Kate motioned for him to enter. "Come in, Lorenzo. I'm sure this will impact you." He looked confused but entered his parents' bedroom and sat on the bed, as his father lit up. It was rare to see his father smoke in the house, so he knew whatever he had on his mind, it was bothering him.

"What's going on?"

Kate sat next to him on the bed. "Your father got a request to see Donatella."

Lorenzo looked angry. "And he went?"

Kate stroked his arm. "He did. She wanted money."

Lorenzo looked at his father. "Are you giving her money?"

Shade wasn't surprised his son still harbored so much anger against the Alizzi. "I did not give her what she asked for. She wanted a loan for a couple of million." He took a long drag on his cigarette before he began. "The house is falling apart around her, and the grounds have had no attention in years. The inside is bare to the bone. She has obviously sold everything that is worth a dime. She admitted as much to me. I went there thinking she wanted to sell the territory, but she isn't budging on that."

He stood and walked to the window, opening it, exhaling the smoke as he stood and looked out over the gardens. "I offered to pay her servants' wages. She only has two. That is all, nothing more. At least she will not be left alone in her villa. She has been shunned. And somehow, I feel responsible for that."

Kate followed him with her eyes as he paced. "Why should you feel responsible? She's suffering the consequences of her own actions. She betrayed the people who befriended her, she betrayed

Lorenzo. How could we ever trust her again after that? How many years had she planned to trick him? Did her ruse start as soon as he came here as a child? Was she plotting even then? You have been more than generous, offering to pay the salaries of her staff. At least she's not left alone."

She looked at Lorenzo. "What do you think?"

Lorenzo shook his head. "I do feel pity, and I wish things weren't so bad for her, but I could never trust her again."

Shade nodded in agreement. "I still don't trust her, son, not after what she did to you, and the way she did it. I will never trust her again. But if she can't pay her servants, they will be forced to leave. They did nothing wrong, and they deserve a decent wage to support and feed their own families. She will never see the money. It won't touch her hands. I will make sure my accountants set it up for them, and she will not have access."

***

Chantal had gotten Grace to sleep and decided to head to the first floor and wait for Lorenzo to return from camp. As she was approaching the stairs, she smelled cigarette smoke, and could feel Lorenzo's presence. She heard voices coming from the bed chamber his parents occupied and headed in that direction. She was picking up bits of their conversation as she approached the door. They were discussing the Alizzi, the mistress whose territory bordered their own. She'd overheard enough rumors over the years to know there had been an alliance that went back to Shade's youth, but something had happened that put a strain on the relationship. In her family, she was raised to never question, so she'd never asked for details, and Lorenzo had never brought it up. She quietly pushed open the door and stepped inside the room. "Am I interrupting?"

Lorenzo held his hand out to her. "Come, *cherie*. We were just discussing my father's visit to the Alizzi. She wanted money, and large sums of it. My father agreed to pay the salaries of her few remaining house staff. I guess I have assumed you were aware my father was originally under contract to mate the Alizzi. It was a contract he didn't wish to honor. The Alizzi had always been our ally until an incident that involved me a long time ago, before I ever met you. I will discuss that with you in private. We used to protect their land, but after the occurrence, my father cut all ties. She was struggling to make ends meet even then, I'm sure she's desperate for money now. Her coven is gone, and she has no businesses, no source of income beyond what her father left her. I don't question her need for the money. We're just surprised after everything she's done; she asked my father for this favor."

Chantal took his hand and listened to him speak. "I am sorry to have interrupted, but I felt your anguish. It concerned me. I have heard a few things over the years but did not know the details."

He kissed her forehead. "We have no secrets, *cherie*. The past is past, and I had not heard from her in all these years. The incident with her is not something I like to talk about. My father has a softer heart, I think. I'm not sure I would have shown the compassion to pay for her house staff."

Lorenzo turned to his father. "So, what next? Do you think it's just a matter of time before she's forced to sell her territory to you? It would make her even more vulnerable. I'll admit, I'm conflicted about it. I have no regard for her, but then again, she is an ally, and her territory does provide us with a buffer between the Medici and the Borgia covens. She betrayed our trust, but she's no enemy and has no power."

Shade put the cigarette out in an ashtray. "Well, I feel no danger from her whatsoever. And she now knows if she wants to sell, I am willing to buy. I believe, in time, it will come down to that. She has no other choice. I think we leave well enough alone."

Lorenzo nodded. In his head, he was remembering the kindness she showed him as a young boy when he first came to camp and missed his mother. He remembered how she had stepped in, and filled the void, helping him through those early days. Was there good in Dona? Or had she been plotting even then. He was a hardened warrior now, and he'd learned the hard way to be careful who he let into his heart. "Then it is done."

17

Kate and Shade had spent several days with their adopted granddaughter, and helping Chantal to get the nursery set up, before returning home to Bel Rosso. As much as she'd enjoyed seeing her children, and grandchildren, it always felt good to be home. Bel Rosso was as much a part of her as Shade was. Kate couldn't imagine living anywhere else.

Gi was there to greet them, and Theresa set to work immediately, getting things unpacked and a load of laundry going. Kate could tell Shade was eager to get back into the camp as well, even though Christoph had things well in hand. She followed him into his office as he prepared to leave.

"The baby will be good for them, don't you think? Chantal will feel like she has a purpose now, and Lorenzo is trying hard to be more attentive."

"*Si, mi amore*, she is much attached already. Lorenzo has made some effort as well, and that helps out greatly. His priorities were a bit confused, to say the least. You can see things are better between them. What are your plans for this evening?"

She sat on the edge of his desk, as he scrambled through papers. She'd have thought that for someone to have lived as long as he had, he'd have found a way to be organized by now, and it brought a smile to her lips. She'd have him no other way.

"I think I should call Natalia while you're in camp tonight. I doubt she's heard the news. Chantal already called the boys, but I'm sure Christoph will be interested in hearing the details from you as well."

He shuffled the papers and opened drawers in his desk, trying to find some legal papers from Jules. "*Si,* they now have a sister, and I expect them to visit her as well."

He stopped what he was doing and looked at her sitting on his desk. "And no, I am not disorganized, it is called organized chaos. And for the record, I miss my Nattie. Damn, when was the last time we even saw her. She needs to come home for a visit. I am so proud of her, but I miss her. I miss Marcello too. I know they have their duties, but I thought this Council would be a bit more lenient."

She leaned over and kissed him as he flipped through several legal documents. "Jules could take care of all of this for you, you know. I'll ask Natalia to come visit us when I call her. Maybe she can get away. Now, get to the camp. The sooner you finish up there, the quicker you can come back to me."

He left the folder where it lay on the heap of papers on his desk. He knew where everything was, and if anyone would organize it...well, it would be like his wardrobe. He'd never be able to find a damn thing. Kissing her, leaning her back over the desk, he growled. "I always come home to you. Now, give Nattie my love, and tell her to get home."

He walked out of the office and off to camp. He still made the walk to camp every single night; it was one of his quiet pleasures every evening. Walking in the night air, under the moon, off to be what he was born to be...a warrior.

***

Kate followed him out the office and encountered Shannon who grabbed her up in a hug. "I heard about the baby. I can't wait to see her!"

Kate laughed as she felt ambushed by her dearest friend. "She's a jewel, Shannon. How anyone could have abandoned her is a mystery to me. I'm sure Lorenzo and Chantal will come for a visit as soon as things are settled. They need to establish a routine for the baby first."

Shannon was giddy with excitement. "I saw the pictures you sent. I can't wait to hold her. It's been a long time since we've had a baby in the house."

Kate nodded. "It has been. You want to hang with me for a while? I'm going to call Natalia."

She shook her head. "No, but thanks. Luca and I are going out for a while."

Kate raised one eyebrow, and Shannon laughed as she turned on her heels and returned to her bedroom to get dressed. Kate took the stairs to the second floor and ran into Christoph, on his way to the camp.

"P Bear home?"

Kate gave him a hug, which he returned, lifting her off her feet. "He's on his way to the camp now. He can fill you in on your new sister."

Christoph laughed. "Who would have thought I'd have a new sister after all this time. Life is never dull with the Medici's."

As he released her and headed downstairs, Kate responded, "I think that's an understatement."

She checked with Theresa to see if she needed any help before returning to her bedroom. She tapped the computer screen that was flush against the wall and tapped in the number for the Council. The Council members weren't allowed to have their own individual phones, but they could be reached. The image came into focus as one of the staff answered the call.

"May I speak with Ivory please?"

The staffer nodded, recognizing Ivory's mother. "Hold on please, while I locate her."

Kate waited patiently, folding a load of clean laundry as she waited for her daughter to appear on the screen. After about five minutes, she saw Natalia, wearing the off-white robe that obscured so much of her beautiful face.

"Is everything okay, Mommy?"

Kate smiled back at her. She noticed whenever any of her adult children were nervous about something, they reverted to calling her mommy instead of mom. "Everything is more than okay. I have some wonderful news."

Natalia pushed the hood from her head, making her thick, brown locks visible. "Really? What's going on?"

Kate gave her a sly grin. "Your brother, Lorenzo, is a father again."

Natalia's face reflected the shock as her mouth formed an O shape, and her eyes were open wide. "What? No one told me Chantal was pregnant! I've had no visions of another birth."

Kate shook her head. "She wasn't pregnant. Someone abandoned a newborn half-breed on the Council doorsteps in Florence. They were going to dispose of the child, as is protocol, but decided since Shade had taken in his own half-breed son, maybe the Medici's would be interested in taking this one. So, it's official,

Chantal and Lorenzo have adopted her, and she's recorded as their adopted daughter, Grace Medici."

Natalia clapped her hands, as the smile spread across her face. "That's amazing! I'm so happy for them. Can you send me some pictures?"

Kate nodded. "I'll send them now. I didn't want to send them from Florence until I could talk to you."

Kate pulled up the photos on her phone and sent them to Natalia, as Kate listened to her squeal in delight with each image.

"Mommy, she's beautiful! And to think she would have been destroyed."

Kate nodded. "But where would they go? Look at how Cory lived before your father found him, and Cory was a survivor. He fared better than most. Can you imagine the life of a half-breed female on the streets?"

Natalia hung her head. "Yes, I can imagine it, and it's an abomination what we do to our own kind."

Kate smiled back at her. "Well, if it makes you feel any better, Lorenzo and Chantal told the European Council that they'd take all of the abandoned half-breeds in the future. The Council doesn't think there are many, but who knows? I mean, no one really keeps track of them. They've never been recognized or recorded as vampire births."

Natalia nodded. "I'm all too aware. It's always bothered me."

Kate looked back at her quizzically. "Then do something about it, daughter. You're the only one of us who can."

Natalia stared back at her, an idea formulating in her brain. "I can't do it alone. Changing the bylaws requires a majority vote by the Council."

Kate winked at her. "I have faith in your powers of persuasion."

Natalia bit at her lip. "Mommy, there may not always be a family that wants to take them in, like Lorenzo and Chantal. I can work to change the bylaws, so the infants aren't destroyed if they're abandoned by the mortal world, but the vampire culture still rejects them as well. Changing hearts and minds takes time. We'd need some means to care for them. The Council would never be able to raise them. I'd need an orphanage or something, and it would have to be staffed, and protected. That takes money, and a lot of it. Not sure the Council even has the funds for that."

Kate looked back at her daughter. "Natalia, if money and protection are your two obstacles, don't you think your father holds the key? I don't know how many more years we will have Cory. He's really showing his age now, but I know your father dearly loves him, and only regrets he didn't find him sooner."

Natalia agreed. "Maybe with the DNA databanks we keep now, we could identify which family sired the half-breed, and work with them to slowly accept the idea of adoption. Yeah, it's worth a try. Is Daddy home?"

"He's in the camp. We just got home, and you know your father, he couldn't wait to get back to the camp. I'll call him." She sent the message telepathically, asking Shade to return to the house.

***

Shade and Christoph were working the new recruits together. He'd planned to head out later tonight and check on the Dead House with Theo, but he needed to assure himself things were running smoothly in the camp first. He kept his eyes on the females, but it seemed their skills now easily rivaled those of the males. The gender mix of warriors was nearing 50/50, and he was proud of that.

He was ready to head into D.C. when he heard Kate's soft voice inside his head, beckoning him home. He teleported inside the house and took the steps two at a time, entering the bedroom to see his daughter's beautiful face on the large screen. He kissed Kate and stood smiling at the screen. "My Nattie! I miss you!"

Natalia beamed back at him. "Daddy, I miss you too. Mom was just telling me about the new addition to the family. So, I'm an auntie once again. I have an idea, and it's going to be a long shot, but I'll need your help to pull it off."

"*Si*, you know I will do anything for you." He raked his hand through his curls. "Let's hear your idea."

"What if I could introduce a new bylaw to the Council, one that would force recognition of the half-breeds? We can't force the immortal family to take the abandoned child, because their life might not be any better than if they were left on the streets. But with our DNA banks, we could find the male who sired the half-breed, and at least give them the option to take the child. If they refuse, we will need an orphanage, staffed with wet feeders, nannies, and tutors. We need a way to prepare the half-breeds for integration into our culture as they aged. I mean, look at Cory, and what a contribution he was able to make. How many have we lost that could have been saved? If I make the proposal and put it up for vote, the Council will need to know I had the funding for an orphanage, or the new bylaw would never be passed. So, what do you think? Can you allocate land, and build us a facility, staff it, and assign warriors for protection? It would be a lot of money, Daddy, and you know not everyone will be happy about it."

Shade sat on the bed, as Kate curled up next to him, as he listened to Natalia explain her proposal. He could hear the excitement in her voice. She'd done some amazing things with Council here in the States that had positively impacted the covens. This was what he'd wanted for his children, to give them the power to change their world and make it better for their kind.

"We have money, Nattie, I am not concerned about that. I will contact Jules. Let's get him involved in resolving any legal issues. He can oversee the funding as well. The proposal to Council I leave up to you. There is a large piece of land adjoining the Council. I have held it in the event Council was to ever need it. It is yours, my princess. Get your plans drawn up as to what you want, and if you get approval, we will see that it is built. Staffing will take some work. They will have to be selected carefully. Of course, the warriors are a given. You handle the Council, and I will take care of the rest, deal?"

She nodded enthusiastically. "Thanks, Daddy! This will change lives!"

He looked at her face, reflecting the excitement she felt for this project. This was what she was born to do, and he'd help her. "*Si*, that is your gift to our world, Nattie. I will contact Enzo as well, he may be able to provide us with tutors once we get established, and we have plenty of contacts for wet feeders. I am so proud of you. Now, on a completely different subject. When the hell are you coming home?"

"Soon! I promise. Maybe I can get away next weekend? Marcello said he had some business to check on in the camp, so he could escort me."

He smiled and squeezed Kate tightly. He didn't miss the fact her voice softened when she spoke Marcello's name. "Well, that would be the best news I have heard in a while, both of you in one visit. I am sure Luca and Shannon will be glad to hear it. I think Luca misses his cousin more than I do. *Ti amo*, princess. Get busy! You have a lot on your plate."

Natalia blew them both a kiss. "I love you so much! And thanks again, Daddy. See you soon." The screen faded to black as Kate slid her arms around him, kissing his neck.

"Thank you. This will change the future for so many."

He snuggled into her neck and lay back on the bed, pulling her along. "Don't thank me yet. She still has to get through Council, and that will be no easy task. If she is successful, I will need your help as well, you know. I can't do any of this without you."

Pulling her on top of his chest, he looked into her eyes, so beautiful and brown. Pushing her crimson hair behind her ears, he smiled. "Do you think Nattie, and Marcello are closer than she lets on?"

Kate pursed her lips. "I've often wondered the same thing. Marcello always seemed drawn to her, but he kept his distance when he was here in the camp. I never asked, but I assumed you saw it too, and it was why you chose him to take the role as Commander of the warriors at Council. Natalia knew from a young age she was destined for Council, and a life of solitude, so she has always held her emotions close to the heart. She's never said anything to me. Does it concern you?"

He felt his heart crack a bit that Natalia might never know the intimacy of true love, might never know the love of holding her own *bambino*. She'd never be allowed to mate. "I accepted a long time ago she would be where she is right now. When the Council requested warriors, I knew exactly who I wanted to go with her. It wasn't easy giving up Marcello. But deep in my heart, I felt better knowing they were together. He will always protect her, no matter what. I have seen the way they both look at each other, their exchanged glances. A warrior needs love too. When Fiamma died, Marcello got a glimpse at losing someone who meant more to him than just a fellow warrior. I think he realized there was much more to life than just defending Medici. It was almost as if their paths were destined to cross. I have no concerns, and if there is something between them, I will be grateful. They both need each other."

She laid her head on his chest, listening to the sound of his heart. "Then I hope they've found each other. If she has his heart, and she's able to help these half-breed children, maybe it will make up for the path not followed. I know she loves what she does, and she's happy, but I want her to know the joy that love brings too, not just the joy of her accomplishments."

He smiled and kissed the top of her head. "You are a hopeless romantic, *bel.* You want everyone to be in love like us."

She looked up at him. "They should be so lucky."

18

Natalia started working on a draft for the revision of the Council bylaws that would make it illegal to abandon or destroy the half-breeds. She knew this would be a tough fight as it was contrary to their history, but preserving their species was vital. Even if the half-breeds couldn't produce new vampires, they could play a role in strengthening the covens. Jules had been working with her to draft the legal language, and she knew she had her father's support in building a facility that would cost the Council nothing.

She finished packing a few things for the weekend. She didn't need much, since her mother kept everything she needed in her bedroom, as if she'd just stepped out for a minute, and still lived there full-time. She heard a light tap on her door, and answered to see Marcello, out of his Council leathers, and dressed in jeans.

"You ready, Nattie?"

She smiled at him. No one called her Nattie, or even Natalia inside these walls. Here she was Ivory, but she loved hearing her name on his lips. "Let me grab my bag."

She went to pick up the small overnight duffel, and he picked it up for her and slung it over his shoulder. Without asking, he slid his arm around her waist and pulled her close as they teleported out to Bel Rosso. As they approached, he circled over the estate, taking in the aerial view of the camp, the vineyards, and the acres of fields where the flowers were cultivated. Everything had been harvested now, but the fallow earth had its own raw beauty as the fields lay dormant in preparation for winter. There were a few horses in the pasture who responded as they passed over them, and Marcello could see Aegis following them from the ground, prancing in a circle from time to time, as she waited to greet Natalia.

Marcello laughed. "Looks like you have a greeting party."

Natalia looked down to see the wolf, with her mate close by. Studying the animals that were attached to her mother, sister, and niece was another area that Natalia was responsible for. The Council had no recorded history of vampires with the gift of animalism. They had all been shocked to discover the animals that bound themselves to their mother were all still alive, as if they too were somehow immortal.

"Let's land here." She pointed to a plot of land in the backyard, near the pool her mother had built for them even before she was born. The pool had been emptied for the upcoming winter, and Natalia wondered if her parents even used the pool. She and her sister and brother had spent long hours playing in the pool and wandering the acres of Bel Rosso.

Marcello landed softly, and set her down, kissing her cheek. Even here, he knew to be discreet. "I have some things I need to do in camp, but once I'm done, I'll let you know. Maybe you can get away."

She winked at him. "Maybe."

He laughed as he headed for the camp. "You're a tease, Natalia Medici, and don't pretend otherwise."

She giggled as she walked inside the house, calling out, "Mommy! I'm home!"

Kate heard her daughter, and ran for the back door, arms open wide as mother and daughter hugged. "I'm so glad you're home!"

"Is Daddy here?"

Kate shrugged. "In the camp. He knows you're coming and said he wouldn't stay long. Want to come in, sit by the fire?"

Natalia looked wistfully out the back door. "You know, I think I'd like to go outside. We never leave Council. I almost forget what fresh air smells like."

Kate nodded. "Okay, let me grab a jacket. There are still some late blooming things in the garden."

Gi was already there with her jacket and asked Natalia if she needed an extra wrap. "I'm good, Gi, thanks."

Kate took her daughter's hand as they walked outside, finding the narrow footpath, lit by the landscape lighting, which wound its way through the garden. "Tell me how things are going."

Natalia shared with her an account of what she was working on for her Council presentation, and how much help Jules had been, as they walked through the garden. They made their way down the path and ended up at the bench that was placed years ago in the spot still called the baby's garden. Kate took a seat, and pulled

Natalia down next to her, as Natalia gave the details of how she planned to change the Council bylaws.

Kate looked at her daughter's face in the moonlight. "Are you happy, Natalia?"

Natalia looked back at her with surprise. "What a strange thing to ask. Of course, I'm happy. Have I done something to make you think otherwise?"

Kate shook her head, "No, of course not. It's just, you're the child I see the least, and I'm always concerned for your well-being. Not your safety, I know you're perfectly safe, it's just...I don't want you to feel lonely, or alone."

Natalia gave her a shy smile. "Well, maybe I'm not completely alone."

Kate nodded. "Well, no, I didn't mean that you were alone. You have the other Council, and your work is important. I meant..."

Natalia laughed. "I know what you meant, Mom, you and Dad both. You think I need love in my life. I don't have what you and Dad have, but I have enough."

Kate looked at her, scrunching up her brows. "Well, that sounds cryptic. What are you telling me, daughter?"

Natalia chuckled, her laughter carrying on the night air. "Who said I'm telling you anything?"

Kate leaned back on the bench. "I know love when I see it, Natalia. And I have watched you every day from the moment of your birth. Do you think I don't see the exchanged glances and secret smiles between you and Marcello? Do you think it's pure coincidence that your father took the SIC of his beloved camp and re-assigned him to Council? Talk to me."

Natalia looked down at her feet, and her mother could see the blush in her cheeks even in the moonlight. "I do love him, Mommy. And he loves me. You know we can't be open about it, but we find time to be together."

Kate slid her arms around her daughter's shoulders and leaned her head against hers. "Then I'm happy for both of you."

Natalia looked at her. "Do you think Daddy would be mad?"

Kate kissed her cheek and whispered, "No, I promise you."

Natalia smiled back at her. "Good, I'm glad you know. I didn't like keeping it a secret from you."

The two women leaned back on the bench, as Kate still clutched her hand. The small garden statue of the angel that marked the grave of the baby she'd lost over a century ago was aged by the weather and covered in moss. After all this time, seeing the small grave still broke her heart.

"Maybe if the old Council had someone like you who was fighting for the half-breeds, I would have had someone to help me with that pregnancy. You need to think about that too, Natalia. The doctors we have specialize in vampire issues only. We had that doctor that Alec and Rissa recommended, and he brought me the pills. Maybe they would have worked if I hadn't taken the extra pills that Rissa poisoned.

As Natalia looked at the small statue, she felt a wave of dizziness, the feeling she got before her gift of third eye was about to reveal something to her. "Mommy, he wasn't real. That doctor wasn't a real doctor."

Kate sat up straight on the bench. "What? What do you see, Natalia?"

Natalie placed her fingertips at her temples. The visions she received always caused a mild headache. "Rissa hired him. He was an actor. She gave him the pills to give to you. They were all poison."

Kate felt a wave of nausea as she remembered that time in her life. They'd let this imposter into their home. Even after all these years, she felt violated. Her voice cracked when she answered, "I don't understand. Why would she do such a thing?"

Natalia pushed hard against her temples, as the headache throbbed. "Alec didn't want Daddy distracted."

Kate looked startled. "Alec? Alec knew?"

Natalia nodded her head. "He told her to bring the feeder. Does that mean anything to you?"

Kate felt her anger rise at the memory of the voluptuous feeder that Rissa had brought to the house. "Alec told her to do that?"

Natalia nodded again. "You were still mortal then. He was hoping you'd leave Daddy if you saw him having sex with the feeder."

Kate felt the wave of nausea again. "What else do you see?"

Silent tears fell down Natalia's cheeks for the brother she never knew. "He wanted the baby gone. He needed Daddy to focus on what was happening in D.C. and not be distracted. He told Rissa how to make the pills."

The wail that came from Kate was as fresh with pain as the day she'd lost the baby, the day she'd looked for his tiny body in the blood-stained sheets. "No! My baby!"

***

Shade looked up when Marcello walked into camp and their eyes met across the field. He'd felt both Marcello's and his daughter's arrival. The other warriors responded immediately, surrounding their old friend, gathering around to talk and catch up. Shade joined them, listening and laughing along with the warriors. Once the greeting party was over, he shouted out orders to get to work. He and Marcello walked inside the office and were just getting down to business when Shade sat straight up in the chair, Kate's emotional pain and plaintive wail screaming through him. "It's *bel!*"

He teleported out instantly and was immediately at her side. Cradling her in his arms, he had no idea what the hell had sparked her pain. He looked with confusion at Natalia. "What the hell happened? What the fuck is going on?"

He saw Marcello appear at Natalia's side, his arm around her, comforting her.

Kate sobbed on his shoulder and was amazed this new information about the death of their first child could hurt this bad after all this time. She answered him through her sobs. "Alec. We thought it was only Rissa who brought the pills, but Natalia has seen it all. It was Alec."

Shade felt his beast rise to the surface. He should have known from the very beginning. How could he not have realized this? He was so wrapped up in himself and Kate and the baby at the time, he couldn't have imagined an ally would work against him. He threw back his head and roared in pain and anger. He heard the camp grow quiet, as they heard his roar, and he was aware of the arrival of Luca and Shannon.

"I will have his fucking head for this! That black-hearted bastard!" He covered Kate with his body, holding her, as if he could shelter her from the pain.

Luca had felt Kate's pain and had teleported to the garden to find her on the bench in tears, and his master in a rage. Shannon landed softly behind him, and he took her hand and spoke to Shade. "Master, how can I help?"

Luca saw Marcello with his arm around Natalia and thought to himself, *Well, that's one cat out of the bag.* He knew instinctively whatever had caused Kate's pain had nothing to do with Natalia and Marcello. Luca had long suspected a connection between those two, and though he never spoke of it, he knew Shade was aware of it as well.

Shade tried to calm himself down, realizing he could be of no help to Kate otherwise. He informed Luca of Alec's deceit before issuing instructions. "Luca, get over to camp, let them know everything is fine with their king and queen. We are safe, just a personal crisis. All the damn years I have had Alec's back. The hell I went through to protect him and that bitch he called a mate. And all along, he was laughing behind my back, knowing he had destroyed our child. We will not tell anyone until we decide how to take this bastard down."

He tried to breathe through the pain and anger. He needed to get a hold on himself. He couldn't comfort Kate in this condition.

"Marcello, I need to be with Nattie alone for a few minutes. Take Shannon back into the house."

He watched as everyone moved to carry out his orders. He took Natalia's hand, wanting to comfort her as well. "Come, it's cold, we need to get inside the house."

Picking Kate up in his arms, the three of them teleported back inside the house. The fire was roaring when they landed in the living room, and Gi was wringing his hands, having heard his outcry.

"We are fine, Gi, just bring us some Midnight immediately."

As Gi went off to get their drinks, Shade sat down on the sofa, with Kate curled up in his arms. Natalia sat at his feet, her head resting on his knee. "Tell me all you know, Nattie. What else had Alec done?"

She looked up at him. "I don't know details, Daddy. I just see glimpses. I don't know why the visions came to me tonight. I usually see what's ahead, not past. But I saw something about a feeder that Alec had asked Rissa to bring here. Alec hoped it would make Mommy jealous or hurt enough to leave you. And the doctor Rissa sent was not a real doctor. Alec told Rissa to send him and told her how to make the poison pills. They were meant to kill the baby and maybe Mommy too. Alec didn't want you distracted from what he needed in D.C., and he thought Mommy was too much of a distraction."

Laying his hand on her head, he closed his eyes. His youngest daughter had brought them a new revelation that would change everything. Alec had killed one of his own, and he'd pay with his life. He felt his daughter's pain as well, not only for the loss of the brother she never knew but the physical pain she experienced from the vision.

"Is there something you can do for the pain, Nattie? Something we can get you? I'm not thinking straight. Do you want to be with Marcello? He is in Luca's suite."

She stood up from where she was sitting on the floor, putting her glass on the table. "I'm fine, Daddy. The pain from the visions pass quickly. I think you and Mommy need to be alone. I'll be in Luca's suite if you need me. Don't worry about me."

"*Grazie*. It is a shock to us both. *Ti amo*, princess. Don't worry about us. We take care of each other, your mommy and me. Let Marcello comfort you because I know he will."

Natalia kissed him on the cheek, and he felt as if the wound that had long ago healed, had been ripped open once again. He waited as she walked from the room, knowing she'd seek comfort from Marcello. He stood up with Kate in his arms and grabbing a blanket from the back of the sofa, he lay down on the rug in front of the fire with her. Gently wrapping the blanket over them, he cuddled her close to his chest. She was in so much pain.

"Just let it out, *mi amore*. I'm here and we need to get through this together. When we lost our sleeping warrior, it tore at us, almost let it come between us. I am not going to do that again. I love you, and I promise you, with all my heart and soul, I will kill Alec for you."

She looked up at him, the blood tears on her cheeks. "Not this time, lover. This time, we kill him together."

19

Natalia was back at Council after the weekend at home. Marcello had, of course, heard all the commotion over her vision involving Alec and the lost baby. He looked at her as she stood with her back to him, lost in her thoughts. "What do you think he will do?"

Natalia was looking out the window, dismayed by what she'd just learned. "What?"

Marcello repeated the question, and she shook her head. "He'll do what he always does; seek retribution for Medici, in his own time, in his own way. I don't know any more details than you do, and I can promise you, he won't share his plans with me. We'll both hear about it when it's over."

He stood close behind her at the window, slipping his arms around her waist as he nuzzled into her soft hair. It pained him he'd never feed from her, but he also knew she belonged to no other. She turned in his arms and kissed him lightly.

"I have stuff to finish up, and Emerald will be looking for the draft on the half-breeds. I need to get back to work."

He gave her a soft smile. "That makes two of us." They never had enough time together, every minute stolen. As he turned to leave, he told her, "I'll check in later."

She pulled the hood back over her hair, obscuring her face as she peeked up at him from under it. "I sure hope so."

He could see the soft smile on her lips. He returned to the warriors, and she returned to the data center where she spent her nights.

Natalia had worked with her nephew, Jules, on the legal draft for the bylaws. Jules was her sister Sophia's only son, and he wasn't born warrior. Natalia had always enjoyed his company, since, like her, he was drawn to more intellectual pursuits and had decided to become a lawyer. He visited her from time to time here at Council and had been useful in helping her prepare arguments for various issues. They felt they had a common bond in that they both didn't quite fit the pattern. She knew that Jules had always felt a little like the black sheep of the family since he was the only male not born warrior, but he was born beautiful. Natalia was always struck by his beauty whenever she saw him. There was nothing feminine about him, he was definitely all male, and his sexual preference were female, but his features were strikingly beautiful. He had Alfie's light brown hair, and Sophia's piercing blue eyes and soft complexion. His lips were full, and he had eyelashes any female would kill for. Like her, he grew up with his head in a book. She knew Alfie worried about not siring a warrior and wondered if Shade harbored any ill feelings about that. It was a secret her sister had shared with her, but she and Sophia knew Shade adored all his grandchildren. If there was any disappointment, he'd never shown even a hint of it. Both Lorenzo's and Sophia's children were doted on equally by their grandparents.

She and Jules had worked late on the final document, and she was gathering up all the notes and was ready to schedule her hearing with the Council. There was only one last thing to accomplish before presenting her draft, and that was to notify Malachi. She owed him that. Malachi shared her gift of the third eye, and had been a strong mentor for her, preparing her to take on her role in Council. If the U.S. Council adopted this change in their bylaws, then the European Council would be forced to consider the proposal as well. She wanted him to be aware of what she was about to do.

Natalia moved to the conference room to the phone monitor and tapped the screen. She saw the image appear on the monitor mounted in the wall. It was one of the runners that worked at the European Council. He knew her only as Ivory and acknowledged her.

"Could you please find Malachi for me? It's imperative I speak to him."

The runner nodded and left his seat, as a soothing picture of a waterfall and soft music played. Ignoring the image on the screen, she sorted through her notes until Malachi appeared, his eyes covered by the green hood. Still, she'd recognize him anywhere.

"Ivory, what can I do for you?"

Natalia settled herself against the edge of the table, preferring to stand. "Thank you for seeing me, Malachi. I'm going to be making a plea to my Council for a change in the bylaws, and I wanted to make sure you were aware of it before I do."

Malachi slipped the hood back further on his head, his eyes now visible as he stared back at her. "A bylaw change? You understand that is quite rare, and not something any Council should take lightly."

She nodded her head. "I'm aware."

He couldn't hide the look of concern on his face, but he knew she was levelheaded, and if she was proposing a change, it was something she'd thought out at length. "Go ahead then, let me hear it."

She picked up her notes. "Well, it's sort of your fault. I mean, you started it when you gave the half-breed to my brother and his mate."

Malachi had a smile on his face. "Ah, so you will lay this on my shoulders then."

She suppressed her own smile. "This is serious, Malachi!"

He crossed his arms over his chest. "Proceed."

She cleared her throat. She didn't need his permission to present this amendment for consideration, she had as much power in her Council as he had in his, but his approval had always mattered to her.

"I want to make it illegal for the vampire community to destroy the half-breeds. If the infant is rejected by the mortal and abandoned, then Council will take in the child, and use the DNA databanks to find the male who sired it. If the male refuses to take the infant, or no other family agrees to adopt, then the Council will house and care for the child, teaching them a trade or skill, providing for their education until they can be integrated into a coven."

Malachi sighed and closed his eyes. "Ivory, that is very noble, but how would your Council ever care for these infants? I took a chance that your brother would be open to the idea of adopting this half-breed only because he had grown up with a half-breed brother."

She held up her hand. "I've thought of that. I know we can't take them in. I spoke to my father, and he was willing to allocate more land to the U.S. Council. He said there is a large parcel adjacent to where we are now. He will pay to build the facility and staff it. I told him we would need wet feeders, and nannies, and, of course, tutors. He is already speaking to Enzo, to find good tutors for us."

Malachi tapped his finger to his lips. “It could work. It will take time to change attitudes, but trust me when I tell you, everyone has watched Cory's progress. He was the first and only half-breed brought into our community, before Grace. No one thought it would work."

Natalia shook her head. "Because no one ever tried, Malachi. We need the half-breeds. They have something to offer the covens and leaving them to fend for themselves does us harm. It risks our exposure. We have to take care of our own."

He chuckled. "You make a sound argument, Ivory, and I would love to be a fly on the wall when you present this amendment. Go, you have my blessing, not that you need it."

She beamed back at him. “Thank you, Malachi. I love you like a father."

He smiled. "I know you do, child, and it makes this old heart fill with joy."

20

Chantal was excited and busy making sure Grace looked beautiful in preparation for her son's visit, although Grace needed little help. She was the most adorable and perfect baby to Chantal. She was anticipating it would be a wonderful night. Henry was coming to meet his little sister. Chantal and Lorenzo had informed both of their sons about the adoption, letting Christoph know they'd visit Bel Rosso soon. She laughed out loud thinking about how Kate, Shannon, and Natalia were all so excited for them to come visit with the baby. Chantal would have such a grand time showing off her Grace. She loved Kate, and her sisters-in-law, but she'd never felt like she fit in. They were each so strong and independent, and she'd been raised to defer to the males in her life.

Chantal had been busy, shopping for only the best for baby Grace. Her wardrobe was full already with the most delicate and expensive items. Lorenzo was always teasing her about how much could one small baby wear, but he did it with love. She picked Grace up and held her gently in her arms.

"Now, you must be on your best behavior, *mon ange*. You are going to meet your big brother Henry. He is so handsome, and a warrior, just like your *papa*."

Grace looked up at her with large eyes that seemed to twinkle with understanding. Chantal made her way down the grand stairs and headed for one of her favorite rooms, the sitting room. It was elegant and yet had a comfortable, relaxed atmosphere. As she passed Antonio, he announced her son was waiting for them in the sitting room, as she'd requested. Chantal was beaming as she entered the room and saw her Henry sipping a glass of Red Moon.

As she approached him, she stopped in her tracks and the smile on her face disappeared. Her mother was standing off to the side. Chantal was completely taken off guard. She looked from her mother to Henry.

"I don't understand. You are not welcome here, *Maman*, Lorenzo made that clear to you and *Papa*."

"Chantal, Henry told me he was coming to see you and Grace, and I asked if I could join him. Your father doesn't know I'm here. I have tried to ignore this baby, but my heart is pulled to her. I beg you to not send me away."

Chantal felt her heart breaking all over again, the pull of her parents against her mate.

Chantal instinctively pulled Grace closer to her chest. "Henry, you should have told me you were bringing your *grand-mere*."

She moved to sit, and Henry was immediately at her side to assist her. Chantal was still confused. Her mother had never taken a stand against her father in her life, and she remained suspicious of her mother's motives.

As Henry settled in next to her, he peered at the small face looking back at him from the pink blanket. He answered his mother as he took the infant's hand. "*Maman*, I wasn't aware *Grand-mere* wasn't welcome. I don't understand."

Amelie stepped in closer to get a look at the baby. "I didn't tell him, Chantal. He knows nothing of the dispute. Please don't admonish your son. If you wish me to leave, I will, but I am asking you to please let me stay."

Chantal felt torn, but this was her home, and her baby, and Henry was her son. She was mistress inside these walls, and she'd play no games with her mother. "Henry, please understand. *Papa* has decided to have nothing to do with Grace. He forbade her entrance to the chateau in Paris, but said I was still welcome there. *Maman* did not stand up for me nor Grace. I was forced to choose between my birth family, and the family I have created with my mate, and I have chosen. Someone has to fight for this infant. I told *Papa* if he did not accept Grace, he did not accept me. He stormed out."

Grace began to squirm in her arms, fighting the close hold she had on her. "Now, now, *mon ange*, it is all right, *Maman* is right here and so is your big brother Henry."

She put Grace on her shoulder, rubbing her back softly, whispering soothing words in her ear. Grace turned and looked at Henry, cooing loudly. Chantal didn't look at her mother but spoke with confidence.

"I do not wish you to leave, *Maman*. But do you see the position you have put me in?" Her eyes locked then with Amelie's. "Can't you see how this makes me feel? I love you and *Papa*. But I also love Lorenzo, my sons, and Grace. How will you ever keep this a secret from him?"

"I have been dealing with your father long before you were born. He is a proud and stubborn male, as are most, *oui*? Do not concern yourself with that. Your father will not hold you accountable for my actions. He loves you dearly, and he already regrets his harsh words, although he is too proud to back down. He misses you. I have told him I do not plan to have my daughter in exile, and he must see reason. It will take time, but he will come to love this baby."

Chantal could feel her mother and the aching she had to hold the baby. She stood and placed Grace in her arms. "*Maman*, please listen to me. The Medici's are part of the change for good for our kind. I like being part of that change. There are no secrets between Lorenzo and me. He talks to me about his plans as warrior and master of this coven, his vision for the future. I rarely heard *Papa* share his thoughts with you. Lorenzo and I grew up in circumstances more different than similar. We were both of royal blood, but the similarities end there. I am learning our love can bridge those differences and bring us together. You need to make *Papa* not only accept Grace but accept the rights of all half-breeds. Fight for us, *Maman!* How do I explain to Grace, once she is older, that her *Grand-pere* abhors her existence? I need your help. It is all I can ask of you."

Amelie sighed. "I can't push him into anything, Chantal, he is much too stubborn for that. But he will follow in time." She felt the warmth of the small bundle in her arms. Grace looked back at her with wide eyes and Amelie smiled and stroked the infant's cheek. "Look at you. You are growing already, and your cheeks have such a healthy glow." She rocked the baby gently in her arms. "My granddaughter will not be an outcast, at least not for long. I promise you will never have to explain to Grace why her *grand-pere* is absent. By the time she is able to notice such things, Henri will have come around."

"You make it seem so easy, when I know it will not be so." Chantal sat next to her son. "As for you, my son, how is it that every time I see you, you become more handsome? So, what do you think of this new sister of yours?"

Henry laughed. "I think my new sister will take some of the pressure off me. Perhaps you will stop asking when I plan to settle down and mate and give you grandbabies."

Chantal smiled then. "She does make me happy. But I do think it is time you at least started to look for a proper mate, *oui*? You are no longer the baby of the family."

She stood and walked to her mother, who appeared in her element holding Grace. "How do you intend to pull off these secret visits?"

Amelie responded, "Do you think your father keeps such close tabs on me? I tell him I am going shopping, or I have a charity event."

"*Oui*. *Papa* never makes notice of schedules." Reaching down, she stroked Grace's face. "But this little one is taking much of my time. She feeds very well and is such a good baby. I think I will like very much having you back in our lives, *Maman*. But make no mistake, if I am ever forced to make a choice, it will be for Lorenzo, and for Grace."

Amelie leaned her head against her daughter's, as they both looked down at the innocent face of the baby in her arms. "I understand, and thank you, Chantal. It was breaking my heart to feel the separation between us. Do not worry about your father, leave him to me."

21

Shade stood in the office used by Micah at the inn in the Napa Valley. He and Kate had spent a lot of hours talking since their discovery of Alec's involvement in the death of their first unborn son. Alec had served his sentence to spend one hundred years underground that was issued by the Council and had been free for some time now to move about freely. Shade had protected him, given him the land to build L'Adventure, provided warriors for security, and during that time, Alec had made a lot of money. He still had no territory, no warriors, and no coven. He had nothing but the club and had decided, given his limited options, to continue to run the club rather than start from scratch to rebuild a coven.

Knowing what he knew now about Alec's involvement in the loss of their first child, Shade would never let him live, and neither would Kate. The first phase of the plan was to dupe Alec. Shade wanted neutral ground for this discussion, so he'd chosen their inn at Touch of Tuscany and was waiting for Alec's arrival. He'd decided not to meet Alec at L'Adventure, nor would he ever have him back inside Bel Rosso. The inn wasn't too far from Alec's club, and a neutral place to have this conversation.

Micah had stocked the office with Midnight, at Shade's request, and the office was sequestered far enough from the main part of the house that they wouldn't be seen by any of the guests. Neither Micah nor Raven had any idea of what the meeting was about. Shade didn't like hiding things from his warriors, but until the plans were in place, he preferred secrecy.

He sat, waiting impatiently, checking his watch, sipping his Midnight. He wanted his mind clear and focused on the objective. He stood and paced, trying to relax. He was dressed casually, so as to blend in with the mortals at the inn, and he knew this was how Alec would arrive also. At last, he heard the light rap on the door, as Micah opened it, announcing that Alec had arrived. Shade nodded and watched Alec stroll in as Micah closed the door quietly behind him. Shade greeted him. "Long time no see, brother. Can I pour you a drink?"

***

Alec had been in a rush to get to the inn. He rarely left the confines of L'Adventure, even though his sentence was officially over. He'd traveled a few times to London, where there was a similar club, to get new ideas for expanding the services he offered. He was surprised when he got the request to meet Shade at his inn in Napa, but then Shade told him Kate didn't want him visiting L'Adventure without her. That was easy to believe. He'd always thought Kate's sexual adventurism was a little too pedestrian for his taste and could never understand how she'd managed to keep Shade entertained all these years. "Please. You know I find teleporting tiring. A drink will be welcome."

He accepted the drink and took a seat in the plush armchair. "So, what did you want to meet about? Your message was rather cryptic."

After Shade poured Alec a drink and refreshed his own, he took a seat opposite him. "I need your help, a favor, actually. Life has gotten routine for me, and I need a bit of a diversion, one that only you can help me with." He sighed for emphasis, while keeping an eye on Alec. *This should get his damn curiosity up!*

Alec took a sip of the wine as he listened, looking up with some surprise. "A diversion? Of course, how can I help?"

"I brought Kate to the club once before, although it was a long time ago. She enjoyed it a lot. I admit, it has been a struggle to convince her that I need a bit more, sometimes, to keep me satisfied, that we need to venture out, explore other paths."

Shade set his glass aside as he stood and paced, raking his hand through his hair. "You know how it is Alec, once in a while you need something more than vanilla. Don't get me wrong, she's great, but I've finally convinced her to try something different. She has agreed to a *ménage a trois*, but not with a stranger. She would only go forward if it was with someone, we both knew. Someone she could trust. I need your help, brother. So, I am asking if you would be interested to do this with us?"

Shade sat back down in his chair, and leaned forward, his arms resting on his knees. "It would have to be at your club of course, private, very private."

Alec smiled to himself as he sipped from the glass, unable to suppress the chuckle. "I'm surprised you lasted this long, brother. I know your sexual preferences better than anyone. I've never been asked to join a client before, but for you, I'll make an exception. And of course, it will be private. L'Adventure is known for its discretion. We wouldn't be able to maintain our clientele if we weren't able to guarantee every master's privacy. Do you need me to set up the room for something special, or are you just winging it?"

Shade settled back in the chair, crossing his leg over his knee. "Well, I think some bondage is a good mix in a threesome. Mild, though, I don't want to scare her. I want her to come back again. Something with a little master/slave sex play. We have done that before with just the two of us. I think a St. Andrews Cross would work well. She can be immobilized without feeling too out of control."

He stood and refilled his drink and refilled Alec's glass as well. "It took me a long damn time to convince her to do this. I have wanted a *ménage a trois* for some time. I would have preferred a female, but she wasn't going for that." He chuckled as he sipped from his drink. "Appreciate you doing this for me, brother. I think you will enjoy her; I want you to enjoy her, but don't push it too far too fast. I want to introduce her to these things slowly, understood?"

Alec nodded. "I'll follow your lead. She'll be reassured to see that you're in control, and the one calling the shots. I can hang back and watch in the beginning. Knowing someone is watching can be a very powerful sexual stimulant in itself. You can let me know when you want me to engage, and how much. And if it doesn't work out, if she changes her mind, you can ask me to leave. No problem, brother."

Shade's smile was wicked. "*Grazie*, brother. I appreciate this. She is very curious, and that's a good place to start. Appreciate you taking the time to come up here. Everything going well on your end?"

Alec lit up a cigarette and took a deep drag before exhaling the smoke. "Business is strong. I leave when I need to or want to. I have more than enough money. Life couldn't be better."

Shade laughed softly, knowing Alec had swallowed the bait. "Glad to hear it. I will contact you soon with a date and time. Thank you, brother."

"Happy to oblige. I wouldn't have L'Adventure if not for you. It's the least I can do."

Shade acknowledged his words. Alec would have nothing if not for him. He shook his hand as Alec stood to leave, teleporting out. *Well, perhaps not the least, brother.*

22

The hour of midnight was approaching, and Shade was dressed and ready to teleport out to L'adventure. He'd never before taken Kate into a situation that he knew would end in violence, and he couldn't help but feel some concern, despite her determination. Tonight, would also mean the end of a centuries' long association with someone he'd considered an ally. He'd been thinking about the many adventures he and Alec had shared, not all of them positive. There was a time when he'd lost his way, when his soul was dark and depraved, and Alec had gladly accompanied him on that journey. But that was before Kate, before he knew how love could heal, before he discovered how having a mate he wanted to spend eternity with, would change him. Alec had never outgrown that depravity.

Grabbing his third glass of Midnight, he worried whether his sweet *bel* would be able to go through with this plan tonight. He was watching her carefully and could feel her nervousness. But there was something else inside her as well, a level of determination he'd not witnessed before. They both had their minds set, this had to be done. He sipped at the drink and then pulled his hair back behind his head into a loose ponytail, a few curls hanging loose around his face. "I think you should have a glass of Midnight, *mi amore*. It will help relax you."

Kate was standing in her closet, staring blankly at the outfits hanging there, when she asked herself, *What do you wear to kill someone?* He handed her the glass of wine, and she took a swallow, feeling it burn inside her belly. She had no illusions about what they were about to do. She couldn't continue to walk this earth and pretend she didn't know what Alec had done to them. She couldn't let Alec live without paying for the consequences of his actions, but that didn't make her less nervous.

In the end, she selected a simple black dress, and a pair of ankle strap black heels. Black was always appropriate for a funeral. He was dressed in his leathers, and if he was nervous, it didn't show. He'd killed many, but her list of kills was short. She'd killed Cuerpo, to save her own life, and she'd killed the two Asian feeders. She knew they were innocent of any wrongdoing. They were doing what they'd been bred to do, what they'd been ordered to do by Max, but killing the feeder's brought retribution against Max, and helped heal the pain of betrayal that Shade felt in his heart. It wasn't a kill she was proud of, as the feeders were defenseless, and they were sacrificed as a means to an end. Fiamma had been with her then and had said nothing as she beheaded the feeders. Her last kill had been Jacks, although her death didn't come by her hand, but by her command, when Aegis and the others had torn Jacks from limb to limb. She swallowed down the rest of her wine, as it calmed and soothed. Locking eyes with him, she nodded. "I'm ready, lover."

Shade watched as she downed the Midnight, and knew she was ready. They'd planned carefully for what they were about to do. He'd never let harm come to her, but she had a part to play and so did he. Tonight, they'd avenge their sleeping warrior. Ever since discovering Cory, he'd tried not to focus too much on the loss of their son. He was aware now that the boy could have survived in this world, and could have had a place in their lives, just as Cory and Grace had. He was comforted in his sorrow and anger by the thought that Natalia was changing things for their kind, and the half-breeds would now have a totally different future.

"Remember to just breathe, *mi amore*. Stay calm. Come, it is time we leave."

He took her hand and they teleported toward San Francisco. He'd contacted Alec prior, setting the date and time. He told Raven he was coming, but to keep the information to himself to minimize their exposure. They had teleported directly inside the club, landing inside the lobby and bypassing the warriors who stood guard. Shade tipped the face of his queen to his and kissed her on the lips. He locked eyes with her. "**This is for our sleeping warrior. You are safe with me**."

She stared back at him, feeling comfort in his words. He'd never failed her, and she knew he never would. "You lead and I follow, in all things, lover, in all things."

Bree approached them in her sprayed on latex bodysuit and a smile. "Welcome back. Haven't seen you two in a long time. Alec told me what you wanted, and I have your room ready. Follow me, please. I've already informed Alec you're here. He'll be joining you shortly."

Bree turned on her five-inch heels and strutted like a model on a catwalk down the long corridor of private suites. They followed behind her, and Kate cleared her throat when she noticed his eyes had settled on Bree's tight ass, intentionally swaying for his pleasure. He chuckled as he looked down at her and winked.

She looked up at him. "Stay focused. We have enough to attend to tonight."

Bree inserted the key card in the lock and pushed open the door, handing the card to Shade, her hand lingering in his a little longer than necessary. Looking back at him, she flipped her blonde hair and purred. "The Red Moon you requested is on the table. Be sure to call me if you need anything."

Kate intentionally walked between them, as Shade took the card, and she grabbed his hand, leading him into the room. "We've got it covered, thanks. You can leave now."

Bree flashed her a cold stare before closing the door and heard the lock click into place. Kate heard his soft chuckle, amused as always by her jealousy. She looked around the room at the equipment that had been set up for them. They'd discussed, in great detail, how they'd carry out their plan. Alec was no warrior, but he was a master, and he wouldn't go down easy. Shade had said they'd have to have him restrained and sedated, and that would be no easy task. Alec was a dominant, not a submissive. He wouldn't be so eager to allow himself to be bound to St. Andrews cross. Shade opened the bottle of Red Moon and dropped the tranquilizer inside. The cross sat at a slight angle, like a giant X in the room, thick leather straps at each point of the cross. It made Kate shiver to look at it.

Shade wasn't nervous about what he was about to do, or how to do it, that was the easy part. He was more concerned about Kate, and carefully leading her. He saw her look at the equipment in the room. He knew she felt out of her element here, but she'd have to move with some confidence if they were going to pull this off.

"I know this isn't easy, but he thinks you are interested but also conflicted. Your nerves will not be unexpected. Use them to your advantage. Be curious."

He removed the leather jacket and quickly pulled the tee-shirt off over his head and threw it to the corner. Walking toward her like she was his prey, he pulled her body hard into his, and kissed her long and passionately. "If you feel frightened, remember to just look into my eyes, and forget he is here."

Taking her hand, he led her on a tour of the objects on the walls and tables. "Floggers, whips, chains...play toys. Touch them, don't be afraid." He led her to the cross placed in the center of the room.

"St. Andrews cross, you remember our discussion?" He ran his hand across the leather strap and looked into her eyes. "See, easy. Just buckle the straps tight around my wrist and my ankles. That's all there is too it, *si*?"

He leaned over and unlaced his boots, kicking them off before unzipping his fly and stripping from his leathers.

***

Alec slid his own key card into the lock and opened the door of the dimly lit room. Shade was already naked, and his fully clothed mate was strapping his wrists to the two upright arms of the cross. Kate turned to look at him over her shoulder and dropped her hands. It was clear she wasn't familiar with the equipment.

Alec smiled. "Well, I didn't expect this, brother. Since when you become the submissive?"

Shade chuckled. "I'm her teacher. How better to let her get familiar with the equipment than to let her use it on me? It will calm her nerves to let her take control. Will you give us the pleasure of just watching from the shadows for a bit?"

Alec huffed to himself. He would never have allowed his mate to lead him around like this. He poured himself a Red Moon and took a seat in a chair in the corner of the room. Pulling out a pack of cigarettes from his pocket, he lit up, keeping his eyes on the female. "Your dime, brother."

Kate squatted down and strapped Shade's ankles to the lower limbs of the cross, acutely aware of Alec's presence. She reminded herself why they were here and tried to stay focused. As she stood, she slowly ran her fingers up his legs, across his muscular thighs, and stopped at his hips, as she gripped him tight. She locked eyes with him and read his thoughts for her to stay strong. She stepped back, staring at his body, looking chiseled from marble, and strapped to the cross. Even restrained, he looked deadly and dangerous.

She reached down and grabbed the hem of her dress, and pulled it over her head, standing before him in a black lace bra and thong, and her strappy black heels. She swallowed hard, trying to ignore the second set of eyes on her.

Alec watched from the corner as the dress came off, feeling more relaxed than usual. He settled into the chair, eager to watch. Her skin was flawless, and her paleness was exaggerated by the black undergarments. She was small and delicate, even by mortal standards, and it was easy to see her appeal.

Kate walked slowly around the cross, her hand trailing across Shade's tight abdomen. She stood before him and rose on tip toe to kiss his lips as he tilted his head forward to her. Her kisses were soft and gentle, and she moved to his jaw and nibbled his ear, her tongue following the curve of his neck onto his muscular shoulder. Her hands brushed against him with the lightness of a feather. She wouldn't torture him with floggers or leather straps; she'd torture him with softness and gentleness. Her mouth found his nipple, and her tongue flicked over it before sliding down his belly to the throbbing cock that waited for her.

Shade wasn't surprised that she ignored all the pleasurable and painful vices she had at her disposal. He knew his *bel* like no one else. Her tongue unleashed its own brand of torture, warm and wet, as she explored his body, hardening his nipples with the flick of her tongue. She left a heated trail down his abdomen, and he knew where she was headed, and he tugged against the leather straps with anticipation. His blood was rushing faster as her tongue explored his abs and teased his cock.

He would command her from this position, showing Alec that being strapped to the cross didn't diminish his station as a dominant. He could still control her. He told her what he wanted, and how he wanted it, and ordered her to her knees.

Kate knelt before him. He may be the one subdued, but she remained, as always, his. She cupped his balls in her hands as he'd asked and heard the sharp intake of his breath. Her tongue lashed out, as she tasted the salty, musky, maleness that was his scent. She sucked his balls into her mouth, and slowly slid them out, blowing her breath on them, and watching the goose bumps rise on his thighs. Her hands glided up and down his thighs, before returning to his cock, encircling him, and guiding the bulging head to her mouth. She slid the smooth head into her mouth, and across her tongue, before she took the full length of him deep into her throat.

Shade struggled against the straps, responding to the pleasures of her mouth. His hands begin to sweat. He wanted to run them through that crimson, feel her silky mane between his fingers as he guided her head. His growl rumbled through the room and his eyes lit up, his fangs punched through. "*Cazzo, mi amore*."

His fangs already ached to sink deep into her soft flesh, but he knew that wouldn't happen tonight. They had other things to accomplish. He flung his head to the side and caught Alec in his gaze. Alec's attention was on her, and the magic she worked with her mouth, as he knew it would be. Sending Kate a message, he entered her thoughts. **"When you are ready, sink your nails into my thighs and draw blood. The smell of my blood will light him up. Keep focused."**

She telepathically acknowledged his instructions, and knew she had him on edge, just as she could hear the uncomfortable squirming from Alec as he shifted his weight in the chair. She slid his cock slowly in and out of her mouth, her movements deliberately seductive. She felt his cock throbbing, growing more rigid with each slow stroke, and she lightly drew her nails over his balls and felt them tighten. She moaned as his cock pushed deeper, and the vibrations of her moan traveled the length of his cock, triggering his orgasm. She saw his whole body go rigid on the cross as his head thrashed and he released into her. She sucked him dry, as her hands clawed down his thighs, drawing thin trails of blood. She licked her lips, and then ran her tongue over the fresh blood. She looked up at him, before turning to look at Alec. "You're next."

From her kneeling position, she released the straps around Shade's ankles and gently rubbed the chafed skin before standing before him, kissing his lips, and releasing his wrists. They locked eyes, knowing what they must do. She mouthed the words, "I love you."

Getting his breathing under control, Shade's body felt alive, wanting her, and wanting the kill. Alec stood and stepped up beside him, and Shade noticed he was more than ready to get his hands on Kate. He could see from the look in his eyes Alec would much prefer to strap Kate on the cross. Quickly getting his mind in the game, they needed to get Alec's ass strapped on the cross so he could be kept under control.

"Damn, brother, why are you still dressed? Cooperate, *si*? She is still skittish with another male. Let's not lose the pace!"

As Alec smirked, he stripped bare, and Shade nodded to him to take the position on the cross. Alec hesitated for a second, and Shade knew he didn't like this move. Alec was the one heaping out the abuse. Shade roughly grabbed his wrist, slamming Alec hard against the cross as he raised his hands over his head. He strapped his wrist in place before licking his vein and growly softly. "Play along, brother."

Alec grunted, feeling sluggish, and allowed his arms to be strapped down. Shade bent down to his ankles, strapping them in, pulling the straps tight. As he stood, he moved in close and grabbed Alec's hard cock in his hand and squeezed hard as he stroked him. "My Queen is in control now. Whatever she wants, she gets. Hope you are ready, brother."

Alec was hard already from watching her perform. He'd hoped to take a more dominant role in this little threesome and show her what it really felt like to be controlled by a master. He wasn't entirely pleased to be strapped on the cross. He consoled himself with the thought that it may be worth it to feel her mouth around his cock. "Let's see what your queen can do."

Shade leaned in close, nose to nose. "Oh, I would say she can do quite a lot."

Shade stepped back to admire his work then turned to Kate. He kissed her like there was no tomorrow. **"Give me one moment, *mi amore*, and the promise I made to you for revenge will be yours."**

Shade telepathically called out to Raven. **"I need you at L'Adventure immediately. Bring me a sword, sharp and true, and one that your queen can handle. Come directly inside, take no shit from anyone. Come to Room 17. Knock, your queen will come and take the sword. Remain on standby outside that door until further instructed. Move it!"**

Shade ran his hand along her cheek. "Get dressed, my Queen. Raven is bringing you a present." Winking, he smiled and turned to Alec. "Sorry for the delay, brother, but I do believe you will quite enjoy this special delivery."

"What the fuck?" Alec didn't like the direction this was going and struggled against the straps as he heard Shade tell her to get dressed. He watched as she picked up the dress from the floor and pulled it over her head, shaking out that mane of red hair. He felt sluggish and shook his head to remove the cobwebs. "Not sure I'm interested in your games, brother."

He heard the tap at the door, and Kate opened it wide enough for him to see Raven standing on the other side, handing her a sword. He yanked at the straps, reinforced to restrain the strength and resistance of a vampire, and his heart pounded as he realized he was at Shade's mercy. "Enough of this!"

Shade watched his futile struggle to release himself from the straps. He turned his back on him and walked back to Kate. Kissing her softly, he took the sword from her hands. Spinning it around in his hands, he flexed his muscles. He looked over his shoulder at Alec. "How does it feel to be immobilized, knowing you face the wrath of your past? The King of Medici has a score to settle with you."

Shade approached him slowly, as Alec continued to try to pull free from the straps, his brain feeling clouded, and he was wondering now if Shade had slipped something in his drink. Shade touched the tip of the sword to Alec's abdomen, above his cock, which had now gone limp. He drew a small trickle of blood as he left a razor thin opening in his skin.

"I wouldn't struggle too much if I were you. You might lose that infamous cock of yours."

Alec's eyes glowed red, and he bared his fangs. "Is this part of your game? I will rip your throat out, Medici!"

Shade's beast flared in anger and hatred over what Alec had done. His eyes blazed and his fangs grew long. "You will rip *my* throat out? And how do you propose to do that?"

Shade stepped in closer, as he roared and slashed the sword across one cheek, marring that face Alec was so fucking proud of. "You killed my son, our son. You and that fucking bitch of a whore you called a mate. You planned the whole, black-hearted thing. You even planned the feeder, and for what? So, I would not be distracted from your plans to take the White House? I should cut your cock off and shove it up your ass while you watch, but that isn't good enough for me. You are staring at the dealer of your death, but unlike my son, you will see it coming."

Alec struggled against the restraints and was wondering what the fuck he was talking about, when the memory of that long-ago pregnancy came back to him. Kate was still mortal then, and he'd sent Rissa to give her pills that would kill the baby, and quite possibly, Kate. *That was ages ago! The only person who knew was Rissa, and she was long dead. How had he discovered this?* He needed to stall for time. "What are you talking about, brother? I never killed your son."

Shade roared, raising the sword above his head. "Don't play the fool with me."

He got in Alec's face, his fangs dripping, as his eyes glowed red. "My son died, and my mate almost died. I hope you meet the bloody bitch you connived with in hell, and the two of you burn for all eternity together."

Shade spit in his face and turned his back on Alec once more, walking back to Kate. He handed her the sword. "My Queen, this honor belongs to you, to our son. Take it. Let us be done with the black-hearted bastard."

Kate took the sword from his hands and slowly walked to stand in front of him. He snarled at her, his fangs bared, saliva dripping. He'd kill her where she stood.

She spoke softly. "You killed our child."

He spit back at her. "Your half-breed!"

She nodded slowly. "Yes, our half-breed son. You took his life, and now I'll take yours."

She slowly drew the tip of the sword down his other cheek, leaving a deep wound, as she watched him grimace. "That is for the feeder you sent." He spit at her again and stared back with so much hatred she knew he'd kill her in seconds if he was freed. She placed the point of the blade at the base of his throat, and locking eyes with him, slowly dragged the sword down his chest, across his abdomen, and stopped at the base of his cock. The wound opened up as the blood poured forth, running down both of his legs and pooling at his feet, as he struggled to free himself. His growl was loud, a mixture of pain and anger, when she raised her voice, making sure he heard her. "And that is for the poisoned pills. The ones I so desperately took in an effort to save the life of my child; the pills that almost killed me."

Alec struggled against the restraints, growling and shaking the cross violently in an effort to free himself, but the straps he'd had designed to immobilize an immortal held firm.

It had been over a hundred years since Luca had taught her how to swing a sword, but they were lessons she'd never forgot. Grasping the hilt with both hands, extending her arms, she swung the sword in an arc, and in a single blow, removed his head. The sound of his roar, as he saw the blade glint in the dimly lit room, was cut short as he felt the blade slice through his throat, severing his skull from his spine. His world went dark, as his head rolled across the floor and landed at Shade's feet.

She stared as his headless body went limp on the cross, his weight supported by the straps. "And that is for our infant son, who never lived to draw a breath."

He never heard her last words. His life had ended, as the blade of the sword removed his head.

Shade watched as Kate took the swing and, with one clean stroke, she beheaded Alec, and logged another kill under her belt. He looked down to see the severed head, in a wobbly, rolling path land at his feet. He kicked Alec's head across the room and heard the dull thud, as it hit the wall. He'd lost count of the number of times he'd wanted to splatter his fucking brains across the room. No longer would he have to deal with his bullshit.

He heard the sword clatter to the floor, as she dropped the blade and turned to walk into his arms. "I love you, my Queen. But right now, there is still work to do, and I need to give Raven instructions."

He opened the door to allow Raven to enter, and quickly closed the door behind him. "Raven, you will speak of this to no one, ever. Find Bree, and together with our warriors, have the place evacuated. Tell them there is an unforeseen emergency, and they must leave immediately. Then burn this fucking place to the ground with Alec in it."

Raven nodded, looking with some surprise at the severed head, recognizing the identity of the victim on the cross, but he didn't ask questions. "With pleasure, boss-man." Shade knew Raven would handle any loose ends.

"Let's go home, *mi amore*, I think we have dealt enough death this night."

He lifted Kate in his arms as they teleported out. Shade grinned as he heard the sounds of Nickelback's "Burn it to the Ground" blaring out into the night, and the skies lit up with the flames from the fire.

23

The teleport back to Bel Rosso was a swift one as many things rolled through Shade's mind. He kept Kate close, to calm her and keep her warm in the chill of the night air. She was vampire, but not accustomed to the kill, and it had been a night of releasing pain and exacting revenge upon someone they'd both known a long time. He felt her shiver in his arms and knew it wasn't all from the cold. It didn't matter how long she lived, she didn't have the heart of a killer, even if the kill was justifiable.

He landed gently on the path to the baby's garden and set her down. Hand in hand, they walked down the path through the garden that was swiftly going dormant for the coming winter. As they approached the stone marker, aged and covered in moss, Shade envisioned the infant had he lived and grown to be a man. He could have grown up in their home, with their other children, and like Cory, found his own path. He sat down on the bench and looked up at the moon. It was a clear night, with twinkling stars above them. He took a deep breath, feeling the crisp, cold air hit his lungs. She sat next to him, her head on his shoulder, and he felt the softness of her hair along his cheek.

"You were brave tonight. I know it was not easy for you. Talk to me."

Kate stared blankly at the small statue of the angel, nestled among the lavender plants that had long lost their bloom. "I didn't feel brave. I was driven more by my anger, I think. I felt fear when he looked back at me, and I knew if he could free himself from his bonds, he'd kill me in a heartbeat. I could feel his hatred wash over me."

The tears fell silently down her cheeks, tears of grief for the child she never held, and tears of relief that now both people responsible for the baby's death were dead. "I still don't understand. How could this baby ever have mattered to them? How could this tiny life, this half-breed, who would have had no power in our world, how could he have been such a threat that they wished him dead?"

Shade shook his head and sighed. He would do anything to take the pain away from her, and he wished he could kill Alec all over again. He turned slightly and kissed her tears as they ran down her cheeks. "You and the baby were a threat to them both. Alec wanted my undivided attention, focused on his goals, and he was willing to pay any price to get where he wanted. In the end, it cost him everything, his coven, his territory, his power, Rissa, and eventually his life."

She wrapped both arms around him. He was her anchor in a storm, her rock in times of doubt, her strength in times of fear. He'd been there for her every moment of their lives, just as he'd promised. The early years had been challenging, while they both found their way, and had to figure things out as she learned to live in his world, but he'd tried hard to never let her down. There had never been a day when she felt unloved. "You will always have me."

He snuggled into her, and felt her love wash over him in waves. He never tired of that feeling. "Tonight, we did what was needed. They are gone now, Kate, both of them gone from our lives. They can't harm us or what is ours. Our children and grandchildren are safe."

He kissed the top of her head. It was time to tell her what he had done. "When you were so sick during that pregnancy, I feared I would lose you both. I made some choices that have haunted me, and yet to this day, I know I could not have chosen differently. I still would have let him go to save you. I didn't know the pills were poison, but I could see they were killing you. I knew you would never stop taking them if you thought they would save the baby. I had Gi switch out the pills. I have always felt conflicted about that, but I can't live without you, Kate. It was never an option."

"Lover, you did what you thought would save me for our future. For the children that would follow and the life we have shared. If the roles were reversed, I would have done the same. Never apologize for that."

They both looked up when they heard the crunch of gravel underfoot, and she felt Luca approaching, his bond to her never broken. In the pale light of the moon, they could see Luca and Shannon, walking hand in hand toward them. They both had known the reason for the trip to California. Luca had offered to go with them, to kill Alec for her, but she had turned him down, knowing this was something she had to do for herself.

Luca sat on the ground at her feet, and Kate scooted over, making room for Shannon on the garden bench.

Luca took her hand. "You okay?"

Kate nodded. "It's over."

Shannon laid her head on Kate's shoulder. "I'm so sorry, Kate."

Kate laid her head atop Shannon's. "He can rest in peace now. It took a long time for the truth to be revealed, but his death has been avenged."

Shade took comfort in being surrounded by the people he held most dear. He'd chosen well when selecting Luca as her protector, and Shannon had been a perfect mate. "Funny thing, as I am sitting here, memories flooding my brain of how far we have come together. We have come through a lot. This is where we belong, right here. It was our fate to be here together. Strange the things you learn as you get older. Hell, when I first went out on my own, I thought I fucking knew it all. But *Madre* was right, my life was just beginning, and the lessons would never end."

24

Lorenzo was dressed in the tuxedo that Antonio had laid out for him and was fussing with the bow tie in front of the mirror, cussing under his breath when Chantal entered the room. He could see her reflection in the mirror, wearing a ball gown of deep blue. The Grecian style gown was draped over one shoulder and had blue beading at the waist. The skirt fell in soft folds to the floor. She'd chosen a magnificent sapphire and diamond necklace and earrings that he'd given her and had piled her hair in a loose construction of soft curls on top her head. The color complimented her eyes and her peaches and cream complexion. She was a vision of loveliness and sophistication.

"*Cherie*, I don't know what I ever did to deserve you."

She smiled at him in the mirror. She knew he loved her in blue, and he'd been bringing her a steady supply of sapphires and diamonds. She'd need to expand the vault soon. She laughed softly as she answered. "I'm not sure you do. My *papa* says smart men always mate above their station."

Lorenzo laughed out loud. "For once, I completely agree with your father. Can you help me with this tie?"

He heard the soft whistle of the voluminous fabric as she walked towards him and tied his bow tie perfectly as she clucked her tongue. "My warrior can weld a sword, yet he cannot handle a simple swatch of fabric at his neck." She winked at him playfully, and he gave her a kiss when she finished his tie.

"How is our daughter? Is Grace settled in for the evening? I know for a fact my mother would prefer to stay here with her new granddaughter than go to this affair."

Both Shade and Kate had flown in for this event and were staying with them at Castello. They'd all received the invitation to the official ball following the mating of Master Farnese's daughter, of the Sicilian coven. The Farnese family had been long time allies to the Medici, and Octavio and Maria Farnese were eager to share the joy of their only daughter, Aurelia, mating a powerful master from

Spain. It was considered a slight of the highest order to miss such an occasion. Lorenzo had been to many such formal affairs and could only imagine the number his father must have attended. Sophia and Alfie would also be there, to represent the Medici's.

Chantal brushed off his shoulders and walked around him, inspecting him in the tuxedo. He hated wearing them, but she loved how handsome he looked in the tux. Besides, she enjoyed the chance to get dressed up and wear her expensive jewels. She quickly took another look at herself in the mirror.

"Well, if the nanny can get her from Bebe's grasp to put her down for the evening that will be quite something. I don't think your mother has let go of her since they arrived. I admit, I am looking forward to this grand occasion, but I do feel a pang of guilt leaving the baby behind." Checking the time, she turned to him. "Lorenzo, we must leave now, we do not wish to be late. The plane is waiting."

***

Kate had reluctantly left Grace with the nanny and now needed Theresa to help her get dressed quickly in the red strapless gown. The soft silk was ruched at the waist and fell in a straight column to the floor. She had secured the waist with a ruby and diamond broach and wore a pair of ruby and diamond earrings that dangled almost to her shoulders. She checked the time, and knew they should be leaving soon, but couldn't resist the impulse to check on Grace one more time. Slipping into the nursery, she scooped the baby up from her crib and held her against her shoulder. Grace has fed, and her eyes looked heavy with sleep. Kate sung her a lullaby as she walked with her to the window, singing a song she made up on the spot about the moon looking down on baby Grace.

Shade had finished dressing. His hair had been pulled back and tied loosely at the nape of his neck. He wondered how many times he'd attended these damn events in his lifetime. At least this trip would be made with much of his family, and he could spend the evening dancing with Kate, and socializing with masters he rarely got to see since moving to the States. He'd noticed when Kate slipped out of the room a short while ago, and now Theresa quickly came back in the room to fetch a shawl.

"Let me guess, she is with Grace."

Theresa smiled at her master. She'd been with the Medici family since his parents' time, and yet Castello was no longer home to her, it was Bel Rosso that was in her blood. Besides, coming back here was always a bit painful since she'd lost Marco. She could still feel his presence. "I am afraid getting her to leave tonight will be difficult. She is singing Grace a lullaby to get her to sleep."

Shade shook his head and took the shawl from Theresa. "I will deliver this. Go on, take the night off and visit with your friends."

He walked to the nursery and stood leaning against the doorjamb as he watched her with the baby. It brought back memories of her with their own children. She looked like a beautiful confection, and still made his mouth water. She seemed oblivious to him as she gently rocked the little one in her arms again. Her voice was soft as a whisper as she sang to the infant. He stepped quietly into the room and leaned over her shoulder.

"You look quite beautiful, *mi amore*, holding that angel in your arms."

She turned quickly to face him, gently rocking the infant in her arms. "Look at her, Shade. How can anyone have abandoned her? She's so beautiful. I'm so happy for Chantal and Lorenzo to have this gift. I think Grace is just what they needed. She's healed a lot of wounds already."

Kate kissed the baby's forehead, as Grace blinked her eyes, finding it hard to keep them open. "She's almost asleep. She's fighting it, just as Sophia used to do."

Shade chuckled. "Ah *si*, Sophia was never still for long, she viewed sleep as a waste of time. Come, *mi amore*, we must go. Chantal and Lorenzo are already downstairs waiting for us."

Reluctantly, Kate turned the baby over to the nanny, and slipped her arm into Shade's. "You look rather dashing tonight. You'll charm all the females at the ball, so be sure to let them know your dance card is already filled for the evening."

"*Si*, my queen, you have nothing to worry about. My eyes will be glued to your ass in that dress. Come!" Putting the shawl around her shoulders, they headed downstairs where Chantal was silently pacing. Shade laughed to himself. She was so very different from his *bel*. Chantal was a prominent social butterfly, whereas Kate had always been a home body. He grinned as Lorenzo was already pulling at his tie. Some things never changed. Sophia and Alfie had arrived and were waiting as well. Alfie was fidgeting even more than Lorenzo. Unlike Lorenzo, who'd been raised to understand his obligation to these social celebrations among their covens, Alfie had been raised solely in the camps and always felt a little out of his element among all the pomp and circumstance surrounding these events.

Dante was waiting for them outside in the limousine, as they all piled in and headed toward the airport. They'd fly to Palermo, on the island of Sicily, and then Dante would drive them to the estate. Lorenzo had made all the travel arrangements, and as usual, the Medici's were running late.

As they approached the old-world Sicilian castle, the place lit up the night sky. Dante navigated the long narrow drive to the door, and the staff led them inside. The ballroom was already crowded with guests as soft music played and the sound of light conversation and laughter carried over the sound of the music. Shade and Kate were the first to be announced to the room, as they were the patriarch and matriarch over all of the Medici covens.

"King Shade Medici and Queen Katherine."

As they entered the ballroom, the sound of conversation ceased, and all eyes turned in their direction.

"King Lorenzo Medici and Queen Chantal."

Lorenzo and Chantal followed behind them to the designated table.

"Prince Alphonso Medici and Princess Sophia."

Each of the men stood behind the chairs of their respective mates, until all of them had arrived at the table. Once the females took their seats, the males sat down next to them. Immediately, crystal urns of Midnight and Red Moon were set about the table, as the low murmur of voices resumed.

Shade looked about at his family. "Well, that was quite an entrance, *si*."

Chantal checked her phone and Kate leaned over and reassured her. "Grace is fine, she has her nanny, and Theresa is there. Stop worrying and enjoy the evening. You look beautiful, by the way."

Chantal slipped the phone back in her evening bag. "Thank you. Do you like the jewels? Lorenzo picked them out."

Kate smiled at her. “My son has excellent taste, in all things."

Chantal blushed at the compliment. A butler appeared and poured the wine into the goblets, and the family raised their glasses in a toast, "*Per sempre*, Medici."

They each drank from their glass before setting them back down on the table. Sophia leaned in and began a conversation with Chantal about the baby, and the two chattered away. Lorenzo was locked in conversation with Alfie, as the two laughed easily together. Kate slid her arm into Shade's as she looked at her children and their mates and took joy in their happiness. She kissed Shade on the cheek. "We did good."

"Oh, we did more than good.” He leaned in and kissed her and admired how the candles reflected back the light in her eyes and gave her skin a soft glow. "Damn, you are the most beautiful treasure I have ever seen." She smiled back at him with a smile that traveled all the way to her eyes, and it made his heart sing. He took a long sip of his Midnight, as his eyes roamed the room. His attention was caught by the unexpected appearance of Donatella at a nearby table. He hadn’t seen her since his offer to buy her land. She nodded to him, and he nodded back.

Kate followed his gaze as he nodded and turned to see the woman who’d betrayed her son. Shade could see Kate’s spine stiffen, as he responded. "That is a bit of a surprise."

Kate answered him softly, hoping not to draw attention. "I wish they hadn’t put her so close to our table. I don't think Lorenzo has noticed her yet. Please, let's not make a scene. We can be cordial...we should be cordial. There are too many eyes and too many gossips in this room to do otherwise."

Shade winked at her. “A wise decision, my queen.”

25

Shade looked around the ballroom, not really focusing on any one person. There wasn't anyone present who wasn't aware of the rift between the Medici and the Alizzi, but that wouldn't stop the gossip. *"Mi amore*, perhaps for protocol's sake, I should be cordial and go speak with her. Would you care to join me?"

Kate sighed, swallowing her pride. "I prefer not, but all eyes are on us, so let's get this over with." He stood and pulled out her chair as she took his arm and walked with him to the nearby table.

***

Dona had been seated at a table that had been set for four, but she was the only person seated there. She'd been surprised to receive the invitation from the Farnese's. Most of the masters had come to ignore her presence altogether since she no longer held any real power beyond her birthright, and the invitations to social occasions gradually disappeared. It was just as well, she'd convinced herself. She no longer had the funds to buy new gowns for such grand ceremonies. The gown she wore tonight was old, but her Lady in Waiting had reworked it to make it more presentable. Her jewels had been sold off years ago. Shade had made good on his promise and had continued to pay the wages of her butler and Lady in Waiting. Had he not, they would have had to leave her as well. She was acutely aware of the number of eyes on her, and the fact that no one else was assigned to sit at her table. She squirmed uncomfortably in her seat, sipping at the Midnight. There was a full carafe on her table, and she planned to drink all of it. The wine was expensive, and she rarely bought it anymore. She heard the rustle of a long skirt behind her and turned her head to see Shade and his mate approaching.

Shade stood at her table, Kate on his arm, and he had no intentions of sitting. "Good evening, Donatella. It is good to see you out. I am sure, as are we, you are most happy to see Aurelia has mated Master Diego Flores. It will be a good union indeed, for Italy and Spain."

Dona was taken aback by his sudden appearance. "I... yes, thank you. It should be a good union, I would think. It is always wise to align well with your matings." The words were barely out of her mouth before she realized she may have offended him. "I mean, my father always said that... you look well, Medici. Would you care to sit down?"

Shade felt Kate bristle as Dona stumbled over her words about wise matings before she quickly corrected them. There were quiet mumblings from the other guests, and he could feel all eyes on the King and Queen of Medici. "No, thank you, Donatella, I have a care to take a few spins around the dance floor with my beautiful mate, but I wish you a good evening." He nodded to her without a smile, and quickly led Kate out onto the dance floor, which now held several couples.

Lorenzo had noticed when his parents stood and left the table, and he looked over his shoulder to see his father talking to the Alizzi. He felt his temper rise, even after all this time.

Sophia saw his face getting red and kicked at his shins under the table. "Cool down, brother. Dad is just being cordial. We're under a microscope here."

Lorenzo turned back to the table and downed his Midnight. "Well, I'm not fucking going over there. I don't care who's watching."

Chantal turned discreetly to look back at the woman seated alone at the nearby table. She was tall and beautiful, even if her fashion was dated. She could hear the anger in Lorenzo's voice. She turned to him, keeping her voice low and speaking softly. "Who is that?"

Lorenzo took a deep breath. "That's the Alizzi; the Mistress whose territory borders ours."

Chantal felt her heart race. She knew Lorenzo's history with this woman. He'd explained to her that the Alizzi had betrayed and tricked him into having sex with her when he was much younger. "Are we not the King and Queen of all of Northern Italy, Lorenzo? Your father was performing his duty in being cordial. Are you ashamed to introduce me?"

Lorenzo dragged his hand across his face. "Chantal, please, it's hard enough for me to sit here when all I want is to choke the life out of her and watch her struggle for her last breath. Why would you want to meet her?"

Chantal was shocked by his anger. She had underestimated the level of hatred that ran through him for this female. "I apologize. It is not my place to counter your actions. But I was raised to be cordial even in the worst of situations within a social environment. My name required me to do so. If you will excuse me, I think I will use the powder room and check on Grace."

He quickly placed his hand over hers. 'I'm sorry. I didn't mean to take any of my anger out on you. You did nothing wrong." He leaned over to kiss her cheek. "Forgive me, *cherie*. I don't want to spoil our evening. When you return, will you dance with me?"

She locked eyes with him and smiled. She was grateful he wouldn't make a scene. "*Oui*, my king, we danced the first night we met, and I would like very much to feel as I did that night."

He leaned over to kiss her before he stood and pulled out her chair for her, as she left the table.

Alfie poured more Red Moon into his glass and filled Lorenzo's as well. "You sure as hell talked your way out of that one. Good come back." He noticed Sophia staring at him. "Look, I'm not going out on the dance floor. Your brother is the twinkle toes at this table. I hate this damn stuff. I'm just trying to smile and pretend I'm having a grand time."

Sophia raised one eyebrow. "I know you think you wear the pants in the family, Alfie Medici, so don't make me make a scene. You're dancing with me, and that's all there is to it."

Lorenzo laughed. "I suggest you not rile my sister. I promise it won't end well."

Alfie shook his head. "I should know better than to challenge her by now." He stood and pulled out Sophia's chair. Taking her hand, he led her to the dance floor. He grinned at her, as she gave him 'the look', and it made him laugh. He loved her spirit, and always had. It was what had attracted him to her in the first place.

Chantal returned to the table to find Lorenzo sitting alone. He immediately jumped to his feet and extended his hand. "My dance card is empty. I hope you'll give me the pleasure of your company."

Chantal smiled and took his hand. "I would be most honored."

She danced with him, and he moved her gracefully around the dance floor. He was handsome, and his demeanor commanded attention. Chantal held her head high, proud to be in his arms. She never felt more like a queen than when she was with him at a social event. Lorenzo had never lacked confidence.

The floor wasn't crowded, but the ballroom was huge. She continued to scan the crowd as he moved gracefully with her, when her eyes caught sight of an unusual vampire at one of the tables. He was sitting alone, but his dress distinctly defined him. His coat was of the finest maroon velvet, and white lace cuffs reached out below the sleeves, covering his hands to the joints of his fingers. She couldn't help but notice the many jeweled rings that covered each hand. It wasn't modern attire, and he appeared to have stepped out of time. As they danced around again, he was looking directly at her and she was a bit startled by the attention. His hair was long, well past his shoulders and black as a crow's wing. His eyes were dark pits and he looked at her as if he could drop her where she stood. He smiled at her, more a sneer than a smile. His whole demeanor was evil, and a small shiver ran through her. She quickly avoided his eyes and realized the dance was over. Lorenzo escorted her back to the table, as Shade and Kate joined them. Once seated, Shade filled everyone's glasses. Chantal nodded her head in the direction of the strange vampire, as she spoke to Shade. "Who is that vampire sitting back to your left? He is very different in appearance."

Shade turned his head to see who she was referring to, and his expression turned sour. "That would be Master Rodrigo Borgia, one of our greatest enemies. The Borgia's are no ally to the Medici. The feud that exists between us has been going on since my *padre's* day. Borgia is based in Rome but owns all the territory of southern Italy. The only thing that separates us is the land owned by the Alizzi. If he had his wicked way, he would have all of Medici territory as well. But that will never happen. He is one black-hearted bastard, Chantal. Stay close to Lorenzo when he is around. He is a great warrior, but not an honorable one."

Shade downed his glass of Midnight. He knew Rodrigo would probably be here given the scope and importance of this occasion. He took note that Rodrigo was alone. Neither Rodrigo, nor his brother Soren, had ever mated. They'd built an empire but not a legacy. They both had a reputation for unscrupulous behavior, and no master would approve of mating their daughters to the evil Borgia's. Shade was glad he had his family here tonight, a show of Medici greatness and strength.

Lorenzo looked to the table where Rodrigo was sitting. He'd heard his father speak about him all his life. In camp, all the warriors had been trained on the tactics used by the Borgia's, but he'd never crossed paths with him before. "So, that's Rodrigo?"

Shade huffed. "Son, that is one vampire that will give you a run for your money. He is older than I am, and one of the best warriors I know. His army of warriors can easily rival our own, and they are not trained to be honorable. Let sleeping dogs lie, there has not been any incidents between our families for many centuries and I don't intend there to be."

Chantal shivered again. "He looks completely wicked. He made eye contact with me when we were dancing. I got the strangest feeling from him. I had to look away."

Shade nodded. "Stay clear of him, all of you. He can be very charming, and he knows how to manipulate every situation to his advantage."

***

Rodrigo had watched as the Medici entered with his warrior son, one of his daughters, and their mates. His daughter looked much like the Queen, and he sensed a fire inside her that rather intrigued him. He sneered when he laid eyes on Lorenzo. He looked like his father, not quite as tall, but he had a long way to go to earn the same credibility as a warrior his father held. Still, it was known that the son was a fire-thrower, and that was something Rodrigo knew he had to respect. Rodrigo had always kept close tabs on the Medici lineage. They were all shocked when he mated the mortal, but then all was forgiven when she was reborn with the rare gift of animalism. No one had dared challenge the Medici for territory since the Battle of Bel Rosso and her gift was on full display. She had a reputation of killing deadly vampires. Rodrigo had heard the news from abroad that Canton was dead now as well, and Rodrigo had no doubts, that blood was on Medici hands.

The rumor mill kept him well informed, and he'd heard of their love for the half-breeds. Rodrigo huffed in disgust. The half-breeds were useless and should all be dead. He and his brother had slaughtered countless numbers of them. A deep, deadly chuckle rose up in him as he eyed the prominent daughter of Henri Valois. She was a beauty, and another alliance Medici had nailed down. Rodrigo had heard that Henri didn't take well to hearing the news his daughter had adopted a half-breed, and he was hoping it would drive a wedge between the Valois and the Medici. He'd welcome anything that would weaken Shade Medici's power.

As if he didn't have enough, the other Medici daughter sat on the Council in the United States, and Rodrigo was sure Shade Medici thought he couldn't be touched. Medici coins weren't the only coins that flowed into the Council's coffers. The Borgia had contributed greatly as well. Rodrigo looked down his nose at him. He'd been allowed to rise too high, gaining much land and power, and if anyone needed to be knocked down, it was Shade Medici.

He let his eyes roam and found Donatella sitting alone. What a pathetic beauty she was. Her fate had been tied to the Medici early on and look where it got her. The covens had watched as Dona had tried to regain his affection, to no avail, and then had switched her attention to the son. The rumors were rampant when Shade broke his alliance with her, and there were whispered stories that she'd tried to seduce the young Lorenzo.

Her territory bordered the Medici's and had been left unguarded. Her financial state was well known, as the covens watched the slow deterioration of her villa and her land. What a shame, but what an advantage for him. Dona needed funds, and he needed a better way to monitor the Medici. She was the perfect target, penniless and vulnerable, and her land would give him the perfect advantage. If the Medici had turned their back on her, perhaps there was an opening he could fill. She would fall subject to his charms, and then he'd take it all. Let the Medici strut his grandeur with Borgia right next door. His mouth watered at the thought. He watched Donatella as she drank heavily of the Midnight. She was hopeless and weak, and easy prey.

The Council and the covens revered the Medici, and it sickened him. Soon, they would all understand he'd own all of Italy. Standing, he nodded to the guests at the other tables. As he picked up his jeweled walking stick, he made his way to Donatella. It was time to begin the takedown of the Medici.

"*Scusi* Mistress, may I sit and talk a while with you? You are looking most lovely this evening, *bella*."

Dona had been pouring yet another glass of wine from the decanter when she was startled by his sudden appearance. She looked up at him with surprise. "What? Oh...yes, of course. Sit; may I pour you a drink?"

"*Grazie*."

He took the seat beside her and turned to face her. She was a rare beauty and could still take most men's breath away. He could easily fuck her into submission and get whatever he needed, without her being the wiser. Raising his glass, he offered a toast. "To *Italia*, and to the beauty of the creature beside me." As they each took a sip, he held her gaze over the rim of her glass.

"I am sure you remember me, Donatella, we have had a few encounters in our day, *si*?"

"I remember you well, Rodrigo. It has been centuries since our paths crossed. I was a young girl at the time. Even then, my father warned me about the Borgia's. You must know my fate. I'm sure it is no secret that I own nothing of value now. What brings you to my table?"

Lifting the decanter, he refilled her glass to the brim. "*Si*, you were young and beautiful. The Medici was a fool to let you go. Now he sits with the once mortal Queen. Just look at them, such a display. Not all gloat about you, *bella*. Some of us have long memories and ache for the days of long ago when things were much simpler. We took care of our own. We did not gloat with the size of our coven, nor the number of our warriors. Medici had nothing when he started. Borgia still has more, my dear."

He sipped his wine and let her take in his great strength and elegance. He let his words sink in. "I only wished to be cordial, and let you know that not all of us look down upon you. You were not treated fairly. But enough of this sad talk, I don't wish to spoil my evening. Why not dance with me? It would be a shame for you to come out on such a night and not dance, *si*? Would you oblige this master with such a simple request?"

She felt light-headed from the alcohol and was confused by his invitation. It was clear no one else was going to stop at her table, let alone ask for a dance, and she might as well enjoy herself. Besides, what's the harm in a dance? "I would be most pleased to dance with you."

He laid his hand across his heart. "I am honored."

Standing, he pulled out her chair and reached out his bejeweled hand, as the white ruffle of his shirt brushed against her hand as she laid it inside his. She staggered slightly as she stood, full of Medici liquor, and he steadied her. They gracefully walked to the floor and he began to dance with her, holding her close.

"We shall give them something to talk about. Imagine if your *padre* had aligned you with me, *bella*. Your fate would have been so different. Your life would be easy and carefree, full of love and not a care. All of Italy would have bowed at your feet."

Dona listened to his words. Was he mocking her? She wasn't sure. She knew her father hated the Borgia's, as did Shade's father, which was why they had both pushed so hard for Shade to mate with her, joining their two territories. Had Rodrigo called on her when she was a young girl and been turned away by her father? Was he interested in her still?

"Perhaps, but that is in the past. There was a sizable dowry once, but that is gone now. I have nothing to offer any male of my station."

Rodrigo didn't miss that several couples had removed themselves from the dance floor once they began to dance. He cared not. He had one thing in mind and that was to lure this helpless creature to him. "Well, we cannot change the past, *si*? I am saddened that it has come to this. But you have much to offer, *bella*. You are intelligent and beautiful; you would make any master a wonderful mate. Alas, I have not mated myself. I often wish I had. Once you become my age, there are no more wild oats to be sown, and it would be nice to have the company of an intelligent and beautiful female to enjoy, one who shares my old-world values." He smiled at her as he danced and led them around the floor, making sure he passed the Medici table several times. As the dance ended, he bowed to her slightly and escorted her back to the table. "You dance with such a light foot and as gracefully as ever, my dear. Would you oblige me one more thing this night, *bella*?"

"If what you ask is within my power to do so. What is it you seek, Rodrigo?"

"My heart is saddened that this has befallen you. The Medici is a brute to put such a hardship upon you. Would you allow me to call upon you? A simple evening of talk and company, or perhaps a trip into town, a café, or anything you would wish. Please, I must insist. I would enjoy your company."

Dona could think of no reason to turn him down. She hadn't had guests in her house in years, and many of her fine things had been sold off. She'd hate for him to see how she lived. "Perhaps I could meet you in town? I'm afraid my villa is not what it used to be."

"Of course, whatever arrangement pleases you." He retrieved an elegant calling card from his jacket and placed it discretely on the table. He bowed and took her hand, kissing it lightly. "I await your call, my dear. I am looking forward to it with much joy. I bid you a good evening."

He grabbed his walking stick and made his way onto the balcony before lighting up a cigarette. *Ah yes, my little bitch, you shall fall right into my hands.* He laughed out loud into the night air.

26

It was the day after the ball, and Lorenzo was pleased to see how much Chantal had enjoyed the evening, even though she'd missed Grace, and checked on her well-being often during the evening. He made a mental note to be sure he took her out more often. In the meantime, he received a call from a jeweler in Florence who'd been looking for a special piece of vintage estate jewelry for him. It was a grand, one-of-a-kind piece designed by Cartier, a panther bracelet, covered in diamonds, with sapphire eyes. He walked to the camp in search of Alfie, to see if he'd like to go with him. "You busy, or can you turn this over to one of the lieutenants and go with me to Florence?"

Alfie was rubbing his eyes, feeling a little sluggish after all the drinking last night. He lit up a cigarette as Lorenzo approached and tossed him the pack. "I'm not that busy, easy enough to turn it over, brother. What the hell is in Florence that needs your attention?"

Lorenzo caught the pack of cigarettes from him and lit up before tossing the pack back. "I had a jeweler looking for an estate piece for me, and it finally went on auction. He grabbed it up, so I need to go pick it up and pay for it. Won't take long."

Alfie shook his head and grunted. "You bought her more jewels? She can only wear so damn many at once, brother." Alfie blew the smoke up toward the sky and looked at him. "You know, she told Sophia that she needs to get a bigger vault because you've given her such a selection. Fuck, brother, you're making me look lame."

Lorenzo exhaled the smoke and laughed. "I have a lot to make up for. You've been a more attentive mate to my sister than I've been to Chantal. She was feeling alone and isolated, and I should never have let that happen. So, what do you say? You want to join me?"

Alfie shrugged as he slapped Lorenzo on the back. "Let's go then." As they teleported out, he shouted over to his friend. "I better get a drink out of this at least."

Lorenzo laughed. "I'll buy you a drink as soon as we pick up the bracelet."

They landed in the city center of Florence near Ponte Vecchio and pushed their way through the throng of tourists to get to the bridge that crossed the river Arno. The jewelry stalls lined both sides of the bridge and the crowds made it almost impossible to move. Florence was known for its high-quality gold jewelry, and tourists were pushing at each other, looking for a deal. Lorenzo saw his contact look up as he was finishing a transaction with a tourist and wink at him, nodding his head upward, indicating he'd meet him in the passageway above the covered bridge. Lorenzo nodded his head and nudged Alfie to follow. Lorenzo led him behind one of the jewelry stalls and up a hidden staircase to the Vasari Corridor that extended the full length of the bridge. The private corridor was built in 1564 for one of Lorenzo's mortal ancestors, Cosimo, so he could travel around the city without danger, hiding him from his enemies. The passage connected directly to the Medici Palace in Florence and extended all the way to the Boboli Gardens. He leaned against the wall and waited patiently for the jeweler who appeared within minutes.

"Sorry to keep you waiting, Lorenzo."

"No problem, old friend. Did you find the piece I was looking for?"

The man gleefully reached into his pants pocket and pulled out the diamond studded bracelet set in platinum gold, the blue eyes of the panther shining bright. Lorenzo smiled. "That's the one. How much did you have to pay?"

The jeweler winced. "Two-point-five million. I hope that's okay. If not, I can find another buyer."

Lorenzo took the bracelet and gave him a wide grin. "My accountants will bring you the money within the hour."

The jeweler nodded. "*Si, grazie*. Anytime you need anything, you call me, *si*?"

Lorenzo shook his hand and slid the priceless bracelet into his jeans pocket, as he and Alfie returned back down the stairs to the main corridor across the foot bridge.

Alfie was astounded at the price tag attached to the piece. He laughed softly. "I know Chantal's a queen, but damn brother, that was one hunk of change you just dropped back there. I hope to hell you get your money's worth."

Lorenzo draped his arm around his shoulder. "She's worth it, and like I said, I have a lot to atone for. Come on, I think I have enough money left to buy you a drink."

They left the Ponte Vecchio and made their way into the city and found a bar that was frequented by locals. Lorenzo slid into a booth and lifted two fingers to the bartender, who caught his signal and poured two Red Moons for them. A waitress picked up the order and delivered it to the table.

"Here you go, gentleman. Lorenzo! I haven't seen you in a while."

Lorenzo quickly scanned her face and tried to remember if she was on his list of conquest, but he'd been mated too long, and those faces were a blur. "Yeah, don't come in much."

Alfie bit his lip. He could see his brother trying like hell to come up with a name to the face and knew it was a useless exercise. The list of women they'd both gone through was far too great to remember. As the waitress winked and left, he couldn't let that one go. "We can't go anywhere, you know that. Now I know how Shade always felt. There's one of them always lurking around, waiting to pounce. We can't fucking remember them all, but they remember us."

Alfie raised his glass and Lorenzo followed suit, as the glasses clinked, they laughed. "Here's to the ladies that had us while they could." Alfie downed the Red Moon. "Did you see Borgia dancing with Dona last night? Think it's anything to keep an eye on?"

Lorenzo turned serious. "I saw it. I'm not sure if it means anything or not. She arrived alone, which is no surprise, but he was alone too. May just have been a coincidence, you know? I mean, it's not like Rodrigo could have asked to dance with the mate of any of the other masters there. I don't think he has any allies in that group. I'm trying not to read too much into it."

***

Vanni walked into the bar and immediately felt the presence of other vampires. He scanned the bar as his eyes quickly settled on Lorenzo, the bane of his existence. He noted the ever-present Alfie, sitting across from him. He still blamed Lorenzo for ending his time at the

Medici warrior camp, and for setting him on fire in front of the other warriors. His own father, a Medici warrior, had denounced him as his son, and made sure he understood he'd shamed their entire family. He'd been kicked out of his home and left to make his own way in the world. He had self-trained on the streets and now he was a mercenary warrior for hire, and a damn good one. He'd vowed to one day show Lorenzo he could rival his skills at any turn. He spent most of his time in Rome and Naples, seeking out any master willing to hire a mercenary. The Borgia had been extremely good to him, hiring his services whenever they were in a conflict. He still had a few contacts in Florence who hadn't shunned him, so he'd visit on occasion. He never expected to see Lorenzo and Alfie here. It had been well over a hundred years, but his seething anger over how that bastard had taken away his life dream still ate away at him. He slipped onto a bar stool and ordered his drink, trying to ignore their presence.

***

Alfie shrugged. "I noticed Shade didn't really seem to be bothered by it, so just thought I'd ask your thoughts." Alfie turned to get the attention of the waitress for another drink when he saw him. It wasn't unusual to run into vampires in Florence at this time of evening, the city offered a ripe feeding ground, but he was surprised to see Vanni after all this time. "What the hell is he doing in here?" Alfie nodded towards the bar.

Lorenzo looked up from his drink and followed Alfie's nod towards the bar. He saw Vanni sitting there, occasionally casting a sideways glance in their direction. "Vanni, haven't seen him in years. No coven patch on his leathers, must be a mercenary now. Besides, what kind of asshole wears his leathers around mortals?"

Alfie looked at him with a scowl on his face. "Is that all you have to say? What the hell is he doing in Medici territory is what I want to fucking know. I thought he was long gone out of the country. Father threw him out. Just looking at him makes me want to smack the hell out of him."

Lorenzo shook his head. "Let's not start anything inside the bar. I don't want to draw attention. Wait until he leaves. I'm not looking for a fight, Alfie. I just want him to move on."

Vanni took his time with his drink, checking out the female tourists that were milling about the bar. He was far from home and needed some company. He was keeping his eyes on the two Medici's but knew Lorenzo would never confront him in public. Vanni huffed to himself. Lorenzo would always ride on his daddy's coat tails. After a good hour, he got up and retreated outside, wondering if they'd follow. He strolled easily through the night, keeping his eyes peeled for easy prey to relieve the ache in his stomach for feeding.

As soon as Vanni left, Lorenzo tossed some money on the table and nodded to Alfie. "Let's go." The two of them got up and followed him outside. They looked up and down the darkly lit street, and could see him nearing a streetlight where a mortal female stood alone. "Better move fast. Looks like he's out to feed."

Alfie agreed. "I'm going around the other side of the street, come up from behind the girl. Staying in the shadows, but if he makes a move, I got her."

Alfie looked around to make sure they weren't being observed, then teleported over the buildings and landed quietly behind the girl about half a block away. She wouldn't notice him, but he could still listen and see all that Vanni would do. Vanni looked like he was going for the kill, and not just to feed.

Lorenzo moved quickly, coming up from behind as Vanni approached the girl. "Hey, Vanni."

Vanni spun on his heels and faced Lorenzo. Bastard was going to ruin his night of fun! He wasn't in the mood and decided to stand his ground. The spoiled king wasn't going to thwart his plans. "Well, if it isn't the spoiled little prince. Or should I say king? Slumming it?"

Lorenzo ignored the jab. "What are you doing in Florence? This is Medici territory. You run out of victims?"

The young girl's attention was drawn to the two men who appeared confrontational, and she started looking around to see if anyone else was nearby.

Vanni laughed in his face. "Just traveling through, thought I'd stop and see if your ass had any control over here. But then again, I guess Daddy makes sure you do a good job. What are you going to do about it, spew some fire at me?"

Alfie watched closely as Lorenzo kept Vanni occupied and Vanni's back was turned to the girl who seemed paralyzed with fear.

He stepped out and made his presence known to the girl as she turned, looking back at him with fright. Holding up his hand, he spoke in a calm voice. "No need to be frightened. I mean you no harm, but it looks like things could get ugly between those two, so go on ahead and move down the street, don't look back and go quickly. I won't let anything harm you."

The girl glanced back at the two men who appeared to be facing off against each other, then back at Alfie. She had no idea what was about to go down but was smart enough to take advantage of an opportunity to leave. As she quickly skirted down the street, Alfie stepped out in the light of the streetlamp. He took a stance that clearly communicated he was taking no bullshit from anyone.

Vanni turned his head and saw him standing in the halo of light cast by the streetlamp. "So, I see you still have your lap dog protecting your ass."

Alfie growled. "That would be Prince Medici to you."

Vanni stood facing Lorenzo once again. "Yeah, I heard the rumor that you were banging his redheaded sister. Good move, Alfie. That's one way to advance your career."

As Alfie stepped forward, Lorenzo held up his hand. "No need to let things get out of hand here. Just move on, Vanni. Not a request."

Vanni sneered. "Yeah, that's what I thought. Still more mouth than action. I'm done dealing with your two lame asses." He lifted straight up, teleporting back out to Rome. He was done with Florence, for now.

Alfie kicked the street with his boot. "Damn, I want to throttle him, he's one mouthy bastard."

Lorenzo laughed. "I could see you frothing at the mouth for a fight, but I've got a two and a half million-dollar bracelet in my pocket that is vintage Cartier. Chantal would have my ass in a sling if I brought it home broken."

Alfie chuckled. "Okay brother, I'll give you a pass on that one. But now that I'm all worked up, it might be a good idea to get back to camp, so I can take out my anger on some young warriors."

Lorenzo slapped his back. "Good idea, brother. My sister thinks I get you in too much trouble as it is."

"Well, she'd be right!" As they both took off back to Castello, their laughter was caught in the night wind, traveling in the air over Florence.

27

It had taken Natalia several months to get the Council members to agree to change the bylaws regarding the care of half-breeds. The new law stated the half-breeds could no longer be destroyed by Council, and any vampire who sired a half-breed child could relinquish the child to Council, where the child would be raised and educated in safety, and returned to the respective coven, if known, when they reached maturity, to become a contributing member of the coven. Once the U.S. Council adopted the new law, the European Council followed suit. The Eastern Council in Asia had not agreed and remained with their original law.

Natalia had been busy overseeing the development of the orphanage, and hiring the staff of nanny's, wet feeders and tutors. The Council communicated the new law to the covens, and they'd barely opened their doors before the first children were dropped off there. Sometimes, the mother stepped forward, brought by the male vampire that had impregnated her, and they relinquished the child together. Other times, the child was left at their doorstep. Regardless of how they arrived, the Council had agreed, there could be no punishment or admonishment for the vampire or the mother, or it would discourage them from coming forward.

The facility was built to accommodate ten children, with the capacity to expand. There had been no records of half-breed births, and they really had no idea what to expect. They had seven children already, ranging from infants to adolescents. The infants were the easiest, because they could work with them from birth to integrate them into the vampire culture. The adolescents were more difficult, as they had grown up trying to fit into two distinct cultures, neither of which had accepted them before. The older children were often angry and sullen and took extra attention.

Natalia had already ordered that the expansion of the orphanage begin and had added some therapists to the staff to assist the older children, but all in all, she was quite pleased with how things had evolved. Of course, until the children had grown to be adults and integrated into a coven, they wouldn't really be able to judge the success of the program. Natalia had a unique perspective, having grown up with a half-breed brother, she felt confident the program would work. She'd call her mother at least once a week to give her an update, and both Kate and Shannon had let her know if she needed any volunteer staffing to help with the children, they'd both be available. The European Council was following her model and duplicating her methodology in their orphanage.

The change wasn't without controversy, and there were many who still looked down on the half-breeds and thought this was a waste of time. Natalia knew she had a lot riding on this. As she made her way back to her private room, she felt bone tired. She was caught off guard when she entered her room to see Marcello waiting for her. "Marcello! What are you doing here? Did anyone see you come in?"

He chuckled as he stood to hug her. "Now what kind of warrior would I be if someone saw me enter? You don't sound very sure of my skills, Natalia."

She allowed herself to be enveloped in his hug, his muscular arms enfolding her, pulling her tight against his hard chest. It felt good to be comforted, instead of the one always giving comfort. "Mmm, this feels nice."

He kissed the top of her head. "I can make it feel much nicer."

She laughed as she broke free. "Can I take a rain check on that? I need to call my mother."

He kissed her mouth, with the promise of what was to come. "A check I plan to cash, and soon. I'll be back after next rounds." He winked at her and left as quietly as he'd entered. Natalia fell back on the bed, releasing a big sigh. She'd never planned to mate and yet, she had the love of her life with her every day. She'd never planned to have children, and here she had an orphanage full of them. It's funny how life worked out sometimes. She got up and splashed some cold water on her face, and looked at her image in the mirror, noting the dark circles under her eyes. Her death slumber would pull her down soon, so she rushed to the only conference room with a phone and asked the sole monitor there for some privacy. He exited the room as she sat before the big screen and spoke to the computer to call her mom. She listened to the soft trill of the phone, and within minutes, her mother's face appeared on the screen. "Mommy!"

Kate beamed back at her. "You look tired, Natalia. Are you getting enough rest? Are you feeding enough?"

Natalia laughed. If her mother only knew how often she was with Marcello. "Mommy, I'm fine. I never appreciated how much work this would be, but I love it. We got another infant today, bringing us up to seven. I'm glad I'd already ordered the workers to start on the expansion."

Kate shook her head. "Seven! Natalia, that's wonderful. That's seven children who would probably never have survived their childhood. I'm so proud of you, daughter. Do you need my help?"

Natalia nodded. "Yes, please. Maybe if you and Auntie Shannon could help with some of the older kids. They don't adapt as well, and they have a lot of anger. Maybe if you had a regular schedule where you visit?"

Kate smiled back at her. "Of course, we'll be happy to. I'll talk to Shannon, and we'll work out what days work best for us, and I'll get back to you."

Natalia's smile spread across her face. "Thanks, Mommy! Oh, and how is Grace doing?"

"She's fine. Growing like a weed. She'll be walking soon."

Natalia nodded. "Give them all my love. I have a lot to do, but I wanted to check in. Tell Daddy I love him."

Natalia blew her a kiss, and Kate caught it. "I love you, Nattie. Get some rest!"

As the image faded from the screen, Kate sighed. Shade would be in the camp a little longer, so she headed downstairs to find Shannon and Luca, so they could pick what days they could go together to the orphanage.

***

Shade had left the camp in Christoph's hands. Spring always brought new recruits and busy nights at camp, but over the years, he'd tried to step back and let his SICs and lieutenants take command, so they too could gain more experience in leading. Tonight, he'd decided to make a few rounds in D.C. He'd do this every few months, making sure things were running smoothly and Theo had everything under control. He flew low over the bustling life in Georgetown, and then further into the heart of the capital. They hadn't seen a skirmish in D.C. in a very long time. He changed his route and headed over to the Dead House, entering the old Victorian building. The house had served them well throughout the years, and they had modernized the command center to provide them with the latest in surveillance technology. He walked to the control room and found Theo busy on the computer, as his eyes scanned the numerous screens. "Well, I am glad to see you are so damn busy."

Shade sat in one of the office chairs and propped his feet up on the desk. "Just made a few rounds over the city and found it crowded but boring."

Theo nodded, keeping one eye on the screens. "Weather is getting warmer. That always brings out more tourists and things start to pick up this time of year. Haven't had any problems, so far. How are the new recruits? You get a good batch to work with this year?"

Shade answered him as his eyes moved from screen to screen. "It was a slightly smaller turnout this year, but it is the very first year that the camp took in more females than males. I have to tell you; I think half of it has to do with my grandson. The word gets around, the camp is being run by a new generation of Medici, and he's unmated. That worries me sometimes, but so far, he hasn't shown any favoritism." Shade shrugged and shook his head.

Theo laughed. "Well, there's something about that Medici charm that definitely appeals to the females." He picked up a pack of cigarettes and pulled one free with his teeth before tossing the pack to Shade. As he lit up and exhaled, he looked around the room to make sure they were alone. "So, how's that orphanage thing working out?"

Shade took the offered pack of cigarettes and lit up his own before shifting his eyes to Theo. It seemed an odd question for him to ask. "Nattie has it up and running and they already have about six or seven children in there. The expansion is still in the works. I am really proud of her, *and* Lorenzo, they have made a big difference for the half-breeds. It is long overdue, in my opinion."

Theo nodded then leaned his head back and exhaled the smoke slowly. "So, there are no consequences for the vampires? I mean, if they bring in a half-breed, they can just, you know, leave the child there, and... walk away?"

Shade looked at him quizzically. "None. The point of all of this is to stop this ancient belief that the half-breeds must be destroyed." Shade paused a moment, taking a drag on his cigarette, to see if Theo responded. When he was silent, he continued. "I would hope that any vampire who knew he had sired a half-breed would want to take responsibility."

Theo avoided his eyes. "Well, I'm not sure what you mean by take responsibility. I mean, a warrior without a mate can't very well bring home a child, like you did." He held up his hand. “You know I have no ill feeling about half-breeds. We have all had Cory in our lives too long not to see that the half-breeds can be an active part of the coven. So, when these kids are grown...they join the coven then, assuming you know where they came from?"

Shade stood to his full height and stretched his arms over his head, before leaning down, placing both hands on the desk and looking at the screens. He wasn’t sure what the hell this was all about. "They will be well educated and raised in a safe environment. They will have clean feeders and learn how to survive in our world. And yes, it is my hope that they will be able to return to the original coven from which they were sired. If the coven refuses them, then Kate and I will take them into Medici." Shade glanced over at Theo. "So, which one of my warriors has a half-breed?"

Theo nervously shuffled some papers on his desk, afraid to look his master in the eye, not wanting to disappoint him. He answered in a voice barely above a whisper. “I do, master."

Shade stood up slowly. Theo? He knew he had to set the example for every master and acknowledge the courage it took for any vampire to step forward. He sat down and spun the chair, so it faced Theo. "Look at me."

Theo turned in his chair and locked eyes with him. Theo had been an honorable and trusted warrior. "It is okay. I think no less of you. Actually, I would expect nothing less from you. We will help you. How old is this half-breed and where is he?"

Theo shook his head. "I just found out. I met this girl in one of the clubs, and she used to show up a lot, and she was willing, so, you know, I kept going back to her. Hadn't seen her in a while though, and then, this week, I saw her in the club. She came up to me and told me she had a baby...my baby. She was already overwhelmed. Asking me questions about what to do."

Shade could feel the uneasiness inside Theo, but he felt something else as well, a need to know that his own flesh and blood would be taken care of. Shade laid his hand on his shoulder. "Relax, we are going to take care of this right now. Get whoever you need back in here to take over command. No explanation is needed. Then you and I are going back to Bel Rosso. We will call Natalia and see where she guides us. You know how to contact your girl?"

Theo nodded. "Yeah, I put her number in my phone. I told her I'd figure out something and get back to her. Not sure she believes me."

"Then she is in for a huge surprise, because Medici coven takes care of their own. Not sure how much she can be involved in raising this child, if at all. That's why we need to get Natalia on the phone immediately."

Matteo appeared in the Dead House, having been summoned back by Theo. "You need me, Theo?"

Theo nodded. "Leaving for a while, and I need you to take over command until I return." Theo tapped the screen. "Everything is here, just scroll through the screen." He flipped through several screens, showing him the grids and who was assigned where. A bright red spot glowed on each grid. "All the warriors are micro-chipped, so you can see exactly where they are."

Matteo nodded. "Got it," he responded as he slid into his chair.

Having left Matteo in charge, they both teleported directly back to Bel Rosso. Gi was immediately there, and Shade directed him to find Kate and have her come to his office. As they walked inside the office, Shade headed to the small bar and poured them a Midnight. "You need this more than me right now. Your duties are over for the night."

Theo nodded and accepted the drink. Shade slid into his huge leather chair behind his desk and smiled, feeling his *bel* approaching, her curiosity piqued.

Kate entered the office, surprised to see Theo. "Theo! What a pleasant surprise." He was one of the quieter warriors. Shade had kept him assigned to the Dead House for a very long time, and she rarely ever encountered him.

Theo jumped to his feet when she entered, almost knocking over his glass of wine. “My lady."

Kate laughed, still amused that these massive warriors still got nervous in her presence. “Please, sit down." Kate looked at Shade questioningly, wondering why she’d been summoned to this meeting with a warrior, as she took a seat.

"Sit down, Theo. Relax. *Mi amore*, Theo has come to me with a dilemma. He has just discovered he has a half-breed infant. He is in contact with the female, but I am not sure what we should do next, beyond contacting Nattie. I know Theo has some very important questions, so I think it would be advisable to get her on the phone. Thoughts?"

"Yes, call Natalia. I don't think there are any rules to follow. But she can help guide Theo." She turned her attention to the warrior who looked uncomfortable in his own skin. "You did the right thing, by coming to us. Your child will have a chance now."

Shade dialed up the number to the Council and his call was answered immediately as the image appeared on the large, televised screen hanging on the office wall. "This is Master Shade Medici. I wish to speak with Ivory, it is of extreme importance." He was told that Ivory would be summoned, and he waited to see his daughter appear on the screen.

Natalia heard the tap at her door and the messenger told her there was a call. Perhaps it was Malachi. She pulled the hood over her head and hurried to the conference room. When she saw her father's face on the screen, she was confused. "Dad?"

"There is my princess. Sorry to disturb you, Nattie, but as you can see, I have your *madre* and Theo here. We have something we need your help on. You remember Theo, do you not?"

Natalia pushed the hood back slightly from her face. "Of course, I remember him. He used to chase me and Sophia through the hay barn when we were children. We would try to hide from him, and he’d pretend to be the monster." Natalia laughed at the memory. "How can I help you?"

Shade looked over at Theo and grinned. Theo was sitting there nervous as hell but nodding his head in remembrance. "Nattie, Theo has just found out that he has a half-breed infant. Theo has posed some questions to me that I truthfully cannot answer. But before I turn this over to him, a few things I am concerned about. One, is there a test that is conducted so that Theo can be assured this is his *bambino*? His female is a clubber." Shade turned back to Theo. "No offense, Cory's *madre* was a clubber as well, and we will take this child no matter, but I want to make sure this one is definitely yours if possible." Theo nodded. Turning back to the screen, Shade continued. "Please tell me there is room available, because I want to make sure that, if this *bambino* is his, he becomes part of the Medici coven."

Natalia nodded. "We have room, and yes, we can test for paternity. That's not a problem. He needs to bring the child to us at the orphanage, and they'll get DNA samples from the child and from him. We don't allow the mortals inside because we don't expose the identity of the other vampires who live and work here taking care of the children. We know there are mortals who speculate on the Council, but of course, they have no way to prove what goes on inside these walls. Unfortunately, while we were able to get both Councils to agree to take in the half-breeds, they wouldn't agree to allow the mortals to stay in contact with their children. The children become ours. Theo may visit the child if he wants to, but it's totally up to him."

Theo nodded his head, glad that he'd not have to give up all rights to his son. As a warrior, he'd never mated, and never expected to have children. He found his emotional bond to this child unexpected. "I can bring him. No problem. His mother was already at wits end, because he wanted to feed. She has to hide him from her family. I can pay whatever it costs to keep him there, and I will be happy to visit, and make sure he knows who his father is."

Natalia shook her head. "There's no charge. We wanted no barriers to bringing the children here. The sooner you bring him, the better, Theo. He's at risk in the mortal world. You don't need an appointment. Someone is ready to receive children at any hour of the night or day. Okay? Bring him soon, please."

Theo nodded, assuring her he would.

Shade was proud that Theo was stepping up. It was good for all his warriors to understand there was no longer shame in this procedure. "Thank you, Nattie, I am so proud of what you have done. It is good to know we can finally save these souls." Shade spun in his chair and looked at Kate. "You are too quiet in this."

Kate stood and walked to the chair where Theo sat and kissed the top of his head. "You did the right thing. Your son will grow up safe, and receive the best education, and when he reaches maturity, he'll come here, and live near you in the camp. Cory helps out at the orphanage, training the children who are interested, in leatherwork. Others are taught weapons skills, and how to care for and maintain weapons, so they can help out in the camp. Angelo also works with them, training them to care for horses. If they want something formal, like lawyer, or accountants, they are given that education. The future is their own."

Shade blew a kiss to Nattie and then disconnected. He was glad Kate was here to offer comfort to his warriors. "Theo, you need to contact your female and arrange to pick up the child. You need to make this female understand that her child will be cared for, and given a good life, but she can't be involved. You should be sure she understands that you will be a part of this child's life. Once you have the baby, Kate and I will go with you to the orphanage. Any questions?"

Theo shook his head. "I don't think it will be a problem. She was in tears when she came to me. I can go to her anytime. I can go tonight if you want me to."

Shade looked to Kate. "What do you say, *mi amore*, you willing to do this tonight?"

Kate nodded. "Of course, yes. We'll make the time."

Shade stood from his chair, directing his comment towards Theo. "I think, warrior, you need to go get your son."

Theo stood, and they fist bumped.

"Just bring the child back to Bel Rosso, we will be waiting, and then we will all go to the orphanage."

Theo left immediately, and Shade took Kate in his arms, grateful for her warmth and constant support. "I think this coven will never stop growing."

28

Theo teleported to the mortal's apartment building and knocked on the door. He could already hear the wails of the newborn inside. The young woman answered the door, looking frazzled, and gave him a hard stare. "Can I come in?"

She pushed the door open and turned and walked away from him without answering. Theo stepped into the small apartment, already feeling cramped for space, and closed the door behind him. The small one-bedroom efficiency apartment wasn't designed to accommodate the needs of an infant. The attractive woman he'd bedded already looked older, and it was clear she wasn't sleeping, her eyes red from frequent crying. She'd let the infant feed from her, and she looked pale and anemic. He heard someone banging on the wall of the apartment next door as they shouted, "For god's sake, make that baby shut the fuck up!" She broke into tears again, and he tried to take her in his arms, offer comfort, but she broke free. She had only anger in her heart now.

"I have a solution. I found a place for Noah."

She looked at him with a mixture of confusion and anticipation. "What do you mean, you found a place?"

He sat down on her ragged sofa and lifted the newborn from a drawer on the floor she'd pulled from the dresser to use for a cradle. The infant appeared impossibly small in his strong hands, but stopped crying immediately, and looked deep into Theo's eyes. The woman dropped into a chair, exhausted, but happy for the silence.

"What place? What are you talking about, Theo?"

He rocked the baby gently and laid him over his shoulder. "We have an orphanage, for half-breeds. They'll be given a good home there, with nannies who will take care of them, and feeders, and tutors. When they're grown, they'll be assigned to a coven, where they'll have a job, a role to play to support the coven."

She cocked her head to the side. "Are you just making this up?"

He shook his head. "No. I'm telling you the truth. I want what's best for him too, you know."

She laid her head back against the chair, closing her eyes and not speaking. For a moment, he thought she may have fallen asleep, when she finally spoke. "Will I be able to see him?"

Theo's voice was soft when he answered. "No. I'll see him. I'll make sure he's okay, and when he's grown, he'll come to my coven. But you'll have to let go. The others can't risk being exposed."

She nodded her head as she stood and started to gather his meager belongings, carefully folding them into a diaper bag. "Then do it now, before I change my mind." The tears fell silently down her cheeks.

He took the bag from her and leaned down to kiss her, but she turned away. His heart broke for her. "I'm sorry. I never meant to hurt you."

She answered in a whisper. "I know. Just go now, please."

With the infant on one shoulder, he slipped the blue diaper bag over his other shoulder and teleported back to Bel Rosso. When he landed in the expanse of grass in front of the Tuscan-style house, Aegis moved forward to greet him, sniffing at the infant. Theo scratched the wolf behind the ears as he knocked on the door. Gi answered, and welcomed him in.

Kate heard the commotion in the foyer and headed for the front door to see the warrior, holding an infant and a blue diaper bag, looking completely out of his element. "Here, give him to me."

Theo slipped the baby into her arms, and said, "This is my son. This is Noah."

Shade could feel Theo's presence inside the house and heard the voices. Quickly leaving his office, he walked to the living room where he found Kate holding an infant. Theo stood near her, looking uncertain.

"I never get tired of seeing you with a *bambino* in your arms, *mi amore*." He smiled as she looked down at the bundle in her arms. Shade turned his attentions to Theo. "Any problems?"

Theo shook his head. "No. I think she was relieved that we had a solution. I still feel bad, though. She didn't look healthy. I'm not sure either of them would have survived if we hadn't taken him."

Shade nodded. "Her body will replenish the blood she has lost but keep an eye on her. She did give birth to your son. If she needs help, find a way to help, with or without her knowing. You are a

Medici warrior, and I expect you to do what is honorable." Walking to Kate, he looked down at the baby wrapped in a thin cheap blanket. "You know you have to give him up, *mi amore*."

Kate rocked slowly back and forth with the infant in her arms. "Well, not really. Natalia has asked that Shannon and I help out, so I will probably see him every week. I'll have the best of both worlds. Like grand-children, I can leave them for someone else to take care of when I come home."

Shade grunted. "Well, this is the first I am hearing of this. You will make sure Luca escorts you both and stays there with you. No argument. Even though Medici warriors protect the orphanage, it is still a new concept and incidents may occur. I know you can take care of yourself, but I insist Luca is with both of you. Now come, we must get to the orphanage." Holding her close with the infant in her arms, he looked down at her. "I do believe it best, *mi amore*, if Theo takes his own son, *si*?"

Kate smiled back at him, "Making you nervous, is it?"

He chuckled at her response. "I know how quickly you get attached. The longer you hold him, the harder it will be for Natalia to pry him from your arms." Shade turned to Theo. "And you, does this *bambino* have a name?"

Theo nodded. "His mother named him Noah."

Shade looked back at the infant. "Well, Noah, welcome to Medici. Let's get you settled into your new home and get your life started." He smiled as Kate handed Noah back to Theo, who looked like a bull in a China shop. Nudging Kate, he laughed. "He reminds me of Marco. That time you handed Lorenzo to him before we went out on the balcony, and he screamed bloody hell for Theresa!"

Kate giggled at the memory. "Well, warriors and infants aren't always the best combination. Let's get going. It's chilly out at night, and I don't know how much immunity the half-breeds have. I want to see him safe and secure in the orphanage."

"*Si*, queen bee, let us be off." They all teleported to the orphanage located in northern Virginia. The orphanage sat on a beautiful, secluded plot of land far from any main roads, and within sight of the Council. As they came to the entrance, Shade immediately recognized his warriors on duty. "Warriors, we have come to make a delivery, please direct us where we are to go." Shade turned to Kate. "Any chance Nattie might be here?"

She shook her head. "I doubt it. She checks in from time to time on the operational needs of the orphanage, but she has her own duties to Council. I'm sure she'd come if you call her though."

"I wish she were here. I think I will do that." Shade telepathically called out to his daughter, asking her if she'd come immediately to the orphanage, explaining that he was there with Theo and his son. One of the warriors led them to a large waiting area and instructed them that someone would be right out to assist them. Shade paced the floor, hoping his daughter arrived soon. He watched Theo put Noah over his shoulder and bounce him a bit as he began to cry.

Natalia appeared in her white robe at almost the same time as one of the facility nannie's rushed forward to take the infant from Theo. The nanny looked at him, understanding without asking, that he was the father.

"We'll give him the best of care, don't worry. First, we'll assign him a wet feeder. After feeding, and a bath, he will be examined by a doctor. Did you want a paternity test, or no?"

Theo nodded. "Uh, yes, we want the test."

The nanny turned and said, "Follow me then. We'll get him settled first, then take a DNA sample."

Kate, Shade, and Natalia watched as Theo followed the nanny down the long hallway. Natalia shook her head. "That's eight now, in just six months. Glad I ordered the expansion."

Kate looked around the facility. It was spotless. "Do you know where they're from? The children?"

Natalia pushed the hood from her head, revealing her full face. "So far, all of them have been from the surrounding areas of Virginia, Maryland, Delaware, and D.C. I know the law was communicated to everyone. I assume we'll get children from other regions eventually."

Kate went exploring down the hall as Natalia walked alongside her. Kate looked into the rooms, some set up for teaching, some for play. She'd seen the plans for the building and knew there was a center courtyard where the children could play outdoors, away from any observing eyes. She stopped and turned toward her daughter. "Maybe, or maybe it's too far. The concept is new, and giving up a baby is hard, Natalia, even when that baby is a half-breed. Maybe we need more facilities, located across the country near the big cities where we have a heavy vampire population. Maybe one isn't enough."

Shade followed them down the corridor, listening to their conversation. "Your *madre* makes a good point, Princess. No vampire will travel a great distance for a *bambino* that is half-breed, they will destroy it first. We are working against an ancient way of thinking and trying to change attitudes will take time. The process must be convenient. We have to remove all obstacles. We need more facilities. Coordinating the building, the land, the faculty, and the funding is going to take some doing."

Natalia answered her father. "I can handle the planning and coordinate with contractors to duplicate the building. I just need the land, and the money. Maybe you can get other masters to give us some land within their territories, but the money to keep the places running? That's a tall order."

Shade paced back and forth in the hallway, his hand running through his curls. "I think there are masters who would donate territory. Not all will be so flexible. Not all masters think like I do. If Council can get them to agree to allocate the land, we can fund the building and all that goes with it." He stopped pacing and looked up at the ceiling and sighed. "I have been changed by the circumstances of my life. Kate has changed me, Cory has changed me. All of my children have changed how I see our world now. You will have your work cut out for you, to have the other covens give up territory to build."

Natalia gave him a stern look. "*I* have my work cut out for me? I was thinking you could take care of that. You know all of them, and who better than the Medici to make a request for their land. If you're agreeing to fund the facility, maybe they'd be willing to pay a fee when we return the children to their covens once they're adults. If not, so be it. I don't want to make their transition to the coven contentious. I understand it will take time for all of them to come to terms with this change."

Shade stared at this child of his own blood, as her temper flared directly at him. He locked eyes with her, his hands on his hips. She was passionate about this, and wanted what she wants, and demanded he make it happen. It suddenly hit him she was addressing him not as his daughter, but as Council. "*Si*, as the Medici, I will convince my fellow masters and use this facility as a guideline. It is as you wish, Ivory." He nodded to her just as he heard Theo approaching.

Kate turned her head and bit her lip hard to suppress the smile, as she watched their daughter take charge, issuing orders to her father in her role as Council. She heard the echo of a warrior's boot heels clicking on the floor of the long hall and saw Theo returning to the group, rolling down his sleeve.

"They took my blood. They said it would be a few days before they got the results. They'll let me know. They said not to visit for a while. They want Noah to get acclimated to his new routine and new surroundings." He looked from one to the other. "Did I miss something?"

Shade cleared his throat. "Well, you can be assured that Noah will receive the best of care. We were just discussing the issue of more orphanages across the country, near high population areas, just a Council to master meeting." Shade looked down and shuffled his feet before looking up at his daughter. He'd been taken aback by her assertiveness but was secretly pleased. She was a warrior in her own way. "Is there anything else I can assist you or Council with tonight?"

She smiled back at him, suddenly aware that she'd slipped into her authoritative role with him. It wasn't easy being the only female Council, and she'd had to learn to stand her ground among the males. "Sorry, Daddy. I didn't mean to be so harsh. With all the males here, if I want to be heard, I can't be timid, or they'll walk all over me. I'm thankful for your help."

"Well, you have earned the right to knock me off my perch. I tend to forget that your duty at Council is something I need to pay heed too. Malachi would be proud, and so am I." He lowered his head and mumbled. "You do have a bit of your *madre* in you."

She laughed. "And a bit of my *padre* too. I've seen your temper as well."

Shade threw back his head and laughed. "Well, I will take that as a compliment. I will be in touch. I love you Nattie, nothing will ever change that." He went to Kate and threw his arm around her waist, pulling her close. "I think it is time we head back to Bel Rosso. Noah is safe now. And besides that, the sun will soon be rising, and it has been a very busy night. What do you say? May I escort you home?"

Kate gave her daughter a quick hug and kiss and reminded her that she and Shannon would be coming back soon, before slipping into his arms and teleporting out. Theo remained behind for a second, shuffling his feet, and looking uncomfortably at Natalia, as she raised the hood back over her head.

"Uh, thanks for doing this."

Natalia nodded. "No thanks necessary, warrior." She turned to leave and walk back to her private quarters at Council, leaving him standing alone before he too teleported back to Bel Rosso.

29

The night was crisp and clear. Teleporting high above the Medici territory in Northern Italy, on his way to the Alizzi, Rodrigo could feel the power from the Medici camp in the air. He made the rounds of the Alizzi's territory. Donatella had been reduced to nothing in their world. She no longer held any power, and even her position as Mistress and Queen no longer had any value. She was an immortal who had failed miserably in keeping what she'd been given by birth. He sneered at what he saw of her estate. She'd let everything fall to ruin, but the locale itself was vital. He landed at the front door, making sure his elegant coat and long dark hair were presentable. A smile crept slowly across his face, and the sound of the chuckle that left his mouth was wicked and dripping with menace. She'd be such an easy target. He knocked and waited as the man servant answered the door and showed him into the drab, empty parlor. He was offered a glass of Midnight, which he accepted, and slowly took a few turns around the room as he waited for her.

***

Dona was in a bit of a panic as she quickly changed clothes and her Lady in Waiting brushed out her hair. Rodrigo had said he'd visit, but his arrival here was unplanned and she wanted to make sure she looked her best before greeting him. She finished her makeup, and applied some lipstick, looking at her reflection in the mirror. She admired the face looking back at her, her exotic beauty still intact. Satisfied that this was the best she could do, she waved her hand at her maid, dismissing her, as she rushed down the stairs and to the parlor to meet him. As she entered, he was walking around slowly, taking in the meager contents of the room as he sipped on the Midnight.

"Rodrigo! I apologize for keeping you waiting. I wasn't expecting you so soon."

He turned to greet her and smiled so gloriously; it could easily light up the dim room. "My dear, you look as charming and beautiful as ever."

Setting the glass down on the table, he walked to her with his hands held out before him. He took both her hands in his and lifting them to his mouth he kissed each palm. "I do beg your forgiveness, for I must admit that I have missed your company." Holding on to her hands, he looked at her face and smiled. "You are such a treasure to these old eyes. Come, let us sit and talk." He led her to the settee and sat down beside her. "Do say you forgive this old master for being such a rude brute. I should have given you notice of my arrival."

Dona smiled back at him. "I am always thankful for company, Rodrigo. Of course, you are forgiven."

He gently slid his arm behind her along the back of the settee, as his hand played with the silky dark hair that was her treasure. She was a beautiful female. There was no denying that. Dona always had an exotic face, and dark, alluring eyes. "*Grazie*, my dear. You have no drink. Please take a sip of mine. I fear I am quite comfortable, and do not wish to leave your side."

He handed her the glass of Midnight and nodded, prompting her to sip from it. "Come, relax, it is only me, the Borgia. You have nothing to be embarrassed about. I have been aware of the lack of financial stability in your life." His eyes scanned the room. "It saddens me to think you spend your time here, alone, in such a place. It is one of the reasons I have come without invitation."

She took a small sip from his glass. She kept the wine for guests only, unable to afford to drink it regularly anymore. "Well, yes, I do spend much of my time alone, but do not pity me, Rodrigo. I have grown used to it."

He watched her red lips along the rim of the glass and heard her sip and knew she'd kill for a vampire of his stature to feed upon. "Not pity, my dear, just a sadness that you have become used to such. You deserve better." He turned slightly so he was facing her. "Donatella, I have come to ask you something. It will be a great favor to me, and I hope, a wonderful escape for you." He slid his finger along her cheek, tipping her chin to look at him.

Donatella looked back at him, wondering what he could possibly ask of her. "What is it you wish to do?"

"I am hosting a very intimate gathering and hope you will consider coming to the Borgia estate and joining us. I would wish for you to stay a few nights. Enjoy my home, the grounds, the horses, and my company." He stood then and refilled the glass with Midnight. "Of course, my younger brother will be joining us. You do remember Soren, *sí*?"

"Soren, of course, I remember your brother. I can't recall the last time I saw him, though. So, this gathering, it will be formal?" She was already wondering what she could possibly wear for a multi-day event. She'd remade the dress she wore to the Farnese's in Sicily out of an older gown.

He could read her mind working out what to wear. "Do not fret, Donatella, I shall provide all that you need. It would be a pleasure for this old soul to get you away from this drab atmosphere for a while. Come and enjoy some time in luxury amongst friends. Ride with me, peruse my elegant gardens, drink my Red Moon and Midnight, dance, and enjoy the company of others without a care. I will prepare the grandest guest room at my estate for you. I'll send a car to pick you up. You need bring nothing. Will you oblige me?" He went down on one knee, taking her hands into his. "Will you give the Borgia much happiness by agreeing to share my company? Say yes, my dear."

Her mind was a whirl of thoughts. The Borgia had always been an enemy to her family, and to the Medici. But as hard as she tried, she couldn't think of a single incident involving the Borgia's in over a century. Old feuds did die over time, and certainly, they'd had no contact or reason to have conflict. She couldn't think of any reason to turn down his invitation. "I would be honored to be your guest, Rodrigo."

He had her right where he wanted her. He'd show her she couldn't live without him once she got used to the finer luxuries of life again. He leaned over and gently kissed her lips, letting the kiss linger. He pulled back slightly, and could feel her breath on his face, his eyes locked with hers. "You have made me quite happy."

Dona was no fool. She'd been on this earth long enough to know nothing came without a price. While she was eager to accept this invitation, she knew he'd expect something in return. He was a man of much wealth and power, and used to having what he wanted, when he wanted it. She didn't find him unattractive, but she felt no desire for him. She smiled and backed away slightly after his kiss. She knew he'd expect more from her if she went with him to his estate for several days, and she was wondering how much she was willing to compromise. "Well then, I am glad I can still make someone happy with just my company. I am looking forward to it, Rodrigo."

He stood, feeling her doubts. She wasn't desperate enough yet to return his advances, but she would be. "As am I, my dear. One week from Friday, I will arrange the car to pick you up. And please do not worry yourself; I will arrange everything, Donatella." Bowing slightly, he smiled. "I will not take up any more of your time. I have enjoyed your company and once again, apologize for arriving unannounced. I do look forward to your visit."

Her manservant appeared at the door, and escorted Rodrigo out. Dona followed behind him, watching him leave. She was filled with a mixture of anticipation and dread. How was it she'd come to a place where her best option for survival was Rodrigo Borgia? She closed the door behind him and felt too ashamed to make eye contact with her manservant.

30

Chantal held Grace in her arms as the infant slept soundly in the limo. The plane ride had been a long one, but very comfortable on the Medici private jet. They were going to Bel Rosso for Grace's first visit there. Grace was a few months old and seemed strong and healthy. Chantal felt like she was strong enough now to take her on the extended trip. She felt both nervous and excited for the rest of the family to meet Grace, and she could feel Lorenzo's eagerness to be back in his childhood home, so different from where they lived now. Lorenzo spoke often of his years growing up here, and having free reign of the property, along with his sisters. It sounded so beautiful and simple. Chantal had never lived with such freedom, or anything so simple. She was charmed by her first visit long ago, of the house, the vineyards, and the vast fields of flowers, the horse pastures, and the mountain range on the horizon. Bel Rosso was a paradise, and now their eldest son, Christoph, resided here, and he loved it as much as Lorenzo. Lorenzo's childhood had been so different from hers. She'd been raised in such a closed environment, under strict guidance. She rarely saw her papa and played alone inside the chateau. The Medici's were loud and boisterous, and their affection for each other was on constant display. She always got nervous before a visit, as they tended to overwhelm her with their laughter and affection. They had an ease of how they approached life that she'd never felt.

Dante pulled onto the long private road that led to the house, and she looked out over the sprawling property, lush and green with the spring growth. She loved the stables and the horses grazing in the pasture. Soon, the fields would be in full bloom with the color of the sunflowers and lavender. It always smelled delicious here and made her want to go outdoors, which was very unusual for her. As they pulled up in front of the house, she saw Kate standing outside, anxiously waiting for them, Aegis and Night Stalker by her side. She knew Shade would still be in his slumber. Grace suddenly yawned and stretched, as Chantal smiled down at her small cherub face.

"Wake up *mon ange*, your Bebe is waiting for you. She will be disappointed if you are snoozing." Looking over at Lorenzo, she smiled. "I am so eager to see our son. We haven't seen Christoph in so long."

Lorenzo smiled back at her. It was always good to get back to Bel Rosso. It held a lot of memories for him. "I talk to him at least once a week, but I haven't seen him in a long time, either. He should be waiting for us."

He looked up toward the house, and saw his mother in the doorway, and Aegis and Night Stalker romping with joy, like young playful pups, and it made him laugh. They had come out to greet him. Dante got out and opened their door. Lorenzo exited, and then helped Chantal out with the baby. Grace had come to them so frail, and now she looked robust and healthy, her cheeks plump with a nice pink glow. Lorenzo calmed the wolves as they walked toward the door. His mother gave him a hug, before turning her attention to Chantal and the baby. Gi appeared in the door, quickly followed by Theresa and Shannon, all straining to see the new baby. They made their way into the foyer, the women clamoring to hold the newest member of the Medici coven as Luca appeared, all smiles, and exchanged a fist bump with Lorenzo. "Congratulations, brother." Gi herded them into the living room, as the women excitedly talked over each other in their eagerness to see the baby.

Chantal took a seat and Grace instantly began to cry in response to the noise and excitement of everyone around her. Chantal quickly unwrapped the blanket from around the infant and calmed her. She had dressed her in the palest pink from head to toe. Shannon was immediately at her side. "Would you like to hold Grace? She is a bit overwhelmed, I believe. She is not used to so much attention."

Shannon nodded. "I'd love to hold her. It's been a long time since we've had a baby in the house." Shannon lifted the baby to her shoulder, and bounced her lightly, as Grace lifted her head to look curiously around the room. Shannon made eye contact with Luca, and they exchanged a smile. They'd made the decision, years ago, that they'd have no children, but it wasn't an easy choice. Luca's role as protector to the queen already demanded divided loyalties between Kate and Shannon and adding their children to the mix didn't seem fair. Seeing her hold the baby now reinforced for both of them what they'd sacrificed. He mouthed the words, "I love you", and she beamed back at him.

They heard footsteps as Christoph bounded downstairs and rushed into the room. He encountered his father first, and he and Lorenzo exchanged a hug, before he headed in Shannon's direction. "So, this is my little sister." Grace looked up at him, her eyes wide, and then broke into a toothless smile. The crowd laughed as Christoph took the baby in his arms.

Gi heard the door opening at the rear of the house, and hurried to help Cory, who was assisted by Hyde. He was old now and walked with the aid of a cane. "Heard there was a new member of the family."

Gi took his elbow and escorted him into the room with the crowd. Christoph proudly showed off the baby. "Grace, meet your Uncle Cory."

Cory reached out to touch her, the knuckles on his hands stiff and swollen, and the baby grasped his forefinger. The noise level rose, as everyone was talking and laughing, and Gi left to get enough wine for everyone. Kate had been patient enough, when the baby started to squirm in Christoph's arms, and she approached. "This is my granddaughter! Give her to Bebe." Once again, Grace was passed off, as Kate took the infant.

Chantal took note of Cory's appearance. She found it hard to believe how he'd aged over the last hundred years. It gave her a small pain in her heart. She knew she'd easily outlive Grace, and it would be hard to watch her grow old and frail. Gi maneuvered through the room with Midnight, and Chantal quickly grabbed a glass and sipped at it. She looked at all the faces of the people admiring Grace, and wistfully wished she'd grown up here, with all of this love surrounding her, and brothers and sisters to keep her company. She sat quietly, feeling almost invisible at times in their chaos. Her eyes kept returning to her son, he looked so much like Lorenzo, and Shade.

Once Kate took the baby from him, Christoph turned and saw his mother sitting quietly. She'd always been somewhat remote, and often felt overwhelmed around the loud and boisterous Medici clan. He made his way through the crowd to stand in front of her.

"*Maman*? You are happy to see me, *oui*?" He held his arms open for her.

Chantal felt her heart leap over a million times. She stood and softly ran her hand across his cheek. "*Oui,* my son." He wrapped his arms around her, and she laid her head on his chest. "I have missed you so much. Isn't Grace beautiful, she is *mon ange*, and I am so glad you will love and protect her."

"With my life, *Maman*. I would protect her with my life. She is Medici, *oui*? We stand as one."

Chantal looked up at him and beamed. Her royal Valois blood was in his veins as well, but he was definitely a Medici. And somehow, deep inside her, she knew she wouldn't want to be anywhere but with them in this life. She gently pulled away and went to find another glass of Midnight. Gi was there quickly offering her another glass. "Thank you, Gi. I seem to be a bit emotional today. Do you know if Natalia will be visiting us tonight?"

He shook his head. "She was not able to join us. She had obligations to Council, but she did say she would get here at some point during your visit. She is most eager to meet her niece."

***

Shade heard the familiar whir of the blinds as they opened. He'd felt Kate leave his side earlier in preparation for their son's visit. He laid there quietly and felt the energy inside the house. His son was home, and the powerful energy of love and happiness was enough to blow the roof off this house. A huge grin slid across his face. The joy and love rolled over him and took his breath away; he could feel Kate's joy with Grace in her arms. He rose and took a quick shower, running his hands through his still wet hair. Pulling on a pair of jeans, a tee shirt, and boots, he rushed down the stairs. The laughter and rumble of voices sounded like music to his ears. Bel Rosso would always be home for all of them.

He entered the living room, still towering over everyone in the room, his son and grandson included. He spotted Lorenzo and their hug was one that he cherished. No one could have asked for a better son. "Well, isn't this one happy ass meeting!" He spotted Cory and was so glad he'd joined them. Walking to him, he put his arm around his fragile shoulders. "So, what do you think about that beauty in Kate's arms? You have a new niece."

Cory smiled back at his father, who looked the same as the day he'd met him well over a century ago. He was not unaware that he looked like he could be Shade's great-grandfather, and not his son. He answered his father, his voice now soft and gravely with age. "I think she's very lucky that the Medici found her." He accepted the hug from his father, who held him gently, aware of his frailty.

"She isn't the only lucky one, Cory. Thanks to Natalia, we are making a difference for all the half-breeds, and you are the biggest reason it is happening. Come, let me help you sit down. It's like a pack of rats in here." As they both laughed, he helped Cory to sit and Gi got him a drink immediately. Grace suddenly gave out a loud shout and Shade grinned, making his way to Kate. "Come to Papa Bear. Give her up, Bebe. My turn, *si!*"

Kate handed him the baby, as Shade quickly lifted her over his head, and Grace giggled. The sound of her laughter made everyone in the room laugh with her. Kate stepped back and looked at the faces of all these people she loved so dearly.

Shade laughed along with his family. This plump bundle looked like a cake confection. Grace grabbed at his curls and tugged, holding on as he chuckled. "You are not the first one to grab onto those locks!"

The infant cooed as he laid her over his shoulder, her small hand still clutching a strand of hair. The noise level in the room was deafening when Jules walked in. His long brown hair hung over his shoulders, and those trademark blue eyes shining. He set down his briefcase and eyed the tiniest female snuggled into Papa Bear's neck. His Uncle Lorenzo was the first to spot him and the hugs began. He made the rounds, greeting his family one by one, and saving his grandmother, Bebe for last. She was the love of his life. He adored his own mother Sophia, but Bebe was the one who seemed to understand him the best. He wasn't born a warrior, in a family that prided itself on warriors, and she'd helped guide his path, making sure there was a place for him in the business, working with her and Auntie Shannon. He hugged her and kissed her cheek. "Full house tonight, Bebe."

Kate beamed back at him. "Not full enough. I wish your mother and father could have joined us too, but I understand Lorenzo needs

Alfie to keep an eye on things in Florence. Did you see Natalia today?"

"Yes, I saw her briefly at Council to review some employment contracts for the orphanage. She's really busy and shared that she was already working on expanding. But she said she'd be here hopefully tomorrow evening. She's really excited to get her hands on Grace. She's interested in talking to Chantal and Lorenzo, as well, about raising a half-breed. You know Nattie. She's going to explore all avenues when she tackles something." He took her hand and squeezed it tight. "You look really happy tonight, *bel*. I wish all of us could, for once, be in one place at one time." He looked over and saw Shannon, Uncle Luca by her side, waiting impatiently. "Did Auntie Shannon get her share of Grace yet?"

Kate nodded. "I think everyone has held her, and good luck getting her away from Papa Bear."

Shade was in his heaven with the infant half asleep on his shoulder. He didn't miss the arrival of his youngest grandson, Jules. Jules walked up to him and smirked as Shade responded. "Don't even think you can steal this female from me. She is mine!"

Jules laughed at him. "Papa Bear, don't you have some warrior business to tend to, in fact, doesn't half this room?"

Shade loved Jules, as he did all of his grandchildren. He was intelligent like Nattie and had one hell of a head for business. "Smart- ass."

Shade eased Grace from his shoulder and Jules took her in his arms. "But you're right. We have a camp full of new recruits that need to be whipped into shape. I think we need to roll out. We'll be back before the sun rises." He made his way to Kate and kissed her. "Christoph and I need to get the new recruits into their assignments. I'll be back as soon as I can." He turned to Lorenzo. "You joining us in camp, son?"

Lorenzo nodded. "Hell yes. I'd love to see everyone again."

31

Rodrigo sat and planned in the massive palace he'd occupied for centuries with his younger brother, Soren. Their palace was outside of Rome, and its grandiosity would put Versailles to shame. The many house staff were preparing for a small and intimate gathering of his friends to be held at the palace the next evening. The palace was made up of four separate wings. He had his own private wing and living quarters, almost a castle unto itself and Soren occupied the opposite wing. They could go for months without crossing paths. The third wing was reserved for guests, and entertaining, and the fourth wing housed the massive staff required to keep things running. The palace was surrounded by elaborate gardens. The Borgia controlled all the southern part of Italy from the tip of the boot to the border of Umbria. Just as the Borgia had gradually conquered the other smaller covens in the south, and assimilated them into their own territory, the Medici had been doing the same in the north. There were only four territories in Italy now. Besides his own, there was Ottavio Farnese, who controlled the island of Sicily, the Medici in the north, and the small region of Umbria, still owned by the Alizzi. He would have taken Dona's territory years ago, had the Medici not given her protection. He'd been busy taking other covens, and now hers was the only thing standing between him and the Medici. He could just take it. After all, the Alizzi had no warriors and no way to defend her land, but what would be the fun in that? It would be so much more entertaining to drag this out and humiliate both the Alizzi and the Medici at the same time.

He'd sent the car for her, and she'd arrive before sunrise. Unlike the Alizzi, neither he nor Soren were day-walkers, and he cursed the sun and the restrictions it placed on his life. Still, he was eager for her arrival, and anxious to show her all the riches and luxury he could bestow upon her. She'd lived in poverty for so long. She would have forgotten how it felt to be surrounded by such opulence. He would court her, and spoil her, and it wouldn't be long before she would be eating out of his hand. That bitch would be his, and with it,

Umbria. After that, there would be no more barriers, and he'd start the slow and progressive access to the Medici. It was well known, far and wide, that the Borgia and Medici were enemies. The Medici had remained the only coven large enough, and powerful enough, to stand in his way of ruling all of Italy. Their two covens had been quiet for far too long. It was time for the Borgia to rise, and take what they felt was rightfully theirs, and Dona was going to help him get there.

He sat quietly, fingers steepled together in front of his face, as his brain worked through the elaborate plan. His grin grew wider and more wicked with each thought. Soren would play a huge role, as always. He couldn't have achieved all he had without the aid of his younger brother. He didn't fear the Medici warriors. He had his own army, as big and as powerful as anything the Medici produced. Of course, the Medici did tend to hold sway with the European Council, and that had always stuck in his craw. There seemed to be nothing Malachi wouldn't do for Shade Medici, and now his own daughter was part of the American Council, and a pet of Malachi. No matter, Rodrigo felt confident that, with careful planning, he could defeat the Medici, and send him what was left of his coven to the States for good.

He felt the energy shift as his brother approached, and he was glad for the interruption. He wanted to give his brother some last-minute instruction for the arrival of the Alizzi. Soren must be on his best behavior.

Soren had made his way across the marbled floor, barefoot and shirtless and wearing his leather pants slung low on his hips, the laces on his fly half undone, and blood still on his chin. It was clear he'd been playing and feeding. Rodrigo chuckled deep in his chest, as Soren looked at him nonchalantly. Soren's eyes were a deep, dark brown, bordering on black, and held a hypnotic quality. He'd taken to outlining his eyes in dark kohl eyeliner, which only intensified his look of pure evil. His dark brown hair hung tangled past his shoulders, the tips of his hair stuck together and wet with blood. Rodrigo watched as his brother swiped his hand across his mouth, wiping away the blood on his lips and smearing it across his cheek. There were spatters of blood covering his bare chest. Soren was skinny and lanky, not built like a warrior, but he could fight. Physical strength was not his best weapon, his gift was his power. Soren was a dream-walker, and it was a gift he used with great frequency. As far as Rodrigo knew, Soren had never used his gift to bring pleasant dreams, but only dreams of pain and torture. Rodrigo's gift was sin-eater. He was able to absorb the sins of the dying, and as the centuries passed, his soul became a black abyss of the entire world's evil. They were two of the most feared and evil masters in the world.

"It looks as though you have had your fill of fun this night, my brother." Lowering his eyes, his mouth curled up on one side in a lopsided grin. "You are dripping blood upon the marble."

Soren shrugged. He could care less about the mess or his appearance. He curled up in the corner of the elegant and ornate Louis XVI settee, upholstered in red damask. He looked completely out of place seated on the delicate piece of furniture. He closed his eyes and sighed. He'd taken his fill of blood and sex, with partners both willing and unwilling, and his eyes felt heavy with sleep now. "My soul is full for now. My favorite snack was on the menu tonight, since tomorrow you will expect me to behave in a more civilized manner. The heart of the half-breed was still beating as I swallowed it. The blood was so delicious and fresh." Licking his lips, he rolled his eyes to his brother. "There is still another in the cage if you are up to it."

Rodrigo shook his head. "I am sure they are becoming harder to find, since the laws have now changed. Not all are happy about it, but I am sure you can pay some mercenary enough money to find you the half-breeds, so you won't starve for lack of them."

Sitting upright, Soren grunted. "Too bad my scouts couldn't have stolen the little bitch the Council gave to the Medici. But I never give up hope. They are paid well to get to them before they are dumped at Council's feet." Leaning back against the settee, he extended both arms across the back of the furniture. "Besides, the babies are just appetizers for me. I prefer them a bit older. I can satisfy my sexual appetites, as well as my hunger for blood, and of course, the torture. I love seeing the fear in their eyes, as they realize they are about to die soon, and eventually, beg me for death's release. They are all useless skin and bone, put on this earth to satisfy my hunger only."

Standing, Rodrigo began to walk about the room, his walking stick at his side. "The Alizzi will be arriving tomorrow. It will be of the utmost importance that you behave and conduct yourself as a gentleman of high breeding and refined taste. I want her to see and absorb the wealth and luxury of the Borgia. She is playing hard to get, and I will continue to play her games for a while, and court her as I should. The hatred of the Borgia by her pathetic *padre* still lingers in her mind. It was his mistake to align with the Medici and look what that got her."

Soren cocked his head to the side, his thoughts rambling. "Why do you bother with such effort? Just fuck her and be done with it. Why play these games? Take her, and her land. She has no army, and Medici will never come to her aid."

Rodrigo growled. Soren had no patience. "I want her to come to me, not the other way around. I want her to crawl to the Borgia on her knees, beg with open arms. What fun is it to run head long into this when time is on our side? Besides, I rather like the game. It amuses me."

Soren stood. He was bored now and wanted only to shower and retreat to his bed. He was tired of Rodrigo's games. He'd known his brother had wanted Portia, and he'd never gotten over the fact that she'd chosen Christofano. His anger over her loss still seethed inside him, and Soren knew it only grew with time. He remembered well how Rodrigo had chased Portia, but she only had eyes for Christofano, leaving Rodrigo to pine over the bitch for centuries.

"You do intend to share her. I would be offended if you did not. She is quite a good fuck, so the rumors say. What good is having a whore if you do not share?"

Rodrigo laughed and banged his cane against the marble floor. "You must learn patience, Soren. All in good time, my brother, all in good time."

***

Dona was trying to relax and enjoy the three-hour drive to Rome. She was wearing a simple dress and had packed the same gown she'd worn to the Farnese event. She knew Rodrigo said he'd 'take care of everything', but she wasn't sure what that meant. If he had other guests, she was well aware she'd stand out like a sore thumb in her remade gown. She was having second thoughts about accepting his invitation. She had no illusions about how the other covens looked down on her. She settled in the seat, and took a nap, and was startled when her driver said, "We're here, mistress."

She woke up, feeling groggy, and shook the sleep from her eyes. She'd seen pictures of the Borgia Palazzo, but they couldn't do it justice. The palace was massive in scale. She'd heard it had over 700 rooms, and more than 60 staircases, with a capacity to hold 20,000 people. Her villa would probably fit inside a single ballroom! The driver opened her door and helped her out. When she turned to retrieve her luggage, he reminded her that he'd take care of it and see it was delivered to her room. She straightened her skirt and looked about nervously. "Have the other guests arrived?"

He shook his head. "No mistress, my master wanted you to have time to rest before the ball." She sighed with relief, glad at least she wouldn't walk into a ballroom full of people. He led her to the door, his hand on her elbow, and the majordomo swung the door open, and bowed to her. "Mistress Alizzi. We are honored by your presence. Please come in."

Dona nodded her head slightly in his direction. It had been a long time since she had been treated with such deference. He escorted her to a receiving parlor to wait for his master.

Rodrigo was informed of the Alizzi's arrival and entered the room, elegantly attired with his arms wide open as he bowed his head slightly. "Welcome to Borgia Palazzo, my dear. It is so good of you to come and join me." He went to her, taking her hands into his and kissing her cheeks softly. "I do hope your trip was a pleasant one. Please, let me lead you to my living quarters. I occupy one wing, and my brother is in another. We can easily settle down, talk, and have a refreshing drink without being disturbed."

Dona felt overwhelmed by the opulence surrounding her. She'd always thought Castello was magnificent, but it looked like a humble cottage by comparison. The gardens took up eight acres around the palace. Castello had more land around it, and covered more acreage, while the Borgia had built their palace to cover most of the land. Rodrigo took her arm and led her down a hallway filled with gilded mirrors and sparkling chandeliers. "You have a lovely home, Rodrigo."

"*Grazie,* my dear. It is at your disposable, I assure you, any time you wish. I want you to make yourself comfortable while here, I wish this visit to be a joyous and relaxing one for you. It is a beautiful building, *si*? It was built to survive the ages, just as I have done."

Easily leading her through the palace, he could feel her every breath. She was impressed, and he was quite sure, by the end of her stay, she'd be eager to come back again and again. She'd be a fool if she declined his attentions. As they entered his wing, he led her to the opulent parlor where he entertained privately. "Please, sit, we shall have some Midnight."

Immediately, a servant appeared with a tray of drinks. Rodrigo sat opposite her, so he could gaze at her face. She was looking around the room, admiring the beauty of the lush furnishing and rare art. "I hope you did not go to too much trouble preparing. I have taken care of everything for you, Donatella."

He was appalled at the hideous dress she wore. She looked like a peasant. But he knew he could revive her into the beauty she once was, with little effort once the new garments and jewels graced her body. She'd find it hard to give that up.

Dona gratefully accepted the Midnight. She rarely drank it anymore, keeping it only for her guests, which were rare. The wine tasted good and felt even better as it soothed her. "I didn't want to presume anything, Rodrigo. I did bring a gown with me."

He shook his head. "Nonsense, you should be dressed as the queen and mistress you are. Never let them see you down, always appear in control, Donatella. You are a beautiful woman, with an ancient and royal bloodline. I will be most proud to have you on my arm." He watched her over the rim of his glass as he sipped. She still wasn't so sure about this, and he wasn't going to push. She'd succumb to him. They always did. "And please, do not fret over your safety. My personal guards surround the palace night and day. They are well armed and the best of my warriors. No harm shall come to you. I will be at your beck and call should you require me."

"That is most generous of you, Rodrigo. And your brother, Soren, he is doing well? I have not seen either of you in such a long time."

"Soren is well, *si*. He will be joining us later with the other guests. He is most anxious to reacquaint himself with you. We had a most delightful conversation earlier discussing your anticipated arrival. He is much younger than me, of course, but a master in his own right. It takes the two of us to control such a large territory and coven." Standing, he reached for her hand. "Come, let me show you to your quarters. I am sure you will wish to rest and have time to prepare yourself before our gathering."

She took his hand, as he helped her stand and led her through the palace. They walked for what seemed like miles before he escorted her to a bedroom appointed in gold. The light reflected off every surface. She couldn't imagine how bright it would be in the daylight hours, but then, she knew both Soren and Rodrigo were called to their death slumber and had never seen this palace in the light of day. "What a beautiful room, Rodrigo."

"I am pleased you like it, Dona. This entire suite is for you. Make yourself comfortable." Leading her further into the room, he clapped his hands several times and Giada appeared. He had assigned her specifically to the task of being Lady in Waiting for Donatella, while she was here. She'd been drilled to listen for anything the Alizzi might say that could be useful information and to pry into her private business as well. Rodrigo made sure Giada understood if she didn't comply, her life would be ended in a most torturous way.

"Donatella, this will be your Lady in Waiting for your stay, her name is Giada." He turned to Giada, giving her a look that made her blood run cold. "Giada, may I present Mistress Alizzi. I expect you to treat her with the utmost respect and honor."

Giada curtsied and kept her head down. Rodrigo noticed the packages, beautifully boxed from all the designers he'd contacted, and stacked on the bed. He waited for the Alizzi to speak before he presented her with the fine gifts.

Dona nodded to the maid. "Oh...that is most kind of you. I didn't bring my Lady in Waiting. I am sure she will be most helpful in aiding me to get dressed for the evening's affairs."

Rodrigo smiled at her, and with the wave of his hand, shooed Giada from their presence, as if she were a fly he could easily swat away. "Please, let me know if she does not suit your tastes. If she is in any way rude or incompetent, I will punish her accordingly."

He walked farther into the room toward the elegantly stacked boxes on the massive bed. "And these, my dear, are all for you. Consider it a gift, in return for your gracious acceptance of my invitation." He held up his hand, anticipating her rejection of such an opulent gesture. "Please, do not argue, it is what you deserve. Now come, I wish for you to open them and see if they appeal to you. I have taken the liberty of picking out what I think will please you."

Dona opened box after box, containing everything from fine silk underwear and silk stockings, to a one-of-a-kind designer gown and shoes. The gown was a gold beaded sheath dress that was sleeveless, cut low in the back, and falling in a straight line to the floor. The metallic gold shoes were matched perfectly in color. The gold would look splendid against her dark bronze skin tone. Another box contained a gossamer shawl of gold, so sheer and light, it looked like it could float on air. She opened the remaining boxes to find large pear-shaped diamonds for her ears, and a large diamond pendant for her neck. She would glow like Aphrodite in this dress. "Rodrigo! This is too much."

He was pleased as she opened his luxurious gifts. Her face said everything. She'd look elegant and refined, and she'd soon be reminded her life could change dramatically, if she'd only let him. Taking her hands into his, he stepped closer into her. "It is nothing, Dona, you are a beautiful female, and you should be spoiled."

He kissed her on the lips. She was still a bit skittish, but he persisted, holding her hands firmly and not letting her back away. She was resisting him less but didn't return his affection. He broke the kiss and stepped back. "I must leave you now. It is almost time for my death slumber. Tomorrow, we will be greeting the guests at midnight. Giada is close at hand; the bell pull will bring her rushing to you. Spend the day how you wish. Enjoy the gardens or ride the horses. Just be sure to get some sleep. The closets are full to capacity of everything you will need, clothing, shoes, riding gear and sleepwear, as well as lingerie and jewels. Giada will draw a bath for you. Please feel free to use the scents and anything you find in the suite. It has all been put here for you. The bar is full as well."

He made his way to the door. "Do not lift a finger, Donatella, I pay my staff well to do their job. Use Giada to the fullest. I wish for you to be well rested and prepared for a lovely evening on my arm."

He left her alone, and she could hear the sound of rushing water from the bathroom. Giada was on her knees, checking the temperature of the water when she entered. She jumped to her feet. "Let me help you disrobe, mistress."

She unzipped Dona's dress and helped her out of it. Giada carefully folded her clothes, as if they were actually of some value. When Dona was nude, Giada held her hand, as she stepped into the tub and lowered herself into the steaming hot water. Giada pinned her hair up, so she could lay her head back against the tub. Without asking, Giada took a sea salt scrub and started to rub Dona's skin briskly, until it glowed.

"You will look beautiful, mistress. My master will be so pleased to have you on his arm. Is there another who courts you?"

Dona had her eyes closed, as Giada ministered to her. “No, there is no one."

Giada made a clucking sound. “Foolish men, to leave you alone." She proceeded to talk to her, as Dona relaxed, and Giada plied her with more questions.

32

Chantal woke abruptly, feeling momentarily disoriented until she remembered she was at Bel Rosso. Sitting up, she called softly for Lorenzo, but he wasn't in bed with her. The room was dark, and the electronic blinds were open. Lorenzo must have gone to camp. They were both day-walkers, but they frequently slept during the day as Lorenzo preferred being in the camp at night. She'd slept during the day with him, as she was tired from their journey and all the celebration surrounding their arrival. She was rubbing the sleep from her eyes when she heard Grace crying. She grabbed her robe, quickly pulling it over her shoulders as she ran down the hall to the nursery. Bebe had never dismantled the nursery once her own children started having children. She said there was no need because there would be grandchildren soon. Chantal barreled into the room ready to soothe Grace when she found Bebe, cuddling and cooing with her, as she walked with the infant on her shoulder.

"Oh, I am so sorry, I hope she did not wake you. I must have been in such a deep sleep. You must think me a terrible *maman*."

Kate cuddled the baby close, softly bouncing her, shushing the infant. "Chantal, we have nannies and wet feeders because we cannot do it all ourselves, and of course, she has her Bebe. You needed your rest, and I was awake."

Kate took a seat in the rocker where she had sat and rocked all her children, and her grandchildren. "Sit down, daughter. You have done this before, with boys no less. No need to panic. See, she's quiet already. Besides, Natalia is coming tonight. She's eager to see her new niece."

Chantal relaxed as she saw Grace settle comfortably on Kate's shoulder and took a seat on the daybed that stayed in the room for the nanny. "I am glad Natalia is visiting. I have a few things concerning Grace I wish to speak to her about. She is probably my best source to learn about half-breeds." She looked down at her hands and sighed. "Lorenzo says I worry too much. But I have so many questions. Do you think she will mind?"

Kate rocked the baby slowly, watching as Chantal nervously wrung her hands. "Natalia will be glad to help you in any way possible. Why are you so undone? Do you regret your decision to keep this child?"

Chantal snapped her head up and looked at Kate with surprise. "Oh no, never! I have not for a minute regretted my decision. I am hoping there will be more to follow, and I will gladly accept them all. I feel very strongly on this issue." She unconsciously twisted a strand of her hair and bit her lip, unsure if she wanted to reveal all to Kate. She felt so inept at times and wondered if she was doing right by Grace. "It is nothing serious, just a few questions is all." She stood and walked to the window of the cheerful nursery. "I suppose Lorenzo went to camp; he loves coming home. Maybe someday I will be able to go back home again."

Kate followed her with her eyes as she walked to the window. "Yes, Lorenzo went with Shade, as soon as the sun set. They both love being in the camp. It's in their warrior blood. I don't know what Shade would do if there was no camp to run." She stared at Chantal's back as she looked out the window in the direction of the camp. "I'm sorry your parents have been remote. I know how hard that must be for you. Give them time. I can't imagine your mother would be able to stay away for any length of time. They'll get past this, as they see the infant grow, and how much you and Lorenzo love her. Things are good with the two of you, yes?"

Chantal turned to her. Kate was the glue that held this entire family together. She'd never truly confided in her. "Well, my *maman* and I have made amends. She secretly visits Castello to be with Grace. I feel horrible about keeping it from *Papa*. But she promises me she is working on him, to make him understand."

She walked to the rocking chair and knelt beside it, letting her hand play softly in Grace's hair. "You know I love Lorenzo so much. He spoils me with jewels and flowers. He makes sure I have everything I want, and he has never tried to exercise control over me. He is trying very hard to be more attentive, spend more time with me. He is a romantic and considerate mate and a wonderful *papa* to Grace. I know he is doing all he can to make me a priority in his life. I understand the warrior in him, as much as I can." She stood again and walked to the crib, folding the blanket that had been tossed aside. "I never have you alone, so I wanted to tell you something, but please don't tell Lorenzo or Shade."

Kate felt torn. She was asking her to keep a secret from her mate. "If I can, Chantal. I try very hard to be open with Shade, to share everything. If your secret doesn't involve him or affect him, then I'll keep it to myself."

Chantal nodded in understanding. "Lorenzo told me that his grandparents live in the spirit realm at Castello. He said he and his sisters can hear them, but cannot see them, but that you can. I have never felt or seen anything, but since Grace has arrived, I have a strange feeling sometimes. I sense someone watching. I know they both accepted Cory, but he was Medici blood. Grace is not, and I often wonder if Portia would approve of me. I am the Queen of Medici now, in her castle. I wonder if they would have accepted Grace. Is it true that she comes to you, and you can see her and speak with her?"

Kate listened to her daughter-in-law, concerned after all this time whether Portia and Christofano had accepted her. She felt sympathy for this woman who had been raised with so much self-doubt. "Chantal, I see them both, and speak with them, as does Shade. Castello is where their spirits will remain for all eternity. It's where they lived and loved in life, and where they remain in the spirit realm. Portia has an unconditional love for Shade and all of his children and grandchildren. She loves him without reservation. Christofano was very strict with Shade and wasn't one to express his emotions, but he too shows his love and affection in his own way. I assure you, their concern is for your happiness. If you and Lorenzo are happy, then their spirits are at peace with you."

Chantal shook her head. "You must think me such a fool. Or perhaps that I have too much time on my hands to think about such things."

They both turned their heads toward the door as they heard Natalia enter the room, Marcello behind her. Chantal thought her sister-in-law was beautiful and stunning in her own right, and Lorenzo had mentioned he thought his sister was close to Marcello, in a way that exceeded his role as her protector. Chantal had watched them together, and it was evident in their eyes they were in love. Chantal looked down and felt the heat rise to her cheeks as she was still in her nightgown and robe. As Natalia rushed to her mother and Grace, kneeling to get a better look, Marcello leaned over and softly kissed Kate on the cheek. He laid his hand gently on Natalia's shoulder, telling her he was leaving for camp, and to call if she needed him. Neither Chantal nor Kate missed the gentleness of his touch on Natalia's shoulder or the look of love in their eyes when she acknowledged him as he left.

Natalia returned her attention to Grace and tickled the infant under her chin and watched as she smiled back at her. "Mommy, can I hold her?"

Kate stood from the rocker so Natalia could sit, and placed Grace in her arms. "Of course. Let her know she's loved by everyone in her family." Kate moved to take a seat on the nanny's bed, as Natalia turned her attention to Chantal. "Has she been feeding okay? And sleeping? Does she have a routine? I've found that establishing a strong routine for the children in the orphanage is crucial. They have never known structure."

Chantal glanced quickly from Kate to Natalia. "Well...I have a problem. I was hoping we'd be able to discuss Grace. She seems to have difficulty with the feeder at times. She goes to her fine, but at least once a week, she refuses. She fights her and fusses terribly. I seem to be the only one to settle her, and she feeds from me instantly at these times. My boys did not do this. They transitioned easily to their feeders. I have had Dr. Bonutti to the house several times, but he is not schooled on half-breeds and is little help. She sleeps fine but loud noises bother her. It is as if she is overwhelmed with too many voices or noises. I have nowhere to turn for help. I do the best I can, but I feel as if I am failing her in some way. Does the orphanage keep records of their health and growth? Do they have physicians that are more schooled on this?" Chantal tried to calm her hands as she became aware, she'd been wringing them in her lap as she spoke.

Natalia took note of her nervous behavior. "Sit down, Chantal. The good news is, we're all learning here. We've neglected the half-breeds, denied them a place in our culture, and as a result, none of us knows much. We're learning as we go. I don't see a problem with the fact that Grace seeks you out to feed from time to time. She should begin to wean herself away from you though as she bonds more with her feeder. You need to remain calm. She'll feel what you feel, and if you're nervous and unsure, then she feels that, and she's nervous and unsure, and needs extra comforting. We're keeping detailed records at the orphanage, trying to learn as much as we can, but we're finding our way as well. Just love her, make her feel safe in her environment, and she should calm down. Is my brother spending time with her? She needs to know she has a mother and a father."

Chantal sat next to Kate and bit her lip nervously as she began to wrap the sash of her robe around her hand. "Well, when he can. Please do not take that wrong, he does love her so much. He has so many duties. I know he feels conflicted about making sure he spends enough time with me as well. I never want to pull him from his duties, they are important."

Natalia rolled her eyes. "Chantal, my brother is a warrior, a *Medici* warrior. He's a king, a master, and leads the largest coven in all of Europe. You don't need to protect him. You do him no favors by keeping things from him. He can't fix what he doesn't know about. You have a responsibility to him, and to Grace. Tell him. Stop cowering behind your own shadow!"

Kate placed her hand on Natalia's knee. "Natalia, you don't need such harsh words."

Natalia sighed, her impatience showing. "I'm sorry, Chantal, but you must be strong. Our coven demands it of you."

Chantal stood, her face filled with pain and hurt. "How dare you." She felt her voice crack. "I was hoping you could help me, not point out how inept a queen and *maman* I am. I raised two sons, gave them to this coven as warriors. You know nothing about raising a child. Never judge me or how I raise my own. I was born Valois and I know how to be a queen." Her fists were balled up at her sides and she stared down Natalia. "Give me my daughter."

Kate stood up from the bed. "Stop it! Both of you. This is about Grace, and what Grace needs. This isn't a contest about who makes a better mother. Chantal, if Lorenzo isn't engaged with the baby, then that's a problem. Let him know what you need from him. He loves this child. I can see it in his face every time he looks at her. But he'll always be a warrior first, just as Shade is always a warrior first. I would have to remind him from time to time that he needed to re-access his priorities. That's not a criticism of you. I know my son, perhaps better than anyone. He's exactly like his father. Tell him what you need, daughter, and he'll come through for you."

Chantal nodded. "I am sorry, Natalia, there is no excuse for my behavior. I did not grow up with a voice. I was not allowed to have an opinion of my own. But since Grace has come into my life, I have found I *do* have a voice and I will *do* anything for her. I feel so helpless at times. There is no one to help these children. I keep a journal of everything that happens with her. It may help the future generations. I just want her to have everything my sons had." She looked at Kate with a sad smile. "He tries so hard. I guess we both need to try harder, together, to make sure she will be fine. I admit all of my energy has been spent on Grace lately." She turned to Natalia once again and laughed softly. "By the way, you sounded just like your sister when you said that. I never realized you had a temper like Sophia."

Natalia laughed out loud. "Not hardly. My sister would have just said, 'Suck it up and quit whining!' I apologize if I spoke harshly. In our family, my mother always encouraged us to speak our minds. I understand you have your hands full, and we're charting new territory here. We're both learning as we go. Keeping the journal will be invaluable for the future, as I'm sure there are more half-breeds out there than we ever realized. I'm already expanding the first orphanage, and we're planning to build more across the country."

Grace began to struggle, her arms flailing. She needed feeding, and soon. Chantal took her from Natalia's arms and put her on her shoulder, as the infant snuggled into her neck. "Are there any plans to build orphanages in Europe? I think, perhaps, we should consider that."

Natalia shook her head. "That's not my call. I have no authority in Europe. Malachi is aware of what we're doing here, and the European Council did follow in our footsteps, making the same changes to the law in regard to destroying the half-breeds. I'm hoping they'll decide to build orphanages as well. The European Council is very old, and they're reluctant to change their ways. It was a big step forward for them to change the law. In time, perhaps, they'll see the light, and build the orphanages."

Chantal could feel Grace rooting at her neck. "So, it would take Council's approval to do this. Well, I am the Queen of the Medici, which must carry some weight. This would take a great deal of funds. I know that Shade is funding everything here. I think, perhaps, it is time I speak with my *papa*. All I can do is try, and hope that enough time has passed that he will see Grace in a new light, as well as our cause."

She stepped to the door and turned to look at the two women. "Thank you both for your encouragement and acceptance. I promise you I will do much better with *mon ange*, and with Lorenzo. I love them both so much." She walked out of the nursery and back down the hall to their guest room. She had a lot to discuss with Lorenzo when they got home, as well as a plan to visit with her *Papa*. She'd do anything for this child in her arms.

Natalia looked questioningly at her mother. "Will she always live in fear of her own shadow? No wonder she and Lorenzo were at odds."

Kate looked back at her daughter. "Be patient, Natalia. She's finding her way, and she deeply loves your brother, and this child."

Natalia sighed. "Patient? Mom, it's been…"

"Stop it, Natalia. I'll not have it. Chantal will find her path."

33

Rodrigo had been informed the guests had arrived, and they'd been served drinks. They were well into their cups awaiting his arrival. He loved making a grand entrance, and tonight would be no exception. He knew the tongues would be wagging when he showed up with the Alizzi on his arm. His mouth watered to see her in the finery he'd chosen for her. She may be poorer than a church mouse, but Dona could still turn heads. He sent his personal manservant to fetch her, and bring her back to his suite, so the two of them could enter together.

As the manservant arrived at Dona's door to escort her to Rodrigo, Giada had been working frantically to help her dress and had followed Rodrigo's instructions as to how she was to look, and what time she should be ready. Giada gave her one final inspection before turning Dona over to the manservant. Dona followed the servant down the long hallway and down a flight of stairs until they arrived at Rodrigo's private suite of rooms. Tapping lightly on the door, the servant called out, "Master, I am here with Mistress Alizzi."

Rodrigo smiled to himself. *Let the show begin*. He opened the door and for a mere second, his breath caught in his throat. She was stunningly beautiful, like a butterfly escaping the cocoon. "My dear, you do look simply stunning. Please turn, let me see all of you." He took her hand and held it up to watch her turn slowly. "I must say, you will turn many heads this evening. Does everything suit you?"

Dona blushed with the compliment. "More than you could possibly know. I can never repay your kindness, Rodrigo. It has been ages since I've had a new frock to wear. I do hope you won't leave me to my own devices once we go to the ball. I'm afraid I will not find many who will show me the same kindness you have extended."

He smiled at her, thrilled she was seeking his protection. He slid his hand along the diamond necklace, its large pear-shaped pendant nestled perfectly between her plump breasts. He let the polished gemstone roll softly between his fingers and then leaned down and kissed each fleshy orb peeking over the bodice of her gown. "You deserve much more, Donatella. They will see that you are a gem hidden from view for far too long. Let us join our guests."

He took her arm and placed it around his elbow, as they walked regally to the wing of the palace designated for entertaining. "This will only be a small gathering, a few masters from Greece and Spain, one or two from the States. You won't be overwhelmed. I always provide a few mortals who are here for the pleasure of my guests, both male and female. If you see anyone in particular you would like to enjoy, do let me know, my dear, they will be yours."

She was being offered to feast upon guests brought here for that purpose. It was an extremely old world custom that very few vampires practiced anymore. These types of activities had been relegated to a few exclusive sex clubs. She wasn't surprised to learn that Rodrigo and his brother, Soren, still indulged in such debauchery. "I'm sure I will be fine." She tried to calm the butterflies in her stomach, concerned about making an entrance, and wondering if she'd be accepted, or discreetly snubbed.

As they walked down the stairs, they made their way to one of the many ballrooms. There were several grandiose ballrooms inside the Borgia palace, but Rodrigo has chosen this smaller ballroom for the guests tonight. He stopped abruptly outside the doors and turned to her, taking her hands in his. "Donatella, I must give you a vital piece of advice. Not all of my guests tonight are aware of your situation. Do not enter with your head down or appear ashamed. You must conduct yourself as a queen, a mistress of high standing, and they will accept what they see. Present yourself as you once were, strong and courageous. Smile, and enjoy what is my pleasure to give you."

Taking her arm, he placed it once again over his own as his doormen opened the doors wide. The room was lit as if by the sun, and every surface gleamed. Rodrigo wore a smirk on his face, as he took in the surprised looks on the faces of his guests. All eyes were on the goddess in gold on his arm. "Welcome to Borgia Palazzo, my friends. May I present to you, a dear friend, who has obliged my old soul by agreeing to accompany me this evening. Mistress Donatella Alizzi."

Everyone nodded in her direction. The few who knew her were shocked by her presence and wondered what Rodrigo was up to, although they wouldn't dare to ask. The guests who didn't know her were shocked by her astonishing beauty. They all raised their glasses as a greeting before Rodrigo told them to carry on, and the guests resumed their conversations. Rodrigo chuckled to himself; it was always rewarding to know his money and power still held sway over so many.

Dona's nerves were set at ease as the guests in the room seemed not to mind her presence there. They appeared accepting, if not welcoming, and she could deal with that. She did take note of the few males who stared a little longer than decorum would dictate, and she was flattered by the attention. A waiter appeared with glasses of Red Moon on a silver tray, and she accepted a glass. "It is all quite lavish, Rodrigo. I can't remember the last time I was at a gala as grand as this."

Patting her hand as it lay on his arm, he smiled. "Oh, Dona, this is not grand, just a few friends gathered for a quiet evening. But stay with me, and I will show you grand. Come, let us mingle and I shall introduce you to my guests."

Leading her amongst his guests, he was pleased with her gracious manners. She was feeling confident among the strangers, as he made her introductions. Rodrigo noted the lingering stares from the males, as well as the looks of jealousy from the females.

Soren stood to the side, the drink flowing easily down his throat. He watched the Alizzi as she glided alongside his brother. He couldn't help but be taken in by her beauty and knew he'd enjoy fucking her and feeding from that long, elegant neck. She was beautiful and his imagination was running wild with all the things he could do to her. But for now, he had to be patient. Let his brother reel her in. She wasn't stupid. She'd managed to survive all these years with no mate, and no warriors. He made his way slowly around the room, quietly watching her. Her voice was as melodic as she was beautiful. He grinned, knowing it would sound tantalizing as she lay screaming underneath him. Making his way toward the two of them, he waited for the proper moment to interrupt.

"Brother, did you intend to make me wait the entire night to introduce me to the beautiful Alizzi?"

Rodrigo chuckled and nodded. "Ah, are you jealous, brother? I told you she was a beauty, with charm and wit. Dona, may I formally introduce you to Master Soren, my younger brother."

Soren extended his hand, and she placed her hand in his. He bowed slightly in her direction. "It is my pleasure."

Dona smiled back at him, her skills at coquetry returning quickly. "The pleasure is mine, I assure you. I've heard so much about Rodrigo's younger brother. I can't believe our paths haven't crossed before."

He smiled at her and leaned in to whisper in a softer voice. "Ah, but I do believe perhaps we may have met once at Carnivale, but then, one never knows who is behind the mask, *si*?" He winked at her and loved the momentary flash of shock that crossed her face. He'd never been with the Alizzi, but he was well aware of the rumors of her little escapade with Lorenzo. "So, tell me, how is Umbria these days? Cannot believe the Medici has not swooped in and charmed that territory right out from under your feet. He is such a land mongrel."

Rodrigo cleared his throat. "Soren, this is not the place to discuss such, we are here to entertain and enjoy the company of the Alizzi."

Soren mocked him with a 'tsk', and looked around the room, as if to check if anyone overheard, before turning back to Dona, his voice dripping with sarcasm. "I do apologize, mistress, if I offended you."

Dona laughed nervously, not quite sure how to take Soren. "Of course not, no offense taken."

Rodrigo was quick to pull her away from Soren, he should have known he'd never behave himself. "I wish for you to meet someone else, my dear. Ah, now where has he gotten to? Ah yes, there he is."

He strolled with her across the room to one of his lead warriors. He'd risen in the Borgia ranks over the years, but for one reason and one reason only. He'd been a mercenary, formerly employed by Shade, and he knew every inch of the territory in Virginia. "My dear, I wish for you to meet one of my finest warriors, he is vital to my coven and my army." As they approached the male, he was easily identifiable as a warrior. He stood taller than the other vampires, and his strength was evident in his stance.

"May I present Mistress Alizzi of Umbria. Dona, this is Tomas."

Tomas bowed before her. "I'm honored to make your acquaintance, mistress. As you are an honored guest of the Borgia, I'm at your service in all matters."

Dona nodded her head in a slight bow. He was a warrior, after all, not royalty, or even a master. She didn't extend her hand. "Tomas, I am happy to meet you. Have you been with the Borgia for very long?"

"I have been with him a short while, perhaps fifty years now. I was a mercenary warrior, and I have traveled the world. But the life of a mercenary can be a difficult one, so I have pledged to the Borgia. Italy is my land of birth, and I have been happy here." He eyed her closely. So this was the Alizzi. Tomas was aware of Rodrigo's plan, to use the Alizzi in his goal to take over the Medici. He'd not forgotten the long ago deception he'd coordinated with Max when they'd plotted to used Cuerpo to kill the then mortal Queen Katherine. The plan had failed, and now both Cuerpo and Max were long dead. He'd escaped, however, and the Medici had never known he had been a spy in his ranks. He smiled at the memory. He'd ingratiated himself to the Medici, and his skills quickly earned him a promotion to SIC of his Dead House. That was long ago when the Medici had first settled in Virginia. Now, he'd made himself invaluable to the Borgia, and once again was playing a role in bringing down the Medici.

Dona had never owned warriors herself, but she'd grown up practically living at Castello. She knew about mercenaries, and how rare it was for them to settle down, pledging their allegiance to a single master. "Well, that is quite rare as I understand it. The Borgia must be fair masters for you to choose to stay."

Tomas looked her up and down. She was one fine piece of ass, one that was well above his station and he'd never be allowed to enjoy, but he knew his master's plan was to have her and convince her to align with the Borgia. "My master is most fair, and I'm a warrior in one of the largest armies in the world. The Borgia knows what he wants, and he gets it. He is wise beyond his many years, my lady. He is a leader amongst vampires, held in fine regard. You are most fortunate to be chosen by him. His taste in females is highly discriminating. It speaks volumes that he seeks you out."

Dona smiled back at him, her cheeks turning bright pink as she blushed. It had been a long time since she'd received compliments from men. Rodrigo whisked her away onto the ballroom floor as the music filled the air. He was light on his feet and easily led her in a waltz. The crowd made way for them, clearing the center of the ballroom, and looking on in admiration at Rodrigo, and the beautiful female in his arms. Dona took note of the approving stares. She'd been shunned for so long, ignored for so long, that she'd forgotten what it felt like to bask in the envious looks from others.

They spent the evening dancing, drinking the wine that flowed plentifully, and listening to the music of the live orchestra, hired for this occasion. Rodrigo introduced her to his circle of friends, all of whom welcomed her into the fold. She gossiped and exchanged social banter until the sun was about to rise. Not all of the guests were day-walkers, but Rodrigo and Soren both were being called to their death slumber. The crowd began to thin, as the guests took their leave.

Rodrigo told her he was hopeful she'd stay and sleep here in the guest room he'd set aside for her. "It is a long drive home, Donatella, and we have partied the night away. If you wish to be taken home, I will summon the driver, but I hope you will stay. It would please me greatly to be able to see you when I wake."

Dona did feel tired. She'd not had a social life in years, and the prospect of a soft bed with luxury linens was appealing. "I'd love to stay, Rodrigo."

He gave her a gracious smile as he summoned Giada, who seemed to appear from nowhere. "Giada, take Mistress Alizzi to her room, and see that she has everything she needs."

He took Dona's hand and kissed it. "Thank you my dearest, for making this night so special for me. Now, if you excuse me, my death slumber calls."

He quickly left the ballroom, leaving her in the care of Giada.

"Mistress? Let me take you back to your room, where I'll run your bath, and prepare your bed." Dona nodded silently, looking at the strong, muscular back of Rodrigo as he exited the room.

34

Shade made his way back from camp and took in the rich scent of the night air. It was mid-summer and things were in full bloom. The air was fragrant with the heavy scent of the many flowers that filled the gardens and lined the path to camp, as well as the acres of sunflowers and lavender planted nearby. He even loved the smell of the freshly mowed grass. He loved this aspect of summer, but he hated the longer hours of daylight. His death slumber was longer, and it made his nights so short. Looking toward Bel Rosso, he could see lights shining through the windows in the house. Lorenzo and his family had returned to Florence, but Sophia and Bianca had come for a short visit, and Kate was in her glory. Natalia had planned to visit again tonight so she could see her sister and niece as well. He stepped onto the back patio and flopped down in a lounge chair near the pool. Laying his head back, he stared up at the stars. He could see millions of them in the Virginia sky. He knew Nattie was inside, waiting for him, to discuss his progress on the orphanages, but he wanted to take in the peace and quiet after leaving the noise of the camp, before entering the clamor of activity going on inside.

Natalia was enjoying the company of her sister and her niece. It was rare for Sophia to visit Bel Rosso, so the sisters looked forward to having this time together. The three generations of Medici women had been up talking all night. Natalia stood up to stretch. As she walked to the window, she saw her father walk up to the house and take a seat in a lounge chair by the pool. He looked into the night sky, and she wondered what he had on his mind. "Excuse me," she told the other women, lost in their chatter, as she slipped from the room and poured her dad a glass of Midnight, and carried it outside to him. As she approached him, she could see he had closed his eyes. “A penny for your thoughts, Daddy."

He smiled to himself as he heard the soft voice of his youngest daughter. He opened his eyes but didn’t move. "Well, I was contemplating if I should enter that house and all the chaos, or sit here a while in the quiet. I am sorry if I kept you waiting, Nattie."

He sat up then and saw the glass in her hand. "Tell me that is for me, and instead of a penny, a kiss will work well for your old man."

She handed him the glass and leaned forward to kiss his cheek. She took a seat across from him. "You look tired, but I was wondering if you have an update for me? We started on building the second orphanage in California, but have you had any luck in getting any other masters to allocate land from their territories?"

He smiled. "You are definitely my daughter, getting right down to business." He took a long drink from the Midnight and looked at her. She was right, he was tired. "I have all the paperwork ready for you on the transfer of that land in California. Like the plot here, it will officially be transferred over to Council. As to the other locations, I got a few refusals, but I have two more locations that masters have agreed to allocate if you are interested. Keep in mind, Nattie, I had to do some fast talking to convince them this was a good idea and would benefit their covens in the long run. Bastards hate giving up territory."

"I understand, Daddy. It will take a while for our culture to change its views on the half-breeds. On top of that, I have been pushing through bylaws that give our females more power. It's not some fluke of nature that I was born to Council, and Malachi agrees. It's a sign of our evolution as a species, and time to recognize these changes in our culture are important to our future survival. We have centuries of history to overcome. Everyone is set in their ways, and they won't change overnight. I didn't expect it to be easy. Where have you gotten permission to build?"

He loved her and her enthusiasm for this project. He was so proud of what she'd accomplished in shifting the balance of power in their male-dominated culture. "Well, I had to visit the master of Texas personally. He isn't easy to move. Honestly, I was expecting a no. That coven has always been somewhat isolated and live by their own rules down there. They take hell from no one. But he agreed and I have the papers inside. There is a huge piece of property outside of Dallas that is yours now." He drained his glass and set it on the small table. "Illinois is on board as well. The master in Chicago is female, and she is an old friend. She is smart, and believe it or not, she was interested in the progress we had made here already. She has been paying attention to your venture with the half-breeds and appreciates the laws you have pushed through granting females more power. She was already considering trying to do something similar, and I convinced her to let you run this, you are the expert, and she heartily agreed. But she has one condition."

Natalia leaned forward in her chair. "What is it? I'm sure we can accommodate her."

Shade smiled back at her. "You know, you look just like your mommy when you get excited about something." He reached over and took her hands into his. "Well, it was not a request of you, but more for me. A long time ago, we decided to train warriors for other masters. I did this only for the masters I knew and trusted, so warriors I had trained did not come back to attack me. She is one of those masters. But there are many rogue gangs in Chicago, and she says her warriors have their hands full keeping that city safe. She said she would agree to transfer the land, as well as paying for everything that was needed to run the facility if I would agree to come to her aid when needed. Provide the assistance of my warriors at no charge. She has some good ideas of where she wants to place the half-breeds once they are grown and can be reintroduced into our culture. She says she knows they have a lot of half-breeds on her streets, older children though. She's not sure about infants. Tell me your thoughts. I didn't agree to anything yet, this is your project, your decision, but if you want Chicago, I'm willing to do what she asks."

Natalia's face lit up. "Yes, of course! We have a few older kids in the D.C. orphanage. We have tutors ready to accommodate any age group and to do remedial work because a lot of the older kids dropped out of school really early. We can help her with that. That's not a problem."

"Good. I think then, for right now, we have the bases covered. Let's get all this rolling before we branch out any further. You will like working with Mistress Colette. She is very intelligent and full of ideas." He stood up and stretched. "All the papers are in a huge folder on my desk with your name on it. Take it with you and get busy. You need money, you know where to come. So, let us put business away for a moment. It is rare for me to have you to myself." He walked to her and laid his hand gently on her shoulder. "How are things at Council and with Marcello?"

Natalia reflexively looked over her shoulder to see if anyone was about when he asked about Marcello. "Council is good. They've been very supportive of the orphanage project and have been good about enforcing violations when they're brought to our attention. It looks like Malachi is having good luck with the European Council as well. They aren't as far along as we are, but they're making progress." She looked down at her hands. "Marcello is doing well." She had become used to protecting both of them from scrutiny.

He knew what she was doing. They would protect each other. He crouched down in front of her, so they were face to face., sliding his hand along her cheek. When the hell did she grow up so fast? "My sweet Nattie, have you forgotten how to talk to your daddy? I am not blind, and you know you can tell me anything. Are you happy? Are you in love?"

She leaned her forehead against his. "I am happy, Daddy. I'm doing something important with my life and making a difference for our kind. I love my family, but I wouldn't have been happy if I'd followed in Mommy's footsteps. I mean no disrespect, but I wasn't meant to be subservient to my master. I do love Marcello, and he loves me. He understands that this is important to me and makes no demands. I know he'll always be a warrior first and foremost. We've both found a way to have love in our lives, without compromising what we both need to achieve."

"Good, it is important to me, knowing you both take care of each other. I know your work is important, and you will never know how proud I am of you, but it brings my heart such joy to know you found a way to have love in your life. We all need someone to listen to our hopes and dreams and love us for who we are."

He heard the rustle coming from the side of the house and leaned back to see Riparo slowly creeping his way toward them. It was a bit unusual to have him this close to the house, but then he heard the door onto the patio opening and his granddaughter was running toward him.

"Papa Bear! You're home!"

He stood and gathered Bianca into his arms. "*Si!* And I know I promised you a game of chess before I took my death slumber. But someone is here to see you." He turned toward Riparo who was standing in the clearing near the pool. Bianca broke free of him and headed for the mountain lion. He looked at Natalia and shook his head. "I got dumped over a big cat."

Natalia laughed. “Don’t take it personally.”

35

The house at Bel Rosso felt empty now that all the children and grandchildren had returned to their lives. Kate missed all the noise and clamor of the family being home. She and Shannon had spent a few hours going over their businesses, all of which remained highly profitable for the coven. The house was feeling increasingly warm when Gi interrupted them to say the air conditioning wasn't performing properly, and he'd summoned for repair. Kate laughed. "Good, for a minute, I thought it was just me. Let's call it a night, Shannon. We covered a lot of ground already."

Shannon relaxed back in her chair, lifting her long hair off her neck. "Fine with me. Luca was painting. Maybe I can talk him into taking us out on the bike. That would cool me down."

Kate was shutting off the computer and stuffing documents back in the drawers. "Yes, go! There's nothing else going on here."

Shannon stretched as she stood and prepared to leave the room. "You want to come with us?"

Kate smiled. "Uh, no. Now, get out of here."

Shannon laughed as she made her way back to her suite. As she entered the room that comprised his art studio off of their living room, Luca was standing with his back to her, shirtless, and wearing his trademark white drawstring pants that hung low on his hips, as he painted. His golden skin had a soft glisten from the sweat. She approached him from behind, sliding her arms around his waist and laying her chin on his shoulder, admiring the picture that was emerging from the canvas.

"*Mia belleza*."

She kissed his neck and tasted the salt on his skin. "Wanna be bad?"

He chuckled softly. "What did you have in mind?"

"Gi said the air conditioning was out."

He nodded his head. "I noticed."

"I was thinking maybe you could take us for a ride on the Harley."

He laid down the pallet and wiped his hands on a rag before turning to place his arms around her. "I'm on duty right now, you know that."

Shannon made a pout which only made him smile. "But maybe, since it's quiet, you could ask Shade if you could go? Kate said for us to just go. He can send someone else from camp here for the night."

He looked back into her face, a mixture of innocence and mischievousness. He'd never tired of looking at her. "You win, *mia belleza*." He sent a message to Shade telepathically, letting him know all was quiet, and could he take the night off with Shannon.

***

Shade was roaming around the campgrounds, sizing up the progress of this season's recruits. They were several months into their training now and had already made a few cuts. He wandered through the groups, keeping his eyes open for anyone who needed instruction or correction. He took a stand beside Aislynn as she barked out orders to the group of females who were trying to refine their shuriken skills. He heard Luca in his head asking if he could take the night off and would it be possible to send another warrior in for protection. Shade chuckled, he knew Luca and Shannon deserved some time together. He scanned the camp and saw everything was running well and decided he really didn't need to be here tonight. Christoph, as usual, had everything under control. He let Christoph know he was leaving and sent Luca the message to get the hell out for the night. Besides, the humidity was unbearable, and he'd like nothing better than a cool air-conditioned night in bed with *bel*.

Kate made her way upstairs, passing Theresa in the hallway, fanning herself. "It is hotter up here, my lady. You may want to stay downstairs. I was just coming down myself."

Kate nodded. "I'll change into something cooler."

She entered their bedroom and stripped out of her clothing, standing nude in the closet exploring her options for something cooler to wear. "Fuck it," she muttered under her breath. She pulled on a light silk robe and stepped into a pair of slippers and made her way back downstairs and out the back of the house to the pool. The pool lights were on, as well as the landscape lighting in the gardens surrounding the pool. She let the silk robe slide from her shoulders in a puddle at her feet, as she stepped out of the slippers. She walked to the pool, entering by the stairs at the shallow end. The water felt cold as it hit her skin, and she walked deeper into the pool until she was shoulder deep in the water. She could hear the roar of the motorcycle as Luca left the garage and knew that Luca and Shannon were heading out for a night drive.

Kate moved near the side of the pool, and dunked down, submerging her head, and re-emerging, running her hands over her face, and pushing her hair straight back. She allowed her body to float face up in the water and rested her neck against the edge of the pool. She could hear the soft panting from Aegis and knew the wolf was close by. Closing her eyes, she let the water support her as she moved with the gentle waves of the water.

***

As Shade got closer to the house, the lightweight tee shirt clung to his chest and back with sweat; still, he'd take the heat over the cold any day. The tight leathers were stuck to him as if they were his own skin. He stopped on the path and pulled the tee over his head, hoping for a cool breeze, but the air was still. As he got closer to the house, his eye caught a passing shadow in the pool lights. He smiled wickedly as her rose scent reached him. He quietly made his way to the pool and stood in the lush landscaping, out of her view, watching as she dropped her robe, and stepped into the pool. She was still the most beautiful female he'd ever laid eyes on, and she was all his. His breath caught in his throat as her robe glided to the ground, the light reflecting off the water bounced off her lily-white skin. His heart pounded as he watched her from behind as she seductively disappeared under the water, and emerged as a beautiful mermaid with crimson hair, her face up to the moon. She still had the power to drop him to his knees. She glided effortlessly to the side of the pool, and resting her head and neck on the lip, allowing the water to cradle her body as she floated on her back, her nipples turning hard from the cool water. He ached for her, and wanted everything about her, still.

He walked slowly to the edge of the pool, standing over her. He knew she was aware of his presence now, but her eyes remained closed.

"I see the water nymphs are out this night. I do beg your pardon, my queen, but I was summoned to your side as protector for the remainder of the evening. I do hope you will not mind the changeup."

Without opening her eyes, a smile crept across her face. "Aw, and I was so hoping for Skelk!"

She opened her eyes to see him standing over her, his shirt already gone, and the leathers glued to his skin, looking ten feet tall from her vantage point floating on her back. She heard the low chuckle rumble up from his chest as he bent to unlace his boots.

He pulled off his boots and began to strip the leathers from his skin, not an easy task now that his cock was raging, and his blood ran hot. "Skelk, is it? Didn't know he was your type, but I'll do my best not to disappoint." Tossing the leathers unceremoniously, he stood naked over her, his powerful legs straddling her head as she lounged on the lip of the pool, and his cock standing at attention. Diving into the pool, the cool water hit his skin and invigorated him. He swam underwater and spied her legs outstretched before her. Reaching up, he spread them easily and emerged between them, shaking his curls, as the water splattered them both. He heard her giggle and grinned back at her.

"It has been a long time since we played in the moonlight, *mi amore*."

She lowered her feet to the bottom of the pool and wrapped her arms around his broad shoulders. "Too long. Are you getting too old for me?" She bit at his chin, feeling the rough stubble against her tongue.

"Did you just call me old, woman? Because if you did, I think maybe I need to prove to you that age has nothing to do with how efficiently I can make wild passionate love to you."

She nipped at his skin, arousing him even further. "I wasn't looking for efficiency, old man."

He grabbed her ass under the water and lifted her to his waist. He felt her legs straddle him, as she wrapped them around his hips. He dipped down in the pool until the water was up to her chin, and her hair floated out behind her in waves of red, lit from beneath by the pool lighting. His moan was louder as she nipped at his neck, her tongue like fire against his throat. She kissed his neck and shoulders, slowly and methodically, leaving no inch of him unexplored. They were practiced lovers and knew every curve and crevice between them. He didn't need to direct her to what he liked. She knew exactly what that was. How she nipped at his ear, and ran her tongue around its shell, the spot on his neck that always sent shivers down his spine, the way she gripped his hair or kissed his jaw. The way she pulled his bottom lip into her mouth and sometimes nipped it to taste his blood. He was happy to let her play and loved when she led.

His cock grew more rigid with her teasing, and he could feel the heat of her sex even in the cool water. He wanted nothing more than to be inside her. "I love every inch of you."

She clung to him as he held onto her in the water, her lips close to his ear, she nibbled at his earlobe, and whispered, "And I love you." Kate relished this alone time with him. There was nothing routine about their life, and especially not their sex life, but it had been a while since they'd played outdoors. When the children were young and living at home, sex in the pool wasn't an option. She heard his words of love and felt the goosebumps rise on her skin. She'd always loved him to the core of her being and still marveled that, with all this time, she only loved him more.

He kissed her then, passionately and with abandon. Long, slow kisses, playful kisses, open mouth kisses where their tongues danced and darted around the other. As he broke the kiss, he nipped at her lip and let his tongue slide over her chin to her neck where he snuggled and growled. Her vein pulsed against his tongue, and called out to him, igniting his primal need for her. He didn't want to move too fast. It was rare to have the whole night with her. He moved in the water, swirling them around together, as if in a dance. "You feel so fragile in my hands, but you are still the only one who can make me toe the line."

He dipped beneath the surface of the water, letting it cool their heads before re-emerging. "Do you ever wonder what your life would be like if we had never met?"

Kate laughed, her laughter carrying on the night air. "Besides the fact that I'd be long dead by now, I imagine I would have spent my life in a cubicle, working next to Shannon, as we shared our mutual disappointment over the men in our life."

Her laughter was a melody to his ears. "I think some mortal would have come along and stolen your heart. For me, I can't imagine what path I would have taken. Perhaps I too would be gone by now. You have changed everything, *mi amore,* my family, my businesses, and my coven. I would not have changed anything in our lives together."

"Nor would I, lover." She stared back at him. His eyes even bluer than the pool of water they stood in. She'd never tire of him, could never tire of him. His hands cradled her hips, as her legs remain wrapped around him, and they needed no words to communicate what was in their hearts. She leaned forward and kissed him again, as he responded more aggressively, his mouth covering hers. She could feel his fangs punch through, and ran her tongue over the sharp tips, hearing the moan that started deep in his chest. His hands gripped her hips more tightly as he repositioned her, easily sliding his warrior's sword home. She momentarily broke the kiss as she gasped, closed her eyes, and dropped her head back.

He felt the heat that surrounded his shaft and heard her gasps as if taking her for the first time. He saw the look of wanton anticipation on her face, as he relished in the pleasure of claiming her. She was forever his walking sin. His fingers pressed deeper into the soft curves of her hips, as he watched her run the tip of her tongue over those full red lips. He thrust his hips forward, pushing his cock deep, nestled hard and pulsing inside her heat.

She looked at him, beads of water clinging to his long, dark lashes, and water dripping from his dark curls. They stared into each other's eyes, no words were needed, and he felt what was in her heart, as she felt what was in his. They were bonded as one, hearts, minds, body, and soul. He moved to the side of the pool where he could press her back against the side, his cock still buried inside her. Her hands gripped handfuls of curls and tugged with an urgency.

"Impatient nymph." Sliding his tongue along her pulsing vein, he began that timeless rhythm, rocking his hips against hers as he felt her respond. The water made a soft, lapping noise as it splashed around them, her breasts, playing peek-a-boo with him, as they bobbed up and down, first in, then out of the water. He leaned down, and she laid back against the side of the pool, as he drug his fangs over her shoulder and down her flawless skin. Gliding his fangs over her erect nipple, he drew no blood but felt a soft shiver run through her. He sucked the hardened nub of her nipple into his mouth and rolled it with his tongue as her nails clawed into his muscled back and it felt as though he'd die if he didn't taste her. His lips returned to her neck, and she turned her head, welcoming his advance as he sank his fangs into her delicate flesh. Her blood splashed over his tongue and ignited that familiar raging fire in his body. She was his, forever his.

She continued to ride his cock, as he penetrated deeper, aching for that moment of completeness. She reveled in the sensation, when she felt the sweet sting of his fangs in her flesh, his lips sealed around the wound, as he drank from her. Her moan was soft, as she felt the transfer of energy between them, and the heat between her legs built. He broke away long enough to beg her to feed, and she leaned her head on his shoulder, biting deep into his flesh. His hand tangled around her wet crimson, guiding her mouth to the spot on his neck that drove him to insatiable ecstasy. He returned to feeding, and the bond was complete.

The power of his blood hit her like a lightning bolt and drove the fire that burned in her belly. Her hips thrust hard against him, taking all of him, as their bodies created a series of waves that splashed against the sides of the pool. She felt the orgasm hit her, as she threw her head back, his blood still on her lips, and her cry of passion echoed in the night.

He watched as the orgasm took her, his blood on her lips, a trickle escaping down her chin. The glow in her eyes and the sound of her cry of passion was for him and only him, and something he'd never had the words to describe, even after all these years. She was the only one who'd taken his blood, and he knew if he ever lost her, there wouldn't be another. He leaned over her and licked the small trickle of his blood from her chin and swirled it in his mouth before kissing her.

Their hearts pounded in sync as their breathing returned to normal, and he cradled her in his arms, holding her close to his chest and smiling down at her. "Still think I am too old?"

"The night is still young, ask me again at sunrise."

He laughed loudly as he held her tighter, and she wiggled free. Swimming backward away from him, she smiled back at him mischievously. As she reached the side of the pool, she turned and climbed up the ladder. He watched as her body emerged, the water cascading down her perfect form, like a statue carved from marble.

Standing on the edge of the pool, she lifted her arms above her head, and pushed back her crimson locks, wringing the water from her hair. He could stare at her for all eternity, and never tire of the view. "Don't leave me, *mi amore*."

"Never." She lowered herself to the edge of the pool and sat down, her legs dangling over the side, her feet in the water. He swam slowly in her direction, the lights from the pool dancing on his face. As he reached her, he slid his hands up her thighs and nibbled at her knee. She bit her lip, and he heard the sharp intake of her breath, as the heat of his mouth made contact with her flesh, cooled by the water. He gently opened her legs, and moved between them, as she draped her knees over his shoulders, and leaned back, supporting her weight with her arms. He grabbed her hips, and scooted her to the lip of the pool, and buried his face between her legs. The moisture clung to the tight red curls and he nuzzled into her heat and heard the soft moan escape her lips. His tongue playfully explored her depths, as his lips tugged and teased. He was savoring the taste of her on his tongue and coaxing her to the next level of sexual arousal. He could hear her breathing as it became more ragged, and she crossed her ankles around his back, drawing him closer. His tongue explored every surface, teasing the hardened nub nestled in the soft folds of her sex, sending an electric shock through her system each time he flicked his tongue, as his fingers dug deeper into the smooth soft flesh of her hips, holding her firmly in place. He read her responses and pulled back every time she reached the edge. He could read her body like a book and played it like a fine instrument. His mouth and tongue expertly brought her to the brink of orgasm again and again, until she cried out, and he knew the teasing had gone on long enough. Plunging his tongue into the depths of her, tasting the honey that was his alone, he felt her body spasm as she lurched forward, her hands in his hair, gripping tightly. He sucked at her delicate petals and stroked her clit with his tongue until the last wave of her orgasm subsided, and he felt her pull away, the intensity of the sensations too much to bear.

He lifted her from the side of the pool, and lowered her back into the water, holding her close as she laid her head on his shoulder, her body still shaking in the aftermath of her orgasm. He held her quietly as her body sought to find normal again. Walking with her, she wrapped her legs around his hips, and he made his way to the shallow end of the pool and up the steps. He carried her over to the lounge chairs by the pool and set her down. He opened the storage chest that held the pool supplies, and pulled out a big beach towel, and wrapped it around her.

She watched as he moved, water dripping from his skin, completely confident in his nudity. He'd always moved with the same power and grace, whether he was clothed or unclothed, and she'd always admired that in him. She draped herself in the large beach towel, starting to dry off as he sat in the lounge chair next to her. He pushed the dark wet curls back from his face, and tilted his head back, shaking the water from his hair.

"Do you need a towel, lover?"

He gave her a crooked smile. "I'm good."

Standing, she moved to his lounge chair, pushing him back until he was lying down, and wedged in next to him, wrapping the beach towel around the both of them. "I wouldn't want you to get cold."

He chuckled. "It is probably seventy degrees out here, *bel*. I don't think I will get cold."

Kissing his neck, before moving to his chest, she looked up at him from under the towel. "Better safe than sorry."

Her kisses started in the middle of his chest and worked their way down across his steel hard abs, and she slid her body down his. She could feel the heat of his erection, as his body responded to her. She heard him whisper, "*Bel,*" as his hand slid into her hair, and the towel slid to the patio. She positioned herself between his legs, as he opened his thighs to accommodate her. She buried her nose into the thick patch of hair above his cock, but the chlorine from the pool had washed away much of that musky scent she loved. She encircled his cock with her hand, slowly stroking him as she flicked her tongue over the smooth head. She felt the muscles in his thighs tighten, and she slid his cock into her mouth, savoring the taste and feel of him in her mouth, letting her tongue explore the textures between the shaft and the head of his cock. His moan was guttural and emanated from deep in his chest, and she slid his cock deep into the back of her throat, feeling it pulsate and throb. She too knew the art of the tease, and how to take him to the edge, how to make him beg her for release. She slid his cock in and out of her mouth, swirling her tongue across the head, and increasing the pace until she felt both of his hands gripping her hair, holding her still while he thrust his hips forward and took control, releasing his seed as his head was thrown back in ecstasy, his cry of passion loud in the still of the night.

Sitting up, she licked her lips and smiled at him salaciously as he struggled to catch his breath. “Now we’re even.”

They heard the compressors for the cooling system kick in, as the air conditioning had been repaired. Shade raised himself to his elbows and stared back at her. Sitting up, he scooped her up in his arms and carried her back inside. “Never even, *bel rosso*, as you said, the night is young.”

36

Dona had stayed over the extra day in Rome and had been treated to gracious attention from Rodrigo before reluctantly packing her things, including the new garments and jewels he'd so generously given to her, and taken the chauffeured driven car back to her humble villa. She woke early in her bed to the sound of some heavy equipment working outside her window. She slid from the bed and rushed to the window to see an army of people working on the grounds. They were pulling up dead shrubs and clearing parcels of land that had been overcome with weeds and overgrown trees and brush. "Mario!"

Her manservant rushed into the room, and grabbed her robe, carrying it to her at the window. "Yes, my lady?"

He helped her as she struggled to put on the robe and point out the window at the same time. "What is this?"

He shook his head. "I don't know, my lady. They showed up early this morning, at sunrise, and started working in the gardens. I assumed you had summoned them."

She tied the belt of her robe as she turned from the window, agitated. "Me? How would I be able to afford them? Of course, it was not me! Get out there. Find out what they're doing."

He turned to leave the room, feeling chastised. "Of course, my lady."

As he left, her maid entered, and helped her bathe and dress. Dona was in a rush to be finished with her routine. Just as she was leaving her bedroom to go downstairs, Mario returned. "So, what is it? What's going on?"

He wasn't sure if his news would make her happy or angry. "The workers were sent by the Borgia, my lady. They say they have been instructed to return the gardens to their original glory. All the old and dying plantings will be removed, and new plants and trees installed. The foreman said it should only take two days because he has a very large crew."

Dona looked confused. "Rodrigo? Rodrigo did this?"

Mario nodded. "So, it would appear, my lady."

Dona started down the stairs, followed by her manservant and maid, her only company through the last many years. "I should call."

He answered her, even though her comment seemed directed at no one in particular. "Yes, my lady."

Dona didn't have the latest technology in her home, she didn't have the vision phones or the computers that deftly managed everything from temperature to lighting and responded to the sound of her voice. She retrieved the old tech cell phone from the office and dialed Rodrigo. He may not be able to see her, but at least she could express her gratitude, and let him know this was too much.

The majordomo at Borgia Palazzo heard the phone ring and answered it quickly. Both Borgia masters were typically deep in their death slumber by the early dawn. He was quite shocked when no visual of the caller appeared on the screen. "Borgia Palazzo." There was a silence on the line at first and he wondered if the caller had hung up.

Dona paced as she waited for someone to answer. "Oh. Yes." She was realizing the time and thinking that perhaps Rodrigo has already taken to his death slumber. "This is Donatella Alizzi. The call is not urgent. I do apologize. Has Rodrigo gone to his slumber?"

"Ah yes, Mistress Alizzi. If you will hold for a moment I will see if Master Rodrigo is still awake." Pushing a button, he put her on hold and then pushed the personal intercom system inside the Palazzo, connecting to Rodrigo's manservant. When he answered, the majordomo informed him that the Alizzi was on the line and would Master wish to accept the call. He waited only a few moments before the manservant returned to say the master would take the call.

Rodrigo was still awake in his living quarters. The electronic blinds had sealed him in against the sun, but he had switched on a lamp as he continued to read. He'd sent the workers to the Alizzi home to begin work at sunrise, and he was anticipating her call. He was anxious to hear her voice and hoped he'd find that she was pleased with his gift. He'd struggled against his death slumber; certain he'd hear from her. It was only the beginning of what he had planned. His manservant informed him she'd called. He smiled a wicked grin. He spoke to the computer, "Connect me, please." He wasn't surprised when he didn't see an image appear on the screen. She lived in the dark ages with her technology.

"*Buongiorno*, my dear."

Dona had continued pacing with the phone in her hand as she waited and was caught off-guard when she heard his voice. "Rodrigo! I hope I did not disturb you."

"It would not matter if you did, my dear, I would always take a call from you. Please, is something wrong?"

"I was calling to thank you for the gardens, but really, this is too much! I can't accept a gift of this magnitude. I have no way to return such a gesture."

The wicked grin spread across his face, the evil in his eyes would drop any normal soul to their knees, begging for mercy, but fortunately, she couldn't see him. "It is but a mere gesture, to show my appreciation. You have already paid me by gracing me with your recent visit. It is the least I can do after sharing your company with me. Besides, I want you to be able to go outside, enjoy the summer season, and take pleasure in the gardens. No need for you to shut yourself inside any longer."

Dona was beginning to wonder about all the rumors she'd heard over the years about the evil rule of the two Borgia brothers. He'd shown nothing but kindness and sympathy for her situation when other covens had shunned her. "Your generosity is overwhelming, Rodrigo. I do hope you will visit when the gardens are complete. I would enjoy your company, and a garden is so much better when its beauty is shared."

"My dear Donatella, that would be such a sweet pleasure for me. My foreman tells me he should have it completed fully within a few days. I would be delighted to visit you and share in the garden. Of course, I can't join you in the daylight, but I look forward to smelling the sunlight in your hair. I dread these long days apart from your beauty. When I am there, we must look into getting your technology updated, my dear. If I am going to court you properly, I wish to see your smile whenever we speak by phone, *si*?"

She was taken aback by his words. Court her? He was courting her? It had been so long since a man paid any attention to her. In her culture, a master's or mistress's value was judged by their power and wealth, the size of their coven or their armies, and their ability to wield influence. She'd lost all of those things. She had no more power than her manservant or her maid, who were only able to stay because the Medici still paid their salaries. "Oh, Rodrigo that isn't necessary. Honestly, I rarely make a call."

"I beg to differ, my dear, it is most necessary. You are being courted by the Borgia, and I can't have you living like a pauper. I refuse to argue with you. My gifts are given from my heart, and I hope they are received with openness and love. Are you declining my affections, Dona?" The tone of his voice shifted slightly and was more commanding. She would begin to slowly understand, he'd have her and he'd be in total control.

She heard the slight change in his tone, more challenging, as he took control. It wasn't unwelcome. She'd been raised under the old values, and even though she was a mistress, born of a royal master, she too had been taught she'd defer to her mate, had she ever had a mate. "No, of course not. I certainly have no intentions to offend you. I am most grateful for your attention and your kindness. I did not want you to feel...obligated."

Rodrigo smirked. She'd heard him, loud and clear, and understood that to offend or rebuke him was a mistake. No one messed with the Borgia. "I feel no obligation other than to make you happy, Donatella. It fills me with joy to see you smile. I will see you in a week, until then, enjoy the garden."

He hung up then, not waiting for her response, as he chuckled to himself. Oh, she would be his.

37

Alfie was busy inside the office at camp working on some long-overdue changes in the location assignments for the warriors. They tried to keep the warriors in rotation, so they gained experience in other parts of Italy, as well as their covens in Greece and France. He sat at the computer, looking over charts and graphs when he heard the office door open. The sound of the warriors training on the campgrounds was suddenly deafening inside the office as the door opened when Alfie looked up to see one of the warriors assigned to border patrol standing in the doorway. "What is it?"

The warrior stood with his arms behind his back. "Something is going on at the Alizzi place."

Alfie stopped typing and gave the warrior his full attention. "Explain to me what you're talking about, warrior."

"When we reported for border duty over there tonight, there'd been some big changes made to the property. She's landscaping the gardens, clearing out all the dead brush, and planting flowers and trees, adding sculptures and walking paths. The entire grounds are being restored."

Alfie scrunched up his face in disbelief. How the hell did that happen? Dona could barely afford to keep the lights on in that place. "*Grazie*, wait outside until I speak with Master Lorenzo, he may wish to question you."

The warrior nodded and stepped outside, closing the door behind him. Alfie telepathically asked Lorenzo to come to the office immediately.

Lorenzo was walking the training field, making a mental note of each of the recruits, assessing their development when he heard Alfie summon him. He motioned to one of his lieutenants to take over and teleported into the office. He took a seat across the desk from Alfie and threw both feet on the desk; his legs crossed at the ankles as he pulled a pack of cigarettes from his pocket and lit up. "You need help typing, brother?" He tossed the pack in Alfie's direction and watched as he quickly snatched the pack from the air.

Alfie lit up and leaned back in the chair. "No help needed with the paperwork, even though you seem to always assign it to me. I just had a visit from one of our warriors on border patrol. Seems some changes are happening at the Alizzi's. He said there's major landscaping going on and the gardens are being restored. What the fuck is that about? She has no way of paying for that kind of restoration."

Lorenzo inhaled deeply before blowing out the cloud of smoke. "Interesting. I had heard some rumors that she'd attended some event Rodrigo held at his palace in Rome. Has to be him, we know she can't afford it. I hadn't given it much thought when we saw them at the Farnese ceremony. They didn't attend together, but he was definitely attentive to her. This is an escalation, though. Doesn't make a lot of sense. The Alizzi knows the Borgia. She knows they haven't been our allies for centuries. Still, this is a little too close for comfort. My dad probably needs to know about this."

Alfie looked back at him with concern. "You really think Borgia has something to do with this? She has to be aware of the carnage he's caused. I agree, you better get the old man on this."

Lorenzo dropped both feet to the floor, requesting the call to Bel Rosso, and the computer responded. As the phone rang, he looked back at Alfie. "May be nothing, and I know little of the Borgia's, but I know that in Christofano's time, the battles were intense. My father says they could never prove it, but it was felt the Borgia had a hand in the bonfires that killed Christofano and Portia."

As the screen came to life, it was Gi's face he saw. "Gi! Is my father in the house or the camp?"

Gi nodded to him. "He is in the house. I will transfer the call to his office."

Shade slammed the desk drawer closed and was about ready to head outside when he saw the computer screen flash that there was an incoming call. "Fuck!" He hit the button and immediately his son's face appeared. "Well, this can't be good if you're calling me in the middle of the night from camp. What's going down, son?" Shade took the last sip of Midnight from the glass on his desk.

"Maybe nothing. Just thought you should be aware, though. Remember when we saw Rodrigo dancing with the Alizzi at the Farnese ball in Sicily? Well, I've heard through the grapevine that he held some gala at his palace in Rome about a week ago, and she was his guest of honor. Heard she stayed at his palace for several days. She was decked out in a new gown and covered in jewels. Now we just got word that her gardens are being restored. The old gardens at her villa covered several acres. It would cost millions to recreate. No way Dona is paying for all that. Not sure what's going on here. I know, in the past, Dona held no affection for the Borgia, but if she's now relying on him, that puts him a little too close for comfort."

Shade listened intensely, running his hands through his hair. "She is definitely not capable of paying for a damn thing. What the hell is she thinking? She knows that Borgia is the closest enemy we have had for as long as I can remember. If it *is* Rodrigo, he is up to something, and you can bet it is not to help Dona. I don't like it. Before we do anything, we need to be sure Rodrigo is involved. Can we get any information on the people out there working?"

Lorenzo could see his father's agitation. "Our warrior heard the workers weren't local, they were from Rome, but we can probably find out more."

Shade slammed his fist on the desk. "That stupid fucking bitch!" He stood and paced, his anger building. "I have no doubts it's Borgia if they are from Rome. Keep an eye on the place. If you see that bastard there, I want to know immediately. In the meantime, I think I need to make a visit to the Alizzi. She knows better than this. Hell, Borgia is responsible for way too much pain and loss in this family." Shade sighed out loud and shook his head. "You do know he was after your grandmother for a long time. I would bet my life he was the one that set the fires that took their lives, he fucking hated my *padre* for taking *Madre* from him, not that she ever had an interest in him. Rodrigo would tell my *padre* if he could not have her, then no one would have her. My *madre* never left the grounds without my padre's personal protection."

Lorenzo knew the hatred for the Borgia's ran deep and crossed generations. "I understand, Dad. We'll get warriors back on the border, and we'll put feelers out in town. If anyone sees or hears anything, we'll know immediately. Is there anything else I should do?"

Shade leaned in close to the screen and raised his voice. "You listen to me, and you listen good, son. I want no one to confront him.

That's what he wants. Do not give him any reason to come after us. Am I understood?"

Lorenzo nodded, surprised at his father's sudden outburst. "We'll stay low-key and off the radar. No problem. I'll let our warriors know they aren't to do anything to instigate trouble. Observe and report only."

"Lorenzo, you need to understand, Borgias will take the smallest thing and make it a fucking war. Rodrigo and Soren are two of the evilest vampires that ever lived. Rodrigo is a Sin-Eater, and you sure as fuck don't want to tangle with that. Rodrigo likes to provoke, and hope his opponent responds. Then he can claim he was just defending himself. There is no reasoning with these two. They are the most dangerous coven in the world. And Soren...he eats half-breeds alive for fun. Stay low but keep tabs on Dona. I am going to go see her personally, find out what the fuck is going down, and set her ass straight. She will listen to me."

"I've got it under control, Dad. I'll keep you informed if I hear anything else. Tell Mom I love her. See you soon."

***

As the screen went black, Kate was walking past his office on her way to find Shannon when she overheard his agitation. She made a detour into his office. She'd heard him ranting about Rodrigo and Soren. "Who were you talking to, Shade?"

He sat with his head in his hands. He had to get to Dona before she did something he couldn't mend. How far had she already gone with Borgia, and why couldn't she see he was manipulating her? He looked up as Kate walked in. "Our son."

She went to him, brushing the hair back from his face. "Is everything all right? I heard you speaking of Rodrigo and Soren."

Closing his eyes, he took a deep breath. A simple touch from her hand could calm him. "I don't want to scare you, but I want you to know what's going on. One of the border patrol warriors saw that the Alizzi grounds are being restored. Lorenzo called to tell me. He also says Dona has been at the Borgia Palazzo to a ball he held there, wearing a new gown, and covered in jewels. Rodrigo is behind this, and it reeks of no good. They are so fucking powerful, always have been. It rattles me as to why she is giving him the time of day."

Kate sighed as she slid into his lap. "She's lonely, and she's lost everything. Her prospects for the future aren't promising. If he's showing her attention, I can see why she'd respond. I saw them together at the Farnese ceremony in Sicily. She was seated alone at the table, like an outcast. No one even acknowledged her presence, except Rodrigo."

"No, *mi amore,* he does nothing without cause. He could care less about her. Let me tell you some things. Rodrigo was in love with my *madre* once. He wanted her, and the alliance that would come with being mated to her family. *Madre's family* never cared for him, nor did she like him, but that didn't matter to Rodrigo. He was angry when she mated my *padre* and hated them both for spoiling his plans. I believe in my soul that he was responsible for their death. He knew I was gone and that I could never get to them in time. We believe he took advantage of the chaos in Florence during the time of the bonfires and used the mass hysteria of the mortals to his advantage, leading the raid on our home. Unlike the mortal Medici family, we had tried to remain low-key and out of the public eye. The rivalry between the Borgia and the Medici is legendary in our culture. That is why *Padre* pushed me so fucking hard to mate the Alizzi, to keep the Borgia at a distance. Across the centuries, it has always been a battle between our two covens for who would eventually control all of Italy. The Borgia are powerful, and they have great gifts. If you only knew about the things these two can do."

Kate looked at him with question. "Their gifts? What is so unique about their gifts? You're a dream-walker. We have three Medici who have the gift of animalism and two fire-throwers. What gift could they possibly have that could defeat us?"

Shade laid his head back on the chair. He needed for her to understand the evil of these two vampire masters. "Rodrigo is a sin-eater. Very dangerous. He consumes the sins of those he kills and takes on their darkness. Do you have any idea how many he has slain? Imagine the black abyss that is his soul. Soren is a dream-walker, like me. I do not use my gift for much evil; I have used it as a weapon as a last resort. But Soren is an expert at it. He loves to torment and torture his victims in their dreams, where they can't escape from him. They are both old-world, they practice ancient customs. Soren eats half-breeds alive, famous for it. He has warriors who roam the streets and clubs looking for them. I am told the entire underground of Borgia Palazzo is a playground of death and fun for them both. They rape and kill and drain for pleasure. I need to nip this thing with Dona in the bud before it spirals out of control. I need to go to Dona and talk with her, convince her that this is insanity. Make her see sense. I have no choice at this point. The Borgia does nothing out of goodness. She is weak, and he is jumping on that with both feet. He wants that territory."

Kate felt a chill run down her spine as he explained a sin-eater. "I haven't met a sin-eater. I can't imagine how black his heart must be. Be careful. We've been lucky in that our coven hasn't had to defend itself since the battle with Max, and that was a small battle. We don't want to bring war down on our people."

He lifted her from his lap and walked to the doors of the office that led outside. Opening the door, he let the night air cool his agitated heart and soul. "Dona has no idea what she is dragging us into."

Kate watched as he stood with his back stiff, and she could feel his anger. She feared the talk with Dona might be too little too late. "Then go. Do what you must do. Don't let this nightmare into our lives."

38

After making arrangements to cover the camp, and leaving Luca in charge at home, Shade teleported straight from Bel Rosso to Florence. He teleported over his own territory in Tuscany, past Castello and the campgrounds and into Umbria. As he neared Dona's villa, he breathed deep, as he tried to detect any presence of the Borgia before he landed. Picking up nothing, he landed on the rooftop of her home and stood looking out over the grounds. The moonlight shone down like a spotlight from above to give him a great view. Everything in the gardens had been replanted and replaced in fine detail. He could envision the vibrancy of the colors during the daylight hours, now that everything was in bloom again. He growled deep in his chest. He knew Dona didn't have two lira to rub together, and could never afford to do this on her own, and was even more convinced, seeing the massive scale of the renovation, that this was Borgia's doing. If Rodrigo had taken an interest in her, Shade knew this wouldn't be the last of it, and he'd stop at nothing to lure Dona into his web of wickedness. She'd allowed herself to be blinded by his gifts, and Shade was here to make sure she got her sight back.

Swooping down to the entrance, he pounded his fist heavily against the thick wooden door, rattling it on its hinges. Mario answered quickly with a surprised look on his face. "Master Shade, we were not expecting you, please come in."

Shade brushed past him and scanned the house, finding the inside of her home still barren. "Get the Alizzi, now! I need to speak with her!"

***

Dona was relaxing in a hot bath, enjoying the bath products she'd brought home with her from the Borgia Palazzo after her visit there. Rodrigo had insisted she take them as they'd been purchased for her visit, and he had no use for them. She was soaking in a sea of bubbles that came up to her chin, when she heard her maid, Marie, tapping frantically at her door. “My lady! The Medici is here to see you. He is waiting in the parlor."

Dona sat straight up in the tub. "What? What does he want?"

"I have no idea, my lady. He is waiting for you in the parlor."

"Come help me, Marie. Hurry!"

The maid rushed in and helped Dona from the tub. She was briskly drying her off as Dona tried to quickly apply some make-up. Marie helped her into one of her dresses that had been re-worked to look more modern, as Dona slid on a pair of shoes. "How do I look?"

Marie fluffed out her hair, running her hands through the sides. "Beautiful, my lady."

Dona rushed from the room and down the stairs to the parlor to find Shade pacing impatiently. “I am so sorry to keep you waiting, Shade. I did not expect you. Mario! Bring him a drink, please!"

Shade stopped his pacing and turned to glare at her. "Sit down, Dona, we need to talk. I do not like to be kept waiting, and I don’t have much time.”

Mario carried a tray of drinks to them, and Shade took a glass, throwing it back in one gulp. Placing the glass back down on the tray, he walked to where she sat and leaned down to her, nose to nose. "Do not even think about lying to me, I want the truth from you, *si*?"

She was taken aback by his anger, and her own anger flared. "Then I suggest, in the future, if you do not wish to be kept waiting, you notify me in advance of your intentions, instead of dropping in unannounced! It may not be grand, but this is still my home, not yours, Shade Medici! And I am still the Mistress of Umbria. You would do well to remember that. And for the record, I have never lied to you. Not even with the incident involving Lorenzo. I have always spoken the truth. What is it you wish to know? Because I will remind you, my life is no longer any of your business. You washed your hands of me years ago."

His fangs punched through as he growled. "Need I remind you, mistress, I pay your servants’ wages? Careful who you step on in your way to dig yourself out of the hell you brought upon yourself."

He backed away from her and stood to his full height, retracting his fangs. He took several deep breaths, calming himself as he took a seat opposite her. "You and I need to talk about what the hell is going on around here. My son calls me in the middle of the night and tells me your gardens have been restored. Rumors are circulating about you and the Borgia." He locked her in his gaze. "What the hell are you doing with the Borgia?"

Dona was indignant that he'd come here to confront her in her own home about her personal affairs. "What am I doing? I assure you my behavior is above board, not that this is any of your concern. He showed me kindness at the Farnese ceremony in Sicily, which is more than I can say for you. He invited me to his home for a gala that he hosted, and I awoke one morning to find that he had restored my gardens to their original glory. He has asked for nothing from me and understands I have nothing to give him in return. No one, not from your coven, or any other, has shown me a single ounce of respect in the last century, so do not lecture me, Shade."

Shade shook his head. "Dona, what the hell has happened to you? Can you not see it? When did Borgia ever do anything for anyone without cause? He isn't the type to show kindness to anyone. If he is showering you with attention, then there is something he wants."

He stood, restless, agitated, and tired as his hands raked through his hair. "I didn't come here to insult you, I apologize. But I am concerned. Dona, listen to me, please! Do you not remember the hell he inflicted on our people? The debauchery he and Soren both engage in? Your *padre* and mine wanted our mating because of the Borgia. Look at how powerful he is now, and yet, he is charming you for what? Think, Dona, think!" He went to her, crouching down, laying his hands on her knees. "Look at me and tell me you haven't forgotten the evil the Borgia has brought to both our families, that you haven't forgotten all the things your *padre* told you about them."

She looked away from him, unable to make eye contact. Rodrigo wasn't an unattractive man, but he had a sinister look about him. Something inherently evil, that seemed to have become a physical part of him. He was imposing, and he ruled through intimidation and fear. Few, if any, dared cross him. He was a sin-eater, and the souls of those he'd killed had been dark. He'd absorbed them all, becoming more evil with time. She knew all these things as they'd been drilled into her by her father. She'd been warned to steer clear of the Borgia.

"I remember everything, Shade. Perhaps, if you had listened to the advice of our fathers, perhaps if you had mated me, I would not be left here alone. Our fathers both knew the power of the Borgia's, and I was told from the time I was a young girl that I would be mated to you, so our families could join forces, and protect both our covens. I remind you, it was you that turned your back on that contract."

Her words struck a chord in him, as he realized he'd had a role in this outcome as well. He had to take the conversation in a direction he hadn't wanted, but he was desperate to make her see what was happening. He took her hand in his and rubbed his thumb across her knuckles. He watched as her face turned back to him, and he could see her holding back the tears.

"*Si*, it was I who turned my back. I was not ready to mate, and I did not love you, Dona. You have been a friend, a companion. We grew up together and spent much time together. You welcomed me to your bed, and I accepted your invitation, but I could not envision my life with you. I could not envision being mated for eternity to a female I did not love. It would have been unfair to you, and me. Things have been bad between us for a while now, but you led my son into something evil, you hurt me and my child. I don't expect you to understand the depth of the betrayal I felt, since you have no children of your own. But you need to move past all that and be careful where you step. Borgia will drag you down and crush you in an instant. I don't want that to happen to you. I care enough to care about how this ends and he will destroy you." He stood and paced slowly around the room, his back to her when he posed the question. "Has he made you an offer for the territory?"

She looked at him as he stood with his back to her, and the image of him standing in her parlor sent a spike of pain through her heart. She'd loved him with every cell of her being and had done everything she could think of to win his heart. When they were both younger, he'd spent so much time with her, had fed from her, and slept with her at his side. But he'd never said the words she'd longed to hear from him and knew she never would. She thought, with time, the pain of losing him would subside, but it never did. "He has not made any offer or made any demand. He has asked nothing of me, Shade. His advances have been most gentlemanly. I assume you have heard I was at his palazzo in Rome. I was given my own room. He did not visit my bed or invite me into his. Your concerns are unfounded."

He turned then to look at her. Borgia was slowly getting to her. He could see it in her face. "Dona, he will try. I assure you, he will come to your bed. He is a sin-eater, and you are so vulnerable now, you can't tackle that kind of wicked. Please be careful, that is all I can ask of you."

He walked slowly to the door, turning before he left. "I apologize for coming unannounced. I am begging you to keep your wits about you. You have always had good instincts, Dona, listen to your gut, never ignore that."

Her eyes followed him to the door. "You're leaving? You just got here!"

"*Si*. I have teleported from Bel Rosso. I am tired and need to get to my slumber soon. I will need to stay at Castello, I won't make the teleport back in time before sunrise." He looked at her then and knew she was still desperate and vulnerable. He could never forgive her for what she'd done to Lorenzo. He wished it had never happened, but it had. Had it not, he would still be in control of Umbria and its safety.

She stood and followed after him. "You could stay here if you wish. I could have Marie get a room ready for you. You would not be disturbed."

"*Grazie*, Dona, but I honor my mate. Besides, I wish to visit my granddaughter." Dona nodded her head and gave him a sad smile. "Yes, of course, your granddaughter. Give my best to Lorenzo and Chantal on their new baby. I am happy for him." She could think of no way to delay his departure. "You know you are always welcome here. I hope you will return again, perhaps under different circumstances."

She was standing right in front of him, and he could smell the bath salts on her skin. "My offer still stands. I will buy Umbria and you can be free of all of this."

She shook her head no. "This is the only home I know."

He needed to make her understand that Borgia was no friend to her. Reaching out, he took her in his arms and hugged her, his voice soft in her ear. "Remember my words; remember those of your *padre*. When your instincts tell you something is wrong, please heed them. Please, I beg you to step lightly. It could mean your life, Dona." He pulled away and didn't look at her, leaving swiftly out the door and teleporting back to Castello.

Dona had closed her eyes as he held her, laying her head against his chest. She remembered his scent and the sound of his heart. It was almost more than she could bear. And then he was gone. She stood quietly in the parlor as a single tear ran down her cheek.

39

Shade returned to Castello just in time to beat the sunrise. Antonio had a room ready for him, informing him that Master Lorenzo and the family were already in their slumber. Lorenzo and Chantal were both day-walkers, but Lorenzo spent most nights in the camp, so they'd both adjusted their schedules to sleep during the day. Shade didn't want to disturb them, and even though he was tired, his frustration with Dona wouldn't allow him to lie down quite yet. He made his way to the office and called Kate to let her know he was all right, and he'd be taking his death slumber at Castello. He planned to return once the sun set, and he had a meeting with Lorenzo and Alfie. Antonio appeared again, with a large glass of Midnight which he drank down quickly. "Master, allow me to show you to your room. You need rest now." Shade offered no argument as he followed the butler to his room, already sealed in darkness, and he climbed into the bed. He was acutely aware of Kate's absence from his side, as he slipped into his slumber.

When he woke, he could hear the rustling about of others in the castle, as everything came to life at sunset. He quickly showered and dressed before making his way into the long hallway and heading out to find his son. The whole idea of Borgia moving in on the Alizzi disgusted him and had him on edge. He needed for Lorenzo to be forewarned of any impending danger and raise the level of alertness within the warrior camp. They were dealing with evil incarnate, and nothing could be taken for granted. He heard the most adorable giggle coming from the library and knew it was his newest grandchild, Grace. He followed the sound and as he walked to the door, he saw Lorenzo holding her on his lap, reading her a book. Lorenzo was making gestures with his hands and making funny faces, as he changed his voice for each character. Shade felt his heart skip a beat. He'd cherished the smallest moments with his own children when they were younger, and he was grateful to see Lorenzo taking the time to bond with this child. "I remember that story, your *madre* used to read it to you."

Lorenzo looked up at him. "It was one of my favorites." Grace smacked at the page, gurgling her intent for him to read more. "How did the visit with the Alizzi go?" The nanny appeared, and took the baby away, leaving the two of them alone.

Shade sighed and shook his head. "I'm not sure. Maybe you should have Alfie join us, so we can go over this together. Let's go to the office and have a smoke and drink while we wait."

Lorenzo called out to Alfie telepathically to meet them in the office, as the two of them made their way through the castle. "Sounds serious. Should I put extra protection on the family? Rene is always here in Castello with Chantal, and Nicola never leaves Sophia and Bianca, do you think that's enough? We can order more warriors to guard the homes."

"That's part of what I want to discuss. But before Alfie gets here, Dona said to give you, Chantal, and Grace her best regards, she wishes you all well."

Lorenzo huffed. "She wishes me well?" He was pouring three glasses of Midnight when Alfie appeared in the room. Lorenzo handed his best friend a glass as he passed a glass to his father. "Those are well-wishes I could do without. Everything from Dona has strings attached."

Alfie took his glass and settled into a chair. "So, what's up?"

Shade sipped at the Midnight and flopped down in a chair. He chose not to sit behind the desk at Castello, that chair belongs to his son now. "As you know, I visited with the Alizzi last night, and you both need to listen. I need you to make some changes, keep the warriors informed."

Alfie draped a leg over the arm of the chair as he sipped at the wine. "So, what's she up to now? We've all seen the gardens. How far has Rodrigo managed to insert himself into her life?"

"She tells me he has made no offer for territory, but I can tell she is enamored by his attentions. She is vulnerable and he is moving in on her, I can feel it. She claims the gardens were a gift, and he has asked for nothing in return." Shade grumbled. "That bastard does not give favors. He wants something. He is courting her, trying to convince her he is interested in her. All I have are theories based on his past. I think he wants Dona's territory. I offered to buy it from her again, but she refused. Rodrigo would have to kill her, or mate her, to get it. He is either trying to intimidate us or worst-case scenario, push into Medici territory." Shade stood and paced, just the thought made him boil. "There are times I wish Marco was still here, he knew the fucking hell Borgia could stir up."

Lorenzo winced. He couldn't hear Marco's name, even after all these years, without feeling some sense of responsibility. The bullet that took out Marco was a clean shot, and it was clear Marco had been the target, but still, Lorenzo felt like if he'd acted faster, maybe Marco would still be with them. Neither he nor Alfie had any experience with the Borgia. They were enemies, but enemies that had maintained a distance from the Medici, avoiding conflict at all cost. A battle with the Borgia coven wasn't good for either the Medici or the Borgia. They'd both suffer heavy losses, and both covens knew it. "So, are we in danger here or just being cautious? What are you advising we do?"

Shade leaned against the desk. "My first concern is for the family. I think the women need to be sequestered indoors. I hate to do it, and I know they will balk at the lack of freedom, but at least until we have a better idea of what Rodrigo is up to, I'd rather be safe than sorry." Shade locked eyes with Lorenzo. "Soren loves half-breeds. He eats their hearts while they are still alive. Do not let Chantal take Grace out for any reason. I want warriors guarding Castello and Alfie's villa. I know they have protectors, but I think we need to escalate. I don't want the females going out at all, none of them, even escorted. Have everything brought to them by an appointed warrior. Borgia may already have spies watching our routines. The only advantage we have is neither Rodrigo nor his brother are day-walkers, so we know they will only come at us during the night. They rule through fear and intimidation. I want the border between our territory and the Alizzi's patrolled, and I want to know every damn detail of what happens there, night and day, *si*?"

They both nodded, as Lorenzo spoke up. "We can lay out a detail for more coverage of Castello and the villa. Chantal won't object to being grounded and will certainly have no problems with keeping Grace close at hand." He looked at Alfie. "Sophia, on the other hand."

Alfie shook his head. "She won't like it, nor will Bianca, but they'll stay put. Fuck, they both have the gift of animalism. Any fucking Borgia would be a fool to get too close to either of them."

Lorenzo had to chuckle at the thought, he knew Sophia would call out the hounds and ask questions later. "I'll put the patrol back on the Alizzi border. At least we'll know if anyone from the Borgia coven is visiting her. Do you want her followed if she goes out?"

Shade nodded. "I want Dona followed, but only to her borders. Do not go into Borgia territory. Do not give him a reason to escalate. That needs to be clear to everyone. Keep all the warriors aware of any changes immediately. I want the smallest thing reported, I mean even if it seems ridiculously insignificant, check it out."

He refilled his glass and lit up a smoke, continuing his pacing. "The first thing we need to find out is who is leading his warriors. We need to know names. If we know who is running the show, we may have some history on how they will respond. Starting today, we close down any new recruits coming into the camp. Borgia will stop at nothing to infiltrate." Shade sighed. "I want no regrets. I know this must seem over the top. The Borgia has already done much damage to this family, and I'll be damned if I will let him take anything more. Anything else you are concerned with?"

Alfie spoke up. "I know one of his warriors. Vanni. His family disowned him when he was thrown out of our camp. He worked as a mercenary for years, and eventually ended up with the Borgia. He's pretty high up in the ranks. I'll see if I can find someone who knows his rank."

Shade took another drag from the cigarette. "Get our warriors together. Ask them if they know anything about the Borgia warriors. Try to get information. I will make phone calls as well. Should be easy enough to find out who the hell is in charge over there. As for Vanni, his *padre* has remained with us, but you can bet he knows something. See what he can share. Do you doubt his allegiance to Medici?"

Lorenzo shook his head no. "His father was shamed, sent him away when he was still young, soon after he was thrown out of camp. His family doesn't speak his name. I have no doubt that in a battle, the father would strike down the son, but I'd never ask that of him. He's given enough."

Shade nodded. “We have no proof of anything yet, this is just precautionary. Let’s raise the alert level in the camp and have them prepared. I do not want to be the one that starts this thing. If we can avoid it, we will, but treat it as a deadly threat. It doesn’t help that he has Vanni. Vanni knows our camp and our methods. Nothing we can do about that now.” Shade hung his head, as his memories invaded his thoughts. "There is no doubt in my mind Rodrigo was behind your grandparents’ deaths. Remember that."

Lorenzo sighed. He always felt the spirit of his grandparents in Castello. History was pretty clear on the fact that the Borgia had a hand in the bonfires, and he had no doubt Rodrigo would have used the opportunity to flush out the Medici. His own father could have been killed had he not been out on his own at the time. They were stronger now, with more offspring, but no coven should ever consider itself invincible. "We'll remain vigilant. You have my word."

Shade stood then, ready to head back home. He knew his son and Alfie had received the best training, and both were fierce warriors in their own right. He had no doubts about their abilities to manage things here. "I need to get back to your *madre* and make some adjustments in the camps in the States, just as a precaution. Keep me informed. I will come in any circumstance if you need me, and if the sun is high, I will send Christoph or Skelk. We are Medici, and we will not be defeated."

He hugged Alfie with a slap on the back and then hugged his son. "Take care, son. *Per sempre*, Medici."

He walked from the room feeling better, and ready to do whatever it took. It hit him that if they went to battle, this time, his son would be by his side, and he liked those odds.

40

The teleport back to Bel Rosso was an easy one, and the night was clear and beautiful. He couldn't enjoy the night, however, as his head was filled with thoughts of Dona and the Borgia. He had real fears that his family or even his entire coven could be facing serious danger if Dona didn't stop this foolishness with Rodrigo. He landed in the foyer and Kate came to greet him immediately, wrapping her arms around him, squeezing him tight. He felt her love, but he also felt her concern, and he knew she felt his unsettled thoughts.

"Lover, you're home." He carried the scent of clean, fresh air from his teleport. "Please tell me you were able to work things out."

He crushed her to his chest, burying his face into her neck. He always tried to limit his time away from her, as he tended to go a little mad when he was away too long. A night away from her felt like an eternity to him. He kissed her neck softly. "It feels like ages since my arms have held you."

She returned his hug, her head against his chest. She could feel his concern. "Come, sit down with me. Tell me what happened."

He led her to the living room where he sat on the large sofa and pulled her down next to him. She curled up close, her head on his shoulder, and that brought a smile to his face. He loved protecting her and feeling her at his side. He turned serious as he began to share what he'd learned on this trip.

"Visiting Dona did not relieve my fears of the Borgia, it only heightened them. She is confident he wants nothing from her, that his attentions hold no strings. She didn't refute anything I confronted her about, going to his ball or that he paid to have the gardens restored. She is so blind, and she won't listen to me. She won't see reason. He is masking his true intent with her. I have no doubts. Rodrigo is clever and will bide his time. I stayed the extra day so I could meet with Lorenzo and Alfie."

With her head against his chest, she listened to the deep rumble of his voice which always had the power to soothe her. "And how did that go?"

He sighed as his hand played in her crimson locks, a habit that he performed unconsciously. "They are both ready. They know what they need to do. The camp is on high alert, and we will patrol the border. I put all the females on lockdown and ordered warriors to patrol both homes. I also ordered a lockdown on the camp. We won't take in any new warriors until this thing is over."

Kate closed her eyes. She didn't have a good feeling about this one. "That's wise, sealing off the camp at Castello. I'd suggest we take no recruits from Europe into the new training sessions here, only warriors born in the U.S., just to be safe, especially as the news will travel fast that the Castello camp has temporarily stopped taking new candidates."

"*Si*, I will tell Christoph. I found out something else. Remember Vanni? The young kid who used to bully Lorenzo when he first went to camp? He was a mercenary, but it seems he has sworn allegiance to the Borgia coven. Alfie is going to see if he can find out where he ranks, but regardless, it is not good. He grew up inside the Medici camp. In the meantime, I need to try to find out who his leaders are. I have to make some phone calls and do some investigating, but I don't want to draw his attention either. Perhaps if I know them, I can anticipate how they will respond, maybe have some idea of what is coming. It may all be for nothing. I *hope* it is all for nothing. I informed Lorenzo we will not make the first move. Last fucking thing I want to do. But this is the Borgia, I can't let my guard down."

She lifted her head from his chest, locking eyes with him. "Would Natalia know? Would there be records of that stuff? She said they kept a census of every coven."

"Indigo is only in charge of the coven census records in the States, he doesn't have access to the records in Europe. I'm not sure he can help." He laid his head back on the sofa and sighed. "If I go to Malachi, he will know something is up, I can't be snooping there. Malachi would never betray me, but I can't risk asking him for the information." His head snapped up as he looked at her. "Do you think Nattie could find out without stirring too much suspicion?"

Kate shrugged. "I know Malachi has been her mentor and confidant. If she asked him to look into it, Malachi would be the one approaching Agathian, not you, or Natalia. I doubt Malachi would say why he was asking, and Agathian wouldn't ask. Malachi would keep her secret."

He thought a long time before he answered, his mind was in a whirl. "I don't trust the phones at Council, this could be tricky for both of us. I will need to speak with her one on one. Perhaps I could go through Marcello, call him on his private cell. No one would know. I know this sounds like I am being paranoid, but I don't want Borgia to have any hint that I am making inquiries."

She read the concern on his face. "Then do what you need to do. I know Natalia will help in any way she can."

He smiled down at her, the face he loved more than life. "Can you do something for me?"

"I can do anything for you. You only have to ask."

"When I told Lorenzo and Alfie about keeping the females inside, Lorenzo was absolutely certain Chantal would comply. But Alfie laughed, saying he'd do his best. I want you to call Sophia, make the point clear to her. You know how headstrong she can be. I know she has your gift, but I do not want her overconfident."

"Of course, I'll call Sophia tomorrow, and make sure she understands."

"And one more thing, can you talk to Aegis? I want the wolves and all your warriors to scout far and wide within our territory. If they sense anything unusual, I want them to come to you. Will they oblige me?"

Kate nodded. "Yes, Aegis will direct them. And I'll tell Sophia and Bianca to have their warriors on alert as well. No one will get through."

"*Grazie,* my beautiful Queen." He stood and lifted her in his arms, "Now, I have one more request. Will you come to bed with me and fuck me until I scream for mercy? Because I have missed you and I need my woman!"

With her arms around his shoulders, she kissed him, as he carried her up the stairs. "You didn't even need to ask."

41

Rodrigo teleported to Umbria. His smile genuinely wicked as he noticed the heavily armed Medici warriors on her border. He found it quite amusing. The restoration of her gardens had attracted some attention. He looked forward to the stir he'd create with the Medici when he began to restore the entire estate. He'd make her villa finer than it had ever been. As for Dona, he'd make sure her wardrobe was replaced with the latest designer fashions, and she'd feel spoiled again. She'd be able to hold her head up whenever she left her estate.

Tonight, he intended to sit with her in those gardens and sip Midnight and continue the ruse of romancing her. He knew it wouldn't take long for that bit of news to reach the Medici. He was nothing if not patient, and he was enjoying the cat and mouse game with Dona, all the while keeping the Medici on edge, leaving him to wonder what was going on. Rodrigo loved the wickedness of it all, and it made him happy.

He glided slowly around Dona's villa and saw her already sitting in the garden, waiting for him. He landed easily with grace, and she stood immediately to greet him. "Donatella, you look quite beautiful sitting out here under the moon. I hope I have not kept you waiting." He walked towards her, his arms open, with every expectation she'd come to him.

Dona stood from her seat on a marble bench under an olive tree that overlooked lush flower gardens. She accepted his hug with some reluctance. She was more than grateful for the gardens, and his attention, but she was aware that nothing came for free in this world. As Shade had made a point of reminding her, there would be strings attached to Rodrigo's generosity, and she was still waiting for him to reveal what that would be.

"Rodrigo, come, join me on the bench. Enjoy the gardens with me. Mario brought us wine." The small table by the bench had been set with a bottle of Midnight and two mismatched crystal wine glasses.

Rodrigo still felt her hesitation. He knew, with time, she'd become addicted to all he'd lay at her feet. Dona had grown up in luxury, she was born of royal blood, and she wouldn't be able to resist the temptations of having everything her heart desired at her fingertips again. Once she was hooked, he'd own her, and she'd never go against him. He sat next to her, leaving no distance between them. He watched as she poured the Midnight and handed him a glass. He tipped his glass to hers. "To us, Dona."

She looked back at him, trying to decipher the meaning behind his words, and reluctantly responded, "To us."

His arm slid around the back of the bench, brushing against her long dark hair. "It is a beautiful night, my dear, but nothing in this garden could be as beautiful as you in the moonlight. So, tell me, have you been enjoying my gift of the gardens? What have you been up to since last we met? I am most interested to know if you are happy."

Dona sipped from her glass, aware of his arm on the bench behind her. "I love the gardens. I take a walk through them every evening, as the sun sets. The air is beginning to cool then, but the light is so beautiful, casting a rose gold glow over the gardens. But you ask if I am happy? I don't know if I am happy, Rodrigo. I am grateful to have the gardens, so please don't think otherwise. And I am happy to have your company. I have had so few visitors since my fortunes have dwindled. It is hard to come to grips with the reality that I am nothing but a commodity in our culture. As a female, I have no real power. My value was my title, my dowry, my land, my coven, my inherited wealth. As those things have dwindled in value, I too have dwindled in value. It is a hard reality to face."

He toyed with her hair as he inhaled her scent. She was wearing perfume for him, always a good sign. He inhaled deeply and had visions of riding her long into the night. His thoughts went deeper and took a more violent turn, and he shook them off. It was way too soon for that. "Donatella, you have not dwindled in value, just been pushed down. You are still very much in power, and I intend to restore you to your rightful place in our community."

Leaning in close, he kissed her neck softly, his voice a bit softer. "Do not fret, my sweet Dona." He leaned back and drained his glass, setting it on the small table. Standing, he strolled about, taking in the view. “I noticed when I came in, the Medici appear to have taken their stations on your border." He chuckled. "It would seem my appearance in your life has rattled the young king. I find it amusing. They do not wish to help you, that is obvious, and yet they would begrudge me lending a hand. Why would he want to keep you down, Dona? After all, your families go back for several generations. One would think he would be eager to see you back on your feet, reigning over a strong coven. I can only imagine the thoughts going through Shade’s mind. He is quite a curious character, is he not? He refused to mate you and left you to struggle alone out here. Yet, he still takes great interest in your life." He walked behind her then, bending over her shoulder. "You told me he has nothing to do with you, my dear. Are you so sure?" His jeweled fingers dug slightly into her shoulder as he squeezed.

Dona winced slightly under his firm grip. "Shade did call on me, but it was not a cordial visit. He had been informed of the gardens and came to see for himself and to warn me. I sent him away, Rodrigo. You have nothing to worry about."

Rodrigo felt his anger flare. He knew it wouldn’t take long for Shade to hear of his involvement with Dona, but he resented his intrusion so early. He stepped back in front of the bench, and took her hand, tucking it into the crook of his arm, as he strolled with her through the gardens. "So, the warrior came for a visit. I find that quite curious. I can’t tell you who to let inside your home, my dear, but I would give you warning."

He stopped and pulled her close to him, gripping her chin and locking eyes with her. “Are you playing us both, Dona? It is not my fault the fool mated a mortal and tainted his royal bloodline. But I will warn you, I will not tolerate your involvement with him if I am to court you."

Dona was caught off-guard by his sudden change in mood and the menacing sound of his voice as he gripped her chin. She questioned the implications of being courted by Rodrigo. The idea rolled around inside her head. It had been so long since any male paid attention to her. Why now? Why was he courting her? "Rodrigo, I assure you, I have no interest in him, and he certainly has made his intentions clear as it relates to me. You know the relationship between our families goes way back. He was warning me of the past.

I tried to tell him things have changed, but you know Shade. He is a stubborn man, just like his father. I assure you, I have no involvement with him."

He saw the look of fear flash quickly across her face, and he knew she'd heed him. "*Si*, I believe you, Donatella. You are a good mistress." He kissed her softly on the lips, letting the kiss linger for a few moments. She was hesitant but responded. "You are not afraid of me, are you? I have the best intentions, I assure you. We are both of the old ways, Dona, and I value that in you. There have been so many of our kind that has abandoned the old ways. Come, let us stroll more, I have some things I wish to speak with you about."

He led her through the gardens, asking her questions about specific flowers and plants. "I have decided that tomorrow, I will have my workers come to your villa. Now that we have finished the gardens, I think it time we work on the house. We will completely refurbish it, top to bottom. It needs much repair, and then we will replace all your fine things, bring this house alive again with fresh paint, new rugs, and furnishings. I will pay for it all, my dear, and I don't want to hear protest. If you are going to be on my arm, I can't have you living in this hovel, can I? How would that reflect on me? And look at you, Dona. You are a beautiful female, but you have let yourself go. I will have a new wardrobe designed for you, dresses, and shoes, all that you shall need to properly present yourself as the Mistress of Umbria."

Her head was swimming. This was moving much too fast. "Rodrigo, this is too much! I can't possibly repay you for your extreme generosity. You can have any female in Italy, why me? I bring nothing. If anything, I bring you scorn and ridicule."

Throwing back his head, he laughed. "Oh, Donatella, no one dares to scorn the Borgia. I am drawn to you, and what male would not be? If I am generous, it is because I enjoy you. What is wealth if you cannot enjoy it, watch it bring happiness to others. It gives me pleasure to watch you blossom into your true self. You have always enticed me, but our fate seemed to pull us in different directions, *si*? But times have changed, the past is past, as they say. I wish to know you better. Please, my dear, it makes me happy to make you happy. Don't deny me this pleasure." He stopped as they got closer to the house. "I find myself thinking about you often and wishing I could be in your company. Tell me you feel the same, and you don't still carry the same animosity for my family from the old days."

"Of course not, Rodrigo, I hope I have never given you that impression. You have been the only person to show me kindness."

Dona was feeling a mix of emotions that she couldn't sort out. She'd been raised to hate this man, and yet, she was grateful for the kindnesses he'd shown to her. She was happy to have his attention, but she wasn't physically attracted to him. She couldn't say with honesty that she felt drawn to him, and his kisses still felt invasive. She knew a man like Rodrigo would only be patient for so long before he expected more from her, and she was unsure of how to proceed with him. She was already in debt to him now, with the restoration of the gardens. "I do think of you. I think of you often." That wasn't a lie, she did think of him, but her thoughts were confused ones, wondering what he could possibly want from her.

Taking her in his arms, he kissed her with great passion. He wanted her, but only to gain a means to an end. He held her gently, but he wanted to crush her tight to his chest, he wanted her to yearn for his cock and his blood. His patience was beginning to wane, but he must go slowly. "Go inside, my dear, the night air is chilly. The workers will be here tomorrow, choose whatever you wish to make you happy. It is such a small thing to me, considering how happy I am to have you in my life. I will come and check on you, and the progress with the house. You must call me if you have any problems. If the Medici begins to harass you, I will come to your aide. I am more than willing to protect you. Now, get inside. I would come in myself, but I do not wish to push myself upon your company. We will talk soon."

Kissing her once again, his body tight against hers, his hands tangled in her hair, he left her breathless. He kissed her cheek softly and teleported out, heading for Rome. His laughter rang through the night. He had her, and he'd show the Medici his grave mistake of not mating the bitch.

***

Dona stood in the garden as he teleported out, leaving her alone with her thoughts. Her lips felt slightly bruised from the forcefulness of his kiss. He was claiming her, marking his territory by restoring the gardens, and restoring her home. It was a visible message to all that the Borgia had staked his claim, and Dona wasn't sure how she felt about that. A chill ran up her spine, and she hugged her arms across her chest as she rushed inside the safety of her home.

42

Marcello had taken the call from Shade about the increasing threat of the Borgia. He was glad to be of service to help his brothers outside the walls of Council. It was his duty to provide protection to Council and understood it was his sole responsibility now, but he still felt the bond to his brothers in the Medici camp. He patrolled the halls, as he did every night, checking the security of the building. Protecting the Council was an honor. Like warriors, vampires were born to Council, but unlike warriors, they were a rare breed, the rarest among their kind. Because the Council was sequestered, they lived for many centuries. If a Council member were to die before his time, it may take several hundred years before they were replaced. He was careful and made sure every entry was secured and took note of anyone or anything that was out of place. Finishing his rounds, he made his way to Natalia's quarters. He'd given her a heads-up earlier that he needed to speak with her alone. He tapped lightly on her door, and immediately opened it, slipping inside.

"Everything is secured. We need to talk."

Natalia had been pacing when she heard his key in the lock. As he entered her bedroom, she slid the hood back from her face. "Is everything okay? Your message sounded urgent? Is my family okay?"

He took her into his arms, his hands sliding up and down her back. Kissing her softly, he could feel her concern for her family. "Everyone is safe. Shade called me because he needs your help with something. He didn't want to call you on the Council phone, as those calls are probably recorded. It's a delicate matter. Borgia is moving in on the Alizzi. Shade was certain that Borgia is courting her and has reason to believe he's deceiving her to gain access to her territory. Right now, he's trying to gather information, and that's where he needs you."

Natalia looked at him with confusion. "Me? I don't know anything about the Borgia's other than what my father has shared with us growing up. What does he want me to do?"

"He wants you to get to Malachi and ask him if he can get you some information. Malachi needs to understand this must be kept quiet. Your father wants no suspicion that he is seeking information. He needs to have someone check the census records for the Borgia coven, and find out who's in charge of the warriors, his SICs, his lieutenants, anything at all. He's ordered the females in Florence to be sequestered, and Lorenzo isn't taking in any more warriors at camp. He's re-assigned the warriors to cover the borders between Tuscany and Umbria. This is serious, Natalia, Medici is getting ready for war."

Natalia's expression changed from one of confusion to concern. She couldn't remember a time in her life when her father had ordered a lockdown. "Of course, I'll talk to Malachi. But, if my father fears the Council phone conversations are recorded, how can I reach him?"

Marcello pulled out his cellphone. "I have a counterpart in the Florence Council. I'll ask him to give his cell to Malachi. You call from my phone."

Natalia nodded. "The Council never wants a war between covens. It's one of the main things we work to prevent. I'm sure if Malachi has information that can be of help, he'll provide it to me. He knows my father is honorable and would only be seeking the information as a defensive move. I'll contact him as soon as possible. And don't worry, Malachi is discreet. He'll tell no one."

"Be careful, Natalia, but do whatever you can to get the information. I'll bring you my phone as soon as I have set things in motion. Do you wish me to stay?" His smile spread across his face and his blue eyes shone with anticipation.

For a moment, she let her concern melt away as she laid her head on his chest, and felt his arms encircle her. "I have to get back to the data center, but perhaps when we're both off duty you can come back?"

"*Si*, I'll be here. I love you, Natalia." He kissed her softly. Turning to leave, he listened carefully before opening her door. He snuck out quietly, checking the hall passage before exiting her room.

43

Natalia woke from her death slumber to find Marcello still asleep in the bed beside her. She rolled on her side and watched him sleep. She was the only member of the U.S. Council who wasn't a day-walker. Her suite of rooms was designed to seal itself off during the day, plunging her into darkness. The steel door to her suite of rooms, just like all the other Council members', locked immediately when closed. It was an added security measure. There were only two keys, she had one and Marcello had the other. She knew no one would try to enter her suite during the day, and had always felt safe having Marcello stay with her when his schedule would allow. As the electronic blinds opened, letting in the pale evening light, she brushed the hair back from his face, when he opened his eyes, with their long lashes. He smiled back at her. "Sleep well?"

She nodded, her fingers still tangled in his hair, "I always do when you're here."

He stretched and slipped from the bed, checking the time. "I better get going. My shift starts soon. I need to get out before people start stirring around too much." He pulled on his leathers and leaned to kiss her goodbye. "I'll leave my phone. You can call Malachi tonight."

She sat up on the side of the bed, wrapping the sheets around her. "Yes, that's the plan."

He finished buttoning his shirt as he tucked it into his waistband, "Let me know if you need anything."

He scrolled through the contacts lists for her before placing the phone in her hand. "Here, call Amici. He's one of the warriors from Florence assigned to protect Council. We grew up together in the Florence camps. He'll recognize my number when you call. He'll get Malachi for you." He kissed her one last time, whispering, "I love you, and no one will be capturing you, not from me."

"Thanks. And I love you too, Marcello."

He stood at her door and listened to insure there was no activity, then opened the door and disappeared. Natalia climbed from her bed, showered, donned her hooded robe, and hurried out. She checked the data center first to make sure her staff had their assignments and then slipped out to find an unoccupied meeting room. The warriors all carried cell phones, but the Council staff had little contact with the outside world and had only the one vision phone, which was manned by an operator. She'd never wondered before if the calls were recorded or monitored. Slipping inside a vacant room, the lights automatically came on as she entered. Locking the door behind her, she took a seat as far from the door as possible. Pulling Marcello's phone from the pocket in her robe, she dialed up the number of Marcello's friend and waited for him to answer. The screen came to life, and she could see the warrior's face on the other end.

"Hey brother, what..." Amici paused in confusion as he looked back at the hooded face of a Council member, calling from the States. "What's going on? Where's Marcello?"

Natalia pushed the hood back from her face so he could see her. "I'm Ivory, and Marcello loaned me his phone. He said I could trust you."

He nodded in recognition of her name. "Ivory, yeah, you're Lorenzo's sister. I've heard of you. How can I help you?"

"I need to speak to Malachi, please. Tell him in private. Tell him it's urgent. Have him call me back from your phone please."

The warrior nodded. "Yeah, sure. It will take a few minutes to track him down. So, hang tight." He disconnected and Natalia waited patiently while the warrior searched the old Gothic mansion for Malachi. It took about five minutes before the phone in her hand rang, and Malachi, his face partially obscured by his green robe, appeared on the screen.

"How can I help you, child? What's with all the cloak and dagger. Are you in danger?"

Natalia smiled to herself. She realized she'd always be a child to Malachi. "I'm safe, Malachi, but I do need your help with something. Are you aware that the Borgia has made contact with the Alizzi? He appears to be courting her, or at the very least, trying to influence her. My father has reinstated his warriors along the Umbrian border. He hasn't received any threats from the Borgia, but you're aware, I'm sure, of the bad blood between our covens."

Malachi sighed. "The Borgia. They have been quiet for a long time now. I guess I had come to hope the feuding was over. What do you need, child?"

Natalia leaned toward the screen, keeping her voice low. "Can you check with Agathian, check the census records? If you could give us some idea of the size of their coven, and the number of warriors, that would be helpful. Also, if you can find any information on his leaders, his lieutenants, his Second-in-Command, which would be helpful. I promise you, my father won't make the first move. His interest is purely defensive. He's ordered a lockdown of all the females and has stopped taking new recruits into the camp."

Malachi nodded. His eyes still not visible from under the hood. "I will see what information we have. It is imperative that this not escalate, you do understand that *si*? The Borgia, the Medici, they are two of the largest covens in Europe, a war between them...well, I do not even want to think about it."

"I know. It's not my father's wish to go to battle. He understands both sides would suffer greatly."

Malachi lowered his head even more, placing his whole face in shadow. "It will take me a few days, child. I will get back to you as soon as I know something."

"Thank you, Malachi. And one more thing? Please don't divulge to Agathian that you are requesting the information for the Medici. I'm sure he's loyal, but information has a way of getting out. I'd be grateful."

He looked up at the screen, making eye contact at last, and nodded. "I can be discreet. Be alert to your vision's child, as I will be to mine. I will need to know if you see anything."

Natalia stared back solemnly. "I will, I promise." She sat and stared at the screen as it faded to black. She couldn't help but think back on the discovery she'd made in her family's archives when she was a young woman. The information had haunted her all her life, a curse that had clung to each generation. She shook her head as she pocketed the phone, and slipped out of the room, whispering to herself. "Not now."

44

Several weeks had passed and Rodrigo had not yet contacted Donatella, nor had he heard from her. He had intentionally left her alone and allowed her to oversee the remodeling of her villa. Now that the work was near completion, he'd decided to make an unannounced visit. If there was any nonsense brewing with the Medici, he'd soon find out. Teleporting out from Rome, it was a warm night. He was dressed in his leather pants, but he'd left his shirt open, his chest bare. He'd braided his long hair into a single braid down his back, tied with a black silk ribbon.

As he circled above her villa, the lights were aglow, and he could see her manservant scurrying around. He landed softly at the front door and discovered a newly installed doorbell which he pressed to make his arrival known.

Mario answered with a smile, greeting their benefactor. "Master Rodrigo! How very good to see you. Please come in. I'll escort you to the parlor and notify the Alizzi that you are here."

Mario was wearing new clothing, his black waistcoat tailored to fit him exactly, and his crisp white shirt and black bowtie impeccable. He was clearly proud to be wearing a new uniform, as he turned on his heels and escorted Rodrigo down the hall to the newly appointed parlor with large hand-knotted rugs, beautiful antiques, and the artwork adorning the walls. "Please, have a seat. May I get you a drink?"

Rodrigo had to stifle a laugh. How wonderful it was to have money. It could buy you literally everything, including a territory at the Medici's doorstep. "Please, attend to the Alizzi, I will pour myself a drink."

Mario nodded and took his leave, as Rodrigo headed for the bar and poured himself a drink. Leaning with his back against the bar, he took in the changes that had been made to the room, and they pleased him. It couldn't compare to the opulence of his palazzo in Rome, but it would do nicely. He admired the new hand-cut crystal tumbler in his hand, and the abundance of Midnight and Red Moon stocked behind the bar. Dona had excellent taste and had not spared a penny of his money in making the restorations.

***

Mario rushed out to inform the Alizzi of her visitor. As he entered her bedroom, she was with Marie, arranging her closet, now filled with the latest fashions. "Mistress, the Borgia is here to visit. He is waiting in the parlor."

Dona appeared flustered as she left the closet and checked her appearance in the mirror. "Do I look all right?" She was wearing a dress from her new wardrobe, as she admired her reflection.

"You look beautiful, my lady."

Dona flashed him a smile and headed down the stairs and into the parlor to greet Rodrigo. "Rodrigo, what a surprise! You should have told me you were coming. I would have prepared a better reception for you."

He turned to look at her and for a brief moment, he wanted to drop all pretense and take her where she stood, make her his. His smile was one of admiration. "My dear, you are reception enough. Let me look at you. You look stunning. Come, give me a kiss, and let me see you walk in that beautiful garment. Did you choose this yourself?"

Dona smiled at him, accepting his compliment, but was reluctant to offer a kiss. He'd always taken a kiss, and she'd complied, allowing his advances. Not once had she initiated any show of affection towards him. She swallowed her pride as she walked to him and planted a chaste kiss on his lips. "I'm glad you approve. I went shopping in Florence and Milan, of course. I should not need anything new for a while. I thank you again for your generosity."

"You are most welcome." Handing her a Midnight, he smiled at her reluctance. Most females he met were more than happy to toss their scruples aside in exchange for his generosity. But not this one, she was who she was, and he'd brought her back from the dead. "You should come and shop in Rome. I am sure you will find the best of the best there. And, of course, you are always welcome to stay at the palazzo, if you wish." He walked to the wall where the large screen was mounted for the modern phone system. "I am certainly glad to see this. Now I can speak with you and see you as well. I shall call every evening, *si*?"

Every evening? He expects to talk to me every evening? "Oh yes, the new phone. Mario was showing me how it worked. Apparently, it controls all the functions in the house as well. I guess I have really fallen behind the times. I have spent so much time alone here, and really had no need for a means to communicate with the outside." She settled herself on the new sofa, straightening her skirt and crossing her legs at the ankle. "Do you like the room, Rodrigo? I think it turned out well. Please, have a seat."

He chuckled lightly. "You will learn to use the system, my dear, because I wish for you to. It is important you maintain appearances." He sat close beside her, her skin smelling of fine oils and perfumes, the best money could buy. Her hair had been brushed to a high sheen, and her skin was glowing. "I admire your taste, and I think what you have done with the villa suits you, tasteful, not overly done. I do hope you will be giving me a tour of the entire villa?"

Dona smiled back at him. She was quite pleased with the outcome of the renovations and glad to have his approval. "I'd be happy to. Most of the work has been completed. They are still renovating the baths. Perhaps you would prefer the tour when the work is complete?"

Laying his hand on her knee, he leaned in close, and his wicked smile wasn't lost on her. "I will be returning often, I assure you, to ensure the work is done properly. But I would love to see what has been done so far." Kissing her gently on the cheek, he stood and held out his hand to her. "Please, let me see what you have accomplished thus far."

Dona led him from room to room, pointing out the renovations and repairs to the house, as well as the new furnishings and expensive art. "Do you wish to see upstairs as well?"

"*Si*, of course. Please lead on, my dear. I am most impressed so far." Rodrigo pretended to be interested but he could have cared less. If Dona was happy, then he was pleased that his plan was working so well.

Dona had never taken him upstairs into her private quarters before and she felt some reluctance to do so. "Well, come this way please." She led him up the stairs and showed him the completed rooms, as well as the many bathrooms which were being renovated with more modern plumbing. She had avoided showing him her room and hoped that he wouldn't notice.

"The rooms are all lovely. Now, which one is yours? I would like to see where you lay your head when you slumber, so I can envision you there when we are apart." Cocking his head, he smiled at her.

She laughed nervously. "Of course, I was just saving it for last. It is the biggest room, after all, and the bath has been completed." She led him into her suite where Marie was busy folding some of her new purchases and placing them in the wardrobe. She was thankful for Marie's presence. "So, this is my room, I am quite comfortable, as you can see. And the bath is here. It was completed first. I admit, I am enjoying my new things."

He nodded his head at Marie. "You are dismissed." He heard Dona's small intake of breath and watched as the maid scurried off like a frightened mouse. He turned to Dona and slid his finger along her cheekbone. "Such fine bone structure, strong cheekbones. It makes you look regal. Your royal bloodline shows, my dear." She blushed, and he removed his hand, looking around her room. "The room is quite feminine and beautiful, just as you are. Tell me, Donatella, do you not wish to thank me for all that you have received?"

Dona stepped back slightly. "I, of course, Rodrigo, I do thank you for everything you have done." She was well aware of his meaning and knew all along his gifts and generosity came with strings attached.

His hand was quick to wrap around her waist and pull her toward him. She struggled very little, and he let her know as he squeezed her tightly, just how much stronger he was. "Remember that I am the Borgia, and I have chosen you for my own. I return you to your rightful status, because no one else will, certainly not the Medici or his young king. I will have every male and female in this land bowing at your feet. I would suggest you at least act as if you are grateful, not only with words but with actions. I mean you no harm, Dona, but I do expect your respect, if not your admiration, and to remind you with whom you are dealing. Now, think again, do you not wish to show me something in return for the great kindness I have shown you?"

Dona felt conflicted, knowing all along that the day would come. She should have stopped it in the beginning, when he first started showing her his attention. But she'd been lonely, and eager for his complements. But what did he want from her now? To perform her duties, like a feeder in a compound? Play the role of a seductress to please him? "What is it you want from me?"

He sighed, games, she wanted to play them still. "Let me make this very simple for you, my dear." He looked deep into her dark eyes. "Do you find anything about me attractive? Do you not wish to show me some affection? I have tried to please you, and I have moved slowly, as a gentleman should. But you have not shown me anything to indicate that you care for me. I am not asking you to lie naked on the bed and let me have my way with you. I simply want something that acknowledges my attentions, and show you care for me in return. Show me, Donatella."

She swallowed hard and closed her eyes, as she slid her arms around his broad shoulders and leaned into him, kissing him. Her response was mechanical, and she knew he would feel it. She let her mind wander until it was Shade's face she saw in her mind. It wasn't Rodrigo's lips she was kissing. It was Shade's. She blocked her thoughts from him, as her cold kiss turned to one of passion, as in her mind, she kissed the only man she'd ever truly wanted.

He felt her initial hesitancy but was aware when her reluctance turned to passion. His heart raced, her lips were soft, and he felt her tongue as it tentatively began to explore. He returned the kiss, letting his tongue slide inside her mouth, tangling with hers. Her arms felt perfect around his shoulders, as he pulled her tight against his chest. He broke the kiss, and slid his mouth to her neck, inhaling deeply. Her vein was pulsing strongly, and he'd have to be patient, but it wouldn't take much longer now. He kissed her vein lightly as his hand tangled in her hair. His breath was hot against her neck as he whispered, "You will be mine, Donatella. You will be my one and only." He pulled from her then, smiling softly at her. "That was not so difficult now, was it? Now come, I must return to Rome before sunrise."

Taking her arm, he led her back downstairs and outside into the garden. Taking both of her hands into his, he kissed her softly on the lips. "Remember, you will call me every evening. I will return when I see fit to visit. If you care to shop in Rome, I will accompany you to your heart's content. The Borgia sees well to his female, my dear Donatella."

His female. If she'd had any doubts before, then that simple comment erased them. He was clearly claiming her, and she felt her heart sinking. "Yes, of course. I will call every evening."

He winked at her, knowing she now understood, he'd rule her. "That is my good pet. Now run back inside. Put away all your treasures." He kissed her once again, this time with a bit more passion and force. "I will miss you, my pet." Teleporting out, his plan was falling into place. It wouldn't be long now.

45

Rodrigo returned from the Alizzi, happy with the progress on the house, but concerned over her continued reluctance to respond to him. He'd hoped Dona would have been more demonstrative in showing her appreciation. Soren walked into the room and stretched his long arms. He was at least dressed, a sign to Rodrigo that he'd been outside the palazzo, playing his usual games.

Soren draped himself across the velvet couch. "Have you mated the bitch yet? I am tired of this game, brother."

Rodrigo sat down across from him. He was an old vampire, comfortable in his power. "Soren, my brother, it is one of your most unattractive attributes, you have no patience. She needs to be reeled in slowly, but she is coming around. The gardens are completed, and now the house is remodeled. It pleases me to have a house we will use to spy on the Medici as a place of comfort. Give it some more time."

Soren grumbled and stared at his elder brother. "You have never played games with any whore this long. I know it is important to our coven, but I am becoming extremely bored with it all. Why not just force her and be done with it? She means nothing to you, take what you want, and demand her compliance. Once you mate her, she will understand, soon enough, her role is to obey, provide fucking and feeding, all any of them are truly good for."

Rodrigo stood and poured himself a drink. He could feed on anyone, fuck any female, but he needed this one specifically. "She is not yet willing, and to push my advances on her may only spark more interference from the Medici. He has already placed his warriors back along the border. Let him sit on his haunches, the lot of them, and wonder. The situation calls for patience." He slung back his drink. "I have to play them both. I don't want Shade coming to her rescue. That bastard is making her second guess me."

Soren threw back his head and laughed. "I find it amusing as hell that you let Shade Medici bother you so very much. He doesn't want her, but you do, so take what is there for the taking, fuck if she likes it or not. The Medici has to know we are aware of their warriors on the border. The show of force is not for Dona. It is for us."

Rodrigo sat back down facing his brother. "Of course, it is for us, but they don't know our intentions, and I prefer to keep it that way."

Soren gave him a smile filled with wicked intent. "I think it is time I join in the fun. Let me do what I do best and get inside his head. Do a little dream-walking with our oldest enemy. My skills are unsurpassed. I don't need to travel to him to invade his sleep. Let me have some fun, brother!"

Rodrigo thought about that for a few minutes. It was what they had planned to do, but he wasn't ready to go there yet. "It would be interesting to see what he is up to, and what he thinks we are up to, but it is too soon. He too is a dream-walker, and he will know immediately you are in his head."

Soren smirked. "You bore me so. He rarely uses his gift, and when he does, it is often for good. He has never perfected his gift for evil. It is like any skill. It must be practiced. I use mine often, and only for evil, and I have more power in my dream-walking than he can ever imagine. Let me walk and find out." Soren felt his heart race. He was tired of always being second in line to greatness.

Rodrigo sensed the rise in Soren's energy. He knew there was probably not a more powerful dream-walker than his brother, but that didn't change the fact that Shade would know immediately that Soren was controlling his dreams. Once Soren was inside his head, the game was up. The Medici would know exactly what their goal was at that point. But maybe it was time to turn up the heat.

"Walk with him, find out what he knows, what his plans are. But behave, Soren, leave the true power until it is needed. We want them to sit up and notice, but nothing more. He will not strike first. He is much too cautious. He knows we are equally matched in battle. Do not get yourself riled up. You will have ample opportunities to torture him, so move slowly, brother."

46

Marcello entered the data center, looking around the well-lit, all-white room, with the latest in technology. Natalia almost blended into the environment in her off-white robe, as she leaned over the shoulder of one of the workers, checking the entries on the screen. "Ivory?"

Natalia looked up in surprise. Marcello rarely came into this room. She excused herself and walked over to Marcello, who nodded his head in the direction of the door, indicating he wanted her to step outside. Natalia looked over her shoulder, but the staff that managed the massive pools of data all had their backs to her, as their faces were glued to their monitors, and their fingers flew across their keyboards. Stepping into the corridor with Marcello, she carefully closed the door behind her, as she looked at him questioningly.

"Amici called me. He said to track you down, and have you call Malachi."

They walked silently to the nearest conference room. Marcello handed her his phone as she entered the room alone and left him standing guard outside the door. She slipped into a chair and hit dial and watched as Malachi's face appeared on the screen.

"Ah, there you are, child. I hope I did not interrupt anything too important."

She shook her head. "Just my usual routine. Did you find anything for me?"

He held up several pieces of paper. "As a matter of fact, I did. You must be careful, child. When we check the census records, it can be misleading. The size of the Borgia coven in Italy is significantly larger than the Medici. However, the Borgia are confined to Italy, unlike your family. Overall, the Medici is larger, but it means including your covens from France, Greece, and the United States. Pulling your warriors from those locations to fight in Italy would be hard to manage in a battle, not to mention it could leave those other covens vulnerable. Something your father needs to think about. I hope it will not come to that."

Natalia nodded. "He intends to avoid battle at all costs. What else did you find?"

Malachi looked back at the notes scribbled on the paper. "Two items of note. Rodrigo's Second-in-Command is a warrior named Vanni. From what we can tell, he started as a young warrior in your father's camp in Florence. We do not have any information on how he ended up with the Borgia. Are you familiar with him?"

Natalia ran the name through her head, but it meant nothing to her. "Not to me, but I wasn't exposed much to the camp in Florence. My father will know him, I'm sure. Anything else?"

"One other warrior had an interesting history. A mercenary named Tomas who took the blood oath to the Borgia family and joined their ranks is also a SIC. He showed up in our census as working for your father a long time ago, before you were born. It is probably nothing. Mercenaries move from coven to coven all the time. But your father will probably remember him."

Natalia wrote down both names on a scrap of paper. "Thank you, Malachi. My father remains in your debt."

Malachi pushed his hood back and stared back at her. "I do this in hopes of avoiding conflict, you understand. Council here wants to remind you that we must avoid a battle between these two covens."

Natalia looked back at him, his eyes imploring her to understand the seriousness. "I promise you, Malachi, a battle is the last thing my father wants."

Natalia watched as the screen went dark, and Malachi's face disappeared. She pursed her lips as she dialed her father's cell number. She knew he'd most likely be in camp at this hour of the night. It only rang twice before she heard his voice.

***

Shade was in the camp office with Christoph. They'd brought a warrior, wounded during training, into the office to get a better look at his wounds. It wasn't uncommon to have injuries during training, as they trained with real weapons. Christoph had finished examining him when Aislynn appeared. "Let me take him to a feeder. He'll be fine." As Christoph and Aislynn assisted the wounded warrior down to the tunnel that connected to the feeder compound, Shade felt his phone vibrate in his pocket. He looked to see it was Marcello's number and answered immediately, but it was Natalia's face on the screen. "Nattie, did you hear from Malachi? Did he give you anything?"

Natalia laughed. "Uh, hello, and I love you too." Her father was in warrior mode, and she was used to his all-business approach to things when he was in the camp.

Smiling, he blew her a kiss. "Sorry, daughter, my mind is busy with everything that is going on here and in Florence. You know I love you."

She smiled back at him, pushing the hood off her head so he could see her face. "I have some information, some of it you probably already knew. Malachi reminded us that his coven in Italy is larger than yours, but we have more warriors if we include the vampires from all of our covens. He did have some info on who leads his warriors. The names meant nothing to me, but you'll probably know them. He said one of the SIC's was named Vanni, and he'd started in the Florence camp. Do you remember him?"

Shade already knew Vanni had sworn allegiance to the Borgia, but he had no idea he'd made SIC. "*Si*, Alfie informed me that Vanni was in the Borgia camp, but I had no idea he was that high in rank. Vanni was a young warrior in our camp when your brother was first sent to Florence. Vanni antagonized him relentlessly and your brother torched his ass before he learned to control his gift and his temper. Marco dismissed Vanni from camp, and that brought great shame on his family. They disowned him, and Vanni went to the streets, became a mercenary. His *padre* remains one of my most valued warriors."

Shade sat back down in his chair. "I am damn well aware that Borgia's warriors would give us a real run for our money, probably in more ways than we could imagine. I hope to end this before anything happens. Did you tell that to Malachi because I am not looking for a battle?"

Natalia nodded her head. "Malachi was quite clear in his request that we try to avoid conflict. I assured him that was your intention. The other name I have for you is a warrior named Tomas. Malachi said he'd been a mercenary and had worked for you some time ago in the States. He's taken the blood oath to the Borgia now, and has also risen in the ranks to be a SIC."

Shade felt his beast rise slowly and he growled. "*Cazzo*! Son of a bitch." He slammed his fist hard on the desk. "I hate to hear that. Tomas was originally one of the mercenaries in Alec's ranks when I first came to the States. He was one of the very few who had any skills. I made him my SIC over the Dead House. He was valuable to me when we were cleaning the band of rogues called Aries out of D.C., turned out the rogues were led by that mercenary, Cuerpo, who your mother killed. When things settled down, Tomas moved on. He wasn't ready to settle down. But this is not good news. Tomas knows far too much about how we operate and is one hell of a warrior. Borgia has two warriors leading his army who know Medici methods, and he will be sure to use that advantage." Shade closed his eyes, taming his beast. "*Grazie* for sticking your neck out for us, Nattie, I owe you one. As always, you have come through for me."

Natalia saw his angry response and took it in stride. Her father's temper was legendary, although she'd never seen it directed toward her or her siblings, even though Sophia had a knack for pushing his buttons. "Anything else you need? I'm not sure if I can help, but I'll try."

Shade took a deep breath, and looked down at his booted feet, avoiding her gaze on the screen. His voice was softer, but he had to ask her. "Nattie, have you had any visions? I need to know."

She heard the concern in his voice. "No, Daddy, and neither has Malachi. You know I have no control over what I see or don't see. Malachi has already said he'd let me know if he has any visions and share what he thinks they may mean. And I'll do the same. I remind you, our visions can be vague and open to interpretation, but I'll tell you what I see, when and if I see it."

Shade was nodding his head unconsciously, confirming he understood her words. "*Grazie*, I won't hold you up any longer. You keep your instincts about you, be careful. And tell Marcello to watch out for you. I love you so much."

She blew him a kiss as the screen went dark. "I love you, Daddy. Tell Mommy I love her too."

Natalia sat silently in the conference room. She'd been truthful with him, she hadn't had any visions, but she couldn't get the curse out of her head.

47

Shade sat a moment after hanging up with Natalia. Lorenzo had called him at sunset, before he even got to camp, and told him they'd seen workers going in and out of Dona's villa, most likely to restore the inside of the house. There was no doubt in his mind now. Borgia was moving in, and not without a purpose. The noise from the warriors outside in the camp yard was muffled inside these walls, and he barely heard it over his own thoughts. Nattie hadn't had any visions, nor had Malachi, and he wasn't sure if that was good or bad. Was he being overly cautious? He had confirmation of what he'd already suspected, and that was the Borgia army was bigger than his. Although, if it came to war, he could always pull his warriors from France, Greece, and the States, but that would leave his territories vulnerable. "Enough!"

He stood up and teleported back to the house, landing inside his office. Grabbing a bottle of Midnight, he headed up the stairs, shedding his clothes as he went. Stepping inside the shower, he let the hot water fall over him, before he slid down the wall, sitting in the corner of the shower stall, the steam enveloping him as he tipped the bottle to his lips. Everyone depended on his decisions. His son was a great warrior, but he'd never faced a battle of this magnitude, and Shade knew it would fall on his shoulders to make it right. He needed to get his head together, but how the hell did you do that when you had no idea what the fuck the enemy was up to. He'd put on a brave face, but he'd fought enough battles to understand the brutal reality of what was at stake here. His legacy was in place, but he could lose it all.

***

Kate was walking through the garden, a basket on her arm, as she used a small pair of shears to snip at the flowers in bloom that she'd bring inside the house for an arrangement. The scent of the roses, mixed with the lavender, was calming. The landscape lighting lit the path, and the garden took on a different feel at night. She felt him when he teleported over her and headed inside the house. She continued her stroll, thinking he'd join her soon, but he didn't appear, and she could feel his turmoil. She tuned her senses to him; it wasn't anger he felt, but concern, confusion. Turning back toward the house, she entered, set the basket aside, and made her way upstairs. She could hear the water running in their bathroom and opened the door to a steam-filled room. Through the mist, she could see him sitting under the shower, his face turned upward, letting the hot water flow over him as he held the bottle of Midnight in his hand. "Lover? Tell me what has you so troubled?"

Her voice traveled to him through the fog of steam. He laid his head back against the tiles. "I just got a call from Nattie."

Reaching out, he turned off the water and stood up, stepping out of the shower. Looking at her, he realized how long it had been since he'd fed. No damn wonder he was out of sorts. Grabbing a towel, he began to dry off, then used the towel to vigorously dry his shaggy mop of curls. "Lorenzo called me at sunset before I even got to camp. I'm not in the best mood, I guess. I apologize."

She rarely saw him mired in doubt. "So, talk to me. What's going on with our children that has you so upset?"

He pulled the towel from his head and stared at her. "I am not upset with our children." He threw the towel in the corner and strode past her. "It is the news they deliver that has me pissed off and wondering what the fuck I'm doing, and if it is the right thing or the wrong thing. *Cazzo*, I am the damn Medici, feared warrior and master, and I stand here feeling like old age has addled my brain. Fucking Borgia's."

Flopping down on the bed, he laid back. "I just need to get my head clear, that is all."

The Borgia, she should have known. He grew sullen whenever their name came up. She followed him to the bed and lay down beside him. "So, I'd take it Lorenzo had bad news for you. Are things escalating in Florence? Is our son in danger? I haven't felt his fear. Tell me why you're so concerned."

He rolled toward her and pushed the crimson hair from her neck. He breathed in heavily and nipped at her shoulder. His hunger for her grew increasingly. The soft lightweight shirt she wore hindered him from feeling her skin. He growled softly and grumbled.

"I will tell you if you get naked and lie next to me. I need to feel your skin."

She was aware he hadn't fed, preoccupied with the events in Florence, and spending more time in camp with the recent arrival of some of the warriors from Italy. The camp was at capacity, and Christoph had been working long hours too. She sat on the side of the bed, and removed her top, dropping it to the floor, before standing and releasing the skirt that puddled at her feet. Kicking her feet free of her sandals, she climbed back on the bed. "You haven't fed, and you're working too much. Feed from me. Take your strength from me."

He didn't hesitate as he pushed her down and slid on top of her, holding his weight on his elbows. He moaned, feeling his skin touch hers. Being with her was still like having a light switch flipped on in the dark. "I have missed you; it feels like a million years."

He sank his fangs into her neck and immediately felt the calm and light enter him. She was the answer to everything in his life. He felt her body respond as he fed and her movement beneath him begged for his attention. Grinding against her, he felt her hand slide over his cock and he moaned against her throat as he continued to feed. She slipped his steel hard rod inside her, and he broke from her neck. He glided inside her easily; she was wet and pulsing for him. He matched her rhythm. There was nothing he needed but her and her alone.

Kate felt the familiar burst of heat between her legs, demanding satisfaction. She felt him break away, the skin on her throat feeling the cool air after the hot, wet sensations of his mouth. He hadn't fed enough, yet exposed his neck to her, inviting her to take him. Lifting her head slightly from the pillow, she felt her fangs punch through and bit hard into the flesh at the nape of his neck and shoulder. He always bit the tender, soft flesh of her neck or the soft, silky flesh on her inner thigh. She preferred the feel of the strong muscles of his shoulder on her tongue. As she fed, she placed one hand behind his head and drew him back to her.

Shade felt the rapid beating of his heart. There'd been nothing to compare to the erotic sensations of her feeding from him. He sank his fangs once more and rode her hard, thrusting deep inside her as she gripped him and her nails raked down his back. They exploded into a riot of passion and she broke from his vein, but he continued to feed from her, his cock still nestled deep inside her. He always needed more of her. He retracted his fangs and laid his forehead on top of hers. "You still taste like the most erotic fruit on the planet, with a bit of feisty added."

Kissing her long and passionately, he finally rolled off of her and lay at her side. She snuggled into him, her head on his shoulder and one leg thrown over his. His hand immediately went to that beautiful ass of hers. They lay there quietly, as their heartbeats returned to normal.

She waited for him to talk, but he was silent. She brushed the hair from his face as he lay with his eyes closed. "Talk to me, lover."

Without opening his eyes, he answered. "Lorenzo says that Borgia is restoring Dona's house, and she's been seen shopping and buying clothes, perfumes, jewelry. Then Malachi informs Nattie that the Borgia army is larger than ours, but that isn't the worst of the news."

She lay with her head on his shoulder, her hand on his chest, and listened, remaining calm, because calm was what he needed from her. "What's the worst news?"

The sigh that escaped him was heavy. "He has two SICs in place. We are familiar with them both. One is Vanni, you remember him. He is the young warrior who used to torment Lorenzo. I knew he had ended up with Borgia but did not know he had risen to that high rank. The second is Tomas. I am sure you remember him as well, from when I first took over Alec's warriors. Both of them know Medici and how we work, one from inside the camp in Florence, the other from inside the States. This isn't coincidence, *mi amore*. Those two mercenaries were sought out because of their connections to the Medici. And I have no idea of what he is planning to do."

Kate lay quietly, absorbing what he'd shared and feeling his concern. He'd always felt confident, almost cocky, when taking on an adversary, and the fact that he felt so much concern about a potential confrontation with the Borgia worried her. She rose on her elbow so she could see his face. "But we're Medici. We have gifts and powers that others don't possess. Lorenzo and Christoph are fire-throwers. None have dared to take them on. Sophia, Bianca, and I, can call forth every creature to our defense. Natalia may not have seen anything yet, but she will, and what she sees will give us an advantage. Borgia may have more warriors, but they aren't Medici. They aren't trained like the Medici. Borgia has his brother, but you have me, and Lorenzo. You have Sophia and Bianca, Christoph and Henry. There is more power in the Medici blood than all the Borgias."

He looked into her eyes and pushed back the crimson that had fallen around her face. He reached up with both hands and cupped her beautiful face. "*Si*, we have gifts, but he has much more evil. Listen to me, his army is much larger than ours, and they are well trained. If he wants Medici land and attacks, I will have to draw almost every warrior from France, from Greece, and even some from the States to fight him. That leaves much vulnerability. *Si*, we have gifts that he can't match, but you must understand something. There is so much hatred between our covens, it goes back centuries, and it is like a ticking time bomb. I don't understand why he wants to come after us now. After all this time, why now, *mi amore*? We have done nothing to him, nothing! I try to convince myself that he is only after Dona, but my intuition tells me otherwise. I need to know what he wants, so I can fight, or leave it alone. I can't stand the waiting. I don't want a war with him. It will cost us too much. If I bring all my warriors together, I feel we can defeat him, but not without great loss. Look at how many we lost in the Battle of Bel Rosso, and this will be on a much larger scale. I do not like losing my warriors, leaving families alone to suffer their losses. We could lose Lorenzo or Alfie. We could lose our grandsons. Do you see my struggle?"

Kate closed her eyes and bowed her head. "Of course, I see your struggle. We won't lose our children, or our grandchildren. We won't. We lost one. I couldn't survive the loss of another."

He realized he'd brought back memories of their lost baby, and he was scaring her with his vision of the future. He pulled her tightly to his chest. "Do not worry, *mi amore*. We do have a secret weapon. We have love. Borgia can't touch that, nor fight it. And I promise you, I will fight with all I have to save this legacy we have built. I will not give up my territory or my *familia*." He stroked her hair, the slumber pulling at him. "Rest now, sleep with me. We will tackle it as it comes. I will always protect and love you. No one will take you from me." He closed his eyes and let everything go, the arms of his death slumber pulling him under.

48

Soren didn't wait until his death slumber was upon him; he was ready to see what the Medici knew. He liked to perform his dream-walking when he was able to control every moment of it. He knew Shade was also a dream-walker, but he rarely used his gift. Still, unlike most of his victims who didn't possess this gift, Shade would know that Soren was in his head. Soren used his gift regularly and was anxious to see if the Medici could handle his skills. It would give him a view into how future dream-walking sessions with Shade would go.

He wandered through his private wing back to his bedroom. The room was large and held massive, dark gothic furnishings. He hated light and bright colors. The heavy and ornate wood furnishings were almost black. The heavy velvet drapes and all of the upholstered pieces were a deep burgundy red, so dark, that the red was only visible in the light of day, which was something Soren never saw.

He lay down on his bed, flat on his back, and simply closed his eyes. They had obtained a detailed floor plan of the house at Bel Rosso, thanks to Tomas. Soren had studied the floor plans intently. He'd refined his dream-walking skills such that he no longer needed to teleport. If he knew the whereabouts of the victim and could envision their space and was able to mentally place himself there and enter their dreams. He'd refined his gift after centuries of study and practice.

Soren took a few deep relaxing breaths and cleared his mind of all other thoughts. Bringing up the images of the Bel Rosso vineyards in his brain, he traveled in his mind's eye over the beautifully landscaped estate located in White Hall. He could see the house that held the warrior he sought, and easily entered, placing himself inside the darkened bedroom. Shade Medici lay deep in his death slumber, his mind an open book, as his mate slept close at his side. As his eyes adjusted to the darkness, he admired her red hair, and pale skin, and thought to himself, maybe another time. Soren stayed calm and relaxed, as he focused on what he needed to do as he silently slipped inside the Medici's head.

Lying in his bed in Rome, a smile crept across his face, as the visions of the Medici fucking his queen played out before him. As entertaining as it was, this wasn't why Soren was here. It was too soon to alter his dream and reveal his presence. He needed to see what the Medici knew. Soren sorted through Shade's memories, looking for anything of value, anything that could give them an advantage in war. He saw that Shade dream-walked most often with his female, whom he adored. Soren looked for signs of other females, to see if he kept mistresses on the side, but he was faithful to his queen. What a pity, he thought, to miss out on such fun. Soren found himself licking his lips at the sight of his queen. She was beautiful and Soren was fascinated by her dove white skin and the contrast of her bright red hair. He could envision cutting into her flesh, and how brilliant the blood would look against that alabaster flesh. He needed to stop this train of thought, and finish what he'd come here for, which was to find out what the warrior knew about the Borgia. He pushed past the most recent memories, diving deeper into the psyche of Medici. He stumbled on Shade's thoughts about the Alizzi, and his longtime relationship with her. He saw their early friendship, and Shade's resistance to mate, and his refusal to honor the mating contract arranged by their two fathers. Yet he stayed close to her, had even slept with her through the years, and fed from her. He'd protected her borders until the betrayal. His affection turned to anger, and he'd never forgiven her for what she'd done to Lorenzo, and yet he still felt bound by a sense of honor, and strong feelings of guilt about not following his father's request to mate her, to provide a stronger line of defense for the Medici. He saw the anger mixed with pity that Shade felt for the Alizzi now. He thinks she's weak to let Rodrigo in her life. He's aware of the restorations taking place in her house, but he doesn't know what his brother is up to. The Medici was confused, and at a loss as to what to do.

Soren looked further and found that the Medici knew about Vanni and Tomas. He saw a woman in an ivory robe and recognized the Council garb. This would be the Medici's daughter. Soren had never seen her before, but everyone knew the Medici's daughter was the first female ever born to Council. He saw the female in the ivory robe confiding with Malachi, receiving the news that the Borgia army was larger, and how the Medici was even more conflicted now. Shade's mind was a web of questions with no answers. There were so many doubts, and Soren found this amusing, the great fucking Medici in a whirl of confusion. Soren was ready to push the boundaries and find out if the Medici's gift were any match for his.

Soren took a deep breath and let it out slowly and made himself visible inside the Medici's mind. He laughed with that wicked crooked smile and then he began to give the Medici a few visions of his own. He felt the fight slowly build in his victim, the anger, and the frustration, as Shade tried to shake Soren from his dream, but his gift was too weak. He'd left it dormant for much too long and Soren was going to make sure he knew it. He marched thousands of Borgia warriors through his dream, led by Vanni and Tomas, their Borgia battle cries screaming inside his head. He splattered the blood of the Medici far and wide, while Borgia warriors sliced their throats, and beheaded them with ease until there was nothing left. He played this dream, tuning the intensity of the vision and the clarity of the sound until it was overwhelming. He could feel the Medici struggling in his death slumber, trying to lead his warriors to fight and the Borgia kept coming, no matter how many they slew, over and over again, without end. The sound was deafeningly loud inside the Medici's head, when Soren left him with a vision for battle's end. He left the great warrior alone on the field of battle, knee-deep in Medici blood, staring at Castello, burned to the ground, and the Borgia flag planted where the castle once stood. The bodies of his slain Medici warriors floated atop a river of blood. Soren appeared in front of the Medici and spoke, dropping the body of his slain queen at his feet. "We took you bastards once. We will take all you have this time."

Soren let the screams of the battle repeat again, the high-pitched wails pounding inside the Medici's head. He walked out of the dream and opened his eyes, back in his bedroom in Rome. Shade Medici hadn't used his gift for evil for too long. He'd spent years, wasting his gift to keep dream-walking inside the dreams of his queen. He was weak and couldn't take the power of Soren's dream-walking. He lay in bed and howled with laughter. It was just as he knew it would be. No contest.

***

Shade felt his heart pounding as a vision of Soren Borgia raged through his mind. He could see Soren and yet, he couldn't break the hold he had on his psyche. The blood-shed abounded, and as fast as Shade took down an enemy, five more would appear. He couldn't escape from the pounding noise inside his head of clashing swords and the screams of the dying. It became louder and louder. The screams of his warriors and the battle cries of the Borgia tore at him. He felt his body break into a cold sweat as he saw the complete devastation of his skilled warriors, seemingly helpless against the Borgia. Soren couldn't be stopped. He saw Soren approach him, carrying the limp, lifeless body of his *bel*, and his knees buckled. He fought to remind himself this was a dream, and Kate was safe, but Soren was pulling all the strings. As the dream started to fade, he looked at the empire and legacy he'd worked so hard to build, and it was completely gone. He stood alone in the field of death, his *bel* was gone, his children gone, and he didn't have the strength or the will to begin again, to rebuild his coven from nothing. Without her, he was nothing. He was sinking into despair, when the sounds began again, louder this time, as the dream sequence started to recycle. He sat up in the bed, holding both sides of his head, his body covered in sweat, screaming for the dream to stop. The wailing cries of his fallen warriors, his children and grandchildren slaughtered, and the never-ending flow of blood that rose around his knees. But the horror he couldn't bear to look at was Kate's lifeless body at his feet. His body was shaking beyond his control.

***

In a deep sleep, Kate began to feel the turmoil that boiled over inside his head when he sat up suddenly, his body shaking and covered in sweat, as he cried out. She sat up quickly, reaching out to him. "Shade! It's a dream! Look at me. Wake up! Now! We're safe. We're fine." Her mind quickly scanned for any fear from her children, and she felt nothing, and knew they were all safe.

Shade heard her voice through the chaos in his mind. He quickly jumped from the bed and spun around to look for Soren, even though he knew it had been a dream and Soren was long gone. Shaking his head to clear the images, he fell to his knees, grabbing his head to block the stabbing pain coursing through his brain. It was a pain like nothing he'd ever felt before. "Make it stop, make it stop!" He fell forward, face down on the floor. "It was Soren in my head, dream-walking."

She ran to his side of the bed, dropping to her knees beside him as the door opened and Luca appeared. Kate looked up at him with confusion. "Tell me what to do!"

Luca knelt next to them as he reassured Kate. "A dream-walker. When they wreak havoc in your dreams, they can also leave their victims in pain."

Kate massaged his temples and the back of his neck. "Relax, lover."

Theresa appeared in the doorway, holding a jar. "Valerian root." She opened the jar and picked out a single dried root and handed it to Kate. "Make him eat it, now. It will ease the pain and calm the anxiety the dream produced."

Kate took the root in her hand and held it to his lips, closed tight against the pain. "Eat this, Shade. Now."

Shade growled through the pain, but took the root, and chewed on it, swallowing the pulp. "Fuck, what the hell is that? Pain, fucking pain. Why can't I fight this?"

He could barely move, but as the valerian root was absorbed into his system, he began to feel some relief, but he was exhausted. He leaned against Kate, his body covered in sweat, his curls plastered to his face. "Luca, they're coming for us. Borgia is coming for us all."

Luca laid his hand on his master's back. "Then we will fight them, and we will win. Soren has shown his hand. He did you a favor. Our warriors will be ready."

"Help me back into bed, Luca."

Luca easily helped him get back in bed. Shade lay with his arm over his eyes, his head still pounding. "Call Lorenzo and Alfie, tell them what has happened. Have them escalate the patrols. Tell Henry. I don't know where they might strike. Tell Christoph... and Raven. "

He grabbed for Kate and she was there beside him in an instant. "I feel exhausted. I can't hold on much longer. The dream weakened me, and I will be pulled back into my slumber. I need our children protected. Soren is powerful, his gift much stronger than mine. I won't let them win. I won't let them take my family from me again."

The death slumber pulled at him, trying to take him down, but he fought against it. He didn't want Soren to return. "Let me hold you."

Kate slid into his embrace as everything went dark for him, the pull of the death slumber winning out. The dream didn't return. Soren had left, at least for now, and all he felt was Kate's warmth, curled up beside him, her lightness and love healing him, as he fell into a deeper slumber.

49

Rodrigo was up early and waiting for his brother to wake from his death slumber. He was anxious to hear the details of his dream-walking with the Medici. He was hoping his impatient sibling had followed his orders. As he walked through the labyrinth of hallways winding through the palazzo, he made his way to the wing that Soren occupied. He couldn't help but think about the Alizzi. He'd made a point of checking in with her every night, as a means of keeping her on a short leash. He demanded an accounting of her day, and she seemed to understand his warriors monitored her comings and goings. But like Soren, he too was becoming impatient with her. Her reluctance to have sex with him wasn't something he'd expected, and he thought he'd been patient, and generous, enough. It was well beyond time for her to show her appreciation.

***

As Soren woke from his death slumber, he was in a delightfully wicked mood. He'd taken the Medici down hard and won the first battle of dream-walking. Big ass warrior was probably still curled up in a ball of pain. He knew his elder brother was awake and could feel his eagerness to hear the details. Soren got dressed and made his way to his brother, meeting him halfway and steering him to the dining room. The table stretched out across the room and could easily accommodate a hundred people. Soren and Rodrigo met here at sunset every evening for breakfast. It had been their tradition. They never feasted on food, of course, but had the servants waiting on them, pouring out pitchers of thick, dark red blood.

The Borgia warriors were responsible for capturing young mortals and half-breeds from the streets of Rome and bringing them back to the palazzo, where their bodies were drained. The fresh blood, and the victim's heart, was served to them every evening. Soren sat across from his brother and picked up his full glass, holding it up to the light. "Ah, this will be exceptionally filling after my journey last night." He tipped his glass to Rodrigo and drained the contents in one gulp. It was immediately filled to the brim again.

Rodrigo smiled and chuckled low. "So, you were successful then. Tell me, brother, how much did you find out?"

Soren sipped slowly from his second glassful, savoring it. "I can tell you one thing, brother, the Medici does not fuck around on his queen. I looked through his head, sure I would find who else he shared his bed with, thinking we could use that against him, but he only has eyes for her. What a fool! He has no further interest in the Alizzi either, but he is angry with her for associating with you."

Rodrigo nodded. "Well done, brother. I am glad to hear of it. What else have you learned?"

Soren shook his head. "Who is being impatient now?"

Rodrigo slammed his fist on the table, rattling the delicate crystal and china. "Do not play games with me, Soren. I have no patience for your play."

Soren sat back in his chair, tilting it on its back legs and just grinned. He loved riling his older brother; it was justice for having always lived in his shadow. "Do not throw your commands at me, Rodrigo, you need me now more than you ever have. Piss me off and I will leave."

Rodrigo growled as he leaned forward over the table. "Leave? And where would you go, brother? Now, tell me what else he knows!"

Soren tipped the chair back and forth, casually sipping on the blood. "He had no idea what the fuck we were up to. He is confused and not sure what our intentions are. He knows about Vanni and Tomas and is pissed off about it. He is aware that you have restored Dona's villa, and that doesn't sit well with him either. His gift is weak. He could not fight me off in the least."

Soren rocked his chair forward on all four legs and laughed in a most hideously wicked sound that echoed in the large room. "He will not be a problem. I can invade his dreams any time."

Rodrigo listened carefully and observed his brother's cockiness. He was much too full of himself. He knew without asking that he'd overstepped his bounds in dream-walking. "What have you done? You do not fool me, brother. You are much too pleased with yourself to have just looked around inside his head."

Soren stood and sighed with a grin. He casually walked around the room, examining its contents as if he'd never seen them before.

"I left him with the sight of his precious Castello in ruins, his queen dead at his feet, and our Borgia flag claiming its territory. His head will still be screaming with the sounds of the battle cries of Borgia."

Soren could feel his brother's anger as he walked behind him and leaned into his ear. "He knows our intentions now, brother, so I suggest you quit fucking around and put our plans in motion." He stepped back quickly and disappeared, teleporting out of the room.

Rodrigo roared and swiped his hand across the table, clearing it of its finery as the dishes and crystal flew across the room, smashing against the walls and floors, the pitchers of blood splattering everything. "You fool! I did not want him to know this yet."

He stood abruptly, knocking the chair back as he threw his head back and howled. He calmed his raging beast. He needed to keep his wits about him, now that his brother had divulged everything. There'd be no more doubt in Shade Medici's mind. Ready or not, it was time to move forward with the plan.

50

Alfie was finishing up with camp, and his ass was dragging. They had remained on high alert, and everyone was on pins and needles with this Borgia ordeal. He understood it was a serious matter, and to make it worse, Lorenzo had informed him about the dream-walking incident. Alfie had never had a dream-walker in his head, so he wasn't exactly sure what the experience would feel like, but it couldn't be good. Lorenzo had asked him to join him at Castello as soon as they got off duty. Lorenzo wanted to talk to him, but he wanted to be sure they were away from camp when he did.

He saw Lorenzo wrapping up with the warriors he'd been training, so he flagged down one of their lieutenant's, and had him take over. Alfie would like nothing better than to head home to his mate and his daughter, but he figured he'd have to wait at least another hour. He and Lorenzo met daily to review their progress, assess any new intel on the Borgia, and commit their battle plans to memory. As much as Alfie would love a battle, he understood that this wasn't a battle they'd want to take on. Walking into Castello, he was immediately led into the office to find Lorenzo already there.

"You didn't have time before we went on duty to fill me in. What the hell happened at Bel Rosso, brother? Is your father all right?"

Lorenzo was standing at the window, staring into space, his mind preoccupied when Alfie walked in. "Yeah, I think so. Luca said Dad would be fine after his death slumber." He plopped down in the chair and spun it in Alfie's direction. "You remember Vanni, that kid that was in camp when I first came here to train? He used to bust my ass all the time, and I finally lost my cool with him, threw fire."

Alfie nodded, how the hell could he forget that episode. "Yeah, of course. He's with the Borgia now. What about him?"

"He's more than with the Borgia, he's their SIC. Luca called me, after Dad went back into his death slumber after the dream-walk, to tell me what Natalia had been able to find out. He mentioned another mercenary, Tomas, who'd worked for my dad once. I never knew him, but apparently, he settled down too and took the blood oath with the Borgia. Luca said Dad is concerned that Borgia has two warriors who have been inside our organization at some point, one here in Florence, and one in the States. We'll have to keep that in mind as we plan."

Alfie was surprised, he had no idea Vanni had advanced to the level of SIC. He pulled out his smokes, lit up, and threw the pack at his brother. "You should have taken the bastard out that night we went into Florence to pick up those jewels for Chantal. So, now we have this Tomas as well. Borgia must have a pretty big army to need two SIC's. You talk to Shade yet?"

Lorenzo shook his head. "No. I'm sure he'll call as soon as he's awake and has some time to gather his thoughts. Luca said to keep the family on lockdown and have the warriors on high alert. We still don't want to instigate. He made that clear. Dad doesn't want to go on the offense, at least not yet."

Alfie sighed. "Shit, I know he's up to no good. Did Luca say much about the dream-walking? That takes some balls right there. This news is going to go over like a ton of fucking bricks with Bianca and Sophia." Standing, he poured himself a Red Moon. "You want one of these?"

"Pour me one, brother." Lorenzo spun back and forth in the chair, as Luca's words rolled through his brain. "Luca didn't give me much detail. You know, my dad's gift is dream-walking, but he rarely uses it as a weapon. Luca said Soren uses his all the time and is very skilled at it. Dream-walkers of equal power can often block each other, but Dad wasn't able to block Soren. Theresa gave Dad some valerian root, to help him sleep, so Luca didn't get all the details of the dream. My dad would dream-walk in my head when I was a boy, but only with good dreams. He did it with all of us growing up. I've never known another dream-walker, but I've read the stories. When used for evil intent, once the dream-walker puts the dream in your head, it is hard to get rid of the images. They plague your thoughts, even when you are awake. They leave the victim almost immobilized with pain when they are done. What if this isn't the last time? Soren can get to him any time he sleeps."

Alfie slid the glass of Red Moon across the desk to Lorenzo and flopped down in the large armchair across from him. "I don't know a lot about dream-walking, but I have talked to Henry about it once in a while. It can be damn powerful, I know that. And you can bet your ass, Soren won't be using it for good. To be honest, I'm less concerned about the dream-walking and worry more about what their plan is. Will they just come at us here in Florence? Or will they try to hit the other territories as well? I go over alternative plans whenever I'm not in the camp. I sent you copies of what I've worked on so far. I worry they will strike all territories at once, so I have drawn up a few plans to counter that. Something else is bothering me as well. It's my son, Jules."

Lorenzo creased his brow. "Jules? Why? He's probably the most removed from this."

Alfie nodded. "Weakest link in the chain, brother. Jules is no warrior, yet he travels to all the territories between Europe and the States. We've never assigned a protector to him, and I never thought we needed to, until now. I want a protector to be with him, Lorenzo. He can't fight something like the Borgia's." He stared at Lorenzo, "Are you worried at all about Grace?"

"Brother, if you want a protector for Jules, just name it. Whoever you want, and we'll assign them today. And yes, to answer your questions, I'm terrified for Grace, and for Chantal. Chantal was raised protected by warriors, but neither of her parents was warrior-born. She's lived a very sheltered life. And Grace? Based on her sleep patterns, it appears she's a day-walker. She'd have no defenses against dream-walking. I can't even let myself go there. I have no way to protect her from that."

Alfie felt some relief that Lorenzo was worried about the same things. He was comforted to know they were on the same page. When he lay beside Sophia, he worried about being able to protect them all, if things got out of control. He was born a warrior and became a Medici warrior through training and taking the blood oath. It was everything he'd aspired to be. He'd never expected to fall in love with Sophia, and his mating with her had elevated him to the position of Prince. He'd die for any one of his family, here or abroad. "Tristan is good, he'd make a fine protector, assign him. He's itching for a new assignment anyway. I'll let Jules know. He'll tell me it's not necessary, but I'm going to insist. My ass is dragging, brother. I should head home to my beauties."

Lorenzo drained his glass before setting it back on the desk. "Good idea. You go home to your family, and I'll take care of Tristan."

Alfie stood and stretched. "Thanks. You know, you have a family too. I try not to get so wrapped up in this I forget to take care of them. I'm more aware than ever that I need to spend as much time as I can with them. Do the same, brother."

He left the office and stepped out of the castle, looking at the early rays of sunrise. He stood there for a moment and acknowledged the sense of foreboding. There was a dark evil coming, they just didn't know when. Teleporting to their villa, he was anxious to hold Red in his arms.

51

Rodrigo had demanded that Dona call him every evening to give him an accounting of her day, and she had complied, never missing a single night. He was glad to have implemented this little bit of control and took pleasure in knowing she followed his commands. He wasn't unaware of the Medici's daughter on the Council, who was working to change the power base between men and women in their culture, but Dona was old school, and he felt sure he could keep her under his thumb. Tonight, he'd decided he'd surprise her, and drop in for an unplanned visit. He liked keeping her off-balance, unable to predict when he might appear.

Her home had been renovated for some time now, and her wardrobe replaced. Rodrigo would occasionally send some of his own staff to help with the house and gardens and, of course, to report back to him on Dona. It hadn't taken long for her to quickly become accustomed to her old life of luxury, where whatever she desired was at her fingertips, and she was waited on hand and foot.

Dressing in his finery, with a lace collar and cuffs peeking out from his heavy velvet jacket, he added many jeweled rings to his fingers and teleported out into the night, landing gracefully at her doorstep. Rodrigo preferred the fashion of his youth and enjoyed the pure foppery of it. His wardrobe created a certain shock value among both mortals and vampires, which he also enjoyed. He acknowledged he was vain and loved the attention. Let the other vampires blend in with the mortals. What was the point of being a rare and beautiful creature if he couldn't draw the stares of everyone he passed?

He rang the newly installed doorbell, waiting for a servant to answer. He always enjoyed the momentary sense of panic his unexpected visits caused, and how frantically Dona worked to pull herself together. She'd need to get used to that.

Mario scrambled to answer the door, aware that Master Rodrigo had arrived, once again unannounced. Dona's head might still be in the clouds, but Mario had no illusions about who was calling the shots around here now. Opening the door, he bowed his head slightly. "Master Rodrigo. We were not expecting you. Please, come in, and I will notify my lady that you are here. May I bring you a Midnight? Or do you prefer Red Moon?" Mario led him to the newly furnished parlor, now splendidly decorated.

Rodrigo strolled past him as if he already owned the place. He was already suspect of Mario. He'd served Dona a very long time, and no doubt was loyal to her. That could be a problem. Mario may have been here too long to be trusted. Rodrigo would have to get rid of him, and Marie, but there was still time. He'd make sure all of her servants were from the Borgia household.

He walked around the new parlor, nodding with approval. "Midnight will be fine. Is my pet upstairs?"

"Yes, master." Mario poured the wine into a crystal glass, careful not to spill a drop. He could feel the tension in the air and didn't wish to anger Rodrigo. "She is in her bedroom, putting away the many dresses you sent over earlier. I will let her know you have arrived. I'm sure she will be eager to thank you for your continued generosity."

Rodrigo looked down his nose at him, as he prepared his drink. "No need. I will tell her myself. Pour two and give your mistress and me a few moments alone before you bring them upstairs."

Rodrigo strode up the stairs, his silver-tipped walking cane making a distinctive click against the stairs, as he admired the new art hanging in the staircase. He could hear the soft chatter of the two females coming from her bed chambers. Making his way to her door, he stood, silently watching them. The maid caught his eye and gasped, dropping an elegant gown to the floor. His voice boomed with authority, startling her. "You may leave us now."

Maria looked hesitantly at Donatella then scurried past him in the doorway. He walked inside the room, as Dona was gathering the gown from the floor. Opening his arms, he smiled. "Do I not get a kiss or a proper greeting from my dear pet?"

Dona felt like she'd sold her soul to the devil himself. She knew she should have stopped this madness when it first started. She should have run outside on the first day when the workers showed up to restore the gardens and called a halt to the work, but she didn't. She should have said enough when the workers showed up to restore her home to its former glory, but she didn't. And now, he replenished her closets with the latest fashions and covered her in jewels. He'd expect much from her, although he'd never expressly stated his intentions. She wasn't stupid. She knew his actions had strings attached.

"Yes, of course, gifts as generous as these deserve a kiss." She laid the gown across her bed, straightening the skirt, but didn't take a step toward him, but rather let him come to her. She accepted his kiss and the probing of his tongue, but it was revulsion she felt.

Rodrigo felt her reluctance, but he let that slide for now. He kissed her passionately, even though the kiss he got in return was reserved and cold. As he broke away from the kiss, his hand slid along her cheek, his eyes locked to hers. "I take it that you enjoy my gifts and appreciate my taste in the gowns. You will need the new wardrobe, for we will be attending many events and you must look worthy to be on my arm, but enough of this."

Rodrigo took a seat on the chaise lounge, stretching out his long legs, and laying his walking stick on the floor beside him. "Come closer, pet."

She walked with some hesitancy in his direction when he grabbed her around the waist and pulled her down into the space next to him.

"So, are the renovations complete?" He snuggled softly into her neck, taking in her scent.

She was taken aback by his familiarity in her private space as he stretched out on her chaise lounge, pulling her down next to him as if they were lovers. She had no doubt as to where this was leading. She could only deny him for so long. She lay next to him, uncomfortable with the closeness of his body. "*Si*, they are almost complete. There are a few rooms that are rarely used that were saved for last. They expect to finish up within the week."

He kissed her neck, disappointed that she showed such a lack of response. "I am very happy to hear that. I have something very important to ask you." He placed his hand on her jaw, turning her face towards his. "I would wish to ask you to move into the Borgia palazzo with me. We will keep your villa as a beautiful country retreat for us both. We will live in the city, in the heart of Italy, and come here when we need to get away from all the hustle and bustle of Rome, where I can enjoy a little peace and quiet. But you must be with me. It is most torturous not having you near." He took her hand in his and played gently with her fingers. "I will not beg, my pet. So, think carefully of your answer."

She was caught off-guard by his request. Leave her villa? She'd come to accept that she might have to occasionally allow him into her bed in exchange for his generosity, but leaving her home? "Oh, Rodrigo...that is most generous. But this is my home. I was born here. This is all I have left from my father's legacy, this house, this territory. You know you are welcome here anytime. Come and go freely, no invitation required, of course. Besides, what would I do in your palazzo in Rome? I don't know anyone in Rome, and I am not familiar with the city. I have spent my entire life in the countryside."

Rodrigo knew she'd balk at the request, but he wouldn't give up easily. Mario entered the room, carrying a tray of two crystal wine glasses filled with Midnight. He approached them both as Rodrigo accepted a glass. Donatella dislodged herself from his embrace and stood, straightening her skirt before taking the glass of Midnight. She stepped away from him, sipping at the wine, her back to him. He watched her closely. She wasn't going to give in easily. He threw his legs over each side of the chaise as he straddled it and sipped the Midnight.

"Dona, I have lived alone for so long, without the comfort of a female. Being here with you, this is what I miss; watching you move about the room gracefully, your perfume hanging in the air, the soft rustle of your garments, the sound of a woman's voice."

He stood up and strolled around the room. "My dear, I am not asking you to leave permanently. This is your legacy. I will, of course, protect the territory. You will find plenty to do in Rome. Come now, you will be with me, and we can do whatever you wish. I will show you the city and all it has to offer."

He stepped up behind her, his hand clinching her waist. "I know you have spent your life here, perhaps you need a change. Just come stay with me for a while. We have many engagements coming up that I wish for you to attend with me. Do you not agree it is much easier to be in Rome than travel back and forth for such occasions? Come, my pet, do not be so difficult. It is a simple request."

Dona felt trapped. She knew he'd extract payment in some form, and she'd prepared herself for the day when she'd lay on her back beneath him and wait for him to spill his seed inside her, and drink from her throat. But she assumed it would be here, in her home, and he'd leave when he was finished. She figured he'd toy with her until he was bored and move on to someone else. She hadn't expected this. "Well, I suppose I could come for a visit. Maybe stay for a short while, and then return to my home?"

He heard the hesitancy in her voice, and his anger rose. After all he'd done for her, his request seemed like such a simple one. She clutched the wine glass in one hand, so he took her free hand and led her to the window, the moon shining down on the now thriving gardens. He stood behind her, his arm tightly around her waist, his lips close to her ear. "What is it that holds you here, my pet? Tell me. You have no coven, no warriors to lead. Other females would die to have the slightest bit of attention from me. I have given you so much, and I ask so little. I wish to be with you, enjoy time with you. I can give you the world, Donatella, but you seem to hold back."

He quickly spun her around and kissed her hard on the lips. He heard her wine glass hit the floor. He roughly cupped her ass and moaned with unbridled lust into her mouth. He let the kiss go on for some time, leaving her breathless for air. When he broke away, he laid his forehead against hers. "I expect you to make arrangements for a visit, but I know, once you are there, you will not want to return to this loneliness you live."

She fought back the tears. She had no excuse to give him, other than she didn't enjoy his company, and she recoiled at his touch. "Of course, Rodrigo. I'm sure you are right. Give me time to close up the house, and I will come for a long visit in Rome."

He smiled then. He didn't like to lose. Stepping back, he retrieved his glass of Midnight and emptied it of its contents. "I am most fond of you, Donatella. I truly am. You are always on my mind. I will expect you on Friday evening. I will send a car for you, bring as much as you wish. I will expect you to stay for some time and join me for some entertaining evenings. Do not fret, if there is anything you need, I will provide it." He looked at her then. "I will send my warriors to protect your borders while you are with me in Rome."

Dona was processing his demands, and make no mistake, they were demands coated in courtesy. "Protect my borders?" She looked confused. She hadn't had warriors in more than a century, and the Medici had withdrawn their protection. No one had bothered her. They treated her as if she didn't exist. "I doubt I require it, Rodrigo, but do whatever you see fit."

Rodrigo nodded. "It is necessary, my pet, and I'll take care of it. Now, your servants stay behind, you will be attended to by the Borgia staff." He beckoned to her. "I must return to Rome, come, give me a proper goodbye, Dona."

She composed her face going to him, knowing in her heart she was defeated. She had no real power against the Borgia. "Yes, of course." She went to him as he commanded and reluctantly slid her arms around his waist. She couldn't bring herself to initiate a kiss, but he took what he wanted, and she passively complied.

He liked the feel of her body against his. She would be a pleasurable fuck. He extended his fangs and slid them across her neck. He dare not break her skin, for he'd take her then and there, and that would destroy his plan. He knew he'd made his intentions clear. Retracting his fangs, he kissed her gently this time, without force. Hugging her, he reluctantly let go, grabbed up his walking stick, and headed for the door, pausing before he exited. Keeping his back to her, his voice was stern. "A piece of advice, Donatella, when you come to the palazzo, I expect you to appear happy at all times. Look at me as if you want to be with me. It is the least you can do for this master who has given you much. I suggest you learn to pretend to enjoy it. See you on Friday."

He walked out of her room and down the stairs, past Mario who stood, awaiting orders. Turning to the butler, he looked down his nose. "Assist your mistress. It seems she has had an accident with her Midnight." Without another word, he walked out the front door and teleported into the night.

Dona stood alone in her room, looking at the puddle of Midnight on the new rug, as the tears flowed down her cheeks. *Act happy? He expects me to act happy to be in his presence? How did my life come to this?* She turned to look out the window as Mario entered the room and rushed to clean up the mess. She stared out in the direction of Tuscany and wondered if there was any appeal she could make of the Medici that could save her from this nightmare, but she knew those bridges had been burned a long time ago. She was on her own.

52

Luca had kept a close watch over him ever since the dream-walking event, and Shade was clearly not himself. He'd been quieter and somewhat withdrawn. Luca had felt the effects of a dream-walk once, although it had been years ago. A good dream-walker created an experience that made it hard for the dreamer to distinguish between their dream state and reality. A pleasant dream left no aftereffects, but a dream meant to attack, to weaken the dreamer, was designed to fill the dreamer with fear and doubt and leave the dreamer in pain. Shade hadn't spoken to him about the contents of the dream, but whatever it was, it had him shaken, and that wasn't something he often saw in his master. Luca stood in the door of Shade's office and watched without speaking as Shade leaned over his desk, his head in his hands. "Master?"

***

Shade's head hurt like hell, still. Soren had not only left him in physical pain but with a pain in his heart and soul. Shade had never been afraid of battle, he was born a warrior, but even without the images placed in his head, he knew a battle with the Borgia would mean a massive loss of life on both sides. He sat with his head in his hands, the pain pounding behind his eyes, as the sounds of the battle echoed in his head, over and over. The worst part was knowing Soren could come at him again, enter his dreams and wreak havoc. He looked up slowly to see Luca at his door. "*Si*, is something wrong?" He sat back in the leather chair, leaning his head against the chair. He felt like he was a million years old.

Luca entered the room, dimly lit by a single lamp, and took a seat in a chair near his desk. "Nothing is wrong, master. I was checking on you. I can see the dream still haunts you. But you, better than most, know that's the whole purpose of the dream-walker's gift. How can I help you?"

Shaking his head, he winced slightly as the motion caused more pain. "My loyal Luca, always observant. I feel..." The words stopped mid-sentence. He knew he should talk to Luca, and unburden himself, but he felt embarrassed to a fault. He was the warrior's warrior, master, and king, a dream-walker himself. But he hadn't been able to fight Soren in the dream-walk. Borgia must be laughing his ass off knowing how easy it had been. "I don't think I want to talk about it." He stood and walked to the open doors of the patio and stepped outside, hoping the night air would clear his head as he lit up a smoke.

Luca followed him outside, pulling his cigarettes from his pocket and lighting up. He stood quietly, watching the smoke drift away with the soft breeze before he spoke again. "You must talk about it. I've felt the power of a dream-walker before. I know how vulnerable it leaves you, how filled with doubt. I'm a warrior too. I'm trained to stand in the face of death and show no fear. So, I know what you are feeling. Soren caught you off-guard. You haven't had your dreams invaded in centuries, and you rarely use your gift for evil. You walk through Kate's dreams, and the dreams of your children and grandchildren, and you fill them with love and hope. You've created a paradise for those you love, and you forgot the many ways that the evil in our world can slip in. You must talk, and you'll have to prepare. If he visited you once, you know he'll visit again."

Shade listened and knew every word Luca uttered was true. "Words from a seasoned warrior. You are right, I have forgotten what it feels like to have someone make me feel vulnerable and weak. I don't like this, Luca. Fuck, I am the damn Medici. How dare that bastard walk in and just roll me over like I am nothing. He left no doubt there will be a battle between our covens, and it will be the biggest battle we have ever encountered. There will be many losses, I have no doubt. I know we can prepare, but he has advantages as well. He is bigger in numbers. They have inside information, they have Vanni and Tomas. Lorenzo is going to face his first real fight to defend his home and *familia*, and our coven. Is he ready to face that evil? Have I trained him well enough? I keep asking myself those questions, over and over."

Luca let him talk without interrupting. He saw Aegis and Night Stalker moving closer to the house, curious about their appearance on the patio. He watched them both sit quietly in the grass, waiting and watching. "Lorenzo will rise to the occasion, just as you did. He has as many reasons to fight as you did, maybe even more, because there is more to defend now. He doesn't speak of it, but he understands the weight of the burden he carries and his responsibility to the coven. His SIC is mated to your daughter. They will stand together, as you and Marco stood together. Every battle involves sacrifice. Every warrior knows it, and every warrior stands ready for whatever his or her fate dictates. We have faced worse and won. The Medici always wins. When Soren comes again, and he will come, call out to me, call to Marcello, and Raven. Call to Theo, Matteo, and Skelk. You have the power, master. You've forgotten how to use it. Pull us into your dream, and together, we will fight the Borgia. It's how we will defeat him in your dreams, and it's how we will defeat him on the battlefield."

Shade looked at this warrior he loved as much as he loved his own children. He'd known him since birth, his *padre* giving his life for Medici. Luca had dedicated his life to him, protecting his mate, and his children. His words held wisdom. "I will never call Marcello. He protects Nattie, and she can dream-walk as well, and there is not an ounce of evil in her. She is vulnerable. She may need him."

He looked out at Night Stalker and Aegis. They were drawn close to the house by his anxiety. They didn't understand what was ahead, but they felt his concern and doubt. "This will be my first fight without Marco. I have never fought side by side with my son, so many firsts. Borgia wants Medici land, he wants it all, Luca. Soren made that very clear. The Borgia flag was staked in the ground of the Medici ruins. Make me a promise, right now." He turned to face Luca. Their eyes locked. He placed his hand on Luca's shoulder and was close enough to feel Luca's breath on his face. "No matter what happens, don't let *bel* come out to battle. Keep her safe in case anything happens to me. She is a strong queen, and Lorenzo will need her to help rebuild."

Luca stared back at him. "Of course, master, but don't be so quick to assume this is your fate. That isn't the Medici I know. You've already let Soren plant a seed of doubt in your head. He's already convinced you that you can't win. I would say that Soren wouldn't be working so hard if he didn't fear the Medici. Turn the tables. It's what you always do. And don't underestimate the power of the fire-thrower. Your son and grandson's gifts are rare ones, and not many would dare to confront it. You have three females with the gift of animalism. We saw that power in the Battle of Bel Rosso. The Borgia don't have these gifts."

Shade smiled and punched him softly in the shoulder. "Spoken like a Medici warrior. *Grazie*, for everything, Luca. I know I don't say that often enough. I will not make the first move, if that is what the Borgia wants. He will have to do more than walk inside my head. I know Lorenzo and Alfie will fight with their hearts, just as I will. But this dream-walk showed me that the battle is inevitable, and that is something I was hoping to avoid. My sons have been sending me battle plans, one after another, for every contingency. Marco taught them that." Shade raised his face to the moon. It had been over a hundred years, and still, his heart ached for his best friend and brother. Fiamma had been gone even longer. He thought about all the warriors he'd lost through the years, the warriors who'd sacrificed their lives, so he was still standing, and to keep the Medici coven strong. There was no doubt in his mind that the Medici would still be here when this was over. The only question was what would be the price of that victory? "*Per sempre*, Medici."

Luca draped his arm over his master's shoulder. This was the master he knew, the one who never backed away from a challenge.

53

Marie was helping Dona pack up her things for a long stay at the Borgia palazzo in Rome. Dona wasn't sure how long she'd have to stay there and was dreading having to go. She could only avoid Rodrigo's touch for so long before he'd become tired of her unresponsiveness. She was biting back tears, as she slowly folded her clothes and carefully placed them in her luggage. She looked around the room, seeking anything that would help her delay the process, as Marie packed the last of her toiletry items.

"There you go, mistress. I think we have everything you need."

Dona looked back at her absently. "What? Oh, yes, of course. Have Mario help you bring my luggage downstairs. Rodrigo was sending a car for me."

Marie nodded. "*Si*, the car is here already. We will load the luggage in the trunk. Do you know when you will return?"

Dona bit her lip as she shook her head. "No, a week, perhaps? I will let you know."

She left the room and walked down the stairs, feeling like a prisoner being led to their death. How had she let this happen? She watched as her staff loaded the luggage in the car, and the driver opened the door for her. She climbed into the back seat, and laid her head back against the leather, preparing for the long drive to Rome. She didn't look back at her villa, resplendent now after its recent renovation. She wondered if she'd ever see it again, or if Rodrigo would hold her captive in Rome. A tear ran down her cheek as she quickly swiped it away, not wanting the driver to see her dismay. *"Shade, why did you forsake me? I could have loved you as much as she loves you."*

She let her mind drift as the car moved through the night, and she was eventually lulled into a light sleep. She woke when the car stopped suddenly, in front of the massive mansion that had been built by the Borgia's. The driver got out and opened her door, as the staff rushed from the mansion to unload her luggage and carry it inside. The butler greeted her and let her know she'd have the same room as before. She was at least grateful for that. She'd worried that Rodrigo may move her into his bedroom. She followed the butler into the mansion, through the long hallways, and up the curved staircase to her room. Her luggage was laid on the bed, and the same maid had been assigned to assist her. Dona stood silently as the maid unpacked, hanging her dresses in the wardrobe, and putting her things in the drawers. Before she departed, she reintroduced herself. "Perhaps you remember, my name is Giada. I have been assigned to serve you. Will there be anything else, mistress?"

Dona shook her head. "No, thank you."

As the maid closed the door, she replied. "I will let master know you have arrived."

***

Giada informed Rodrigo that Donatella had arrived and was in her designated room. He smiled and nodded. "As before, Giada, tell me anything you hear from her. I want to know everything she does and says to you. You are dismissed."

He checked himself once more in the floor-length mirror before making his way down the long hallway to her room. He grinned to himself. She wouldn't be spending much time in there. He found that her door was shut, and he didn't bother to knock before he entered. It was his palazzo and he'd do as he pleased. She looked up in surprise when he entered unannounced, and as he approached her, he thought she looked rather forlorn.

"My pet, you have finally arrived. You do look a bit grim. Did you not enjoy the trip here?" He kissed her as if they had been together for years.

She allowed his show of affection, trying hard not to show her revulsion. "It is a long drive, Rodrigo. Perhaps I should rest a bit, and maybe a bath? I know it will be light soon, and you will be drawn to your slumber."

He smiled but he wasn't happy with her response. "Of course, Donatella, it is a long drive. I can't say I'm not disappointed as I have been looking forward to your visit." He kissed her cheek softly. "You would smell so lovely bathed in the most luxurious bath products I have supplied for you. Perhaps you would allow me to wash your beautiful hair. I can assist you. Then we can have some time alone, just the two of us."

This wasn't the answer Dona had hoped for. She thought he'd leave her, but now he wanted to bathe her! "That is most kind of you to offer. But I'm sure you have much more important matters to tend to. Surely, Giada could help with my bath."

Releasing a low growl, he ran his hand through her raven-black hair and gripped its silky strands into a fist. "You play such tempting little games, my pet." He chuckled low and released the grip on her hair. Strolling casually around her in a circle, his eyes bored into her. Standing before her, he roughly gripped her breast and squeezed lightly. "Do not continue to temp me, Dona, for I will only play this game for so long. You rile my blood and my beast." He bent his head forward, as his long tongue slowly licked the ample cleavage exposed by her dress. Sliding his hands up to her shoulders, he pulled the garment free and watched as it dropped to the floor, exposing even more of her breasts, cupped in a black lace bra. His breathing increased and his body ached to fuck her until she was unconscious. "Take it off for me, pet, let me see the temptations you hold from me."

Dona swallowed hard. She couldn't play his game. She couldn't find it in herself to play seductress for him. She knew what was coming, and steeled herself to get through it, as she reached behind her back and unhooked the bra, letting it drop to the floor. She fought the urge to cover her breasts with her hands, knowing it would anger him.

He stepped back and stared at her. She was stunning, even more than he'd anticipated. He licked his lips slowly. "*Grazie*, my pet, you are so beautiful. It has been a long time since any male has admired your treasures."

He delicately took her hand and helped her step from the dress as it lay in a puddle at her ankles. Walking her to the huge mirror framed in gilded gold, he stood behind her, as he slowly fondled her breasts, rubbing the nipples to hardness. "Look at how beautiful and tempting you are, my pet. Look at how we will look together, the master and his beautiful toy." His voice became stern as he noticed her eyes were closed to the reflection in the mirror. "Look! What do you see? Is it not what I see?"

She opened her eyes and stared at their reflection, his hands cupping her breasts. Her body betrayed her as her nipples hardened at his touch. "I see a powerful master and an unworthy mistress. You can have anyone you choose, Rodrigo. I am humbled." She dared not enrage him. His reputation for brutality was well known. Dona had been with enough masters to know, when faced with their dominance, it was best to play submissive.

"Ah, *si*, my pet, I *could* be with anyone, but I have chosen you. I am happy that you are humbled, and you remember to whom you speak. It is important that a female always knows her place."

He dropped his hands and walked away from her as if she was suddenly nothing. He wouldn't force her yet, but he did love to torment her. Her breathing revealed more fear than passion, and Rodrigo found that even more enticing. He poured them both a glass of Midnight and returned to her where she stood. Handing her the glass, he smiled. "Do not play the innocent with me, Donatella, your reputation precedes you. You are known to be a devilish dish in the bedroom."

He raised his glass to her and drank the Midnight straight down. Walking to the door, he spun on his heels. "Tonight, I shall let you rest, my pet. We will have many nights to entertain each other in many fashions. I will send Giada back to you. I suggest you rest well." He walked out, closing the door firmly behind him. His wicked laughter could be heard throughout the floor of the palazzo as he made his way back to his room.

Dona sobbed as she listened to his laughter echo in the hallway. Giada entered, ignoring her distress, as she made her way to the bathroom, and started running the hot water in the tub, filling it with the expensive oils. "Your bath is ready, *mistress*."

54

Sophia stood at the window and sighed. Lorenzo had ordered them all on lockdown and she was getting antsy cooped up in the villa. She remained in touch with Luciano, overseeing all the vineyards, but missed the day-to-day activity of running the business. Nicola had taken up residence inside their home whenever Alfie was out, and she'd noticed the animals that bonded to her; the wolves, the lynx, and the eagles had all remained close to home. She felt perfectly safe here, which made the lockdown harder to cope with. They'd seen no evidence of the Borgia warriors trying to infiltrate Tuscany, and certainly none close to the camp. Alfie had been at camp longer, and spending more time with her brother, as they remained vigilant, and developed plans for every contingency. The lynx saw her at the window and crept forward, curling up in the shrubbery just outside. She turned away from the window and searched the bookshelves for another book. Hardbound books were rare, and many of these came from the larger library at Castello. She pulled a book on vampire mythology from the shelf. She and Natalia used to read this book when they were children and laugh at how the mortals viewed their species. She curled up in a chair to read when Bianca entered the room.

***

Bianca was bored. She'd been restricted to the villa now for weeks. She knew her mother was feeling the same, but she rarely complained. Her father was never home, and when he was, he was exhausted or continued to work in his office with the door closed, his signal that he didn't want to be disturbed. Bianca couldn't remember the last time they were all together, laughing and talking, or going out to shop, or even visiting her aunt and uncle at Castello. She missed visiting with little Grace. Other than her pet kittens, she was finding it hard to amuse herself. Deciding to seek out her mother, she roamed the house and found her in the library, reading. "Is Daddy ever coming home to be with us? I'm so tired of being penned up. Why don't they do something?"

Sophia folded the book cover into the pages of her book and looked up when her daughter entered. "Bianca, you've never lived through a battle for territories. We hope the Borgia do nothing, not something. I know you're bored, we're both bored. I'm sure Nicola would prefer that we were free to leave as well. He's a warrior, like your father, yet he must remain here, cooped up with us. Your father will be glad when this is all behind us as well. Come, sit down, and tell me about this young man you're so interested in. And don't pretend I haven't noticed."

Bianca flopped down on the sofa beside her mother and sighed heavily. "Momma, he's probably forgotten about me by now, it's been so long since I've seen him. I hate it. And for once, I think I've found someone who really likes me." She ran her fingers through her long red hair, the same shade as her mother's. "Not that it matters. Papa Bear won't like him, he won't be old enough, or from the right coven, or any of the other excuses. And Daddy doesn't seem to notice at all. He just smiles whenever I want to talk about it. How did you put up with that when you were at Bel Rosso?"

Sophia laughed as she set the book aside. "Daughter, haven't you figured out it's the duty of the patriarch to scare off any suitors? In your father's eyes and your grandfather's, no male will ever be good enough for you. They'll have a lot to live up to. And this boy...this man, you have your eye on, Amondo... he's a Farnese, Italian, and that's good, at least as far as your grandfather is concerned. The Farnese coven in Sicily has always been an ally to Medici, so he'll get a pass on that. He's royal blood, and a warrior, but that doesn't mean he won't have to prove himself to your father and your grandfather. He'll inherit the crown of king someday, and rule Sicily. He's a good match, Bianca. You danced with him all night at his sister's wedding in Sicily. He couldn't take his eyes off of you. If you like him, if you feel drawn to him, I'll support you."

Bianca blushed and kissed her mother's cheek. "I'm glad you like him, Momma, he's handsome but also smart and funny, and really kind." Sighing, she flopped back on the sofa. "He adores Uncle Lorenzo and Papa Bear. He talked about being a warrior all night, and how much he admires the Medici warriors. He has called me several times, but I swear, all this Borgia uproar even has the Farnese warriors on edge. So, he's been busy as well. What's a girl to do in these situations? Do you think Daddy would let me go to Bel Rosso and stay with Papa Bear and Bebe? I mean, I'd be safe there. At least I could leave the house."

Sophia shook her head. "You're moving too fast. You better get your father's approval before taking off with some male to visit Papa Bear! When all this business with the Borgia is behind us, perhaps we'll invite him here, so your father can get to know him better. Then, I'm sure he wouldn't mind if you visit Papa Bear. In fact, he and Lorenzo would insist on it."

Bianca laughed out loud. "Momma! I didn't mean to take Amondo with me to Bel Rosso. Papa Bear would eat him alive! I just meant me." She stood from the sofa and walked to the window. She could see the wolves close to the house. "The animals are restless, Momma. I can feel them, and it frightens me. I'm not blind; I see the extra warriors on guard around the villa. Nicola is always close at hand. I practically bump into him. I'm scared for Daddy. I know he's a great warrior, but I'd never admit to him I'm scared. We will be fine, won't we?"

Sophia bit her lip. She didn't really know the answer to that question, but she answered with confidence. "The Medici always prevail in battle, Bianca. We have paid for it heavily sometimes, but we have always prevailed, always emerged the victor. Besides, there may not be a battle. Your grandfather has insisted we won't make the first move. He'll force the Borgia to bring the battle to us. A battle of this magnitude would take a massive toll on both sides, regardless of who wins. Your father thinks it may not be a risk the Borgia are willing to take. Let's hope he's right, yes?"

***

Alfie was leaving the camp and heading home. Lorenzo had insisted he take the rest of the night off. Both of them had been working nonstop lately. As he entered the house, he picked up the tail end of Bianca's conversation and heard she was scared for him. Heading to the library, he stood back and listened carefully as Sophia answered their daughter, and he smiled. Sophia was so much like her mother in many ways. Kate never let her doubts or fears be known but was always positive.

Bianca looked up to see her father and grinned from ear to ear. "Daddy! Please tell me you're staying home tonight. I miss you so much!"

Alfie smiled as she gave him a huge hug, and he held her tight in his arms. "*Si*, I am home for the night. And I don't want you to worry about the Borgia, we are simply taking precautions. It's standard protocol, okay? We're all fine, and we will remain so. But I need to talk to your mother a minute. Could you give us some privacy?" He held up his hand when he saw she was about to protest. "A few minutes please, Bianca, then you'll have my undivided attention, I promise."

Bianca grinned, happy to have him home. "Well, I intend to make you keep that promise, Daddy. Besides, I have some things to tell you." She wiggled her eyebrows and kissed his cheek before leaving the room.

Alfie shook his head as she left the room, and he turned his attention to his mate. "So, our daughter is scared for me. What about you, Red?"

Sophia laughed. "I'm scared for the person who stands in your way, especially when you stand side by side with my brother."

She stood up to greet him, accepting his warm hug. "I'm glad you're home. You've worked too hard lately. I was about to complain to Lorenzo. So, what's on your mind that you needed to send our daughter out of the room?"

"I asked Lorenzo about assigning a protector to Jules. I picked Tristan, he's a good warrior, and he was eager for a new assignment. Jules is fine with it. He didn't seem to mind in the least."

Sophia nodded. "Jules told me about his protector. They get along well, and I told him I thought it was a good idea."

He kissed her, and she laid her head on his chest. She felt so good in his arms. "There's something else that's happened. But I'm sure Kate's already told you."

Sophia looked up at him. "Something happened? Is it Jules?"

Alfie was shocked, he was sure Kate or Lorenzo would have told her about the dream-walk. "Jules is fine. It was your father. Soren Borgia went dream-walking with Shade. It was pretty ugly, from what I understand. Soren created a battle that wiped out the Medici, and your father wasn't able to block him. It left him drained, and in much pain, apparently. Luca called to tell us, but he's all right." He took her face into his hands. "Red, we don't know what Soren will do. You need to tell me if he tries anything with you or Bianca. His powers are strong."

Sophia looked confused. She couldn't imagine anyone getting the upper hand with her father. "You think Soren would try to dream-walk in my head? I'm not a warrior. Do you think it's because of my gift? Does he understand I could send my warriors any time I please? That Bianca, and my mother, the three of us have the power to wipe him from the face of this earth, and never leave our homes? The Borgia better remember who they're up against, Alfie. I wasn't born warrior, but I was born Medici."

Alfie burst out laughing. "I pity that bastard if he attempts anything with my Red. And I suppose if he pulls this bullshit with me, my Medici woman will come save me and kick his ass!"

He loved when her temper flared. She was still his fiery red, and he loved her with abandon. "Now, come take a shower with me. I'm starving for you, and I doubt we'll have much time before Bianca holds me to my promise."

55

Dona woke from a fitful sleep, despite the comfortable bed and being surrounded by luxurious linens. She knew Rodrigo would be waking from his death slumber soon. She'd taken a long bath before sleeping, and Giada had massaged her shoulders, helping her relax. Giada had tried to engage her in a conversation, asking her if she found her master handsome, but Dona had been careful with her answers. She had no doubts Giada would have been ordered to report back to Rodrigo the content of their conversations. Giada had helped her into bed and pulled the heavy drapes over the windows to block out the daylight, but Dona found her dreams had been troubled, and she woke often.

As she sat up in the large bed, Giada appeared on cue, and Dona wondered if he had cameras in her room, filming her. "Mistress, may I help you dress this evening? Master usually begins the night in the parlor, with a glass of Red Moon and a cigar."

Dona reluctantly slid her legs from under the sheets, and Giada was there to place the slippers on her feet. "Would you like me to pick out a dress for you, mistress?"

Dona nodded. She could care less what she was wearing. Giada went to her closet and selected a dress Dona had never seen before. It wasn't among the things she'd packed. "That's not my dress."

"*Si*, it is. Master purchased some things in anticipation of your visit. I think he would be pleased to see you wearing it."

Dona sighed heavily, giving herself over to the process. She allowed the maid to rub a silky lotion on her bronze skin, making her skin glow and then spritzing her with an expensive perfume. She laid out black lace underthings Dona noticed were also not from the items she'd packed. She put on the garments, feeling like a sacrifice being prepared as an offering to the gods. Giada slid the slinky black dress over her head. There was nothing subtle about the dress, it emphasized her curves, cinching in at the waist, and clinging to her hips. The dress was cut low in the front, displaying her ample cleavage, and even lower in the back. Giada removed a pair of strappy stilettos from a new shoe box and fitted them on Dona's feet. Leading her to the vanity table, Dona sat down while Giada applied her makeup, using dark black kohl to outline her eyes and a deep red lipstick. The maid brushed her hair to a high sheen and ran her fingers through her lush, thick locks.

"Master will want your hair down."

Dona stared blankly at the reflection in the mirror and answered with a bit of sarcasm. "Well, we would not want to displease master."

Giada gave her thick hair a sharp tug. "I suggest you not, my lady. I can tell you I have been with him a long time, and those who displease him do not fare well. My master has been most generous with you. Be sure to show your gratitude."

Dona was startled when she was dressed down by a servant, but then again, it only emphasized she had no power here, not even over the house staff.

Giada stepped back with a smile as if the confrontation had never happened, "There, you look beautiful for master. Are you ready?"

Dona was thinking, *Do I have any choice?* She kept her thoughts to herself. "Of course, lead the way."

***

Rodrigo waited for Giada to deliver his newest pet to the parlor, where Soren had joined him. Rodrigo was pleased his brother made some effort at making himself presentable for their guest tonight. Rodrigo, on the other hand, had dressed elegantly and was puffing casually on a cigar, a glass of Red Moon in his hand. He'd informed Giada of his preferences and had faith she'd deliver what he requested.

Soren sighed and paced slowly around the room. "Why the hell do you wait patiently for her? If she were here as my guest, I would have woken her my way."

Rodrigo gave him a look. "There you go, brother, no patience. Females need time to prepare. They feel more confident in themselves, and it also gives her time to think of what waits for her." He chuckled. "And in the Alizzi's case, what awaits her is not pleasant. I prefer she be on edge. It amuses me to feel her heart race with fear. It riles my beast. Now, keep a civil tongue in your mouth when she arrives, and do not linger long."

He could hear the clicking of her heels as she approached the parlor, and Rodrigo stood to greet her, as Soren stepped up beside him.

Soren chuckled. "Like a lamb to the slaughter." He plastered a wicked grin to his face as Giada left Donatella at the parlor door.

Rodrigo made eye contact with Dona, holding her gaze for a full minute before approaching her. She looked delicious in the dress he'd requested, as it emphasized her curves. Walking to her, he bowed slightly. "My dearest, please join us for a drink and some conversation. You look quite ravishing, and I am most pleased."

He took her hand and led her to a velvet chair. Soren appeared before her with a glass of Red Moon, the wicked grin still plastered to his face. He bent low to hand it to her, his face close to hers. "Welcome back, Mistress Alizzi, please drink up, there is more where that came from."

Rodrigo cleared his throat. "Soren, my brother, please bring me some drink."

As Soren refilled his glass, the two brothers raised their glasses to Dona. Rodrigo smiled at her as if he could eat her alive given the smallest provocation. "To the Alizzi!"

Dona lifted her glass, accepting their toast, as she sat on the edge of her seat.

The men downed their drinks and took their seats across from her, as Rodrigo addressed her solicitously. "I do hope, my pet, your sleep was a comforting one. I found my death slumber was most refreshing."

Dona took a generous swallow from her glass and allowed the wine to soothe her jangled nerves. "The accommodations are excellent, Rodrigo. I could not ask for anything more." She wouldn't tell him her sleep was fitful. He'd only take pleasure in it.

"As it should be, we provide only the best accommodations. You seem on edge, Dona. You must understand, nothing will harm you here. You are well protected inside these walls. Let me offer you something that perhaps will energize you more. I find the Red Moon can be lacking when it comes to satisfying the true hunger of a vampire." He looked to Soren and nodded.

Soren opened an elaborate antique cabinet and removed the case inside. Unlocking the case, he removed a crystal decanter. Holding it with both hands he walked toward the Alizzi, a smile on his face. "Blood of a half-breed, the best cure for your hunger."

Rodrigo sat back and watched her face. She looked as if she might faint. He chuckled. "Soren, mind your manners and pour my pet a glassful."

Soren did as he was told, artfully pouring the blood into a wine glass, careful not to spill a drop. He poured himself a glass as well. He carried the glasses to her and handed her one. "The blood is sweet and clean, freshly drained, just for your visit, mistress."

He laughed out loud and tilted the goblet to his mouth, draining it, before licking the inside of the glass with his long tongue.

Dona watched him in horror as he drank down the blood. "So, not from a feeder?"

Dona had been raised on feeders and had never been trained to hunt. She wasn't a warrior, and her father thought it improper. She'd fed from both immortal and mortal males, but never a half-breed. "This is the blood of a half-breed?"

Rodrigo laughed at her innocent questions. "My dear pet, you look as if you have seen a ghost! Of course, it is half-breed blood, still warm. It is my preference. I do not hunt often. They either come willingly to the Borgia, or my warriors see to my needs. Soren, of course, prefers to find his own enjoyments."

He knelt before her, taking the glass from her hand, and holding it to her mouth. "Come, taste, my pet. It will energize you for our night together. Or did you wish to feed from a live one? That can easily be arranged."

Dona was horrified! *Feed from a live half-breed? One that is not willing?* She couldn't imagine it. "No, this is fine. I will drink this." She tipped the glass to her lips and drank. The taste of the half-breed's blood was very different from both the mortals and immortals. She could understand the attraction some vampires had for the half-breeds. Still, she feared this half-breed was no longer alive and didn't offer up their blood willingly. She emptied the glass and handed it back to him. "Thank you."

Soren took the glass, winking at her. "I shall leave you two alone. Enjoy all the pleasures of the Borgia palace, mistress." He chuckled loudly as he strolled from the room.

Rodrigo leaned forward and kissed her, licking her lips, a small taste of the half-breed's blood still lingering. "You look so enchanting. I do hope you will avail yourself to the pleasure of Borgia Palazzo. Perhaps our ways seem strange to you, but I am sure you will adapt easily. I want you to accustom yourself to our ways, learn what I like, better for you to please me, *si*?"

Dona stared back at him wide-eyed. *Open to his ways? What are his ways? What other things will he want me to become accustomed to?* "Yes, of course, Rodrigo. You know, I can only stay a short while. The villa, the renovations, there is so much to be done. Taking this break is a wonderful diversion from it all, don't get me wrong. And your palazzo, it rivals every castle, every mansion I have ever seen. I am pleased to be a guest here, but I will need to return home soon."

He stood abruptly and yanked her from her seat, pulling her tight against his body. "You have just arrived. You will leave when I decide for you to leave, and not before, my pet. I expect you to stay and enjoy the comforts and pleasures my hospitality holds. I will accept nothing less. Your title does not give you *carte blanche* to come and go as you wish. You will not make me look like some fool who can't hold your attention or your passions."

He cradled her head in both hands and kissed her hard, his tongue pushing deep inside her mouth, demanding control of her. His hands explored, cupping her breasts roughly, squeezing hard, to the point of pain. His cock ached for her, and if she thought she could walk out on her own accord, she had best think again. He lifted her off her feet as music began to play. It was a waltz and sounded incongruent with the times. The lights were dimmed as the candles lit up in every corner of the room. He began the dance, the smooth swaying motion of the waltz, as he gripped her tightly against him. His hips were pressed hard against her, his cock thick and bulging against the fabric of his satin pants. His fangs punched, and he licked them slowly. "You enchant me, my pet, everything about you. I want this visit to be pleasurable for us both. Do as I ask, and you will enjoy everything I have to offer you."

She looked back at him as he danced with her around the room, her feet barely touching the floor, as she tried to keep the fear from her eyes. "I didn't mean to upset you, Rodrigo. Of course, I will stay." She scanned her brain for someone she could call out to but realized there was no one. She had burned her bridges, and there was no one who would come to her rescue now.

He felt her fear and it only whetted his appetite for more. She was intimidated and knew he was in complete control. Still, he wasn't ready to force her. He was hoping she'd come to him willingly. "I did not mean to frighten you, but you are in my home, and I rule here, with all things. Relax. I mean you no harm. But you are with me now, and it excites my blood to have you so close to me."

After a few songs, the music stopped, and he took her hand and walked toward the gardens. He explained the history and layout of the elaborate and intricate designs of the formal gardens. As they approached a stone bench, he offered her a seat and sat by her side. "Tomorrow evening, I wish to take you riding. Giada will see you are dressed appropriately. I can show you more of the property. Besides, I know you were quite the horse-woman in your day."

"That would be lovely, Rodrigo. It has been a long time since I have been riding. Please choose a horse that is not too spirited for me. It will take me some time to regain my skills."

"I have already chosen for you, my pet. You are quite safe with this one. And I will be with you. My warriors will ride at a distance from us, giving us privacy but protection. You will be surprised at how quickly your skills will come back to you. It is much like making passionate love, once you straddle a stallion, you remember quickly how to bring it to your ways, *si*?"

Laughing loudly, he stood and took her hand. "Come, it is chilly, and you have no shawl. I do not wish for you to take a chill."

They walked back to the palazzo, where he escorted her back to her room. It was still early, but he liked he'd leave her alone to wonder about what might lie ahead. "I will have Giada come to you now. Enjoy the evening, my pet. If you wish my company, Giada will bring you to me. My door is always open to you." He kissed her softly, and turned on his heels, walking away. He could feel her eyes staring at his back.

Dona wasn't sure which she preferred, this endless torture to what she knew was inevitable, or just having sex with him and getting it over with. She had no illusions as to his intentions. This man didn't love her, she was just another toy in a very long list of toys, and he'd quickly grow tired of her and move on... and the sooner, the better.

56

Natalia had been upset ever since she spoke with her mother and learned about the dream-walking incident. Her mother had reassured her everything was fine, but Natalia knew her mother too well. She always found the silver lining, and never wanted her children to worry. She stepped from the shower, dried her hair, and put on her lacy undergarments. It was the only thing feminine about her wardrobe, and Marcello was the only one who knew what lay hidden under her robe. It was one of the many secrets they shared. She was sliding the robe over her head when she heard his key in the lock, and he slipped into her private quarters.

"Nattie?"

"I'm in here," she answered as she stepped from the bathroom into her bedroom.

He smiled at her as she entered the room but lost the smile quickly when he saw the expression of concern on her face. "What's wrong? And don't tell me 'nothing'. You wear your emotions on your sleeve."

She gave him a half-smile. They'd been together a long time, and he could read her like a book. She loved their bond, and how easily they fit together. He'd been such an unexpected blessing in her life. She loved her work and knew she was making a difference. She didn't want the domesticated life her mother and sister led, but she was grateful, every day, for Marcello's love. "Well, according to my mom, it's nothing to worry about, but Soren Borgia dream-walked on my dad. She was being evasive, not giving me too many details, and trying to reassure me. She wanted me to know in case I heard about it through another source. I'm not so sure, though. I mean, why would Soren dream-walk with my dad unless it was to weaken him? Do you think you could talk to Luca? The two of you are close. He'd tell you what was going on."

Marcello wasn't sure how much he wanted to tell her. Natalia was strong, but he still worried about her, and always would. She was a dream-walker as well, but he knew, for sure, she'd never used her gift for evil. "Natalia, come lay down with me, let's talk. I have already spoken to Luca."

He lay on the bed and held out his hand to her. She curled up next to him, and she smelled of soap and water, clean from her shower. "You're right about your mom. She won't tell you anything she thinks may worry you. She protects us all, and especially her children. Luca said your father was caught off guard. Your father is like you, in that he rarely uses his gift for evil. I'm aware he's used it a few times to manipulate a situation, but it's rare. He'll be better prepared if it should happen again, and Luca has reminded him he can pull any of us into his head to help. Your father was left drained by the event, but right now, I think he's fine. I'm more concerned about you. It's my job to protect you, Nattie. Dream-walking is a very draining experience. You know how you get headaches when you get a vision? The pain from a negative dream-walking experience is much greater. The dreams are meant to leave the victim with doubt, to plague the mind. They linger, and work on the victim's psyche."

Natalia bit her lip. She wasn't born a warrior and had never used her skills of dream-walking to inflict pain and doubt. She'd read everything available in the Council archives about her gift, and knew it had the power to severely weaken an enemy. "So, I hear you saying two things to me. The first being, my father suffered more than my mother wanted me to know, but I also hear concern Soren might attempt to dream-walk in my head. Why would he do that? I represent no threat to him."

He pulled her close and stared into her eyes. Marcello knew he could never have her fully as a mate, it wasn't allowed. If their situations were different, had she not been born to Council, she would be his in every way possible. "You're Medici, and that is all Borgia needs. If Rodrigo and Soren think they can get to your father through his children, they will try anything. Soren showed Shade a battle where the Borgia emerged as the victors, and there was much bloodshed, destruction. It leads us to believe only one thing, they plan on coming for us, and when they do, they plan to take down the coven."

She shook her head. "A dream-walk is not a forecast of the outcome. Soren may be a dream-walker, but he doesn't have the Third Eye, like me. He doesn't know the outcome of any battle. He puts those dreams in my father's head to create doubt. But my father knows this. The Borgia may be planning something, but I've seen nothing of this battle. Perhaps I'll call Malachi. Maybe he's seen something. In the meantime, what should I do? If Soren decides to dream-walk in my head, I can't stop him."

He'd thought about this as soon as Luca had informed him of what had happened to Shade. "You pull me into the dream, and call on your father, on Luca, on every damn Medici warrior you know. We can take him out. Your father was caught off-guard, but you are forewarned. Don't forget, you are a dream-walker too. You have the power to shape the dream as well if you don't let him get the upper hand. Stand up to him, Natalia, it is but a dream-walk. I know you aren't a warrior, but you're intelligent, you could easily outwit him. In your dream, you can transform yourself into a warrior, with an army behind you." He kissed her softly. "He may never come. It would be foolish of Soren to attack Council, but if he does, pull me in, pull us all in."

Natalia was comforted to know she called to pull the other warriors into her dream to combat Soren. She may not be a warrior, but her gifts were unique, and she was strong. She didn't fear an encounter with Soren. "I'll call upon you, and all the Medici warriors, if he attempts to get in my head. I don't fear the dream-walking. If Malachi had seen something, he would have told me. Still, I think I will give him an update on what's happening here. The visions we see are not clear. Their meaning must be interpreted, so having a base of knowledge about what's going on would impact how he'd interpret any visions he might have, with regard to a battle between covens." She lay quietly beside him, listening to the sound of his breathing, comforted by his nearness. In the safety of this fortress, it seemed impossible to imagine a serious threat to their way of life. "Are you concerned, Marcello? Do you fear for the Medici?"

He hugged her tight. He'd never had to hide his thoughts from her. She was the daughter of one of the greatest warriors of their culture, and she understood warriors. "I was born to ignore my fear, to confront fear with my strength, my courage, and my convictions. I was born with skills that were perfected in the warrior camp and trained to fight to the death. I will still lay down my life for Medici, and so will every warrior under his command. That is why we always win. There is no other coven that has warriors as committed as the Medici. I can't tell you a battle with the Borgia will not cost us. You would know that's a lie. But I believe in my heart the Medici will prevail."

Natalia nodded, her head against his chest. "I feel strong in my heart. My father has spent his life defending what is his. He and my mother have gifts that have been shared with their children and grandchildren, which will give us advantages in any battle. I don't fear the Borgia, Marcello. I may not be warrior, but I know what my father teaches; fear is the first step to failure, and we will not fear the Borgia."

57

Rodrigo sat across from her, watching her sip slowly at the refreshing Midnight. They had spent the night hours riding on his vast estate. He admired her riding skills and gave her the grand tour of his property surrounding the palazzo grounds. He enjoyed watching her ride, sitting astride the saddle, her back straight, and her long hair blowing in the night breeze. He could tell she enjoyed the experience of riding again and didn't miss the ease of her smile as she accompanied him. Her attitude was much lighter this evening, and she didn't seem to begrudge his company, but he knew it was simply the freedom of riding.

He went to her and took the crystal wine glass from her hand, setting it carefully on the table. Sitting next to her, he laid his hand on her thigh. Her tight riding pants accentuated her fit body and voluptuous curves. Squeezing her thigh, he smiled at her. "I do hope you enjoyed the evening, my pet. I always find riding helps to re-energize me and clears my head."

Dona was a bit leery of his hand on her thigh, but she tried not to squirm. She'd been keeping her eye on the sky and knew it was almost sunrise, and he'd be going to his death slumber soon. So far, he hadn't suggested she join him, and she thought maybe he even preferred it that way. She had noticed Soren had numerous women shuttled in and out of the palazzo, but none of them ever stayed to join him in his slumber. "It was a beautiful way to spend the night, Rodrigo. It has been years since I've been riding. And you picked the perfect horse for me. She has such a wonderful disposition, not at all skittish."

He inhaled deeply, she smelled of the clean night air. Moving his hand from her thigh, he placed it around her shoulders as his hand toyed with her hair, twirling it through his fingers. "Ah, you are a marvelous rider. Your skills are just a little rusty. You will regain them in no time. You are such a beauty, and you look so regal mounted on that steed."

He lowered his face and snuggled into her neck, inhaling her scent again. "The outdoors suits you. You smell like the sun and the moon. A perfect match for me, for I can never feel the sunlight on my skin."

The majordomo appeared at the door, clearing his throat, and apologizing for the interruption before announcing Tomas was waiting for him in his study. Rodrigo growled low in his throat, having forgotten his appointment, and hating to see this evening end with Dona.

"I apologize, my pet, but business beckons me. You have such a great effect on this vampire. I got lost in your beauty and completely forgot my meeting." He stood and took her hand, helping her to her feet. "Are you able to find your room, or shall I have someone escort you?" He pulled her body into his, holding her close.

She was relieved to have the interruption. "I am fine, Rodrigo. Do not worry about me. I can make my way back to my room. I am tired, and I am sure you are as well. You will need your slumber. I will see you when you wake."

He kissed her with authority before releasing her from his grip. "I shall wait for that moment, my pet. Now, run along. It is bath and sleep for you, and I will see you at sunset." He walked with her to the stairs and then made his way to his study, leaving her on her own.

Dona sighed with relief and watched his back as he made his way down the hall. She turned and started up the stairs, leaving the wing that belonged to Rodrigo, on her way to the wing reserved for guests, when she heard voices. She slowed her pace as she neared an open door she hadn't noticed before. The door was surrounded by heavy brocade velvet drapes, and Dona realized the drapes were usually closed when she passed. She had assumed it was a window and not a door. She recognized Soren's voice and was afraid to pass in front of the door. She slipped behind the velvet drapes and pressed her back against the wall. She was distrustful of Rodrigo, but she feared Soren. She'd do most anything not to draw his attention. She remained still, barely drawing a breath, and could hear him issuing orders to one of the Borgia warriors, and what she heard made her blood run cold.

Soren faced his warrior, one of an elite group whose sole task was to find half-breeds and bring them to the Borgia palazzo. Soren had his own, personal playroom, located in the bowels of the palazzo, where he held the half-breeds, caged like animals until he was ready to play. "Bring the half-breed in and scout out the other mother with the small child. Pay whatever she wants. It usually doesn't take much. They are eager to get rid of the half-breeds. As before, drill her to find out if she knows of others. The more we steal from the Council the better."

He paced slowly in a circle, his energy building in anticipation of fresh bodies. It never changed for Soren, there was always a rush associated with knowing they were being held captive for him, and he fed off their fear. "Make sure the new one is secured before you leave. I will be down soon. I need to have a small snack before my slumber. Leave me!"

Dona held her breath as the warrior exited the room, and she could hear the sound of his heavy boots as he walked away. She bit her lip and closed her eyes tightly. She had no idea if Soren would leave the room now, but if she left her hiding space, she must cross in front of the open door to get to her room. She was contemplating whether to come out from behind the heavy drapes and head back to Rodrigo's wing when she heard Soren exit. She pushed her back hard against the wall, trying to flatten herself as much as possible, and dared not breathe.

Soren chuckled to himself as his warrior left the room. "The Council will never outwit me. I am Borgia, and I will have my half-breeds. If I can't snatch them from the streets, I will buy them!" He shouted his words out to no one, venting the sheer exhilaration he felt at having a fresh catch. He left the room and turned to go down the corridor when he stopped suddenly. He picked up the whiff of a clean, outdoors smell and his body tensed up. He smiled then, remembering the Alizzi was in residence and his brother had informed him they'd be riding tonight. He blew it off as her scent lingering in the corridor as she'd gone to her room for the night. He picked up the pace once again, bounding down the staircase to the lower floors.

Dona released her breath when she finally heard him depart. Peeking around the heavy drapes to make sure the hallway was empty. She darted from her hiding place and practically ran back to her room. Giada was waiting for her when she arrived.

"My lady, you seem flustered. Is everything all right?"

Dona nodded. "I just need a hot bath before I sleep. Could you get my bath ready, please?"

Giada assured her she'd have it ready as she left to draw her bath. Dona placed her hand on a chair to steady herself. *What did I just hear? That Soren has his warriors capture half-breeds?* She'd seen the new edict that had been issued from Council, stating half-breeds were to be left at the Council doorstep. *Is Soren having them stolen away before Council can find them? Is he buying them from their mothers before they can be turned over to Council? Is that where he found the blood she had shared with Soren and Rodrigo?* Dona had never met a half-breed that she was aware of, but she had lived among mortals her whole life. She knew the Council's code, to do no harm. It wasn't meant so much as protection for the mortals but protection for the vampires, so they didn't draw attention. Besides, she'd found the mortals to be a rather peaceful lot and had never encountered any problems with them. *Is Soren killing half-breeds for pleasure?*

Giada interrupted her thoughts. "My lady, your bath is ready."

Dona looked up, startled, having already forgotten her request for a bath. "What? Oh, yes, of course."

Giada looked at her with her brows furrowed. Dona brushed past her, undressing, and dropping her riding clothes to the floor as she sank into the hot water of her bath. She laid her head back against the tub, and closed her eyes, trying to relax her muscles, as she thought to herself, *Dona, what have you gotten yourself into?*

***

Soren made his way to the oldest part of Borgia palazzo, deep under the main floor. The atmosphere of the dungeon gave him almost as much pleasure as dream-walking. He was addicted to the blood of the half-breeds, and like any addict, he'd stop at nothing to get his high. Their blood held sweetness and an earthy tang that was unique on the tongue and always gave him a rush. He walked the stone pathway lit by oil lanterns on the walls. Not much had changed underground at the palazzo. He approached the huge arched wooden doors, where two of his warriors stood guarding it. They nodded and opened the doors for him. He walked inside and heard the doors close behind him. He stood a moment and breathed in, taking in the scent of fear, hanging thick in the air. He stepped into the dungeon that held the half-breeds and scanned the walls of the many tools and weapons of torture at his disposal. He puffed out his chest as he approached the cages holding the half-breeds, carefully stepping around the noose hanging from the vaulted ceiling and weaving his way around the tables for bloodletting. His heavy boots created an echo as he approached, his steps slow and purposeful. He smelled their fear increase as he walked through the dungeon, knowing who he was and why he was here. He loved their fear; he absorbed it like a lover. He approached one cage that held a female. She'd been caged for several days now. He crouched down on his haunches and cocked his head to the side, staring at her. She curled herself into a ball in the corner of the wire cage, shaking in fear, feeling helpless and naked. She didn't know if she'd be his choice tonight, or what her fate would be. It only made Soren breathe heavy with delight. He was the master of this dungeon. It was the one place he had complete and total control. He ran his fingers along the cage, and she jumped at his actions. His eyes were shining bright as he chuckled.

"I think I will keep you a bit longer."

He stood then and moved onward, hearing her sobs of relief as he moved past. He headed to the newest arrival, wanting to inspect his latest victim. As he made his way along the rows of cages, holding males and females of all ages, he'd stop and glare, feeding on their fear. Sometimes, he'd kick their cages as he walked past and laugh as they scurried to the back.

He found the newest cage that held a small child, perhaps only five. She was undernourished and had the face of a cherub. Her terror was evident as she wailed for her mother. If she only knew, her mortal mother had sold her child to the Borgia. Soren was intrigued with the little one. He reached into his pocket and pulled out a small treat and offered it to her through the cage. She quickly took it with her little fingers. Although she was scared, she had no idea of her purpose here. He opened the cage and reached out his hand.

"Do not be frightened, my little cherub, I shall take care of you. Come, we shall go play a game."

He led her from the cage, further into the depths of the dungeon. She'd do nicely for the evening as his thirst was beginning to give him an ache. He chuckled as the others remained silent, happy to have been spared another night.

58

Shade had left camp and taken Pavi out for a long ride alone. His mind was filled with so many thoughts, most of them concerning the Borgia. The pain from Soren's dream-walk had left him, but the images still lingered. There hadn't been a re-occurrence of the dream, and for that, he was thankful. As he rode the expansive acreage of Bel Rosso, he relaxed a bit. Pavi always had a way of helping him to center himself, allowing him to release his negative energy and get his mind straight. He ran the conversation with Luca over and over in his mind. He'd been out of sorts, and everyone knew it. His family and his warriors were unable to hide their concerns. There was only one person on Earth whose attention he wanted, who could soothe him when no one else could, and that was his *bel*.

Deep in his gut, he knew the battle with the Borgia was inevitable, and the more he thought about it, the more he understood he had to get his mind in a better place. As he approached the stables, he decided what he needed was time alone with her. They needed to get away for a while before things escalated and he had no time. He felt better now, having a plan. They'd get away and have some time together, without interruptions. He approached the stables and dismounted, handing Pavi off to Angelo, and headed back to the house. There were still a few hours before sunrise.

Strolling into the house, all was quiet, and the peaceful energy of their home surrounded him. Where the hell was she? He stood still and listened and heard her humming a song to herself. What was his woman up to now? He headed toward the sound, hoping to find her in a good mood as well.

***

Kate was cleaning out her closet, tossing aside articles of clothing she hadn't worn in a while. Shannon had cleaned out her things and was planning to have them taken into town to be donated, so Kate wanted to take advantage of the timing and clear out her own things as well. She was humming “Into the Mystic” to herself when she heard him enter their bedroom. "I'm in the closet," she called out to him.

As he entered the bedroom, he smiled as he recognized the song she was humming, and knew she was in a good mood. He made his way to the closet, finding clothes strewn in a pile on the floor. She had her hand on a red dress and he shook his head. "Don’t even think you are throwing that on this pile, woman. That dress hugs you like a glove and is one of my favorites." He folded his arms over his chest. "Are you having a good clear-out?"

She laughed as she placed the red dress back on the hanger and returned it to the rod. "I was until the supervisor showed up. How was your ride with Pavi?"

He reached across the pile of clothes between them and lifted her to his chest. "That is master, to you!" His hand slid up and down her back, before resting on her ass. Kissing her softly on the lips, he stared back at her. "I will tell you how my ride went if you promise not to have a field day in my closet without consulting me. I may not be able to find half of what I own, but I know what I like." His grin was huge as he stepped back out of the closet, both hands gripping her ass as she clung to him.

Kate giggled. "Lover, your wardrobe is unchanged, jeans, leathers, and black t-shirts. And you wear your jeans until they’re falling off of you. I wouldn't think of donating your things, and not sure who could use them unless our warriors shop at Goodwill."

He laughed and backed them up to the bed before flopping down, sitting on the edge as she settled on his lap. "I thought you liked my faded jeans!"

They laughed together and he loved that sound. He lay back on the bed, his leather-clad legs hanging over the side. Her crimson fell across his face and mingled with his black curls. "So, tell me, since you are having a good clear out, maybe we should go shopping to fill all the space left in that huge ass closet."

She loved his mood had improved with the ride. She’d felt a little hurt when he hadn’t asked her to join him but knew the dream-walk and the battle was heavy on his mind, and he needed time to sort things out on his own.

"We? Since when have you had an interest in shopping unless it's for weapons or cars?" She laughed with him, kissing his forehead as he lay beneath her.

"My ride with Pavi helped me sort some things out in my head, and I was thinking about taking a trip. I would prefer to have you all to myself, but with the battle on the horizon, I think it best I bring Luca. We need some time together, *mi amore*, just me and you. Let's sneak away." He wiggled his eyebrows at her. "You in?"

They hadn't taken a spontaneous trip in years. She couldn't even remember the last time. They both had so many responsibilities that getting away took a lot of planning, but she knew him like a book and knew he needed this escape. "Of course, I'm in. I'd like nothing better than to have you all to myself."

Snuggling into her neck, he moaned softly. "I want to go to Paris, *mi amore*. You love it there, and you are so happy there, *si*? We could shop, take some moonlight strolls. When was the last time we did the galleries?" He pushed her hair from her face. "I will inform Luca. He can bring Shannon if he wishes, but I am nervous about what Borgia might pull, and I am not taking any chances." He closed his eyes, there was nothing he'd like more than to be completely alone with her, and he hated having to take these precautions.

She softly kissed the lids of his closed eyes. "They have their own suite in the Paris house. We'll still be alone, and the trip will be good for all of us. Go talk to him, I'm sure they could use the time away as well. I'll start packing some things."

The softness of her lips against his closed lids melted his heart. She always knew what he needed, when to be soft and when he needed a bit more romp and roll. His eyes flashed open as she was getting ready to get up, and he rolled her over in a flash, so she lay beneath him. "No, you don't! I have a few hours yet before my slumber, and if you think, for one damn minute, I am wasting them talking to Luca and watching you pack, your ass will need a good hiding. You don't need to pack, no one needs to pack, that house is filled with enough clothes and shoes to outfit a small country. I have something else in mind."

Lifting her off the bed with ease, he flung her over his shoulder. "But first, a shower, I smell like Pavi. Tomorrow is soon enough to talk to Luca." Heading for the shower, he was damn sure everyone else in the house could hear her delightful giggles.

59

Dona slept fitfully, in fact, she really couldn't recall a single night since being here she'd slept well. All she could see in her head were images of half-breeds kept locked away in some dark dungeon as they awaited their fate. She drank their blood the evening the brothers had her join them for breakfast, and the blood was still warm. She didn't think about it at the time, but knowing what she knew now, it had to have been blood from a fresh kill. She was lying in bed, curled up in a ball, the covers pulled over her face. She was trying to think of some excuse for not getting up and joining Rodrigo and Soren for their 'breakfast'. She didn't think she could force down the drink now, knowing where it came from.

She heard Giada tap at her door before she opened it and entered. Giada never waited for her to say it was okay to enter, something her own maid would never consider doing. Dona stayed curled under the covers, as Giada approached and lightly shook her shoulder. "My lady, master waits for you in the parlor. You must get up now. I will get your clothes ready for you."

Dona reluctantly came out from under the covers and slid her feet to the floor. Giada looked at her with concern. "You look pale today, my lady. Do you wish for me to bring you a feeder later?"

Dona nodded her head. "Perhaps." *Yes, a feeder, anything besides drinking the blood of some poor slaughtered half-breed*! Giada helped her dress, as Dona stepped into her shoes. Once her make-up was on, and her hair was brushed, Giada took her elbow.

"Come now, my lady. Master does not like to be kept waiting."

Dona allowed herself to be led down the long hall to the wing that belonged to Rodrigo.

***

Rodrigo paced in the sitting room in his suite. Tomas had brought him news the night before and now he must be away on coven business for several nights. He was distraught he'd have to cut his visit with Dona short. Although he loved his brother, he didn't trust Soren to be left alone with her in the palace. Soren was willful and didn't always abide by Rodrigo's rules. His only solution was to send her back home.

Hearing the knock at the door, Giada left Dona inside the room. She looked drawn and a bit piqued. Her olive skin didn't glow as it normally did. She seemed tense, and her smile forced. "Come in, my pet, please, come sit down with me."

He carefully took her in his arms, kissing her soundly, as if it was their normal evening routine. He escorted her to the large sofa and his servant was instantly there with drinks for them both. "You look a bit drawn, my dear, did you not rest well? Drink up, it will have you feeling better in no time."

Dona reluctantly took the glass and sighed with relief when she saw it was filled with Midnight. "Thank you. I do think this will help." She took several deep swallows of the wine and felt it soothe her frazzled nerves. She closed her eyes as the sweet elixir calmed her system. Lifting the glass to her lips, she continued to sip more demurely.

Rodrigo noticed she gulped down the first few swallows of the Midnight. "I have summoned you early this evening for I must reluctantly inform you I have been called away. I must attend to some coven business I fear will keep me away for several nights. Leaving you without company would be extremely rude of me. Therefore, I have made arrangements for you to return to your home. I promise to make it up to you in the future, my pet. Are you upset with this news?"

It was all Dona could do to keep the smile from her face. "Oh, of course, I understand, Rodrigo. You manage such a large coven. I can't imagine the responsibility you must bear. It is no problem at all. I have a beautiful villa to return to, thanks to you, and there will be much to attend to there. You have been a most gracious host."

Cocking his head to the side, he smiled at her. "Not as gracious as I could have been, my pet. It seems the Midnight has given you a lift. Your color is improving already. I regret having to let you go so early, but these things can't be helped. Giada is, at this very moment, packing your bags. My driver waits at the main entrance to return you home. Would you like for me to assign a warrior to ride with you for your safety? I understand the Medici now has warriors along your border. Perhaps it would not be such a bad idea to have a show of my power, *si*?"

Dona looked back at him confused. The Medici would never harm her. They were his enemy, not hers. "I feel perfectly safe, Rodrigo, but thank you. I believe the appearance of the Medici warriors along my border has much more to do with your appearance in my life. I have never feared the Medici. I will be fine."

He knelt before her, grasping her chin tightly, pulling her face close, and his voice low and venomous. "You will be my good pet now while I am away? Do not make me assign a warrior to watch over you in your home." His grin reached from one ear to the other, his eyes dark and glaring. "I have a warrior who knows the Medici territory well. He was even trained by him during his early years. He would be perfect to protect and watch over you. Do nothing to make me force his presence, *si*?" He stood up then and reached for her hand, his mood instantly lightening. "Come along, my pet, I shall escort you to Giada and you shall be on your journey."

Dona was always caught off guard by his rapid mood changes, one minute scolding her, the next treating her like a treasured guest. He took her hand and helped lift her from the couch as he led her to the door. She quickly polished off the remaining Midnight in her glass and set the empty glass down on a table as he led her out the door and down the long corridor to the main foyer.

Giada was waiting at the door, assuring her that her things had been packed and loaded into the trunk of the car. Dona nodded and started to speak to her, but Rodrigo dragged her along, on his way to the waiting car. The driver stood with the door open, as Rodrigo helped her inside, in a hurry now to have her gone.

"Goodbye, Rodrigo. Thank you for your kind hospitality. I don't know how I can ever repay you for all you have done."

Kissing her hand, he smiled. "The day will come, my pet, when you will find a means to repay me. Until then, it is always such a delight to have your company. You are always welcome here." He closed the door of the car and watched as it drove away.

"Oh, you will find a way to repay me, Alizzi, more than you could ever imagine." He laughed as he retreated to his palazzo, one step closer to the destruction he planned on laying at the Medici's doorstep.

60

Kate pulled back the heavy drapes and opened the French doors onto the balcony to air out the house in Paris. It had been a long time since they had visited. There was staff that came in and cleaned regularly, but the house still had an air of stuffiness to it after having been closed up for so long. Luca and Shannon were getting settled in their private suite on the floor below. Kate stepped out on the balcony overlooking the Champs Elysees and listened to the sounds of the traffic and the voices of the people on the broad sidewalk below. She took a deep breath, as she looked out across the city she loved.

***

Shade had gone downstairs to speak with Luca, before returning to their suite of rooms on the third floor. He'd informed Luca he wanted no one to know of their whereabouts or when they'd be returning. He was to stay in contact with his SIC's, and if anything should come up, then let him know. Other than that, he wanted Luca and Shannon to enjoy the trip, just as he and his *bel* planned to do.

Making his way up to their suite, the house had been prepared for their arrival, and the fresh roses filled the house with their scent. Entering their bedroom, he saw her on the balcony, and he could feel her happiness over being here. He walked up behind her, wrapping his arms around her, his head on her shoulder, and a smile on his face. "This feels good already, alone with my *bel*, back in the city of love. We never seem to spend enough time here."

Kate leaned back against him, feeling the solid strength of him, and the protective cage of his arms around her. She smiled to herself. "We have so many memories of this place. I remember the first time I renovated and bringing the children here over the years. They loved playing in the courtyard. And this view...I could never tire of this view." The Eiffel Tower twinkled with lights in the distance. She already felt more relaxed. "This was a good idea. We needed to get away for a while."

He gave her a squeeze. "And I could never tire of you. Makes no difference where we are, as long as we are together. You are my reason to live and breathe, *mi amore*." Kissing her neck softly, he spun her in his arms and kissed her mouth, his tongue probing gently as his hands slid along her ass. "Anything specific you want to do while we are here?"

"Perhaps, visit the Louvre? I don't have anything in mind, really. I love just walking the streets, watching the people in the cafes. I am just happy to have your time, and not have to share you with a camp full of warriors. It isn't often I have your undivided attention."

"This is true. So, let's both make the most of it. Care to take a stroll with me, get a drink?" He slapped her ass lightly. "Let's stroll to the Pont de Arts, shall we? We haven't been there since Nattie was little."

She looked up at him. "I'd like that. I'd like it a lot. Let me change into flat shoes, and we can walk all night."

Stepping back inside the bedroom, she quickly kicked off the heels and found a pair of ballet flats in the closet. He grabbed her hand, and they ran down the stairs like giddy young lovers on their first visit to Paris. Shade yelled out, "We're out, Luca. Don't wait up!"

Once they hit the streets, they casually strolled the sidewalks, sharing smiles and glances at one another. They passed other couples who were behaving much the same. As they made their way to the Pont de Arts, Shade stopped suddenly and looked inside an old but quaint café. It housed a great restaurant, with an old-fashioned bar. "Do you know, *mi amore*, this is one of the finest cafes in this section of the city, and I have never been inside. Would you accompany me on a date tomorrow evening?"

She paused as he peered through the window. "What have I always told you? You lead, and I will follow." She really didn't care where they went, as long as they went together.

His grin was wide, and his eyes gleamed in the moonlight. "You have always followed, *mi amore*. Not once have you questioned our path."

They finally made their way to the Pont de Arts and crossed over the bridge. They both knew where their lock was located, engraved with their names, and bearing four small metal tags, one for each of their beloved children. They came here every time they came to Paris, as a reminder of their commitment to each other, made so long ago. Shade felt a greater urgency to share it with her this trip, knowing what might lay ahead for them.

"Here it is." He sorted through the mass of locks, finding theirs, and holding it in his hand. He felt her hand cover his own as he looked into her eyes. "*Ti amo*."

61

Dona was relieved to arrive back home and was greeted by Mario, who started to unload her luggage from the car. "My lady, we did not expect you."

Dona smiled back at him, "It was not planned, Mario. Something came up, and Rodrigo had to be away for a few days."

She entered the villa, to be greeted by Marie. "My lady, can I get you anything? We were not expecting your return. I can draw a bath for you."

Dona paused, she'd been thinking about the situation with the half-breeds during the car ride back from Rome. "Just bring me a Midnight, please. I need to make a call." Marie scurried off to pour her a glass of the thick wine, as Dona made her way to the library and the newly installed visi-phone. Marie returned with the drink, and Dona gratefully accepted it, taking a sip to calm her nerves. Walking to the screen mounted on the wall, she asked her maid, "How does this work again?"

Maria stepped forward, "You just touch the screen, or you can activate it with your voice. Shall I call up someone for you, my lady?"

Dona shook her head no. "I can do it but thank you. If you'll excuse me a moment?"

Marie nodded. "Of course, my lady."

As Marie exited the room, Dona stepped up to the screen and could see her reflection on the polished black surface. There were no buttons to push, and she assumed the darn thing was on. In a soft voice, hoping not to be overheard, she said, "Call Malachi at Council."

The screen came to life, and she could hear the soft ringing, followed by an image that appeared on the screen. "How may I help you?"

Dona stared back at the male whose face had appeared on the screen. "Is this the Council?"

The male nodded. "Yes, my lady. How may I help you?"

"I am Donatella Alizzi, and I wish to speak to Malachi."

"Yes, my lady, I know who you are. Hold on, please. I must find him." The male disappeared from the screen, and Dona paced as she continued to sip at the wine. She'd never called Council before and wasn't sure of the protocol. The minutes ticked by and seemed like hours, when the green-hooded figure appeared, his face partially obscured from view.

"Alizzi, this is an unexpected pleasure. How can Council be of service?"

Dona recognized the green robe. She couldn't recall the last time she'd seen Malachi and doubted she'd even recognize him if he weren't in the robe. She set down her glass and faced the screen, speaking in a soft voice. "Malachi, I am so sorry to disturb you, but I was hoping you could pay me a visit? I know it is not customary, but I'm afraid my activities are being monitored."

Malachi was aware of the situation playing out between the Alizzi and Rodrigo Borgia. The Council had been informed of the extensive renovations that had taken place at her villa, but he had the distinct impression from the circulating gossip that the Alizzi was more than happy to have the attention of the Borgia, even though this relationship had renewed the tension between the Borgia and the Medici covens.

"It is not typical for Council to leave our fortress, Alizzi. I must ask you provide me with more detail. Who is monitoring your activities?"

Dona looked down at her hands and twisted one of the new rings on her finger. "You are aware I was seeing Rodrigo?"

The hooded figure nodded. "I am, my lady. Council was informed of the generous renovations that have been made to your property."

Dona looked over her shoulder before responding to him. "Rodrigo's attentions are not exactly...I mean, he has been nothing but kind to me, I don't mean to imply...it is just, I mean, I did not seek out his attention..."

Malachi sighed. He had a busy schedule, and the Alizzi was calling him with quandaries over her love life? "My lady, how you conduct yourself with the Borgia is of no concern to the Council. You are a mistress, born of royal blood. Who you choose to spend your time with is not our business."

Dona shook her head, "No. I am not being clear. I overheard something. Something I am quite sure was not meant for my ears. I fear repeating it. I am sure Rodrigo monitors my comings and goings. If you could please, come here, and I could speak with you in private. I know I am asking a lot."

Malachi picked up on the fear in her voice and thought for a moment. "Fine. I need to wrap up a few things here. I shall visit before midnight."

Dona looked back at him, her eyes reflecting her relief. "Thank you, Malachi. I would not ask if I did not think it was important." He nodded at her as the screen went blank.

Dona called out to Marie, who rushed into the room. "You can draw my bath now. We will have a visitor later."

"Yes, my lady."

Dona left the library on her way to her bedroom, followed by Marie. As Dona undressed, Marie drew her bath. Dona was already worrying as to whether she was doing the right thing. What if Rodrigo found out? Maria stepped forward, letting her know her bath was ready, and Dona directed her as to what clothes she'd like laid out for her as she stepped into the tub, and briskly scrubbed away at her skin, trying to remove any scent of the Borgia. She felt close to tears. She should have stopped this in the beginning. She should have rushed outside when the workers first showed up in her gardens, and called a halt to it, sending them away. She was well aware her loneliness and her greed to have her old lifestyle back led her to make some very bad decisions, and now she had no idea how to extract herself. Rodrigo made her skin crawl, and she knew it was only a matter of time before she'd be forced to lie beneath him. His brother, Soren, sent a chill of fear down her spine every time she saw him. She should have kept the lessons of her father in her head. She should have listened when Shade came to visit her, but her pride got in the way.

She stepped from the tub, and Marie rushed to help dry her off and assisted her with fixing her hair and make-up before she pulled on a dress purchased with Borgia money. As Dona prepared to go back downstairs, she stopped Marie from following her. "Please, stay here in my suite unless I call for you."

Marie looked at her with some confusion. "But your guest?"

Dona nodded. "I'll take care of it, thank you." Dona left, closing the door behind her, and leaving Marie inside. She made her way down the stairs and informed Mario she wished for him to leave Midnight and glasses in the parlor, and then he was to retreat to his private quarters. Her servant of many years merely nodded and carried out her instructions.

"As you wish, my lady."

Dona waited impatiently in the parlor, pouring herself another glass of Midnight, and frequently checking the time. When she heard the tap at the door, she rushed to answer it herself. Malachi stood in his green robe, with a warrior standing a few feet behind him. "Please, come in."

Malachi entered, as the warrior took up his station just inside her door. "May we meet in private, Malachi?"

He nodded, his eyes still obscured by the robe. "Of course, my lady. My warrior will remain here at the entrance."

Dona turned, inviting him to follow as she led him to the parlor and closed the door behind them. She poured him a glass of Midnight as he took a seat in her newly appointed parlor. Sitting across from him, she wrung her hands. Malachi took a sip as he waited for her to speak. "I don't have all night, Donatella. What is it you wish to speak to me about?"

Dona kept her voice low and looked over her shoulder again as if expecting Rodrigo to appear any minute. "I am aware of the new edict from Council, about the half-breeds, and I know Lorenzo and his mate had taken in one of the infants left at your doorstep."

Malachi nodded. "*Si*, that is no secret, Donatella. Why am I here?"

Dona spoke even more softly, barely above a whisper. "When I was at Borgia palazzo, the brothers have a ritual they share every night upon waking from their death slumber. They drink the blood of a freshly drained half-breed. I was forced to join them one evening and share in this ritual. And on the last night I was there, I overheard Soren speaking to one of his warriors. I think they capture the half-breeds and hold them captive. He spoke of paying off the mothers, and watching the Council fortress closely, to retrieve any abandoned half-breeds before Council finds them." Dona almost choked on her words. "He keeps them alive, I think, and locked beneath the palazzo, until he is ready to drain them."

Malachi sipped at the Midnight while she spoke, her fear evident in her voice. Her news didn't surprise him. He knew the new edict providing protection to the half-breeds was reversing centuries of tradition, where the half-breeds were ostracized. Still, there was a difference between neglecting the half-breeds and killing them. Killing a half-breed wouldn't draw as much attention as killing mortals, but it still risked exposing them if not conducted discretely. He was also aware he couldn't issue any sanctions against the Borgia without exposing the Alizzi as his source of information and putting her life at risk. Setting his glass down on the table, he pushed the hood back from his face. "Have you told anyone else about this?"

Dona shook her head.

"Good. For your own safety, Alizzi, I beg you not to speak of it."

Dona asked him in a timid voice, "What can you do?"

Malachi rubbed the bridge of his nose, feeling a headache coming on, the early signs of a vision, and he wasn't sure it was a vision he wished to see. "I'm not sure what we can do that will not put your life at risk. I have no doubt that if we approach the Borgia, he would know immediately the source of the information. I fear, my child, that he has intentionally exposed their practice as a test of your loyalty. Speak of this to no one, and I do mean no one. I will discuss this with my brothers. We will increase the surveillance of the activity around our fortress, and at least try to make sure those half-breeds are left for us reach safety. Other than that, I fear we must wait." He stared back at her, as she looked at him wide-eyed. "I take it from this conversation the Borgia's attentions are not exactly welcome."

She slowly shook her head no. He looked back at her as a tear ran down her cheek. "Are you not able to extract yourself from this relationship?"

She blinked her eyes several times, feeling the hot tears on her cheeks, and answered him in a whisper. "I am in too deep. It is too late for me."

Malachi sighed heavily. "Surely, if you appealed to the Medici..."

Dona shook her head. "Rodrigo is using me. I am his pawn. Shade warned me and I would not listen. If Shade were to interfere now, it would only escalate to what I fear is inevitable. If I am complacent, if I go along, maybe I can appease him."

The visions in Malachi's head told him otherwise but telling her all was lost served no one. "Of course, my child." Her fate was sealed, and there was nothing Malachi could do to stop it.

62

Malachi had been brooding ever since the meeting with the Alizzi. He'd called the Council together and informed them of the situation, and they had increased the surveillance outside their fortress. The warriors had even installed more cameras and motion detectors. He didn't worry for himself, or his brothers. The Council hadn't been attacked since the 14th century, and even then, it was by mortals who thought they were some sort of heretic religious order. He paced his room, thinking about the information the Alizzi had shared with him. She'd called herself a pawn in Rodrigo's game, but Malachi was unsure of exactly what the game entailed. He was well aware of the increased tension in Italy, which was bleeding into the other European covens as well. A battle between covens could upset the balance of power, and impact all the covens, whether they were involved in the conflict or not.

The Borgia had never played by the rules and consistently thumbed their nose at Council. The snapshot of a vision he'd had while visiting with the Alizzi showed him things not ending well for her, but it didn't show him why. It was clear during his visit, Donatella felt trapped in the relationship now. Did Rodrigo only seek to take her territory? Or did he seek to set himself up for a border war with the Medici? Malachi shuddered to think of such an outcome. It would be devastating, and the loss of life immeasurable. He sat down and placed his head in his hands. The decree that the Council had issued about the half-breeds had been met with mixed feelings, but the Council had been prepared for that. Changing hearts and minds took time. Still, to learn the Borgia fed on the half-breeds like they were some culinary delicacies, was an abomination. Malachi was wondering if their actions to provide better protection for the half-breeds might have provoked Rodrigo in some way. He couldn't imagine Rodrigo would attempt to take the half-breed Lorenzo had adopted, but he couldn't be sure of anything these days. It was better to be safe than sorry.

Standing up, feeling every year of his age in his bones, he made his way to the call center. Shuffling his feet down the long, dark corridors, he pushed open the massive door to a room filled with high-tech equipment. He shook his head and sighed, wishing for the simplicity of the older days. "I need to speak to Lorenzo Medici, please. Can you dial him up, then give me some privacy?"

The vampire manning the room silently nodded as his fingers tapped at lightning speed across the screen. As soon as Lorenzo's image appeared, he stood from his seat, and offered it to Malachi, before leaving the room, and closing the door behind him.

***

Lorenzo finished dressing in leathers as he readied himself for another night in the camp. Chantal sat in a rocker in their bedroom, cooing softly to the baby. Grace had grown quite plump and looked the picture of health. He kissed the top of Grace's head, before kissing Chantal. "Remember, *cherie*, you are not to leave, under any circumstances. And keep Rene close, understood?"

"*Oui*, I understand. Let me put Grace down, and I will meet you downstairs before you leave." Getting up from the rocker, holding Grace in her arms, she stood on tiptoe and kissed him. "May we just have one drink together before you leave for camp?" She stared into his icy blue eyes and smiled coyly. "Please, for me?"

He knew he was already running late, but between his demands in the camp, and her demands with the new infant, he understood he needed to make time for her. "Of course, I need to pick up some files from my office. We can have a drink before I leave."

Summoning Rosa, she appeared almost immediately, taking the baby from Chantal's arms. "Do not worry, my lady. She is such a good baby. I will put her down for a nap now."

As Rosa left the room, Lorenzo extended his arm to her and led her from the room, and down the marble stairs. "Tell me, *cherie*, have you heard from your mother?"

As they glided down the stairs, she knew it would be another night he strived to keep their coven protected. "*Oui*, *Maman* is not happy her visits with us are so infrequent, but she understands our safety takes priority. And before you ask, she is trying to work on *Papa*. I do not envy her that task. He is proud and stubborn, as are all of the elders when it comes to the half-breeds. I have accepted our fate, Lorenzo. If he chooses not to have either of us in his life again, then so be it, but I have learned my *maman* is more stubborn than I ever imagined."

Lorenzo chuckled. "It seems Medici males are drawn to stubborn females, *cherie*, and I would have it no other way. If I were to bet, I would place my considerable fortune on your mother. She'll wear him down with time. You'll have your father back in your life, I'm sure of it."

He pushed the door of his office open, allowing her to enter first. As she took a seat, he willed a fire in the massive fireplace to take the chill off the room and poured two tumblers of the wine for them. He handed her a glass and tipped the edge of the crystal against the glass in her hand, creating a melodic clink. "To us, *cherie*."

Chantal would take every second she could with him. It was the smallest of moments, but she'd learned to store them in her heart. They kept her warm when he was on duty. "To us." She smiled and sipped when suddenly, the large screen came to life, and she stifled the sigh over yet another interruption.

Lorenzo noticed the second the screen flickered, and the image of Malachi appeared. Getting a call from Council wasn't an everyday occurrence, and Lorenzo was troubled by the fact Council was calling. He downed the drink and moved to take his seat behind his desk. His brow was creased as he spoke to the image on the screen. "What is it, Malachi? I can't imagine you've called with good news."

Malachi sighed. "Maybe someday, young Lorenzo, my appearance can be met with joy and not trepidation. But you are right. I fear I don't have good news. I am not sure I have any real news, to be honest, I just have an uneasy feeling, and thought I owed it to you to at least share what little I do know."

Lorenzo glanced in Chantal's direction. She was aware of the conflict with the Borgia, but he hated to subject her to more things to worry about. "*Cherie*? I leave this to you. Do you wish to stay? I hide nothing from you, but I hate you have to bear more than is necessary."

Chantal felt the knot in her stomach. Malachi calling wasn't a good sign. She left her spot curled up on the couch and stepped behind Lorenzo as he sat in his chair. Placing her hands on his shoulders, she stared at Malachi on the screen. "*Bon soir,* Malachi. Whatever your news, we will hear it together." She gently squeezed Lorenzo's shoulders.

Lorenzo laid his hand over hers. "Tell us why you have called, Malachi."

Malachi pushed the hood back from his face, exposing his eyes. "I must demand you keep this information in the strictest of confidence, Lorenzo, on your honor as a Medici, as a warrior."

Lorenzo nodded. "Of course."

Malachi continued. "I met with the Alizzi at her villa. I do not need to tell you, she is in a relationship with the Borgia, but you should know, it is not one totally of her choosing. I went to her villa because she fears Rodrigo, and retribution from him if he were to find out she spoke to me. I do not wish to place the Alizzi in greater harm. I know your relationship with her is strained, but I will not be a party to making her path more difficult than it already is. Understood?"

Lorenzo nodded. "I bear no malice toward Dona. We've gone our separate ways, and I leave it at that. I and my queen will keep this confidence."

Malachi locked eyes with Lorenzo's, looking so much like his father's. "Then I will proceed with what I know. Donatella shared that the Borgia dine on the half-breeds. Their warriors are trained to capture them and return them, alive, to the palazzo in Rome. Dona thinks they are held there, beneath the palazzo. She said she was forced to drink the blood of a half-breed, still warm in the chalice, as their nightly ritual, and Soren eats their hearts. They have been patrolling the fortress around the Council, looking for any infants that may be dropped off. We have increased our surveillance, to try to prevent this. I felt I should warn you. I know you are taking extra precautions, but the Borgia knows you have a half-breed infant. I have no reason, and no information, to suggest the Borgia would come for this infant, but I thought it better you at least know of the danger."

Chantal felt several emotions flow through her. Her first was one of absolute disgust, followed by fear. Then she was overcome with anger. "Malachi, how do you know the Alizzi speaks the truth? This could be some ruse to arouse anger from the Medici. The Alizzi knows of our efforts on behalf of the half-breeds, both here and in the States."

Malachi shifted his attention to Lorenzo's mate. "Her message was delivered to me in private, and in the strictest of confidence. She had no idea I would decide to share it with you. Also, my lady, I felt her fear and it was genuine. The Alizzi understands she has stepped into the web of a very dangerous spider, and she is trapped. She thought maybe I could help her, but there is little the Council can do, and nothing the Borgia would abide by, anyway. I did not bring you this information to instigate a conflict but rather to warn you to keep special guard."

Lorenzo squeezed her hand as he felt her fear spike for Grace's safety. "We thank you for the warning, Malachi. I'll discuss the situation of additional protection around Castello with my warriors, without divulging anything about the Alizzi. I appreciate you came to us. Our children are our legacy, and we know from my brother, Cory, how much of an attribute a half-breed can be to a coven. If you hear of anything else..."

Malachi pulled his hood forward, obscuring his eyes again. "If I hear of anything else, I will let you know, young Lorenzo."

The screen went black, and Lorenzo swiveled in the chair, so he was facing Chantal, placing his arms around her hips, he kissed her firm abdomen. "No harm will come to our children, *cherie*. This, I promise you. I will burn down everything before I would let the Borgia take my family."

63

The sound of the Paris night came to life, echoing gently through the open balcony doors. Both of them lay awake in bed, talking before they must get up and prepare for the evening ahead. Shade had already made reservations at the popular bar, but Paris nightlife didn't get started until much later, and it would be several hours yet before they left. His *bel* slid out of bed and put on her robe before going through the large wardrobe. Both were excited to have a night out together. His cell rang and he grabbed it from the table and stared at it. Growling softly, he grumbled, "This better be good."

Their grandson, Henry, was on the line. As he listened to Henry, he knew his plans were going to be interrupted, and he'd have to leave her, at least for a while. "Fine, give me thirty minutes, I'll be there." As he held the phone in his hand, she turned and looked at him.

"You're leaving?"

"Problem. It seems we have early indications of a possible blight in our vineyards in Burgundy. Luciano is on the west coast and can't get back until tomorrow evening. Henry thinks I should take a look, see if I have a solution. Why did I ever think I could get away?"

Kate couldn't hide her disappointment. "So, our evening is off?"

He shook his head. "Oh, hell no. Nothing is spoiling our time together. This will just be a delay. Would you mind meeting me there, *mi amore*? I can have Luca escort you, stay there with you until I arrive. We have warriors from our French camp guarding the house. One of them can come inside and stay with Shannon until Luca returns. I will make the trip, return as quickly as I can, take a quick shower and meet you there." He walked to her and took her into his arms, his hands sliding up and down her back. "Henry was very apologetic, but he fears we could lose the vineyards if the plants aren't treated quickly."

"Lover, I understand you need to go. A blight could destroy the plants and affect the yield for years to come. Go ahead. I'll take my time getting dressed. Are you sure you want me to go? I can wait here for you?"

Bending down, he kissed her softly, letting his tongue play with hers. "You go ahead, I won't be long." Walking to the armoire, he grabbed some leathers and boots. "We have reservations. I don't want to lose them, so go ahead."

"Be careful then. I'll see you at the bar. Just look for the redhead with the look of anticipation on her face." She gave him one last kiss. "Now, go. The quicker you resolve this, the quicker you come back to me."

He laughed as he walked out the door. "Then I must make sure I don't disappoint. I will inform Luca of what's happening." Making his way down the stairs to the second floor, he encountered Luca. He saw Shannon coming up the stairs from the main floor with her arms full of shopping bags.

"I hate to interrupt any plans you have for the evening, but Henry needs me at the vineyards, we may have a blight spreading. I am going to take a look. I need you to escort Kate to the bar and stay with her until I can get there. Choose whomever you want from the warriors outside to stay with Shannon while you are gone." Shade slapped Luca on the back. "I shouldn't be long."

Luca nodded. "Yeah, sure, no problem. It will take Shannon a while to put all her purchases away. Take your time. You want one of the warriors to go with you? They'd probably like a break from the monotony of guarding the house. It might be good for you, too, with everything going on."

"That's not a bad idea. I'll grab one to follow me. You assign one to be with Shannon and take another one with you to stay behind at the bar."

"Go. Don't worry. I got this."

Shade headed down the stairs and out the front door, but shouted back to Luca, "She is my life, brother, all I got. I'll be back as soon as possible." Shade flagged down one of the warriors from the roof of the Paris house and together they teleported to Burgundy.

***

Luca escorted Shannon to their second-floor suite. She was disappointed he'd be leaving but had come to accept the interruptions to their life, and understood that, for Luca, his loyalty to Shade would always come first. She dumped the shopping bags down on their bed, before sitting down and kicking off her shoes. "Do you think you'll be gone long?"

He knelt in front of her, and lifted her bare foot, massaging it. She leaned back on the bed and closed her eyes, as he applied pressure to the ball of her foot. "I don't think so, *mia belleza*. Put your things away, take a hot bath. I will be back before you know it."

He kissed her foot, and nipped at her toes, and watched as the smile spread across her face. "When I get back, we will have the house to ourselves, and I will make up for my inconvenient departure."

She opened her eyes and looked at him, his smile was devilish, and her breath caught in her throat as she felt the heat of his tongue along her instep. She knew he'd make good on his promise. "I can never stay mad at you."

He chuckled, "I count on it, *mia belleza*."

She giggled as he pulled on her leg, dragging her closer, and kissing her mouth. "Let me run upstairs, check on Kate, see what time she'll be ready to leave. I'll be back in a few minutes."

He stood to leave, taking the stairs two at a time to the third floor where Shade and Kate had their suite of rooms. He tapped on her door and heard her call out to come in. Opening the door, he stood half in the doorway. "Just checking on your timeline. What time do you want to leave?"

Kate stepped back into the room from the balcony. "Our reservations are for ten. I'm going to take a bath, then get dressed. I'll come down and knock when I'm ready. I'm sorry if we've messed up your evening."

He smiled back at her. "You haven't messed up our evening, only delayed it. Come down when you're ready. I'll make the arrangements with the other warriors for protection."

Closing the door, he left her to get ready. Kate ran the tub full of hot water and poured in the rose-scented bath oils. As the tub filled, she pinned up her hair before lowering herself into the water. Laying her head back against the high-backed tub, she closed her eyes and let the heat from the water work its magic. They rarely traveled without the house staff, but she found the solitude soothing. Using a sponge, she gently scrubbed away, until her skin was soft and scented by the oils. Stepping out of the tub, she dried off and wrapped the towel around her slender form. Taking a seat at her vanity table, she expertly applied her makeup, and finished with red lipstick, before letting her hair down and brushing it out. She spritzed on her rose fragrance before leaving the bath and walking to the closet. Dropping the towel to the floor, she ran her hand across the outfits hanging there. Many of the items were too formal, or too casual. She looked annoyed with her options.

"I knew I should have packed. I need something more than jeans, but less than evening gowns, please." She finally settled on a plain white silk blouse, and a black pencil skirt. She grabbed a pair of black heels with an ankle strap. Carrying her selection to the bed, she tossed them down and applied a lotion that contained crushed pearls and diamonds to her skin, giving her pale skin a soft glow. She selected a white lace bra, knowing its outline would be slightly visible beneath the silk blouse, and a barely-there white lace thong. She decided against wearing any hosiery, given how warm it was outside, and kept her legs bare, as she slid into the skirt, tucking in the blouse and zipping up the back. She sat on the bed, and slipped her feet into the shoes, wrapping the straps across her feet and around her ankles before securing the strap. Her fingers and toes had been freshly manicured and painted a bright red. She added a pair of large diamond stud earrings, and a simple diamond pendant at her neck. She opened a few buttons on the blouse, allowing the diamond to fall just above her cleavage. She wore the diamond ring he'd given her that had belonged to his mother and decided it was enough. Standing before the mirror, she made one last check. The outfit was simple but elegant, and besides, it would have to do. Making her way to the second floor, she tapped at the French doors that led to Luca and Shannon's suite. It was Shannon who answered.

"Wow, *chica*! Got a hot date?"

Kate laughed. "We'll see. I may get stood up over a bunch of grapevines."

Shannon laughed with her. "Then find the hottest guy in the bar. You look too good to go home alone."

Kate shook her head. "I'm pretty sure the only other hot guy in that bar will be Luca."

Shannon slapped at her arm. "Well, in that case, forget what I just said."

Luca heard their voices and joined them. "What are you laughing about?"

Shannon winked at him. "Nothing. Just girl talk. Now, take Kate to the bar, so you can get back to me."

He kissed her as he extended his arm to Kate. "Walk or teleport?"

Kate smiled at him. "Can we teleport? These shoes weren't made for walking any distance."

Luca looked down at her feet and smiled. "No, they weren't. Those are fuck-me shoes if I ever saw them."

Shannon howled with laughter. "Well, don't be subtle, Luca! Take Kate to the bar, please, so you can get back home."

He kissed Shannon and teleported out. They landed in an alley near the bar and slipped unnoticed into the crowd on the sidewalk. Luca checked their surroundings and noticed the two warriors he'd assigned standing in the crowd outside the bar. They both acknowledged his presence with a slight nod of the head, letting him know they had scoped out the bar and everything looked good. Luca led her into the crowded space, where the voices of the crowd all blended to an indecipherable mumble. Luca looked around. "You said you had reservations?"

Kate nodded. "We do, yes. Let's check in with the maître d'."

When Luca checked them in, Kate informed the gentleman she was waiting for another party to arrive. He asked if they'd like to go to their booth or wait at the bar.

Kate surveyed the room, taking in the crowd of mortals. "Let's sit at the bar. Down there at the far end, where I can see Shade when he arrives."

Luca nodded and led her through the crowd. She was completely unaware of the fact, as they passed through the crowd, the men stopped talking to look at her, but Luca noticed. They reached the far end of the bar that was curved, so they were now facing back toward the door. She took a seat on a barstool and crossed her legs. He slid onto the seat next to her. The bartender saw her when she came in and hadn't taken his eyes off her. He was immediately in front of them, asking for their order. Luca leveled him with a stare, "Two Midnights."

The bartender blinked a few times and looked surprised. The wait-staff had all heard rumors about the patrons who ordered Midnight and Red Moon. "Coming right up."

He returned with the filled glasses and placed them in front of them. He tried to catch the redhead's eye, but she paid no attention to him. He sighed and went back to his job of serving drinks as fast as he could. Luca lifted his glass to her, and Kate smiled back at him, clinking her glass to his.

"Well, you're not the date I expected tonight, but you'll do, warrior."

Luca laughed. "We have history, that's for sure."

Kate sipped at the wine. "Yes, we do have history." Kate was silent a few moments as she scanned her memories. He'd been at her side through it all, just as he'd sworn to. Luca knew as much, if not more, about her relationship with Shade than she did. "I'm not sure we would have survived it all without you."

He watched the expression on her face become more serious. "Yeah, you would. I know you, and I know him. You would have always found a way through. Besides, he loves you more now than the day he found you."

She gave him a soft smile. "Yes, he does. Although, I know he always worries he hasn't done enough, hasn't spent enough time with me. But he has always made sure I knew I came first in his heart."

Luca took a deep swallow from the glass. "He has no regrets, Kate, none. I can promise that."

She looked at him over her glass. "And how about you? Do you have regrets?"

He looked up with some surprise. "You're kidding, right? I have a life most warriors can only fantasize about. No regrets. Not one."

She smiled and sipped at the wine. "Good. That makes me happy."

***

Shade had finished up with Henry. It was a common blight, and it had been caught early. He gave directions to Henry and knew

Luciano would have it under control when he arrived tomorrow. "Now, if you will excuse me, I have plans with your Bebe."

Shade chuckled at the crooked grin and shoulder punch from his grandson who laughed and said, "Spare me the details please." Teleporting back to the house, he quickly showered and tried to manage his mop of silky dark curls. He wasn't much for cologne and preferred his masculine scent. As he came out of the shower, the bedroom still held the fragrance of her signature rose scent. A soft smile spread across his face. He was anxious to get to her. Opening the wardrobe, he stopped and laughed out loud. There hanging inside the door was the outfit she'd left for him. She knew him better than he knew himself. It didn't matter where in the world they were, what house they occupied, he could never find a damn thing. He pulled the jeans draped over the hanger and stepped into them, commando as always. They were soft and worn and fit him like a glove. He slipped on the crisp white dress shirt, leaving a few buttons undone at the top. Tucking the shirt into the jeans, he slid on his Italian leather belt and slipped his feet into his dress loafers. She'd left him a navy-blue sports jacket. Slipping it on, he looked in the mirror and brushed his hands through his hair.

Leaving, he headed downstairs and took note of the warrior stationed outside Luca and Shannon's suite. He nodded as Shade passed and continued down the stairs, and out onto the street. Shade scanned the street and saw his own warriors from the French camps strategically placed and blending into the surroundings. The lieutenant approached and offered Shade a cigarette, which he accepted. The warrior lit the cigarette for him as he gave him a report, letting him know the night had been quiet. Shade took a deep drag on the cigarette and exhaled, slapping the warrior on the back. It was exactly what he wanted to hear. He informed the warrior Luca would be returning shortly. Teleporting directly out to the bar, he landed, well hidden from the busy nightlife. He walked about a block, weaving through the crowd, and ignoring the stares he drew from the women on the street as he checked the surroundings. As in any big city around the world, the immortal community congregated in the target-rich environment. The hunting was easy. He sensed their presence but felt nothing unusual or distinctly evil. As he arrived at the entrance to the bar, he knew his warriors were nearby.

Stepping inside, his eyes adjusted to the dim light, as he looked around for her. Over the mixture of the scents from the humans, perfume, cigarette smoke, whiskey, and wine, he picked up the distinctive scent of roses. It wrapped around him and made his heart swell. She was here, his mate, his love. He made his way to the end of the bar closest to the door, shouldering his way through the crowd, when he saw her, his gait faltered as his heart skipped a beat. She was at the far end of the bar, sitting beneath a recessed light in the ceiling that cast a glow on her red hair. He felt as if there was a ton of weight on his chest, seizing the breath in his lungs at the sheer beauty of her.

Her hair was down, and the crimson surrounded her face. His eyes raked across her like she was his prey and he wanted her at that moment like nothing before. The white silk blouse complemented her alabaster skin. Her blouse was open just enough to show a hint of cleavage, as well as the outline of the delicate lace bra she wore beneath it. The diamond pendant nestled between those beautiful orbs and he was envious, wanting to touch her there, feel the soft warmth of her skin. Her black skirt hugged her tight as she sat on the barstool, her legs crossed. His eyes followed her shapely legs, her skin seeming to glisten in the light from the bar, as he took in her slender ankles and the strappy black heels that covered her feet; one foot hooked on the rung of the barstool, the other dangling, as she unconsciously tapped her foot lightly to the music in the background, talking to Luca. She was fucking stunning, and she took his breath away. He was struck by the realization this was similar to the outfit she'd worn the first time he saw her at the cocktail party at Alec's. She'd stopped him in his tracks then, and tonight was no different.

Shade looked around the bar and noticed he wasn't the only male who was staring at her. He could feel their envy of Luca, as they watched carefully for an opening, looking for any reason to approach her. His urge to protect her overwhelmed him. His beast was beating down the door to claim her and let every bastard in the place know who she belonged too, but he resisted the impulse. In an instant, he decided not to approach her, but to win her all over again. He took a seat at the far end of the bar from them and slid onto a barstool. He telepathically let Luca know to get the hell home to his mate and leave the warriors outside. Now, all he had to do was get the damn bartender's attention; another lusting bastard thinking he could land the crimson-haired goddess. *Think again, punk, she belongs to me.*

***

Kate was instantly aware of when he stepped inside the bar, picking up his scent, but was puzzled when he stood in the crowd, observing them before he slipped into the seat at the far end. She saw Luca acknowledge him and knew Shade had communicated something to him. He turned to her, "Have a good night. I'm out."

Luca slid off the barstool and muscled his way through the crowd, leaving the bar. Kate turned her attentions back to Shade, giving him a questioning look, and saw the playfulness in his eyes. **"You want to play, lover?"**

She picked up her glass, and took a sip of the wine, never taking her eyes off him. Setting the glass down in front of her, she ran her forefinger slowly around the rim, before dipping it in the wine, and placing her finger in her mouth, licking away the wine. She slowly removed her finger from her mouth. The bartender almost broke his leg trying to get over to her. "You need a refill?"

Never taking her eyes off Shade, she pushed the glass in the bartender's direction. "Yes please, and would you do something for me?"

He leaned over the bar, getting as close to her as the bar allowed. "You name it."

"Deliver a Red Moon to that gentleman at the far end of the bar."

The bartender looked over his shoulder, his sigh of disappointment audible. "Which one?"

Still staring at Shade, meeting his gaze, she answered, "The one who looks like he could eat me alive right now."

He looked back over his shoulder at the man who had his eyes locked on her, and she was right, he did look like he could eat her alive. "You know him?"

Kate smiled. "Not yet."

The bartender shook his head and left to pour the Red Moon. He carried it to the other end of the bar and placed it in front of the man with dark hair and piercing blue eyes. "From the redhead. Looks like it's your lucky night, my friend."

Shade was mesmerized by her teasing game and realized she was more than ready to play. He answered the bartender, "No luck, watch and learn."

Her eyes were still glued to him as he lifted his hand and slid it through his hair, pushing the curls from his eyes. Lifting the glass of Red Moon, he locked eyes with her and nodded. His eyes bored deep into hers as he took his first sip. He lowered his head and licked his lips as he gave her a look that could burn down the city.

Kate watched him with a seductive smile on her face, as he acknowledged her from across the bar. When he stared back at her, she placed one elbow on the bar, and slowly twisted a thick strand of her red locks around her finger. She uncrossed her leg, and slowly shifted her position, before re-crossing her legs, and running her hand along her calf. She couldn't help but notice she was drawing stares from other men now, as she sat alone at the bar. The bartender returned with her Midnight, sliding the glass in front of her. She looked over his shoulder, her eyes locked to Shade's ice-blue stare.

"Can I get you anything else?"

She looked at the young bartender, a mortal, probably no more than twenty-five. "As a matter of fact, you can."

His eyes lit up with anticipation but were quickly extinguished when she continued. "Ask the man if he'd like to join me."

He sighed. "Yeah, sure... happy to be your dating service," he answered sarcastically, but turned and made his way to the far end of the bar. Stopping in front of Shade, he leaned his elbow on the bar. "Pretty sure I know the answer, but the redhead wants to know if you'd like to join her?"

***

Shade hadn't missed how she seductively uncrossed and crossed her legs, and neither did his beast, and he wasn't sure how long he could sit there. *Damn woman!* She knew exactly what dropped him to his knees. He heard her request of the bartender and smiled to himself, but he knew she was far from done playing with him. Shade locked eyes with the bartender when he delivered her request. He pulled out several hundred euros and placed them discreetly in his hand.

"Refresh our drinks, over there. And keep them coming until we leave."

He slid off the stool and stood, sliding off his jacket and slinging it over one shoulder. It was evident by the bulge in his jeans he was more than entranced by the delicious morsel at the other end of the bar. He walked to her as if he owned her, his eyes shimmering with anticipation and lust as they locked onto hers. He stepped up close to her and hung his jacket over the back of the empty barstool. He propped one foot on the footrest and leaned his arm over the back of the chair, as he smiled at her.

"*Buonasera, mi amore*."

She smiled back at him. "Italian? An Italian in Paris. How interesting. Please tell me you speak English. I'm afraid my Italian is rather limited to few very inappropriate curse words."

"*Si*, I speak English and French, and several other languages. *Scuzi*, my manners, I'm Shade. Shade Medici."

He slid onto the empty barstool, his arm going immediately to the back of hers, brushing softly through her crimson locks. The softness of her hair made him fist his hand. He wanted to fucking kiss her lips until they were swollen and pink.

She tilted her head down, looking up at him through red locks, as she slowly repeated his name. She turned slightly on the barstool until her knee barely brushed against his thigh. "Shade Medici. I've never met anyone named Shade before."

She extended her hand, "I'm Kate. Kate Reese. Am I going to be pleased to meet you, Shade Medici?" Kate laughed to herself, remembering how lost for words she'd been, the first time she saw him.

He loved how she teased him. His heart was beating out of his chest, he wanted to touch her, kiss her, but he loved the delicious agony of this game. He shook her hand gently and lifted it to his lips, before placing a soft kiss in her palm. He didn't let go of her hand as he smiled back at her. "Kate Reese, beautiful name. American, *si*? Suits the beauty that sits before me."

His eyes quickly glanced down at her blouse, and his chest heaved at the paleness of her skin, and the hint of cleavage. Raising his eyes back to her face, "I am most pleased to meet you, and I promise you, I have the most honorable of intentions. May I ask if you are in the city for business or pleasure, Kate?"

Kate stared at his lips as they kissed her hand, and she felt his hot breath on her skin. It sent goosebumps up her arms and a shiver down her spine. "Oh, Mr. Medici, I assure you, I'm here for pleasure, so I hope your intentions aren't too honorable. What brings you to Paris?" She pulled her hand free and dropped it to his knee.

He smiled wickedly at her response. Her hand landed on his knee, and he could barely breathe. No other female on this planet could light him up like she could. His desire for her had never waned in all their years together. He placed his hand on her thigh at the hem of her skirt and slowly slid his fingers beneath the fabric, gently gripping the inside of her thigh. He leaned into her neck and whispered, "My intentions can be as dishonorable as you desire, *mi amore*. If it is pleasure you seek, I promise I can deliver it." He kissed her neck, along the pulsing vein, in the exact spot where he usually sank his fangs. As he pulled away, he could feel her heartbeat faster and he tipped up her chin, looking into those dark eyes that teased with their innocence, but he knew better. "Now, please don't disappoint me by saying no."

She held her breath as his hand landed on her thigh and slid just under the hem of her skirt. When he leaned forward, she thought he was about to kiss her lips, and she parted them in anticipation, but he nuzzled into her neck instead, pushing aside her thick hair, and kissing her neck. She took a sharp intake of breath when she felt his lips against that tender flesh, and her body ached to feel that sweet sting. When he tipped her chin up to look at him, she was already dizzy with lust. In a breathless voice, she answered, "Well, I would never want to leave you disappointed. You don't strike me as a man who'd be reluctant to let his wants go unspoken." Kate was aware they were drawing a crowd of onlookers, watching, and listening to the interplay between them.

Removing his hand from under her skirt, he pushed the glass of Midnight in front of her, picked up his own glass, and took a large sip. He was parched, his mouth dry, aching to kiss her. He watched her do the same, and he couldn't resist any longer. Setting his glass back down, his hand slid along her neck, and he pulled her into him, letting his tongue snake out and lick the wine from her lips, and then he went in for the kill. He kissed her with passion and lust, allowing his fangs to punch through, and felt her tongue glide over them as a guttural moan escaped from him. *Cazzo*, he couldn't handle much more of this damn cat and mouse, she'd kill him dead with the biggest fucking hard-on he'd ever experienced. Breaking the kiss, he instantly put a finger over her lips. "Shh, so now you know. I have a secret. Vampire. Are you frightened, *mi amore*?"

She'd felt his fangs punch when he kissed her, and she raked her tongue across them, knowing it pushed his beast. It excited her. He never exposed his fangs around mortals, and he was playing a dangerous game. Her heart pounded with excitement. She whispered, "Vampire. I've heard about vampires." She leaned in close to his ear, her tongue teasing before she answered. "I've heard their sexual appetites are insatiable." She slid her hand up his inner thigh until it settled on his crotch. "I heard they are hung like horses, and I can feel that much is true. Do you want to fuck me... vampire?"

Her hair slid across his face as she whispered to him and he fisted his hand hard. She liked this dangerous game, and he'd never seen her so brazen and so sure of her sexuality. But he knew her passion ran deep. He'd known since the first time he locked eyes with her over a century ago when she stumbled over her words. Her eyes spoke to him even then and told him there was a deeper passion buried deep in her soul; she'd just never met the man who could pull it out. He became that man and had won her heart and her soul. "*Si*, fucking you deep and hard is just the beginning of what I want to do to you, *mi amore*. Tell this vampire you want to understand the true meaning of insatiable."

He fisted her hair as she fondled his crouch, and his beast was fast losing control. He needed to get them out of there. He softly yanked her head back, and leaned in, whispering, "Leave with me. Now."

Shade stood and helped her from her bar stool, wrapping his jacket around her shoulders. He took her arm, and all eyes were on them as they made their way for the door. He didn't miss the stares, a mixture of envy and lust. He'd seen it all before, but she was his. He'd played for keeps, and she'd be with him for all eternity.

Kate snuggled into him, his arm around her, as they hit the Paris streets, the sounds of the bar left behind as other sounds assaulted them. The streets were teeming with people, and the traffic was heavy. Her heels clicked on the sidewalk as he led her away from the crowd, his hand at the small of her back. She leaned her head on his shoulder, as he slid his hand south, cupping her ass. "Those heels give your nether region an enticing sway, Miss Reese."

Kate smiled at his comment. She noticed the placement of his hand on her ass, as they walked down the streets of Paris barely drew any attention. "And you, sir, are quite bold. I am wondering what you have in mind for the evening. These heels were not made for long walks."

He chuckled, enjoying the game. Dropping his hand from her ass, he grabbed her hand and spun her around to face him, pulling her close. He cupped her face in his hands and stared into her eyes; he was lost. He kissed her with abandon, right in the middle of the sidewalk, as the people made their way around them. He was oblivious to everything around him, except her. His tongue explored her mouth, and he felt her lean into him, her soft hair blowing gently across his face. Breaking the kiss, he looked down at her, her eyes closed, and her lips still parted. He took her hand, leading them down the sidewalk.

"Miss Reese, those heels were meant to set a man's heart ablaze, and I no longer feel so honorable. Do you trust me?"

Kate cast a sideways glance, still breathless from the kiss, as the wind picked up her hair, blowing it across her face. She raised her hand, and slowly brushed it away. "Trust you? I barely know you, sir, but I'll admit I'm intrigued. I'd hate to waste a night like this with a man of honorable intentions."

He glanced at her and gave her a grin. "I assure you my thoughts are quite dishonorable right about now."

Cazzo, how he loved her! Steering them forward through the crowd, he saw the hotel ahead. "I do believe, Miss Reese, you need to remove those shoes and relax a bit, and if this male gets lucky, you may remove a few other items. Come."

She looked up at the hotel entrance and smiled. "I'd say your chances are based more on skill than luck, so we'll see how far you get. But I would like to slip out of these shoes."

Opening the door for her, they proceeded inside. He took her to a seat in the lobby while he went to the desk inquiring about a room. The clerk looked up, "*Bonsoir, monsieur*."

Shade slid the credit card across the counter. "*Bonsoir*. Your best room, please, a suite if it is available."

"*Oui*, how many nights?"

"Just one."

As the clerk entered the data and slid a key across the counter, he looked at the beautiful woman seated in the lobby. Raising one eyebrow, he looked up at Shade. "And will you need help with your luggage?"

Shade pocketed the key and stared back at the clerk. "No luggage."

Walking back to Kate, he dangled the key in front of her. "Care to accompany me to my room? I will enjoy helping you remove those shoes."

Kate uncrossed her legs, letting the skirt rise before standing and taking his arm. "By all means, please lead the way. I'll gladly let you remove these shoes, and then we'll see what else you can talk me out of. Like I said, skill, not luck."

He chuckled. "Challenge accepted."

He led her to the elevator, and they stepped inside, pushing the button for the top floor. As the door closed, he backed her into the corner, their image reflecting on the mirrors that lined the three walls of the elevator, creating an illusion of many men and women, from different angles. He bent down to kiss her, as her arms slid around his shoulders. When the door opened, he picked her up and carried her to the door of their suite. Setting her down on her feet, he inserted the key into the lock and pushed the door open for her. He willed two bottles of Midnight along with crystal wine glasses on the bar. The room was airy and light, decorated in white. The bed was huge, covered in beautiful crisp white pillows, and a plush duvet, where he wanted to throw her and make love to her until sunrise. The window gave a panoramic view of the city, with the Eiffel Tower in the distance.

Slipping his jacket from her shoulders, he hung it on the back of a chair. "May I interest you in a drink, Miss Reese? I fear I am parched. Besides, the drink may help eliminate any hesitation you may feel. I would hate to be rejected."

She took a seat on the foot of the bed and accepted the glass he handed her and took a sip, looking at him over the rim of the glass. "I doubt you've ever experienced rejection. You don't strike me as a man who accepts no for an answer." She ran her foot along his well-defined calf. "I think you promised to remove my shoes. Do you keep your promises, sir?"

He loved watching her own her sexuality. She'd never understood how damn beautiful she was. He downed the Midnight and set the glass down. "*Si*, I always keep my promises."

He lifted her leg to his chest, letting her foot rest there, massaging her calf. His eyes never left hers. He began to unbuckle the ankle strap, unwinding the strap and letting the shoe slip from her foot. Pushing her back on the bed, he lifted her bare foot to his lips and kissed each red painted toe, sucking them softly, one by one, into his mouth. He kissed her instep, her skin soft and lily-white, and he wanted to eat her alive, every inch of her. His warm kisses proceeded along her calf and up the back of her leg. He blew gently on the back of her knee and left behind a wet kiss.

Kate had locked eyes with him and watched as he slipped each toe into his mouth, and sharply inhaled when his tongue raked over her instep. Dropping her head back, her eyes closed, she felt his mouth explore as he moved up her calf and to her knee. In a strangled whisper, she told him, "other foot".

Letting her foot drop softly, he crouched and lifted her other foot, watching the look on her face. "*Si*, as you wish."

Repeating the process, he removed her shoe, and massaged her foot and calf, before his tongue followed the same path as his hands. He kissed up to her knee, and then slid both hands under her skirt, caressing her thighs. Sliding his hands behind her knees, he pulled her to the edge of the bed. He could smell the musky scent of her sex as his eyes peered at the hidden treasures under the skirt. Standing, he leaned over her, placing his hands on either side of her face, as he went nose to nose with her. "I do believe, Miss Reese, your shoes have been dutifully removed."

She stared back at him breathlessly, supporting herself on her elbows. "A job well done, sir. And as a reward, I'll allow you to remove another article of clothing. Your choice."

He stood tall then, between her legs as they dangled over the side of the bed. "I am honored."

His hands tugged at the white blouse tucked inside the skirt, freeing the silky fabric. His hands slid ever so slowly up her sides, the material so white against his dark olive complexion. He cupped her breasts, running his thumbs over her nipples, before gripping the blouse and giving it a quick yank, as buttons flew. Leaning down, he suckled her nipples through the lace lingerie until they were hard and erect. His fangs punched through, and he bit into the lace bra, biting through the delicate lace as her breasts were freed. He nuzzled his face between her breasts, licked and sucked as her body responded.

Kate was caught off-guard by the suddenness of his movements, as she heard the sound of the buttons being torn free. She struggled to free her arms from the blouse as his mouth explored, letting the garment drop to the bed behind her. She gently pushed him away. "My turn."

He stood upright, as she sat up on the bed, placing his belt buckle at eye level, and she slipped the belt free. Laying the belt on the bed, she looked up at him. "Don't lose this, we may need it later."

She loved the wicked smile that spread across his face, as she un-tucked his white shirt, and slowly opened each button, starting from the bottom. As each button was opened, she exposed a little more of the hard-muscled abdomen beneath the shirt, and she planted a kiss as she went. Not able to reach the top buttons without standing, she yanked at the shirttails and watched as the shirt opened. "Take it off for me."

Oh, the vixen wants to play. At her command, he shrugged his broad shoulders and let the shirt slide off his arms. He grabbed the shirttail in each hand and looped it around her neck, pulling her gently to him and leaned down, kissing her lips. "Anything else you wish removed, Miss Reese?"

She accepted the kiss that spoke of things to come. "We're just getting started, Mr. Medici. I may need help with my skirt. It zips in the back...so hard to reach."

Licking her lips, he whispered, "Let me assist you."

Stepping back, he dropped the shirt to the floor and took her hand, lifting her from the bed. As he walked around her slowly, his eyes took in every inch of her. He ran his hand across her back, her hair caressing the back of his hand. He dragged one finger down her spine, from her neck to the waist of the skirt. As he gripped the zipper, he snuggled into her neck, kissing it gently. Sliding the zipper down slowly, he planted a string of kisses along her spine. Crouched behind her, he slid the skirt over her hips, and down her shapely legs. Her ass was calling his name as he stared at that tiny thong. Biting gently on one cheek, he snapped his palm against the other, before squeezing it. "If you will step from your skirt, Miss Reese, I await your next command."

His hands steadied her, as she felt the skirt drop to the floor, and he nipped at the firm rounded flesh of her ass when she felt the sharp sting of his slap. Her gasp was audible, as she absorbed the blend of pain and pleasure. He was always careful with her to never cross the line. She'd seen the savagery vampires were capable of when having sex, and knew he'd gone there many times, but not with her. He worshiped her, and his devotion hadn't dwindled with time. She stepped out of the skirt, and kicked it aside, as she turned in his arms.

He stepped back to admire her, his eyes taking her in, from the top of her red head to her feet. She was stunning, standing before him in only a diamond pendant and a white lace thong. He remembered watching her when she was mortal, and how mesmerized he'd been by her flawless pale skin and the sharp contrasts of her bright red hair and dark eyes. He found her no less tantalizing than the first time he saw her naked. She'd stolen his heart and soul and held it still. His breathing was heavy with lust and his heart hammered. His eyes bored into hers, as he watched them turn from dark brown to beautiful amber. He slowly unzipped his jeans, and slid them down his hips, letting them drop to his ankles. He stepped out of his loafers and kicked his jeans aside. His cock was rigid as he stood in front of her in all his male glory.

She stared back at him as he removed his jeans and gripped his rigid cock in his hand. Looking up, she locked eyes with him. "Mr. Medici, you saved the best for last. Or at least I hope you did. Are you sure you know what to do with all that?" She knelt before him, and slid her hands up his thighs, placing her hand over his, before flicking her tongue over the bulging head. She looked up at him. "May I?"

Her tongue was hot as hell on his cock. He may be a warrior, but with one flick of that tongue, she made his knees quiver. He had to remind himself this was all about the seduction and tapped his beast down. Her eyes showed a mixture of lust and playfulness, of teasing and love. Reaching out, he slid his hands through her hair. "I can most assuredly say, Miss Reese, I know exactly what to do with it. Please, proceed." He gripped a fist full of her hair, resisting the urge not to guide her, but let her go at her own pace.

She smiled back at him, seeing the beast behind his eyes, itching to be freed. "I must say, I admire your restraint, sir." He dropped his hand, as she slid his cock deep into her mouth. Stroking slowly, sucking gently, as her tongue played across the smooth, slick head. She cupped his balls in her hand, feeling the weight of them. Then she gently scraped her nails across his balls and heard him hold his breath.

His head dropped back as she took him deep into her throat. He felt the beast rise to the surface. "*Cazzo*!" His voice was raspy and raw as his eyes turned red, casting a glow over the white room. His fangs punched through, and he growled as she swallowed his cock and he felt it hit the back of her throat. He gripped her hair tightly, and slowly withdrew his cock from her mouth, his breathing ragged.

His beast was hungry after being held down for hours, and now he was hard to control. Reaching down, Shade picked her up and carried her to the bar in the corner of the room and sat her atop it. Grabbing her skirt from the floor, he ripped a strip from it and walked behind the bar. Using the fabric torn from her skirt, he covered her eyes and tied it behind her head. "Miss Reese, you temp me mercilessly. Now, it is my turn."

Pushing her hair aside, he kissed her shoulder. She turned her head to the side, and he kissed the corner of her mouth. "Patience, my *bel rosso*."

His hand trailed down her spine, and he watched the goosebumps appear on her skin. Returning to the front of the bar, he placed a hand on each knee and gently spread her legs before removing his hands and stepping back from her. Her pulse beat faster, and her breathing was fast and shallow. He looked at her with the black cloth secured over her eyes, and her lips slightly parted. With the back of his forefinger, he gently touched the tender flesh of her inner thigh and watched as she jumped, startled by the contact. He placed his hands behind each knee and slid them over her shapely calves and back up again. He could feel the tension in her body, as she waited to see where he'd touch her next. Using only the tips of his fingers, he lightly dragged them down her arms, from her shoulders to the hands, where she held on to the edge of the bar as he watched her bite at her bottom lip. "Should I continue, Miss Reese?"

Her answer was barely a whisper. "Yes, please."

His chuckle was low and deep in his throat. Kneeling, he placed his hands on her knees again, and ran them up her thighs, letting his fingertips tug at the thin lace of the thong, and hearing her sharp intake of breath. He kissed one knee, and then the other, before starting the agonizingly slow trail of kisses along her inner thigh. Using his teeth, he tugged at the thong, before lowering his mouth to her sex and sucking the fabric into his mouth. He sucked at her through the fabric, his tongue probing her clitoris until he felt that sweet bud grow hard. He felt her hands on his shoulders, as she steadied herself, and he moaned. He reached up, and with one quick snap, ripped the thong from her body. He nuzzled into those soft curls and her scent covered his lips and nose. He began a long, intense seduction of her sex with his tongue, relentless teasing as his hands grasped her hips, holding her in place.

He knew every inch of her, as his tongue glided in and out, and his lips tugged. Her breathing was ragged, and she clung to him, as he lifted her legs over his shoulders. Her moans filled the room, as he pushed her to the edge, then pulled away, before beginning all over again.

Blindfolded, and waiting in tense expectation for each sensation, wondering what he'd do next, she was about to beg him, when she felt the sharp sting of his fangs into the tender flesh of her inner thigh, and the orgasm hit her hard. She dropped her head back, feeling the power of his feeding.

He felt the orgasm hit her and her blood drove him further, his beast wanting more. He retracted his fangs, her blood still on his lips as he sucked every bit of honey from her, the mixture a powerful aphrodisiac. He stood, removing the blindfold and kissed her hard, his cock still aching to be inside her. Picking her up, he carried her to the bed and laid her down. As he straddled her, lying down on top of her, he kept his weight on his elbows. "Miss Reese, you have brought out my dishonorable intentions, but I must warn you, if you go any further, you may steal something precious to me."

"And what might that be, sir?"

He looked at her with so much love. "My heart." He kissed each cheek softly, then kissed her nose and finally her lips.

When he ended the kiss, she looked back at him. "Then I will steal it, but only if you steal mine, and promise to never break it."

He took her hand and laid it over her heart. "*Si*, I shall steal it, and I vow to never break it." He kissed her then, slow and long, as he rolled them together as one, so he was now on his back, and she sat atop him. He reached up and cupped her face. "What have you done to me, Miss Reese?"

She smiled back at him, "I thought you knew? I thought you always knew. I tamed the beast, lover. He was mine from the start."

He grinned up at her and slapped her ass hard. "Prove it, my walking sin!"

"Is that a challenge, Mr. Medici? Did your mother never teach you to stay away from strangers? This is a very dangerous game, and turnabout is fair play." She slid off of him and retrieved the discarded makeshift blindfold from the floor. She twirled the strip of torn fabric around her fingers. "This was my favorite skirt. You tore my favorite skirt, and I think you should pay for that. That's only fair, don't you think?"

He didn't mind the view of her bare-naked ass climbing off of him. He was happily surprised when she picked up the torn bit of skirt. She was going to kill him before the night was over, in the best possible way. He felt the laugh roll from deep inside him, as he rolled to his side, propping himself up on his elbow, with a wicked grin on his face. "Miss Reese, I think we are on the same page here." He flopped back on the bed, spread his legs apart and stretched his arms across the wide bed. "It is only fair since it was your favorite. I am ready."

Kate chuckled, "You're' very accommodating, sir." She walked back towards him and bound his eyes with the strip of black cloth. "But you did ask me to prove it, so keep that in mind."

Standing over him as he lay spread-eagle on the bed, she took him in. If ever there were a more magnificent man to walk this earth, she'd yet to see him, and she'd lived a long time. She closed her eyes and willed the handcuffs into her hands. When she opened her eyes, she smiled. Willing forth objects wasn't a gift she used very often, and she was glad to see she still had the touch. He lay quietly on the bed, blinded to her actions. She ran her fingers across the palm of one hand, a touch as light as a butterfly landing on a flower. "Do you feel that?"

His breath left him for a second, her touch so light he wasn't even sure he felt it. He tuned in to her. He didn't want to miss one moment of this night. "*Si*."

"Good." She linked her fingers through his, lifted his hand to her lips, and licked his palm, before lifting his arm over his head and handcuffing his wrist to the headboard. The furniture in this room was made by mortals for mortals. If he resisted her, if he wanted free, she knew he could break free without a lot of effort. He'd never cared for being restrained, and tonight, she'd test his limits. She felt his momentary concern flow through her, his instinctive reaction to resist, when she bent low over him, her lips at his ear, as her hair fell across his face. "Shh. Don't struggle."

He lay still, having no idea what was coming. He heard a slight jingling noise of metal against metal, and felt the cold steel around his wrist, followed by the soft click of the cuffs. His instincts told him to resist, and his breathing heightened. He calmed himself, knowing he could break free at any time. He tried to relax, reminding himself this was all part of the seduction. "It is a dangerous game you play, Miss Reese."

"Did I not tell you, Mr. Medici? I'm a dangerous woman." She held his hand, secured by the handcuff, and licked at his wrist as her fangs punched through. She lightly raked them across his skin. "Vampire. Like you."

Her kisses trailed down the well-defined muscles in his arm and skimmed across his shoulder. Standing up, she walked to the foot of the bed, letting her fingers trail lightly across his chest and abdomen; watching his muscles flinch in reaction to her touch. She dragged her fingers down his thigh, and across his knee, making her way to his ankle, where she snapped another pair of handcuffs around his ankle and secured it to the bedframe. She bent over him, letting her hair caress him as she kissed the top of his foot. She could see his breathing pick up, and heard the ragged catch in his throat, his cock still rigid from their play, and waiting for release. She walked around the foot of the bed, and secured his other ankle, before slowly walking toward the head of the bed, trailing her pale fingers across his golden skin. Taking his free hand, she lifted it above his head, and expertly snapped the final pair of handcuffs in place. She stepped back and stood silently, holding her breath, making it difficult for him to figure out where she was. He turned his head, listening, but she remained as still as a statue, making him wait.

He growled slightly. She was taking her damn sweet time torturing him. He could hear in the tone of her voice she was enjoying this, and he'd play along. His beast was screaming inside him, not happy to be restrained. It took a lot of willpower for him to allow her to do this and he knew she meant no harm. He had to fight back the memories of the sex cult, and being with Sabine, whose intentions weren't always as innocent. Damn, he should be over that by now.

He realized he could no longer hear her breathing, and moved his head from left to right, concentrating on any sound to try to locate her. Where the fuck was she? He lifted his knee and felt the cuffs dig into his ankle. "Miss Reese, the vampire, I am impressed. I do believe you have me at a disadvantage. But don't forget, I am twice your size, and have four times your strength."

Kate smiled, despite his brave retort, she felt his underlying discomfort. She willed a feather into her hand and stepped up next to the bed, touching the tip of the feather to his chin, and watching him twitch. She slowly dragged the feather across his chest, and around each nipple. "Mr. Medici, I will have your beast on his knees, begging me for release. The beast has always been mine to command."

She drew the feather down his abdomen, down the substantial length of his cock, and across his balls. "Your beast will do my bidding. He will do what I want, when I want. You are powerless to resist."

He felt the light touch of the feather, teasing and erotic, as she explored every sensitive spot on his body. "He will do your bidding because you enchant him. It is a wicked skill. You must have had a powerful and loving master to teach you such tricks. I know you were mortal, you were turned and not born." When she ran the feather over his balls, he issued a strangled noise from his lips.

She crawled onto the foot of the bed, and slowly made her way to the head, letting her breasts and hair caress his chest. She licked his lips, and then kissed him. "How very astute of you. I was a mortal once, and I had the most powerful master. My master cast a long shadow, vampires bowed at his feet, and other masters cowered in his presence. But I can't find him now. He hides from me, but I will know his beast. He is tortured by my scent of roses and drawn to my red hair. Are you my master? Or must I bring out the beast?"

Her body glided over his like a snake, caressing him. Her hair dragged across his chest, and he craved to grab it by the handfuls and feel it run through his fingers. Her kiss was sensual, luring his beast. He couldn't see her, but her image was burned in his brain, and his mind's eye saw every curve of her body. "He is one lucky master to have had you. He must miss you with an ache that would crush him." His fangs punched and he moved his head back, displaying them. "This master's beast craves you, draw him out, *si*?"

She sat upright, straddling his chest. "But is he my beast? Is he the one I seek?" She willed a candle into her hand, and held it upright, and watched as the flame came to life. Never taking her eyes from the candle, she watched as the wax melted and pooled, before she slowly tipped the candle and let the hot liquid drip onto his chest.

He smelled the acrid smell of the flame moments before he felt the hot wax hit his skin. He felt the pain of the heat, then felt her breath across his chest, as the wax cooled and hardened. He instinctively tried to rise and the cuffs jangled, tugging at his wrists. She continued the slow drip of candle wax down his chest, and he growled, rolling his head right to left.

She slid down his body, until she was straddling his cock, hard as steel between her legs, and let the wax drizzle onto his abdomen. There was nothing she wanted more than to ride him, but that wasn't part of this game. Not yet. "Are you my master?"

Blowing out the flame, she watched as the smoke curled upward in a column in the air before she dropped the candle and willed a knife into her hand. The blade was made of steel, with an edge honed to a sharpness that would split a single hair. Leaning forward, her hair again brushing lightly against his chest, she laid the cold steel blade against his skin, and carefully lifted the hardened wax, one small drip at a time. "I suggest you not move. The blade is razor-sharp. I would hate to cut you."

He took a sharp intake of breath when he felt the cold steel against his bare chest. His beast was pushing hard for release. The sweat beaded on his forehead and slowly ran into the hair at his temples. His hands were fisted, as his beast growled. "Draw blood and you will find out if I am your master."

She stopped as quickly as she'd started and sat upright. "Is that a threat? Do you threaten me, Mr. Medici?"

His chest heaved. Her teasing was driving him out of his mind. He wanted to take her hard and fast. His cock was so rigid it ached, and the pain was mixed with lust. "I never threaten, I command. I am master. You play a lusty game with this beast."

She leaned over him, her lips close enough to brush against his as her hair fell over his face like a curtain. "And I am your mistress." She bit into his lip, drawing blood, before sucking his lip into her mouth.

His beast rolled out, it was the last straw. His voice was a deep growl as he snapped the cuffs and freed his hands, ripping the mask from his eyes and stared at her. "You are mine!"

As he broke free and sat forward, she locked eyes with him. "Yours, always yours."

Lifting her hips, she slid his rigid cock into the hot, wet folds of her sex, slowly sliding down the shaft. "And I will take what is mine." Sliding her hand behind his neck, she pulled him closer, licking at the pulsing vein in his neck before sinking her fangs deep.

He dropped his head back, eyes closed, relishing in sensations his cock had been aching for, as he penetrated her. His beast welcomed her as he drove hard inside her. Her fangs sank deep and his heart slammed inside his chest. He gripped fistfuls of her hair as she fed. Lifting his hips, finding her rhythm, his strokes were deep, and he reveled in the sweet honey that glided it home. She drank from him like she hadn't fed in days, and it drove him out of his mind. The most erotic sensation he'd ever felt was her mouth at his throat, taking the blood that sustained her. His hands slid down her back and gripped her ass, controlling the movement of her hips. His balls began to tighten, and he knew he was close. He gripped her tight, and lifted his hips, thrusting hard into her. She lifted her head and licked her lips, and he struck hard at her throat, biting into that pale flesh, and feeling the electric surge of her blood as it hit his system. He pulled her head to his shoulder and cradled it there, drinking his fill, as he snapped his ankles free from their bonds, giving him more leverage. She whispered to him, "Take us there, together." He felt her fangs sink into his shoulder.

She let her beast grapple with him, reveling in the almost violent exchange, knowing he'd never hurt her. She rode his cock hard, as they both feasted on blood, and she growled as the heat between her legs built. She felt the hard pulsing of his cock inside her and knew he'd waited long enough. Breaking free, she dropped her head back as the orgasm hit her, and she gasped for air, clinging to his shoulders as he pounded hard into her.

He watched the lust on her face, and he felt such a rush of love. Their beasts united, and they met on that plane of pleasure and joined souls no mortal would ever know. His eyes burned into her, as he watched the orgasm wash over her, and he came deep inside her. His growl was loud and filled the room.

He collapsed back on the bed, pulling her with him. Their hearts beat in sync and their souls curled into one another. He rubbed her back as her hair splayed across him and their breathing settled back to normal. Reaching up, he tipped her face to him, his fangs now gone, his eyes their normal fathomless blue. His kiss was so soft and gentle, always letting her know her savage lover was back, and the beast has retreated. "*Ti amo*. Welcome home, my walking sin, my *bel rosso*, my lily-white. You have found your master, Miss Reese, and he loves you with his life."

64

Rene sat across from Chantal and waited. He'd made his move on the chessboard minutes ago, and he was watching her face as she tried to figure out the best move. They played chess more often now that Chantal was restricted to home. He could tell she was distracted, her fingers spinning the chess piece around and around. "My lady, it is your move."

Chantal was thinking about the call from Malachi, and the information about the Borgia taking half-breeds right off the street. The more she thought about it, the angrier she got. Something had to be done! Putting a few more warriors around Council wasn't enough to address the situation. She blinked and looked at Rene. "*Pardon*? Oh, yes, I am sorry, Rene."

"My lady, is there something bothering you, perhaps I can help?"

Chantal smiled, he'd been her protector since she was a small child, and yet, he still called her 'my lady'. She stood up and paced around the room. "Something is bothering me, Rene, and I am not sure how to approach it."

Rene stood as well. "I understand, my lady. If this is personal, I don't mean to pry."

Chantal shook her head, "No, it's not personal. I apologize, but could you leave me for a while, I need to make a phone call."

"Of course, my lady." He bowed his head and left the room. Her mind made up, she headed to Lorenzo's office and stood before the large screen. "Council."

She watched patiently as the screen came to life, and one of the anonymous runners came into view. "I wish to speak with Malachi, please, Chantal Medici calling." He nodded at her, telling her he'd seek out Malachi immediately.

***

Malachi was exiting Council chambers after a long session with his brothers regarding a territory dispute in Spain. They'd taken a recess as Jasperion needed to conduct more research on the land deeds. They'd re-convene tomorrow night. He was making his way back to his private chambers when a runner approached to tell him the Medici queen was on the phone for him. Malachi looked up in confusion. "The Medici queen? Which one?"

The runner shook his head, "Lorenzo's mate. I did not recognize her right away, but the facial recognition software confirmed her identity when she introduced herself as Chantal Medici."

Malachi rubbed the bridge of his nose and took a deep sigh. He couldn't imagine this was good news. He turned in the corridor and made his way to the call center, the runner on his heels. As he entered the room, the runner closed the door behind him and patiently waited outside the closed door. Malachi slipped into the chair and saw the queen of the European Medici coven pacing before him on the screen. "My lady, how can Council be of service to you tonight?"

Chantal heard Malachi's deep voice and stopped her pacing, looking intently at the screen. "I am sorry to bother you, Malachi, but I wish to speak with you alone. Lorenzo is at camp and will be for the duration of the night. It is important I speak with you. I cannot come to you, or I would. All of the Medici females are sequestered, and I will not disobey my king's orders to stay inside Castello. I request you visit me here."

Malachi had been hoping to rest awhile in his chambers but knew the issue must be of some importance. He'd never been contacted by Chantal before, and she rarely accompanied Lorenzo when he visited Council. He was aware the Medici had placed all the females under strict protection, not allowing them to leave the safety of the compound since the tensions with the Borgia escalated. "*Si*, I will be there momentarily. Given the tensions, I will bring a warrior with me. I fear I am much too old to fight these days, my child. Expect me within the hour."

"Thank you, Malachi." She watched as the screen faded to black and left to find Antonio. She informed him Malachi would be arriving and to please take him to the gold sitting room and offer him a Midnight as well. He nodded, and she quickly made her way to the bedroom to change into something more appropriate for meeting with Council and checked on Grace before Malachi's arrival.

***

Malachi arrived with a warrior at his side and lifted the heavy iron knocker on the imposing door to the grand foyer of Castello. He knew without looking about that security cameras monitored his every move. The majordomo answered, and welcomed him in, leading them both to a well-appointed sitting room. His warrior took up position just outside the door as Malachi followed Antonio inside and took a seat, accepting the generous portion of Midnight he was offered. Antonio excused himself and said my lady would join him shortly. Malachi nodded and took a long swallow from the glass, savoring the flavor of the wine, and enjoying the much-needed boost to his energy level. The years had taken their toll, and Malachi felt every one of them. They called themselves immortal because their lives could span centuries, but they all knew, without speaking of it, that they too eventually faded away. It wasn't something Malachi had ever given much thought to, until lately. He was lost in his own thoughts when he heard the Medici queen enter, and he quickly set the glass aside and stood to greet her. "My lady."

Chantal closed the door behind her and went to him, taking his hands into hers. "Thank you for coming, Malachi, I know you are busy, but this is important. Please, sit down."

Taking a seat opposite him, she wasn't going to play games. "I will not waste your time with small talk but get straight to the point. Since your call regarding the information the Alizzi shared about the Borgia I have been bothered with how it was handled. I am going to be extremely frank with you, Malachi. Putting more warriors around Council is a start, but it will not provide protection for the older children who are already on the streets. The Borgia's are a powerful coven and have always found ways to work around the laws. But I too am from a powerful coven, and I will not stand by and watch this horror unfold."

Malachi noted her agitation. "I understand your concern, my lady. I had no illusions the actions of Council would stop the bad behavior from the Borgia, but there are limits to what the Council can do. We are a legislative Council, but our powers of enforcement are limited. What would you have us do?"

Chantal leaned forward and stared at the elder. She couldn't imagine his age, or all the things he'd seen. "Ever since Grace came into my life, a lot of things have changed for me. I can't sit idly by while I wait for our culture to accept the change in attitudes over the half-breeds. My own *Papa* has disowned me for taking in a half-breed. I have thought long and hard about this, and I have a great inspiration and example in my own sister-in-law, Natalia. She is making the changes that need to be made to insure these children have a safe and secure place to grow up and gain an education while being integrated into our culture." She stood up then, retrieving his glass and refilling it, and pouring one for herself as well. She handed him the glass and waited for his response. "It is my calling, Malachi, to save them."

Malachi accepted the glass from her and sipped as she spoke. "And how would you propose to save them, my lady?"

Chantal paced back and forth across the room as she answered. "I want to build orphanages likened to what they have in the States, and I don't mean just in northern Italy in Medici territory, but the whole of Italy, Malachi. Natalia is making great strides on this issue. We are sorely lacking here. I may not be able to save them all, but I can assure you, I can save more by building orphanages and providing a safe haven for them."

Malachi followed her movements as she paced in front of him. He could feel her nervous energy. "What are you saying, my lady? Does the Medici want to fund the operation here, as Shade has done in the States? Are your plans to only tackle Italy, or all of Europe?" Malachi emptied his glass. "Ivory is part of Council, and she has taken on this mission. It is her calling as well. But Ivor, I assure you, he is too old and has little interest. He voted to accept the change in the by-laws because he understands we must start to change our ways, but I doubt he would put much energy into constructing the orphanages and getting them staffed. Then there is the small issue of funding."

Chantal stopped pacing and set down her glass. "Malachi, no empire was built in a day. I want to begin in Italy, and once established and others see our progress, we can expand. I do not expect Ivor, or anyone from Council, to do the work. I only need Council to issue an edict regarding the older children, and not just the infants, to make sure they are brought to the orphanages. I will handle everything else. The Queen of Medici was once a Valois Princess. I have many connections of my own. Medici will fund this, plus I have my own fortune, and I am more than willing to give it all for this cause. I have only one request of you, Malachi. I need you to convince the Council this is the path that needs to be taken. I need your help to make them understand this is what needs to be done for the betterment of our race."

Chantal heard the soft knock on the door and opened it to find the nanny holding Grace. Taking Grace from her arms, she closed the door and walked back to the couch, sitting down with Grace in her lap. "Now, *mon ange*, I want you to meet a great vampire. This is Malachi, from Council."

Chantal raised her eyes to Malachi. "Look in her eyes, Malachi, and tell me you do not see the progress this child has made being in our care. Tell me she and her kind are not worth fighting for."

Malachi had heard the rumors the mate of Lorenzo had been a reluctant queen, but he saw no evidence of that now. He looked at the plump, happy infant she held in her lap and knew the child's life was forever changed when she was taken in by the Medici. "If the Medici are willing to fund this initiative, and to oversee the development, then I can assure you, my lady, I will be able to convince Council to give you its full backing. You understand, not all will be accepting. Like your own father, there will be some who reject the idea the half-breeds have a place with us. You will meet many obstacles. Are you sure you want to take this on?"

She stared into his ancient eyes and she knew, without a doubt, this was all she wanted. "I am the Medici Queen, and the coven is my responsibility as much as it is Lorenzo's. Nothing or no one is going to stop me or change my mind."

Malachi nodded. He'd hoped for a simpler task when summoned here tonight. His visions had become stronger, and he knew there was a conflict brewing between the Borgia and the Medici, but the path that conflict would take had not been shown to him yet. It was an issue that already plagued the Council, knowing if the two covens went to war, it would mean much bloodshed and only one coven would rule in the end. Her timing to take on this mission could not have come at a worse time. "My lady, I can see you are determined to carry this through. I will meet with Council, and you will have your answer before sunrise tomorrow."

Standing up, she felt the relief in her heart. She had a long way to go to see this through, but the first step was accomplished. "I cannot tell you what this means to me, Malachi. I am grateful you took the time to come to me. Your gracious help will not be forgotten."

As she led him to the door, Grace cooed and clapped her hands together. Chantal laughed at the child and was certain she heard a small chuckle from beneath the green cloak. Malachi and his warrior took their leave, and Chantal headed up the stairs with a little lift in her step. "Come *mon ange*, it is time to get you to bed."

65

Lorenzo was glad the night was over and walked back from the camp to Castello. The camp had been on high alert for some time now, and it was wearing on everyone's nerves. Chantal always waited up for him, and together, they had adjusted their sleep patterns to sleep during the day. She was born a day-walker like him and had spent her entire life being able to walk in the sun, and he appreciated her willingness to make this dramatic change. He needed to do it to accommodate the life in camp. She could have maintained her own sleep pattern, but she'd made the decision to change so she could lie beside him, and he was forever grateful. He looked forward to crawling into their bed and feeling her lie, soft and warm, next to him. He knew this was a change his mother had made to be with his father as well and understood how important that was to his father. It was an act of love, and he needed to never take it for granted.

Stepping into Castello, all was quiet. Chantal had worked hard to make sure Grace was usually down for a nap by morning as well, or at the very least, turned over to her nanny. Antonio greeted him and offered to take the sword strapped on his back. Lorenzo shrugged his shoulders, freeing himself from the harness that held the long blade, and handed it over to Antonio when he picked up on the scent of another vampire. "Did we have a guest?"

Antonio nodded. "*Si*, master. Malachi was here to see my lady."

Lorenzo looked confused. Council wasn't in the habit of making house calls, and he immediately wondered what had gone wrong, and why he hadn't been summoned back to the house. "Is everything okay?" Antonio didn't seem disturbed, which confused Lorenzo even more.

"He met in private with my lady, but neither of them seemed upset. He came at my lady's request."

Lorenzo creased his brow as Antonio left to take his sword to the office. Making his way up the grand staircase, Lorenzo passed Rene who was coming down the stairs. "Is everything okay?"

Rene nodded. "*Si*, no problems, master. All is quiet."

Lorenzo was somewhat comforted by the calmness of the house staff and her protector but still confused as to why Malachi would have been summoned in the first place. As he entered their bedroom, Chantal was already in a nightgown and robe, standing up from the rocking chair and handing a sleeping Grace over to her nanny. As the nanny walked past him, she paused, allowing Lorenzo to pull back the blanket, and place a kiss on the infant's forehead. "Sleep well, my little angel."

As the nanny left the room, she closed the door behind her, and Lorenzo went to his mate, wrapping his arms around her. She was fresh from the shower, and he inhaled her scent. "*Cherie*, it's good to be home, but is everything okay? I understand Malachi was here. I was afraid things had escalated with the Borgia, but Antonio said you summoned him. Did something happen that frightened you?"

***

Chantal was waiting for him as she sat, lulling Grace to sleep, rocking gently in the chair. She looked at the infant as she lay in her arms and wondered how any mother could give up a child. She knew very little of the mortal world, as she'd been sheltered from them, but she couldn't imagine a mortal mother would have less love for their child, and there must be a woman out there whose heart had felt broken. Grace moved her fists slightly as she slept. Chantal smiled down at her angelic face. "Sweet dreams, *mon ange*. I hope I can help others like you have those same sweet dreams."

She felt Lorenzo enter the house. It didn't take him long to come to her. He looked tired, and also a little worried. As she handed the baby over to her nanny, he came to her and pulled her into his strong arms. She heard him inhale her, and it was the most wonderful compliment without words. He was home now. It was their time together.

"No, Lorenzo, nothing has frightened me. I would have called for you straight away if I was frightened, and Rene is always close by. I asked Malachi to come and see me as I wished to speak with him personally."

She took his hand and led him to a large comfortable chair. "You are so tense, I am sorry my actions caused concern, but I wanted to speak with him about a project. I wanted his support, and to have him address Council on my behalf."

She went to the small cabinet set up as a bar and poured him a large Red Moon. Handing it to him, she stood behind the chair and began to massage his neck and shoulders.

He gratefully accepted the Red Moon and took a healthy swallow. He stretched his neck from side to side, releasing the tension in his shoulders, as her strong but delicate hands worked their magic. "What was so urgent you felt the need to summon him here? I'm surprised you got Malachi out of the fortress."

Pressing deep into his muscular shoulders, she leaned down to his ear. "You forget I am the Medici Queen, and mother to the future kings. I do hold some rank when I make a call. Malachi was very obliging. He knows our situation, and that I cannot leave the castle."

She moved around the chair and sat on his lap. "Lorenzo, do you promise to hear me out, every detail? This is important to me."

He polished off the glass and set it aside. "Then it's important to me as well. You have my undivided attention. Besides, I'm eager to hear what would draw those old bones away from the fortress."

She nodded before she spoke. "Every time I look at Grace now, I think about what is going to happen with the half-breeds. Ever since Malachi's call about what the Borgia was doing to them, it has angered me. Putting extra security around Council is not going to solve this problem. "

She reached up and stroked his defined cheekbones. "I want to build orphanages here in Italy, and then branch out all over Europe. I want to give them a future. It is working in the States, no reason it cannot work here, but I will need your support and guidance as well. This is my calling, Lorenzo." She stopped talking and kissed him softly on the lips. "Say something, please."

He saw the light in her eyes and knew she felt a passion for this project. "*Cherie*, this is a big undertaking. We have the money, you know that's not an issue, but this is a full-time job. These babies, these children... They aren't all found as early as we found Grace. They're not all as healthy. The older children may have lived on the streets, may have been abused. They'll need special care. You know you can't do this alone, and I don't have much time to help you. I'm on board if it's what you want but be sure it's what you want to do. I fear you'll feel a lot of pain in your heart for these children. If this is your decision, then I ask you talk with my sister. Natalia can help you with what she's already learned."

She sighed, relieved to know he at least agreed with her. Laying her head on his shoulder, she twirled a long strand of his dark hair around her finger. She remembered the first time meeting him, his long hair and strong warrior's body. She was enchanted by him, never having met anyone like him before. "I have not spoken to Natalia yet, but I am sure she will help me. I believe, if I asked Sophia, she would help as well. To be honest, Lorenzo, I think I would be more heartbroken knowing they are out there with no safe haven. I don't expect you to help me, you have enough responsibility, I only need your support. Natalia knows what will work and what doesn't, and I will seek her guidance."

She sat upright and slid off his lap, pacing around the room. "I know with the current situation I can't leave the castle, but I can plan. Much needs to be done before we can even build, and we will need tutors, nannies, feeders, and health care specialists." She stopped her pacing and looked at him. "Lorenzo, this is not a whim. I intend to dedicate myself to this effort. I know what it will entail. I have thought of nothing else since finding out what the Borgia is doing."

He smiled back at her, "I can see that, *cherie*. You have my blessing, and I'm sure both of my sisters will help. Start small, with one orphanage here in our coven. Learn from that, what works and what doesn't, before you expand. That is how Natalia started. The orphanages will provide jobs as well and may help change the hearts and minds of the vampires who still resist the idea of the half-breeds. It will be good for the entire coven. I'll talk with Alfie. You'll need warriors for protection, so we'll need to start planning for that as we recruit. There is just one thing I demand of you."

She went to him, once again sitting in his lap and hugging him. Her smile reflected the joy she felt. "Anything, Lorenzo."

He returned her hug. "We are still in danger from the Borgia. Until this thing is settled between us, I'll continue to insist you stay confined at Castello. You'll need to coordinate everything from here, the builders, the staffing, even how to find and collect the half-breeds. I can't risk losing you, Chantal. The half-breeds are important, and I support this change in our culture my sister started, but I won't allow you to put your life in danger. That's not negotiable."

"I promise to abide by the rules of my king. I can work from here until this situation blows over. But I too worry about you as well, more than I ever say. I have learned one thing being mated to you. The Medici knows about family and love, and it is a powerful weapon. Even though I am frightened, I will stand and fight in any way I can."

He brushed the hair back from her face. "*Cherie*, you'll never see the chaos of a battlefield. That isn't an image I ever want you to have in your head. You fight by staying here and keeping Grace safe. I hope we don't go to war, but if we do, the Medici will rule. My father has spent his life making sure this coven will never fall again. Our warriors are well trained and loyal to their coven. But make no mistake, if we fight, we will lose many, and the females must be protected to ensure our bloodline. If the battle comes, Castello is best equipped to provide protection. Sophia and Bianca would be brought here to be kept safe. My father won't stand idle while a Medici coven is attacked, so he'll come, as would Luca, and Kate and Shannon would be held here as well. Castello would be guarded by a battalion of warriors who stand shoulder to shoulder around its perimeter. None will enter here."

She snuggled into his neck, her arms wrapped around him. She'd not let herself think of this, of what was to come if it came to battle. She held back her tears, squeezing her eyes shut. She didn't want him to see how frightened she was for him. "Promise me, Lorenzo, no matter what happens, you will come back to me. I know we have a huge army of warriors, but I also know you. You will be in the thick of them, fighting."

Lorenzo cradled her head against his shoulder. He hadn't fought as many battles as his father, but he'd seen enough to know nothing was guaranteed. They were well prepared, and his warriors well trained, but he knew this wouldn't be an easy battle. He'd meant what he said when he told her the death toll would be large, on both sides, and no one was immune from injury or death, not even him. Their history was a long one, reaching back centuries, and the stories of battles for territorial gain were legend. The cold, hard fact was, in order for one master to win, another must surrender or fall... And a Medici never surrenders.

"I will always come back to you, *cherie*." He didn't add the words, 'I promise.' He knew it was a promise he couldn't make.

66

Rodrigo drained his goblet. Dona had only been gone a few nights, and yet, she'd not contacted him once. He'd demanded of her that she call him every evening, and she hadn't complied with his rules. He sneered at the idea she thought she no longer needed to do his bidding since she'd returned home. He had plied her with gifts, treated her like a damn queen, and completely refurnished her home and gardens, and still, she showed no signs of being enchanted with him. His patience was running thin. He wasn't accustomed to courting a female, anyway. He usually took what he wanted, but he was hoping he could win her over to serve his greater objective of grabbing her territory. He'd show that bitch who the master was!

Banging his skeleton-head cane hard on the floor, he stood and decided it was time he paid her an unexpected visit. He walked from his private quarters and headed to the main floor, where he found his brother gorging himself on a half-breed. The young boy lay limp across the elaborately set table, as the life drained from his eyes. Rodrigo knew his brother preferred taking the half-breeds alive and relishing in their fear as he slowly drained them.

Soren looked up as his brother approached, the blood dripping from his chin. He could see Rodrigo was agitated. He picked up a linen napkin and delicately wiped his face as if he were seated at a five-star restaurant before giving his brother a wicked grin. "What has your little timid bitch done now?"

He knew his remarks landed the perfect punch on a wound that had been festering for some time. He found it amusing his brother had yet to fuck the Alizzi and take his due.

Rodrigo growled. "You leave her to me. I am heading there now. She will soon learn; I grow weary of her games."

He teleported out from where he stood, leaving his brother to his own devious adventures for the night. He teleported high over the Medici land, knowing they were monitoring for any evidence of activity from the Borgia, and he laughed. He loved how they were on pins and needles, and he'd keep them that way a while longer. He landed at the Alizzi's front door and didn't bother to knock, opening the door and letting himself in. In a normal household, there'd be warriors to guard against such an intrusion, not to mention, entering another vampires home uninvited was one law Council enforced with a death sentence. But Donatella had no warriors, and she wouldn't dare report his misconduct to Council after all she'd accepted from him. She wouldn't have the privilege of someone announcing his arrival. He strode through the front entrance and Mario came rushing out. "Master, we were not expecting you."

Rodrigo snarled. "As planned." He brushed past the insignificant servant and took the stairs two at a time. He could smell her, she was in her boudoir. He didn't knock but pushed the bedroom door open and walked in as if he'd ruled here for centuries.

Dona was startled and couldn't hide her surprise when Rodrigo burst into her room. She knocked over the glass of Midnight and was panicked to find a towel to mop up the wine. "Rodrigo! I didn't know you were coming!"

She clutched the robe she wore over her gown. "I would have dressed for you. If you will give me a second, I can have Mario prepare you a glass, and I will get dressed."

He walked purposely toward her, his mood dangerous and agitated. He liked she was rattled by his unannounced visit. She needed to know who she was dealing with. Grabbing her around the waist, he gave her no time to think and kissed her roughly. Her body was rigid, and she struggled, but his strength kept her planted right where he wanted her. "You have disobeyed me, my pet. Do you not miss me? Why must you disobey and not follow my simple request for a phone call? Do you play games with me? It is a dangerous thing to do."

"No, I... I was busy with the house, Rodrigo. Time just got away from me, and I know you are busy too. I will call in the future, I promise!"

He saw the fear in her eyes, and his sin-eating soul went up a notch or two. Her dark eyes were open wide and staring back at him when he felt the shiver through her body. Grabbing a hand full of her hair, he yanked her head back and felt her breath leave her lungs. "You have nothing but time, Donatella, and you will make time for me. I have given you back your life and yet, you act as if it is nothing."

His tongue snaked out, licking the tender flesh of her neck, feeling the rapid pulse along her vein. Her heart was racing, and a dark excitement rushed through him, one he hadn't felt in a long time. "I can make your life a living hell, my pet, without ever being here." He let go of her hair and pushed her away from him. "You are mine now, and you will do as you are told. I am the Borgia. Do you understand me?"

His? What does he mean by his? Her mind was in a confused muddle. "Yes, of course. Whatever you say, Rodrigo. I'm sorry I have displeased you." Her head hurt where he'd yanked hard at her hair, and she was afraid to anger him further.

He turned and walked away, his back to her as he made his way to the bed, walking around it slowly, his hand sliding along the finest linens his money could buy. He yanked back the duvet. Its softness fisted in his fingers. He lifted the sheet from the bed and held it to his nose. He inhaled her scent but was also looking for the scent of any other vampire that may have shared her bed. Luckily for her, he could only smell her scent on the sheets. He growled with a dark, deep desire. "This is where you sleep, naked, without me. Your scent covers this sheet like a fine wine soothes the pallet. Come to me."

She walked reluctantly in his direction, unsure of his intent. Was he going to force her into bed? She stood a few feet away, just out of arms' reach. She knew the servants wouldn't help her, couldn't help her. He was a master with great power.

He was annoyed when she stopped short. "And still, you disobey the master who wants to give you everything. Why do you tempt me, Dona? Do you not like what you see before you? Do you not appreciate all I have given you? It is much too late to run." His grin was wicked, and his eyes bored into her, holding her on the spot. He walked the short distance to her, her body shaking with the fear of what he might do. He fed from the fear and power he had over her. Grabbing her hand, he placed it on his cock, now rigid and rock-hard against his leathers. "Feel that, my pet. This is how you leave me... Hard and pulsing to pleasure you. Do you not ache to feel it inside you?"

Her heart was pounding, and her mouth felt dry when he yanked her hand and placed it on his crotch. She could feel the rigid steel beneath his pants. Her voice was barely a whisper when she answered him. “Of course,... I thought... perhaps, we would move slowly."

Throwing back his head, his wicked laughter hung heavy in the room, and her level of terror escalated. He snapped his head forward, releasing her hand and grabbing her shoulders, digging his fingers into her tender flesh as he pushed her to her knees. "Pleasure me, pet, show me you will not disobey again."

She looked back at him, trying to hide the fear and revulsion in her eyes. He forced her to her knees, and her hands shook as she lowered the zipper on his pants. He reached inside his pants, gripping his cock, and pulled it out for her. She stared back at his hand, as he slowly stroked his hardened steel, and felt his free hand grip her hair. There was no escaping her fate. She placed her hand over his and slid the head of his cock into her mouth. He dropped his hand from his dick but maintained the grip on her hair. She began the slow, smooth movements of gliding his erection in and out of her mouth and hoped he wouldn’t take long.

Rodrigo felt his power over her soar. As she moved slowly, his hand gripped more tightly around her silky black hair. He felt her hesitancy, and he used his grip on her hair to increase the speed he demanded. He slammed his cock into the back of her throat and his moans echoed off the walls, an eerie sound. She took him higher and sucked him expertly. He increased the speed of his thrusts as he fucked her mouth. He looked down at his cock sliding in and out of her lips, closed tight around his cock. His beast rolled through him, and he knew he was about to spill his seed inside her sweet mouth. "Swallow me, bitch, all of me."

He roughly yanked her head back and forth, faster, until the orgasm hit him, and he felt his seed spill to the back of her throat and his roar of victory rolled throughout the house, and the lights flickered off and on, with the evil that spilled out of him. He pulled her by the hair from the floor and kissed her hard, his mouth taking control of hers, bruising her lips. His tongue drove deep inside her mouth, tasting his salty cum. As he released her from the kiss, he pulled her head back and stared into her eyes. "My sweet pet, never disobey me again. I am your master, *si*?"

She looked back at him, unable to disguise her fear. "Yes, master."

He released her hair that was now tangled around his hand, yanking it free. He slid his finger along her jaw and kissed her vein that pulsed with fear on her long, elegant neck. "Remember who you belong to, Donatella."

Fastening his leathers, he walked out the door that still stood open. Before he left the room, he inhaled deeply of her fear, and his power, a mixture he rather liked, an intense aphrodisiac. He teleported from the landing at the top of the stairs. It wouldn't be long now, this territory would be his and so would she, and then Medici would fall at his feet just as she had moments before.

***

Dona remained standing by the bed where he'd left her, afraid to move. She felt the energy shift as he teleported out and she started to weep, collapsing on the floor. "Shade, what have I done?"

Her maid entered and helped her to her feet. "I need a shower."

"Of course, my lady."

She led her to the bathroom as Dona dropped her robe and pulled the gown over her head. "Burn these."

She stepped into the hot shower, and scrubbed herself raw, using the washcloth to scrub at her lips until they almost bled, spitting his seed from her mouth, and gagging, knowing this wouldn't be the last time, or the worst of what was yet to come.

67

Theo had been out hunting, it was his night off at the Dead House. He'd gone to the club where he'd met the mortal female who'd carried his child, but she was nowhere to be seen. She'd made herself scarce since he'd taken Noah to the orphanage. He'd even made the rounds to her old apartment, but it had been vacated. He felt a sense of loss, he no longer saw neither her nor his son. Natalia had told him to wait a few months before visiting Noah, but he was feeling the loss of his son and needed to make sure he was doing okay. He kept picking up his cell, wanting to touch base with Natalia, but she was Council and ordinary vampires of his stature didn't contact Council. He'd returned to his quarters at the camp and was pacing the room. He didn't think he could just show up at the orphanage and ask to see his infant son without prior permission. He scrolled aimlessly through his contact list until Marcello's name and number appeared "Damn, Marcello!" He dialed and waited, wondering if he'd just end up in voicemail.

Marcello was making rounds in the Council compound when he felt the soft vibration of his phone. He pulled the phone from his pocket to see Theo on his caller ID. Creasing his brow, he hoped this didn't mean they were having trouble in D.C. "Brother... what's up?"

"Yo, brother. Been a while. Don't panic, everything is running smooth. D.C. is thick with tourists, but we have everything under control." Theo stammered, he was nervous and felt like an idiot asking Marcello to intercept for him. "I, uh, need a favor, brother."

Marcello leaned against the wall as he talked. "You got it, brother. How can I help?"

Theo flopped down on the bed, shuffling his scuffed boots on the floor. "Look, I am just going to get to the point. I have a son at the orphanage. Damn sure you already know that. I want to go see him. I haven't been there since I dropped him off, and they told me to wait. Can you ask Natal... I mean Ivory, if she could call and make sure I can go see him?"

Marcello smiled to himself. He knew how important the orphanages were to Natalia, and for some reason, it pleased him Theo felt an interest in his half-breed child. "I know about your son, Theo, and I'll be happy to check if you can see him. Natalia's in the data center. Give me a few minutes to talk with her and I'll call you back."

Theo let out a sigh of relief. "*Grazie,* brother, I owe you one." He hung up and decided he needed to clean up a bit and change his clothes in case he got approval to see his son.

Marcello pocketed the phone and headed to the data center where he found Natalia overseeing the small army of workers. She looked up when he entered, and he motioned for her to join him. She excused herself to the worker she'd been assisting and made her way through the long workstations. "Is everything okay?"

He nodded as he opened the door, inviting her to step outside in the hallway where he could speak privately. "Just got a call from Theo. He wants to see his son. I was hoping you could help him out with that."

Natalia bit her lip. It was still a little early for a visit, but the infant boy named Noah had adjusted well to the structured life in the orphanage. He'd been an anxious baby and cried frequently when he was first brought to them, but the assignment of a permanent nanny and regular feedings had quickly settled him. "It's still a little early, but I like Theo is showing an interest. A warrior like Theo can help change the attitudes of other warriors if they hear he visits his child. You'll have to escort me. I'm not allowed to leave alone."

Looking around the corridor to make sure they were unobserved, he stepped in close to her. "I will gladly escort you."

She smiled back at him, and playfully slapped at his arm. "Behave yourself. Call Theo and tell him to meet us there in an hour. In the meantime, I need to let Emerald know I'm leaving the compound."

As she rushed off, he watched as her ivory robe dusted the floor, concealing the curves that only he knew lay under that robe. He pulled out his phone and returned the call to Theo. "You're in, brother. Meet us in an hour."

***

Theo hung up from the call and felt both excited and nervous. What would he do with a baby? He knew he had a lot to learn. He finished changing and pulled his long dark brown hair back in a ponytail. He ran his fingers through his rough beard before he teleported out to the orphanage. Standing outside the confines of the orphanage, he didn't see any sign yet of Ivory or Marcello, so he lit up a cigarette. He hoped Noah was growing and doing well. He was a little surprised Natalia would meet him personally, and not just call ahead and authorize his visit. It made him nervous, wondering if Noah was all right. Would they contact him if he was sick? All these damn questions he had. How in hell was he supposed to know if Noah needed something, like clothes and diapers and all that baby stuff? He felt useless as a father, but he was determined to learn and be there for his son. He felt the air shift and knew they had arrived. He snubbed out his smoke under his boot and quickly made his way to the entrance to find Natalia and Marcello. "*Grazie* for doing this for me, Ivory. I am grateful."

He looked at Marcello and could see in his eyes how much he loved her. Theo was happy for them, he knew their romance was a 'secret', but all anyone had to do was look at the way Marcello looked at her to figure it out. Besides, everyone knew, it was the worst kept secret ever. All of the warriors acknowledged it, but never spoke of it. "Appreciate your efforts on my behalf."

Marcello slapped him on the back. "Glad I could help."

Natalia rang the bell and was greeted by the warrior on guard at the door, knowing their arrival had been observed on the security cameras. The warrior bowed his head to her. "Ivory." When he looked up, he made eye contact with both Marcello and Theo; he remembered them both from camp. Natalia immediately took charge, issuing an order.

"Have the infant Noah brought to us in reception, and have his nanny accompany him, so Theo can meet her."

The warrior nodded, as Natalia started down the long hall to the reception room, and the two warriors scurried to keep up. Natalia looked over her shoulder as she addressed him. "I'm glad you have an interest in your son, Theo. I think you'll be surprised at how much he's grown. He was quite thin and weak when he was brought here."

Theo followed orders whenever he was around a Medici, and Natalia was much like her father, getting straight to business. "I have a great interest in my son, but I have to admit, I know nothing about being a father. I have no experience with babies. Is Noah okay? I have a lot of questions. Do I ask you or his nanny?"

Natalia laughed. "No new father has experience with babies, Theo. You will be fine. His nanny will be able to answer any of your questions. She is dedicated to him and him alone. That has allowed him to bond with her. He was anxious and cried often when he was first brought to us. You did the right thing. He is a happy baby now."

Natalia led them into the comfortable reception center, filled with plush furniture, and a warm carpeted floor. The room was child-friendly and had several toy boxes against the wall. As they took a seat, it only took a few minutes for the nanny to enter, holding the plump, happy baby in her arms. He had his father's dark eyes and dark hair.

Theo was shocked when he saw his child. He didn't look anything like the last time he'd seen him. He stood up and walked to the nanny, peering at his son wrapped in the blanket. Looking at him now, he could see the resemblance. Huge brown eyes rolled up to his, and he almost lost his breath. This was his son! He fidgeted with his hands at his side. "Hey buddy, you're looking good." Theo looked up and smiled at Natalia. "Can I hold him?"

She nodded. "He's your son, Theo. He'll feel the blood bond immediately. Of course, you may hold him. Play with him. Take all the time you need. Do you wish to be alone?"

Theo wasn't sure he wanted to be alone, but he knew one thing, he wanted to spend some time with Noah. "I know you're busy and I don't want to keep you from your duties, but I would like the nanny..." He paused and turned to the woman holding his child. "Excuse me, but I don't know your name? I'm Theo, Noah's father."

The woman smiled at him. "It is nice to see you are here for Noah. My name is Sarah."

Theo liked her immediately; she had a soothing voice and a polite manner. "Would you stay with Noah and me while I visit with him?"

She nodded and juggled Noah gently into his arms. Theo walked slowly to the sofa, holding Noah as if he would break. Sarah quickly sat beside him. "Let me show you something if I may. It will help you to be able to talk to him, see his face and comfort him." She took Noah from Theo and laid him on his back along Theo's legs, the infant's head resting easily between his knees.

Theo looked down at him, and Noah cooed loudly. "He has some lungs!"

Natalia unconsciously took Marcelo's hand, and then quickly dropped it. "Let's give them some privacy. Come with me, I'll show you around the orphanage." As they left the room together, Natalia addressed Theo. "Take your time, just call when you're ready."

Theo nodded and his eyes returned to his son. "He's really growing. He looks so different. He looks happy. I have questions that plague me because I don't know what I can and can't do. I have a busy life as a warrior, so it's not easy for me to be here. But I want to know if I can make a schedule to come and visit him? And if I can bring him things he needs? What does he need?"

Sarah hadn't seen many parents visit their children, but she knew that was Ivory's hope. She smiled at the huge warrior holding the infant. "He needs nothing but your attention. The orphanage provides everything, clothes, nurturing care, and eventually, an education. He is checked medically once a month, and he is allowed to play with the other children. Of course, right now, his play is limited, but it will help him to socialize as he gets older. We establish a routine of feeding, sleep, play, and eventually physical exercise ad education. The structure is important in their development. Noah was brought to us early, so that's good. Some of the children are older and have been living in the streets. He'll do fine, and grow up to be strong, like his father."

Theo looked over and smiled at her. She was knowledgeable and he felt as if he could easily talk with her. "When he gets older, will I be able to take him out of here to visit where I live? I know all of this is new, but it was something I was hoping I might be able to do." He lifted Noah and let his feet dangle until they found purchase on his strong thighs, then he began to bounce him a bit. Noah smiled and gurgled, and Theo grinned.

"No one has asked that question before, but you're a Medici warrior, so I can't imagine Ivory would deny you that. Would you take him back to the camp at Bel Rosso? I'm sure our queen would welcome it."

Theo nodded. "I want to be involved in his life. Warriors don't have much in the way of families outside of their brotherhood. I like knowing there is a little guy like me in this world. I want him to know what I stand for, what I do, and what my values are as a warrior. I never thought I would know family beyond my warrior family." Theo stopped bouncing Noah and pulled him to his neck, laying him over his shoulder. He stood then and walked around the room with him, feeling the infant's heartbeat against his chest. He rubbed his back gently; Noah smelled sweet, and he was so soft. "I want him to know someone outside these doors...well, I mean, I want him to know I love him."

Sarah smiled at the image of him cradling the infant on his shoulder. "He'll know, and I'll tell him about his father when you're not here. I'll make sure he knows he's the son of a great Medici warrior, and he'll thrive in the Medici coven when he comes of age."

Theo felt his heart burst. He was a father, and he had a son now, one who would never know the streets. He sat back down as Noah had fallen asleep. "I saw how Cory came to life once he found family. Cory was on the streets, and I see it all the time. How horrible it is for them. I never want Noah to see that. Thank you, Sarah, it means a lot to me to know you're here for him."

He gently handed Noah back to her with a bit of regret. "I'll come again soon."

He stood up when she did and watched her walk out of the room with Noah. He felt relief, knowing his son was being well cared for, and at the same time, a yearning loss because he wouldn't see his son every day. He'd make sure to be a part of his life, and he would grow up to be a good man. Theo was determined, now more than ever, to make that happen.

68

Shade woke early and got up from their comfortable bed in their home on the Champs Elysees. His *bel* was still asleep. Kissing her cheek softly, he pulled on some jeans and a shirt, left their bedroom, and made his way down the two flights of stairs, and slipped quietly out into the enclosed courtyard. He took a deep breath, catching the early evening breeze. It had been several nights since their adventure in the hotel. The role-playing had been exciting, and he still got rock hard when he thought about it. He'd teleported her back to the house just before dawn with her clothes in tatters and held her strong in his arms. They'd spent the last few evenings enjoying each other and the company of Luca and Shannon, but he wanted to renew the game. She was a challenging partner, but she always had been. Finishing up his smoke, he headed back inside, and he could hear her moving about inside the house. Before he headed up the stairs, he chuckled to himself and pulled out his cell phone, waiting for her to answer.

***

Kate woke when she felt his absence from their bed. She stretched and yawned, before rolling over and sitting up, grabbing her robe. She stepped out on the balcony, looking at the city lights when she heard her phone ring. Creasing her brow, hoping nothing had gone wrong that would cut their trip short, she returned to the bedroom and grabbed her phone. She smiled to herself when she saw it was Shade on the caller ID. "Hello?"

"*Buonasera*, Miss Reese. Shade Medici here." He waited a moment, listening to her breathing on the other end. Yeah, her heart rate just went up a notch. She was as excited as he was to continue this little game. "I hope you are having a wonderful evening, *si*?"

Kate giggled. "They've all been wonderful evenings, thanks to you. I've needed to sleep just to regain my energy. I must say, you're not lacking in the stamina department."

He didn't stifle the chuckle. "*Si*, never have, but I must say, Miss Reese, you have entranced my beast. I have held you, a willing prey, inside my Paris home for several days and nights now, and I thought, now that we are, how should I say... better acquainted, perhaps you would accompany me out this evening, *si*?"

She twisted a strand of hair around her finger as she walked around the bedroom, and their bed, with its tossed and tangled sheets. "I think I know you well enough to say yes. After all, I'm not sure there are any parts of me left that you aren't already acquainted with. What did you have in mind, sir?"

His heart did a bounce. Oh, he loved discovering her over and over again. It never got old. "Well, I have an interest in beautiful art. And although nothing will be able to touch your beauty, I thought perhaps we could visit a gallery of your choice. Does art interest you, Miss Reese?"

She sat on the bed, pulling her knees up under her chin. "I do like art. There are some wonderful displays in Montmartre, in the artists' colony. Maybe we can find something to remind us of our time together."

"I would be honored to accompany you there. I will pick you up in an hour. And Miss Reese?"

She smiled as he kept up the facade of the game. "Yes, Mr. Medici?"

He grinned wickedly. "I would suggest you do not wear those tempting black heels. I intend to show you Paris as you have never seen. We will be doing a great deal of walking." He hung up, grinning like some damn young pup. He walked inside and teleported to Lorenzo's old bedroom to get ready for the evening.

Kate tossed the phone on the bed and jumped in the shower. When she got out, she dried her hair and did her make-up. Heading for the closet, she picked out a light sundress and a pair of ballet flats. She brushed her hair until it shined, leaving it down, and spritzed on her rose fragrance.

Shade could hear her in their room, bustling about. He was moving his ass as well. He dressed in a pair of jeans, ripped at the knees, hanging low on his hips, and well worn. He slipped on a white dress shirt and rolled up the sleeves to the elbow. He chose a pair of black boots that laced above the ankles and slipped a knife inside his boot. Old habits die hard. He ran his fingers through his hair and shook out his curls, before adjusting the leather braided bracelets that lined his wrists. Checking his watch, it was time. Slipping his cell in his back pocket, he left the room and grabbed a single long stem rose from one of the many vases that filled the house. He listened outside their closed bedroom door and heard nothing. He used his knuckles to tap lightly at the door.

Kate heard the knock. As she opened the door, she smiled at him. "Punctual as always, Mr. Medici. I must say, you look good enough to... eat."

Grinning, he winked at her. "Be careful what you wish for, Miss Reese. You look rather delicious yourself." His eyes took her in from the top of her head down to her little flat shoes. "I see you have taken my advice." He pulled the long stem rose from behind his back and held it out for her.

Taking the rose from his hand, her fingers brushed against his, and she felt the spark between them, their passion as strong today as the day they met. "My favorite." She held the rose under her nose. "I wonder how you knew."

It was damn near killing him to stand there without kissing her, and he was wondering why he'd begun this game of torture. He took her hand and kissed each knuckle. Taking the rose back, he snapped the stem in half and tucked the rose behind her ear. His voice was gravely and thick. "You must know, Miss Reese, the rose is a sensual flower. The vampire's gift to his lover, *si*?"

"Lucky me. Shall we go? Or... I could invite you in? What do you think, Mr. Medici? Do we keep our little tryst a secret, or do we show the world?"

He stepped back and nodded, taking her hand. "Oh, Miss Reese, one thing you should know about me. I am not afraid to show the world the beautiful creature on my arm. Would you care to teleport alongside me?"

Taking his hand, still caught in the mesmerizing blue of his eyes, she answered him. "You lead, and I follow."

"I like how you think, Miss Reese." Hand in hand, they teleported from the house. He telepathically sent Luca a message they'd be out for the night. He had no idea what lay ahead and didn't care, he was with his *bel*. He led them over the beautiful city, taking a few loops, looking at the lights together that seemed to shine just for them. He kept looking over at her face, beaming in the moonlight, her hair blowing in the breeze. How had he ever won her heart? She always made him feel like the luckiest male in the world. He landed them in a discreet alley, away from the crowd. Pushing a stray strand of crimson behind her ear, he smiled. "Are you ready to tackle the world, Miss Reese?"

"Only with you, Mr. Medici." She looked down the dark alley where they had landed. "Do you have a plan?"

Taking her hand, he led her out of the alley into the nightlife that was quite different from their previous cafe date. They had landed in Montmartre, where the artists tended to congregate, and an area known for its nightclubs. In the early beginnings of the twentieth century, many famous artists had studios in or around Montmartre, including Monet, Picasso, Pissarro, and Vincent van Gogh. Ever since, it had been a haven for wannabe artists. "Perhaps we should wander to the artists' colony? It always reminds me of my earlier years living in Florence, flourishing with artists who were waiting for their talent to be discovered. Let's see if perhaps we can find something that interests us both, *sí*?"

She almost skipped beside him in excitement. "I love the art colony! I wondered if the artists were still coming here after all this time." She squeezed his hand, and walked ahead of him, tugging at him to follow.

Cazzo, he loved her smile and seeing her so happy and carefree. "What happened to 'you lead, and I follow'? Turning the tables on me, Miss Reese?" He laughed along with her and would follow her to hell and back if necessary.

She laughed out loud. "I got excited. You may have to remind me if I get out of line, Mr. Medici." Stopping, she turned to face him, and sliding her arms around his waist, she looked up at him coquettishly. "Am I out of line?"

He cupped her face in his hands. "Miss Reese, my hand on your sweet ass will let you know if you're out of line, *sí*? But I must warn you to be aware of your surroundings." He kissed her forehead.

She laughed. "Oh, I'll keep an eye on you, for sure. Don't think I don't notice how the women look at you, and I have no intentions of sharing."

Holding his hand, she led him through the open-air stalls that held the art, some of the artists stepping forward, trying hard for a sale, others painting and ignoring the potential customers. They browsed through the racks of art, some pieces small enough to fit in your hand, others so large they'd be hard to carry. There were pieces done in oils, acrylics, watercolors, and multi-media. They both flipped through the canvases, looking for something that spoke to them. She found a painting of the Pont de Arts with lovers embracing. "This one. What do you think?"

"You would choose a painting of lovers, Miss Reese. Pont de Arts is a famous landmark for lovers."

"Are we not lovers, Mr. Medici? Or am I just another notch on your bedpost?" She cast him a sideways glance. "Will you cast me aside for the next pretty girl that walks by?"

Shade knew she was teasing him, he could see it in her eyes, even as the breeze blew her hair across her face, as she gave him that sideways glance. He moved close to her, laying his hand over hers as she held the painting. "I do not see anything here that could even touch your beauty." He tipped her chin up. "I think the painting is most appropriate. Do you wish for me to purchase this for you?"

"That depends. Does the affair end when you leave Paris? Am I your Paris lover?" She slid her hand up his chest, feeling the hard muscles beneath his shirt.

He felt her hand, the warmth of her touch penetrating through his shirt, and his beast stirred. *Whoa, down boy, public place*. Her hand reached the open neck of his shirt, and flesh hit flesh. Licking his lips, he cocked his head to the side. "I have no intentions of letting you go." Leaning in, he kissed her, and the flame inside him ignited.

She responded to the kiss, her lips soft and receiving, his tongue exploring. When he broke away, she held his gaze. "And I had no intention of leaving."

Placing his hand at the small of her back, his eyes still glued to hers, he pulled her in close. With his free hand, he played with a strand of her hair, twisting it around his fingers before he fisted a handful, uttering a soft moan. "Miss Reese, you are every temptation I have ever dreamed of."

Giving him a coy look, she responded. "Then you're in luck. Temptation is my specialty." The crowd was starting to take notice of the couple who stood seemingly oblivious to everything else around them. "How should I tempt you tonight? With the touch of my hand? With kisses? Soft kisses that explore every part of you? Or long, passionate kisses? Tell me, Mr. Medici."

"Must I choose? What if I want all of the above? What price would I have to pay for such sweet temptations? The painting? My heart? My soul?"

She tugged at the waistband on his jeans, pulling him in close. "Your soul will do nicely."

He grinned. "Let's start with the painting, the soul comes later. You are walking sin, Miss Reese." Reaching into his jeans, he handed her several euros, having no idea how much the painting costs. "Do the deal."

She smiled wickedly at him as she stepped away to find the artist and purchase the canvas. He turned to face the crowd that was milling about and pulled out a pack of cigarettes. Lighting up, he exhaled the smoke and slid one hand into the pocket of his jeans. He saw a young female glancing at him.

***

Giselle had been working the streets all night, without any luck. She approached him and held the cigarette to her lips. "*Bonsoir*. Can I get a light?"

"*Oui*. Your English is good. Local?" Shade pulled out his lighter, flicking it open and lighting her cigarette. She was mortal, very pretty, and quite young. Her chestnut hair flowed easily down her back and her eyes were midnight blue. She wore a dress that matched her eyes and it flowed softly around her, secured by thin straps over the shoulder. Her heels accentuated her long legs.

She cupped her hands around his to protect the flame of the lighter, making sure her hands touched his, and softly inhaled on her cigarette. As she exhaled, the smoke floated away in the breeze. She smiled at him. "*Merci*. I was born here. My name is Giselle. And you are?"

Shade was aware she was sizing him up. "Shade."

"Shade, I could not help but notice you with the girl." Giselle nodded in the direction of the redhead who was bargaining with the artist. She had seen the exchange of money following their playful encounter. "We can make it more interesting, *oui*? The three of us?"

Shade was taken off guard. She was a damn hooker! "Giselle, a beautiful name. You are very attractive, but I do not think my female would be interested." He smiled at her, thinking she'd accept that and move on.

Giselle tilted her head, placing her hand on his arm. He was a strikingly handsome man, and she was experienced at working the streets. "Your female? That is an odd turn of phrase. You gave her money, did you not? Do not be so sure, *monsiuer*. She might surprise you."

Shade had to stifle the chuckle as he realized the hooker thought Kate was her competition, also working the streets.

***

Kate finished up the transaction with the artist and took the carefully wrapped canvas. Turning around, she looked for Shade in the crowd and saw the young girl on his arm. She sighed and shook her head. Women were drawn to him like a magnet. She made her way back to him, watching the conversation between them. "Lover? Who's your friend?"

"Ah, *mi amore*, this is Giselle and she just made me quite an interesting offer." He looked at Kate and winked.

Kate looked at the girl. "Oh, I'm sure she did. What was the offer, Giselle?"

Giselle took a drag on the cigarette. "Considering that you are working my territory, it is quite a generous offer. I suggested a threesome. You have done that before, yes? That way, we both get paid. Otherwise, I will need to ask you to move on. My territory."

Kate realized the girl was a hooker and had to adjust her thinking. "Don't you think the john should choose? I mean, I hit on him first. We've already agreed on a price, and I'm not into a three-way."

Giselle huffed. "Then you will not last long out here." Giselle moved closer to Shade. "What do you say? Can you handle two?"

Shade looked from Kate to Giselle as they talked, and he was amused Kate was playing along. "*Oui*, I can handle two, but I already paid, so this deal has to be damn sweet."

Before Giselle could answer, Kate flashed him a look that said she wasn't playing anymore. "Oh, you want a better deal? I'll show you a deal." She grabbed his hand and dragged him away, as Giselle stood confused.

"What about me?"

Kate looked over her shoulder. "Fuck you, Giselle. This is my territory now!"

Kate led him back the way they'd come, dragging him into the darkened alley. She pushed his back against the wall. "A deal, Mr. Medici? You're looking for a deal?" She propped the canvas against the wall and yanked at the waistband of his jeans, unbuttoning the fly. "I'll show you a deal."

Shade had to bite his lip hard to stop from laughing. He was wondering where that redheaded temper had gone. "Bring it on, Miss Reese."

She felt his cock, hard against her hand as she tugged at the buttons on his jeans. As she freed his cock, she stroked him slowly, teasing. "Oh, I'll bring it."

She dropped to her knees in the alley, sliding his cock inside her mouth. She rolled her tongue over the bulging head and slid her lips up and down the steel hard shaft. She cupped his balls in her hands, feeling the weight. She slowly pulled back, until his cock was released, and ran her tongue over his balls. "Any special request, Mr. Medici? I want to make sure you get your money's worth."

He laid his head back against the brick wall, his heart racing as her mouth worked magic. His beast was screaming to be released as that warm mouth teased and played with him. He looked down and found her looking up at him, her eyes still reflecting a hint of anger and jealousy as she asked him the question. He had a special request, all right. Bending down, he easily lifted her and turned so she was pinned against the wall. Assaulting her mouth, he kissed her, relaying the urgency he felt. Sliding his hands up her dress, he pulled her thighs up to his hip. She responded by wrapping both legs around his hips. Breaking the kiss, he stared into her eyes as they turned amber. "*Si*, I have a request. To be buried deep inside you."

Kate was caught off guard by the suddenness of his response and was only partially aware there were people who passed the entrance to the alley from the street. The lighting on the street was dim, but the ally was dark. She wasn't sure if they could be seen or not, but he was done with playing the game, and his beast had taken charge. Visible or not, she knew he wouldn't stop now.

He felt her slide her arms around his shoulders, as his hand explored beneath her skirt, and with one swift yank, ripped the panties from beneath the dress. He moaned as he heard the ripping silk. His cock was standing at attention, and in one easy move, gripping her thighs, he slid inside her with ease. He heard her sharp intake of breath, as he buried his head into her neck and inhaled her scent. He held her firmly as he slid in and out of her, at first, slow, and then picking up the pace of his thrusts as their urgency built. She was warm and wet, and he felt her move with him.

Kate was aware of someone standing at the entrance of the alley, it was only a silhouette, but she recognized Giselle. She'd followed them and now stood watching. Kate was pinned between the rough brick wall and his hard body. She felt his mouth at her throat, his breath hot against her skin, and heard the familiar growl. Her mobility was restricted, but his wasn't as he thrust into her. She could see the soft glow of red in his eyes when she felt the sharp sting of his fangs, and the moans escaped her lips. She dropped her head back as much as she could, as he drank from her. The burst of heat between her legs was immediate, as she gripped his hips with her thighs, and he pounded hard against her. She clung to his shoulders and looked, again, toward the entrance of the alley. She saw Giselle raise her hand to her mouth, as she spoke the word... "Vampire!" Kate watched as she backed away in horror, turning, and running from the alleyway in a panic. The beast was oblivious to their surroundings, and continued to feed, as they both neared their climax.

Lost inside her, her blood fueled the fire that drove him harder. Gripping her hair, he pulled her head to his neck. He wanted her to feed with him. When he felt her mouth at his throat, and his blood flowing into her mouth, it pushed them both over the edge of the cliff where he'd kept them carefully balanced. They came together, as the waves of their orgasm crashed over them in the dark alley. His growl echoed off the walls of the enclosed space. His beast had taken control, driving his cock deeper inside her, crushing her against the brick wall of the building. As the climax slowly ebbed, he snuggled into her neck as his beast retreated. "*Ti Amo*."

He kissed her, licking his blood from her lips. He chuckled softly, as he put her down on her feet, and helped to straighten the dress that had bunched up around her hips. Adjusting himself back into his jeans, he tucked in his shirt.

Kate was shifting her dress into place, aware she no longer had on any panties, and wondering if she should tell him. They'd lived among mortals and were careful to never expose themselves. The idea of vampires had remained a myth among the mortal community at large, but Giselle worked the streets at night. It was possible they weren't the first vampires she'd encountered. "Shade, the girl... Giselle, she saw us."

He bent over to pick up the painting that was propped against the wall and looked up at her. "*Bel*, this is Paris, lovers have trysts everywhere, including alleys. She's a hooker, she saw us having sex. Not the first time, I'm sure."

She slid her arm around his as they walked out of the darkened alley. "No, I mean she saw the beast. She saw your eyes and watched you feed. She became frightened and said the word 'vampire' before she ran away."

He stopped abruptly and pulled her back into the alley, as he assessed the situation. "She knows I am immortal! I told her my name, but not my last name. But then again, she's a hooker, so what she says may not hold much weight. Still. It is a risk." Closing his eyes, he honed his senses but didn't pick up any danger. "We have to find her, *mi amore*. We can follow her scent. She can't be too far."

Kate looked across the dwindling crowd. The artists had packed up their inventory of art and cleared the square, but there were mortals wandering the narrow streets, patronizing the bars that never closed. Kate pointed, "She ran off in that direction. She's in heels, she can't run very fast."

He nodded. "Follow me. I need to erase her memory. We need to figure out a way to approach her that doesn't frighten her."

Taking her hand, they walked quickly down the street as he picked up her scent. She must be frightened because her path was taking him into areas where there was more of a crowd, as people entered and exited the many bars. "She is close, I can smell her. Walk with me, as if we are just having a stroll."

As they moved through the crowd, he followed her scent and saw her leaning against the wall of a cafe. "There she is, *mi amore*, by the cafe. She is probably still startled and trying to convince herself she did not see what she thought she saw."

Kate smiled to herself. She bet the little bitch wouldn't be as eager to snuggle up to her mate this time around. Still, they had to play it cool. The last thing they needed was some woman screaming vampire and running through the streets.

He read her thoughts and chuckled. "So, we have a decision to make here, do you approach her, or do I? Or do we go at her together? What do you think is most effective?"

Kate bit her lip, trying to remember what Giselle might have seen. "I think she only saw you. Your eyes, and she saw you feed. She may still think I'm mortal. Let me approach her first."

He kissed her quickly. "I am going to approach her from behind. Keep her distracted as long as you can. I just need to lay my hands on her head and wipe her memory, *si*? Unless you think I need to kill her for touching me?" He grinned.

He was making a joke, but she knew this could get out of hand. "Hopefully, it won't come to that."

He left her side, to get in position. Kate decided her best option was to play a distraught mortal who was seeking solace from someone who might be able to appreciate her circumstances. She ran her hands through her hair, leaving it disheveled, and broke a strap on one shoulder of her sundress. She looked down to see her knees were already dirty from kneeling in the alley, and kicked off one shoe, tossing it aside. She saw the girl standing outside the bar, approaching men as they left. Kate headed in her direction and saw the fear in Giselle's eyes when she looked up, recognizing her. Kate called out to her, "Giselle, please. I need help."

Giselle looked past Kate, looking for the handsome man that had been with her, and glad now she hadn't been invited to join them. Giselle was still not sure she wanted to get involved. "Stay away from me."

Kate got closer, knowing if Giselle made eye contact, she could hold her in her gaze, and keep her from running. "Please. Don't run."

Giselle was annoyed, but also a little frightened. "Why should I help you?" She looked at the disheveled woman standing before her, staring into her amber eyes. She felt a calmness come over her as she stood transfixed.

***

Shade moved faster than mortal eyes could see and got behind Giselle, staying out of her line of vision and waiting to see if Kate could detain her. He could overhear their conversation, and he was impressed. Damn, he loved that woman. He'd never allowed her to work the streets, as his warriors, but she was holding her own. He saw the moment she locked eyes with Giselle, immobilizing her, and he moved in quickly behind her. He spun her around, locking the startled girl in his gaze, gripping her firmly. He spoke in a soft voice and watched as she relaxed her shoulders. There were a lot of people around, so he pulled her close, and ran his hand through her hair. "I mean you no harm. Relax, you are safe with me."

He felt her heart rate slow, and reached up, laying his hand across her forehead, as he pulled her to his chest. He quickly wiped her memory clean. She wouldn't remember them, or the events that unfolded in the alley. Dropping his hand, he kept his eyes locked with hers. "Go home, Giselle. Turn around and walk home." He released her and reached for Kate's hand as the two of them disappeared into the crowd.

Giselle stood stunned for only a few seconds and then blinked her eyes, feeling a moment of confusion. She looked about at the people walking out of the bar, then wandered off in the direction of her nearby apartment,

Shade looked over his shoulder to see the girl slowly move through the crowd, looking a bit disoriented. "Well, Giselle won't be making any more money tonight."

Kate looked back to see Giselle walking away from the bar, presumably on her way home. She almost felt sorry for her. She couldn't help but notice how quickly and skillfully Shade had been able to manipulate her. "We should go home now. I think we've caused enough trouble for one night."

He looked her up and down. "*Si, mi amore*, you look a bit worse for wear this evening." Taking her hand, they teleported back to their house.

On the journey home, she wondered how many times he'd fed from mortal women and erased their memories. After all these years, she still felt the pang of jealousy over women he'd known centuries before she was even born.

69

Shade stood on the balcony, taking in the Paris air. He was in a good mood, relaxed and rested. He scanned the beautiful skyline and knew it was time for them to go back to Bel Rosso. It had been a glorious week alone with her and he felt regret over needing to get back to the business of being a warrior. He knew Kate was ready too, he could feel it, Bel Rosso would always be home to them both. He heard the soft tread of her bare feet coming up behind him and smiled, knowing she could feel his hesitation to leave Paris. Her hands slid around his waist, her head lying on his back. "We have to go back home, *mi amore*."

As her head lay against his strong back, she could hear the deep rumble of his voice in his chest when he spoke. Squeezing him, she closed her eyes. It had been so good to escape the tension that had swirled around them with the Borgia. They were able to push it all aside for a few days and pretend everything was fine. He didn't speak about it, but she knew there was the increased activity in the camp and heard the hesitation in Lorenzo's voice whenever she spoke to him. Other than the Battle for Bel Rosso, Kate had never seen a large battle. If they went to battle with the Borgia, it wouldn't be for a few acres of land, it would be for all northern Italy, and she had no illusions it would result in a massive loss of life for both sides. She felt a tightening in her throat. She had lived in their culture long enough to know there would be two primary targets on both sides of the battle. The Medici would be working hard to take down Rodrigo and Soren, and the Borgia would be working equally hard to take down Shade and Lorenzo. She swallowed hard, unable to bear the thought of losing either. Staying in Paris and pretending wouldn't make the problem go away. It was time to go back home and face whatever lay ahead. "Yes, it's time."

He felt his heart constrict with her thoughts. Her worry was valid. He'd always made it clear to her, he'd protect her with his life, and that hadn't changed. He spun around slowly and looked down into her face. "We have survived this long, *mi amore*. We are stronger now, our warriors greater in number, and our bloodline secured through our children and grandchildren. We will fight and win, and our bond can never be broken. We will move forward as always." He cupped her face in his hands. "I confess, I brought us here to escape the chaos in the camp and all the worry over the Borgia. I have no regrets, we both needed this, but it is time to return to reality." He kissed her forehead and pulled her tight into his chest. "Nothing will touch you, *bel*."

She melted into him, enveloped in his arms. She had no fear for herself. He'd always protected her. She'd seen him in battle, and like every Medici warrior, he knew only one code of ethics: no surrender, no retreat. It wasn't her life she feared losing, it was his, and Lorenzo's, and every warrior who bore the Medici crest on his or her leathers. "You always protect me, lover. Come, we have much to do if we're returning home."

She glanced out at the Paris skyline, the lights of the Eiffel Tower twinkling in the distance, and she felt a cold foreboding chill down her spine. She blinked back a tear and rejected the idea this could be the last time she stood here with him. She shook the thought from her head, then turned and walked back into their bedroom to start gathering up the few items she wanted to take back to Bel Rosso with them, including the canvas they'd bought at the artists' colony. In her head, she reminded herself he'd promised her an eternity, and she planned on holding him to that promise. "Do you want to let Luca know?"

"*Si, mi amore*, I am going down to speak with him now." He chuckled as he watched her pick up the painting they'd bought at the artists' colony. "It just struck me, every time I saw Shannon on this trip, she was carrying enough shopping bags to open her own damn boutique. Would you mind if we teleport back and let Luca and Shannon take the jet back with the belongings? Can you manage without your Luca for a day?"

She smiled back at him. "As long as I have you."

He cocked his head to the side, his curls falling into his eyes as he grinned. "Have you not figured out by now you are stuck with me, my walking sin?" He turned, shaking his head, still chuckling, and made his way to the second floor where Luca and Shannon had their private suite. The door was open, and soft music floated from the room. He stuck his head in and found them curled up together on a large sofa. He cleared his throat and Luca's head popped up. "Sorry to interrupt, but want to walk outside and have a smoke with me? We need to discuss heading back."

Luca planted a quick kiss on Shannon's cheek before jumping to his feet. "Right behind you."

As he headed in Shade's direction, he looked back over his shoulder and gave Shannon a wink. She lifted her blouse and flashed him her bare breasts and he had to stifle a laugh as he followed his master out the door.

As they strolled outside, Shade lit up and pitched the lighter to Luca. "I fucking don't want to go back. This has been a relaxing week with no interruptions, and I feel incredible. But it is time." He paced back and forth in the enclosed courtyard behind their house. "You and Shannon ready to head back?"

Luca lit his own cigarette as he watched his master pace the courtyard. He chuckled to himself. "Master, with all due respect, my schedule is your schedule. Shannon and I have enjoyed the break as well, but we both knew it was only a matter of time before we'd need to return."

"Respect noted. I think I need to change our plans. How much damn loot is Shannon bringing back? You two will never be able to teleport all that back to the States. Thinking maybe call Dante, bring in the jet, you two fly back. I fucking hate flying."

Luca inhaled deeply on the cigarette before exhaling. He nodded his head, "Yeah, no way I can carry all that shit." They both laughed. "We'll fly back, no problem."

"Done deal. We are going to head out tonight. I am damn sure, when we hit Bel Rosso soil, I will have enough work to catch up on to last me a month." He sighed. "Back to reality, warrior." He snuffed out his smoke and went back inside. It was time to head home.

***

Kate had the few belongings she planned to take back to Virginia in a tote bag when he returned to their bedroom. Looking up as he entered, she slung the bag over her shoulder. "I'm ready, lover."

For a moment, he stood staring at her, the balcony door open, the breeze catching her hair. The lights from the streets kept her in silhouette, and the noises of the city played softly like a melody.

Their eyes met and deep inside, he was grateful for every single moment they'd had here this week. He burned this image of her into his head to keep him strong and alive on that battlefield. A lump built in his throat, and he swallowed it down. "I love you, Kate. I lead and you follow, *si*? Home sweet home it is, my queen." He reached out and took her hand, and they walked to the balcony, teleporting out fast.

Kate looked back over the city she loved and watched as the Paris house grew small in the distance. Within seconds, they were far from the lights of the city, and she pulled closer to him, as the breeze flowed through her hair, and they soared above the earth, heading to the home they'd built together. She felt the tight grip of his hand on hers. She could teleport freely on her own. She didn't need his assistance, but she loved he still took care of her. She could smell the air and knew they were over the ocean as he sped up, heading back for the States. She could see the lights of the coastline ahead as they approached, and within minutes, they were back over Virginia and circling Bel Rosso. Even in the dark, it was easy to see the layout of their land; the vineyards, the fields of lavender and sunflowers, the open pastures fenced in for the horses, and the stables. From the sky, the camp was visible and well lit. The warriors on the training field. They approached the house, surrounded by the lavish gardens, the pool lit from beneath and looking like a cool blue crystal, gleaming in the dark, the lights from the windows glowed a golden yellow. She smiled to herself. Home was always a welcome sight. He landed them gently inside their bedroom, and Theresa responded almost immediately. "My lady, welcome home. How can I help you?"

Kate looked at Shade and saw his thoughts were already shifting to the issues at hand. "Are you going to the camp?"

"*Si, mi amore*. Just going to change into my leathers and boots."

He headed for the wardrobe and began rifling through his clothes. "And don't give me that look, I know Christoph has things under control, but it never fails... Where in hell are my lightweight tees?"

Kate and Theresa exchanged a glance, and Kate shook her head as she answered, "Second drawer." Turning back to Theresa, she dismissed her. "I'm fine, Theresa, I only have this tote. I'll take a shower and be downstairs later. Luca and Shannon will arrive by morning, they're flying back."

Theresa nodded and closed the door behind her as she left. Kate tossed the tote bag on the bed and climbed on the mattress to sit down, watching him change into the leathers. "Give Christoph my love. I'll see him when he comes home in the morning. I know you'll have a lot to catch up on."

Finding his tees, perfectly folded and stacked in a tidy pile in the drawer, he grabbed one from the top and proceeded to strip and redress. He could feel her eyes on him, and he loved when she did that. "I will tell him to stop and see his bebe before he heads to his suite."

As he finished lacing and buckling his boots, he stood up. "I will have a warrior sent over for protection until Luca gets home. Any requests?" He wiggled his eyebrows and winked, remembering her words spoken to him in that alley in Paris.

She stretched out on the bed. "Oh, I have a long list of requests, warrior, but I fear they'll have to wait."

He grinned at her response and flopped down on the bed beside her, tickling her until she giggled and squealed for mercy. "Feisty vixen, always tempting me from my work and warriors."

Slapping her ass, he kissed her slow and long. "Just remember what warrior will be returning to you at sunrise. Damn, you make it hard to go to work!" He rolled off the bed in one smooth motion and headed to the door. "I will see you later, *mi amore*. Be ready for your warrior when he returns."

He knew her eyes were glued to his ass in the tight leathers that clung to him like a second skin. He walked out and headed to camp, taking his time soaking in home.

The sound of the warriors in camp assaulted him like a glorious welcome home. There was something about that sound he'd always loved. This was his camp and his warriors, and he'd built it from the ground up. He walked through the gates and strolled slowly, observing the groups at work as he made his way to the office. His eyes scanned the field for his grandson, but he didn't see him.

Skelk threw his hand up in welcome, and Shade detoured in his direction. They fist-bumped and Shade smiled. "Looks good out here,

Skelk. We just got back from Paris. Looking for Christoph. Where the fuck is he?"

Skelk nodded his head toward the barracks. "Inside. Welcome home."

Shade made his way to the barracks. Walking inside, the barracks seemed vacant as everyone was on the field. He made his way into the office and found Aislynn speaking to Christoph about the feeder compound. Since Fiamma's death, Aislynn had been the lieutenant responsible for the female warriors, as well as overseeing management of the feeders, and she reported regularly to the SIC on both the feeders and the warriors' schedules.

Aislynn stopped speaking abruptly when she realized her master had entered the office. She bowed her head. "Master." She knew he was here to see Christoph. She picked up her weapon from his desk and told him she'd finish her report later and excused herself.

Christoph stood up from the desk and made his way around to his grandfather, giving him a hug and pounding his fist on his back. "Good to have you home. How was Paris?"

Shade accepted the hug with pride. Christoph, like Lorenzo, was the spitting image of him. "Let me just say, your papa bear and queen bee are glad to be home and well-rested."

Sitting down in a chair opposite the desk, he watched his grandson do the same. "First things first, send over a warrior to stay inside the house with Bebe. Luca and Shannon took the jet back and won't be here until tomorrow. So, let me have it, what happened while I was gone?"

Christoph sent a telepathic message to Skelk to get his ass over to the main house and guard their queen until Luca returned. Skelk was a warrior of immense power, but he was always tongue-tied around their queen. He heard Skelk's mumbled response in his head. Christoph propped both feet on the desk, crossing his legs at the ankle. He pulled open the desk drawer, removing the pack of cigarettes. Lighting up, he tossed the pack to his grandfather. "It's been quiet here. We've taken in the new warriors from Europe, and it's getting a little crowded, but otherwise uneventful. I was thinking we should send some of the warriors out Raven's way, just to ease the crowding and give some of the older warriors a different experience. His camp has capacity."

Shade watched his grandson and chuckled to himself. Yeah, he was just like him. He caught the pack of smokes and listened to the suggestion about sending warriors out to California. "Good idea. Call Raven, let him know we need to relocate some warriors." Throwing his legs up on the desk, he crossed them at the ankle and inhaled deep on his smoke. "Let me know who you want to send. How is the Dead House going?"

Christoph saw his grandfather throw his own booted feet onto the desk, and he smiled to himself, realizing where he'd picked up the habit. "Theo's good. He said everything is quiet in D.C. Come to think of it, Theo has been pretty quiet himself lately. No problems though, he would have said something."

Shade furrowed his brow. "Not like him. You try to talk to him? See if something is bothering him? He has a son now, I hope nothing is wrong."

Christoph exhaled the smoke. "He hasn't said anything. Everyone knows he has the half-breed, but I haven't heard him say much. You know, it's not an issue with any of his brothers, but still, he's a warrior without a mate, and he has a son. Not likely he will bring it up."

Shade dropped his feet to the floor, standing up. "Theo took responsibility, which is what the hell I expect all my warriors to do. He set a good example. I am going to go to the Dead House and see what's going on. I'll check on him while I am there. Anything else need immediate attention, like your damn love life and getting mated? Because you know your grandmother is wondering when the next generation of Medici is going to start rolling in."

Christoph laughed, between his mother and his grandmother, it was the only question they ever wanted an answer to. "You know, it would help if I could get out of this fucking camp every once in a while. I'm working on it, okay? But just between you and me, there's someone I have my eye on."

Shade stopped in his tracks. "Damn. Holding out on my ass, I see. So, are you just eyeing her up, or does she even fucking know you're interested? Which coven is she from? Royal bloodline?" Shade grinned, about fucking damn time the boy got serious about finding a mate!

Christoph wondered if he'd made a mistake by talking. "She doesn't know how I feel. I've kept my feelings to myself. She's not royal blood, and I know that's what you want. But you also told me to follow my heart. So, which is it? This royal blood shit going to be a big deal, or what?"

Shade sat down across from his grandson and stared at him hard, their eyes locked. "I am going to be honest with you. I have learned a lot since I met your bebe, had my own children and watched them find love, and here is my honest opinion. I want the Medici bloodline to thrive, Christoph, but I also know that when your beast sits up and talks to you, listen to him. He will guide you to the mate you are supposed to be with, and that bastard doesn't care about royal bloodlines. Our royal blood is strong, Alfie wasn't royal blood, and neither was your grandmother. She wasn't even immortal. I've had this fight and I never want to repeat it. What I want most is for you to find the person you are supposed to be with, the one whose love will last for an eternity. Listen to your beast. When he taps you on the shoulder, he isn't playing games, it will feel different when she is the one. She will consume you. And he won't let you forget she is around and waiting. Will you just tell me one thing? Is she mortal or immortal?"

Christoph sighed in relief. One hurdle cleared. "She's immortal." He wondered if he should take the next step, he'd been raised under a set of rules that had been drilled into him since childhood.

Shade sat back and waited. He was glad this female was at least immortal. He'd never trade his life with *bel*, and all the hell they'd been through to be eternally mated. But it wasn't an easy journey. Shade grabbed the pack of smokes and lit up another one. "Good. Let me know if you want to take some days off. I will cover for you. I am serious, if you need this, do it. I can call your ass back in if I need you. I know what it feels like to be a warrior and not able to get to your female. Think about it."

Christoph looked at the floor. "I don't need to leave the camp. She's right here."

Shade choked on the smoke he was inhaling. *Fuck it all to hell, a female warrior. How in the hell does this shit keeping happening right in front of me and I never see it.* "Well, I will be damned. Didn't see that coming. But I don't see a lot, apparently. Never saw Theresa or Marco, or Sophia's infatuation with Alfie. So, you want to tell me, or do you want to keep this to yourself?"

Shade saw his grandson staring at his damn boots on the floor. Was he embarrassed, or just wondering if he wanted to give up the name? "Christoph, for hell's sake, look at me. I am not going to rip your damn head off."

Christoph looked up at him. "Okay, well, remember, she doesn't know. I know the rules, so I've kept my feelings to myself, but I have to admit, I think the feelings are mutual. She knows the rules too. We've never been together, never even talked about it. I mean...it's possible I'm only imagining her interest. She could say no."

Shade nodded. "I have rules for a reason. It would be an all-out fuck fest with nothing getting done if I let my warriors go at it. So, I respect you followed the rules. You are honorable, if she says no, are you prepared to let that go? Tell me what your beast does when he sees her?"

Christoph laughed. "My beast practically knocks down the damn door. It takes every ounce of my power to control him. I have to not make eye contact with her, or the beast overwhelms me."

Shade laid his head back and laughed. "Yeah, she's the one all right, damn." He pounded the desk with his fist. "Right there is your answer! You need to let her know, Christoph, your beast will not let it lie. So, what do you think you should do about this?"

He looked back at his grandfather. "What I've wanted to do for a long time, but I was afraid you'd kick my ass."

"*Si*, I like that fear factor. I am the patriarch of this fucking coven and I do tend to kick some ass when things don't go according to plan. But I am learning, the hard way, that love can't be denied. So, I have learned to go with the flow. It all works out in the end."

He stood up and hugged his grandson hard, slapping him on the back. "I am happy for you. Now, you need to tell her. You tell me when and I will make sure you have the time, under one condition."

Cristoph gave him a questioning look. "What condition?"

"Don't fucking give me that look, I do have conditions for your benefit. You treat her with respect and honor. Be a Medici or I *will* kick your ass. You going to tell me who this is, or keep my ass in the dark, because if I have to arrange this, I need to know how to get this female out of the camp at the same damn time."

Christoph nodded, preparing for him to blow a gasket. "She's older than me. Not one of the new warriors."

"Who the hell is it? *Cazzo*!"

Christoph made eye contact, looking into eyes the same color blue as his own. "It's Aislynn."

Shade's mind went blank for a moment as he processed the information. "This changes things a bit."

Christoph stepped back. "You changing your mind?"

Shade stared back at him. "No. But are you prepared if she rejects you? Are you going to fight for her? Win her? Age does not bother me, Christoph, but Aislynn has never once broken the rules. She has never once taken an interest in any of the males in the camp. She is a dedicated warrior, which is why she is in the position she holds right now. I gave her a shot when Fiamma died, and she stepped right into that position without a backward glance. She is not going to walk away from being a warrior. You prepared to tackle all that?"

Christoph nodded. "It won't be your life. It won't be like you and Bebe, I understand that. She's a warrior first and will always be a warrior. We'll train the new warriors, and we'll fight side by side. I'm only happy when I'm inside this camp, and I can't imagine living my life otherwise. She may reject me, but when she looks at me, I see it in her eyes. I know she feels what I feel, but we both knew the rules."

Shade slapped him on the back and headed for the door. Grabbing the doorknob, he looked over his shoulder. "I'm heading to the Dead House. You have my blessing, the both of you. Now, you need to tell her how you feel and find out if that feeling is mutual, but I think you already know the answer. Don't wait too long, we got a monster beating on our door, and I need you to be ready. Trust me on this. If this bond is meant to be, you will both be stronger. I love you, Christoph. I'm proud of you, you handle a lot for your age. Now, get your ass busy, bust some heads out there and figure out when to chase this female your beast is ready to tackle."

Shade walked out the door and took a deep breath. Another love blossomed on the grounds of Bel Rosso. He felt alive and knew in his heart they'd make a good mating, if it was to be. He teleported out to D.C. Now, he needed to see what was on Theo's mind, and hoped like hell it wasn't a problem with a female!

Medici

70

Shade teleported over Washington, diving in low so he could see the warriors on duty as they worked the rooftops. He made a pass over Georgetown for old times' sake. He landed on the roof of the house across from Alec and Rissa's old house. This used to be his old beat when he'd first came here. The house was lit up and people were moving about, passing in front of the windows. Someone else now occupied the house. His memories began to roll, and he shut them down. There wasn't a lot about Alec or Rissa he cared to remember. They had both betrayed him.

He teleported out to the Dead House, walking inside the old Victorian building. The interior had changed drastically over the years to include the most modern in surveillance technology, while the outside remained boarded up, with bars on all the lower floor windows. He made his way to the control room and found Theo sitting in front of the control panel, reading a book. "You decide to feed your brain or just bored?"

Theo looked up, tossing the book on the desk. "Oh, hey. Just passing the time. It's really quiet tonight." He looked over at the large monitor. All of the warriors wore a tracking device, so he could see exactly where they were on the grid. "Nothing to report, which is a good thing, I guess. How was your trip?"

Shade sat down in front of the monitors and kept his eyes on the screen, watching the movement of the warriors. "Good, all good, brother. So, you didn't hear me coming in. That book must be a damn interesting read."

Theo shrugged. "Not really. Just had some stuff on my mind. I guess you heard I went out to the orphanage. Natalia met me there so I could visit Noah."

"Well, since I just got in a few hours ago, can't say I heard that. I have been secluded with the queen for a week." He sat back in the chair and lit up a smoke. "I was just talking with Christoph. We are going to send some warriors from Bel Rosso to the California camp. It's getting a bit crowded since we stopped taking new warriors in at

Castello." He pushed the pack toward Theo. "So, tell me how your visit went with your son? And how did you get Natalia to meet you there?"

Theo accepted the cigarette, even though he had a pack of his own. "I called Marcello. He intervened on my behalf. Natalia set up a visit and she and Marcello met me there. Noah looks really good. I mean, he looks so healthy now. I almost didn't recognize him." He was silent a moment before making eye contact with Shade. "Can I ask a personal question?"

Shade watched him closely. He could see there was something on this warrior's mind. "You can ask anything you want, Theo. That is what I am here for. Shoot."

Theo fidgeted before asking, "I know you adopted Cory when you found out he was your son, but he was a teenager when you found him, he was almost a man. If you'd known earlier...if you'd found him earlier..." He let the question trail off unspoken. "I mean, we didn't have the orphanages then. It's not like you could have taken him with you, but...do you wish you'd found him sooner, known sooner? Would you have found a way to take care of him?"

Shade sat up, leaning his elbow on the control table, and moved his chair to face Theo. "I don't even have to think about that one. It plagued me for a long time once I had found out I had a son that had been roaming the earth for years. I would have sought him out, Theo. I would have found him, given him protection and a home. You are lucky, you found your son when he was just a newborn. And now, we have the orphanages. It will change our whole race, eventually. I think none of that would have come about if Cory had not come into my life. Natalia grew up with Cory, she saw him as her brother, not some half-breed. That opened her eyes to the treatment of all half-breeds, and she was in a position to do something about it."

Theo nodded. "But you're a master, you have more options, more control. I may never mate. Honestly, I prefer being solo, but I can't ignore my son. I thought getting him into the orphanage would be enough, but he's on my mind a lot. So, I guess I'm asking, how do I adopt my son? I know he needs to stay where he is and get an education, but I want to see him regularly, and when he grows up and leaves the orphanage, I want him to be with me. I know he'll never be a warrior, but I can provide for him, help him get started in life... as you did for Cory. I can make sure he has a place where he feels like he fits in."

"I adopted Cory because he is my son, not because I am a master or king. He is my blood, and I wanted to acknowledge that to the world, but most importantly, to him. He was floundering, and he needed roots and a place where he fit in. He needed a male figure in his life, to help him learn how to adapt to our culture. You, on the other hand, have different options. I would suggest you talk to Natalia. You don't need to adopt him, Theo, you just need to record him as your lineage in the Council records. He is already yours. Having his birth documented, officially recognizing him is what is important for the half-breeds, as well as for you. It establishes his legitimacy."

Shade was pleased Theo wanted his son with him. He threw his arm over his shoulder. "I have no problems with Noah becoming part of the Medici coven. He belongs with us. But that is far ahead of us, *si*? Let's face that when the time comes. As for now, you need to make sure you set up a visitation schedule and keep it. As Noah grows up, he will have expectations of your visits. If you start this, you have to see it through, or you cause him more pain. You are setting a precedent for how all of the vampires who wish to claim their own blood will play out in the future."

Theo was relieved his master understood. "Natalia has already told me I can be a part of his life in the orphanage, so I'm not concerned about that. It was more about what happened afterward. I wasn't sure since I didn't have a mate if I would have the same opportunity to continue to care for him. He can live in the camp if he wants. It's too early to know what his skills will be, or what he will be interested in, but I want to help him. I'll talk to Natalia about making sure he is recorded as my son. Thank you, master. This takes a great burden from my shoulders."

Shade pounded him on the back. "Theo, your son can be a source of great joy in your life. After Cory, we all know what a half-breed can accomplish now. We know they can survive, and even thrive, in our culture, and make strong contributions. I know Noah will have that. We will make sure of it. It will not be easy, raising him without a mate. I was lucky to have found *bel* before I found out about Cory. Being a warrior will make it challenging to find the time to care for him as much as he needs. It will be a huge responsibility; there is no book to teach you how. Once you start, you can't just stop and walk away because it's too hard. It is a lifelong job. You understand that, *si*?"

He nodded. "I understand, and I take it on willingly. I know he's in the best place now, because I could never care for him this young. But if he knows I'm his father, if he grows up knowing who I am and knowing I love him and will be there for him when he's old enough to leave, that's all that matters. We'll figure out the rest of it together... as you and Cory did."

Shade stood then and walked around the console, his hands running through his hair. "Cory is getting very old. I do not know how much longer he will live. It is something that worries me all the time, letting him go. I know I have given him a good life, and hopefully made up for all the mistakes I made by not being there when he was young. Noah will pass before you, Theo, unless something happens to you. I will speak with Natalia and Kate, we need to make sure if something happens to you that Noah comes to us, regardless, and we will make sure he is provided for. I can at least promise you that. I am still not sure I am prepared to outlive my own child, and how it will feel to lose one of my own."

Theo nodded as he took another drag on the cigarette. "Yeah, I was noticing how old Cory was getting the last time I saw him in camp. I'm aware I will most likely have to bury my son. Still, Cory has lived longer than a mortal, and he's had a good life, and Noah can too. If you can make sure Noah is protected, if something should happen to me, that would mean the world to me, and ease my mind, knowing no matter what, he'll be taken care of."

Shade turned and looked at him. "Consider it done, Theo. He belongs with the Medici coven. We take care of our own, so rest your mind. If there is ever anything you need to talk about, come to me, come to your queen, we are here for you."

Theo stood and accepted his hug, as they slapped each other on the back. Shade stepped back and looked at him. "I think I have had enough of coming back to reality for one night. I will discuss all the things we talked about with Natalia and Kate. Natalia will see his birth is properly recorded."

“I’ll raise him right, master. He’ll know what it means to be Medici, even if he never wears the sword."

"I would expect nothing less from my warriors. Get your ass back to work, I’m heading home."

Shade walked outside and stood in the night air, lifting his face to the moon. He knew there was much to be done before the Borgia made their first move. He wanted them all to thrive, down to his last warrior. He wanted their future secured, and the Medici name to forever be one of honor and respect, representing the highest standards of warrior and family. He was going to fight to his last breath to survive and protect all that was his. He lifted himself high into the air and headed for home, and his *bel.*

71

Now that Christoph had permission from his grandfather to pursue Aislynn, he'd been wracking his brain to find some excuse to take her away from the camp so they could talk. He'd never voiced his feelings to her, nor had she to him, but the glances they'd exchanged spoke volumes, or at least he hoped they did. He headed to her private room inside the barracks and tapped at her door.

***

Aislynn sat at her vanity, brushing out her long black hair. She usually wore it pulled back, in one long braid down her back, but tonight, she was off duty. She'd use the time to do laundry, maybe take a pair of pants over to Cory that needed mending, and spend the evening in her room, reading. Downtime had been rare, lately. She heard the tap at her door and scrunched up her face. She hoped this interruption didn't mean the end to her night off. When she opened the door, she found Christoph and felt certain her night off was about to come to an end. "Master, good evening. Is there something wrong? Would you like to come in?"

Christoph was taken aback when she opened the door. He rarely saw her with her hair down, and it took his breath away. "Hey, I know this was supposed to be a night off." He stepped into her room and looked around. Aislynn was all warrior on the training field, but he noticed the feminine touches in her room. "May I sit down?"

Aislynn could tell he was nervous, and it made her wonder what had gone wrong. She smiled at him as he took tentative steps inside her room. She couldn't remember him ever coming to her room before. He was so handsome. He could make a girl's head spin. He looked so much like his father and grandfather, but he had a style all his own.

"Of course." She pointed to the two comfortable chairs in the sitting area in her room. The warrior barracks had seen more than a few overhauls through the years. Their queen was always making sure their comfort was a top priority. She felt lucky to have her own private quarters, as did all the leaders in the camp. Unlike Marcello, who'd been the previous SIC, Christoph lived in the main house on the Bel Rosso estate. She pushed the door all but closed, leaving it slightly ajar. It was against the rules to fraternize with warriors of the opposite sex, and Aislynn didn't want anyone to get the wrong idea about having Christoph alone with her in her private quarters.

Christoph noticed she'd left the door slightly open. "I hate to invade your free time, but I had a request from Velia. She said having all the extra warriors here from Europe was causing a problem with the feeders. She knows the situation is temporary, but still, we don't know how long it will go on. She contacted the Matron in D.C., asked if we could maybe bring a dozen feeders here until this whole thing with the Borgia plays out. We'll have to pay the compound a fee, of course. I was thinking, if you wouldn't mind, maybe you could join me? We need to select the twelve, negotiate a price, and arrange to have them transported here. Then maybe we can spend what's left of our night off in D.C. What do you say?"

Aislynn sat down in the chair next to his. His dark hair made her palms sweat from the desire to run her fingers through it. She quickly banished the thought from her head. It was never going to happen. She was a warrior, and he was a prince and master. He'd be expected to bring home the goods when it came to securing the Medici bloodline. She knew she was attractive and could seduce almost any man she wanted, but she didn't fool herself. She couldn't compete with royal blood. "Of course, whatever you need, master. To be honest, I wouldn't mind getting away from camp. It's getting cramped in the barracks with all the warriors from Florence. It's become hard to find a quiet place to hear my own thoughts."

She smiled and bit her lip. They could be alone in D.C. for the rest of the evening? It would be pleasure and torture at the same time. "When are you leaving?"

"Uh...right now, if you're ready. You need to uh, braid your hair or something?"

He took her off guard with the comment. She looked down at her outfit and wasn't exactly sure how she should be dressed. She was wearing jeans and a thin, flowing top that skimmed the top of the waistband, and was still barefoot. She quickly raised her eyes to his. "Should I look as though I'm a lieutenant of the Medici camp? I can easily change into leathers if you want. I don't want to embarrass you."

He laughed. "Aislynn, you could never embarrass me. Besides, I've never been inside another feeder compound. Shade usually handles this stuff. If we're in leathers, we won't be able to hang out in the district later. So, just throw on some sandals. I was planning on just staying in jeans as well. And one more thing...while we're out, away from the other warriors, call me Chris."

She paused momentarily. His family called him Chris, or Christoph. A few of the male warriors who'd befriended him called him Chris. She'd always called him master, except when she dreamt of him. In her dreams, she called him Chris. She nodded and stood up, straightening her top and running her hands through her hair. "Yes, okay...well, feeder compounds are run much the same, Chris."

She quickly went to her closet and grabbed a pair of sandals, slipping them on. "They all serve the same purpose, none are as grand as ours, but functionally, I imagine the D.C. compound will be much the same. The Matron there is Lena. We've sourced a few feeders from her compound before." Reaching up in her closet, she grabbed a knife and slid it inside her jean pocket. It was sheathed, but paper-thin and could easily kill if angled correctly. "Ready."

He smiled back at her. He liked she was low-maintenance, and it didn't take her any time to get ready. That was a reflection of her training as a warrior. "Let's go then." He left her room and could hear her following as they made their way to the training field. Christoph made sure Skelk had everything under control and told him they'd be gone the rest of the evening before the two of them teleported out.

It was a short trip to the feeder compound, which was actually on the outskirts of Washington, in the Virginia countryside. They landed at the guard shack, where the guard stepped out to greet them. Christoph had called ahead, and they were expected. The guard waved them in, and they walked to the compound. Christoph looked at her, "I'm going to let you select the twelve. You have a better idea of who will fit in with our existing feeders. Besides, you'll be the one who has to manage them. That okay with you?"

Aislynn nodded her head. "That's fine." As they walked in, Aislynn took control, and they were immediately taken to Lena's office. Lena showed them into a private room, where about two dozen feeders had been lined up. Aislynn casually walked amongst them, asking them questions as Christoph sat back and watched. She selected eleven females and then turned to Christoph. "You choose the last one. I insist."

Christoph looked over the remaining selection and picked out the girl with long black hair and ice-blue eyes. She looked a lot like Aislynn, but without the definition in her muscles. "Then I pick this one." He knew she had to see the resemblance, and he gave her a wink when he made his choice.

Aislynn was a bit shocked at how obvious he'd made his choice but was secretly thrilled. She didn't miss the wink or its subtle innuendo. Her heart desperately wanted to believe he liked her, but she knew it was against all rules. She'd pushed her feelings down for him for a long time now, since the day he'd walked into the Bel Rosso camp. He was her master, a prince, a future king, and off-limits to her completely. She valued her position and her pride as a warrior. She'd never compromise that for anything. "Good choice." She turned from him then, her heart hammering in her chest as they proceeded back to the office, sealing the deal with Lena. When they exited, she glanced at her watch. "So, what does one do on a night off in the district?"

Christoph chuckled. "Beats the hell out of me. My grandfather hasn't given me much time off, and I rarely get assigned to the Dead House. Theo gave me the names of a couple of bars that serve Midnight. You want to go for a drink?"

Aislynn grinned up at him. "So, let me get this straight, you asked Theo for advice on bars? This should be interesting! I'm thirsty, but I have one condition." She crossed her arms over her chest. "That you don't overindulge, and I'm not seen dragging your butt back to Bel Rosso."

He laughed with her. "Listen, I still have to answer to my grandfather, so that won't be a problem. Hey...there's someplace I wanted to check out first. You game?"

"I'm game. Lead on."

"It's a surprise. May I hold your hand while I teleport us there? I don't want to tell you in advance. I've never been there myself. Just something I wanted to check out." He held out his hand to her.

Aislynn felt her knees go weak. Hold his hand? She looked from his face to his hand and felt her face flush. She stammered a bit, her voice going soft as she looked about, checking to see who was around them. "Sure." She took his hand and felt the sparks fly up her arm and straight to her heart.

He felt the electricity between them and saw her blush, and it pleased him. "Stay with me." He teleported them out in the direction of D.C., and stopped in Arlington, landing on the rooftop of a high-rise condo complex. They were surrounded by other high-rise condos, and he saw the look of confusion on her face.

"Did you bring me to this spot for a reason? What am I looking for?" She looked up at him, staring into those eyes.

He nodded, looking across the street, counting the floors until he found the condo. He pointed at it. "See that condo across the way, count up seven floors. That's where Bebe lived when she was mortal. My grandfather met her at a cocktail party and fell in love with her. He found out where she lived and rented the penthouse in this building we're standing on, so he could be close to her. He told me the story, of how he courted her when she was a mortal before she ever knew he was vampire. He said he never told her he lived here. He didn't want her to know he was watching her, because it would have frightened her away." He looked at the lighted windows as a young couple moved about inside the condo.

Aislynn listened to his deep voice, how it changed to a softer tone when he talked about his grandfather. "I knew she'd been mortal. I've never heard their story before. It sounds romantic. They have a special and unique love. It's truly rare to find a mate that remains as devoted as the day you met them. We've all seen how he looks at his queen. He sees nothing else when she's near. I can't imagine ever having someone that special in my life. It's been hard being a female warrior and fighting against the odds. Some of the male warrior's mate, but it's rare, even for them. For me, it's just a dream."

Christoph kicked at some loose gravel on the flat rooftop, still holding her hand. "Doesn't have to be...just a dream, I mean."

Aislynn was quiet for a moment, not sure she'd understood his meaning. He still held her hand, and she was struck by how protective the gesture felt. She took a shaky breath. "I'm a warrior, in charge of many, as are you. But there's a big difference. You're obligated to mate and carry on your bloodline. For me, I was born to be a warrior. I could never give that up. I'm proud of it. I love being a warrior for the Medici. Being mated isn't my destiny, Chris."

He dropped her hand and slid both hands into his jean's pockets. "And you're okay with that? I mean, it's true I'm expected to mate. That's been made clear to me from birth. But what about you? If you could mate, and still be a warrior. Why wouldn't you want both?"

She looked out over the night lights and shrugged. Suddenly, her heart felt heavy. "I never really thought about whether I could have both. I've worked hard to reach a level of leadership among the warriors. I appreciate that I'm in the Medici camp. When I first came here, female warriors were rare and not exactly popular. But a lot has changed in our culture, and I had Fiamma, as well as Natalia to thank for that. Fiamma took me under her wing and taught me everything she knew, including how to navigate my way through our male-dominated culture. After she died, and I was promoted, all thoughts of any type of relationship went by the wayside. Now, Natalia is working to ensure our equal status, and I see changes for us in the future." She walked in a slow circle around the rooftop. "So, what's her name, Chris? You brought me here for a reason, and you seem to be trying to tell me something. I can only assume you have your eye on someone." She couldn't look at him, afraid of his answer. He wasn't hers, and never had been, but the thought of him being mated to someone else would hurt deeply.

He could feel her nervousness but wasn't sure of the cause. Was she nervous she was the one he was attracted to or the one he wasn't? He tried to read her thoughts, but they seemed as confused as he was. "Wow. I thought I was being subtle, but I guess not. Didn't realize you'd pick up on the fact I had someone in mind. I brought you here for a reason, Aislynn. My grandfather threw the rules out the window when he met Bebe, and that's what I've done. I went where my heart led me, and it led me to you."

Her head spun. He wanted her? The attraction she'd held for him had been mutual, and not just a fantasy? She turned slowly and went to him. Taking both his strong hands into hers, she looked up at him. "I've always felt a connection to you but dared not think it was mutual. I've worked to keep it hidden, knowing it was against all the rules. You'll rule this coven someday, as master and king, and I'm honored you think of me in this way. But I'm not sure your family will feel the same. I'm warrior born, and there's no royal blood in my lineage." She looked deep into his eyes, squeezing his hands. "You deserve so much more."

He returned the squeeze of her hands. "First of all, I think I'm the best judge of what I deserve. I'm a warrior too. This is all I know. I was trained in Florence and have lived in a warrior camp all my life, either here or in Italy. I can't imagine a life away from camp, or my brothers. I know my grandfather juggles two worlds, running the family businesses and overseeing the camps. For me, I have no interest in the business. There are others in the family who will take that on. Secondly, I don't take this lightly. I spoke to my grandfather before I approached you, and he approves of our union. I know your loyalty to this family, and how much of your life you have dedicated to being a warrior. I would never ask you to give that up. You can be with me and still be a warrior."

Aislynn had been a warrior a long time, she was older than Christoph, and had experienced a great deal. She'd felt a mild attraction to other warriors in the past, but nothing like she'd felt for Chris. For the first time, she felt more female than warrior. She ached to be held by him, feel his arms around her, and feel his lips against her. She couldn't fathom what it would be like to taste his royal blood on her tongue. He was all she'd ever wanted. "Then I choose you. I can't imagine being with anyone else."

Christoph sighed in relief. "I was afraid you'd say no. I've been in love with you a long time, but I kept my feelings to myself. Like you, I knew the rules. I thought I'd get pushback from my grandfather, but when I talked to him, he gave us his blessings. That's why I brought you here. This is where it began for the two of them. This is where he was living when he made his own choice to reject the rules. Bebe wasn't royal and wasn't even immortal. If they can make it work, then certainly, we can. I can move slowly, Aislynn, give you all the time you need. I know this is sudden, but I'll wait for as long as it takes. You're the one my heart seeks."

"It won't be easy, Chris. We have a camp to run, and who knows what will happen with the Borgia. I think we both know it's not a matter of if, but when, something will go down." She dropped her hands from his and slid one hand along his cheek. "Slow is good, we have a lot ahead of us, but knowing we can face it together makes us both stronger."

He placed his hand over hers. "We fight side by side. It gives us both the strength to endure. Now, let's not spend our whole night on the rooftop." He slid his free hand into the pocket of his jeans and extracted a key. "To my grandfather's penthouse. It was unoccupied, so I rented it for the night in case you said yes. So, tell me, Aislynn, yes or no, to a night in the penthouse suite?"

She smiled and bit her lip. "Come on, warrior. Let's test those bedroom battle skills. I have a feeling this might be your lucky night. Think you can handle a female trained by the Medici?"

He laughed as he pulled her close. "Trust me when I say, I know I'll have my hands full!" He took her inside the penthouse his grandfather had occupied so long ago. He stood with her for a minute at the large picture window that looked across at the condo his grandmother once owned. There was a clear view into both the living room and the bedroom. Christoph chuckled to himself. His grandfather hadn't given him any details on what he'd observed while he stood in this very spot, watching his grandmother, but it didn't take a lot of imagination to figure it out. "This is where it all started. If P-bear hadn't turned Bebe, hadn't fallen in love with her, I wouldn't be standing here right now. It's fitting, don't you think? That we begin here?"

Aislynn knew at that moment he loved her without a doubt, and she him. He'd brought her to the place where it had all begun. Taking his hand, she led him away from the window and toward the back of the apartment to the bedroom. "I can't think of a better place to begin. I hope it brings us the same good fortune and love it brought to my king." She stopped when she got to the door of the bedroom and spun around to face him. "I didn't speak the words, I've held them unspoken for so long, but I love you, Chris."

"I've always loved you, Aislynn. From the first time I laid eyes on you as a young boy. I was too young for you then, and the other warriors teased me and said all I needed was a good feeder. I kept my distance for as long as I could until my beast wouldn't allow me to walk away any longer. But I wanted you to know that. This isn't some impulsive act on my part. I've waited for you my whole life, and I'll love you with all that is in me to give."

Her heart leaped inside her chest. She looked at him with a devilish smile. "Then show me you can make love as well as you fight."

She led him by the hand into the bedroom, and he kicked the door closed behind him, as he chuckled. "I'm a Medici. What do you think?"

72

Shade woke early and was lying quietly in their bed, her head on his shoulder. He could tell from the rhythm of her breathing; she was still asleep. He was anxious to find out how things went for Christoph. He'd decided not to mention anything to *bel* until he knew for sure Aislynn was equally as interested in Christoph as he was in her. He slipped out of bed, trying not to disturb her, and smiled as she burrowed her face into the pillow. He tucked the blankets around her, and lightly kissed the top of her head, before pulling on his leathers and trying to dress quietly.

Leaving their room, closing the door softly behind him, he made his way to the camp. It was early, and the warriors were just starting to wander out onto the training field, seeking out their assigned stations. As usual, he walked amongst the warriors, shouting out guidance or stepping into their groups and helping them, one by one. He'd assigned most of the authority for running the camp to Christoph, but he still made sure his warriors were the worlds finest. His grandson was already on the field and busy keeping the warriors in line. Aislynn was leading the females in crossbow. He kept his eyes on them, trying to gauge how their time off together had gone. Christoph kept casting long looks in her direction, and the damn grin on his face looked like it may be plastered there permanently. Shade knew that fucking look and laughed to himself. As the warriors lined up into two groups for mock battle drills, he made his way to Christoph, who stood on the sidelines watching. He lit up a smoke as he took up a position standing next to his grandson.

"I am assuming, by that damn grin plastered on your face, the condo saw some action last night."

Christoph laughed, taking a cigarette from his grandfather, and lighting up. "Is it that obvious?"

"*Si*. Let's take a walk. Some things I need to discuss and there are way too many ears here." Shade headed around the mock battles taking place on the field and out the gate, following the footpath toward the stables. "So, let me hear it, she responded to your advances?"

Christoph took a long drag on the cigarette before tossing it to the ground and stubbing it out under his boot. "Yes. Like me, she'd kept her feelings to herself. She said she's a Medici warrior first and had worked hard to earn her station. She knew the rules about fraternizing, but also never thought she deserved to be with me since she wasn't a royal. Taking her to the penthouse, where everything started with you and Bebe, was a great idea. Thanks for suggesting it."

As they came to the pastures, Pavi was out in the field, along with a few other horses. He climbed the wooden fence and sat on the top rail. Christoph followed. "You are welcome, Chris. I thought it might help her to understand your message if she knew how Bebe and I started. I never told Bebe about that place, probably should, don't think it would change anything at this point." Pavi snorted and raised his head up and down in acknowledgment of his master's presence. "Aislynn is a warrior, and a damn fine one. I just want to make a few things clear with you, *si*?"

Christoph chuckled. "You never told Bebe you were watching her?" He almost slipped off the fence laughing. "Well, I guess, at the time, it wouldn't have been a good idea. I mean, she was mortal and didn't know you were vampire. Probably would have ended things pretty quickly. Bebe always talks about the first time she saw you at a cocktail party, and how she wasn't able to have a conversation with you, and the story about the Halloween party when she brought you back to her condo. We never heard much of the story from your perspective."

Shade grinned from ear to ear. He remembered the first night he saw her at the party, she shut him down with her beauty. "I saw her and lost my soul on the spot. I knew immediately it would be different with her. I never hid I could have any woman in the world I wanted without much effort. Hell, my reputation preceded me. Bebe didn't make it easy, and even when she let me in, we had a lot of hurdles ahead of us. I wouldn't change anything, though. She has made my life worth it."

Shade shook his head. "*Cazzo*, I saw her pale white skin, that flaming red hair, and those dark eyes and I lost my mind. I still lose it every time I look at her, nothing has changed. Never will. She is my eternity, my true mate, and I would never change one damn moment of my life with her. She is my light in all the darkness. She showed me what love truly is. I sure as hell never deserved her, and I am one lucky bastard. Here's the key, I have spent every day making sure she knows where she stands in my heart. There is much in my life to manage, with the businesses, the warrior camps, the expanding covens, my children, and grandchildren, but above it all, she comes first. If you want what I have, then you must make Aislynn your priority as well, and always show her that. I expect you to man up and hold her till the end of time."

Christoph listened as his grandfather looked out over the pasture and could see the faraway look in his eyes as he remembered the time over a century ago when he'd first met her. He'd grown up watching them, and their love and devotion to each other was apparent to everyone around them. He hoped he could have something even remotely close to the kind of love his grandparents had, but he also understood the rarity of that kind of love. "I want to have what you have. I'm ready to commit myself to Aislynn. We'll move slowly, give ourselves time to get to know each other before we mate. We both understand we'll have a lot to juggle since we're both warriors. Any advice on that?"

Shade leaned back on the fence and looked at his grandson. He'd been in relationships with female warriors before; both Adriana and Sabine were warriors, although he'd never call what he had with Sabine love. Any relationship with a warrior brought a unique peril, as warriors were the most vulnerable to dying before their time. And he knew better than most, you can't always be there to protect them. "Aislynn is older than you, and an experienced warrior. She won't want to give that up. When you're in the camp or in battle together, you're still her master and must still be in charge." Shade nudged him with his shoulder. "But one piece of advice, once you walk off that field, she must be your equal. When you are working, it has to stay professional, Christoph, you set the example. When you are away from the camp, together, then you make her the focus of your attention. Pay attention to her needs, tune in to her."

He pulled the pack of cigarettes out and lit up another one, blowing smoke rings into the night sky. "Aislynn being a warrior, changes things up a bit for you." He sighed heavily. "You do know, Christoph, there will be times when she may go into battle without you. Have you thought about that?"

He nodded his head. "Yeah, we talked about it briefly. I know I can't command our warriors in battle and be worried about her. I have to trust in her training as a warrior that she'll prevail that her brothers and sisters standing beside her will fight valiantly as well, and they all protect each other. We both know, as warriors, our lives are always at risk."

Shade nodded and let his eyes wander over all the land that was Bel Rosso. "You are like me, Christoph. When I came here, I never imagined this would be more home to me than Castello, but it is. I know you feel the same love for this territory as well. Once you mate, we will build a house for the two of you here, as we did for Cory and Madison. There is darkness ahead of us; this thing with the Borgia will affect us all. I will need to take Aislynn with me into battle. I will need every experienced warrior I have on the battlefield. But you will need to stay behind. Someone must secure Bel Rosso, and more importantly, I have to secure our bloodline, no matter what. I need to know you understand this, I need her skills and knowledge to fight."

Christoph frowned. He'd expected the warriors from Bel Rosso would be called upon to help fight the Borgia, they'd been training for that, but he also expected he'd be among them. "P-bear, I can fight this battle too. I'll feel useless if you leave me behind. I know Aislynn expects to go. I understand that as well, but I expected to stand on the battlefield with her!"

Shade rolled off the fence and paced. "This is not negotiable. Neither you nor Henry will be on the battlefield. Think like a warrior and master. If I take you, who the hell will keep this coven secured and protected? None of my grandchildren will see this battle, I can assure your ass of that. Don't even think you are giving me an argument. You have an eternity ahead of you. You represent our future, the next in line of succession. You must survive to produce the next generation, and the next. But at this point in time, I need every battle-experienced warrior to get past Borgia, and I have every intention of coming home with Rodrigo's head on a spike and emerging with your father as King of all of Italy. Am I perfectly clear?"

Christoph lowered his head and nodded. "I understand." He was disappointed, but he also understood the need to protect the bloodline. The Borgia had never mated, if the Medici could take them down, their bloodline ended, and their coven would fold. The Medici would rule all of mainland Italy. But if their fates were reversed, and the Borgia won, at least the Medici bloodline was protected for the future, so they could regain control, rebuild their ranks, and fight another day.

Shade felt remorse for his outburst, but he knew he had to make Christoph understand the sheer magnitude of what could happen with the Borgia. His grandson had never seen a battle of this size. He climbed back up on the fence beside him and threw his arm around his grandson's shoulders. "I love you, Christoph, you are a great leader and warrior. I do not doubt your skills. I am leaving behind my most treasured property in your hands. I would never leave this much behind for anyone else to be responsible for. I need to go into this battle with my head clear of any doubt that all I leave behind will be protected. You are named after your great grandfather, and his warrior's blood flows within you. Let's show him what we got, *si*?"

Christoph understood his role, and his fate. "Then I'll mate with Aislynn soon. She'll be stronger with my blood in her veins, and I need her to come back to me."

He hugged his grandson tight. "I can't tell you when to mate. You will know when the time is right. In the meantime, let Aislynn move into the house with you. But one of us will need to explain to Bebe what the hell is going on. Do you want to break that news, or do you want me to tell her?"

He laughed. "I'll tell her. You know she can never say no to her grandkids."

73

Tomas sat across from Rodrigo and Vanni, discussing the Medici and the territory Donatella still held. Tomas informed him the Medici had stepped up their patrol along the borders. Rodrigo rather liked this game of cat and mouse. He felt in control, keeping the young Medici king in a state of nervous anticipation. Tomas told him there was an undercurrent of fear inside the Medici coven and Rodrigo's face reflected his joy with his evil sneer. He felt it was time to exert more control over the Alizzi, and his wicked chuckle amused Tomas.

"You have served me well, Tomas, keep them guessing. Soon enough, Borgia warriors will be controlling both the Medici and the Alizzi territories. We will rule all of Italy soon. Until then, let us keep their minds in turmoil."

He turned to Vanni. He was aware of Vanni's feud with the Medici, and his eagerness to engage in this upcoming battle. Vanni shared with him the Medici camp had stopped taking in new recruits, and the information pleased him. He knew they were afraid of being infiltrated. He stood and waved them away, as both warriors left the room.

Rodrigo's mind quickly changed gears. He hadn't seen his pet in several nights, and he wanted her here for the upcoming festivities. He'd command her presence in Rome, and she'd obey. He turned to face the large screen inside his office and spoke her name, waiting for her butler to answer.

Mario heard the familiar tone as the call came through, and he rushed to the parlor to see Rodrigo's face materialize on the large screen. "Master, how may I be of service tonight?"

Rodrigo pursed his lips and stared with a look of no-nonsense at the butler. "Retrieve your mistress at once. I wish to speak with her immediately. Do not keep me waiting!"

Mario nodded. "Of course, Master." He scurried off to find Donatella. She'd been outside in the gardens earlier and thought Marie was now helping with her bath. He rushed up the stairs to her room and heard the soft chatter of their conversation. He tapped lightly at the door before opening it a small crack. "My lady, Master Rodrigo is on the phone. He's asking to speak to you. He seems rather impatient."

Marie stopped her chatter, falling silent, as the look of concern washed over Dona's face. "It's okay, Marie. We can finish up here later. Quick, help me with my robe."

Marie slipped the robe over her shoulders, and Dona slid her feet into the satin slippers. She followed Mario back down the stairs and into the parlor. Mario stopped at the parlor door. "I will be here if you need me, my lady."

She gave him a weak smile as she entered the room and faced the big screen. "Rodrigo. How good to hear from you. I hope all is well."

Staring at her on the screen, Rodrigo furrowed his dark brows. She was dressed in a robe, pulling it closed with her hand, and a fake smile on her beautiful face. Her voice held a tinge of fear and Rodrigo took pleasure in it. "My sweet pet, I hope I did not interrupt your plans. You are looking a bit, what is the word I am looking for? Ah *si*, bedraggled."

"I was not expecting your call, Rodrigo. I had been working in the gardens. I love spending time there. It is very peaceful to me to walk among the flowers and weed and prune. I had just taken a bath and had not finished dressing."

He sighed heavily and paced slowly in a circle. "When will you understand you do not need to ruin your hands? I do not wish to feel rough hands upon my face. I will have a gardener assigned and sent to you today, *si*. Now, I have another more urgent issue. Prepare to spend a few nights here at the palace. You need bring very little with you. As always, I will have everything ready for you."

He stopped pacing and stood with his face close to the screen. "I command to see you. I have a busy schedule, and I have no time to be teleporting."

Dona clutched her robe. The last thing she'd planned to do with her evening was visit Rodrigo! "It won't take me long. Are you sending a car for me?"

Throwing back his head, he laughed. "My pet, do you not understand the meaning of urgent? I want you here within the hour.

I will send a warrior to escort you on your teleport to Rome. I need you, Donatella. You wish to see me as well, *sí*?"

Dona's heart sank. She'd always found the drive time to Rome helpful to adjust her mindset to what lay ahead. Teleporting to Rome would take only a few minutes. "Yes, of course, Rodrigo. I will finish getting ready right away."

He ended the call and telepathically called Vanni to his office. Pouring himself a Midnight, he sat in his chair behind the desk and sipped. He didn't have to wait long before his faithful SIC appeared, more than willing to do his bidding. Vanni was dressed in head-to-toe leather and instilled fear in all who regarded him. His dark hair was shaggy and his body lanky yet muscular. He could fight the evilest of warriors. His hatred of the Medici after being banished from their camp left a deep scar, and Vanni had never made it a secret he wanted revenge. Rodrigo looked him over before he spoke. "I have a duty for you, one that is most special to me."

Vanni nodded. "At your command, master." As Rodrigo motioned for him to sit, Vanni took a seat and waited to hear his assignment.

"I want you to go to the Alizzi, and teleport her back to the palace. Do not let her hold you up, she is a conniving wench, but she must be treated like royalty."

Vanni stood, "With pleasure, master."

Rodrigo smiled at him, pleased he brooked no argument. Rodrigo waved his hand and Vanni immediately teleported out.

Vanni made haste, teleporting north, and pushing past Umbria into Medici territory. He grunted with frustration as he saw the Medici warriors on the border. Their blood would soon be flowing on their land. He headed for the Alizzi's villa, landing outside the door, and rang the bell.

Mario had overheard the conversation between his mistress and Master Rodrigo. He knew without checking the person at the door was one of the Borgia warriors, sent to escort Donatella to Rome. Mario invited the warrior in. "My lady will be down shortly. You may wait in the parlor, and I will bring you a Midnight. She is aware of the urgency. She will not be long."

Vanni strutted in as if he owned the place, looking down his nose at Mario. He wasn't impressed with the house, it was far less luxurious than the Borgia palace, but then, nothing could compare to that palace, not even the Medici Castello. He followed the butler to the parlor. "She should be aware. My master said to remind her he doesn't like to wait, so I suggest she be ready before I finish the Midnight."

Mario poured him a Midnight, and Vanni gulped down half the glass to make his point clear. He hated any vampire of fucking royal blood, they represented one thing to him, and that was making vamps like him feel like dirt under their feet. He'd never forget the feel of the flames that licked his skin long ago and ruined the only chance he'd had for a good life. He played their game for now, but it was only a means to get to the one thing he wanted more than anything, Lorenzo Medici dead. He laughed to himself as the butler scrambled out of the room.

***

Dona hurried to finish getting dressed, already feeling anxious about being with Rodrigo. She couldn't help but remember her humiliation after his last visit here. Marie brushed out her hair, as Dona slipped on her shoes. "I guess I'm ready. He said I didn't need to bring anything."

Marie soothed her. "We will take care of everything in your absence, my lady. I will have a hot bath waiting for you when you return."

Dona smiled weakly. "Thank you, Marie." She made her way down the stairs and into the parlor to see the tall, lanky warrior dressed in black leathers, with stringy black hair, waiting for her. "Are you here to escort me to Rome?"

Vanni stood as she entered. She was tall and beautiful, her long black hair hung down her back and her eyes were entrancing. Her figure was full and luscious. She smelled of expensive perfume. So, this was the bitch that lured Lorenzo to her bed. She'd fucked both Medici's, father and son. He had to admire her for her wicked ways, disgracing Lorenzo, but she was paying for it now. He knew the whole story. Shade had stripped her of most everything, and now she was a pawn for his own master. "Mistress, I am Vanni, Second-in-Command to Master Borgia. You are prepared?"

She nodded her head. "I'm ready."

Vanni detected a note of trepidation in her voice. She feared his master and he liked that. For a moment, his thoughts wandered, wondering if he could fuck her as well, but he knew better. Rodrigo would have his head, and no bitch was worth that. "Then let us return to Rome, I can smell the Medici stench from here."

***

As Vanni left his office, Rodrigo could hear Soren slamming doors within the palace. He headed in the direction of the noise, and found Soren in the parlor, pouring large amounts of Red Moon into a chalice, sloshing it about carelessly. He was clearly agitated over something. Rodrigo addressed him bluntly. "Ah, I am glad to see you are home. The Alizzi is on her way here to stay for a few nights, remember to watch what you say."

Soren looked at him and growled. "When will this game you play be over? Just fucking take that bitch and be done with it. I live here as well. I don't like changing my schedule to accommodate her."

Rodrigo felt his temper rise but remained calm. He didn't want to start anything with Soren with Dona arriving within minutes. "What has crawled into your black soul and stirred you?"

Soren paced as he raged. "The Council has more warriors around their compound, trying to protect the half-breeds. Do they think they can stop me? Old fucking fools. They cannot stop my appetite for half-breeds." He stopped pacing and stared at his brother.

Rodrigo chuckled and shook his head. "The impatient one, always wanting things his way. You have many other sources, brother, many places to find your fix. Besides, I would think a few more Medici warriors are no match for you."

Soren threw back the glass of the elixir and drained it. "Nothing will stop me. Not even you, brother."

Rodrigo smiled. "So, there is fresh blood available, *si*? The Alizzi will be here shortly, and I intend to greet her with a delicious fresh drink."

Soren gleefully headed for the door to the dungeon. "Two fresh ones below, I will make sure your bitch has a fresh glass to soothe her aching bones." Rodrigo watched him walk off and within minutes, a fresh pitcher of warm half-breed blood awaited his female in the parlor.

***

Vanni landed inside the palace in Rome, with Dona at his side. He immediately teleported out, leaving her standing alone in the entrance hall. He telepathically sent a message to his master he had delivered the Alizzi.

Dona could hear the raised voices of both Rodrigo and Soren and was unsure of whether she should even move from her spot. She couldn't hear enough to make out their words, but clearly, the brothers were having a disagreement. Dona looked around the entrance hall nervously, thinking maybe she could get to the room he'd always had reserved for her. If he was preoccupied, it may be hours before he sought her out.

Rodrigo heard Vanni in his head, and picked up the wave of her scent, and knew she was inside. As he approached her, she looked like a scared rabbit, trying to determine whether to take cover or run. "Ah my pet, it is so good to see you. Come, greet your master."

Dona looked up as he approached, and any hope of hiding out in her room evaporated. She put a fake smile on her face. "Rodrigo. It is so good to see you again. I hope I am not keeping you from anything important."

"My beautiful pet, you are the only important thing I have on my mind." He walked the short distance to her, noticing she didn't move to approach him. When would she learn? He took her face into his hands and slid his tongue up her neck, inhaling her. "Your scent calls to my blood. The only thing sweeter will be smelling my scent on you when you become mine completely." He nipped her ear softly and then kissed her, his tongue prying open her lips and assaulting the inside of her soft mouth. She didn't fight him, but she didn't respond to his advances.

Dona was repulsed by him, and it was all she could do to remain passive, and not recoil. He'd just implied he would mate her, and she felt her stomach in knots. She knew better than to reject him.

As he broke the kiss, his mouth remained close to hers. He could smell her sweet breath on his lips. "Must I remind you, Dona, try not to look so forlorn over my advances. After all I have done for you, I deserve more don't you think? Do not embarrass me in front of my guests. At least pretend to enjoy my kisses and my touch." Grabbing her hand, he gave it a jerk as he led her to the parlor. "Let us sit and have a drink. Tell me about this need to dig in the earth like a common mortal."

A butler appeared immediately and poured two glasses from the pitcher of half-breed blood. He presented them to Dona and his master on a silver platter. "Drink up, my pet, fresh blood, still warm, just for you."

Dona accepted the glass. She'd much prefer Midnight. She'd never hunted and had no idea whose blood she drank. She had only fed from lovers and feeders. She took a sip of the still-warm blood of a half-breed, knowing it had to be a fresh kill. She'd seen the announcement come down from Council they had put more warriors on their perimeter and reminded all that killing half-breeds was now illegal. She tried to think of something to say. "You are not worried about Council?"

Chuckling, his arm slid around her shoulders. "I have never worried about Council. They have done nothing in all my years that have ever benefitted my rule. And now, the Medici has one of their own on the Council. They will not show me favor. Are you worried Malachi will storm in here and find you curled up on my couch?"

Dona tried to laugh it off. "No, of course not. Malachi would never dare to confront you, Rodrigo."

"No, he would not. Council can make all the laws they wish, it is all they do. Rules are for sheep. I pay no mind to them. I think we are at a time where the Council has outlived its usefulness. I don't see much need for them any longer. Drink up, Donatella, you will be staying for several nights. I have some business to attend to, but I wish you to be near, and respond whenever I call for you, *si*?"

She drank down the glass, trying not to think about where it had come from, and set the empty crystal aside. "Of course, Rodrigo. Do you wish for me to go to my room now?"

As she responded, Rodrigo telepathically called to his brother, telling him to go to the Alizzi home now and carry out the plans they'd discussed. His brother's response was immediate, and Rodrigo felt him leave the house. "If you don't mind, I have business to attend to and will need my rest at sunrise. I will walk you to your suite, Giada is awaiting you. If you awaken during the daylight hours,

Giada is instructed to escort you at all times within the confines of the palace. You are not to leave unless I am with you, *si*? It is for your own protection. I will call for you at sunset and you will come to me."

Standing, he took her hand and led her upstairs to her suite, and Dona followed him to her room, feeling like she was walking to the gallows.

74

Soren had filled the carafe with fresh blood as his brother had requested, then returned to the dungeon, feeding from his stolen treasures, his energy renewing quickly. He was savoring the feast when he heard his brother call to him telepathically. It was time to go into action and implement the next step in bringing down the Medici, and that meant first, they must gain control of that bitch, the Alizzi. They'd discussed this plan in great detail, and Soren was more than happy to carry it out. He quickly teleported out of the palace, and once again, checked the border between Tuscany and Umbria. He could see the Medici warriors in small groups. He noticed their tension rise when he swooped over them. Soren knew they could pick up his scent. His body ached to take a few of them out, but he needed to stay on course. Tonight, he had another mission to complete. Soon enough, he'd be able to release all that anger and ache in his gut to slaughter the Medici. As he drew closer to Dona's villa, his blood surged, and the very air around him felt charged with wicked intent. This night would grow even darker before sunrise.

Landing outside the door, he lifted his face to the full moon and his chest heaved as he took a deep breath, inhaling the scent of the two immortals that lie on the other side of the door. He beat on the door with fists balled tight, indicating his urgency. The butler opened the door slightly and looked skeptically at Soren. Soren could already feel his fear and it fed his blackened soul.

Mario asked timidly, "May I assist you?"

Soren grinned, taking pleasure in the fear of the butler's eyes. "I am sent by Rodrigo." The door remained only slightly open, and Soren easily pushed it forward, knocking the butler off balance. He strode into the foyer with an energy that filled the entire space with pure evil. He looked around slowly, taking in his surroundings.

Mario regained his balance and stood quietly behind the intruder. He'd never seen this vampire before, but he felt certain he was the younger Borgia. The legend of his wicked deeds preceded him, and Mario wasn't sure why he was here. He was a fearful sight to behold, lean and turbulently dark, but not as tall as his brother Rodrigo. Everything about him gave Mario a chilling sense of danger. "The mistress is not home. May I inquire as to your presence here, sir?"

Soren turned slowly toward the butler and cocked his head from side to side, his beast on fire. He walked toward Mario, and his low chuckle echoed in the room. Mario stepped backward until he felt the wall against his back. He feared he'd made a grave mistake in questioning a Borgia.

Soren reached out slowly with one hand and wrapped it around Mario's neck, lifting him off his feet with ease. "Sir? You call me sir? I am a master. I am a Borgia. I have come to devour your soul. Now, where do you keep the Midnight? I feel quite parched after my trip."

Mario struggled to answer, clawing at Soren's hand around his throat. "The parlor, master. I will be happy to get some for you."

Soren let go of him, as the butler staggered, rubbing his throat, and coughing. "Well, don't take all night! I said I was parched!"

Mario nodded and hurried in the direction of the parlor. His hands were shaking, but he removed the Midnight from the bar and poured a crystal goblet full to the brim for the Borgia. Soren lifted the glass to his lips, and downed the contents, placing the empty glass back on the bar. He closed his eyes as if savoring the drink and Mario watched him closely. "Do you wish for more, master?"

Soren scrunched up his face, as he slowly opened his eyes. "I had hoped the drink would fill the void, but it did not satisfy. I fear I am used to much more." He reached out once more and grabbed the butler by the throat, squeezing tighter as the butler's eyes begin to bulge, his feet dangling free and kicking to be released, as the last of the air was leaving his lungs. Soren fed on the butler's fear, and on his death that lay just a moment away. His growl flowed from him, as he spun the butler above his head, like he was swirling a lasso, and laughed as he heard the snap of his neck. Lowering the limp body, the life leaving the butler's eyes, Soren took his other hand and with one forceful twist, ripped Mario's head from his body. Soren giggled like an insane child as he danced with the headless body around the parlor. Mario's arms and legs were flopping about in a macabre dance of their own, as his head rolled across the floor. The butler's blood continued to spout from his neck, spraying the room in his blood, as Soren tilted back his head, opening his mouth wide, to drink the blood as if drinking from a fountain. He quickly tired of the game, and dropped the lifeless body on the floor, and watched as the pool of blood spread out in a puddle at his feet.

Soren kicked at the head and watched as it wobbled across the floor. "That's not as fun as it used to be. It is going to take more than this to keep me entertained."

A female scream diverted him from his thoughts and reminded him he had one victim left. His beast howled. He turned to see the flash of a white dressing gown disappear from the doorway, and he began to chase after her.

Marie was running up the stairs for her life, when he leaped over her, landing in front of her. She froze in place, her body shaking. She'd witnessed the gruesome death of Mario moments before and had no doubt she was next. Her mind was screaming to run back down the stairs, but her body refused to obey, frozen in terror.

Soren fed on her fear. It rose around him like a devil's halo. She was defenseless against his power as a master. She would have to be his entertainment for the night. He howled with evil laughter, and she crouched down on the steps, trying to make herself small, bowing like an insignificant servant to her sovereign master, as if that would save her. He grabbed her hand and dragged her up the remaining stairs, pulling her behind him to the bedroom. He could hear her whimpering, as she desperately tried to clutch at anything with her free hand, to slow her inevitable end. He stopped suddenly and looked back at her. "Why do you resist? We both know how this ends!"

He dragged her into Dona's bedroom and threw her onto the bed, his beast licking his chops to take her. Marie stared back in horror, and she couldn't control her shaking. She knew she was powerless against him, and he'd do as he pleased before he killed her as well.

Soren stripped from his clothes and slowly climbed atop her, ripping the pure white gown from her body. He raped her, over and over, forcing her body into obscene positions for his pleasure, and her humiliation, leaving every orifice violated. Her struggle was easily overpowered by his strength, and her fear and soft whimpering only feed his appetite to inflict more harm. He fucked her until even his beast had had enough and retreated, and then he rolled onto his back exhausted. He turned his head and looked at her, as she lay, semi-conscious, next to him and he chuckled. "Was it as good for you?" When her response was an involuntary moan, he howled with laughter. "Fucking women senseless is my specialty. I have even been known to fuck them to death. But I have something else in mind for you."

He rolled closer to her, sinking his fangs deep into her throat, and drew deep, swallowing huge mouthfuls of her blood. Marie could feel her energy being drained away and weakly tried to push at him until she felt the darkness close in on her. She understood his intent now. He would drain her, and she was already too weak to fight.

Soren gorged on her blood, letting it run down his chin as he drank from her so fast. He drained her close to death, listening as her breathing became shallow, and her heart slowed. He stopped and looked at her pale face. She looked back at him, her eyes glazed over as she neared her death, and he thought this end was too peaceful. She'd need to serve a more wicked purpose. "Tell me you love me, and I will spare you."

She looked back at him, an evil grin on his face, as she made the vain attempt to save her own life. "I love you."

Soren cackled. "They fall for that one every time!"

Climbing over her, he left the bed and stood on the floor as he willed forth a black rope. He threw it over one of the exposed beams in the bedroom. Picking up her limp, naked body and holding her upright, he wrapped the noose around her neck. She was weak, and found it difficult to stand, and clung to him for support. He chuckled as he stepped away, and she staggered, trying to keep her balance. "Don't fall over quite yet."

She was much too weak to fight, and he grinned. He walked slowly around the room, as if window shopping, until he spotted the perfect object; a large, wide-lipped crystal vase filled with freshly picked flowers. He emptied the flowers and water onto the floor. Tossing the vase on the bed, he pulled a chair to the center of the room and lifted her onto it. He bound her ankles together and balanced her on the edge of the chair, with her toes dangling over the edge of the seat, and her body weight supported precariously on her heels. He bit into her ankles, deep into the arteries of both feet, then climbed back onto the bed, stretching out, his hands behind his head, as he watched the last of her blood drain slowly into the vase. He savored the scent and was mesmerized by the delicate pattern created by the rivulets of her blood as it ran over her toes and dripped into the vase. The blood made the wood under her feet slippery, and she struggled to keep her balance. He chuckled to himself. It had never ceased to amaze him at how desperately a person, mortal or immortal, would cling to life, even when the outcome was so clear. He thought he would just kick the chair from beneath her, and end her suffering, and yet he marveled at how hard she struggled to maintain her balance and remain alive... and for what? For one more breath? One more heartbeat? One more second of blinding fear? He lay naked on Dona's bed, slowly masturbating as he watched the maid die a slow death, and it fed him like heroin to an addict. As the vase was filled to the brim and started to run over onto the floor, he watched her head slump, and he came hard and kicked the chair out from under her. Her body jerked several times in an involuntary fight for life, as his own body jerked with the power of his orgasm, and his cum spewed forth on Dona's bed. He lay sated, breathing hard, as he listened to the slow creaking sound of the rope on the beam, as the maid's body swung lifeless in a silent last stand of service to her mistress.

Releasing a big sigh, his night's objective completed, he rolled off the bed and picked up the expensive vase holding the last of her blood. He walked to the mirror of Donatella's vanity, his reflection staring back at him. He admired his powerful and naked form. He wondered, and not for the first time, why Rodrigo got all the glory. There was no reason why he shouldn't be the master to rule the mightiest coven of Italy. He'd rule all of northern Italy soon, and he'd make sure Rodrigo knew this was to be his reward. He was tired of sharing the spotlight. He dipped his forefinger into the blood, and carefully scrawled a message on the mirror for Dona on her return. 'To Dona, with love, Soren.'

He sucked the blood from his finger and retrieved the flowers strewn on the floor where he'd left them, and placed them back in the vase, their stems now swimming in what remained of Marie's blood. He set the vase back where it had been on the dresser, his laughter filling the room with a chilling sound. He got dressed, and released Maria from the noose, leaving the rope hanging from the beam in the middle of the bedroom. He carried her body downstairs and dumped it unceremoniously in front of the fireplace. He built a great fire, waiting patiently until the flames licked high toward the chimney. He dismembered her, using his brute strength to rip her limbs from her body and tossing them, one at a time, into the flames and watched as the fire burned away the flesh and consumed her to ash. He tossed her torso on the pyre and listened to the sizzle of burning flesh and organs, before placing her head on top, facing out, so he could sit and watch the skin melt from her face, burning away the tendons that held her jaw in place, so the skull was left slack-jawed, in a silent scream.

He was amused by his own handiwork. Placing more logs to fuel the fire, he repeated the process with Mario, as he sat crossed legged in front of the flames, drinking Midnight straight from the bottle. Using the poker, he stoked the fire from time to time, until there was nothing left but ash and bone. He looked about, and picked up Mario's head, and tucked it under his arm. He strolled out the door and into the night, leaving behind him a trail of gloom and death that would greet the Alizzi when she returned. He howled as the moon began its descent toward the horizon, and he quickly teleported back to Rome. How glorious it was to be Borgia! It wouldn't be long now before they'd own all of Italy. They'd return with a vengeance, like nothing Europe had seen.

75

Giada rushed into the room, shaking Dona awake. "My lady, we must get you ready!"

Dona woke abruptly, feeling confused as she got her bearings. "What?"

Giada carefully folded back the blankets and helped Dona sit up in bed. "Master has a grand evening planned. He has invited some of his closest friends. I am to have you ready to join him. Come now, we'll start with your bath."

Before Dona had time to process the information, Giada was placing the slippers on her feet and helping her from the bed. She allowed the maid to assist her to the grandiose bathroom, where the tub had already been filled with steaming water and bath salts. Giada pulled the gown over Dona's head, as Dona kicked the slippers from her feet, and climbed into the tub. Slipping beneath the water, she must admit, it did feel wonderful. Giada loosened her hair and used a hand-held shower to wash Dona's hair. She massaged Dona's scalp deftly, and Dona couldn't help but feel relaxed. After rinsing her hair, Giada used a sponge to scrub Dona's skin until it glowed. "I can do this for myself, Giada."

The maid shook her head. "Master insists you are to be treated like the royal blood you are. He said you were not to lift a finger." As Giada helped her from the tub, she dried her off, and then handed her a fresh new silk robe, tossing the used robe in the trash. Dona objected to the robe being thrown away, when, again, Giada shook her head no. "Master said only new things should touch your skin. Once they are worn, they are to be thrown away. He said he never wants to see you wearing the same thing twice."

Dona felt the extravagance was over the top and a display put on for her benefit to make sure she knew how much money he had. Giada gave her a facial, and applied her makeup, before drying her hair and expertly arranging it atop her head, leaving loose tendrils close to her face. She buffed the nails on her hands and feet, and expertly applied a metallic gold polish. As they left the bathroom and re-entered the bedroom, a butler entered with a stack of boxes and shopping bags.

Giada introduced him, "You're back just in time! My lady, this is Tarleton. He is your butler."

Tarleton bowed his head to her and laid the boxes and shopping bags on her bed. "Master had all of these made for you. I just picked them up from the designers."

Tarleton opened the gift bags and removed the finest handmade lace undergarments. Giada removed Dona's robe, oblivious to her nudity, and started to apply a lotion from head to toe. Tarleton handed her the undergarments and Giada helped her put them on. Dona tried to object once more, "Really, I can do this myself."

Giada shook her head. "Master says no. He says your staff has never been properly trained to serve royalty."

Tarleton removed the fine silk stockings and Dona sat down on the bed, as Giada expertly rolled the stockings up her legs and hooked them to the garters. Tarleton removed the dress, a silk confection in white, that contrasted beautifully against Dona's golden skin. He helped her slip the dress over her head and zipped up the back. It fit her perfectly. Giada removed the heels from the shoebox. They had elaborate gold straps that wrapped around the ankles, and Giada helped her put them on. Tarleton opened the safe and removed a gold tiara encrusted with yellow diamonds. Giada secured the tiara in her hair as Tarleton removed more yellow diamond jewels from the safe: a large ring, a wide choker necklace, and earrings. Once she was adorned from head to toe, Giada stepped back and admired her work, giving a nod of approval. "What do you think, Tarleton?"

He smiled, "I think Master will be most pleased."

Giada nodded in agreement. "Let's go, my lady. He has guests coming, and he does not like to be kept waiting." Both Giada and Tarleton led her out, down a long corridor and a flight of stairs, to another corridor that led to a formal dining room. Dona started to feel nervous as she could hear the laughter and chatter of the guests already gathered.

***

Rodrigo had arranged an elegant and elaborate dinner party for his closest friends. Everyone was dressed to the nines when attending any occasion hosted by the Borgia. He'd also taken special care with his appearance, having chosen his wardrobe to coordinate with of Dona's, wearing a white velvet waistcoat, over a gold brocade vest. His white shirt was ruffled at the cuffs and collar. He wore knee britches in a gold color and white stockings. His shoes were also white, with a slight heel, and a large gold buckle on the top of each shoe. He'd even chosen a white cane with a gold skull handle.

Soren remained dressed in black. He roamed the room, laughing and gesturing with his company. He was on his best behavior and still on a high from his adventures of the night before. Nothing was going to spoil this night.

The tables were set with golden plates and utensils, and gem-encrusted chalices. The blood fountain sat in the middle of the large table, filled with freshly drained blood that flowed over three tiers in the tower. The guests lined up to fill their chalices.

The staff remained standing against the walls, awaiting Rodrigo's direction. He felt her approaching and knew tonight, she'd be shown how life with him could be. As she entered the room, a hush fell across the crowd, and the musicians stopped playing. Dona may have lost her position among the elite, but her beauty was undeniable. She looked like an elegant Greek goddess in the white gown. Walking to her, he smiled, "You look most beautiful, my pet."

He kissed each cheek and then kissed her lips. Taking her hand, he wrapped it around his arm and proceeded into the room. "My dearest friends, may I present to you, Mistress Alizzi, the mistress of my heart."

Dona smiled and greeted the guests as they approached, introducing themselves. She already knew most of them, they had snubbed her for years, and they introduced themselves now as if they were meeting for the first time. She knew, if not for Rodrigo, they wouldn't give her the time of day. She kept glancing at the elaborate table setting, wondering what would be served. Everyone here was immortal, and they were all partaking generously from the blood fountain. A blood fountain would never be on display at a dinner where mortals would be present. She'd attended dinners where mortals were unsuspecting guests among the vampires. Food would be served in small portions to the vampires, who would manage to cut the food, and move it around their plate, pretending to eat, then pushing their plates away, saying they were much too full. It was a well-crafted charade. But there were no mortals here. Perhaps the table was set purely to display all the gold the Borgia owned. She greeted the last guests, and then Rodrigo suggested they all take a seat, as he escorted her to the head of the table to sit next to him on his right.

The butlers leaped into action and immediately pulled out their chairs. The rest of the guests remained standing until the Borgia was seated. Soren took his place, flanking his brother on the left, sitting across from the Alizzi, his face a mask of gentlemanly conduct. Once the Borgias were settled, the others took their seats, looking for their assigned places at the table.

Rodrigo looked down the long table and was pleased to show her off. He nodded to the head butler, who signaled to the staff as they all sprang into action. The wait staff poured Red Moon or Midnight into crystal goblets until every guest had been served. Rodrigo pushed back his chair and stood, holding his glass above his head. "Let us drink to the immortal realm, to those here tonight who grace my table with their presence."

Turning to her, he smiled. "To my future queen, may she reign with a true heart of a Borgia, if she will have me, of course?"

He saw the stunned look upon her face. His proposal was public for a reason. He knew she dare not reject him in front of others. He heard the gasps of the group gathered at the table. Someone called out, 'here, here,' followed by the sound of glasses clinking together in the toast.

Dona was stunned! She thought he'd toy with her for a while, then tire of her and move on. At least that was what she'd been hoping for. She heard the guests call out their approval, as she too raised her glass and then drank reluctantly. Her mind was spinning. She dare not question him, especially in front of his guests. She caught Soren's eye as he sat across from her at the table, and the look of evil in them sent a chill down her spine. Soren had no affection for her, and he'd never made an effort to hide it. But he was as clever an actor as his brother, and no one in this room would ever think Soren felt anything but joy for his brother's decision to finally mate.

As Rodrigo sat down, he patted her hand gently, his voice low. "You are most loved by my guests and brother, my pet. Relax and enjoy the evening, there will be many in our future just like this."

Leaning in, he kissed her valiantly, claiming her to all. He could feel her trying to emotionally absorb the shock of his words, and it pleased him a great deal.

The procession of carts began to roll into the room as the servants rolled their carts behind each guest. The carts held an individual golden serving tray with a domed cover, its contents hidden beneath. The staff coordinated their motions like an elaborate dance and placed the serving tray in front of each guest simultaneously, and then stood at attention behind their chairs, awaiting the Borgia signal. Rodrigo signaled to his staff with a small gesture of his hand. The wait staff moved in unison, lifting the domed lids to reveal the evening's delicacy, the still-warm fresh kill of a half-breed heart lying in a warm gravy of blood.

Soren clapped his hands in glee and smiled with delight. His eyes grew wide, and he stared at the bitch across from him. Rodrigo cleared his throat. "Please, let us all dine on the insignificant and useless hearts of the children of the mortal whores who our Borgia vampires ravage."

Rodrigo cut into the heart with his knife and fork, as if it were the finest filet mignon. Closing his eyes, he savored the first bite. "Come, my pet, fill yourself with the delicacy, this is all for you."

Dona felt the bile rise in her throat, and she tried hard to keep the look of horror off her face. The other guests seemed delighted with the display, and it was clearly not their first time feasting with the Borgia. She tentatively picked up her knife and fork and looked across at Soren, who was positively salivating at the morsel on his plate. Dona tried to keep her hands from shaking as she cut a small slice from the heart on her plate and placed it in her mouth. She felt her stomach twist and turn and had to fight back the urge to gag. She chewed and swallowed, and looked at the heart, wondering how she'd manage to eat the whole thing. The guests were laughing and talking, as their glasses of Midnight continued to be kept filled to the brim, and they ate with gusto, enjoying the rare, and now illegal, delicacy. Dona sliced another very small sliver, raising the fork to her mouth, closing her eyes as she inserted the fork in her mouth once again. She felt like this would be the longest night of her life, and she knew better than to show her distaste for the meal before her.

Rodrigo reveled in the glorious sounds of his guests. He didn't miss Dona's reluctance to eat the heart. Soren devoured his meal before it turned cold. Rodrigo sliced another piece and held it out to her. "Come, my pet, let me feed you, you seem to have gone quite pale. Does this heart not suit you? Is it too cold, perhaps? I can have another for you quickly if this one does not please you."

Soren let out a low chuckle, holding up his last bite on the fork in front of him. "I do believe mine was about nine years of age, female, and perfectly aged for a lovely midnight meal."

Dona couldn't believe she was trapped in this horror. "Oh, mine is perfectly prepared, Rodrigo. I was taking small bites to savor it. It is so rare, these days, for anyone to serve the heart of a half-breed." She quickly placed another bite in her mouth. The last thing she needed was for Rodrigo to feed her more from his plate!

He was pleased she continued to eat. She'd learn she would be expected to obey him in all things. As the meal came to an end, the band began to play. Standing, he took her hand, and the guests toned down their chatter and laughter. "Come, let us move to the ballroom and dance."

Helping her stand, he led her to the ballroom and began a vibrant waltz across the massive room. The guests all left the table, some filling their chalices again from the blood fountain, before following the Borgia into the ballroom. Soren chose a close female friend and they too began to dance, twirling and weaving back and forth around his brother and the Alizzi, as other guests joined them on the dance floor. Once the music ended, some couples retreated to the small tables set up around the room, while others remained on the dance floor. The band struck up another song and Soren turned to Dona. "May I have this dance?"

As much as Dona disliked being close to Rodrigo, it couldn't hold a candle to how much she detested Soren. She looked to Rodrigo to see if he was going to protest, but he said nothing, so Dona had no choice but to accept. In one last effort, she looked at Rodrigo. "I must defer to my master's wishes."

Pulling her close, Rodrigo kissed her lips, his breath still fresh from the meal of the half-breed. "Dance with my brother, you must get used to his undying adoration of my queen." Rodrigo traded partners with his brother, walking away from Dona as he escorted Soren's female friend back into the throng of his guests.

Soren took her hand and pulled her quickly to his body. "Do not be frightened of me, I only wish to enjoy the pleasures my brother seeks, to know what he will soon enjoy."

He held her closer than he should, and his hand slid down her back, pulling her hips in close against his. His other hand gripped hers tightly, holding it against his chest. He was graceful in his movements, and glided with her around the dance floor, drawing the attention of others. His face was next to hers, his lips at her ear. "You are so beautiful, and you will please us greatly."

He spun her around in a circle with one hand, her dress floating out around her. Then he pulled her back against his body once again, dramatically dipping her as the song ended. He kissed her cheek, and whispered into her ear, "Perhaps I will give you sweet dreams of your future as the Borgia bitch. You know, my brother and I are very close, and he has always shared his toys." He winked at her as his brother came forward to take her hand.

Dona couldn't hide her horror and was relieved when Rodrigo came for her. Rodrigo smiled at her, knowing the scene his brother just performed was for his benefit. He didn't mind, he was used to Soren's dark sense of humor. Besides, she might as well get used to it. She would eventually live here with him, and she'd grow accustomed to Soren's black heart and games. He clapped loudly, and the band stopped playing. The guests grew still, all eyes upon him. "I have a gift for my beloved pet which I wish to present to her in front of my dearest friends."

The butler rolled an elegant cart forward. Upon it set a large box, wrapped in gold tulle, tied with a gold satin bow. "Please, my pet, accept this as a gift of my undying love for you and my wish to make your life more Borgia in all aspects."

Still struck by the vile remarks from Soren, Dona sought to regain her composure and show her appreciation for this grand gesture from Rodrigo. She placed her hand at her throat. "Oh,

Rodrigo! I can't imagine what it could be. You have lavished me with so much!"

The guests gathered round in anticipation, as Dona carefully untied the satin bow, and gently pulled the tulle from the elaborately wrapped box. “It’s so beautiful. It’s a pity to open it."

As she lifted the top from the box, she peered inside, and her blood ran cold. She staggered backward as she dropped the lid, staring at the head of her butler, Mario, his dead eyes looking up at her. She placed her hand over her mouth to stifle the scream, as the other guests 'oohed' and 'aahed', as if some great treasure had been revealed. *Why? Why would he do this?* Rodrigo stood behind her, as he steadied her, her back pressing hard against his chest as she tried to put distance between her and the severed head. "I don't understand."

Rodrigo was overcome with excitement, as she opened the gift and swooned with a mixture of fear and grief. "What is not to understand, my pet? Your servants were not worthy of serving a Borgia queen, they have been slaughtered for their lowly status. They will be replaced with Giada and Tarleton when you return home for the last time." The guests clapped loudly, showing their approval.

He spun her quickly in his arms to face him. His hands cradled her face as his eyes shone with pleasure and excitement. "Do you not love this gift from your king, my pet? It is all for you. You must rise to Borgia standards as is befitting your station!"

She knew better than to show anything other than gratefulness, especially with his guests all watching. "It is such an extravagant gesture! I don’t know what to say." Her voice quivered, despite her best efforts to hide her emotions. "You are so kind and generous. And Maria? Is she...also gone?"

He was overwhelmed with pride in her ability to display her acceptance. He knew she was putting on a performance for him, and he appreciated the effort. He could feel her inner turmoil and pain. "Oh *si*, my pet. You will be catered to by Borgia servants only." He felt her stumble and pulled her into his chest. "I am afraid my pet has become overwhelmed with gratitude and love for her master. If you will excuse us, I must escort her to her bed. Please, enjoy the evening, my dear friends. I shall return to join you soon."

Lifting her in his arms, he carried her from the room and up the stairs. He kicked open the door to her suite and laid her on the bed. Giada immediately appeared by her side. He caressed her cheek, and then kissed her long and hard, his hand sliding down to her breast, squeezing softly. "Rest, my pet, you will grow accustomed to my precious gifts as a sign of my devotion to you."

As he stood to leave, Tarleton brought in the box and placed it on a small table inside her room. "Make sure she sleeps. If she stirs at all, send for me immediately. She is not to leave this room for any reason."

Giada nodded in acknowledgment. As he walked out, his laughter was shrill and echoed in the corridor. Game, set, and match. She could have no more doubts about his intentions now, nor would she ever disobey him.

76

There had been parties every night at the Borgia palace, raucous parties, attended by both mortals and immortals. Some of the mortals were clearly regulars and were there to enjoy the sex and be fed upon. There were others though that Soren had brought in, who weren't there of their own choosing. Unfortunately, those mortals never left, at least they never left alive. The festivities would always begin at midnight when the many friends of the Borgia gathered for a night of debauchery that would last until dawn. Soren reveled in the orgy of flesh, sex, and blood, but for the most part, Rodrigo sat next to her, both of them on grand thrones, watching the night's entertainment. On occasion, Rodrigo would throw himself into the orgy, always asking if she'd like to join him. She would shake her head no, and he would only laugh and say she had no idea what she was missing. Once he was done, he would return to the throne beside her, kissing her hard before wiping the blood from his lips.

She had lost track of the days and was wondering if she'd ever see home again, when, one night, Giada entered her suite and told her master said it was time for her to return home. Giada started packing up her things. Dona was both elated and afraid. She knew Mario and Marie had both been killed, and she could only hope it had been done quickly, but knowing Soren that was probably too much to hope for. Rodrigo had told her he'd send Giada and Tarleton back with her. She didn't know them well. They had been helpful to her here, but she'd grown up with Mario and Marie, she'd known them all her life. Dona helped to gather her few things to take back to her villa when Tarleton entered her suite as well. She decided not to ask about Rodrigo, thinking, perhaps, she could leave without having to say goodbye when he appeared at her door.

Walking inside, he stepped up behind her and wrapped his arms around her waist, his face burrowing into her neck. "Do not fret, my pet. Giada and Tarleton have been given their instructions. You will see me soon, for I will not be able to be separated from you long."

Spinning her in his arms, he kissed her long and hard, a moan escaping his throat. Breaking the kiss, he looked into her eyes, "You are mine, my pet, all mine." He gave her no chance to respond and walked out of the room.

Giada ordered Tarleton to carry the bags downstairs. "Come along, mistress, there is no time to dally, master wishes you to be gone."

Dona was all too happy to comply. Rodrigo had left as quickly as he'd come, and she didn't even have time to answer him. She looked around the room one last time, her richly appointed prison cell, and was eager to be gone. "Of course, I am ready."

She followed Tarleton; still not sure she could navigate the labyrinth of hallways to the front entrance. He loaded her things into the trunk while the driver held the door open for her and she climbed into the back seat. She sighed with relief, and then Giada slid into the seat next to her, as Tarleton sat up front next to the driver. Dona was hoping she wouldn't need to keep up a conversation on the trip home. She feigned a yawn, and laid her head back on the seat, closing her eyes. The ride back was a quiet one.

She did manage to drift in and out of a light sleep as she listened to the light banter between the servants and the driver. After the three-hour drive, they pulled up in front of her villa. She woke when the car stopped, and she looked at the refurbished facade. A lump formed in her throat as she thought about the horrors that had probably taken place inside. The driver opened her door and she stepped out, followed by Giada. Tarleton gathered her few bags from the trunk, and they walked to the main door as the driver pulled away. Dona entered the access code to the house, and she heard the door unlatch. She pushed it open and stepped into a nightmare. It was clear there had been a struggle from the start, as there was furniture over-turned in the foyer. Dona held her hand over her mouth as she followed the trail of destruction into the parlor and saw the blood splatter on the walls and furniture, and the large pool of dried blood on the rug. She didn't know which of her servants met their end here. There were charred bones in the fireplace, topped with a single skull, where Soren had clearly disposed of both of their bodies. Dona wanted to cry but was well aware both Giada and Tarleton were standing right behind her. "I need to have this cleaned up. The bones removed and buried in the gardens. I don't want to see any evidence of this when you are done."

Tarleton and Giada stood behind her, neither of them disturbed by the sight of the bones stacked in the fireplace. They were used to much worse in their service to the Borgia. Giada stepped forward as Tarleton carried the bags to the upper level. "Pay no mind, mistress, we know how to clean up such things. Go to your suite, rest, and when you wake, all will be back to normal. Tarleton and I will see to our rooms. Go on, to bed with you."

Dona nodded, fighting back her tears when she turned and left Giada to take care of the mess. She headed up the stairs and into her room, again discovering signs of a struggle and the rope suspended from the ceiling, the over-turned chair, the blood pooled on the floor beneath it. The sheets on her bed were blood-stained and in complete disarray, but there was a clear indentation, a perfect outline of Soren, where he had lain, stretched out, to watch her die. It was clear now to Dona, that it was Mario's blood she'd seen downstairs and Marie's blood that was here in her bedroom. She felt dizzy, reaching out to steady herself on the dresser, and noticed the dead flowers in the vase filled with dark, clotted blood. She looked up at the mirror and saw the message Soren had left to taunt her. She felt her stomach turn and feared she might throw up as Tarleton looked on, seemingly unfazed by the carnage. "I can't stay in this room now."

Tarleton shrugged. "Mistress, it is just blood, nothing that cannot be cleaned and burned. You must understand master wishes you only to have the best. It was obvious these two servants were mediocre in their service to you. You will see a difference now that Giada and I are attending to your needs. It will be cleaned in no time."

Dona couldn't believe her ears! "I'll move to another room. Please remove that bedding and burn it as well. I will take the bedroom down the hall."

She couldn't bear the thought of Soren lying on her bed and wanted anything that had touched him removed from the house. She turned and walked, almost trance-like, to one of the spare bedrooms, stepping inside and closing the door behind her. Marie and Mario had stayed with her when all the other staff had abandoned her, and they had paid for their loyalty with their lives. She leaned her back against the door and silently sobbed, as she listened to the sounds of Giada and Tarleton, working efficiently to clean away all evidence of her butler and her maid ever living here.

Giada had joined Tarleton upstairs and sighed. "Our new mistress is prissy and soft. Soren always makes a mess, usually much worse than this. Strip the room, we will burn it all. Empty the fireplace, throw the contents on the rug and drag it outside, burn it, along with the linens inside her room. Remember what master told us, she is to be watched closely and we are to report everything. He wants to know where she goes, who she sees. I will see to her now, give her a sleeping potion and she will sleep until next sundown."

Giada made her way to the spare bedroom and didn't knock before entering. She found the mistress sobbing on the bed. "Do not fret, my lady, it is just linens and rugs. These things can be replaced, just as your servants were replaced. I will let master know what was destroyed, and he will see to it promptly. I will fix you a sleeping powder to help you sleep. Get undressed, I will return with it."

Dona was appalled at her callousness. She referred to her servants as if they were things to be replaced, like rugs and linens! Dona sat on the side of the bed, more than happy to take something that would make her sleep so she could escape this nightmare. “Would you bring me a fresh gown, Giada? My clothes are in the other bedroom."

Giada stood with her hands on her hips. "Let me make something clear to you, my lady. I am not here to grant your every wish. If you want something from another room, I expect you to get it yourself. I have to make the potion, so you sleep and do not bother Tarleton and me while we clean up this small hovel you call a home." She huffed and walked out of the room.

Tarleton overheard the conversation, found a nightdress in the dresser, and took it to his new mistress. "Forgive her, mistress, she is angry she is not inside the palace any longer. She feels it is a punishment to be sent away. The Borgia treats us well. We are not used to this abandoned countryside."

Dona was stunned to be spoken to in that manner! Giada had always been so helpful when she'd taken care of her in Rome. It was clear, now, the tables had turned. Dona accepted the gown and went to the bathroom to change her clothes in private. She knew it would do no good to complain to Rodrigo about Giada's behavior. Rodrigo had made it clear they 'had their instructions'. She had no doubt her every move would be relayed to him daily. She returned to the bedroom and pulled down the blankets from the bed. When Giada returned, she handed her a chalice. Dona looked hard at Giada, wondering if the maid was going to poison her, and Dona was startled to find the idea wasn't unappealing. At least it would be an escape. She drank down the potion without question, almost hoping she'd never wake again.

77

Henri had returned home earlier than expected and found Amelie wasn't at the chateau. He knew his mate had always been a social butterfly, but she seemed to be away more frequently. He'd heard rumors Amelie had been seen in Florence, but he knew the Medici were on lockdown until this mess with the Borgia blew over, so he couldn't imagine she'd take that risk to visit their daughter. Besides, Amelie had never been one to disobey.

Henri summoned his butler, as he changed from his formal dress, and had him bring a Midnight. "Would you by chance know when my mate will be returning?"

The butler handed him the goblet. "She should be home soon, master. Your grandson, Henry, is stopping by later tonight. She said she would be home in time to greet him."

Henri grunted. He'd be happy to see his grandson but was still a little miffed with Amelie's absence, and concerned over the rumors. "And did she say where she was going?"

The butler tucked his head, "No, master." He and the rest of the staff knew Lady Amelie made regular visits to Florence, but they keep their secrets, as they had always done, trying hard not to land in the middle of any arguments between the master and the mistress. Henri chugged down the Midnight before heading to the parlor, already feeling out of sorts.

***

Amelie arrived back at Valois chateau, happy to have spent time with Grace and Chantal. It was becoming much harder to schedule her visits since the Borgia and the Medici had stirred up their long-time feud, and her daughter was organizing the development of an orphanage for half-breeds. Her daughter already had a lot on her hands with baby Grace. Amelie was proud of her. She'd watched her daughter blossom with this newfound passion in her life. She enjoyed the visits and was able to spend many hours with the baby, so Chantal was able to go about her business unbothered over the safety and welfare of her child. Amelie quickly made sure the shopping bags containing items she'd purchased for Grace were tucked inside her leather tote. If Henri found out, he'd suspect she was visiting, and that was an argument she wished to avoid. She'd tried to cajole him, but he was stubborn, still refusing to see the importance of what his daughter was accomplishing and refusing to acknowledge the child she and Lorenzo had adopted. Entering the house, she was aware Henri had arrived before her, and tried to make her way upstairs to put away her purchases.

Henri heard her when she came in and summoned her to the parlor. "Amelie? Could you join me, please?"

Stopping halfway up the staircase, she paused. "*Oui*, one moment, Henri, I am putting away my shopping, I shall be done shortly."

"Now, Amelie. We have things to discuss before Henry's arrival!"

She turned to descend the stairs and took a deep breath. The tone of his voice told her he was in no mood for pushback. She put a smile on her face, and made her way to the parlor, to find him pacing, drink in hand. She carefully placed the tote beside the chair and went to him. "You are home earlier than I expected." She kissed him on each cheek, smiling at him before she returned to the chair. "Is there something wrong, Henri?"

"I can't help but notice you have been away from home more than usual. I have heard rumors." He sipped at the Midnight and watched her response.

Amelie kept her face blank. "Rumors? What rumors do you speak of, Henri?"

Henri eyed the bulging leather tote and found it odd. Amelie was usually carrying multiple shopping bags from high-end designers. She'd never attempted to hide her purchases or had any need to as he'd given her an unlimited budget for shopping. Moving quickly, he snatched up the large leather tote and rifled through it, pulling out article after article of baby clothing. He held up a frilly dress before her eyes. "The rumor that you have been making frequent visits to Florence against my wishes! You are going there to see that bastard child!"

Amelie never expected him to grab her tote. He moved so fast she was caught off guard, and she looked at him with pleading eyes.

She couldn't continue to lie to him, but she wouldn't back down either. "*Oui*. But that bastard child you refer to is my grandchild. I will not be kept from seeing my own daughter and granddaughter just because you have decided to abandon them. Henri, she is so beautiful. She is smart and such a joy to my life. How can you deny me this?"

Henri tossed the tote and dress aside. "Chantal will tire of this foolishness. She is bored right now and looking for something to fill her time. This half-breed carries not a drop of my blood, nor a drop of Medici blood. We know nothing of her heritage. She is most likely the daughter of some middle-class mortal female and a warrior, and you want me to treat her like my blood? I am fine with the Council's ruling that the killing of half-breeds is now considered illegal. After all, they did not ask to be born. But I will be damned if I will accept one into my home and claim them as my own! We have two full-blooded royal grandsons, Amelie, and Henry and Christoph will mate someday, and you will have great-grandchildren to occupy your time. I specifically forbade you from visiting, and you ignored my commands. I have never known you to be so headstrong! I want an end to this, Amelie!"

She stood against his torrent of anger and hatred, and it sickened her to think that she, too, had once believed as he did. But Grace and Chantal had shown her something amazing. The half-breeds were beautiful, and there were only slight differences from a full-blooded vampire. "I ignored your commands because I refuse to live the rest of my life without my child, without my own daughter. I love my granddaughter as well. You can't tell me who to love, Henri."

She picked up the tote and the delicate baby dresses that were strewn about, and carefully placed them into the tote. "You don't even know your own daughter, Henri. *Oui*, she had been lonely since her sons left home. When Grace came into her life, she found a purpose beyond being Queen of Medici. You should be beaming with pride at how much she has accomplished." She took a seat on the settee. "So, you will go to the biggest ball in all of Europe and shame her in front of them all? I never thought I would see the day, Henri when you would abandon something so precious. I refuse to end my visits and I support her in every decision. It is time you understood, I am not going to let her, or the baby, be absent in my life."

Henri gritted his teeth. Amelie had never spoken out against him before. "Of course, I will go to the annual All Covens Ball. If I were absent, everyone would notice. I would do nothing to publicly shame our daughter, but that doesn't mean I have to like it! We have never aired our dirty laundry in public, and I don't plan to start. We have an image we present to our coven, as well as to all covens. I will not have that sullied. In public, I will smile and pretend to be happy with this ridiculous notion of a half-breed grandchild. No one will see there is a rift between me and my daughter...and apparently, with my mate as well! But don't interpret my good nature in public to mean I have changed my position. Clearly, you intend to continue to disobey me and see Chantal and this half-breed against my wishes. If that is the case, then you will travel with a protector. The last fucking thing we need is to have you abducted by the Borgia and used to manipulate our two covens. I can't believe you have taken these risks!"

Amelie stood slowly, facing the man who'd become her life. Their mating had been an arranged one, but she'd grown to love him, follow his every lead and rule. But he'd overstepped when it came to their child, and she was going to stand up to him. "I would risk my life, my fortune, and everything I hold dear for my daughter, and my grandchildren. And I will risk disobeying you as well. You can surround me with an army if you like, but it will never stop me. Our daughter stood up for an innocent child who would have been slaughtered, for the sin of being born. Now, I will stand up for my daughter. Someday, this anger will haunt you, Henri, and you will regret this time you denied your own daughter."

She picked up the tote and walked away from him. Her heart was saddened he couldn't get past the half-breed child. "I taught her well, Henri, how to be a mother and a queen, and she has surpassed all that I taught. I admire her, respect her, and I only wish I could have been as brave."

Henri slumped down in his chair, drinking another Midnight. He hated to be wrong, but he was starting to wonder if he'd made a mistake. He too missed having Chantal in his life. He had no concern for the half-breed but was second-guessing his decision as to whether he should have banned Chantal from his life. He appeared to be the only one who was suffering from his stubbornness, but his pride wouldn't let him admit the error of his ways. He emptied the glass. Henry would be here soon, and he and Amelie would both put on a happy front as if this disagreement had never happened.

78

Natalia was sleeping next to him. Even in her sleep, she was aware of Marcello holding her, protecting her. She fed only from him now and ached to have him feed from her, but she knew that would go too far. She could never mate him. There was no way they could hide that. He'd continued to seek out the feeders provided for the vampires, staff, and warriors, who resided inside the Council walls. She never knew when he went, he never mentioned it, and she didn't ask. He came to her room every morning at sunrise, having turned over his patrol to another warrior. Unlike her, he was a day-walker and could choose to be in the sun, but like her mother, he'd sacrificed the daylight to lie next to the one he loved.

The doors to her suite locked automatically when the doors closed, as they did with each Council member. She had little fear of their discovery. They were discreet, and like herself, all the members of Council were pulled to their death slumber. She was sleeping soundly when she felt the dull ache between her eyes that signaled a vision. She couldn't control her visions. She had no say over when they'd appear, or what they'd divulge. She frowned in her sleep, as she started to recognize the familiar landscape of Tuscany, as warriors gathered in the hundreds. She felt the tension in the air, as the Medici warriors faced off against the Borgia, and a battle began. Most of the figures in her visions were faceless, much like a dream, but she clearly saw her father and her brother, leading the charge. She became restless in her sleep and moaned softly, as the clash of warriors began, and she saw bodies fall, and the blood soaking the earth. She saw the Borgia brothers, both taking great joy in the carnage, reveling in the blood. She watched the battle unfold as if she were standing in the middle of the battlefield, invisible to all around her. The clanging of swords was so loud she covered her ears in her sleep and shook her head no. She watched as warrior after warrior fell, both Medici and Borgia, until she stood alone on a smoldering field, fires burning around her. She looked around her, and there was no one left standing. She sat bolt upright in her bed, jolted from her death slumber as she screamed out, "Daddy! Lorenzo!"

Marcello woke abruptly, sitting up beside her and pulling her against his bare chest. "Natalia, it's only a vision! I'm right here. Look at me, you're awake now."

He pushed the hair from her eyes, rubbing her back. She was shaking, and a light sheen of sweat covered her. He knew whatever she'd seen wasn't good. Kissing her forehead, he spoke gently to her. "Shh, I'm here for you, nothing will harm you."

It took Natalia a few seconds to orient herself from standing in a smoldering battlefield in Tuscany to being safe in her bed, protected by Marcello. Her heart was still pounding in her chest. She allowed him to hold her and comfort her as she gathered her thoughts and regained her bearings. The memory of the vision washed over her, and she felt devastated. She tried not to jump to conclusions. She'd learned, just as Malachi had taught her that her visions must be interpreted, but how did she interpret this? "The battle. I saw the battle. They were all gone, all of them."

Marcello could feel her heart racing against his chest. She was in emotional turmoil. "All of them? Natalia, do you mean all of the Medici or all of the Borgia?"

He lay back with her on his chest and continued to soothe her as best he could. "Talk to me, let me help you."

She nodded her head as he cradled her on his chest. "Both, but how can that be? I saw the warriors by the hundreds, maybe thousands; I could see Rodrigo and Soren, and my father and brother. But in the end, I was standing on a battlefield of bodies. Everyone was gone. That can't be how this ends, Marcello. I couldn't bear it."

He closed his eyes. He had no idea how to help her interpret this vision. "That doesn't seem probable, but I don't know how to interpret what you saw. I think you should speak to Malachi. Perhaps he'd have more answers." He pulled her closer and kissed her. "No matter what happens, Natalia, I'll always be here for you."

Natalia sobbed quietly against his chest. As much as she loved Marcello, there was only one who could help her with this. "You're right, I must speak with Malachi. I can't go to my father with what I've seen. I can't leave him with this kind of doubt about the outcome. I'm not sure I can live with this myself. My family, our coven, we've all worked too hard to have it taken away, to have everything we've worked to build destroyed." She slid away from him, to the edge of the bed, and stood, looking for her slippers as she grabbed her robe. "I need to call Malachi. I must speak with him now or I'll go crazy with worry."

Marcello followed in her footsteps, as he pulled on his leathers. "Then I'll go with you. You must know that Medici will fight and win. We'll be victorious. You must know and believe that." He helped her slip her bathrobe on. "You know I love you."

She stopped and turned to him, holding him tight. "I love you. I don't think I could face this without you. Come with me, I need to call Malachi now. He'll be awake at this hour with the time difference."

She waited while he hurriedly finished dressing, then she made her way to the door. She listened carefully to make sure no one was in the hallway, then opened the door a crack, and peered out. The fortress that held the Council was quiet as a tomb. "Come on," she whispered.

They made their way through the corridors and down to the main floor where the communications center was located. Entering the room, she asked the staffer to leave them in privacy. He vacated his seat and nodded as he left the room and Natalia settled into his chair. She spoke to the monitor to connect her to Malachi, and Marcello sat on the countertop. In seconds, a staffer from the Council in Florence appeared on the screen and looked at her with some confusion.

"I need to speak with Malachi!"

He shook his head. "Did you have an appointment? I don't show anything on my schedule for him."

Natalia realized she'd left her room in a bathrobe, not the ivory-colored hooded robe she always wore, and the staffer didn't recognize her. "No. I'm sorry. I don't have an appointment. This is Ivory. I didn't have time to put on my robe. Please, I need to speak with Malachi as soon as possible."

The staffer nodded. "Forgive me, Ivory. I didn't recognize you. Let me find him for you." He left his post to go in search of Malachi, and Natalia looked at the blank screen, fidgeting. "What if Malachi doesn't know either? Marcello, I can't bear this not knowing!"

"Natalia, don't jump to conclusions. Wait and see what he says."

Natalia tried to take a few deep breaths and calm herself when she saw the monitor flicker to life and the green hooded figure of Malachi appeared. "Daughter, what has you calling with such urgency?" He noticed the absence of her hooded robe but decided not to mention it. Something clearly had her rattled.

"Malachi, I had a vision of the battle between the Medici and the Borgia. It was as if I stood invisible in the middle of the battlefield, and the warriors fell at my feet. When the battle ended, there was no one standing. Is everything destroyed? Is my family destroyed? I can't make sense of this vision!"

Malachi tucked his head and took a deep breath. "I have had visions of the battle as well, daughter. I can tell you one coven survives."

Natalia brightened. "So, we win? We will be okay?"

He shook his head. "I did not say that. My visions are as vague as yours. I know one coven survives, one coven will rule all of Italy, but I do not know which one."

She shook her head no, "But Malachi, in my vision, I saw Rodrigo and Soren, and I saw my father and brother. They were all on the battlefield, and when it was over, there was no one. Who lives? Who dies?"

He pushed the hood back from his eyes. "I would tell you if I knew, daughter, but I do not. If you have any power to stop this battle, then use it. I fear for us all."

Natalia stared back at him in silence. This wasn't what she wanted to hear. "We could lose everything? My family? They could be destroyed?"

Malachi massaged the bridge of his nose, pushing back against the headache that had plagued him for days from his visions. "Ivory, I never mated, and can't remember a time I did not live inside the Council walls. I have mentored you and love you like a daughter. You have been family to me. If I could spare you this pain, I would. I don't have the answers you seek. I wish I did. I only know that one coven survives, and rises to greater power, and the other is destroyed. I can't see who lives or dies from either side. I can't see if the win comes when the masters are slain, or if one side surrenders."

Natalia looked back at him, as a tear ran down her cheek. "Medici never surrenders."

Marcello listened with a heavy heart. He closed his eyes and calmed his racing mind. He refused to accept the Medici rule would end. He stood up and positioned himself behind Natalia, putting himself in view of Malachi, his hands on her shoulders. "*Per sempre* Medici. This coven will not fall, and I will protect her."

Malachi saw Marcello step into the frame. He wasn't surprised. They were both subtle and careful not to divulge their relationship, but to anyone paying attention, the affection they shared for each other was clear. "I know you will protect her, young warrior, and all of Council, but it is not Natalia's life I fear for. I must leave you now." He paused as he looked at them both. "Take care of each other."

The screen went black as Malachi's image faded, and Natalia was staring at her reflection in the smooth surface on the monitor. She felt numb and hollowed out. She leaned her head back against Marcello. "I can't lose my family, Marcello. I can't."

His fingers slid through her long hair. "You won't lose them. You need to talk to Shade. I think it may help you. No one knows the Borgia as he does. Your vision did give us something. Tell him everything you know, Natalia, tell him every detail. Remember everything you saw. The smallest detail could be important. Let your father handle the rest."

She nodded as she stood and embraced him. "You're right. He'll know what to do. He always knows what to do."

79

It had been several days since the vision, and Natalia couldn't keep this to herself much longer. She wanted to speak to her father in private, and that would be difficult to do if she went home. Summoning him to Council would just raise more questions, and her mother would be concerned. She decided to ask him to meet her on neutral territory at the orphanage. He'd suspect her request to see him would have something to do with the business of running the orphanages, which continued to expand. She coordinated her schedule with Marcello and then asked to borrow his cell phone, dialing her father.

***

Shade was thick into the mock battle with Christoph, both of them going at each other without mercy. It was an exercise to demonstrate their skills for the warriors. The warriors stood around them and cheered them on. Shade was grateful for the skill and persistence of his grandson. He'd be kept from this battle with the Borgia, but it was comforting to see how skilled he was. As they wrapped up, both of them sweating and muscles sore, they hugged, and Shade walked to the sidelines as Aislynn, and Christoph started calling out warriors to pair up and practice what they'd just witnessed. Putting his shirt back on, he felt his phone buzz. Grabbing it, he saw it was Marcello and was instantly worried. "Talk. Now!"

Natalia was momentarily caught off guard when she heard him bark at her, and then realized he'd have seen Marcello's name on his caller ID. "Daddy? It's me."

Shade breathed a sigh of relief. "Nattie! What is going on? Damn, I miss you. Are you coming out to see your old *padre*?"

Natalia paced as she talked, winking at Marcello. "I was hoping you could come to see me. I need to go to the orphanage, and yes, before you even ask, Marcello will escort me. I was hoping you could meet me there."

"Business, I should have known it was not because you miss me or your *madre*." He chuckled as he teased her. "I will be there within thirty minutes."

"Love you, Daddy." She handed the phone back to Marcello, who slipped it into the pocket of his leathers. "Looks like you'll be taking me to the orphanage tonight. He said he'd be there in about thirty minutes. Do you need to make any arrangements?"

Marcello shook his head. "I'll telepathically let my warriors know where I'm going, and that you're with me. I'm ready whenever you are, Ivory." He bowed low. "This humble warrior is at your service, my lady."

She laughed despite her worry. "Humble? I don't think Medici warrior and humble work well in the same sentence. Come on, warrior. We have business to attend to."

Shade let Kate know he was heading to the orphanage before he teleported out and found Nattie and Marcello waiting for him. The orphanage was quiet at this hour of the night. Half-breeds lived like mortals, and all of them were able to walk in the sun, so night hours here meant the younger children were asleep. His smile spread from ear to ear when he saw his daughter and pulled her into his arms. "My sweet Nattie, how I have missed you. I love you, my beautiful daughter."

She returned his hug, feeling safe in his arms. "I'm glad you could make it on such short notice. Is everything okay at home? I know I haven't been in a while."

"I would move heaven and earth for you if you need me. Your *madre* is fine. So, what do you need?"

Natalia bit her lip, as she looked around the hallway. She could hear older kids in the TV room and wanted a place where they wouldn't be disturbed. Taking her father's hand, she led him to the parlor set up for families to visit with the half-breeds. Unfortunately, it was a room that hadn't seen as much activity as Natalia had hoped. Marcello followed them into the room and closed the door behind them. "Why don't you sit down, Daddy? We need to talk." Natalia took a seat on the comfortable sofa, and Marcello stood behind her.

Shade could see the serious look on her face and he took a seat but didn't get too comfortable. He locked eyes with his daughter. "Did someone find out about the two of you?"

Natalia looked over her shoulder at Marcello. "I don't think so. Why? Have you heard something?"

Shade looked down at his battered and dusty boots. "No." He stood up again. "You are both blocking me. Nattie, what the hell is going on?" He went to her, lifting her chin to look at him. "You have had a vision."

She nodded her head. "Yeah. I did. I called Malachi. He's had them too. I'm not sure they're going to be helpful. I'm scared, Daddy."

He crouched down in front of her. "It is vital you are scared. It keeps you aware of everything around you. But you, above all, are protected." He stood and kissed the top of her head. He knew he needed to be strong in the face of whatever news she delivered. He returned to the chair and sat down. "I'm glad you are coming to me. Share your vision. Have you seen anything that will guide me, Nattie?"

She frowned as she looked at her hands. "I don't see anything that will help. But maybe you'll see something. I know the battle is in Tuscany. I know the Borgia comes to you. They initiate the battle. I see hundreds, maybe thousands, of warriors, as far as the eye can see. I saw Rodrigo and Soren, leading their armies, and you with Lorenzo. Those are the only faces I saw. I didn't see you or Lorenzo fall, but I didn't see Rodrigo or Soren go down either, but in the end, there are none left standing. I was standing on the battlefield, the bodies piled high, the earth soaked in blood. There were flames and smoldering bodies. So, Lorenzo must have used his gift of throwing fire. When I talked to Malachi, he said one coven prevails and will rule all of Italy, but he didn't know which one. Daddy, this doesn't fit the curse. I didn't see Mommy at all!"

Marcello looked at Shade and felt the hair on his neck bristle. *A curse? Natalia had never mentioned anything about a curse*. "Whoa, back up, a curse? Someone explain to me what this is about." His eyes never left Shade.

Shade stood up and paced the room, his hand running through his hair. "Ivory, I speak to you as a king to a Council member. Please ask your warrior to leave us."

Natalia turned to him, and Marcello started to protest, but he could see in her eyes there would be no discussion. "You know you can tell me anything."

She shook her head. "Not now."

Natalia heard him sigh as he left the room and cast a glance at Shade who didn't make eye contact with him. Once he was gone, she turned back to her father. She had carried this burden of the knowledge of the curse since she was a teen, and she'd carry it a little longer. "What does it mean, Daddy?"

Shade's mind was running through a thousand scenarios. He didn't doubt the veracity of her vision and knew this would be a battle to the death. The only question was, whose death? He already knew it was going to take everything he had to win. "I have done everything in my power as a master and warrior to prepare for this. I have spent my entire life preparing. I know one thing; I am keeping my grandsons off the battlefield to ensure our bloodline will survive."

He flopped down on the couch beside her, his hands covering his face, his head thrown back. "We will fight, we will win. I can't accept any other outcome for our coven. At least I know now the battle will take place on the land that bore me. We have shed our blood there before, and I wasn't able to stop it the last time. I paid with the blood of my parents. This time, I'll be damned if that black-hearted, soulless bastard Borgia will take everything from me or my coven."

He reached for her and pulled her to his chest. He held her tight. She was his baby, his last born. "You need to stop your worry. We are Medici. Love conquers everything. As for the curse, until you see something distinct, let it go."

Natalia felt scooped up in his embrace. He spoke with confidence, but then, he always did. As for the curse...how could she let it go? She had to trust everything would play out as it was meant to be. Neither she nor her father could alter the future. "I'll try, Daddy."

80

Christoph watched a bit of the action after his grandfather left for the orphanage. He hadn't yet revealed to Bebe that Aislynn was moving into the main house, and he planned on mating her. He'd been busy, and well, the time hadn't been right. He'd asked his grandfather to let him break the news to her, but he knew the longer he waited, the more likely she'd hear something. Brushing off his leathers, he decided there was no better time than the present. He gave Skelk a head's up he'd be at Bel Rosso for a while and had him take over.

He walked up the footpath to the house and slipped in the back door. He loved this house. It had been his home for years now. It always smelled great, with the vases of fresh roses everywhere. He heard laughter coming from the living room, and he recognized his Aunt Shannon's laugh. Shannon wasn't really his aunt, but his parents had called her "aunt" and it had just become natural for the Medici kids and grandkids to address her as such. Gi appeared as he was making his way to the living room and asked if he'd like a drink. He politely said no and followed the sound of voices to his grandmother. He stood in the doorway and saw them sitting on the couch together with their legs tucked underneath them, their heads together, laughing and chatting. Bebe looked up at him and a smile graced her face.

"Are you busy, Bebe? I was wondering if I could talk to you since P-bear is at the orphanage for the night."

Kate looked back at her grandson. The boys all looked so much like Shade. "I always have time for you, Chris. Come sit with me."

Shannon stood up, picking up on Chris's need. "Is this a private party?"

Christoph grinned at Shannon. "I think I hear Uncle Luca calling your name."

Shannon slapped him softly on the shoulder and walked out as Christoph sat down next to the only other woman who'd been as influential in his life, as his own mother. "I'm sorry, Bebe, I hope I didn't interrupt anything important. But I have some news for you."

Kate reached out and brushed the hair from his eyes, just as she'd done when he was a little boy. "You know my babies come first, so does Aunt Shannon. You have good news. I can tell by the light in your eyes. Tell me!"

He loved how she never swayed from caring for him. Since he was small, she'd remained protective. Even now, as a grown male, his skills as a warrior were as great as his father or grandfather, yet she still looked after him. She was always there for him and had made the transition from Florence to Virginia an easy one for him when he left his parents and his brother behind. "I'm in love."

Kate looked surprised. She'd not seen or heard anything about Christoph leaving the camp or spending time away with a female. She smiled back at him. "Really? Have you told your grandfather? Chris, I'm so happy for you! When will I get to meet her?"

He laughed. "P-Bear always said you fire questions a million at a time. So, let me answer each one. Yes, he knows and has given his blessing. And I can tell you this... It sure is a hell of a lot easier telling you than him. I went to him first, because I wanted his advice and I wanted him to know where my heart was. Mom and Dad don't know yet. As for meeting her, well, you already know her."

Kate tilted her head. "I know her? Really? And you think she's the one?"

He nodded his head, as a shock of dark hair fell back across his eyes. "I know she's the one. I've loved her a very long time. Ever since I first came here to camp. She's a warrior, but I knew the rules. I never approached her until I had P-bear's blessing, and I waited as long as I could until my beast was eating me alive. P-Bear helped me and arranged for us to be together for a night."

Kate laughed. "Shade arranged your date? Where did you take her?"

Christoph realized she wanted details about the date, and he hadn't anticipated that. He was going to have to lie or rat out his own grandfather, and he could never lie to his bebe. He smiled. Hell, why not? It would be worth it to see the expression on her face when he told her. "Well, there's this condo in Arlington. P-Bear rented it for the night for me and gave me the key. But the most interesting part was the view across the way. It looked into another building. He used to spend a lot of time looking out those windows."

Kate looked confused. "I'm sorry, what? He sent you to a condo in Arlington? I used to live in Arlington when I was still a mortal." She let his words sink in. "Are you saying he lived in Arlington too? He was across from me? Are you sure? I thought he lived here, at Bel Rosso, long before it was called Bel Rosso or looked anything like this. Never mind... Tell me about this girl."

He looked into her eyes and smiled. "Well, P-bear told me the story. He was in love with this crimson-haired beauty with lily-white skin and beautiful eyes. He was afraid he'd lose her if she knew what he was. He wanted to win her heart, but she was a mortal and had no idea he was vampire, or that he was a king. He hoped she'd fall in love with him before he had to tell her. He couldn't hold back his beast, but he still wanted desperately to protect her, so he watched over her. He told me it was where it all began, meeting the love of his life, his mate. I want a love like that. So that is where we began, me and Aislynn, in the condo where P-bear lived when he was watching over you. "

Kate was trying to absorb two separate pieces of information. That Shade had lived in a condo across from hers in Arlington, and had never mentioned it, and that her grandson was in love with Aislynn! She shelved the first revelation for later. "Aislynn? Our Aislynn? Chris, I had no idea! And she returns your affections? She feels the same?"

He hugged her into his arms. "Yes! I love her so much. I know it won't be easy since we're both warriors." He pulled back and looked into her eyes. "It won't be the same life you have with P-bear, but we're going to make it work. I intend to mate with her soon, Bebe. P-bear has given his blessing, and we both understand our responsibilities to the coven. He also gave his permission for her to move in here with me. I'm asking for your permission as well because you made this house a home and I want her to feel welcome. She was concerned that, because she's a warrior, and not of royal blood, our family wouldn't accept her."

Kate felt his joy and shared in his happiness. "Of course, she's welcome here. Tell her she can change anything in your suite to suit her. Those rooms have seen some changes over the years; for Cory, and then Madison. Then, you moved in. Now, it is time for a woman's touch once again. Tell Aislynn not to worry. I was certainly not royal blood or even immortal, and Alfie wasn't a royal. You know we feel stronger about following your heart than mating for a bloodline. We welcome her to our family. Did Shade mention anything about building a house for you? As you mate, have children? You will want your own home."

"He did. Will you help us build and design the house? We're going to need a lot of rooms, Bebe, we want to give you great-grandbabies." He laughed at the look of joy on her face and didn't know who was happier, him or his grandmother. "There's one more thing. We'll mate soon. P-Bear said I won't be allowed to fight in the battle with the Borgia, nor will Henry. He says we must protect the bloodline for the future, and it's a risk we can't afford to take. I'll be staying here to take care of things in the States, but Aislynn must go to Castello to fight. I want her to have Medici blood in her veins. I want her to be strong, so she can return to me. I've just found her and I'm not about to lose her."

Kate squeezed his hands. "Of course, she'll return. Don't even think otherwise." She spoke the words with confidence, but in her heart, she knew there were no guarantees on the battlefield. Aislynn had moved up in rank when they'd lost Fiamma. The memory of that battle flashed across Kate's mind, and she quickly blocked it out. "Your grandfather and your father will be standing together, who could defeat them?"

"Well, I'm sure as hell glad I'm on the Medici side!" He stood up then and turned to look at her. "Thank you, for always being here for me and supporting me. I promise you, with all my heart, I'll love her as she should be loved. May I ask her to move in tonight?"

Kate laughed. "I hope you've at least picked your clothes up off the floor, but yes, of course. She can move in any time."

He hugged her close, kissing her cheek. "I love you so much." He sent a telepathic message to Skelk, asking him to have Aislynn come to the house immediately. He shook his head laughing. "At least I don't make a mess like P-bear when he gets dressed. It looks like a shredder went through the wardrobe when he looks for a shirt!"

Gi appeared at the door with Aislynn, "My lady, the warrior Aislynn is here."

Christoph lit up like the moon when he spotted her. Walking to her, he softly kissed her. "Come in, I've just been telling Bebe about us." Taking her hand, he led her to his grandmother. " Bebe, may I officially present to you the female who will be my mate." Turning to Aislynn, he grinned. "You're moving into Bel Rosso."

Aislynn could feel the rush of her heart and the heat in her face, knowing her skin looked flushed. She was overwhelmed at how quickly things were moving. "Good evening, my queen. I'm taken off guard with the news, but I'm very happy."

Kate went to the leather-clad warrior, whose hair was pulled back into her trademark single braid. Aislynn towered over her, but Kate gave her a welcoming hug. "First of all, call me Bebe, or Kate, whichever you feel comfortable with. Don't call me queen, and please never call me my lady! Secondly, this is your home. Relax, come and go, as you please. Bring your things here and change whatever you want in Chris' rooms. Gi, Theresa and Emma are all at your disposal. They can help with whatever you need."

"You're very kind. I want you to know I love Chris very much. I've loved him for a long time. I promise you, I'll cherish him and love him, even protect him." She looked over at Chris and smiled.

Christoph shook his head. "Yeah, yeah, big bad Medici warrior, I get it!" He kissed her with love shining in his eyes and his heart full. "Let's get back to the barracks, grab some clothes and you can help me clean my room."

Aislynn didn't miss a beat and fired right back. "You make the mess, you clean it up, that's the rule in the barracks, and that will be the rule in our suite."

He laughed and grabbed her hand, leading her out of the room. "Already bossy, and you haven't even moved in yet."

***

Shade teleported back home to find his grandson and Aislynn laughing and teasing each other. "Well, it looks like your grandmother knows the news." It felt good to come home, but his heart was heavy with the news of Nattie's vision. He didn't want to spoil the joyous mood, so he kept his concerns to himself.

Christoph hugged him, pounding him on the back before he and Aislynn left to return to the barracks and start collecting her things. "P-bear, Aislynn will be moving in tonight."

Shade congratulated them again and then went to Kate, who was beaming with happiness. "Your warrior is home. And I take it, by the look on your face, your evening was a good one."

She smiled back at him. "I don't know how you managed to keep that secret, even knowing Chris wanted to tell me himself. I couldn't be more pleased for both of them. So, tell me about this condo in Arlington, Mr. Medici. And any other secrets you might have."

Shade ran his hand through his hair. "I am going to kill him, the damn snitch!" He grinned at her and lifted her off her feet, kissing her with a desperate need of her, and a love that consumed him. "First things first, Miss Reese, this vampire needs to be bathed head to toe. Then, he needs to lay in a soft bed, naked with you, feeling your heart beating next to his. Then, all of your questions will be answered, but first, there is a question I need to ask of you."

She laughed out loud as he lifted her off her feet. "And what exactly would that be?"

He leaned over her, his nose touching hers, staring into the depths of her dark brown eyes. "Do you love me?"

"More than life. Now, what have you done? You are making me more suspicious by the minute."

He answered with mock innocence, "I have done nothing!" He cradled her to his chest as he carried her up the stairs. "I have loved you since the moment I laid eyes on you. And nothing was ever going to take you from me. *Si*, I had the condo, because I wanted to protect you from all the evils that lurk in the dark. You know them now, but you did not then. I needed to have you fall in love with me before learning the truth of what I was. I deceived you, but for a very simple reason. I loved you and I would have died without you. Still love me?"

She looked up at his face as he carried her up the stairs. "So, you were a stalker? Is that what you're telling me? You watched me in secret?" She laughed, wondering how much he would have been able to see when she remembered the dreams. "You dream-walked, didn't you! Those rose petals in my bed! I thought I was losing my mind. That was you!"

He stopped on the landing of the stairs and looked down at her with a wicked playful smile. "Oh *si,* it has always been me, *mi amore.*" He continued up the stairs with a prideful stride, carrying his world in his arms. "And I think, tonight, I shall show you being awake is far more mind-boggling than any dream I can give you, Miss Reese."

81

Shade had a lot on his mind. There were many things going on at Bel Rosso. His grandson was in love, and this pleased him, but his daughter's vision of the battle had left him scouring his brain for answers. Kate seemed happy, and the news of Christoph and Aislynn offered a bright spot in what appeared to be an inevitable battle. Everyone was pushing harder in the camp, training until exhausted. The camp was overflowing with warriors since they'd halted the intake of any new warriors in Florence. He'd yet to meet with Raven, another thing he needed to get organized. He thought he'd need Raven in Florence and needed to make sure the camp in California was covered in Raven's absence.

He made his way down to the weapon's bunker that had been built inside Bel Rosso, beneath its lively ground floor level, behind the wine cellar. It used to be their primary bunker but now served as a supplement to the other weapon's bunker inside the walls of the camp. It was a yearly task to take inventory, making sure all the weapons were up-to-date and there was enough to meet the demands of the ever-growing camp. Tonight, however, he was here for another reason. He was deciding what should be sent back to Castello in preparation for the battle.

Shade had told no one of Natalia's vision. Luca had volunteered to help him pack up the weapons, and it felt like the old days, when it was only him and Luca, supplying the bunker, keeping the weapons clean and sharp, ready for a night's work on the streets.

As they worked, packing up weapons for shipment, the conversation was minimal, and they stayed with the task at hand. It left way too much time for his mind to work overtime about how best to prepare and protect his family. The battle was coming, he just didn't know when. He went over a checklist in his mind, but one thing kept nagging at him. He felt confident his daughters would be safe, and he even felt strongly about Lorenzo's ability to hold his own in a battle. The grandsons wouldn't see this battle, as much as they'd like to. Henry would remain in the warrior compound in

France, and Christoph would remain here at Bel Rosso with Jules. Bianca would be protected inside Castello with all the females, including Sophia, Kate, Shannon, and Chantal. In protecting his grandchildren, he knew he'd preserve the bloodline. It gave him a sense of security about the outcome and the interpretation of Natalia's vision that one coven would prevail. He knew, in his soul, it was very unlikely he, Lorenzo, or Alfie would come out of this unscathed. They would be the primary targets. It was only logical reasoning to expect at least one of them could be hurt. He didn't let himself think of death. He couldn't. It never helped a warrior to consider that outcome when facing a battle, but in his gut, Shade knew they would lose many.

Luca was watching him, and his mind was clearly elsewhere. "Master? What has your mind in such turmoil?"

Shade looked up, having almost forgotten Luca was in the room. "It is nothing. We are done here, I think. Go on back to your suite. I will finish putting this ammunition back into the locked safe and then I will be up."

Luca nodded but didn't leave, looking at his master.

Shade shrugged him off. "Look, just have a lot on my mind. Don't ask me any questions right now. I just need some time to think."

Luca nodded and headed out. Shade stood and stretched before sitting on the conference table and looking around the room. If these weapons could talk, the stories they would tell.

They had built a family here, a home. Now, he needed to make sure all he'd worked for, survived into the future. In his heart, he felt Lorenzo would be fine. He'd found his mate and had grown to be the Warrior and King, that was his birthright. He smiled when he thought about his red-headed devil child. Damn, if Sophia hadn't tested every nerve, but she too had found her mate. They were both content and happy with their lives and had given him grandchildren to carry on the Medici dynasty. His heart became soft when he thought about his Nattie. She'd been such a quiet child and a special gift. He was proud of her, as the first female born to Council. She'd already altered the course of their future with her work inside the Council to shift the power base for females and provide protection to the half-breeds. But it also brought him worry. His soul still ached that she'd found love but could never mate and had to hide it from the world. He couldn't imagine such a life. He'd have died if he couldn't have mated Kate.

He knew Marcello loved her, but he wondered if it was a love of convenience, since they were both sequestered behind Council walls. He wondered if Marcello would have been drawn to her, and her to him, had they not been so confined. It wore on him that his daughter may never feel that deep connection that could only come with the blood covenant. That blood bond was the greatest gift and bound them for eternity. He shook his head and stood up. "Fuck, old man, you will go insane thinking about this."

Picking up the crate of ammunition, he carried it inside the safe, moving some other crates around to make room. Suddenly, he saw the smaller safe he used to keep in his office. It had been pushed into a corner and hidden behind crates of weapons. He'd completely forgotten about that safe, and its contents.

The answer he was seeking had been staring at him this whole time. It had been there all along. He quickly pushed the small buttons with the combination and heard the click of the safe unlocking. He turned the handle and pulled it open. "You damn stupid fool. It was here all this time."

He reached inside and carefully pulled out the vials of the potion he'd purchased from Alec long ago. He didn't know if the contents of the vials were stable enough to survive all this time, but he still had the formulation, carefully written on the papers inside the safe. Back when they were fighting the Aries coven on the streets of D.C., Rissa had managed to get the vials away from her attacker. It was a unique chemical formulation that masked the vampire's scent and allowed the Aries rogues to move about freely, undetected. He'd held all the remaining vials, and he held the formula. They'd never used it in battle, and quite frankly, he'd forgotten about it after all these years.

He carefully tucked a few vials inside his jacket. If Nattie and Marcello used the potion, they could mate, and no one would be the wiser. They could never have children, but they could have each other. All he had to do now was convince them. He felt like he'd discovered a new world. "Smartest fucking thing you ever did in your whole fucking life, Rissa!"

With a grin on his face, he locked up and headed upstairs to put the vials in his office. Of course, the formula would need to be retested, but it was time to call Marcello. He needed to have a heart-to-heart talk with the warrior who loved his daughter.

82

Shade was in his office when he looked at his watch. It was one in the morning. He knew Marcello would be well into his scheduled shift at Council, and Nattie would be engaged in her job. Pulling out his cell phone, he called the warrior, waiting a few rings before he heard a familiar voice. Besides Luca, Marcello was probably one of the finest warriors that had ever come out of the camp in Florence. "Marcello, you busy? Have something I wish to speak to you about. But I will need you to come to Bel Rosso, *si*?"

***

Marcello felt the soft vibration of the phone in his pocket and pulled it out to see Shade on caller ID. He answered, hoping it wasn't bad news but was surprised by Shade's request. It was unusual for his former master to request a meeting, especially since Marcello had been assigned as Commander of the warriors at Council. His sole responsibility now was the protection of Council. Warriors usually only left the Council fortifications to accompany one of the Council members, and the Council rarely left. Natalia left more than all the others combined, since she visited her family, and now had the orphanages to tend to. He responded, knowing Shade wouldn't ask him to come if it wasn't important. "Yeah, sure. I need to re-assign someone to my post, but I can be there in about thirty minutes."

"I appreciate it, Marcello. I know it is an unusual request. I'll be in my office at the house."

Shade ended the call and went to the bar, pouring himself a large Midnight. He needed to approach this warrior carefully, speaking to Marcello not as a master, but as Natalia's father. Technically, Marcello no longer reported to him. Walking out onto the patio, he sipped at his drink and listened to the night sounds as he waited. It wouldn't be long before fall weather would be approaching. Inhaling the night air deeply, he absorbed this moment of quiet and set his mind to the conversation he was about to have.

***

Marcello let Natalia know he was going to be leaving the premises for a short while and was assigning another warrior to her. He wasn't sure why Shade had summoned him, so he decided not to tell her he was visiting with her father. "I think I should increase the weapons we keep here at Council, to be on the safe side, with this Borgia thing brewing. Doubt it will impact us, but I'd rather be over-prepared. I'm going to the Medici camp. I'll meet with Christoph and see if he can spare some weapons and ammunition and have them shipped here. I shouldn't be long."

The warrior he'd assigned to her was approaching, so he couldn't kiss her goodbye. They rarely showed any signs of affection for each other outside her private suite.

Natalia nodded. "Of course, I'll be fine, don't worry."

The truth was, he did worry. He always worried about her if she wasn't in his sights. He locked eyes with her, as he telepathically told her he loved her. He watched the shy smile on her lips, as she responded. **"Behave yourself."**

He chuckled as he teleported out, heading for Bel Rosso. He circled over the estate and could see the camp at maximum capacity as the warriors practiced on the field. As he neared the house, he could see the soft glow of a cigarette on the patio and knew it was Shade, stepping outside for a smoke. He landed softly near him. "Master?"

"Marcello, it is good to see you. Appreciate you coming so quickly." He put the cigarette out in the small sand-filled urn Kate had placed there for him. "Come inside."

As they both entered the office, Shade refilled his glass. "I would ask if you want one, but I know better. You always follow the rules." Chuckling, he sat down in his huge leather chair. "I wanted to speak with you about Council and preparations for security. We both know what is coming. If you need anything, just ask, it is yours. I would advise you to make sure your warriors are prepared, keeping their skills honed. I expect nothing to happen here, but as always, we should all be prepared for the worst possible scenario."

Marcello took a seat in a leather armchair, crossing his boot over his knee. "I've met with the warriors, and we've reviewed our protocol. We've increased the security level. I told Natalia I was coming here to pick up some extra weapons, and it would probably be a good idea to increase our stock, just in case. Those warriors not on duty are practicing weapon skills, so I think we're in good shape."

Shade nodded. He had no doubt Marcello had everything under control. "I will speak with Skelk, he will arrange whatever you need, and we will make sure it gets to Council." Shade looked at Marcello, he'd grown up in his camp in Florence, and had come to the States with the very first round of warriors here. He'd grown into a man and warrior to be respected. "I do have something else I wish to speak with you about. It concerns my daughter." Shade spun the crystal glass on his desk between his forefinger and thumb. "I am curious, as any *padre* would be."

Marcello squirmed in his seat. Shade was aware of the relationship he had with Natalia, so he was a little confused as to where this conversation was going. "What is it you wish to know? I hope you know I'd die protecting her if that's your worry."

Shade grunted. "I have no worries about that. You took an oath when you signed on with me years ago, warrior, to die for this coven. And you took another oath to the Council." Shade sat forward in his chair, stretching out his long legs under the desk. "I am wondering about your relationship with Nattie. Do you love her, Marcello, a true love? I am speaking to you as a *padre*, not your former master. Is this love out of convenience because you are both sequestered at Council and she is the only female there? Answer honestly, I make no judgments, I am just curious."

Marcello planted both feet on the floor and leaned forward in his chair, his arms resting on his knees. "I love Natalia. I've always loved her. I never approached her when she was living here, and I was in the camp because I thought she was off-limits to me. Besides, I knew you weren't crazy about Sophia's attraction to Alfie in the beginning, so I kept my feelings to myself. Then Natalia left to spend time with Council in Florence, and eventually, came back to the States, and took up residence in the new Council compound. I just assumed that was the end of things. I knew she'd never be allowed to mate then. When you assigned me to Council, to oversee the warriors there, I still never thought anything would develop between us. I admit, I selfishly assigned myself as her personal protector, and maybe because we spent so much time together, the barriers came down. I don't know if she always had feelings for me. We've never discussed it, but I can tell you, we love each other now. She only feeds from me. I changed my schedule, so I sleep beside her in her death slumber. I go to the feeders because I have no choice, but I never hunt. If I could take her blood, I would. Does that answer your question?"

Sitting back in his chair, lifting his drink, he took a long sip. His eyes remained glued to the warrior in front of him. "Speaking of selfish, I, too, am guilty of such when it comes to my Nattie. You do not think it was a coincidence you were sent to Council, do you? You are much smarter than that, Marcello. I chose you because you were my best, and I wanted you to protect her. I would trust no one else with my daughter's safety. But let me ask you something. If Nattie had not been born to Council, and you both had remained here at Bel Rosso, would you still love her as you do now? Would you have asked me to mate with her? Would you have tried to win her love and be with her for all eternity in a blood covenant?"

Marcello looked at the floor. "The answer is yes. If Natalia had stayed here at Bel Rosso and showed even the slightest interest in me, then yes. You know Natalia, she was always the quiet one, and always had a book in her hand. As a young girl, she showed no interest in the warriors. I would like to think that had she stayed here, as she got older, she would have sought me out as well. I can't speak for her. She shares much with me, but your daughter still keeps a lot to herself. I would like to think she'd have chosen me to mate."

Shade stood up then and paced slowly behind his chair. "If you could mate Natalia, would you?"

Marcello looked at Shade, unsure of why he was asking when it was clearly not an option. "I would, of course, but you know Council would never allow it. No Council has ever mated."

Shade stopped his pacing and grasped the back of his chair, staring at Marcello. "What if I told you there is a way for you to mate, without Council consent, nor anyone ever knowing? What would you say to me then, Marcello?"

Marcello furrowed his brow. "Is this a test? My answer would be the same. I would mate her tomorrow if it were possible."

Shade grinned, that was the answer he was seeking. "No test, warrior, but a resolution. Do you remember the Aries coven and how their rogues attacked on the streets of D.C.? Think hard, Marcello, do you remember those nights we could not detect them because..." Shade left the sentence hanging in the air, waiting for Marcello's memory to kick in.

"Because we couldn’t pick up their scent. They’d taken some kind of potion that blocked their scent. Yeah, I remember."

Shade nodded. "Alec sold me the formula for that potion. I paid dearly for it. I held it as a possible weapon in our arsenal, but we never used it. Now, its true purpose has become known to me." He sat down in his chair again. "All my children can know the bond of the blood covenant and what it means to be mated. It has always bothered me Nattie would be denied this. I need this peace of mind, Marcello. If I give you the potion, will you mate her? It will keep you both safe, both of you can fulfill your duties with honor, and still have that bond. I want to know she has you forever."

Marcello was stunned. "I... yes, of course...does she know? Have you talked to her?"

"No, she does not know. But I intend to speak with her alone. She will give argument. I have no doubt. I am expecting that. But I needed to know your intentions with her first." Shade ran his hand through his mop of curls. "Marcello, this is her choice. If she says no, and I cannot convince her, then you must accept her choice, *si*?"

He nodded. "I already have more than I ever expected. I know I have her heart. I hope she’ll choose to mate with me and allow me to seal the covenant. I ache to feed from her and her alone. But if she says no, if she feels the risks are too great, I’ll accept her decision. I won’t pressure her."

Shade approached the warrior he trusted with his youngest daughter’s life. Hugging him, he pounded him on the back. "I would be honored to have you for the mate of my princess. Now, return to your duties. *Grazie*, Marcello, for everything you have done for this family and coven. I hope, with all my heart that soon, you will be my son-in-law."

Marcello was feeling dumbfounded by the revelation that mating Natalia was even an option. "Regardless of her decision, I’ll never leave her side. That, I promise you."

83

As soon as Shade had spoken with Marcello, he called the Council, speaking with Natalia and arranging a meeting. He informed Kate he'd be leaving to see Natalia and would return before sunrise. She was curious about his plans, and he told her he was working with Natalia and Marcello to ensure Council was well protected in the event the Borgia conflict expanded to the States. He was still dressed in his leathers when he teleported out. As he landed, he was met by warriors trained in his own camps, Marcello among them. "Good evening, Marcello."

Neither of them made mention of their earlier meeting, but Marcello knew why he was here. "Come with me, Master Medici, Ivory is waiting for you."

Marcello led him down a long hall, to a reception area. Marcello took him to a closed door. "Ivory waits for you inside, master. Now, if you'll excuse me, I must attend to my duties."

Shade pounded him on the back and watched as he returned the way he'd come. He tapped lightly at the door.

***

Natalia had been working in the data center when Marcello had come to tell her that her father was on his way here. She'd looked at him quizzically. She knew Marcello had gone to Bel Rosso earlier in the night to gather more weapons. "Do you know what this is about?"

He looked down and shook his head no, not making eye contact. "He'll be here shortly. Why don't you let me take you to the private reception area?"

Natalia gave him a look, sensing he knew more than he was saying, but followed him to the reception room where guests meeting with Council waited when they had an appointment. She took a seat and sighed. "You're making me nervous, Marcello."

He chuckled, which made her relax a little. Marcello left her, and within a few minutes, she heard a tapping on the door. She stood up as her father entered, and she slipped the ivory hood from her head, as a smile spread across her face. Regardless of the reason for his visit, she was happy to see him. She walked into open arms. "Daddy, please don't spoil my night with bad news."

Shade was always filled with pride when he saw her in her robe. "Nothing bad, I promise you, Nattie. But there is something I need to speak with you about. Please, come sit down. Get comfortable with me." He led her to a couch, still holding her hand in his. "I have discovered something I wish to share with you, something that could make your life happier, more complete."

She sat next to him and shook her head. "More complete? I don't understand. I'm happy here, Daddy. I hope you know that."

He smiled at her, "*Si*, I know you are happy. It is your destiny to be here at Council. But what if you had an opportunity to fulfill not only your duties to Council but also seal your bond to Marcello? Would you wish for such a life?"

She tilted her head as she looked at him. "You know I love Marcello. He's been an unexpected blessing in my life. He's shown me love and passion, he's my companion, and his loyalty to me is beyond question. But I was born to Council, just as you were born a warrior and a king. This is my path, my calling. I could never give up my life at Council. I feel like I've been given a gift, to have him in my life, but you know we can never mate. I feel blessed to have what we have."

Shade watched her face as she spoke, wearing her heart on her sleeve. He reached out and gently stroked her cheek. "If you had not been born to be here in this place, do you think you would have fallen in love with Marcello, chosen him as a mate?"

Natalia furrowed her brow. "If I'd not been born to Council? It's hard for me to imagine, but yes, had I been like Sophia, and free to choose a mate, Marcello is the male I would have chosen for myself. I know that wouldn't have gone over well with you, both of your daughters mating with warriors. But I love him deeply, Daddy. I knew from an early age the Council was my path, so I tried to put any ideas of mating out of my head. But I always noticed Marcello in the camp, even as a young girl."

He stood up, and let out a sigh, his heart ached for her to accept that she could have both. He paced in front of her. "Nattie, we both know what is coming, you more profoundly than any of the others.

We hold this secret of the curse between us. I love you from the depths of my soul, but I have a wound inside me that refuses to heal, fearing you will never know a blood covenant. There is another secret I can share with you. I can offer you a choice, but it will be up to you to accept or deny. I am begging you, please hear me out and think hard before answering me."

He bent down on one knee in front of her and looked at his daughter with a plea. "I have a potion, a formula that I own solely. It can hide your scent. It can hide Marcello's scent." He gripped her hands, his voice deep and filled with hope. "You can take this potion, drink it. You could mate, seal the covenant and no one would ever know. It was used by a coven that raided D.C. before you were born. Rissa was attacked by a rogue from this coven, and she was able to retrieve the vials. You could remain here in Council but know what it feels like to have the eternal bond of the covenant." He reached up and cupped her face. "I know you love Marcello, but I need to know, in my soul that you will have that eternal bond."

Natalia looked at him with confusion. She'd never heard of such a potion. "What are you saying? That we could mate, and our altered scent would not be detectable? No one would know?" Her mind was running a mile a minute, as the questions flew through her head. "We'd still have to be careful. We'd never be able to have children, but he could feed from me. Only me. Daddy, are you sure?"

“I have never been more sure of anything in my life, princess. I know what it feels like to be in love, knowing this person you feed from must hold back from feeding from you. It is an ache that leaves an empty void inside. I went through that with your *madre*. Listen to me. I have already talked to Marcello about this. He is more than willing. But the choice is yours. *Si*, you would still live here, as you do now, keeping your relationship secret, but the covenant would be sealed. This is your choice, Nattie. Marcello will accept whatever you decide."

Natalia stood up and paced the room. She was already breaking the rules by having a relationship with Marcello. She was fairly certain Malachi was aware, although they never spoke of it. She wondered if the Council was to discover she was mated if they'd force her to leave. Could she be happy if she didn't have Council? Was she willing to risk everything for Marcello? This was a big decision. She'd still have the orphanages. They were paid for with Medici money. She stood at a window that looked out on the dark night. She could see her reflection in the glass, and her father, standing behind her. She realized she was asking herself the wrong question. It wasn't an issue of whether she could live without Council; it was a question of whether she could live without Marcello. He'd made her life meaningful. She was able to share her joy with him, and she realized how empty her life would feel if he weren't here. She could live without Council, but she couldn't live without Marcello. What they had together wasn't a traditional love. It wasn't the love she saw between her mother and father. That was a love that was rare and unique, and she and her siblings all knew it. But still, it was their love, and she didn't want to lose it. She turned back to face her father. "My answer is yes. If you can protect us from being discovered, then yes."

He went to her and crushed her to his chest. Burying his face in her hair, he felt relief, knowing all of his children would be loved and cared for. "I love you, Nattie, my sweet girl." He held her for a few moments, both of them connected. "I know I ask much of you but tell me you do this for you and Marcello, and not just for me."

"It's my decision, Daddy. For Marcello and me." She laughed. "Who knew I had a streak of Sophia in me all along?"

He laughed then, letting all of his emotions out. All of his children would be properly mated, and he could walk onto any battlefield knowing his precious children had found their true mates. "I am no young vampire, and your *madre* has taught me the very essence of what love is. She fell in love with a warrior and mated. Sophia did the same. Chantal did as well. So, I fear, my Nattie, your fate was sealed a long time ago!"

She hugged him. "I think women are drawn to Medici warriors. What's not to love?"

"Oh, *si*, there is no love like that of a warrior. This is my gift to you, Natalia. It is the most precious gift I can give to you. Love your warrior to his core, and he will return that love for all of eternity. You have my blessing to mate Marcello, my Princess."

Natalia clung to him. She was grateful for this gift, but she couldn't help but wonder if it was prompted by the vision and the curse. "Thank you, Daddy."

84

Shade had the vials of the new batch of potion in his desk drawer, hidden well inside a velvet-lined box. He'd arranged for the laboratory to produce a fresh batch and had them make several months' worth. The vials were made of titanium, so no light or moisture could penetrate. He'd sealed the recipe for the formula, and the location and number of the lab, inside the box. Natalia would be able to have it made as needed and sent to her privately. It had been years since anyone had used the formula, and he decided that before giving her the precious liquid, he needed to test it. The scientists at the lab had ensured him it was still effective, but he wanted proof for himself before turning the potion over to Natalia.

He pulled one of the vials from the box and stared at it. This was his daughter's life of happiness inside, a tasteless liquid that would bring her the ultimate gift of a mate for all eternity. But who among his trusted warriors could he rely on to test it? Walking outside onto the patio, he lit up a smoke, his mind running through his options. He could hear the clatter of swords and muffled shouts that carried on the wind from the camp. He didn't want to reveal his true purpose for testing the potion. He scrunched his eyebrows as a sound reverberated in his ears, a deep voice that could be heard above the others... *Skelk*. Skelk was perfect. He wouldn't run his mouth, and he stayed to himself in camp.

His mind was made up, Skelk it was. He sent Christoph a message telepathically, to send Skelk to the house immediately. He needed him to go to D.C. for a few hours. Shade went back inside and slid the vial inside the top drawer of his desk. As he started to pour a Midnight, he heard Skelk outside on the patio. He looked outside to where he stood and opened the door, giving him an unobstructed view of the warrior. "Skelk, come in. Have a seat."

Shade watched the unshaven warrior take a seat. Skelk was tall and lean, but all muscle, his hair always looking as though it had never seen a brush. He'd never been one to care much about his outward appearance. Shade chuckled to himself as Skelk took a seat across from the desk. He'd never felt comfortable indoors. Even after all these years, he looked like he was about to be sent to the gallows.

"You asked for me, Master."

Shade nodded. "*Si*. I need your assistance on something. It is no secret we are preparing for battle. Many years ago, the Aries coven swept into D.C. and we had a mess on our hands because we could not detect them."

Skelk sat with his booted foot resting over his knee and his arms crossed over his chest. "I remember. You think they have returned?"

Shade shook his head. "No, we totally wiped that filth from the earth. But perhaps you did not know I acquired the potion that kept their scent hidden."

Skelk grunted. He'd never heard of this before. "Interesting, but I don't see what this has to do with me, master. I'm not one for small talk. Neither are you. What are you saying?"

Shade grinned. Skelk hated wasting words or time. "I have had a new batch of the potion made. I need a warrior to test it for me. I have never used this in battle, but I will need all the tricks I can pull out of my hat dealing with the Borgia. I want you to test this for me. I need it to be kept quiet, no one to know. It is tasteless and harmless, no side effects, but no one can detect your scent."

Skelk dropped his booted foot to the floor and leaned forward, his shaggy mop falling over his eyes. He peered up through his hair at his master. "So, you chose me as the guinea pig? Am I supposed to be grateful? I will do it but make sure Theresa is close by in case I get sick from that shit. How do you plan on me doing this?"

Shade laughed as he stood and poured a small amount of Midnight into a glass. "Theresa is inside, and your ass is tougher than any small amount of potion." Pulling out the vile, he held it up to Skelk and handed it to him. Skelk took the vile, opened it, and sniffed. It was clear and had no smell at all, it looked like water. "I sure as fuck hope you ain't trying to kill me, master. But if you are, I hope it's painless and kicks my ass instantly."

Shade leaned down and grinned, handing him the glass of Midnight. "Just swallow it and chase it with the Midnight."

Skelk started to do as he was told but paused. "I will do as you ask, but tell me first, what the hell do you plan for me to do once I swallow this hocus pocus?"

Shade sat back in his chair. "We are going to teleport into D.C., then go our separate ways. We are going to play hide and seek. You need to find me. If it does not work, I should smell you coming, but if it does, you will have outwitted the best warrior in the world, *si*."

Skelk grinned from ear to ear. He swallowed the potion and chased it with the Midnight then slammed the glass down on the desk. "Game on, brother." He teleported out of the open patio doors in an instant as Shade's laughter echoed through the house.

Shade immediately geared up with weapons. He had no intention of hurting Skelk, but he never went out on the streets without weapons. He told Kate and Christoph he was heading to the Dead House and would return later. He felt alive as he teleported out, his blood surging. He was the oldest vampire in this camp, and his skills were far superior to Skelk's. But Skelk was a damn sly warrior, he belonged on the streets.

As he teleported around the metro area, he informed Theo that Skelk was in D.C., and not to forewarn the warriors of his presence. He was testing their skills tonight, as well. Shade crept silently along rooftops, and down seedy alleys of the club scenes, but he never detected or sensed Skelk. *Where the fuck is he?* He'd been out there for over an hour when he spotted several of his warriors standing around smoking. Apparently, it was a damn slow night. He saw one of them as he picked up his scent, and looked about. They knew he was there as he dropped to the street right behind them.

***

Skelk had kept himself out of sight of his master. He'd detected him not long after he arrived and stalked him for over an hour. Clearly, his master never knew he was there. He'd purposely put himself upwind from Shade, but never once did he notice him. *This hocus-pocus works*! He watched as his master landed directly behind a group of warriors standing around with their dicks in their hands. *Big mistake, warriors. Boss don't take lightly to fucking off*. He crept silently on a rooftop above them, keeping hidden in the shadows, and listened and waited.

***

Shade scolded his warriors. "I don't pay you to stand around taking smoke breaks. Just because there is no action, does not mean there is no evil lurking."

Three warriors turned to face him, their eyes filled with guilt and surprise, their hands going immediately to their weapons, startled by his sudden appearance. Shade grinned. "Want to take me on, warriors?"

One of them spoke up. "No, master. We were just talking about switching out grids."

Shade chuckled. "Relax, just out here checking the nightlife. Making sure you're keeping your skills sharp. Give me a damn smoke."

The warriors relaxed and one of them pulled out his pack and pitched it to his master, but it never made it to his hand.

Skelk pulled the arrow from his back and loaded it into the crossbow, waiting for the right moment. He didn't have to wait long. His aim was precise as he let the arrow fly and it shot through the pack of cigarettes, impaling them on the arrow as it buried itself into a wooden bench.

Shade heard the soft whistle of the arrow coming at them but never moved. He knew who'd shot the arrow, at least he hoped he did because he sure as fuck couldn't smell him! He stood still as three warriors went into attack mode, pulling weapons and scattering as they scanned the area for the intruder. "You see, you never know when evil lurks around you. This was a test, a very successful one on my end, and your end as well since you are all still alive. I suggest you get to your grids and act like fucking Medici warriors."

Shade teleported high above them and landed on a rooftop across the street. He could see Skelk coming toward him, landing beside him with a grin spread wide across his face. He still couldn't pick up his scent. The potion still held its magic.

Skelk handed him a smoke. "Hocus-pocus still works."

Shade lit up, a grin on his face as well. "And so, do your fucking crossbow skills."

Skelk grunted. "Think I'll head out, have some fun while this is still in my system."

Shade nodded his consent. "Let me know how long it lasts."

Skelk winked. "Sure thing, master. By the way, hide and seek is my favorite."

Shade watched him teleport out and shook his head. He was damn glad that specific warrior was on his side.

85

The courier delivered the package to the Council, and the warrior at the main gate accepted it. They had been notified that the Medici was sending a package for his daughter. The warrior tucked the package under his arm and carried it back inside the fortress and down the long, winding corridors, to the data center. He entered the well-lit room, where the staffers sat in front of computer screens as their fingers flew across the keyboards. His eyes scanned the room, looking for her. The ivory robe almost worked as camouflage in this bright room filled with high-tech equipment. He carried the package in front of him as he approached her. "Ivory. This arrived at the gate. I was instructed to deliver it to you immediately."

Ivory looked up at him, taking the package and thanking him, showing no emotion on her face. "Thank you, warrior. Return to your post now, please."

As he left, Natalia set the package down on the counter and finished giving instructions to the staffer that was entering the data. There were no windows in this room, but she knew the sun would be up soon. Making a final inspection of the staff workers, she gathered up the package and made her way to the second floor which housed the private suites for the Council. She saw several of her brethren making their way to their suites, pulled to their night slumber. She entered her suite and heard the door lock automatically behind her as it closed. Setting the package down on the bed, she carefully opened it and read her father's hand-written note with instructions on where to order the vials in the future, along with a copy of the formulation. He instructed her to store the vials inside the safe in her room, and that she and Marcello must each drink one vial a day. She removed two vials and placed the remaining vials and the notes inside the safe.

Taking the bottle of Midnight from the bar, she poured two glasses and added the potion to each glass before carrying the glasses to the bedside table. She pulled the hooded robe over her head and tossed it on a chair, before climbing into the shower, and scrubbing her skin pink. As she stepped from the shower, she dried off and dried her hair, brushing it to a high sheen. She didn't wear make-up at Council, and she didn't wear a fragrance. They weren't forbidden, but the environment wasn't conducive to behaviors women employed to enhance their attractiveness to men. Wrapping a towel around her torso, she made her way back to her bed and turned down the covers. Dropping the towel to the floor, she slid beneath the sheets and waited for her warrior.

***

Marcello finished his rounds, giving instructions to the warriors taking on the daylight duty. He knew Natalia's schedule well. He always waited for at least an hour before going to her room, giving the other Council members time to get settled and hopefully, slip into their death slumber. Careful as always, he made his way to her room. Unlocking her door, he slipped inside and closed it, making sure it locked securely. The room was dark, except for a few candles. Making his way to her bed, he found her waiting for him. He smiled as she lay beneath the sheets, knowing she was naked and warm. Removing his sword and propping it against a chair, he went to her and kissed her softly. "You look comfortable."

She smiled back at him. "I am comfortable. I was waiting for you. Are you ready to make this arrangement permanent, warrior?"

His eyes grew large, and he couldn't believe what he was hearing. "You've chosen this path for us then?" He sat on the edge of the bed, looking down at her. "Are you sure?"

Natalia lifted herself on her elbow. "I've only been certain of two things in my life. The first was I wanted this life at Council. I knew from the time I was a young girl I was destined for something different, and that I wouldn't live like my mother or my sister. And the second thing is I love you. I've always loved you, Marcello. When I came to Council, I thought I had to sacrifice you in order to have this life. My father wanted me to have the best protection since I'd never mate. You were his SIC at camp. You were Luca's cousin, and only living family. And yet, he decided to send you here, with me. The fact that we've been able to share what we have, has been an unbelievable blessing. But now, for my father to have found a way for us to mate, it's almost more than I can comprehend. But yes, I've never been more sure of anything in my life."

He leaned down and kissed her passionately, knowing that this night would be one he'd only dreamed of. "I love you, Natalia Medici, and I vow to you, I will never leave you. This will bond us for all of eternity, as we should be. I have never craved another as I do you."

He stood up and easily removed his boots before stripping off his leathers. He could feel her eyes on him with every move. He was in his prime as a warrior, strong and muscled. He stood before her, naked as the day he was born. "Do we take this potion before or after we mate? Shade didn't instruct me on its use."

She sat up, holding the sheet over her breasts as she reached for the glasses by the bed, handing one to him. "We take one vial a day, and Daddy has sent over about a two-month supply, along with instructions on how to order more. Tonight, we drink the potion in a toast. To us, Marcello. I pledge to love you till my last breath, and beyond."

He took the glass and tipped it to hers. "For all eternity, my love."

They both drank the Midnight down, emptying their glasses. He took the glass from her and put them back on the nightstand. He lifted the sheet and slid in beside her, his arm around her in a protective manner. "My dreams have come true. My beautiful Natalia will become my mate, and I shall forever remain her warrior."

He snuggled into her neck, leaving small kisses along her vein. He moved to her white shoulders and nipped softly, not breaking the skin. His lips explored her breasts that were full and beautiful, teasing and suckling to his heart's content. He could feel her heart racing, pounding for him. He moved on top of her gently and cupped her face in his hands, kissing her passionately, letting his tongue communicate his need.

Natalia closed her eyes and focused only on the pleasure of his mouth against her skin. He'd slept beside her for years, and they'd made love a thousand times, but this time would be different. She'd drink from him, as she'd always done, but tonight, when her body ached to feel him at her throat, when she could feel him fighting his own desire to feed, they wouldn't hold back. Tonight, their covenant would be sealed. She slid her hand down his muscled back, and over the curve of his ass. She always marveled at his strength. Her other hand was buried in his hair, as she held the back of his head to her breast. She wrapped her legs around his hips, eager to have him. "Take me now, Marcello. Make me yours. We've waited long enough."

Her plea lit his beast and his fangs punched through. His cock was harder than it had ever been, and he knew his beast had chosen her years ago to be his mate. Her legs gripped him like a vice and he easily entered her wet haven. He moaned softly, knowing they must both continue to make love quietly. He rocked his hips against her and felt her respond, but his beast wouldn't wait, he was anxious to have her blood. He thrust faster and deeper, as she gripped his long hair, and it only excited him more. Her body was his treasure. She moved with him, their patterns familiar, and yet new, as they each knew the other's body like their own. Reaching up, he grabbed her hand from his hair and looked into her eyes. "Feed, my love."

When he asked her to feed, her lips found the tender skin of his neck and she brushed back his hair. Her tongue explored the taste of his skin, salty to her tongue before she sank her fangs into his flesh and felt the power of his warrior's blood on her tongue. It surged through her, like an electric current, and the fire burned between her legs, a fire only he could extinguish. She drank from him, as her heart pounded faster, and his hips thrust harder into her. She broke away, his blood on her lips. "Now, Marcello."

She gave him the signal to feed, and his heart damn near stopped. He rose slowly, still inside her, and kissed her neck, letting his tongue slide along the pulsing vein. He whispered softly against her throat, "I love you."

Sinking his fangs into her vein, he felt the surge of Medici blood hit his system. He almost choked, forgetting to breathe as it lit his body on fire for her. Her blood held power, royal and ancient, and was the sweetest blood he'd ever tasted. Closing his eyes, he let it take him to a place he'd never felt before, sheer ecstasy of mind, body, and soul. He drew deep of her gift of life, his whole body on fire to be one soul with her. Sliding his hand behind her head, he lifted her to his throat once again, they must feed together. As her fangs pierced his skin and drew deep, he exploded inside her, feeling her own body convulse around him.

The moans escaped her, even as her mouth was sealed against his flesh, and his blood flowed across her tongue. She'd been raised on feeders, and came to the Council a virtual virgin, having never been with a male. Marcello had been her first and only lover, and the power of their lovemaking always left her sated. She'd always fallen into a deep death slumber in his arms, knowing the depth of his love, and the protection of his arms. But she'd never felt anything like this. When the circle was made complete, and he'd finally fed from her for the first time, the only vampire to ever take her blood, the force of it was overwhelming, and she couldn't hold back the sounds that escaped her throat. She clung to him with both arms, as her thighs tightened their grip on his hips. She would have all of him. He was finally hers, bound in a way that couldn't be broken. She felt the power of the orgasm hit her hard, as she broke away from his throat, her head thrown back on the pillow, and the sounds of her pleasure echoed inside the room. "Marcello!" He was hers now, and she belonged to him.

He unlatched from her neck and looked down at her as he looked at the face of the female that was now his alone. His blood was upon her lips as a testimony of their mating. He remained inside her, spent. Softly licking her lips, he licked away each drop and kissed her with a gentleness no one would believe possible from a warrior of such great strength. "Mine, all mine."

He rolled them gently, so she was lying on his chest, his arms around her, caressing her back. They lay without words for a while, each lost in the other. "I love you, Natalia. I've always loved you. I will forever love you."

She felt their heartbeats synchronizing and knew for all time, her heart would beat in unison with his. She reached up to touch his cheek and felt the death slumber pulling at her, taking her under fast. She smiled in contentment. She understood, at last, why it had been so important to her father she had this bond. She whispered, "And I will forever love you." She felt the darkness take her, but could feel him holding her, protecting her, even as she slipped into her slumber.

86

Summer had started to fade, as the days started to transition to fall, but tonight had been unseasonably warm and humid. Shade stepped outside on the patio and lit up a cigarette. He'd received confirmation his package had been delivered to his daughter. He had no doubt they'd seal their blood covenant soon. He hadn't spoken of his plan to anyone. He'd needed the assurance from both of them that this was something they wanted, and at the same time, understood the need to keep this under wraps. He hadn't even told Kate. He finished his smoke and walked back inside the house, heading upstairs to Christoph and Aislynn's suite. Kate had been there most of the night, helping them to re-design the space. As he entered their suite on the top floor of the house, she sat cross-legged in the middle of the floor, piles of fabric samples and catalogs surrounding her. Aislynn sat on the sofa behind her, leaning over her shoulder, and Christoph was in a nearby chair, his leg thrown over the arm of the chair.

Shade watched her from the doorway. "I don't know how you do all that. I've never been able to figure out how you can look at a bunch of fabric swatches and paint chips and pull it all together inside your head to make something beautiful."

She looked up at him from her seat on the floor, as he towered over her, making him look even taller. Kate laughed. "Maybe I was born with it. It just comes naturally to me. Want to help?"

He laughed out loud, his blue eyes twinkling. "That would be like asking a warrior to dance in a ballet." He walked to her and held out his hand as she grasped it and he lifted her from her seated position. Pulling her into his chest, he buried his head into that crimson and inhaled. "I am sorry to interrupt, but can you break away from all this and come with me?"

"Sure. Most of this stuff has to be ordered anyway. I'm sure Chris and Aislynn can find something to entertain themselves. Now, what do you have in mind for me?"

He growled as he leaned his head down and kissed her. "I want to run away from our responsibilities for the night. Besides, there are some things I want to talk to you about." He slid his hands down her back. "I feel like taking a swim, but not in the pool. I think, on a beautiful night like this, we should take a trip to the grotto and swim buck-ass naked in those cool waters, *si*?"

Christoph laughed as he responded to Aislynn's blush. "Okay, first of all, to Aislynn, you better get used to it, and secondly, to P-bear, way too much information."

Kate laughed. "We better leave. You're embarrassing your grandson."

Shade stared at Kate and didn't acknowledge Christoph or Aislynn. "Imagine that...two bad-ass Medici warriors, blushing and acting as though they have no clue what I am talking about." He took her hand, "Now, you have a choice, we can ride the horses, or teleport."

"Teleport, but only if you hold my hand."

Taking her hand, they teleported out over the fields, rising up the base of the Blue Ridge Mountains and it took them only seconds to find the grotto, nestled deep within the trees, a spot only nature could create. They'd come here many times over the years, it was their private paradise. "Ah, now this is what we both need. It seems we both have been busy, running in different directions lately. I have missed you."

He kissed her neck and licked her vein, a soft growl vibrating through him. He left a trail of soft kisses up and down her neck and began to lift the soft cotton shirt over her head. "Have I told you how beautiful you are this night?"

"You have not." She laughed as she unbuttoned his shirt and helped him out of it. "But then I've failed to mention how handsome you are tonight, so all is forgiven. I'm glad we came here. The water in the grotto is colder than the water in the pool. It's so hot tonight." She dropped her skirt around her ankles and kicked off her sandals as he stripped from his jeans.

He grinned. "Come on." Grabbing her hand, he helped her to walk out on the rocky cliffs above the grotto. "One, two...." He dived off the cliff, still holding her hand. Just before they hit the water, he let go of her hand and they both plunged into the deep, cooling water. He surfaced, shaking his head, and floating to her. "Damn, that feels good!"

Kate absorbed the shock of the cold water against her skin, relishing in how refreshing it felt as she surfaced, pushing her wet hair back from her face, and laughing. "Whatever happened to three?" Looking up at the night sky, the moon was bright, but the air barely moved the leaves on the trees. She swam closer to him and wrapped her arms around his shoulders. "So, what's on your mind? I can tell you've been preoccupied with something the last few days, and there's something you've been waiting to tell me."

"*Si*." He kissed her lips. "I have given a gift to Nattie and Marcello. Something I didn't discuss with you, and I feel guilty about that, but I had my reasons for not telling you."

She looked at him quizzically. "You gave them a gift? Why would you think you need to discuss with me a decision to give them a gift? What did you give them?"

He swirled them around in the water, letting the water lap against their skin, cooling them off. "I don't have to tell you that ever since Nattie knew she was going to Council, I have struggled. It was never easy to watch Sophia and Lorenzo find their mates and know she would never have that. Can you understand that?"

She nodded. "I understand, but she has love. She has Marcello. They've been discreet, but I do think what they have is real and lasting. I'll admit, I've felt better knowing she has Marcello in her life, even though it's technically forbidden. So, you gave them something? "

"*Si*, I was in the bunker, packing up weapons and ammunition to send over to Castello. I found my old office safe. I had forgotten it had even been moved inside the ammunition's safe. It struck me like a bolt of lightning. We have the potion that blocks the vampire scent. I had completely forgotten about it. We never had use for it during a battle, so I had stored it away. I had the idea perhaps Marcello and Nattie could mate, and hide their scent, but I needed to understand how they felt for each other. I talked to Marcello first, to make sure his love was not one of convenience. But ultimately, I knew it had to be Nattie's choice. I went to see her at Council. She loves Marcello, but she is also aware of the risks. So, I had a new batch made for them, tested it on Skelk to make sure it still works. They are going to mate, *mi amore*. Our little Nattie." He watched her face, waiting for the gravity of the news to sink in.

Kate was both thrilled and frightened at the same time, struggling to see which emotion won. "Lover, are they safe? Are you sure? I mean, I'm thrilled if they wish to mate, if that's what they want, but I know our daughter. She'd hate giving up Council. I had no experience with the potion myself. I remember you speaking of it, and how it masked the scent of the rogues. Are you sure, after all this time?"

He grinned at all her concerns. "I am certain the potion will protect them, but we must keep this information to ourselves. I have told no one else, and I think it stays here. I will not even tell our other children. I know Sophia and Lorenzo would do nothing to put Natalia at risk, but I won't even take the chance of them accidentally speaking of it. It is clear Natalia made a choice, and for her, the reward outweighs the risk, but still, she never wishes to leave Council. However, if push comes to shove, she would choose love." He cupped her face in his hands. "Could you live without me, *mi amore*?"

She stared back at him, the water dripping from his hair, the moonlight reflected in his eyes "I would give up everything for you, this all means nothing without you. And for what it's worth, I think she made the right choice. If they should be discovered, Natalia will find her own path, or better yet, make her own path. She's the quiet one, but don't mistake her silence for weakness. She's probably more determined than Lorenzo, and more stubborn than Sophia. If this is what they've decided, then they both have my blessing."

He kissed her then with an overwhelming love he couldn't deny. She was his world, and with the mating of his youngest daughter, he felt at peace. They would win this battle with the Borgia and come home to Bel Rosso, all the more powerful for it. "I am sorry I did not tell you, *mi amore*. I wasn't sure both of them would even agree, and I didn't want to give you concern. Forgive me?"

She smiled back at him. "When have I ever been able to not forgive you? You still hold me entranced. From the first time I laid eyes on you."

He threw back his head and laughed. "The first time you laid eyes on me, you were entranced all right. You could not string two words together without stammering and you could not get away from me fast enough. Good damn thing I love the chase!"

She laughed with him, remembering how he'd left her tongue-tied before she answered him seriously. "You have no idea how grateful I am you didn't bail on me. There were times I was certain I'd lost you with my reluctance to open up my heart again, and how I silently begged you to not give up on me."

His chuckle held a hint of mischief. "I remember begging, *mi amore*, but not exactly in that context." He floated them out to the center of the grotto where the water was deeper and cooler. "I knew, deep inside me, there was so much love and passion caged up inside you. And who better to unlock all those treasures than a warrior? And, by the way, you have done something to this ancient royal bloodline... You have tainted it!"

She frowned at him. "Have I? All our children have two gifts, rare gifts at that. Our daughter is the first female born to Council. I would say this mortal enhanced your royal bloodline!"

Holding her tighter, he chuckled. "Calm down, minx! What I meant to say is, apparently, all the Medici females are now born with an irresistible attraction to mate warriors!"

Kate smiled at him. "I'm not sure you can lay that at my feet. I doubt I can claim any credit for how handsome a Medici warrior looks, and how protected he can make a female feel. From my experience, all females are attracted to Medici warriors, especially mine."

Shaking his head, he gave her that cockeyed grin. "I never hid my past, and once you had me, they all thought they could run you over, but my *bel rosso* showed them a thing or two. You never gave up on me, or us. I would have had a very different life without you. You have always been my greatest strength and my biggest weakness, and I would change nothing."

87

Dona had been miserable in her own home since the death of Mario and Marie. Tarleton and Giada made sure the house was impeccable but they both looked down their noses at her and were dismissive of her requests. Marie had always been a friend and would chat endlessly with her, while Giada only spoke to issue orders. It was as if their roles were now reversed, and Dona was living in their home. Giada didn't help with her bath or getting dressed as Marie had. She'd hear them talking and laughing with each other, but when she entered the room, they'd fall silent and solemn. Dona didn't think it was possible to feel more isolated, and she sank further into a depression every day. She slept longer, and when the weather was good, she'd escape outdoors to work in the gardens, even though Rodrigo had sent her a full-time gardener.

She'd been in the gardens for much of the day and was returning to the house, the dirt under her fingernails. At least working in the garden made her tired. She entered the house and immediately heard Tarleton and Giada laughing and talking. She hurried past the room they occupied and rushed up the stairs to her bedroom, stripping off her soiled clothes and tossed them in the hamper. She ran her tub, letting the water get as hot as she could tolerate, before stepping in. She pinned her hair on top of her head and slid into the tub. As she rested her head against the rim, she closed her eyes, but it didn't stop the silent tears that streamed down her cheeks.

***

Rodrigo sat in his suite of rooms, his mind whirling. He unconsciously tapped his skull-tipped cane on the floor, the sound ominously echoing in the grand scale of the room. He was contemplating his next move. The annual All Coven's Ball was approaching quickly, and he wanted the bitch as his mate beforehand. All of the Medici would be there, flaunting their family and finery. It annoyed Rodrigo that the Medici had bred like rats, and there were so many of them now. For centuries, Shade had been his sole rival, but now, they just kept breeding! Standing, he walked in circles around the room. The Medici legacy was alive and well, but he intended to end it all. They were all too high and mighty.

He licked his lips, his mouth dry. Tarleton and Giada had kept him informed of Dona's every move. She was becoming more depressed and isolated, and ripe for his plans. The Alizzi was primed and ready to cave to his advances. The sound of his low, wicked growl vibrated through him. It was time for a showdown with the Alizzi.

Rodrigo decided on the spot and teleported straight into the Alizzi home. Giada and Tarleton were startled to see him but stood instantly at attention. Tarleton spoke first, "Master, we are glad you have graced our presence. May I offer you some refreshment?"

Rodrigo removed his leather duster and pitched it at Tarleton. "No, make yourselves busy and only come when and if I command, that is an order." Both servants nodded and scurried from the room. Walking to the stairs, he took them two at a time and headed for her private suites. He entered her room and could hear her in the bathroom, bathing. He kicked the door open with a loud bang, and it slammed against the wall, and he grinned at her shocked scream. Walking to the tub, he towered over her. His eyes scanned her from the top of her head to the tips of her toes, peeping out from the bubbles. He leaned over the tub, his face close enough to feel her breath, and inhaled deeply. "You smell of dirt and grime, my pet."

Dona cowered in the water, pulling her knees to her chest, trying to make herself small. "I was working in the garden." She tried to control the quiver in her voice but to no avail.

Her fear sent a rush of power to his beast as her voice cracked and quivered. Grabbing her hair, he yanked her head back to look at him and snarled. "You have once again forgotten whom you belong to. Do you always seek to be a lowlife, dirty bitch, living in this hovel?" His voice rose in volume with each word. "I have given you everything. Pulled you from disgrace and made you look and live like a fucking queen, and this is how you repay me? Digging in the dirt like some commoner? I am the Borgia, and you will heed my every wish and command."

Dona winced when he grabbed her hair. He hated when she worked in the garden and soiled her skin like a commoner. "I'm sorry, master. I will do better."

"*Si,* my pet, you will and shall." He called for Giada and she appeared instantly at the door. He let go of Dona's hair and reached under the water to lift her soiled hand. Speaking to Giada, his voice was filled with disgust. "Look at these hands and nails that of a beggar, *si*?"

Giada nodded. "A total disgrace, master."

Rodrigo flung her hand away from him and stepped back from the tub. "Scrub her hands and nails until they bleed. Scrub her entire body! Prepare her for her master. If I find one spot of dirt on her, I will beat you both until you beg for mercy."

Giada nodded and went to the cabinet, removing supplies. She began with a nail brush and roughly scoured Dona's delicate skin. Rodrigo paced in the bathroom, observing. "Feel free to scream or moan, my pet. I rather like the sound."

Dona struggled to free her hand as Giada scrubbed mercilessly, but Giada's grip was strong. Dona felt embarrassed as he paced the bathroom, watching her every move as Giada unceremoniously scrubbed her clean, handling her as if she were an inanimate object. Once done, Giada opened the drain and let the water flow from the tub, then stood with her hands on her hips, waiting for Dona to stand. Dona had stood nude before many men, she knew her body was a work of art, but they both made her feel self-conscious and ashamed. She reluctantly stood, trying to shield her nudity, and saw the sneer on Giada's face as she tossed her a towel. Turning to her master, Giada bowed her head. "Do you need me for anything else, master?"

Rodrigo snatched the towel from Dona as he passed. "Leave us."

Turning to face Dona, she finally smelled and looked as he wished her to. He lifted her hand, raw from the scrubbing, with a small trickle of blood around her cuticles, and his heart raced. He sucked each of her fingers into his mouth as his moan echoed in the bathroom. "Now, you are fit to accompany me to the bedroom, my pet."

Grabbing her roughly, he led her into the bedroom and pushed her to the floor. "Unclothe your master, and revel in his strength and power."

Dona grimaced as he sucked at her fingers, but at least they healed immediately. She followed him into the bedroom, where she was forced to the floor. She began by unlacing his boots. He balanced on one foot as she struggled to pull the boot free from his foot, then she removed the other boot. She unbuckled his belt and pulled it from the belt loops when he snatched it from her hands, and lashed out at her, the belt striking her hard across the bare flesh of her back. She whimpered, wondering what she'd done wrong, and continued to undress him, hoping not to anger him. Unsnapping his leathers, she lowered his zipper and was acutely aware of the massive bulge in his pants. He was excited by his rough treatment of her, and that didn't bode well for what may be to come. She lowered the leathers down his slender hips and pushed them to his ankles, so he could step out of them. She stood up with some hesitancy, still feeling shame at her nudity, and unbuttoned his shirt, avoiding his eyes. She slid the shirt off his broad shoulders, and let it slide down his arms and onto the floor. She'd seen him nude before. Rodrigo was an imposing figure, he was tall and strong, but he'd never had the same aesthetic beauty as Shade, but then, who did? She stepped back, bowing her head, and meekly asked, "Is there anything else, master?"

He reveled in her meekness, her submissiveness to his commands and he was pleased she understood her place. Her beauty aroused him, as did her fear as her hands shook disrobing him. His body was aching and in need of fucking and feeding. He summoned Tarleton to bring Red Moon to the room. As the servant entered, he poured only one glass for the master. Rodrigo took the glass and downed it instantly. He strolled around the room, picking up things as he moved about, ignoring her completely. He could feel her dread of what was to come, and also felt her embarrassment that he flaunted her nakedness in front of the servants. She recoiled into her own body, trying to hide her nudity from Tarleton.

He chuckled, "I do not know why you hide your body, my pet. You have never been ashamed before. As I understand it, you have fucked every male vampire in Italy, and far beyond. Drop your hands and turn slowly, so Tarleton may see the pet I covet."

She was embarrassed by his request but dared not disobey him. She dropped her hands to her sides and slowly turned so Tarleton had an unobstructed view. "Yes, master."

Tarleton knew his master and kept his eyes on the mistress. He wasn't surprised at how he degraded the mistress. He had gotten used to the cruel ways of both Borgia brothers. As she turned, Rodrigo went to her and grabbed her around the waist, licking her lips before leaving a trail of wet kisses down her neck. "Leave us, Tarleton. If anyone comes near this house, dispose of them immediately. "

"*Si*, master." Tarleton closed the door as he left.

Rodrigo picked Dona up and dropped her unceremoniously on the bed before crawling between her legs. His hands slid up her thighs and he wanted to consume every inch of her. He lifted his head and flung his long hair behind him as his eyes stared into hers, his fangs aching and punching through. "You can make this easy or hard, my pet. But you *will* please me."

It was hard to mask her fear of him. She'd held him at bay for a long time now, and he'd grown tired of the game. He'd take what he wanted, with or without her consent. She knew if she struggled against him, it would anger him but also excite him, and he'd be even rougher. She closed her eyes. She'd submit, but in her head, she'd escape. It wouldn't be Rodrigo who took her, it would be Shade. She'd escape into her memories, to the many times he'd had sex with her, and fed from her, but always denying her the right to feed from him. "Of course, I will please you, master."

He took his cock in hand and stroked himself several times, his head falling back. He drove into her deep, ramming into her hard. She was tight, a sign she'd not lain with anyone in a long time. Grabbing her tits, he squeezed them hard, biting and nipping at her nipples, bringing blood to the surface, and he slurped like a hungry animal. Her skin was smooth and sweet. Grabbing her legs, he lifted them high into the air and over her head, slamming his cock deep into her, setting a brisk rhythm. He leaned into her, his lips against hers, his eyes blazing red. "Feed, bitch, now."

Dona submitted to his rough advances, changing the pictures in her head. It wasn't Rodrigo and his careless advances she felt, but Shade and his slow seduction. She let herself fall deeper into her fantasy, trying to escape the pain he inflicted on her body when she heard him demand she feed. *No!* He had fed from her many times, if she fed, she'd be bound to him. She choked back her fear and revulsion, not sure how to respond. "Rodrigo... we will be mated!"

He tuned into her thoughts and was angered by the fact it was the Medici she fantasized about. *She dreams of the fucking Medici and then denies my request to feed?* He roared. He pulled from her and slapped her hard across the face. "You will do as you are told, bitch. I will wipe Medici from your mind and your body."

Rising from the bed, he dragged her to the edge of the mattress, flipping her over and entering her from behind. His thrusts were hard and bruising, and his fingers clawed at her hips. As he slapped her ass, he came hard inside her, filling her with his seed. In a lightning-fast motion, he flipped her on her back and entered her again. Gripping her wrists, he pushed them above her head and sank his fangs into her neck, drawing her sweet blood into his mouth, drinking mouthfuls as he fucked her hard.

Dona felt tossed about like a ragdoll, while he took what he wanted. She fought the tears, knowing this would always be how he made love to her. No, not making love. This wasn't making love. She could feel the depth of his hatred for her. He'd take his pleasure by hurting her and humiliating her. When she felt his fangs at her throat, she slipped back into her fantasy, feeling Shade's lips instead.

Rodrigo tapped into her thoughts again and saw it was still Shade she escaped to. He was enraged that she denied him his right as master. He stopped thrusting inside her, but his cock remained buried deep as he ceased his feeding and grabbed her face, looking into her eyes. His voice was graveled and raw with hatred and wickedness. "He will not save you. Scream for him, my pet, but I will fuck away every fantasy of him until you learn you are mine now."

Biting her lip hard, he sucked it into his mouth and drew her blood once again as she squirmed beneath him. His body covered her as he pressed her further into the bed, thrusting once again inside her, his beast urging him to take all. Fisting her hair, he yanked hard, nearly ripping her hair from her head. "Show me your fangs, my pet."

She was trapped, and her fate was sealed. She had to force her fangs to punch through, and the unwanted tears flowed. She'd feed from him and seal the covenant. He'd own her now. He lay his body down on top of her and she bit into his flesh. The power of his blood hit her hard, and it was filled with darkness and evil and tasted vile. Her body responded to the power of his blood, despite how much she hated him. The fire built between her legs and exploded in an orgasm with the power to shake the bed. It was done. She was sealed to him, and it could never be undone. In her head, she wept, but she lay still, staring with dead eyes at the ceiling. It should have been Shade.

Rodrigo felt the connection being made as he came inside her. His beast now owned her soul. He roared as he sat atop her, his beast letting the world know she was claimed.

Her blood trickled from his mouth as he rolled off her. He felt powerful and dominant as his ancient Borgia blood, now mixed with the Alizzi's, rushed, and sparked through him. Her blood was sweet, and yet meek and mild. It wouldn't take long for his blood to overpower her beast and bring her to the darkness he enjoyed. He stood up by the bed and grabbed a fistful of her hair once again and towered over her. Snapping her head back, he saw her tears flow. "You, my pet, are now Borgia. I own you and your territory. You will address me as master at all times." Flinging her to the floor, he commanded her to get dressed.

She hit the floor hard, throwing out her hands to break her fall. Getting to her feet, she ran to her closet, glad to be away from him. "What do you want me to wear, master?"

"It matters not to me. Dress, now." He gathered his clothes and dressed before calling Tarleton and Giada to the room. "Your queen will no longer be residing here. You will remain here to take care of the house. I will have warriors here soon. Until then, kill anyone who dares enter the premises. This is now Borgia territory."

Tarleton nodded. "As you wish, master, and congratulations."

Rodrigo dismissed them and turned to Dona. "Now, pet, it is time you go home where you belong."

In her head, Dona was screaming, but she knew better than to object. She put on her underwear and pulled a dress from the hanger, slipping it over her head. She could care less how she looked as she stepped into a pair of shoes. He was taking her away from her home, and she doubted she'd ever see this place again. "Do you want me to pack, master?"

He drew back his hand as if he'd slap her hard across the face again but refrained. Still, he took pleasure in watching her flinch as she prepared for the blow. She'd learn, soon enough, never to ask such ridiculous questions. "You will need nothing from here. You are the Borgia queen now. Come, we're going home."

As he lifted her in his arms they teleported out across Umbria. As they entered Borgia territory, he could hear the vampires of his coven and their celebration. It didn't take long for the news of his mating to travel. He wasn't in the mood for any celebration. She was only a means to an end in his scheme to rid Italy of the Medici.

He landed inside the palace with her still in his arms, his servants all lined up to greet them. He walked past them all without speaking a word or acknowledging their presence. Instead, he carried her straight to his private wing of the palace and entered his bedroom. He opened the door to an adjoining windowless room and carried her inside. The room was elegantly appointed, but not close to the grandeur of the room she'd occupied when visiting. He threw her on the bed.

"This is your room now. You are not to leave it unless you are with me. You will stay here until I have need of you. You will be tended to as I see fit." He turned and left the room, slamming the heavy door as he went, securing the door from the outside.

He headed for his office. It was time to call in Tomas. He could now put the next phase of his plan into play. There would be warriors assigned to the borders of Umbria, which now fell under Borgia rule.

Dona climbed from the bed and stood inside the windowless room, a room that adjoined his private suite. She wasn't his mate. She was his prisoner. She'd heard him lock the door from the other side. She walked around the dimly lit room, exploring the walls of her new prison before returning to the bed and curling into a ball.

She let herself sink into darkness. *I am nothing. I am nothing. I no longer exist.*

88

Lorenzo wiped the sweat from his forehead as he moved through the warriors who were practicing on the field. It was warmer out tonight than he'd anticipated, and he was wishing he'd tied his hair back. He stood to the side of the practice field, his hands on his hips, as he watched. Alfie was in the midst of it all, prodding and pushing them for more. Lorenzo had to smile. He remembered the days when it was Alfie and him, on this field training, while others barked orders at them. Alfie looked up and caught his eye, and slowly weaved his way through the sparring warriors, dodging swords, to join Lorenzo. The two stood together, shoulder to shoulder, as close as brothers, and looked across the field of warriors. They both knew there was no greater force than the Medici. Borgia had numbers, but the Medici warrior was still better trained.

Alfie nudged him. "They look good."

Lorenzo nodded in agreement. "Yeah, don't want to take anything for granted though."

They both turned their heads when one of the warriors from border patrol teleported in, landing only a few feet from them, a look of concern on his face. Lorenzo and Alfie exchanged a glance, wondering what was going on. Lorenzo looked at the dust-covered warrior. "You got news for me, warrior? Not sure I like that expression on your face."

The warrior unconsciously started brushing the dust from his leathers, "Master, there's a shitload of stuff happening on the border."

Lorenzo and Alfie dropped their casual stance, and stood up taller, their senses on alert. "Spill it, warrior!"

The warrior nodded. "We had reports earlier in the night that Rodrigo had visited the Alizzi. That's not unusual. We just keep an eye on his comings and goings. Sometimes, it's Soren who shows up, sometimes Rodrigo. We always log it."

Lorenzo sighed in exasperation. "Get to the point, warrior. I hope you didn't come back just to tell me about Rodrigo's social calendar."

The warrior stood taller. "No sir. Rodrigo left and took the Alizzi with him. Again, that's not unusual. He often takes her to his palace in Rome. But almost immediately, we started seeing the Borgia warriors show up, lining the border between Tuscany and Umbria. They were all laughing and joking about the fact their master had mated the Alizzi. If that's true, then all of Umbria belongs to the Borgia now. What do you want us to do?"

Lorenzo was trying to process what he'd heard. If Rodrigo had mated Donatella that put the enemy at his doorstep. "Get back to your post, warrior. I'll confer with my SIC and we'll get new plans to you shortly."

The warrior nodded and teleported out, as Lorenzo turned on his heels and headed for the office inside the camp, Alfie right behind him. Lorenzo looked over his shoulder. "Don't say anything until we're inside the office."

Alfie nodded. His head filled with possible outcomes. They entered the office and Alfie closed the door behind them. Lorenzo scooped up the pack of cigarettes on the desk and lit up, pacing the floor. Alfie poured them both a drink of Midnight and slid the glass across the desk to Lorenzo. "Fuck! I never thought Dona would mate him. What the fuck was she thinking?"

Alfie settled in a chair and took a big swallow from his glass, his feet propped on the desk. "Don't think we should spend a lot of time on the why, brother. Too late for that. The question is, what should we do next?"

Lorenzo picked up the glass and downed it before dropping into his chair. "You're right. The first thing we need to do is get some of our top lieutenants out there to assess the situation and figure out how many people we need on the border."

Alfie could see the Medici fire boil up inside Lorenzo. Like his father, he was quick to anger, then settled down to figure out the best response. "Both of us need to get out there too, check out what's happening. Also, our warriors have been out there all night. If Borgia brought in his warriors, they'll be fresh. Maybe we should think about changing out a few regiments." Dropping his feet on the floor, he couldn't imagine Donatella mating that bastard. It felt like she was betraying the Medici all over again. He'd never spoken to anyone of his nights in her bed when he was just a young warrior. "Rome is probably lit up as well. Fuck. If this was designed to antagonize us, don't jump the gun, brother. Last thing you need is Borgia rolling in here ready to rock and roll."

Lorenzo nodded. "You're right. Better to see for ourselves, then there's no mistaking what's going on. Last thing we want right now is to provoke them before we have all the facts. Let's have the lieutenants prepare for a second shift to go in fresh. In the meantime, you and I can figure out how many we need and see for ourselves what the Borgia's are up to."

They left the office, and summoned their lieutenants, giving them a quick rundown of the recent events. "Darius, you come with us. The rest of you, stay here. Get a regiment ready to replace the current troops, and have a second regiment on standby. We'll let you know more when we get back."

Darius joined his master, as the three teleported out, and the lieutenants on the ground scrambled to carry out their orders. Lorenzo kept a keen eye out as they flew low across the landscape, making sure there'd been no intrusion of Borgia into Medici territory. As they neared the border, the number of Borgia warriors was staggering. It was clear Rodrigo wanted to send a message, and Lorenzo heard it, loud and clear. The three of them teleported into the center of Umbria and could see the Alizzi villa was crawling with warriors. Dona's home had been transformed into a field camp for the warriors. Lorenzo cursed under his breath and they turned and headed back toward the border, landing on the Tuscan side. His Medici warriors responded immediately to his presence, as a field lieutenant approached him. "Master, their troops have been growing in size all night. No one has engaged. There hasn't even been an exchange of words. I told our warriors to zip their lips. We didn't want to start anything."

Lorenzo nodded. "Good job. Keep a cool head. They may just be looking for an excuse. Keep it tight. I'm going to walk the border, get a feel for their numbers, and then we'll give you your orders. We have a fresh regiment ready to come in and relieve you."

The warrior started to object. "We don't need to leave, master. Reinforcements are all we need."

Lorenzo stared back at them. "We'll see." He started to walk the border, Alfie and Darius in tow, careful not to antagonize the Borgia standing only a football field away.

Alfie kept his eyes peeled for anything unusual, but he knew when he saw the Borgia warriors that this had been well planned in advance. Borgia was letting them know he had Umbria now. Borgia warriors were practically lined shoulder to shoulder. How many fucking warriors did he have? As they walked, he strode side by side with Lorenzo, with Darius close behind. Lorenzo stopped once in a while and stared at them in the distance. Their attention was drawn to three Borgia warriors who stepped out from the others and started walking toward them. Alfie unconsciously put his hand on his sword. He didn't like this at all. He looked at Lorenzo, who'd noticed they were approaching. Alfie growled under his breath. "One step over this border and I will slay them dead."

Lorenzo's eyes never left their approaching enemy as he stood his ground. "Whatever you do, brother, keep your cool."

Vanni walked toward them with a swagger, flanked by two of his warriors. He couldn't wait to get close enough for Lorenzo and Alfie to recognize him. He sneered at the sight of them both. They could never take on the force of the Borgia. But as long as they thought they could that was the ticket they needed to win the Medici territory and make Borgia the most powerful coven in all of Europe. As he came within yards of the dark-haired king, he sneered and spit on the ground. His legs were spread in a stance of authority, his arms hanging by his side, his stringy black hair blowing in the night breeze. "Umbria is now held by the Borgia. Seems that interests you, Medici."

Lorenzo stared back at the warrior who'd once bullied him as a young boy in the Medici camps. "There are many things that interest me, Vanni. You're not one of them. You keep to your side of the border, and you'll have no problems with the Medici. Umbria never belonged to us, nor would we have taken it. The Alizzi wasn't our enemy, nor was she ever yours. I hope Donatella is safe." Lorenzo had long ago let go of any feelings he'd had for Dona, good or bad, but he never wished her harm.

Vanni looked down and kicked the grassy field with his boot, as he chuckled. "I should have known your first interest would be the Alizzi. She's now the Borgia queen and is no longer interested in little boys. She's chosen a true master." Vanni narrowed his focus onto Darius. "Still a Medici, Darius? Looks like you came up in the ranks, another one of his kiss-ass, cock-suckers." Shaking his head, "Sad, you could have become a Borgia, their wealth and power is more than Medici could ever provide."

"I prefer to be a warrior of honor and integrity, unlike yourself," Darius spit back at him.

Lorenzo nudged him, motioning him to be silent. Lorenzo looked hard at Vanni. "Does your master have a message for me, or did he just send you to be a pain in my ass, Vanni? I have things to do, and they don't include standing here listening to you yap."

Vanni casually reached up and drew a sword from the sheath on his back. He let it hang at his side as he gripped the handle. "I think you're smart enough to get the message. We won't be leaving any time soon." He turned to walk away but stopped. He pointed his sword at Alfie as he spoke to Lorenzo. "Don't forget to take your bodyguard, Medici. You might forget where the border is." He turned back and walked toward his waiting warriors.

Lorenzo had to fight every fiber of his being not to lop off Vanni's head. "I hate that asshole. And I really hate he still gets under my skin after all this time."

Alfie took a deep breath. "I've never hated anyone in my life like I hate that punk. I think I actually hate his wicked ass more than the Borgia. If nothing else, confirmation was given that Donatella is mated. We need to increase our presence on this border, and all trips into Umbria will have to be halted. Let's gradually switch out the warriors on duty now. Put Darius and another lieutenant in charge of the schedule."

Lorenzo nodded in agreement and motioned for Darius to start implementing their plan. "In the meantime, you and I need to get back to camp. We need to increase the threat level at Castello and increase the number of warriors on guard at your villa as well. I'll let Henry know. I don't think this will affect France or Greece, but he should be aware, so he can at least be alert for any changes. I'll need to let my dad know. He's not going to like hearing Dona mated Rodrigo. She's betrayed our family again."

Alfie shook his head. "Brother, I don't envy you that phone call. Piece of advice, turn the volume down, cause he's going to blow the roof off Bel Rosso when he hears this." Throwing his arm over Lorenzo's shoulder, he laughed. "He may be my father-in-law, but he's your dad, and I have faced his wrath for the love of your sister. That was enough for me!"

Lorenzo smiled despite the seriousness of the situation. His father's temper was legendary, although it had rarely been directed at his children. "Then I best be the one to break the news, I doubt anyone else would survive."

89

Lorenzo and Alfie returned to the camp, leaving Darius at the border to assess the situation and coordinate an exchange of fresh troops. After a quick consultation with their lieutenants, Lorenzo left Alfie in charge of the camp and made his way back to Castello. Now that they had everything in motion, it was time to let his father know what was going on. He entered the old castle and made his way to his office. He could hear Chantal's voice, ringing with laughter as she encouraged Grace. Lorenzo rounded a corner to see Grace crawling in Chantal's direction. Lorenzo smiled at both of them. Grace had started to pull herself up as well and would be walking soon.

Chantal looked up and was surprised to see him back from camp so early. Despite his smile, Chantal could see the concern in his eyes. He was home early, and her worry for him felt valid as she looked at him. He was dusty and dirty and looked exhausted. As Grace reached her, she picked her up and walked to Lorenzo. Grace was already gurgling in the language only babies understood, her arms outstretched to Lorenzo. "Lorenzo, you are home early, I hope everything is all right." She stood on tiptoe and kissed his cheek. "It looks as if someone else wants a kiss as well."

Lorenzo took the baby in his arms and kissed Grace on her chubby cheeks. He praised her for crawling, and Grace cooed back as if she understood his words. He handed the baby back to Chantal. "She'll get dirty if I hold her. Can you have the nanny take her, please? I think we should talk."

Chantal felt her heart sink. Even his voice told her something had gone wrong, and this didn’t bode well. "Of course, let me get her settled and I will be right back, Lorenzo."

They exchanged a glance, and she knew this was serious. As she left the room, Grace began to whimper, her arms reaching for Lorenzo. The nanny appeared to take Grace, and Chantal composed herself before returning to Lorenzo, taking a deep breath. She would, one day, be the Medici queen and whatever had happened, she’d stand with him. As she returned to him, she took his hand and led him to the parlor. "Relax, let me pour you a Midnight, you look as if you need one." Pouring him a large tumbler full, she returned and sat beside him.

He accepted the glass and took a sip. He didn't want to frighten her, but she needed to be aware. "I don't want you to be overly concerned, but you need to know the Borgia have assumed control of Umbria. For some reason I can't fathom, Dona has mated Rodrigo. Her territory automatically falls to him now. The Borgia has already moved his warriors to the border, and they've set up camp in Dona's villa. As I understand it, Dona is in Rome now. We'll increase surveillance around the castle, and I'll assign a few more to be inside as well. I'll do the same for Sophia and Alfie's villa. I don't want you to leave Castello, not even with Rene. You should warn your mother as well. I know you love having her visit, but I'm not sure it's safe for her to travel here. I'm sorry, *cherie*. I don't mean to upset you with this news, but I think it's for the best."

Chantal laid her hand over his as he spoke. She knew this was just the first of many changes to come. She was aware of Lorenzo's history with Donatella. She'd met Dona and knew her relationship with the Medici family was a long and complicated one. Lorenzo had told her everything, and this mating seemed like one more betrayal. She didn't answer him right away. She took a minute to process what he'd told her. This would slow down the progress of the orphanage even more now. They'd planned to be opening the doors soon, within weeks. "I understand, it is extremely dangerous for our families. I will inform *Maman* she may no longer visit. I am not upset, just..."

He set his glass on the table and took her hand. "What is it, *cherie*? You know I won't let any harm come to you. You and Grace are safe here. I'll see to it."

"It is not that, Lorenzo. I am very confident in our safety inside these walls." She stood then, and took his glass, walking to the bar to refill it. "The orphanage is due to open within weeks. I wanted to be there when it opened. My presence is important, but I will do as you ask." As she returned to her seat, she looked at him. "Does this mean that warriors will be taken from the orphanage?"

He leaned back against the sofa and rubbed his hands over his face. "*Cherie*, I know how important the orphanage is to you, and to our coven. I think we have to take it a day at a time. I don't know where we'll be in three weeks' time. Continue to have the builders work on completing the orphanage, and we'll see what's going on as we approach the opening. I can't promise you I'll let you go. We may have to delay the opening. I know the Borgia target the half-breeds, and I can only spread my warriors so thin."

She sighed with a bit of relief. There was still hope and she was determined to have this orphanage completed. She took his hands in hers. "Thank you." She curled into his chest. "Please do not worry about Castello. Rene has told me of all the plans if anything happens. I have had the house staff preparing the lower levels with makeshift beds, blankets, and supplies. Everything is ready for whatever happens. But I do worry about you, Lorenzo. Let me have a hot bath drawn for you, you look exhausted. You need to feed."

He ran his hand through her thick hair as she rested her head on his chest. "Thank you, *cherie*. I'll gladly accept your offer, but first, I must call my father and let him know what's going on." He kissed the top of her head. "For a female who wasn't raised around warriors, you have learned quickly how to adapt."

She smiled at his words. "I have loved you always, Lorenzo, and I will do whatever is necessary to keep you." She kissed him before standing to take her leave. "Go, call your father, and I will be upstairs waiting for my warrior."

He watched her leave the room before standing and making his way to the office, taking his glass with him. He poured himself a refill as he looked at the time. The sun would be rising here soon, so it was still night in the U.S. He spoke to the computer system to connect him to his father, and heard the big screen come to life as the connections were made. He took a seat in his chair and saw Gi's face appear on the screen. Lorenzo raised his glass. "Gi! Is my father about?"

Gi nodded. "It is good to see you, Master Lorenzo. Hold on, I will find your father for you."

As Gi stepped out of the line of vision, Lorenzo could see the office his father occupied in Bel Rosso, its surroundings so familiar. Lorenzo took a big swallow of Midnight, as he waited for his father to appear.

***

Shade was making his way down to his office. The house had been a flurry of activity lately as they all prepared for the All Covens Ball. He'd pull a tuxedo from the closet and be done with it, but the females had been planning for weeks about what they'd wear. Between Kate, Shannon, and Aislynn, it had become a three-ring circus, as they tried on gown after gown, and discussed hairstyles and jewels. He felt the need to escape all the estrogen. As he hit the landing on the stairs, Gi almost ran into him. "Master Shade, Master Lorenzo is on the phone for you."

Shade felt a shiver of dread and hoped this was nothing serious. "*Grazie*, Gi." Walking into his office, he saw his son's image on the screen. He looked worried, and Shade could see his exhaustion. As he sat down in his chair, he looked his son in the eyes. "Good to see you, son. By the looks of you, this is not a social call. What has happened?"

Lorenzo saw no reason to drag this out. "I just got back from the border. The Borgia has claimed Umbria and has already taken control. It seems Dona made a choice to mate Rodrigo. It didn't take the Borgia long to move in. They have several regiments stationed along the border and have set up a camp in Dona's villa. I've been told Dona has moved to Rome already, and now lives in the Borgia palace. Alfie, Darius, and I went to the border just to check things out. We're already increasing our numbers there, and I'm going to increase coverage here at Castello and at Sophia's. They haven't made any move of aggression, so right now, we're just in a standoff. Our warriors know they aren't to provoke. Is there anything else I need to do?"

Shade showed no emotion. Rodrigo's interest in Dona now was crystal clear; she'd been a pawn in his plan to get closer to the Medici. He sat thinking before he replied to his son. He reached inside the top drawer of his desk and lit up a cigarette, taking long drags. "Do you have enough warriors? We have the over-flow here at Bel Rosso, as well as California. If you need them, we can send them to you. Greece and France can spare warriors as well. I prefer you take warriors from Greece. It will leave Henry with a full house if anything erupts in France near the Valois."

“I think we're good for now. I'd rather save the backup troops in the event we go to war. That way, Borgia never knows our full capacity. By the way, we saw Vanni on the border.”

Shade leaned back in his chair. "Well, it seems he is pushing us in stages. You make me proud, son, you have done a good job. Remember, do not goad him. Keep the warriors well informed of his tactics, and by all means, keep the females in total lockdown. You look a bit worn, Lorenzo. Do you need your old man to come for a while, take some of this load off you?"

Lorenzo leaned back in the chair, a crooked grin on his face. "Nah. We got this. Alfie is an excellent SIC, and our warriors are ready. The Borgia have always been cocky and in your face. Let's just see how it plays out."

Shade nodded. He was pleased Lorenzo had this well in hand. "Relax a bit yourself, son. Rodrigo will draw this out and try to wear you down. There is no doubt in my mind he will throw down the gauntlet at some point, but he isn’t ready yet. The All Covens Ball is coming up. He always wants to show his power and prowess at this event, no doubt with Dona on his arm this year. He won’t make a move before this. There would be too many masters gathered in one place. He is not stupid, by any means. So, relax and take care of your mate. How is my angel doing?"

Lorenzo smiled. "Crawling, and soon to be walking. I remember those years with Henry and Christoph. Chantal will be chasing her through every room of the castle soon."

Shade grinned. "I remember those days well. Make sure you are a part of it, son, they grow up fast. Get your ass to bed and feed. Call me if anything changes. I love you, Lorenzo."

Lorenzo returned that love and the screen went blank. Shade stared at it for a long time. He knew the Borgia’s were scheming, but so were the Medici’s.

90

Natalia was about to leave the data center when a runner approached to let her know she had a call. She thanked him and headed for the communication center, where the staffer had Malachi on hold. She asked the staffer to leave so she could speak privately. As soon as the door closed behind him, she took the seat in front of the large screen and removed the mute option. "Hello, Malachi. I hope all is well."

He pushed the green hood back ever so slightly so he could see her better on the screen. "I am fine, thank you, child. I did want to speak with you before you went to your slumber. I have had a vision."

Natalia sat up straighter in her chair. "About the battle?"

He shook his head, "No child. I have not seen anything further about the battle. Have you?"

Her face reflected her concern. "No, and I don't know whether that's good or bad."

Malachi's face remained emotionless. "It is neither good nor bad, it just is, child. We will see only what we are meant to see, and nothing more. But that brings me to the reason for my call."

Natalia pushed the hood from her head, wondering what he'd seen. "You look… upset."

He frowned slightly. "Do I? I think I am feeling more confused than anything. In my vision, I saw you as mated." He watched her face closely for her reaction.

Natalia was caught off-guard and didn't have a ready response. She felt her face grow hot and knew her blush would be visible to him. She was wishing she hadn't removed her hood. "I don't … mated?" She was struggling for words. She didn't want to lie to him, and if he'd had a vision, she had no idea how much he'd seen. She cast her eyes downward, unable to maintain eye contact. "I don't know how to answer that."

He looked back at her, his face betraying nothing. "Then I suggest we just stick to the truth, *si*?"

Her head was filled with all the possible outcomes at once, but foremost in her mind was that he'd ban her from Council. She looked up at him, and she knew he could see the guilt in her eyes. Not able to bear his rejection, she closed her eyes as she answered. "It's true. I'm mated."

He nodded once. "To Marcello."

She answers softly, "Yes."

"I don't understand, Ivory. How is this possible you have mated, and it has gone undetected? It is the part of my vision I could not decipher."

She looked up at him. "My father had access to a potion he'd acquired years ago that blocks a vampire's scent. He met separately with both Marcello and me, to understand the nature of our relationship, and then he encouraged me to mate. I do love Marcello, and were I not born to Council, he is the male I would have chosen. I didn't do this for my father, I did this for myself, but I can tell you this mating was extremely important to my father. I'm afraid, Malachi. I'm afraid to acknowledge what this might mean, and why my father felt this was an important path to take. I was afraid Council would find out, and I'd be banned. In the end, my love was greater than my fear. So, what happens now? Will Council meet to decide my fate?"

Malachi sighed heavily. "I have been thinking about this for a few days now, ever since I had the vision. I have told no one."

Natalia looked surprised. "You have kept my secret? Why?"

He shook his head. "The visions do not always reveal everything. I knew you were mated even before I asked, and I knew it was to Marcello. I also saw your father in the vision, and his need to have you mated to the male. I did not see anything about a potion. That explains how it has remained a secret to those around you. I have spent hours thinking about this, and why it was shown to me. There is something that nags at me about your father's need to have you mated that has kept me silent. I do not understand it all, and I may never understand it all, but my instincts said it was related to the battle in some way."

Natalia nodded. "Yes, I felt the same way. It was as if he felt I'd be better protected if I were mated, even though I have no role in the battle. I can tell you it gave him great peace of mind."

Malachi thought about what she'd shared. "Who else knows?"

"Only my mother, my siblings weren't even informed."

He nodded once. "Good. Then keep it that way. I wanted to speak to you before making a final decision, but I have decided to keep this to myself."

She couldn't hide the shocked expression on her face. "Really? You'd do that for me?"

He rubbed his forehead. "I do it for you, yes, but also because I don't see the big picture. It plagues me that by exposing your secret I may weaken us all somehow. It does not escape me you are the first female born to Council. That, in itself, means something. You have already made strides in shifting the balance of power, so our females are not regarded as second-class citizens, or merely the property of their masters. You are changing the culture as it relates to our acceptance of half-breeds. These are no small matters. Who is to say how your rule in the Council will shape us as we move forward. I can't say I agree with your decision to mate, Ivory, because I have not been shown all the pieces to the puzzle. I will keep your secret, and I suggest you do the same. "

Natalia looked at him quizzically. "Do you think I'm in danger?"

Malachi paused as he looked back at her, considering her question. "I'm not sure how to answer that, child. I don't feel any sense of physical danger for you, and there was nothing in the vision to suggest that. What confuses me is the appearance of your father in this vision. I don't understand his role. As you have learned, everything in your visions is there for a reason. It is a clue, a puzzle piece, and you must be careful in how you interpret it. I feel I don't fully understand this vision, and so, out of my love for you, and not wishing to do more harm than good, I will remain quiet."

Natalia was struck by his statement of doing more harm than good. "So, you do think this is tied to the battle."

Malachi shook his head. "I don't have the answers you seek, but I felt your father needed to find peace in knowing all of his children were safe somehow."

Natalia felt a shiver down her spine. "Malachi..."

He held up his hand. "I have no answers, Ivory. You are the only sibling that knows the Medici history. You know the curse that has followed each generation. You have known it since you were a young girl and researched the archives at Council. The end has already been written. It was written long before he was born. It is not for either of us to know when."

Natalia felt a sensation like an ice-cold hand squeezing her heart. "But it doesn't mean my mating is in any way related to the curse."

Malachi nodded. "You're correct, it doesn't. Don't forget, your father has known of this curse since he was a young boy. If anything, he has learned to be the master of his own fate. Don't read more into it than is there, but if you should have any visions, please share them with me."

She answered him softly, "I will."

"I also think the information about the curse is something you must keep to yourself. You must not share this information with your mate. The more people know, the more they feel compelled to intervene, and I have found that only makes things worse. We must let fate play out. Your father knows what to do."

Natalia nodded and answered, "Okay," but she didn't feel confident.

"Get some rest, child. Go to your mate."

The screen went black, and Natalia sat and stared silently for several minutes. She was remembering her early exploration of the Council archives in Florence when she was just a young girl. It was her father's secret, and she had carried it all her life.

She stood up and left the communication center, letting the door close behind her as she made her way up the stairs to her private suite. When she entered, she found Marcello already waiting.

He smiled at her. "You're late tonight."

She blew out the candle by the bed as she dropped her off-white robe and climbed into bed beside him. "Got held up in the data center."

91

The night of the All Covens Ball had finally arrived. The annual ball had been held for centuries and was a long-standing tradition among the vampire community. Shade had always attended, as had his parents before him, and he'd taken Kate every year since their mating. As the family grew, and the children reached adulthood, they too, along with their mates, had been expected to attend. Even Natalia had attended in her younger years before joining Council.

In his parents' time, the responsibility for hosting the event would rotate from one coven to the next, but as the size and number of the covens had grown through the years, the Council would designate a different host city in Europe in which to hold the prestigious event. This year, the gala event was being held in Rome, and unfortunately, in the center of Borgia territory. The Grand Hotel Plaza Roma was an elegant old hotel, large enough to accommodate their needs. The family had flown there from Florence and checked into the hotel, as had most of the masters of Europe.

Shade had finished dressing and took a final look in the full-length mirror, his custom-made Italian tuxedo fitting his frame expertly. He had no idea what Kate was wearing tonight. Castello had been a flurry of activity this week, since the females weren't allowed to leave without considerable protection, the designers had been coming to them. They were all keeping their selections secret. He smiled at his reflection, wondering what she'd chosen to wear. They'd been staying at Castello for almost a week now, and the family had enjoyed being together, and having the opportunity to see Grace, as well as to celebrate the union of Christoph and Aislynn.

Shade had also taken advantage of the time to check out the borders of Umbria and he wasn't surprised at the number of warriors posted there. Rodrigo was showing his prowess and strength. He knew Rodrigo would be at the ball tonight, with Dona on his arm. He'd reminded his family to remain vigilant while they were at this event. He doubted Rodrigo would want a confrontation in front of all of Europe's masters, but still, Shade didn't want him provoked. He was determined to enjoy himself and his family tonight.

They'd just received confirmation that both of Chantal's parents would be attending. Henri had been reluctant to accept the invitation, but Amelie had finally won out. He knew Chantal had been both glad and nervous upon hearing the news, as she was hoping for any signs of reconciliation with her father. As he adjusted his cuff links, he called out to Kate in the adjoining room. "What time are we supposed to be down in the ballroom? I want us all to arrive together, *mi amore*."

"I'm almost ready!" Kate finished dressing with Theresa's help. She used to look forward to the ball, but in recent years, their family had grown so large that getting everyone coordinated to attend was a nightmare of logistics. The gown she'd chosen was gold brocade embroidered against a nude-colored net and clung to her body like a second skin. As she looked in the mirror, turning slowly and looking over her shoulder, she was second-guessing her choice. "This really doesn't leave much to the imagination."

The back of the gown was cut low, and the front showed ample cleavage. "Seriously, what was I thinking?"

Theresa laughed. "You look lovely, my lady."

Kate smirked. "You always say that. I think this may be over the top, but I didn't bring a plan B, so I guess I'm stuck with it. I can't believe I let Sophia talk me into this."

She added some large diamond studs and a wide diamond cuff bracelet. Theresa helped place the diamond tiara on her head, securing it in her hair, which had been piled in a mass of loose curls on top of her head. Theresa knelt and helped weave the straps of the gold metallic shoes around her ankles. "There you go, my lady. All done."

Kate stared at herself in the mirror, unsure of how Shade would respond to this dress. Because of the sheerness, the gown had to be worn without any underwear. The embroidery was strategically placed to cover her breasts, her crotch, and portions of her behind, but otherwise, she looked practically nude in the dress. Sophia and Bianca had insisted she buy it when they were selecting gowns, and she had allowed herself to be talked into it, but she was having regrets. "Okay then, let's get this party started."

Theresa spritzed her with her rose-scented perfume and Kate checked her makeup one last time before she tapped on the door into Shade's dressing room in the massive hotel suite and stepped in.

Shade was buttoning his jacket and adjusting his silk tie when he heard the door open and could see her reflection in the mirror over his shoulder, and she took his breath away. He turned to look at her. His mouth watered as his eyes claimed every inch of her. She looked beautiful in the dress, but it wasn't something she'd typically have worn, the sheerness exposing much more than she was normally comfortable with. Her legs were visible through the gold gossamer as she walked toward him, and he couldn't take his eyes off of her. He couldn't recall her ever dressing so provocatively in public, but her beauty was stunning. He placed his hand over his heart, as his eyes raked up and down her body before locking with her beautiful amber eyes. "You make my heart stop beating, *mi amore*."

Kate was watching his face carefully to see his reaction. This dress wasn't really her style. "Are you sure? If you hate it, you can blame Sophia."

He walked toward her and gently took her face into his hands, kissing her softly on the lips. "You are perfection." He took her hand and spun her around slowly, taking in the view of the dress from the back. "*Cazzo*, did they design this dress around that beautiful ass?"

Kate laughed. "It was custom made to fit me. I tried on a prototype from the designer, then he took all my measurements and custom cut the dress. The embroidery is done by hand. I'm still not sure. I feel like I need a big coat."

He grinned, his voice low and sexy. "No coat is needed. That would just mean one more thing I would have to rip off you when we get back to this room tonight." He walked around her again, his eyes not getting enough. He took a deep breath as he realized every male in the room would be wishing she was theirs, and he rather liked the idea. "Just a warning, if anyone asks you to dance, I want to see all hands above the damn shoulders."

She laughed. "Then you best keep my dance card full so I will have no need to dance with anyone else. Come on, I'm sure the others are ready and waiting. We should head to the ballroom."

He bowed to her and took her hand, tucking it around his elbow. "Do you actually think any of our children will be standing around waiting for us? More like the opposite." They both laughed as they made their way down to the lobby. He'd told the family to meet there before entering the ballroom. The hotel had closed its doors to the public for the evening, as the entire facility had been rented out to the covens. Every vampire who held even a small coven in Europe would be in this building tonight.

The hotel had wait staff assigned to the lobby, milling through the crowd with trays of Midnight or Red Moon. Several of the covens were standing around, casually chatting or having a drink before entering the ballroom. Shade didn't miss the heads that turned as they entered the lobby, but it wasn't him they were looking at. He was proud of her as she held her head high and smiled. He chuckled to himself. If they only knew how much she preferred to not be the center of attention and was wishing she was wearing a coat. He noticed Lorenzo first and guided Kate in their direction.

Kate followed his lead through the grand old hotel and saw the whole family gathered in the lobby: Lorenzo and Chantal, Sophia and Alfie, and Luca and Shannon. Christoph was there with Aislynn. It was her first appearance at the ball. Henry, Jules, and Bianca were without escorts, but Kate doubted they'd spend the evening alone. Chantal's parents had joined them, and Kate was surprised to see Henri and Amelie. No one was sure they'd attend since Henri had taken such a stand against Chantal and Lorenzo adopting Grace. Kate smiled at the family. "It looks like everyone is here."

Sophia beamed at her. "Mommy, I love the dress!"

Kate shook her head. "Really, because I feel naked?"

Shannon laughed. "It only took you a century to loosen up."

Kate gave her a mock glare. "I'm not sure I have."

Shannon nudged her shoulder. "Have a few drinks, you'll be fine."

Bianca made a quick move to her grandfather, always her hero. "P-bear you look so handsome. Where's Uncle Cory?"

Shade smiled down at the redhead who was dressed way too grown-up for his taste. "You look very beautiful, Bianca, but when did you grow up?"

She smiled slyly up at him and he realized she had that same glint in her eyes as Sophia used to have when she was up to no good. "Cory wasn't feeling up to making the trip this year. His health is deteriorating more and more. He said this is a bit more than he can handle. Not sure I can handle it myself."

Bianca gave her grandfather a sad smile. “Then give him our love and tell him we missed him.”

Kate looked about at their family, the people she held dearest to her heart. "Shall we go in then? Henri? I hope you’ll be joining us at our table. No point in the two of you sitting alone."

Henri nodded. "*Oui*, we had planned to sit with you. Amelie can be quite persuasive when she sets her mind to it."

Kate looked at Amelie and winked. "Good, as it should be. Lover, would you lead the way?"

Shade took Kate’s arm and led this great coven into the main ballroom. He’d never been more proud. "I will issue my annual advice before we enter. You are Medici, remember your manners, be respectful and above all..."

Before he could finish, everyone chimed in together, "Keep your sword arm free." They all laughed and lined up behind him as they entered the ballroom. Shade gave the name of the Medici and the *maître d’* escorted them inside the massive ballroom, now crowded to capacity, and led them to their table. The men pulled out the chairs for their mates, as the *maître d’* seated the single females. Shade smiled. He had the largest table in this room. Medici was showing their pride and legacy this night. Every year, they grew larger in number. The wine was poured immediately, and Shade started to stand and make a toast, but Lorenzo stood first and Shade nodded to his son and sat back down. He was proud his son was the Medici King of the European covens and taking his rightful stand.

Lorenzo held his glass high, and everyone around the table did the same. "To the Medici and the Valois, our past and present are intertwined, may our future be so as well, and may our great families long reign. *Per sempre*!" The crowd responded with "*Per sempre*" before taking a drink.

Shade sipped his wine, his arm across the back of Kate’s chair, as he looked around the room. He nodded to several of the masters, singling out the Farnese’s and Flores’ tables, and noting the Anjou's were here. He was surprised that Henri hadn’t sat at the Anjou table. The Valois and the Anjou were the two reigning covens of France. He leaned over to Lorenzo and whispered, "No Borgia yet, pompous ass is going to make a grand entrance."

Lorenzo swallowed the mouthful of Red Moon. "Of course. He'll arrive late, so everyone will see him. At least he didn't offer his palace to be used for the ball this year."

Shade grunted. "I would still have gone, but I would have worn my leathers and a full complement of weapons. I am almost looking forward to his appearance. It will be a show of the grandest black-hearted entertainment." He turned to Kate and looked down at her hands in her lap, fidgeting with the ring that had belonged to his mother. "*Mi amore*, you look beautiful, stunning beyond words. Don't think I don't hear every thought going through the minds of every male here tonight. I thought Henri was going to turn purple and choke when he saw you."

She nodded. "I'm trying to tune it out. I fear your mate has become quite comfortable with life at Bel Rosso and wearing jeans or a simple sundress. I don't care to be the center of attention." She looked up at him and smiled. "Unless it's the center of your attention, of course."

Leaning down, he kissed her soundly. "You are always the center of my attention." He slid his hand into her lap and held her hand. Looking across the table, he watched Christoph and Aislynn, both of them entranced with each other. "Aislynn looks quite different with her hair down and wearing a beautiful gown of white. I don't think I have ever seen her like this. Our grandson has good taste in women."

Kate smiled. "She does look lovely, doesn't she? She's holding her own for her first ball. This must be quite a change for her. I remember how intimidated I felt the first time you brought me here."

As Christoph stood and pulled out Aislynn's chair, taking her to the dance floor, Shade shifted his attention to Sophia and Alfie. Alfie was already tugging at his tie, and looked uncomfortable, wishing he was back in leathers. Shade chuckled, you could dress him up, but his warrior always showed through. Shade looked around the table at his family. "I love my *familia, mi amore*. Look at them, just as we dreamed."

She leaned against his shoulder. "More than we dreamed. I could never have imagined this."

He kissed the top of her head when he caught movement heading straight for the table and recognized the young Farnese Prince, Amondo. He was a tall, strong, and respectable warrior in his own right. His dark hair hung in curly locks just past his ears. He approached Alfie and politely asked if he might have the honor of dancing with his daughter, Bianca. Shade looked at his granddaughter's face and saw a familiar look in her eyes. *What the hell is this?* Alfie gave his permission and Shade watched his granddaughter nearly jump from her chair as Amondo led her away. Shade sat up straight and looked at Sophia. "Someone want to explain to me what's going on? Like right now."

Sophia laughed. "Chill out, Dad. Jeez, you get worse as you get older. Bianca met Amondo at the Farnese wedding in Sicily. They've been calling each other ever since, and both of them have been waiting for tonight. You should start preparing yourself because I think it's going to get real serious, real fast."

Henry cleared his throat. "Well, as long as we're spilling our deep, dark secrets, I guess I should tell you I've been seeing Giselle."

Shade was stunned. First, he got hit with the news there might be a mating between the Farnese and Medici and then he heard his grandson was seeing Giselle? *Who the hell is Giselle?* Holding up his hand, he cleared his throat. "One damn thing at a time! So, you are telling me my granddaughter has an interest in the Prince of Sicily, and no one bothered to give me a heads up? Why am I always the last one to know?" Shaking his head, he looked at Henry. "And who the hell is Giselle?"

Kate choked on her wine trying not to laugh. "Lover, they're all adults. They can't stay under your rule forever."

Sophia shrugged. "Why do you get so upset? It's the natural order of things. Did you expect her to live at home forever? Besides, she didn't tell us until recently. I knew you'd have a cow, so I put off telling you. As for Henry, he's on his own."

Henry laughed. "P-Bear would keep us all at home if he could." Turning his attention to his grandfather, he answered his question. "Giselle is the daughter of the royal master of the Anjou coven that borders the Valois. You should be pleased."

Shade leaned back and looked over at the Anjou table and saw a beautiful young lady with long blonde hair and big green eyes. She was regal in her manner, and she was staring straight at Henry. "I never said I was not pleased, Henry, Anjou is a respectable bloodline, and very old. So, my suggestion is you get off your ass and ask the beauty to spend her evening with you, like a true Medici. She can't stop burning a hole in your back as it is."

He sat back and laughed. "Love is in the air, *mi amore*." He stood and took her hand. "Would you do me the honor of a dance, my Queen?" Suddenly, he felt like he could dance the night away with her. There had been a time when he was the sole heir, and he'd wondered if he'd find his mate. He had been concerned the Medici legacy would end with him, but now it seemed his children and grandchildren would ensure the future generations for centuries to come and his heart was soaring.

92

The entire city of Rome was teeming with vampires and their respective families for the All Covens Ball. Rodrigo had estimated there were close to 2,000 vampires not from his coven who were in his territory for this annual event. The ball had a long history, and they had yet to have an incident, but he'd placed his warriors on alert just as a precaution. He may be powerful, but he also had few allies among the other covens. Every master from Spain, Germany, France, England, Italy, and the Scandinavian countries would be in attendance, sitting there like peacocks showing off their heirs and money. He didn't trust any of those bastards. None except the Medici had claimed him as an enemy, but he knew they all held ill will for him. The Medici would be on his doorstep, three generations of Medici blood gathered in one place and he couldn't spill a damn drop of it this night.

Tonight, was all about showing off his new mate, claiming Umbria, and showing the Medici and the other European covens he'd always take what he wanted. His one worry for a spoiled evening was his quick-tempered and impatient brother. Soren was getting more restless of late, even though Rodrigo had finally mated Donatella. Rodrigo had no intentions of ruining his plans for destroying the Medici.

He made his way to Soren's suites to give him instructions for the evening. He rapped hard on the door. He knew Soren was inside. He heard Soren call out to enter and he walked in to find him with a female riding his cock. "Get rid of the whore, Soren. I need to speak with you at once."

The female stopped her wild ride and looked at him with glazed eyes. Soren had plied her with wine and drug. Soren grunted as he quickly tossed her aside and ordered her out. "Your timing sucks, as usual, brother."

A butler appeared at the door to escort her out of the room. Rodrigo waited for the female to leave then made himself comfortable, reclining in a chair. "How many times have I told you,

Soren, no mortal females inside our private suites? We have rooms for these shenanigans."

Soren growled at him as he picked up a bottle of Midnight. "What the hell do you care? And besides, I will wipe her memory clean or kill her before I let her go." He stood naked in the room, his cock now flaccid. "I haven't decided yet on which option. What the hell is so important that you need to interrupt my time?"

Rodrigo watched his brother walk around the room, comfortable in his nakedness, not bothering to pour the wine into the glass, but chugging it straight from the bottle. "I need to give you some instruction for the evening. It is vital you control yourself. Do not instigate any trouble with anyone, specifically the Medici."

Soren slammed the bottle down on the table. *Oh, now he is going to give me instruction!* He'd been patiently waiting for this battle to begin, to finally release all his anger and hatred loose on the Medici. He was tired of Rodrigo's constant instruction and feeling under his thumb. Rodrigo never let him forget he was the second born. "I have attended this fucking ball since I was a child! I am a grown male, with my own fucking mind and you think I don't know how to act? You grow more slow, and dull-witted as you age, brother. I sit back and watch for months on end while you dally with the Alizzi, months wasted we could have taken the Medici by surprise, slaughtered them all. And now they have warriors lined up against us. When are you going to do something?"

Rodrigo stood and bared his fangs, his beast angered. "I rule this coven, whether you like it or not and you will heed my word, brother. I will take you down if you think for one moment, I will let you destroy my plans. Every master in Europe will be watching us, and you will not lay blame at our feet for anything. No tricks, no scheming or dirty deeds. This night is about displaying our power and prestige. Now, prepare yourself to look like a Borgia!"

Rodrigo walked out the door and slammed it hard as he left.

Soren growled and threw the bottle at the closed door. He'd show his brother power! Rodrigo had always been slow to show just how much power the Borgia had, and Soren was tired of waiting! He was anxious to rid this country of the Medici forever. He paced and kicked at the furniture, throwing things about like a child having a tantrum. He stood in the middle of the room, his body covered in sweat and his mind a jumble of wicked thoughts. Tonight, was a perfect opportunity to strike at the Medici, and Rodrigo wanted to throw it away. He rushed to his wardrobe and found the old ruby ring. It was a precious treasure passed down through the generations of Borgia. The ruby stone capped a deep well that had been hollowed out to hold poison and had been used to kill many in its long history. Throwing back his head, he laughed wickedly. How easy could this be? The Medici would all be drinking, and it would be so easy to slip a drop or two into a glass. His brother may be after Shade, but Soren had his eye on Lorenzo, and Lorenzo liked his drink. Suddenly, Soren's night looked a lot more entertaining as he headed for the shower.

***

Dona had remained captive in her suite since she'd arrived. Rodrigo came to her when he needed to feed and took her body savagely. She fed from him in return out of necessity, but she wondered if perhaps she could stop feeding. Maybe she could starve herself. She was startled when Giada entered the room and appeared in a hurry. "Get up and get showered. Wash your hair. I've been instructed to get you ready for the All Covens Ball."

Dona looked at her with some confusion. She hadn't been allowed to leave the room since he'd brought her here, and now he was taking her to the ball?

Giada snapped at her. "Hurry up! Does it look like I have nothing better to do than wait on you!"

Dona slid from the bed and made her way to the bathroom, showering and washing her hair. She'd attended the ball many times in her life, and she knew what a huge event it was. Of course, he'd want her there. The word of their mating would have spread, and everyone would be expecting to see her on his arm. When she stepped from the shower, Giada grabbed her roughly by the arm and shoved a towel at her. "Dry off. I'll need to fix your hair."

Dona did as she was told, and looked about for her robe, but there was none. "My robe, please?"

Giada sighed in exasperation. "No time. Just sit."

She yanked the chair out from the vanity table and Dona took a seat, shielding herself with the towel while Giada dried her hair, and expertly styled it in a formal updo. "Can you do your own make-up?"

Dona nodded. "Of course."

Giada turned to leave the room. "Then do it while I get your gown ready."

Dona fought back the tears as she applied her make-up, then sat back to appraise her work. Her face was beautiful and didn't reflect how she felt on the inside. She heard Giada calling her from the bedroom. "You done yet? I don't have all night!"

Dona made her way to the bedroom. Giada held a strapless column evening gown that looked like liquid silver. It was stunning in its plainness, with no adornment. Giada was careful to slip the dress over her head without disturbing her hair and zipped the dress up the back. Her shoes were also metallic silver, and Rodrigo had chosen her jewelry as well. Giada had brought a large diamond necklace choker that opened in front, the two ends extending down toward her breasts, and capped with two large pear-shaped diamonds that must be 30 carats each. Her earrings were designed to complement the necklace and dangled almost to the shoulder. The gown was clearly chosen to showcase the jewels. Giada fitted the diamond tiara into her hair and expertly secured it in place. She stepped back and admired her work and issued what Dona assumed was a grunt of approval. "Well, I've done my best. Stay put, and don't mess up anything. Master will come for you when he's ready to leave."

***

Rodrigo's manservant helped him dress for the evening. He stood back to admire himself in the mirror. His black dinner jacket was adorned with gold brocade. It was a much older style jacket, harking back to another century, but it was a look Rodrigo preferred. His black tuxedo pants were well-tailored, and he turned to the side to see the gold satin stripe down the side of each leg of the pants. His shoes were Italian in design, a loafer style that had the same brocade pattern as his jacket and topped with gold tassels. He'd placed a jeweled ring on every finger. He'd left his hair down as it brushed his shoulders and made a striking figure of a powerful master. He was satisfied with his appearance and was ready to call on Dona.

He entered her room and she stood tall and elegant before him. He walked around her several times, checking every inch of her. It would do. "You look beautiful, my pet. The others must see I take good care of my queen. Your manners must be impeccable." Reaching up, he tipped her chin to meet his stare. "You will smile and act as though you are thoroughly in love, and happy being my queen. If you do not, you will be punished far beyond anything you can imagine. I expect nothing less than perfection. You will show that bastard Medici it pleases you to be a Borgia."

Her smile was tight and forced. "Of course, master. It will be as you wish." She wouldn't dare to disobey him.

"Then let us be gone." He walked her to the stairs, and they proceeded to make their way to the atrium where Soren waited for them.

Soren smirked as his brother and the bitch entered. As usual, Rodrigo looked like a preening peacock. Soren had chosen a black tuxedo with a red dress shirt to match the ruby ring on his finger.

Rodrigo nodded to his brother. "Have you settled yourself, Soren?"

Soren grinned. "Quite settled, brother, let's get this party started. Everyone should be there by now."

Their car was waiting outside, and their driver took them straight to the front door of the Grand Hotel Plaza Roma. Rodrigo helped Dona from the car, offering his arm as she elegantly placed her hand around the crook of his elbow. "From this moment on, everyone will be watching us, keep reminding yourself you are the most powerful queen in Europe and act like it."

They walked inside and headed straight for the ballroom. The noise level inside the room made conversation difficult as thousands of vampires were dancing and drinking, mingling about. Soren trailed behind them, his brother always taking the lead as the elder. As they entered the ballroom, the *maître d'* escorted them to their small table, as a veritable hush fell across the room, all eyes upon them.

Dona wished she could feel pride at being on his arm, but she couldn't. She held her head high and knew she looked elegant in her gown. She tried not to make direct eye contact with anyone, but rather looked across the room at nothing. She could feel the questioning stares of the people in the room as they all stopped to look at them when they entered. As much as she hated being locked in her room, she hated being here more and was wishing she was back in the safe confines of her enclosed space. She prepared herself for what would be a long night and tried to smile as if there was nowhere else, she'd rather be.

Rodrigo walked with his chest puffed out, his beautiful mate on his arm. His eyes took in the room as masters stared at him, some with envy, and others nodding their greeting. As they passed the Medici table, he looked straight into the eyes of Shade Medici, giving him his most wicked smile. As they reached their table, he pulled out the chair for Dona and as she sat, he tipped her chin up and kissed her, claiming to all she was his. Leaning into her ear, he growled out softly, "Show love and passion, my pet, or you will regret this night for all eternity."

He smiled down at her and then sat beside her. Soren selected the seat that would allow him to observe the Medici table. He didn't stare, but he'd be watching for the right opportunity to poison Lorenzo Medici. As the waiters approached with wine, Soren downed his drink before the waiter could get away and grabbed another. He needed to watch his intake tonight. He needed to keep all his senses on alert, so his brother had no idea of his intentions.

***

As the Borgia's entered the ballroom, Shade heard the haunting hush fall over the room and he knew the Borgia's had arrived. He looked to the door and saw Rodrigo literally strutting with Dona on his arm, their late arrival making them the center of attention, just as Rodrigo had planned. It was no secret to the covens that he now owned Umbria and had mated the Alizzi beauty. Shade felt his body tense up at the sight of them. His beast wanted to reach out and rip Rodrigo's head off and shove it up Soren's ass. He felt Kate grip his hand tightly and squeeze. He locked eyes with Rodrigo as they passed his table, and Shade kept his expression neutral. After they passed, he let out his breath and his beast settled down. "Well, that was as I predicted. You would think the moon shone out of his ass."

Kate shushed him. "Let it go. Things are already strained. You can feel the tension in the air. He'll not try anything here, there are too many masters who'd gladly see his head on a platter. Don't let it spoil our evening, the young ones are having a good time tonight."

Aislynn had just picked up her drink for a sip when Christoph asked her to join him on the dance floor. They had so little opportunity to go out together because of their duties in the camp and they were enjoying the evening. She stopped suddenly with her drink halfway to her mouth when the Borgia's entered. She'd never seen them before, but she did not doubt who they were. She squeezed Christoph's leg under the table, and he gripped her hand. As they passed, she felt a shiver go down her spine. "So, that's the Borgia's?"

Christoph sneered as he watched them pass. "That's them. Puffed up poppycock. I don't see anything to worry about. Rodrigo looks like he got stuck in the 18th century in that outfit."

Christoph turned to his brother, "Henry, are you going to sit there all night, or are you going to grow a pair and go ask that girl you've been staring at all night for a dance?"

Henry took another sip of Red Moon. "Biding my time, brother."

Christoph nudged him. "Yeah, well, keep biding and someone else will move in. Get your ass over there."

Henry downed the rest of the Red Moon and pushed his chair back as he stood and got ready to approach Giselle's table. "Wish me luck."

Lorenzo laughed. "He doesn't need luck. He's a Medici." He looked at his mother. "Right, Mom?"

Kate chuckled. "She doesn't stand a chance."

Henry crossed the ballroom, and bowed slightly to Giselle, taking her hand and kissing it. They'd been seeing each other for some time now, but he'd kept things quiet. With all the family drama around the Borgia, he hadn't felt the timing was right to start up something serious. He stared at the delicate beauty of Giselle, with her long blonde hair, the color of honey and her hazel eyes. She was of royal blood, and her regal breeding was evident. She was delicate and looks frail, a contrast to the female warriors he saw in the camps. "May I have this dance, *mademoiselle*?"

She smiled demurely. "*Oui*. You took your time getting here Henry Medici. I thought you would never ask."

Kate watched them from the other side of the room, as Giselle stood gracefully, and Henry led her out to the dance floor. She leaned over to Shade, speaking quietly in his ear. "Pay attention. I recognize that look. She'll be your next granddaughter-in-law."

Shade looked at the beauty on Henry's arm. "Well, by the way he holds her, I would say he is quite familiar with her. This is not their first meeting, by any means. She is a beauty, and apparently, he can't take his eyes off her. He has been glancing in her direction all night, and she to him. But then, all of us Medici men know the power of seduction. Romancing your female is vital." He winked at her and leaned over for a kiss.

Chantal sat quietly observing the room. Lorenzo had yet to ask her to dance, but he was having a fun evening, chatting with the family. Suddenly, she realized he was speaking to her, asking why she was so quiet. She blinked as his words registered. Turning to him, she smiled softly. "I'm sorry Lorenzo, but this night is not a pleasant one for me. The Borgia's sicken and anger me in their hatred of half-breeds. And I miss my Grace." She glanced toward the end of the table as her father sat quietly with her mother. "Having my parents here is not easy either. My father used to be so proud of me, and we would dance together at the grand balls. Now he sits there with his bruised pride, smiling at me every once in a while, pretending everything is fine."

Lorenzo hated she felt so sad. "Please, *cherie*, don't let them spoil your evening. You look beautiful tonight. You wore blue, and it makes your eyes impossibly beautiful. I couldn't bear it to see them filled with sadness. Come, dance with me."

She smiled at him with such adoration, she was so proud he loved her with kindness and passion. Her mother would never know such a love. "I would love to dance with you."

Shade watched his son and Chantal head for the dance floor. "About time he showed off his queen." He looked down the table at Jules. "Well, Jules, tell me, since both of your cousins seem to have found their future, is there anyone you have been having a liaison with?"

Jules sipped at his wine. "Sorry, P-bear, but I'll have to remain a disappointment to you for a bit longer. I fear I'm more like you than you may care to know. When I've finished sampling all there is, I may find the one I'm looking for."

Kate laughed. "Okay, that is already too much information."

Amondo returned Bianca to the table and bowed his head slightly to Shade. "I hope you don't mind sir, but I have asked your granddaughter to join my family at the Farnese table. Since her father is on the dance floor, I thought perhaps you would give your permission."

Shade stood and reached his hand out to Amondo, as they shook hands. Shade liked the firm grip and the manners of the young Farnese. He would be an excellent mate for his granddaughter. "It is good to see you, Amondo. I give my permission whole-heartedly, under one condition." He looked over at Bianca who rolled her eyes at him.

Amondo nodded. "I'll meet any condition you require, sir."

"Good because I would expect no less from a warrior of your standing. I will let my precious Bianca sit with you at your table, if you give your word as a warrior to protect her. This night, I am keeping a close eye on my family with the Borgia present, *si*?"

Amondo looked back at him, locking eyes with the fierce warrior. "I assure you, Master Medici, the Borgia's are no friend to the Farnese. I've been raised to be alert to their evil ways. Bianca will be safe. I'd lay down my life before I'd see her harmed. You haven't yet spoken to my father tonight, but you should know he's already stated if there's a battle between the Borgia and the Medici, he'll stand and fight with the Medici. Our warriors are at your service."

Shade was impressed beyond words. Amondo was a true warrior, and his heart burst with joy. He knew, without a doubt, Bianca and Amondo would mate, he felt it in his bones. "Then enjoy the evening with my Bianca."

Amondo bowed slightly to the Warrior King before returning to his table with Bianca. Shade watched them walk away arm in arm, and he turned to Kate. "They will be happy together, *si*?"

She smiled back at him. "Maybe as happy as us."

He lowered his head, knowing their love would be impossible to match, but if his children and grandchildren came close, then that was good enough. "I recall when I would attend this ball with my parents, there would be many connections made that ended in matings. Thank the damn moon and stars, I didn't take that shit seriously."

Kate sipped at the Midnight. "I suppose you'd like me to compliment you on being such a playboy that it took you so long to get to me?"

Jules chimed in. “See, that's what I'm talking about. Don't make snap decisions!"

Kate couldn’t help but laugh at both of them.

93

Rodrigo was putting on a show for the crowd and Soren paid no attention to his over-the-top antics. He'd fawned over the bitch all night. Even Soren could tell she wasn't thrilled with his overt attentions. He hoped his brother punished her later. Besides, Rodrigo and Dona seemed to have captured the attention of the crowd, allowing him to move about without much notice. He fidgeted with his hands, sliding the ruby ring containing poison up and down on his finger. He was anxious, waiting for the right moment to dump the poison into Lorenzo's unguarded drink. He was finding the task more difficult than he'd expected. The Medici table was crowded, and even though they were dancing, it seemed like someone was always at the table. He cursed under his breath. The bastards bred like rabbits! There were too many of them, but soon, there'd be one less if he could get a chance. He noticed the servers were ever-present, busy trying to keep filled glasses in the hands of every guest. He decided on a change of plans. The full dose of poison would easily kill Lorenzo, but he couldn't get close enough to their table without being unobserved and pouring the poison in a glass carried by a server would never ensure Lorenzo received it. Perhaps he'd set the bar too high.

He refocused his attention and was able to see the pattern to which each server was assigned in the ballroom and could single out the server that covered the Medici table, along with nearby tables. He now had a chance of at least crippling one of the bastards.

***

Shade excused himself from Kate and walked outside on the large veranda, milling with vampires from the many covens throughout Europe. He lit up a smoke and stood taking in the night air. He felt someone walk up beside him and turned to see Ottavio Farnese. He watched, as Octavio lit up a large cigar. "These damn events get bigger and bigger every year, Farnese. It is good to see you here tonight. We haven't seen you since the ceremony in Sicily, to celebrate your daughter's mating to Diego Flores. I hope she is happy."

Ottavio spit a piece of tobacco leaf to the ground. "*Si*, she is very happy. It has been a good union for her, and of course, it unites my coven with a powerful coven in Spain. I was pleased with my daughter's choice for a mate. We miss her, of course, but she visits when she can."

Shade took a drag on his cigarette and exhaled the smoke. "And now, it would appear my granddaughter has taken an interest in your son. I am impressed with Amondo, he has grown into a warrior with a solid reputation. They would be a good match, Ottavio, would you not agree?"

Ottavio puffed at the cigar, the thick smoke hanging in the night air. He and his family had known the Medici for centuries. "I would say a mating between the Farnese and the Medici is long overdue, *si*? My son is quite taken with your granddaughter. She is all he talks about. A union of our covens would be a good thing, Shade. The covens have grown larger, and the Borgia keep absorbing the smaller covens within their own, wiping out the weaker master. Whether or not our families are joined by mating, I wanted to speak with you tonight. Everyone knows the Borgia is targeting you, and it will not be a battle without massive causalities. I wanted you to know I will stand beside you in battle, as will Amondo. Our coven is not as large as yours, but our warriors are fierce. We can't let the Borgia win. If the Medici falls, it would only be a matter of time before he took down the Farnese. I can't hold him off alone. He would become too powerful then. You have my word. We will stand with you when the time comes."

Shade wasn't surprised by the offer. The Farnese had been a long-standing ally of the Medici. "I am honored and grateful for the support, Ottavio. This mating with the Alizzi places the Borgia on our doorstep. He borders our territory now and has moved his warriors along our borders. We are prepared to battle, and there will be one. It will take strategy and wit to beat him."

He let out a sigh and looked up at the moon. "Ottavio, I am a powerful master, I have lived a long time, and fought enough battles to know nothing is guaranteed. As a powerful master yourself, you will understand my concern for my lineage to move forward, no matter the outcome of battle." He turned and faced Farnese. "I would like to see my children and grandchildren secure before this battle begins, to know their futures are established. Will you do me the honor of drawing up a contract between Amondo and Bianca? I would like to see it signed before this blows up. I know Alfie and Sophia will have no objections. Alfie will gladly sign, and I can witness it. It will lay out my granddaughter's dowry, and what she will bring with her to the Farnese, then we can sit back and let them choose their own time. It would be a great comfort to me to know my granddaughter will be happy and protected in her future."

Ottavio shook his hand. "Consider it done. I will have a contract sent to Alfie in a few days' time. I assure you I have no hesitation, and Amondo is chomping at the bit."

Shade laughed. "It seems both of them have a bond already, and our families shall unite in mating. It will be cause for a grand celebration!"

They walked back into the ballroom together. Shade was uplifted by the thought of his family growing, even with the overshadowing of an upcoming battle. As he headed back to the table, he caught sight of Kate as she laughed and talked with Shannon and Chantal. It lifted his spirits even more to see her happy. She was as beautiful as her heart, a vixen in an angel's disguise. His eyes caught Dona sitting at the table with Borgia. She sat up straight, her back rigid, with a forced smile on her face. He'd known her all his life and he knew the smile was for show. He shook his head; he couldn't believe she'd mated the one vampire master who'd been an enemy to both of their families for centuries. He felt no regret for the beautiful woman who'd once been an ally and friend.

***

Dona held her glass to her lips and sipped, smiling at all the right times, and nodding at the clever remarks Rodrigo or Soren made. She greeted any well-wishers who came to their table. She was playing her role, and it was exhausting. She sighed heavily as Soren and Rodrigo had their heads together, deep in a conversation and she felt safe to let go of the fake smile she'd held until her cheeks hurt. She looked around the room and saw Shade returning to his table, rejoining his family. He barely cast a glance in her direction. She knew he was angry, and probably thought she made the decision to mate with Rodrigo willingly. She regretted she couldn't go to him and explain this mating was not of her choosing. She looked at Kate and found she was looking back at her. Dona flushed, giving her a nervous smile before casting her eyes down in shame and embarrassment.

Kate had been watching her for some time and she wasn't fooled by the practiced performance. She saw Dona's smile, but it did nothing to hide the pain in her eyes, and she didn't miss the fact that as soon as Rodrigo's attention was drawn elsewhere, Dona's smile would fade. The woman looked miserable. Her "happiness" was an act, put on for Rodrigo's benefit. At first, Kate thought Dona was getting what she deserved if she mated Rodrigo for his power and money, but the longer she watched her, the more she saw. Dona flinched slightly when Rodrigo reached for her. She pulled away from him, almost imperceptibly, perhaps unconsciously when he showed affection. She observed Rodrigo and saw he was putting on an act as well. His affection toward her wasn't genuine. He was acting out a role tonight as much as Dona was. Kate watched Soren, and his contempt for Dona was just beneath the surface. He hated her, and he hated her intrusion into their life. He didn't like his brother had a distraction, and Soren was no longer the focus of all his attention. As Kate observed the threesome, it dawned on her Dona hadn't gone willingly to this mating and she was being held against her will. Dona looked up again, and the two women locked eyes. Kate read the pain and torment in those eyes but knew there was nothing she or any of the Medici could do to intervene. **"I'm sorry."**

Dona looked down and quickly swiped away a tear before Rodrigo could notice. **"I do not want your pity. I want your help."**

Kate didn't look away from her. **"It's too late for that now. Our fates are sealed. This battle is inevitable. We can't help you."**

Dona nodded subtly, unnoticed by anyone other than Kate. **"Can you forgive me for doing the unforgivable? I have apologized to Shade and Lorenzo so many times, but it falls on deaf ears. I know I brought this on myself. Can you at least forgive me?"**

Kate stared back at this broken woman who'd lost everything. She'd hated Dona for so many years, and maybe that hate had driven her to this end. **"All is forgiven, Dona. I hope you can find some peace."**

Dona squeezed her eyes shut, fighting her emotions before she looked back up at Kate. **"Thank you"**

***

Shade stopped several times, as he made his way back to the table to Kate. As he reached the table, he noticed she was staring at Dona and her mood had shifted. He stood behind her, his hand on her shoulders, and leaned into her ear. "Would you give me the pleasure of this dance, *mi amore*?"

She looked up at him. "I was wondering where you wandered off to. I would love to dance."

She stood up from the table and placed her arm in his as he led her through the crowd. He pulled her close as they swayed slowly to the music. "I take it your conversation with Ottavio went well?"

"Very well indeed. Farnese is drawing up a mating contract between Bianca and Amondo. He will send it over to Alfie for his consent. It will lay in wait until they are ready."

“Shade, that’s wonderful! I’ve been watching them tonight, and I have to say, I don’t think it will be a long wait.”

He snuggled gently into her neck. "Now, you want to tell me why the hell you had a stare down with the new Borgia Queen?"

She looked up at him, reading his mood. He seemed more concerned than angry. "I think you should know Dona didn’t go to Rodrigo willingly. He’s taken her against her will and abuses her still. I know it’s too late, and we can't intervene, but I want you to acknowledge her intentions...or maybe better stated, her lack of intentions. She didn’t do this to hurt us, and I’ve forgiven her. It won't change the outcome of things. I know this battle is pending, as much as you try to keep it from me. What's done is done, but perhaps you could ease her pain by forgiving her as well. It’s you she loves, not Rodrigo. It was always you."

Shade was quiet at first. Her statement took him off guard. He’d noticed earlier Dona didn’t appear happy, but he didn’t give it much thought. "I am aware Dona has always loved me, but I could never return that love. We grew up together, I saw her as a friend, I slept with her, and perhaps that was not wise. It may have given her hope of something that would never be. I cannot say all my decisions and actions were good ones. But the Medici coven remained loyal to her and provided protection until she betrayed us and took out her anger on our son. I regret what has happened to her, and I certainly don't condone the abuse, but my heart is not ready to forgive. She made her own destiny."

Kate laid her head against his chest and wasn't unaware of the irony. After so many years of feeling jealous of the women in his past, she was the one asking him to forgive the female who'd betrayed them both. "Yes, she did. I don't deny that. But I think she's paid dearly for that mistake. I'd ask you to consider if maybe our harsh response, even though it was warranted, perhaps played a role in driving her to the Borgia. She's asked for forgiveness. If it brings her some peace of mind, what harm can it do? She's bound to Rodrigo now, and I doubt he'd ever release her. He'd see her dead first. If you don't feel forgiveness in your heart for Dona, then I ask you to do this for me."

He pulled back a bit and stared down at her face. She'd never asked for much from him in their entire lives together. And truth be told, he could deny her nothing. He knew deep within his soul this was the honorable thing to do. He was the Medici, and integrity and honor was the lesson he taught to every warrior. He kissed her softly, knowing deep in his warrior soul, it was the right thing to do. "For you, *mi amore*, I will do anything, even this. You have rarely asked anything of me, and I see your heart is unsettled over this matter. Consider it done." He saw her smile as he pulled her close again. "But don't think I am going to go over there and ask for a dance."

She hugged him closer and laughed. "Don't get frisky on me. If you ask her to dance, I'd break both your legs." Getting serious, she looked up at him. "Thank you. This means a lot to me."

Kissing her nose, he grinned. "And you mean the world to me, *mi amore*."

As the dance came to a close, he led her back to the table, a smile gracing his face. When they settled back into their seats, he felt Dona's eyes on him. He glanced up and she looked away quickly. She was sitting alone at the table, as Rodrigo and Soren worked the crowd. He sent his thoughts to Dona. **"Don't turn away, Dona. I know this is not how you wanted things to end."**

Dona glanced about nervously before looking in his direction. She had no doubts the punishment from Rodrigo would be severe if he caught her communicating with Shade. She'd seen him take his mate to the dance floor, and it appeared now she had been the topic of their conversation. She looked at him hesitantly. **"I am sorry, Shade. I made a lot of mistakes, and I caused you great pain. You are not mine to love, but I never stopped loving you. I beg your forgiveness for what I know is unforgivable."**

He took a deep breath and locked her into his gaze. He realized the depth of sadness and hell buried in her eyes. **"All is forgiven, Dona. I cannot intervene in your relationship with Rodrigo. What happens between a master and mate is off-limits, but I will wish for you a place of peace in my heart. Be brave and strong, as your *padre* taught you. You are still the Alizzi."**

Dona felt a weight lift from her shoulders, a burden she'd carried for years. She bit her lip as a tear fell and she wiped it away. Their forgiveness changed nothing, and yet, changed everything. At least they knew she wasn't part of this plan to bring down the Medici, she had been used as a pawn on a chessboard to bring down a king. At least she had that. She mouthed the words, 'Thank you', before looking away. She dared not hold him with her eyes much longer in case Rodrigo or Soren should take notice.

Kate leaned over, placing her head on his shoulder. "And I thank you as well."

94

Soren made his way to the side tables that lined the ballroom where the servers refilled their trays. He walked nonchalantly, looking about, stopping to talk to a few vampires he knew. He bided his time, the Medici server in his sights. His brother was occupied with other masters and it was perfect timing. He kept his eyes peeled as his anxious beast awaited the deed. He saw the server replenishing his empty tray at the server's table, so he made his way to him. He created a diversion with the servers, accidentally bumping into one of them, and sending the glass-filled tray crashing to the floor, as the other servers scrambled to assist. He quickly made sure no one was watching him as they were all working to clear up the mess, and the Medici server set his tray upon the table and rushed to help his coworkers. Soren passed by the table, flipping back the ruby stone that covered the well filled with poison, and put a single drop of the poison into each glass. He could only hope it would be enough to drop one of the Medici's, and that the server approached their table before running out of drink.

He stood idly by as the server returned to collect his tray. His beast howled inside him as the server grabbed the tray of poisoned drinks and made his way around to the Medici table. Soren moved about so he could keep his eyes on where the server went and who took the glasses. Several were swept off the tray by passing guests, and Soren had no concern for the collateral damage they'd do. He watched as the server approached the Medici's and Lorenzo grabbed the last glass.

Soren quickly made his way outside for some fresh air and to calm his roaring beast. At least the night wouldn't be a total waste of his time. Maybe this would speed up the timeline for the battle. He'd long grown tired of his brother's drawn-out approach. He stayed outside, waiting for the fast-acting poison to hit the random guests and the young Medici.

***

Chantal and Lorenzo had been dancing the night away and she couldn't be happier. As they finished the dance, he led her back to their table and found Aurelia and Diego Flores were standing nearby. Diego and Lorenzo started up a conversation and Chantal chatted with Aurelia. The daughter of the Farnese had been a friend of Chantal's for some time and she had missed seeing her since her mating to Diego. They now resided in Spain, and since Chantal's confinement to Castello, she rarely saw anyone.

Lorenzo had taken the last glass from the tray as the waiter passed when Diego suggested they go outside for a smoke. "Of course." He set the drink down on the Medici table and leaned over to whisper in Chantal's ear. "I will be outside, *cherie*. I won't be long."

Chantal smiled back at him and nodded, continuing her conversation. He was glad they'd come. The females needed a night away having been sequestered for so long, and he loved that Chantal was enjoying herself.

Chantal returned her attention to Aurelia. She was thrilled to have an adult her own age to engage in conversation. She had missed the gossip of the outside world. "I am so glad you are here, my friend. Please sit with me. I am confined to Castello, and with Grace to care for, and the plans for the orphanage, I have been too busy to keep up with what is going on in the covens. Tell me, how do you like mated life? Is Diego a good mate?"

Aurelia grasped her hand. "He has been a wonderful mate. It has required some adjustment, living in Spain and being away from my family, but he works so hard to make sure I am happy. My mother has told me about the conflict here in Italy. I hope your family is okay. Are you safe?"

Chantal squeezed her friend's hand. "I am mated to a warrior king. I am more than safe. I am surrounded day and night by warriors." She chuckled. "I make light of it, but I am grateful beyond words. Who could have imagined I would have mated a warrior? To be honest, this whole ordeal with the Borgia is quite stressful on our family, Aurelia, but we'll get through it. And then I have Grace! She is the most beautiful gift I could ever have been given. She is such an angel. You have probably heard I am working diligently on behalf of the half-breeds and have been building an orphanage like the ones in the States. It means the world to me. I intend to build more facilities all over Europe, with time. The orphanage in America is run by Lorenzo's sister, and I have used it as my model. They are making such a difference in these children's lives."

Aurelia nodded. "Yes, we have all heard of your progress with the half-breeds. Diego and I have discussed adopting. We will have our own of course, but at least it will help to spread the concept into Spain. Perhaps when things settle down with the Borgia, I could visit the orphanage?"

Chantal's heart leaped. "Oh, that would be wonderful. It would mean so much to me. Of course, you must come. I would love to give you a private tour once all this Borgia mess is over. I still hear resistance from the elders. They are still not convinced we should allow the half-breeds into our culture. I want our generation to show them this change can work and is good for all of us. You are a good friend, Aurelia. I'm happy you and Diego understand this."

Chantal reached for her glass and found it-empty, so she grabbed Lorenzo's full one and began to sip the Midnight. She was parched from the dancing, and the talking, and emptied half the glass. "Excuse me, I am so parched, Lorenzo loves to dance."

Aurelia lifted her own glass and sipped at her wine. "We both have much to be thankful for. I will speak with Diego tonight."

Henri couldn't help but hear the conversation between his daughter and the daughter of the Farnese. He rolled his eyes when Amelie squeezed his knee in protest.

"Do not say anything to spoil your daughter's evening, Henri. The integration of the half-breeds into our culture is inevitable. The younger generations don't hold the same views as we once held."

Henri grunted. "I don't have to like it."

Amelie looked at him, her eyes sad. "No, Henri, you don't. But your stubbornness keeps you from our only child, and I think that is a high price to pay for your pride."

Henri knew her words held the truth, and he needed to let go of his anger, but he wasn't ready. "Do not push me, Amelie."

She sighed and turned her attention back to her daughter.

Chantal continued to sip at her drink as she noticed her father's annoyance at the conversation. He was still holding on to his old views, and she only wished he would let go of his pride and show her the support she craved. She returned her attention to Aurelia. "I am so glad you will speak with Diego. It is good to know that there are other strong covens that support our efforts with the children."

As she drained her glass, she heard a loud wail across the ballroom. Chantal looked in the direction of the noise to see what was going on and saw a female had fallen from her chair to the floor just two tables away from them. People were beginning to crowd around her when another vampire fell to the floor. She quickly looked about for Lorenzo in a moment of fright, when the room began to spin. She grabbed the edge of the table, thinking perhaps she'd had too much to drink when she felt the sharp pains in her belly. She tried to stand, and she felt her peripheral vision fading. It was like looking through a dark tunnel, but she could hear all the commotion around her. People were crying and screaming, and the orchestra stopped playing. *Where is Lorenzo?* Her whole body was encased in the pain, and there was a trickle of blood running down her chin. Chantal tried again to stand up straight to look for Lorenzo but grabbed her stomach as the pain became increasingly more intense before she began to fall. "Lorenzo! Lorenzo!"

Aurelia was startled by the cries from the other tables when Chantal grabbed her stomach and looked unwell. "Chantal? Are you all right?"

Luca had been talking with Shannon when he heard the commotion and looked up to see Chantal trying to stand, gripping the table. He was at her side immediately, catching her as she collapsed, and helping her to sit back down.

Henri rushed to her end of the table. "Chantal? What's wrong?"

His daughter looked pale, and she'd broken out in a sweat. There were others around them who'd fallen to the floor, wincing in pain.

Lorenzo felt the stabbing pain in his own gut when he heard her cry from the balcony, and rushed back indoors, leaving Diego standing alone. "Something's wrong!" He was immediately at Chantal's side, looking at the chaos around him. "Chantal. Talk to me." His mate looked pale, and her eyes were glazing over. He looked around the table. "What the fuck happened?"

Luca lifted her glass and sniffed at it. He'd been drinking Midnight all his life, and the change in the bouquet of the wine was very subtle, but it was there. "Poison. They have all been poisoned."

***

Shade and Kate had been dancing and began to make their way back to the table when all hell broke loose. At first, Shade thought someone had just had too much to drink, but then he felt the ripple of fear as it flowed through the crowd. He saw several people down as he and Kate made their way back to their table when he was hit with Lorenzo's fear and he grabbed Kate by the hand. "Move fast, we have trouble."

He saw Henry ahead of him as he dragged Kate through the crowd, sending out a telepathic message for everyone to report to the table immediately. As they reached their table, Lorenzo was holding Chantal and he heard Luca say the words poisoned. "Fuck!"

Alfie and Sophia appeared in an instant, and he looked up to see Christoph and Aislynn barreling toward the table, Jules right behind them. "Get Bianca, now! Everyone, teleport immediately to Castello, I want the entire family there right away! Lorenzo, take Chantal, we need to move out of here. Go in pairs, teleport together, in case someone else is poisoned. Move out!"

Amelia turned to Henri. "I'm going with my daughter back to Castello, whether you follow or not."

Henri looked back at her. "Of course, I am going!"

Chantal felt herself losing consciousness, and the pain was unbearable. She could hear the others around her, but she had no strength to talk. She felt Lorenzo's arms around her and immediately felt safer. She moaned softly into his chest and felt the blackness overtake her and then there was nothing.

As Shade issued orders for them to leave, Jules looked around and didn't see Bianca. He rushed over to the Farnese table and grabbed her hand, not giving her time to say goodbye to Amondo. "Gotta go, now."

She looked over her shoulder at Amondo as Jules dragged her away, and he was shouting to her. "Go! I will come to you later!"

They reached the table as the family was teleporting out, Chantal in Lorenzo's arms.

***

Aurelia looked about in a panic but saw Diego approaching. "Are you all right, my love?"

"I am fine, it is Chantal. But I think we should all leave as well."

Diego nodded his head, "Come with me, we will find the rest of your family and go back to Sicily." He hurried her away as others were leaving the ball, teleporting out immediately, while others helped the fallen.

***

Soren waited outside on the crowded veranda, smoking. He began to hear the ruckus inside and the others that had gathered on the veranda, started rushing back into the ballroom. He chuckled under his breath. It had begun. The poison had taken hold. He walked inside, feigning curiosity, asking a few people what was happening. He stood back and watched with a gloriously wicked feeling of victory. Vampires were scrambling, and there was panic at the Medici table. He maneuvered himself closer and watched as Lorenzo picked up his luscious little French mate in his arms, and Soren could see both anger and fear play across Lorenzo's face. The poison had not found his intended target, but his mate would do well. Perhaps if he was lucky, she would die a horrible and painful death right before Lorenzo's eyes. He stared as the brood of Medici brats rushed to the table, and Shade bellowed out orders for them to leave. He felt disappointed he wouldn't get to see how it played out. Soren looked around and saw his brother's eyes boring into him, the Alizzi bitch on his arm, looking like a scared rabbit.

Rodrigo had been as confused as all the guests when the chaos broke out, but it didn't take him long to figure out some of the vampires had been poisoned, and Soren was at the root of it.

He saw his brother standing nonchalantly, as the other guests scurried about in panic. He knew Soren had done this, and it wouldn't take long before everyone would assume it was the Borgia. His temper flared, but he needed to keep it under control. Before leaving the table, he instructed Dona not to drink anything, then quickly ran to each fallen vampire, seeing how he might assist, and checking on the well-being of others. As the ballroom started to empty, he walked slowly back to his brother, who seemed completely unconcerned. In a voice filled with anger, he made sure

Soren knew he was displeased. "We shall leave now. Say nothing until we are back at the palace."

Teleporting out, Dona beside him, they returned immediately to the palace.

Soren was laughing as he landed inside the Borgia palace walls. He couldn't hold back the glorious feeling of victory over his brother. He was still hoping he'd hear news of at least one Medici death. Strolling to the bar, he poured out a fresh glass of half-breed blood, still warm and delicious. "You seem beside yourself, brother, you should be celebrating."

Rodrigo rushed at him with eyes flaring, his beast wanted blood for the careless act. Soren faced him, his own beast now engaged, his fangs punching through as he defended his actions. "The perfect opportunity is laid at your feet and you piss it away to show off that fucking whore you call a mate. Be careful, brother, you may be powerful, but killing me only leaves you weaker."

Rodrigo stood rigid, his body shaking with anger. He told Dona to return to her room and not come out until summoned. He could hear the soft swishing of her gown as she ran up the stairs for high ground to his private wing. Rodrigo approached his brother, his teeth clenched. "What in hell have you done? You fool! They will all know who has done this. The poison could kill them."

Soren didn't back down, his eyes locked with his brother. "I did something you were too afraid to do. I took control, we are Borgia, we take what we want. Besides, there wasn't enough poison to kill them. I couldn't get to Lorenzo, so I had to spread out the dose to ensure at least one of them would go down. The victims were so random, no one can place blame."

Rodrigo snarled his contempt. "You achieved nothing! The Council will hear of this, the Medici will push them to investigate and bring retribution. Have you gone mad?"

Soren laughed in his face. "I am not the one mad, brother. You are the one completely insane. The Council can prove nothing and since when have you become so damn afraid of their ruling? Has the Medici weakened your resolve? Are you running scared now? Has that bitch addled your brain with tales of his prowess and power?"

Rodrigo's rage spiked as Soren taunted him about the Medici. He knew Dona thought of Shade every time he fucked her, and hearing his brother throw the Medici in his face sent his anger through the roof. He leaped forward, grabbing Soren by the throat, as they both grappled with each other. Their fighting was fierce, as pieces of furniture crashed and splintered, littering the path they made through the room. The palace thundered and shuddered with the ferocity of their fight, but no one dared interfere.

Blood was spilled on the walls and carpets as they tore at each other. This wasn't the first time the brothers had fought, and they both doubted it would be the last. They fought until their anger subsided, and they had released their aggression, then they both stopped as suddenly as they'd begun, covered in blood, and sweat.

Rodrigo grabbed Soren by the neck. "No more! You will do no more until instructed. I will continue to rule this coven as I see fit. We have come this far and now are so close. Do not push me, or I swear I will kill you myself, brother. I can do this with or without you, have no doubt!"

Soren had pushed him far enough for now, but if his brother thought his patience was unlimited, he could think again. He had no intentions of letting those Medici bastards live much longer.

95

Once back inside Castello, Shade took charge, his first concern getting immediate help for Chantal. As they all entered the castle, Shade shouted out orders. "Lorenzo, get Chantal upstairs at once. Make her as comfortable as possible." He turned to Kate. "We need Theresa, she is an expert on poisons and remedies."

Looking about, he started issuing assignments. "Alfie, get down to the camp, I want all warriors on high alert immediately. Make sure that fucking border is covered from one end to the other. Anything goes down, I want to know."

Alfie nodded and kissed Sophia before he teleported out.

"Henry, I need you to do the same in the French camp, get back there now. I don't expect any trouble but would rather have the warriors on alert. Check out everything just to be sure." Turning to Christoph and Aislynn, he issued more orders. "Call Bel Rosso, inform the lieutenants of what is going on. I want every camp on full alert, make sure someone contacts Raven as well. This is a precaution, but they need to know what has happened. I want you here with me, both of you. If Borgia is going to strike, it will most likely be here. Jules, find Rene, post him outside Chantal's door. Luca, make sure we have the warriors shoulder to shoulder outside Castello. We have the whole family here, and no one comes in without my permission."

Shannon turned to Luca. "Can I help?"

"Not now, *mia belleza*. Stay inside, help Kate."

Shade watched them scramble and found Shannon, Henri, and Amelia looking befuddled. "Come, let us go to her."

***

Kate rushed off to find Theresa in her private quarters. Theresa looked startled when she looked up to see Kate at her door. "My lady! I didn't expect you back so soon."

Kate shook her head. "No time! Chantal's been poisoned. Hurry!"

Theresa leaped from her bed and started digging through the contents of her wardrobe, pulling out the old apothecary box. "Do you know what kind of poison?"

Kate was frantic, feeling like this was taking much too long. "No! Theresa, please!"

Theresa lifted the entire box and tucked it under her arm. "Okay then, take me to her."

Kate turned on her heels and rushed back through the castle to the grand staircase, lifting her skirt, and taking the stairs as fast as she could, Theresa on her heels. They made their way to the bedroom shared by Lorenzo and Chantal, where the family had gathered, and Rene stood guard. Kate could see Chantal, lying on her back in her blue gown, Lorenzo, Shade, Shannon, Henri, and Amelie all crowded around her. Her face looked deathly pale.

Kate shouted at them. "Move! Give her air."

Lorenzo held his ground, as the others reluctantly took one step back, making room for Kate and Theresa. Theresa placed her hand on Chantal's face, which felt cold and clammy. "Tell me what happened. Tell me how she reacted."

Shannon spoke up, "She was just laughing and talking when she tried to stand, and she looked pale and was gripping her stomach before she collapsed. There were others in the ballroom as well, all responding the same way."

Theresa felt for a pulse in Chantal's neck and found it slow and weak. Lorenzo was looking at Theresa's face, trying to read her expression. "You can help her, can't you?"

She nodded her head once as she opened the apothecary box and sorted through the old bottles, extracting one dark brown glass bottle whose label was no longer legible. "I think so."

Lorenzo looked angry. "You think so?"

Kate shushed him. "Lorenzo, stop. Let her work." Kate looked up to see Amelie in Henri's arms, sobbing quietly on his shoulder, and Henri comforting her. She was struck by the fact it was the only time she'd ever seen any display of affection between them but quickly dismissed it with her concern for Chantal. She watched as Theresa bent over Chantal's lifeless body, gently lifting her head, and placing the bottle to her lips. Theresa looked up at Lorenzo. "Help me, please. I need her to swallow this."

Lorenzo used his fingers to gently part Chantal's lips, as Theresa poured a few drops of the foul-smelling elixir into her mouth. Lorenzo could see Chantal swallow, and grimace at the taste. He looked up at Theresa. "How long? How long before we know."

Theresa hardly paid him any mind. "Quiet, child." She checked Chantal's pulse again, leaving her fingertips resting on the artery pulsing slowly in Chantal's neck, and detected the slightest change in rhythm. She closed her eyes and concentrated, as she mentally scanned Chantal's body, and saw the antidote flowing through her veins. Chantal's pulse beat faster and stronger, and Theresa breathed a sigh of relief. Sitting upright, she looked at Lorenzo. "She will be fine. Do not move her, and do not feed from her for four days. Do not let Grace feed from her for at least ten days. The infant's body will be more susceptible to any remnants of the poison. But you must force her to feed from you. She will resist. Feed her from your wrist, and make sure she drinks well. Understood? She will be weak, but she will gradually regain her strength."

Lorenzo nodded. "Yes, of course, anything!" He leaned over Chantal's pale face and kissed her gently on the forehead. "*Cherie*, do you hear that? You will be fine. You will come back to me."

Kate heard a soft sob from Amelie and went to comfort her. "She'll be fine now, don't cry. Theresa is a healer."

Amelie nodded as the tears flowed. "We could have lost her!" Turning to her mate, she looked at Henri. "We could have lost her!"

Henri nodded silently, a tear on his cheek. "*Oui*, but we did not, my love."

***

Shade had stood back and let Theresa do her work. He felt his son's heartbreak. He remembered when Cuerpo attacked Kate and the intense fear he'd felt when he found her. The sobs from Amelie brought his attention back to what needed to be done. He went to Kate and held her against his chest. He wasn't sure which of them needed it more. "We should all leave Chantal to rest now. There is nothing more we can do. She just needs to rest and let the elixir work through her system. Amelie, stay with your daughter, you can help Theresa get Chantal out of that gown and into something more comfortable for her. Henri, let us go downstairs and have a drink, I think we could use it." He went to Lorenzo and laid his hand on his shoulder. "Son, come on, she will be fine; there is nothing more you can do."

Lorenzo shrugged off his father's hand, and glared back at him, shouting, "There is plenty we can do! Why aren't we doing it?"

Kate gave her son a stern look. "Lorenzo! Not here!"

Luca had returned and joined the family just in time to see the friction break out and started to usher Lorenzo from the room. "Not the place, brother." Lorenzo broke away from him and stormed out the door and down the stairs, waiting for the others to follow.

Shade backed off. He kept his mouth shut. He understood the intensity of Lorenzo's anger and that he wanted revenge, but Shade would need to keep a steady hand at calming him. "Let him cool off. Now that he knows Chantal will be all right, other emotions will take hold. *Mi amore*, come, I need to get out of this damn tuxedo. I have told the house staff to arrange a room for Amelie and Henri here in Castello."

Turning to Henri, he nodded. "You should remain here as our guests for as long as you wish, Henri. Anything you need, we will have staff assigned to you. There is room for everyone to stay here at Castello until I know for sure what is going on."

He walked with Kate down the hall to their bedroom. Once inside the room, Shade quickly undressed, tossing aside the tuxedo and grabbing a pair of jeans and a t-shirt. He sat down on the bed to lace up his boots. He stopped and took a deep breath, running his hand through his hair. "I need to keep Lorenzo under control, *mi amore*, he will want revenge."

Kate had removed the tiara and let her hair down, shaking it out. She tossed the expensive earrings and choker onto the dresser and turned with her back to Shade, so he could unzip the dress. As he finished lacing his boots, he stood and unzipped the dress for her, kissing her neck as she shimmied out of the skintight gown. "He should want revenge. You know it was Rodrigo. Who else could it be?"

The dress fell in a puddle at her ankles, and she stepped out of it, pulling on a robe as she turned to face him. "We have no enemies among the other covens. Don't expect Lorenzo to give up so easily. He's the only person I know more stubborn than you."

"*Si*, he may be stubborn, but right now, we don't have all the facts. There were many covens present, and Chantal was not the only one poisoned. We can only assume it was Rodrigo, but there is much that doesn't make sense. Get dressed and meet me downstairs. I need to have you with us as soon as you can. You will need to take control of the household with Chantal ill."

He kissed her then, holding her beautiful face in his hands. "I love you, *mi amore*, but I can't rush into a full-scale battle without all the facts." He walked out the door, leaving her to find something to wear. He headed straight to the office where he knew he'd find Lorenzo and discovered Luca and Sophia there as well. He went straight to the bar and poured a drink, giving Sophia a stare. "You need to be with Bianca. Leave us, Princess."

Sophia's temper flared. "Are you kidding me? I'm the daughter of a warrior king and the mate of the Second-in-Command, and you dismiss me because you have things to discuss? I'm not some delicate fucking princess!" She turned on her heels and barreled past Luca, knocking him off balance as she passed. As she exited the door, she turned and snarled sarcastically, "Let me know if you need a snack or anything." Slamming the door behind her, they could hear her stomping off down the hallway. Despite the seriousness of the situation, Luca fought to suppress his smile. "Like father, like daughter."

Shade ignored her outburst. Everyone was on edge and he remained as calm as possible. He looked at Luca as he lit up a smoke. "She will get over it. And don't start with me, not in the mood." He sat down across from Lorenzo who was already sitting behind the desk. "I know you are angry, son, you have every right to be. And if you have something to say to me, let it out. Let's get all this aggression out now. Because your mate is upstairs ill and will need to feed from you."

Lorenzo slammed his fist on the desk, raising his voice. "Why are we just sitting here? We know who did this! You send Alfie to the camp to elevate the alert level when we should be knee-deep in Borgia blood about now. This was my mate! Would you be so calm if this had been Mom? This is bullshit, and you know it."

The Midnight slushed out of Shade's glass when Lorenzo slammed his fist on the desk, and Shade answered him calmly. "First of all, no, I do not know who did this. You are assuming without facts. Jumping the damn gun is no way to win this, son. Strategy and wit are what will be required. That means brains and patience. Are you so anxious to be knee-deep in the blood of the Borgia, along with your warriors? I am not. And if this was your *madre*, I would be sitting here thinking about how and when and why, before walking into a possible Borgia trap and the largest war this coven has ever seen."

Lorenzo swiped his hand across the desk, sending everything crashing to the floor, as he stood and paced. "This is a fucking waste of time! This is my coven! I am king here, not you. I've sat here for almost a year now, keeping my family locked away while they taunt us. I'm not hiding in here anymore!"

He started for the door, and Luca blocked his path. "Calm down, Lorenzo. Your father is right."

Lorenzo shoved him in the chest. "Shut the fuck up, Luca! You'll always take his side."

Shade understood his son's anger but needed to get him under control. "Lorenzo! Get your ass settled down now. Look at me, damn it!"

Lorenzo turned and faced his father, his eyes already glowing red as he spat out his answer. "You have my attention. Now, what do you want from me? You trained me to fight. But here we stand, while the Borgia are back home having a good laugh."

***

Alfie quickly informed Darius about what had taken place at the ball and placed the whole camp on alert. They had gone over the plans a thousand times, but they reviewed them once more. Once they had the warriors assigned, Alfie headed for the camp office where he could strip out of the formal clothes, and back into leathers. After he dressed, he teleported back into Castello. Making his way to the office, he heard the voices getting louder and louder. He stood outside the closed door and listened as Lorenzo went off on Shade and Luca. He rapped on the door and opened it as Luca stepped aside and let him enter. Alfie saw this situation could come to blows and gave Luca a look.

Shade locked eyes with his son. "Have you fucking learned nothing being a warrior? Think, Lorenzo, think! We have our entire bloodline inside this castle. If you go after Borgia now, you play right into his hands. Are you ready to unleash the hell that could destroy your entire fucking family? Settle the fuck down or I will do it for you!"

Kate had changed clothes and was coming down the staircase when she heard the commotion. She was on her way to the office when Henry teleported in, landing in the grand foyer. She turned to him. "Is everything okay?"

He nodded. "We have everything in place as a precaution, but the warriors said there had been no activity in France."

Kate shook her head. "Wish I could say the same for here."

Henry joined her as she walked in the direction of all the commotion in the office. "How is Chantal?"

"She'll be fine. I'm not so sure about Lorenzo though." Kate could hear Shade's response shouted back at their son and she cringed as their tempers spiraled out of control. As she opened the door, Lorenzo was shouting back at his father.

"Oh, you'd like that, wouldn't you? You want to take me on? Show me who's the better warrior?" He moved forward, ready to go after his father, when both Luca and Alfie sprinted forward, each grabbing an arm.

Kate shouted at him. "Enough! Lorenzo, enough! Save your anger for your enemy and stop this now!"

Lorenzo turned and looked at her and dropped his head. He knew she was right, and he'd let his anger get the best of him. He'd forgotten one of his earliest lessons as a warrior by letting his emotions rule.

Shade felt his heart racing. He didn't want to take on his own son and was relieved when Lorenzo was calmed when he heard his mother's voice. He stood with his hands on his hips, looking up at the ceiling. *How the fuck did this get out of hand so fast? This is exactly what Borgia was banking on, a rift between father and son.* He went to Lorenzo and pulled him into his arms. "I know how you feel, son, I honestly do. This is not easy. I love you so fucking much. I am proud of you, but we can't fight yet. We work as a family. It's the one thing we have that will take down the Borgia."

Henry sat on the edge of the desk as the drama played out. He was used to the Medici temper and knew it blew up fast but was quickly extinguished. "I called Giselle to make sure her family got home safely, and to see what they may have seen at the ball. No one saw anything unusual that would indicate who did this, but she said Rodrigo was quick to jump in and help everyone. Soren was stand-offish, but Soren has always been an asshole. I mean, would Rodrigo help if he was the one who put the poison in the drinks?"

Kate looked at her grandson. "Maybe Soren put the poison in the drinks."

Henry shrugged. "Maybe. Wouldn't put it past him, but would he go against his brother? I mean, Rodrigo was there like a peacock tonight. He wanted people to notice him, and Dona. I don't think he would have tried to draw so much attention if he went in knowing he planned to poison the guests. Besides...they have covens in that room who are allies. The poison was random. They couldn't have known who would pick up those glasses. On the other hand, who else would do it if not the Borgia? Poison is their trademark."

Shade listened to the conversation and saw Lorenzo had calmed and was listening too. "The allies of the Borgia could have even done it. Everyone there knows the hatred between our covens. They could have been hoping it would spark a feud. I know one thing about Rodrigo. He is no fool, he is one smart master, he did not get where he is by being stupid. If he was after one of us, he would have found a way to get to his target. The randomness is not his style. I know enough about poisons to know the amount given could not have killed anyone who drank it. Whoever did this, placed the poison into many glasses. Does that sound to you like someone ready to take us on in the middle of a fucking ballroom full of masters who would come to our aid? I think not. So, we are left with questions, and to be honest, I am not ready to risk the slaughter of so many because we think we know the answers. Perhaps it was Soren, but what was his game? What was he setting us up for? Lorenzo, tell me what you think, *si*? Talk to me now."

Lorenzo flopped down in his chair, his head in his hands. "We wait. We increase the vigilance, and we wait to see if they make a move, but I'm not fucking happy about it."

Alfie walked over and poured Lorenzo a Red Moon, a damn big one. He slid it across the desk in front of him. "There's only one thing that is going to calm you tonight. You need to go shower, check on

Grace, and then get your ass in bed with Chantal. She needs you, brother, as much as you need her. Go get some rest. We got your back. Anything happens, we'll come and get you."

Kate nodded. "That's a good idea. Your heart is with her. Go be with her, and you can think more clearly tomorrow."

Lorenzo stood up, taking the glass with him, as he kissed his mother on the cheek. "Sorry for the drama."

She smiled back at him. "Drama? My darling boy, please. I can show you drama. Now, go to your mate."

Lorenzo chuckled as he left the room. Alfie looked about for his mate. "Did anyone see Sophia?"

Luca smirked. "Follow the trail of smoke."

Alfie laughed. "So, it was a full-out Medici family blow-out."

Luca chuckled. "Pretty much."

Alfie left the room, shouting back. "Call if you need me."

Shade shook his head, knowing all was going to be all right for the time being. He watched as Luca and Henry headed out as well. He was left alone with Kate. "I am sorry our beautiful night was ruined, *mi amore*."

Kate went to him and wrapped her arms around him. "We won't let them destroy us. Not after all we've gained. The Medici will always rule here."

Shade smiled down at her. "I have no doubt whatsoever, *mi amore*. Now come, woman, let's see what we can salvage from the rest of this night."

He led her to the door and started to close it behind them when motion caught his eye. He turned his head to look back and saw his *padre* sitting in the leather chair behind the desk, and his *madre* behind him, her hands on his shoulders. They were both looking at him, a smile on their faces. He knew, no matter what happened, they would always rule here. He felt secure his progeny would carry the legacy forward. He smiled back at his parents before closing the door and leading Kate upstairs to their room.

96

It had been a few days since the poisoning, and Lorenzo had remained close to Chantal. Sophia, Bianca, and Alfie had returned to their villa, and Alfie had taken over the duties at camp, so Lorenzo could stay with his queen. Henry had returned to France, and Christoph, Aislynn, and Jules had returned to the States. There had been no further incidents since the poisonings at the ball, and the Council had reported no one had died, but a total of five vampires, all from different covens, had been poisoned. They had launched an investigation, but so far had found nothing to indicate for certain who had committed the crime.

Shade had sent Luca and Shannon back home in case Christoph needed any help with the camp in the States, but Kate and Shade had stayed, as had Henri and Amelie, both insisting they wouldn't leave until Chantal was on her feet again.

Lorenzo was lying on the bed next to her. She'd regained consciousness on the second day but had been confused and groggy. Theresa continued to administer to her, and each day, Chantal spent longer and longer periods of time awake. She was still weak, and Lorenzo had made sure to feed her, biting into the flesh of his own wrist, and holding it to her lips. He watched now as her eyelashes fluttered slightly before she opened her eyes, the color of cornflower blue. "*Cherie*, how are you feeling?"

Chantal awoke slowly, like rising from the bottom of a pool. It had been getting easier, as each day passed, to wake up and stay awake. Her brain felt muddled, and she felt constantly exhausted. She was aware Lorenzo had been forcing her to feed, and it had helped her recover. Still, she felt like, if she could just get up and move about, her energy would return much quicker.

She was vaguely aware of the people who'd been tending to her the last few days. Besides Lorenzo, Theresa had been ever-present, along with her mother, and Kate. She'd tried to get up a few times but had learned quickly, you didn't argue with Theresa. She could feel Lorenzo lying beside her in the bed. He'd spent so much time with her, always speaking to her in soothing tones when she woke, helping her to orient herself. She was grateful knowing he was there for her. Her eyes opened slowly, and she adjusted to the dim light in the room from the small lamp. She turned her head to look at him, and he greeted her.

"Lorenzo." She rolled toward him and sighed. "I slept well, I think. My sleep does not yet feel completely natural. I still feel drugged."

She sat up and made herself comfortable, as Lorenzo arranged some pillows behind her. "I sincerely need to get out of this bed. Grace needs me, and there are things to be done at the orphanage."

He smiled at her as he propped himself up on his elbow. "Not so fast. First of all, between my mother and yours, Grace is well taken care of. The nanny has been wandering around the house, looking for something to do. My father took your father out to see the orphanage and to make sure the building was ready. Did you hear what I said, *cherie*? Your father visited the orphanage. It was empty of any half-breeds, as there were only workers there, and some of the staff, making preparations, but still, that is a big step for him. You are much better, but Theresa says she wants you to remain quiet for a while longer."

Chantal was trying to comprehend what Lorenzo was telling her. Her father, the master of the Valois coven, was visiting the half-breed orphanage? She shook her head a bit, still lost in the fog of the poisoning. She must have been staring at Lorenzo with a look of confusion because he repeated it twice. "Lorenzo, I could never have imagined my *papa* visiting the orphanage. He barely looks at Grace. Tell me I'm dreaming."

He smiled. "It's not a dream, *cherie*, and your mother has placed Grace in his arms several times. He seems a bit uncomfortable, but I think it is more from the fact he is holding a toddler, not a half-breed. The poisoning scared him... Of course, it scared all of us. But, for him, I think he realized he could lose his only child, and she would have left this world never knowing how much he loved her."

Chantal felt the tears run down her cheek and she swiped them away quickly. "I want nothing more than to have my *papa* back in my life."

She moved slowly and swung her legs over the side of the bed and stood up, walking to the window. She stared out as the moon was reflected on the Arno River. "I love my home here, but there are times I miss Paris, too. I wanted to be able to show Grace the château where I grew up and teach her the history of Valois, but most of all, to feel loved and wanted by everyone in this family, so she would never feel like an outcast. I want her to be able to see all of the things I have accomplished for half-breeds. But I suppose, deep inside my heart, I wanted my *papa* to see it as well, to know there is so much more to me than being your queen."

Lorenzo followed close behind her as she was still unsteady on her feet, and stood with her at the window, his hands on her shoulder. He never tired of this view from their window. "He never stopped loving you, *cherie*, He's a man with great pride, who didn't know how to find his way back. Don't judge him too harshly."

There was a tap on the door, and Lorenzo recognized the soft, timid knock. "Come in, Theresa."

Theresa entered, surprised to see Chantal up and about already. "My lady! You must be feeling much better. Allow me to help with your bath, and then your family has asked to visit if you are up to it."

She heard Theresa's request but didn't respond, turning instead to her mate and laying her head against his chest. "I won't know for certain until I face him, if he is just putting on airs for the sake of your family, or if he truly intends to love and accept Grace."

She took his hand to steady herself and turned to Theresa. "I would very much like a bath Theresa, and may I please be out of these nightgowns. I would like to look my normal self as much as possible." She leaned up to Lorenzo and kissed him softly. "Would you be offended if I spoke with my family alone?"

"Of course not, *cherie*. Theresa usually throws me out anyway. I'll check on the camp, and I'll be back by the time Theresa is done." Lorenzo kissed her and dressed quickly as Theresa drew her bath. He let her to her bath and headed to the camps.

After her bath, Chantal was specific in her wardrobe choices. She was so tired of nightgowns, and she had Theresa style her hair. She sat to do her makeup while Theresa rushed around the room effortlessly, making the bed and picking up things. Chantal watched her in the mirror and wondered how many times she'd straightened this room in her lifetime. "Castello must feel very much like home to you Theresa, but I know Kate would be lost without you at Bel Rosso." She stood up and presented herself to Theresa. "Do I look a little bit like myself?"

Theresa was folding up garments and placing them in the dresser when she stopped and looked around the room. "*Si*, I worked here when Portia and Christofano ruled. I was just a housemaid then. I was the midwife at Shade's birth and watched him grow up. I hardly remember a time when I was not part of this family." She shook the memories from her head. "And you, my lady, you look much better."

She reached into her pocket and removed the brown glass bottle. "You must take the elixir now. I have given you a few drops every day to purify your blood, and Lorenzo has continued to feed you, to help your body heal. I would say another two days and you can resume your routine, slowly, of course."

Chantal nodded. She could see Theresa had many memories here. She scrunched up her nose when Theresa offered the elixir. "There must be some way to modernize this liquid, so it does not smell so offensive!" She swallowed it and shook her head, the taste bitter. "Give me a few moments to compose myself, and then let the family know I am ready to receive them. Thank you, Theresa, you saved my life, and have been such a comfort to everyone here."

Theresa bowed her head. "It is my honor to serve you, my lady." Theresa left the room and sought out Kate. She found her in the parlor with Grace and Amelie, sitting before a large fireplace. The fall weather had taken a turn and left a chill in the air. She was about to announce Chantal was up and about when Shade and Henri teleported in. "Master Valois, my lady, Chantal is up and has bathed and wishes to visit with her family. She is looking much stronger today."

Amelie stood immediately, ready to visit when Henri held up his hand. "Not this time, my love. I think I need to see our daughter alone." He paused before leaving the room, "Almost alone." He returned and took Grace from Kate's arms. Amelie looked on in surprise as Henri left the room with the child. Henri carried the little curly-haired blonde toddler in his arms as he made his way up the stairs. Grace was looking at his face with some confusion. He looked at the child, "*Oui*, I am your *grand-pere*, and I know I am a stranger to you."

Grace grabbed his nose and gurgled. He tapped at the door of the bedroom and waited for Chantal to answer.

Chantal had remained standing at the window, holding one hand over her stomach to quell the butterflies, her nerves a bit frayed. When she heard the knock, she put a smile on her face. "Come in."

Her father opened the door and peered inside. "*Ma petite fille*? Do you feel up for a visit from your *papa*?"

Chantal felt her breath leave her. "*Oui Papa*, do come in."

Henri stepped inside the room, the toddler held in one arm. Grace saw her mother and immediately reached out for her. "You are looking well. Theresa said you were much better. You have color in your cheeks again, and a light in your eyes. I have brought you...my granddaughter." He walked toward his daughter and gently handed her the wiggling child.

Chantal had dreamed of the moment she'd see Grace in his arms, accepting her with love in his heart. She took Grace, and cuddled her to her chest, laying her head on top of Grace's. "*Maman* is here, *mon ange*. I have missed you so."

She sat down on the settee with Grace in her arms. "Please sit, *Papa*. You seem to have had a change of heart. I hope it has made you realize every life is precious, even for a half-breed."

Henri looked at his only child. "My daughter, I was paralyzed with fear that I had lost you, and all I could think of was you would leave not knowing how much you were loved. I let my anger and pride blind me. I have had this time to think about what is important in life. I don't want to continue with this foolishness. I want you to be welcome in your own home, with my granddaughter. I have seen the orphanage, and I am so proud of you. I will tell you what I have already told Shade. The Valois family will match the funds of the Medici in caring for the half-breeds. We will make sure this orphanage, and any others you should build, will be successful. I beg you to forgive me, daughter. I beg you to not be as stubborn and prideful as your father, but more accepting and gentle, like your mother, and open your heart to me again."

Chantal felt all the anger and frustration with her father leave her. Besides Lorenzo, he was the only man she'd ever loved, and she knew how much it took for him to swallow his pride. "*Papa*, I am so glad for this. I grew up proud to be a Valois, I loved my childhood, it was so happy, and I was so loved. My sons grew up, having your guidance and love, and they carry that with them. I only wanted Grace to have the same. When you denied Grace, you denied me. I love Lorenzo, *Papa*, I love my sons *and* my daughter. This is my family and my coven. You taught me to be a queen. I am the next generation, and I have to learn to trust the old ways but mold them to fit modern times. The things you taught me have served me well, but I needed to leave my own legacy. Now our Grace will have a childhood knowing Valois and Medici, just as her brothers did. I am proud of you, *Papa*. I forgive you."

Henri wrapped his arms around her. "*Merci*, daughter. You are so much like your mother, kind and loving, and so gentle in spirit. In trying to punish you, I only punished myself. All of your children will carry the pride of being both Valois and Medici and will be loved equally."

Chantal felt her heart lighten. Her family was complete now. Grace began to wiggle and had had enough of being still. "*Oui, mon ange*, I know you are restless. Let us show *Grand-pere* what you can do, how big of a girl you are."

Chantal put Grace down and she took off crawling across the floor, chattering as she went. "She is so precious, *Papa*, and so beautiful. I cannot wait for you to get to know her."

He smiled back at his daughter and her pride in raising this child. "And she will have another *grand-pere* to compete for her attention. I can't let Medici have all the fun."

Chantal smiled at her father. Laying her head on his shoulder, she kissed his cheek. "Thank you, *Papa,* for stepping up, it means a great deal to me, and it will mean we can build more facilities. By the way, the orphanage will be called Grace House. It will be an honor if you will come with me on our opening day. I will be proud to have you beside me. "

Grace had crawled almost to the door when she stopped and rolled onto her butt, sitting up. She clapped her hands, looking at Chantal and Henri. Chantal and her father burst into laughter at the precious child who'd now grow up to know the love of both the Valois and Medici.

97

Castello was finally returning to a normal routine, and Kate and Shade were starting to make plans to return to Virginia. Grace had grown so fast and was sleeping exclusively in her crib now, the ancient hand-carved wooden cradle pushed into a corner. Kate sat rocking the sleeping child when a male servant entered and picked up the cradle. "Excuse me, my lady."

Kate looked at him quizzically. "Where are you taking it?"

"Back to the attic, my lady, until it is needed again."

Kate looked at him a moment. "The attic? You know, in all the times I've been in this castle, I've never been in the attic?"

The servant paused. "Would you like to go, my lady?"

Kate nodded. "I think I would."

She stood and placed Grace in the crib, tucking the blanket around her before following the servant. He led her down the corridor to a back staircase and up to the attic space. "Be careful, my lady, there is not a lot of light."

Kate stepped into the cavernous room, filled with trunks and boxes, discarded pieces of furniture, old chandeliers, and even racks of clothing. She smiled to herself. It would be an antique dealer's dream. She wandered through the dust-covered relics of prior generations of Medici, wondering how far back in time some of the pieces went and to whom they belonged. She spoke softly to herself, "If only they could talk...the stories they could tell."

"Excuse me, my lady, were you talking to me?"

She looked up, "No, sorry, just talking to myself."

"If you don't need me, my lady... I have other duties to attend to."

Kate waved him away. "No, of course, go ahead, I'll be fine."

She picked her way through the treasures, exploring each item before moving on, discovering an old clock, its hands holding steady at 3:40. Kate wondered if the time held any significance. She found a strand of broken pearls in a decorative bowl, perhaps set aside to be re-strung and forgotten by their original owner. There were delicate porcelain figurines, elaborate hats, with hatpins still attached. Kate felt like she could spend a year up here and never get through everything. She found a big trunk and opened it. It was full of a young boy's clothes. She carefully picked up the garments, yellow with age, and wondered if these were Shade's things. She smiled as she folded them and placed them back in the trunk. She sneezed as she brushed the dust from her jeans and moved forward, recognizing the oil painting of Adriana that had hung in Shade's room the first time she'd visited Castello well over a hundred years ago. She stopped in her tracks as she stared at the painting. "So, there you are."

She stared back at the woman in the painting who had caused her to feel so much jealousy, feeling only curiosity now, and sadness at knowing how her life ended. Had Adriana lived, would he have finally mated her? It would have changed everything about Kate's life. She would never have met him, and certainly wouldn't have mated him, or been turned. She would have lived as a mortal, and have died already, like Madison. She rarely thought about the path not taken, because a life without Shade, at any cost, seemed hollow and empty.

She stepped back and her foot hit a large shoebox, tied with twine. Bending over, she picked up the box and blew the dust from the top, as she found another trunk to sit on. As she started to pull on the twine, it was so old it fell apart in her hands. She opened the box to find it filled with letters. She carefully removed a handful, the paper old and brittle. Each letter had been carefully folded, and originally sealed with wax. Through the musk, she picked up the fading scent of violets, as she held the letter to her nose. The wax seal long broken, she flipped over the folded paper to see each letter was addressed to Shade and in the same delicate handwriting. The broken seal, when held together, showed an elaborately embossed letter A. They were all from Adriana. Kate took the last letter placed on top of the stack and slowly unfolded it and turned slightly toward the light, so she could read the faded ink.

> *"My dearest Shade,*
> *I am so sorry. It seems that is all I ever say anymore. All we ever seem to do is fight. I have*

> *loved you since the first time I saw you, but no matter how much I try, my love never seems to be enough."*

Kate stopped reading and closed her eyes. This letter wasn't meant for her. She felt guilty for even reading these few words. She could feel Adriana's pain, even after all these years, for she could imagine loving him and not feeling like she was enough; loving him and knowing he couldn't return that love in full. She folded the letter and placed it back in the box along with all the others.

These were Adriana's secrets, not hers. She placed the lid back on the box and set it back on the floor as she stood, looking one last time at the oil painting. There was a look of wanting in Adriana's eyes, a look of sadness, as if she already knew the outcome. Kate spoke softly to the woman whose ashes had blown across a battlefield centuries before Kate was even born. "I'm sorry too. But if you had won his heart..." She left the words hanging in the air.

She was hit with how much she'd struggled with her own jealousy, and it had all been such wasted emotion and drama. After all this time, she'd finally come to realize her jealousy had never been based on his actions, as he'd never shown her anything other than complete devotion. It was her own insecurities, her fear of not being enough, or not fitting in, or failing him in some way that brought on the jealousy. She knew he'd never leave her now. His love was unconditional, and always had been. She turned and walked away, winding through the path of discarded items of lives lived, and making her way back downstairs, finally leaving the past in the past.

98

The ball was long over, but the tension between Rodrigo and Soren remained a living, breathing thing inside the Borgia palace. Everyone could feel it, including Tomas, when he came to Rodrigo's office to accompany Vanni. They were there to provide an update on activity at the border. Rodrigo looked like a walking time bomb. The gossip about the rift between the brothers, and the poisoning at the ball, had been all anyone had been talking about.

Tomas decided to cross the line and speak his mind to Rodrigo. "This thing between you and your brother has begun to spread to the warriors. I only speak to you about this because you need to know their mood. I have seen you two at odds before, but this is something more."

Rodrigo stared at his SIC. Everyone was speculating on the events at the All Covens Ball, and while the Borgia seemed to be everyone's culprit of choice, there had been no proof found that could be laid at their feet. Rodrigo was annoyed by Tomas's remarks. "It is not their place to question me or my brother. They are paid to kill at my command, and if you cannot relay that to them, you no longer serve my need as SIC. I handle my own affairs, and those of my brother, as I see fit. Get out!"

Rodrigo stood suddenly, knocking over the chair, as the two warriors left his office. Rodrigo stormed through the palace, looking for Soren when he found him lounging in one of the parlors, his leg tossed over the back of a couch. Soren looked as though he ruled the world. It only inflamed Rodrigo's anger more.

Soren was bored, and his patience was waning. They had Umbria now, what the hell was his brother waiting for, a damn written invitation? He looked up when he heard his brother enter the room. "Why do you keep her? Dona is useless now. Why not lop off her head and deliver it to the Medici doorstep? He may even be grateful."

Rodrigo growled at him, but Soren didn't back down and continued to prod his brother. "We own Umbria, and our warriors stand ready. You only need issue the command. Have you no stomach for it, brother?"

Rodrigo had heard enough, and went straight for Soren, knocking him to the floor. "I have warned you who rules this coven, who gives the orders. You will do nothing! Go to your dungeon and play your games there, leave the seriousness of running a coven and winning Italy to me!"

Soren rolled onto his back and laughed. His brother was seething with anger. Soren stood up and faced him with a vengeance. "Running or ruining? You dragged Dona to that ball and paraded her for all to see. Do you think that impressed anyone? She is nothing, she came from nothing! The money you spent to attempt to make it appear she was back in the good graces of high society was for nothing! You impressed no one. You gained a scrap of land that means little to anyone, just to get access to the Medici border. To what end? Just to taunt him? Our ancestors would never have wasted time with such useless tactics but would have attacked by now. Have you forgotten how to battle, be a warrior and draw blood? Are you too damn busy ordering others around and making my fucking life hell to have the balls to battle? Go play with your useless whore, while you give your enemy more time to plan."

Rodrigo felt his body shake in anger, holding back the beast. His fists were balled at his sides as he screamed back at Soren. "Your words mean nothing! Antagonizing the Medici is part of the plan, pushing them to a point of no return, so he attacks out of frustration. Think before you act, fool! Besides, if the Medici attacks first, who can blame the Borgia? We would be protecting what is ours, as is our right. You have never had the patience required for the strategy of battle. Your anger and impatience drive you to act first and question later, overriding your common sense! You will listen and obey, Soren!"

Soren watched him walk away as he headed back to his office. He stood rigid, gritting his teeth, his eyes flaring red. *Who the hell did he think he was talking to?* He was Borgia too, and he was tired of his elder brother dictating to him through the centuries. He both loved and hated his brother equally. But for a simple turn of fate, Soren could have been the firstborn! He still had ways to best his brother, he always had. Perhaps, one day, he'd be the Borgia who ruled inside this palace.

***

Rodrigo slammed into his office, poured himself a Midnight, downing it quickly. He wasn't satisfied, and he'd allowed Soren to get under his skin again. He'd always been able to keep Soren in line, but lately, he was growing bolder and more intolerable. The more Rodrigo thought about his words, the more agitated he became. He strode to his private suites, stripping quickly, no care for the expensive garments. He made his way to Donatella's door and unlocked it, entering, and slamming the door closed behind him. She lay on the bed like a rag doll. She was beautiful, but she no longer moved him to passion. "Get undressed. I have need of you."

Dona could feel his anger and dared not do anything to provoke him further. "Yes, master." She rolled off the bed and started to remove her dress.

He walked to her before the dress hit the floor and grabbed a handful of hair and yanked her head back, kissing her hard. His tongue was deep in her mouth, but she stood before him as if she were a statue, never responding to his touch. He picked her up and pulled her legs to his waist while walking her to the wall. Her back slammed hard against the solid plaster as he drove his cock deep into her sex, pounding his hips against her over and over. He sank his fangs into her neck and drank, but he was growing weary of this non-passionate exchange. She didn't respond to pleasure or pain, and the game had ceased to be fun.

Dona endured the abuse he heaped on her, and escaped as she always did, inside her head. In her mind, his rough and careless grappling became Shade's slow, seductive touch. His brutish kiss and intrusive tongue became Shade's soft lips, and tender nibbles, and the hot, wet feel of his breath at her throat. It was so easy to remember Shade. She remembered every detail of every time he'd made love to her, and she replayed it in her mind. Thankfully, Rodrigo didn't linger. He always took his own pleasure, fed, and left. If she could just hold out...ignore the pain...she could get through another night.

Rodrigo knew she thought of Shade and his beast growled in frustration. It was always the same, no matter how much he hurt or degraded her, she thought of the Medici. After he came, he pulled from her and let her drop to the floor hard. Lifting her by the hair, he wrapped his hand tightly around the raven tresses and shook her hard, back, and forth, lifting her off her feet. "Still, you think of him! You disrespectful bitch! I am your master! My birthright dates back centuries and includes a legion of famous rulers and passionate warriors. How dare you bring shame to the Borgia name!"

He tossed her on her bed, and strolled out, locking her inside the room. He didn't stay to let her feed. Let the beauty starve. Let the bitch dream of Shade Medici all she wanted. He was tired of this nonsense!

Rodrigo showered and dressed for a night on the town. He'd been sequestered inside this palace with only his brother and his ungrateful mate for company for far too long. He needed to feed properly and feel a female respond to his sexual prowess. He craved to feel passion again, on top of a female who wanted his attention. He teleported into the night. Rome had a few underground clubs where he could feast on a bevy of willing females, a virtual smorgasbord to appease his aching appetite. He headed straight for the most elaborate house of debauchery, where his prowess and powers were well known. The private club held beauties from all over the world in every size and shape, all waiting to provide pleasure, available for feeding and the most outrageous acts.

As he entered the club, the matron lit up with happiness. He'd not called here in some time. They would make a lot of money tonight. "Master Borgia, we are honored that you have chosen to visit us tonight. We have missed you. How may we be of service?"

Rodrigo grinned wickedly. "Ah yes, it has been some time. Bring them forth, all of them, I wish to have several at once. Quickly, I feel rather wickedly in need."

The matron nodded and scurried quickly behind a closed door, as a servant offered him a drink as he waited. He didn't wait long. She returned and escorted him inside a large room filled with at least a dozen delectable females. He walked among them, caressing their smooth bare skin, and running his tongue along their neck, as they wiggled and squirmed, casting seductive glances. He couldn't decide which one he wanted, they all looked delicious. "To the Borgia room my lovelies, I shall have you all!"

The matron nodded and led the females to the room set up exclusively for the Borgia master. A petite little Asian beauty giggled as she clung to Rodrigo. "What wicked pleasures do you desire this night, Master Borgia?"

Rodrigo picked her up into his arms as her naked body straddled him. "Let us find out, my lovely, shall we?"

He carried her toward the largest suite inside the club. Let that unappreciative whore he mated have her dreams of the Medici, he was the Borgia and this night, he'd wallow in passion and wicked debauchery in any manner he chose.

99

Rodrigo returned from his pleasurable evening in the underground club, his sexual appetite and his bloodlust satisfied and his beast peaceful. He'd enjoyed the evening of debauchery and had forgotten how enjoyable it was to take pleasure in any manner he chose. He enjoyed that there was no pretense, and the females reveled in the sexual debauchery as much as he had. He went to his bed, his death slumber calling to him. Glancing at the locked door that held the inattentive bitch inside before he slipped into his slumber, he sighed loudly. Soren was right about one thing, she'd served her purpose, and had now become a tedious bore to deal with. She'd never returned his attentions as he'd hoped she would and had proven to be a less than satisfying mate. Perhaps it was time to send her off. It was rarely practiced, but a master had the option to release or exile a mate. He'd never release her, but exile was a different matter. To exile a mate showed the vampire community at large that the mate had proven unworthy. He felt the pull of the slumber overcome him. He'd think more on this when he woke, but for now, he just wanted to remember the night of fucking and feeding and the thrill it had brought him.

***

Soren was up before his brother and waited for his arrival at the dining table. It was their habit to drink half-breed blood together when arising for the night. Soren had felt his brother come home just before sunrise. He'd wondered where his travels had taken him and was eager to find out.

Rodrigo strolled into the dining room and was immediately served as he took his seat. Soren couldn't help but notice how much calmer his brother was. *He has been to one of the clubs!* He hadn't done that since he'd mated the Alizzi. Soren sat back in his chair, casually sipping at the blood in his crystal goblet. "You got home extremely late, brother. Does she not satisfy your needs?"

Rodrigo didn't take the bait. "It is none of your concern, Soren, what I do, or with whom I do it. She was mated for a purpose that purpose has been completed."

Soren took a sip of the blood and grunted. "Then why do you keep her? Why not get rid of her?" His thoughts ran wild. He'd love for his brother to assign that duty to him, disposing of the beautiful Alizzi. How he'd enjoy that little deed!

Rodrigo looked back at him and could see the wickedness in his brother's eyes. He wasn't about to give Soren what he wanted. "I have actually decided to exile her. I will send her back to that hovel in Umbria. She will have no servants. I will schedule a feeder for her."

Soren licked his lips, at least this was something. He still didn't understand why his brother didn't just dispose of her, kill her off, and be done with the worthless bitch. "So, you want to send her back to Umbria, just like that? The house is occupied with warriors. They use it as a command center on the border. You are going to throw her to the warriors for pleasure then? I rather like that thought, brother."

Rodrigo picked up his goblet and stood up from the table. His brother had neither couth nor sense, and if left to him, the Borgia coven would have died off years ago. "Soren, once again, you do not think. You jump into the first thought that comes into your head. I had already ordered the construction of a warrior camp on the grounds of her estate. It will provide more appropriate barracks for the warriors and provide a stable fortress for battle. Her exile will be humiliation enough. She was the Borgia queen. Once I exile her, all will know she has displeased me and is being punished. It shows she did not obey my will and commands and is not worthy to wear the crown nor drink my blood. Let her watch the fortress being built and filled with warriors of the Borgia. Let her see what we will do to that Medici she dreams about still."

Soren smiled to himself. He'd be glad to be rid of her. He didn't like the competition for his brother's attention. He drained his glass before standing. "You have made a wise choice, brother. As for now, I have business to attend to. That fucking half-breed orphanage is almost ready to open. They will be coming far and wide to journey there, perhaps even across our territory."

Rodrigo growled and slammed the goblet down on the table. "Do not be such an imbecile! That orphanage is watched closely by Council and under the protection of the Medici warriors. Council will have no doubts if anything happens near that orphanage that fault lies with the Borgia. We are already under scrutiny from the poisoning, thanks to you! There will be plenty of time, once we have taken the Medici territory, for you to raid the orphanage. Do not jump the gun and destroy this plan. Stay clear, Soren! I will only warn you once."

Soren sneered at his brother. Rodrigo's fear to face the Council and the wrath of a few warriors, all over a few half-breeds disgusted him. He'd let it go for now, but he'd make damn sure to hold him to his word when the time came. "Of course, brother, oh high and mighty Borgia. Hell could be on fire and you would still sit with your balls in your hand."

Rodrigo didn't respond, he refused to be riled tonight by his brother's taunts. He wasted no time in putting his plans into action, and within a week, the camp was functional, and he was able to move the warriors out of the Alizzi's villa. It was a solid building with a high turret that allowed for the warriors to look out across Umbria. He'd chosen several feeders for Donatella and had set up a schedule for them to visit her. He'd made sure the house had been stripped of everything, down to the bare necessities. Now it lay bare of rugs, linens, paintings, and much of the furniture. He'd removed all the fine clothing and jewels and left her with enough to live a peasant's life. He even had the gardens stripped as well, removing the flowers and trees, destroying the beauty that surrounded her home. She'd not be digging in the flower gardens any longer. He'd teach that bitch to mess with the Borgia. She thought she'd known poverty, but she had no clue as to the level of squalor he'd leave her in. She'd find no solace there. He'd removed the supply of Midnight and Red Moon, and she'd starve and feel the pains in her gut until he would send a feeder. How dare she even think about denying him his right as her master?

The time was ripe, and he'd dressed in his leathers, his hair hanging down past his shoulders, a sword strapped to his back, as his boot heels echoed in the hallways. He made his way to her cell. He wondered if she'd be strong enough to teleport. She'd grown weak as he hadn't allowed her to feed from him and had sent feeders infrequently. She'd have to get used to that. He had no intentions of spoiling the bitch with feeders once she was exiled. He unlocked the door and strolled in. "Get dressed. Now!"

Dona was shocked by his sudden entry into her room. She hadn't seen him for days. She slid off the bed, keeping her eyes cast downward, afraid to look him in the eye, afraid to anger him. "Yes, master. Is there something you would like for me to wear?"

Removing his leather gloves, he strolled around the room, slapping the gloves against his palm. "I care not a damn what you wear. I am taking you back to Umbria. You are being exiled. I will have a feeder come to you at my will and pleasure. They have been instructed, on pain of death, to not pleasure you. If you do not want to fuck me, then you do not get fucked. You take nothing with you, you deserve nothing, you are dirt under my boots. Dress!"

Despite his hateful words, Dona felt only relief. She'd be free of him and return to her own home. She dug through the closet and pulled out a clean dress. Tossing her nightgown aside, she put on the dress and stepped into a pair of shoes. Grabbing a brush from the dresser, she ran it through her hair. She sensed he'd be too impatient to wait for her to apply any makeup. Stepping from the closet, she answered meekly. "I'm ready."

Turning to look at her, he sneered. He saw the relief and joy in her eyes, but she had no idea what waited for her. He couldn't wait to dump her useless ass back into the stripped bare home. He picked her up and easily tossed her over his shoulder and teleported out. It took them only minutes to arrive in Umbria. He swooped in low along the border to let her see the warriors that would destroy her precious Medici, and then did a few turns around the property. He wanted her to get a damn good view of the stripped gardens. There wasn't even a blade of grass to cover the turned soil. He landed outside the door, dumping her unceremoniously to her feet. Stepping up to the door, he graciously opened it and held out his arm for her to enter, grinning with the anticipation of her discovery. "Welcome back home, my pet."

As they had teleported across her villa, she'd seen the gardens had been stripped bare. She was disappointed, but not surprised. When they landed at her door, she walked in to find her home almost bare. The furnishings had been removed, and she realized she really didn't care. She'd be rid of him, and that was all that mattered. She'd take her old home and meager lifestyle any day over his lushly appointed palace and her lavish prison cell, if it meant she could escape the Borgias. "Will I be here alone?"

"Quite alone, my pet. I will send a feeder when I see fit. She will be escorted by a warrior, so don't get any ideas. If you step one foot off this property, my warriors have been informed to immediately escort you to my presence. I do not think you are stupid enough to challenge that command. This is your home now. I care not if you rot inside it. You have served your purpose to me. Do you understand?"

She walked around the once familiar parlor. "Yes. I understand. You have exiled me."

He stood before her in the shell of a home, looking at the female who'd briefly been his queen. Her cheeks had become a bit hollow without the regular feedings. Her hair was losing some of its sheen. The once beautiful Alizzi didn't look so alluring to him now. He felt no remorse. He loathed her. "You are exiled, never to be taken back into my graces. You could have had it all, Donatella. You wasted your life chasing after the love of a Medici, a male who never wanted you. How pathetic."

He grasped her face into his hands, locking eyes with her. "I would have given you so much, but you made so many mistakes. It was your last chance at survival. I care not if you die here. I never want to see or hear from you ever again. Scream and beg for Shade, he will not come. But know this, if the master you crave to pleasure you...if he steps one foot over that border to help you, I will deliver his head on a platter."

He pushed her away from him, walking toward the door. "Their death is imminent, along with their children and mates. Just as yours is, my pet. You can't survive here for long on your own. It is just a matter of time before I take it all, Dona." He looked at her with disgust. "You were such an easy mark. You fell right into my hands, a useless dried-up whore to the Medici, and yet, here you stand now, still panting for his cock." He spat at her. "You disgust me to my core." He teleported out, leaving her standing alone.

Dona stared at the spot where he'd been standing, listening to the silence. His words had bounced off her. She hated him, and was glad to be rid of him, and felt no pain from his words. A small smile spread across her face. She'd lived alone for most of her life and could be happy here. She made her way upstairs to her bedroom. It wasn't the opulent room she'd left but held only the bare essentials; an old bed, a table with a lamp, a chair that looked like it had been salvaged from the attic. She opened the closet door to find the clothes she'd left here were gone, with the exception of a few garments. She didn't care. She walked to the window and opened it wide, breathing in the fresh air. She closed her eyes and inhaled deeply. She could smell the freshly turned earth. He'd destroyed her garden to punish her, to take away any pleasure she might find there, but what he didn't understand was what a gift he'd given her. She was free. Free from him and his abuse. Free from Soren. She didn't care where she lived, as long as she was free from the Borgia.

100

Dona woke and looked around the dimly lit room, momentarily confused by her surroundings. She turned on the small table lamp by the bed and recognized her old bedroom in the family villa in Umbria, and a big smile spread across her face. He'd taken all her fine furnishings, all the things he'd brought in when he re-decorated the house for her, along with what few things of value she had owned, but that meant nothing. She was free of him!

She climbed from the bed and took a long, leisurely bath before dressing in a simple frock, and leaving her bedroom to explore. She made her way through the second floor, checking each room. Many of the rooms had been stripped bare of any furniture, and others had a few pieces remaining. She headed down the stairs, checking each room, finding much the same. The parlor had an old sofa, and a few chairs, no art on the walls, and a bar. When she checked the bar, it was void of any Midnight. She smiled to herself. She'd lived for years without it, keeping only a small amount on hand for the rare guest. To Rodrigo, this may seem like he'd plunged her into hell, but she'd lived meagerly for years. He thought she'd feel ashamed she was exiled. It was a rare thing for a vampire to exile a mate, and it was done to show the vampire community at large that the mate had been discarded as unfaithful or unworthy. Dona had lived for years being snubbed. She could care less what the other masters thought of her.

The Medici had shown her sympathy at the ball. Perhaps if she could get word to Shade, he'd provide some assistance again. He'd helped once before by providing the salaries for her small staff, perhaps he'd be willing to do that again. She wouldn't ask for much. She stepped outside the villa and onto the grounds. All the plantings had been removed, and the ground tilled. When it rained, it would be a sea of mud unless she could get some grass planted. There was a warrior camp on her property, within plain view. She could see the warriors coming and going and hear the ruckus inside the camp walls. It struck her then this was no longer her land. Umbria no longer belonged to her. She was on Borgia land and living in a house owned by the Borgia. Still, she'd take this over living under Rodrigo's thumb any day.

She stood and watched the activity in the camp and wondered how she could have been so stupid. This had been Rodrigo's plan all along, to place himself on the Medici border. At least she took comfort in knowing the Medici warriors weren't far off. Shade and Lorenzo would both have made sure the border was well protected, and she knew, even though she couldn't see them, the Medici stood a thousand strong in Tuscany and were aware of every move the Borgia made. She smiled again and turned to go back inside. "It will be a cold day in hell before you ever destroy the Medici, Rodrigo Borgia, a very cold day, indeed."

***

Darius had been keeping Lorenzo informed of the activity he saw taking place in Umbria, and on the Alizzi's property, in particular. It had become clear they were building a warrior camp, even though he dared not move in close enough to examine it. Vanni was in charge of the warriors on the border, and he made his presence known nightly. Darius couldn't stand the sight of him. Darius would like to gather more intel on the camp to take to Lorenzo, but they had strict instructions to do nothing that could potentially provoke the Borgia warriors. "Fuck! That bastard is just taunting us. I can see the manned turrets from here!"

A few of his warriors gathered around him. "Lieutenant, we heard some of the Borgia warriors talking. It seems Rodrigo has exiled the Alizzi back to her estate."

Darius took in the information. "Exiled? Good work, brothers, keep your ears and eyes open. I know everyone is tired of waiting, but we cannot falter now. I'm returning to report to the master. Carry on!"

Darius took off for Castello. "Just what I need, more bullshit to deal with!" Landing at camp in a cloud of dust, he scanned the field and didn't see Lorenzo or Alfie. He marched straight for the office and tapped several times before entering. Lorenzo was seated in the chair behind the desk, but Alfie was nowhere to be seen. "We got trouble, master."

Lorenzo looked up as his lieutenant walked in. He used his foot to push an empty chair back from the desk, so Darius could take a seat. "Take a load off, warrior, and tell me what's happening at the border."

Darius sat down. He hated delivering news that wasn't positive. "Borgia has exiled his queen back to her home in Umbria, and he's already returned to Rome. The warrior camp he built on her property is pretty much completed now. You know his warriors had been using her home as a command base. But they have vacated the house for her and constructed a fully functional camp. They have turrets tall enough to scan the border, and they have them constantly manned."

Lorenzo opened the drawer and pulled out a pack of cigarettes and lit up, offering the pack to Darius who shook his head no. Lorenzo shrugged before tossing the pack back in the drawer. "Bad habit, I know." He thought about the news Darius had delivered. "He's elevating. Maybe they'll make the first move. Make sure our warriors on the border are alert to this."

Darius stood to leave before sitting back down. "Master, can I be frank with you? There are a few things that concern me."

"Speak your mind, warrior."

Darius had second thoughts about speaking out but decided this was in the best interest of the coven, and he needed to make sure Lorenzo was aware of everything. "I've been out there every night. The Borgia seems to rotate their warriors frequently. I see a lot of different faces. I know his numbers are larger, and he is interchanging them a lot. Vanni keeps a steady rotation."

Darius stood and walked behind the chair, his hands gripping the back of the chair as he looked at his master. "We've been keeping the same warriors on guard duty for some time now, and they're getting tired. I don't mean to complain, we're trained to wait, but I worry about them becoming lax. Our warriors pull long shifts. Don't think the Borgia hasn't noticed. Is there any way we can get some warriors from the States in here, just mix it up a bit? If we need to call in reinforcements in a battle, wouldn't it be to our advantage to have those reinforcements familiar with the area and what they face?"

Lorenzo listened to his lieutenant. His father had always taught him to listen to the warriors who were on the ground; they were your eyes and ears. "Good idea. We have a lot of warriors in France too, and a few in Greece. I'll talk to Henry and call my dad. We'll see what we can arrange. Good job, warrior."

Darius nodded. "*Grazie*, master. It would be a welcome relief to the warriors to have some fresh faces, perhaps even some more experienced warriors to talk to. The days and nights are fucking long out there."

He walked out and closed the door behind him. Lorenzo was a great master. He'd been taught by the best in the world. Darius wanted to believe they could win, but he knew they'd need every advantage they could think of to pull it off.

101

Shade and Kate had spent a few weeks in Florence, making sure Chantal had finally returned to full health, before returning to Bel Rosso. Chantal had asked them to stay until the opening of Grace House, but Shade wanted to get back and check on things at home and promised her they'd return soon. He knew Lorenzo still felt there was unfinished business with the Borgia's and wanted revenge for Chantal's poisoning, and he understood that all too well. He'd put himself in Lorenzo's shoes and knew it would have been difficult to control his impulses if Kate had been the one affected by the poison. He'd checked with Malachi several times since the incident, and there still seemed no conclusive evidence as to who had placed the poison in the glasses.

He took Pavi out for a ride. He felt he'd neglected his warrior on four legs for too long, even though he knew Angelo saw to it all the horses got exercise. Riding gave Shade a release, it always had. It gave him time to clear his head and untangle his thoughts. He felt his phone buzz and shook his head, reigning in Pavi. "We can't escape them, can we, Pavi?" He grabbed his phone and saw it is Lorenzo. "Everything okay, son?"

"Hey, Dad, hope I'm not interrupting anything. You got a minute?"

Shade swung his leg over Pavi as he dismounted, letting the horse wander in the pasture as he talked on the phone. He could see a few of Kate's warriors in the forest line, their eyes reflecting the moonlight. "Just out riding Pavi. What's on your mind, Lorenzo?"

Lorenzo propped his feet up on the desk, crossed at the ankles, a position he'd seen his father sit in many times. "A lot going on at the border I think you should know about. Borgia has built a fucking fortress and has a camp on Dona's old property. He's increasing the number of warriors along our border, so he's definitely escalating. Darius also heard Dona has been exiled. She's back in her villa. Darius thought it would be a good idea if we could rotate some of our warriors off the border. I thought I'd call Henry, bring in some of the warriors from France. What do you think? You want to send any of your warriors over from the States?"

Shade listened carefully. "So, he put Dona back in Umbria. That can't bode well for her." He lit up a cigarette and paced the field. "A fortress means he is showing his power, he has upped his game. How are our warriors responding? Any conflict? Sometimes the tension and the waiting causes conflict among the troops."

Lorenzo shook his head. "Nah, nothing like that. I think they're just bored and ready to get on with it. But if they're bored, they're less attentive."

"Agreed. Talk to Henry, see what he can spare, let's change it up a bit. Schedule their guard duty with some downtime. We need them fresh for battle. I will talk to Raven, see what he can spare as well. For now, I'd like to keep the warriors at Bel Rosso*,* just in case he makes a strike here. It's a long shot, the bastard has never stepped foot in the States, he would be lost here. Raven has a big camp out there now. Let's see what we come up with."

Lorenzo dropped his feet to the floor, his boots making a loud thud. "Sounds good, Dad. I'll call Henry. Tell Mom I love her."

"Will do, son. Give our angel and Chantal our love. Stay in touch." Shade hung up and looked up at the night sky. This battle was going to move fast when it started. He whistled for Pavi and Shade heard him whinny loudly as he sauntered back toward him. "Looks like we need to head home, old boy. I know it was short, but it was damn sure sweet."

102

Dona was still enjoying her newfound freedom and wandered outside the villa into the night. She wrapped the plain shawl around her shoulders to ward off the evening chill. The grounds were barren of any foliage, but she'd been kept inside the palace in Rome, so she enjoyed the fresh air. She could hear the ruckus from the warrior camp that was near her home but paid it no mind. As she walked around the corner of the villa, she was startled by a young warrior leaning with his back against the wall. He jumped to attention as soon as he saw her. Dona pulled the shawl close around her throat. "You startled me!" She recognized the Borgia insignia on his leathers. "Are you my protector?"

The young male looked embarrassed. "Uh, no, my lady. I've been assigned to make sure you don't leave the premises, and no one visits."

Dona looked confused. "Where would I even go?"

The young male shook his head. "I don't know, my lady."

Dona sized him up. He was extremely young for a warrior. "So, you were raised in the Borgia camp then?"

He nodded. He felt awkward, and probably wasn't supposed to spend his time talking to her, but he was bored. "Yeah, since I was ten. I've only recently taken the blood oath. This is my first assignment."

He'd been on duty all night, and there had been nothing moving. He was glad to have her company. He knew he'd gotten this assignment because his skills and experience were limited, and it was considered a shit detail.

Dona adjusted the wrap around her shoulders, "Well, I guess you should walk with me then if you're supposed to be guarding me. I just want a little night air."

Dona continued her walk around the property and the boy started walking beside her. "So, what is your name, warrior? You know mine. Seems only fair I should know yours."

"It's Tito, my lady."

Dona turned her head slightly and smiled at him, "That's a nice name. How old are you?"

He shrugged. "About nineteen, I guess."

Dona could see how inexperienced he was and was already wondering if she might be able to win him over. "You must be very good at what you do to get this assignment then."

Tito looked at her and chuckled. "Nah, I don't think so. They needed the other warriors on the border."

Dona looked him in the eye, turning on the charm. "I understand. I may be in exile, as I have displeased my master, but I am still the Borgia Queen. Guarding the queen of the largest coven in Italy would not be given to a warrior without great skills."

Tito considered her words and puffed out his chest. "Well, yes. I mean, I have been well trained."

She nodded her head. "Of course, you have. I have spent my life around warriors, not all are trained with such discipline and skill. You will do well, young Tito. I am sure of it."

She walked the grounds, steering clear of the warrior camp before heading back to her villa. Before returning inside, she turned to him. "Thank you so much for the company, and your kindness. I sincerely hope I will see you again."

He nodded, pleased with her compliment. "Well, I'm not a day-walker, so I've been permanently assigned this night shift until further notice."

She smiled brightly at him. "I can't tell you how happy that makes me. I will feel so much safer knowing you are here protecting me."

He kicked his boots in the dirt. "Well, not officially protecting."

She shook her head as if it were a mere detail. "I feel protected, Tito, and that is all that matters. I hope the rest of your night is quiet, and I'll see you again tomorrow evening."

He nodded his head. "Yes, my lady."

Dona returned inside and smiled to herself. With a little cultivation, maybe she could win him over. It may take some time, but time was something she had plenty of.

Tito resumed his position at the corner of the house. He liked the female that lived inside and was wondering why his Borgia master would ever exile her.

103

Raven was walking back to the beautiful Spanish-style house that had been renovated into the elegant inn called A Touch of Tuscany. It sat in the middle of the 5,000-acre vineyard in the heart of Napa Valley, California, and it had been home to him for a very long time. He and his mate, Mica, still lived in the large apartment above the converted garage.

Over the years, as Medici acquired California, and then Nevada, they had added and continued to expand the second warrior's camp. The camp was established on property away from the vineyards, and the prying eyes of the tourists. It now housed several hundred warriors that protected the Medici territory on the West coast. Raven was SIC here, and he never took his good fortune for granted. He was walking back from camp when his cell rang, and he recognized the number. "Yo, boss-man, what's shaking?"

Shade chuckled and shook his head. "Your ass will be shaking shortly, warrior. I need to speak with you, and I would prefer it be in person, if at all possible."

Raven grinned. "No big deal, boss, let me give Mica a heads up and I will blast over."

Raven hung up and picked up his pace to let his mate know he'd be going to Virginia. Raven's curiosity was piqued. Things were quiet in California, but he knew there was tension around the impending battle with the Borgia. He grabbed a few things from the apartment, and let Mica know he was heading out and would return as soon as possible. Mica handed him a file and asked him to deliver it to Kate. Raven kissed him goodbye, tucking the file under his arm as he teleported out for Virginia. "Come on, Poe!" The large black bird saw him leave and started to follow.

Raven swooped in low around Bel Rosso. It was starting to look like Fall here and he loved the smell of it. The warriors were out on the field, training, and he grinned when he saw the light inside Cory's workshop. Raven knew his old friend was aging, and they would be faced with losing him soon. He'd slowed down dramatically in the last few years, his fingers no longer so nimble. Raven had stopped asking him to make such extravagant leathers for him and settled for more standard designs.

He landed outside the main house and found Aegis and Night-Stalker leaping all over him. He had a special fondness for the wolves. Raven looked skyward and knew Poe would be there shortly. Gi opened the door and nodded for him to come in. Raven made his way to Shade's office and walked in through the open door. Not much had changed through the years. Boss-man was always up to his elbows in paperwork. "Damn, boss-man, do you ever catch up? Get with the times, it is called electronics, lightning speed electronics."

He dropped into the leather chair opposite Shade's desk and flipped his long hair over his shoulder.

Shade looked up as he strolled in. "I have moved with the times, does not mean I have given up all the old reliable ways. How is Mica?"

Raven crossed a booted foot over his knee. “Oh fine, handsome as the day I met him and still hotter than a firecracker, considering his age."

Shade shook his head. "Watch the age comments, brat. I can still kick your ass."

Raven laughed out loud, "Yeah, yeah, yeah. So, what’s going down, boss-man?"

Shade stood up and poured them both a Midnight. "Borgia has built a camp on the Alizzi property, which is now his territory, as you know. He has exiled Donatella back to her villa. Lorenzo feels perhaps we need to rotate some of our warriors along the border. We have been at this stand-off for a long time now, and it would be good to get some fresh blood into the mix. I don’t want to take anyone from the Bel Rosso camp if I can avoid it." Shade pushed the glass across the desk toward Raven, and sat back down in his chair, lighting up a smoke. "So that leaves me with your skinny ass."

Raven picked up the glass and took a sip. "Well, I can spare quite a lot, not much moving in Napa Valley. I could maybe send about a hundred to the cause. Matteo has capacity from the Nevada camp as well if you need them. He could probably spare about fifty."

Shade took a long drag on his cigarette. "Lorenzo is going to speak to Henry as well, see what the French camp can let loose. And we have the Greek camp. I think that will be fine. I don't want to empty out any camps at this point. I need all our territories covered."

Raven raised his eyebrows. "Well, Borgia is one sick fucker that's for sure. And if he's looking for an ass-kicking, we'll be happy to oblige."

Shade chuckled, even though the situation was deadly serious. He was amused Raven was still full of cock and kick-ass attitude. "Send them on over then. Have them report to Lorenzo. Send some of your more experienced. I want the Castello warriors to learn from our U.S. warriors and vice versa. It will be good for both camps."

Raven stood up, remembering the file tucked inside his jacket Mica had asked him to deliver. "Sounds like a plan. I'll get on it as soon as I get back. I want to see Cory before I go back, and might I have an audience with the queen? Mica asked me to give her something."

Just as Shade was about to answer, there was a loud squawking outside the patio door. "What the fucking hell?"

Raven laughed and looked at the door. "What took you so long, buddy? It's just Poe, boss-man. He'd probably like to see the queen as well."

Shade shook his head; some things never changed. He spoke to Kate telepathically, asking her to come to his office.

***

Kate was coming down the stairs when she heard Shade call to her, and she made a detour for his office. She saw Raven and opened her arms to him. "Where have you been? I thought you had forgotten me!"

Raven gave her an exaggerated bow before embracing her. She was the closest thing to a mother he'd ever known, and he loved her. He'd die for her in the blink of an eye. "Well, the king keeps me tied to Napa Valley. Blame him, he never lets me go anywhere! I've missed you!"

She squeezed him tight. "I'm sorry I haven't been out to check on things at the inn. We've had our hands full here. How is Mica?"

Raven reluctantly released her from the hug and pulled the file from under his jacket. "He's pretty damn hot, that's for sure. The inn is always busy. I can't imagine my life without him. There's something else we haven't told anyone yet."

They were interrupted by a loud ruckus at the closed patio doors as Poe pecked and batted his wings at the door. "Damn, someone else is missing you."

Shade looked at Raven and grunted. "You better open that door before that bird breaks the damn window!"

Raven laughed. "He's a warrior, boss-man, not a bird" Raven went to the door and opened it as Poe flew straight to Kate and landed on her shoulder.

As Poe settled on her shoulder, Kate spoke softly to the large bird before turning her attention back to Raven. "So, what's your news?"

Raven looked to both Shade and Kate. He handed the folder to Kate. "Well, Mica and I want to adopt one of the half-breeds. We haven't contacted Natalia yet, but we filled out all the applications. We don't think we want an infant, maybe a child a few years old. After getting to know Cory, we both feel like we want to share our lives with a young half-breed. Mica and I have talked about it a lot. What do you think, my lady?"

"I think Natalia will be delighted to help you find the right child. It's a wonderful decision. You may need a bigger place though, so take care of that first."

Raven grinned back at her. "We're working on that." Holding out his arm, Poe flew to him and squawked. Shade shook his head, there was nothing ordinary about Raven, never had been and never would be.

Shade lifted his glass to him. "There are a lot of things for a young half-breed to learn. It will be a good place for them to grow up. I like this idea."

Raven nodded. "We think so. Who knows, he may even like working at the inn. Mica will make a good mentor." He smiled sheepishly at Kate. "Well, Poe and I are going to visit the camp and see Cory."

Shade stubbed out his cigarette. "Think I will join you."

Raven smiled at Kate. "I'll see you before I leave, my queen. Give our love to the family." He looked at Shade. "See if you can keep up, boss-man, I don't have all damn night."

104

Dona had been carefully crafting her relationship with Tito over the last few weeks. She made a point to go out every night to take in the air and have him walk alongside her. It was clear he was bored with his assignment, and it had made it easy to draw him into a conversation. She was aware he kept an eye on the front door of her villa, and frequently looked in through the windows, checking for any activity, waiting for her to come outside every evening. He talked freely about his childhood before coming to camp. He told her about his family in Naples, and how many siblings he had. He was the only male child and was warrior born, so he was always destined to end up in the Borgia camp. Dona asked him if he'd met Rodrigo and Soren, and he admitted he'd only seen them from afar. Neither of them worked with the warriors in the camp but left all the training to their SICs, Vanni and Tomas.

She regaled him with stories about their palace in Rome, and how big and beautiful it was, careful to never speak ill of either Borgia. Tito seemed fascinated and peppered her with questions. If she didn't know the answer, she made one up for his entertainment. Of course, she knew very little about how the Borgia spent their time, as she hadn't been included in their lives. The information she knew, about the half-breeds held captive in their dungeon, and the dinner parties where the hearts of young half-breeds were served up as a delicacy, was information she kept to herself. She was smart enough to know she wouldn't win Tito's trust by speaking ill of his masters. She gave him a lot of details about the All Covens Ball, and who'd been in attendance, and how grandly everyone was dressed. Tito hung on her every word, fascinated with the details. It was a life far from anything he'd ever known and completely out of reach for him. "I wish I could see the palace! I've heard Vanni and Tomas mention it when they must go there, but they've never told us about what the palace looks like. If I'm a good warrior, perhaps, one day, I can have such an assignment!"

Dona smiled at him, always encouraging him. "Oh, I'm sure you will! You are still so young. There will be many assignments for a warrior of your caliber."

Tito puffed out his chest. She always had compliments for him, and he rarely received feedback of a positive nature in the camp. He liked being around her and waited anxiously every night for her to leave the villa for her walk.

"Could I ask you a personal question, my queen?"

Dona looked at him in the moonlight. "Of course, Tito. You may ask me anything."

He tucked his head, unsure of how to proceed. "You're so nice. I don't understand why my master would have exiled you."

Dona looked sad for his benefit and sighed heavily. "I displeased my master. I fear I was too outspoken for him. He has sent me here as punishment. I hope he will forgive me soon and allow me back into his good graces once again."

Tito consoled her. "Oh, I'm sure of it. I've heard both brothers have a bad temper. I'm sure once he's had time to cool off, he will want you back in Rome. I know, if you were my queen, I would want you back for sure!"

She smiled back at him. "You are so kind. And if you were my king, I would be begging you to allow me to return."

She saw him stand taller, a smile spreading across his face. She wondered if she should seduce him. He would be an easy mark but decided against it. Better he see her as a queen who was loyal to her mate, and gladly doing penance for displeasing him. "You are so kind to me, Tito. I don't know what I would do here without your protection."

He held onto her elbow as she walked. He was her guard, not her protector. She always referred to him as her protector, and he rather liked the idea he was protector to the Queen.

105

Tito returned to camp at the end of his shift, the note folded tightly, and tucked into the pocket of his leathers. What Donatella had asked of him was dangerous. He had, on occasion, been asked to fill in on border patrol, so he could hang on to the note and wait for the next time he was assigned there again. Then he would have to be extremely discreet to break away from the others, get across into Tuscany, slip the note to one of the Medici warriors, and ask them to deliver it to Lorenzo. He had no illusions about what would happen to him if he was caught. He'd grown fond of Dona and couldn't understand why his master had exiled her. There had been no gossip in the coven about Dona being an unfaithful mate. In fact, no one could even recall seeing her outside the palace, with the exception of the All Covens Ball. As Tito entered the camp, he saw a group of warriors, standing in a circle in the middle of the field, and made his way there to see what was going on. Nudging his way into the crowd between his fellow warriors, they were all gathered around Soren, who was regaling them with stories of past battles. Tito stood fascinated. He rarely saw Soren in the camp.

***

Soren was speaking loudly, using his sword as a prop as he recounted his victories on the battlefield. It wasn't often he came to camp and mixed it up with the average warrior, he felt it was beneath him, but he thought they were fascinated with his life and past. He noticed when the extremely young warrior nudged his way into the small crowd, and his eyes never left Soren. He was like a sponge taking in every word.

Tomas began to bark out orders for the warriors to begin their nightly training, and Soren noticed the young warrior was reluctant to leave. Soren approached him, re-sheathing his sword. "I am not familiar with you, warrior, your name and your duty assignment?"

Tito was almost dumbstruck when Soren approached him. "Uh, Tito, master. I grew up in the camp in Rome. This is my first outpost. I've been assigned to guard the villa where the exiled queen resides."

Soren took his measure and wondered why his brother would send such an inexperienced pup to guard the wretched whore. "Tito. My brother must think highly of you to give you such a post. So, tell me, how does the queen fair, being back in her home?"

Tito processed the question quickly. He'd told no one he'd grown fond of Dona, and he wasn't stupid enough to tell that to his master! "I've worked very hard, master. She's been complacent and doesn't put up any resistance, but she does come outside every night to take in the air and get some exercise. I watch her closely and listen for any negative gossip she may be trying to spread about the Borgia."

Tito felt like Soren could see the note tucked in his pocket, and his heart beat faster. He was torn now. The task of getting the note across the border was always going to be a long shot but handing the note to Soren could mean a promotion for him as a warrior. "I've been working to win her trust, so she'd speak freely around me."

Soren listened closely and could sense the young warrior was nervous, the vein in his neck pulsing faster. "And has she extended you her trust? Has she tried to escape? Anything you care to tell me?"

Tito made his decision, slipping his hand into his pocket. "She's never tried to escape. She knows she wouldn't get far, but she has expressed her need to have the Medici know her fate." He held the folded paper in his hand. "She wrote a note and asked I try to get it to a Medici warrior on the border. I took the note and told her, "Of course." Stupid female! Does she understand nothing? Does she think our warriors just stand at the border and chat with the enemy? I haven't read her note, but she wanted it delivered to Lorenzo."

Soren quickly grabbed the note from Tito's hand. "You have done well, Tito. This must be kept confidential, of course, say nothing to anyone. I will deliver this note to my brother. You will be heavily rewarded for your loyalty to the Borgia." Soren stuck the note inside his leather jacket and smiled. "Say nothing, return to your duties, if the queen asks about the note, inform her it was delivered."

Soren could feel his beast rising. He watched the warrior walk away, a proud swagger to his walk. He chuckled to himself. He had no intention of sharing this note with Rodrigo. He headed back to the palace, it was time to read and plan his next move.

Soren got home right at sunrise, his brother already home and sequestered in his private wing of the palace. He chuckled and made his way to his own suites. He grabbed a Red Moon and sat himself down to read the note. As he read, he laughed, pathetic bitch. She was asking Lorenzo for a source of Midnight to curb her hunger and perhaps a small weapon. "I assure you, my lady, you will have your choice of weapons." His beast began to plan, now he just needed to bide his time for the perfect night to launch it. He'd show his brother how to get things done and begin this fucking battle.

106

Soren bided his time, waiting for another night when Rodrigo decided to hit the clubs, and he'd have the whole night to himself. He woke later than usual from his death slumber, the moon already high in the sky. As he made his way to the first floor, his brother was up and dressed in his finery. Soren poured the warm half-breed blood into a glass and sipped delicately as he addressed his brother. "It looks as though you are enjoying your new freedom. Her exile apparently suits you."

Rodrigo raised his hand to halt any insults and whatever else was about to spill forth from his brother's lips. "Do not start with me this night, Soren. I am heading out to enjoy the pleasures of the clubs."

Soren lifted his glass to him. "As you should, brother, Borgia males should never be shackled to one female. Good riddance to the bitch, I say!"

Rodrigo watched as Soren downed the last of the blood in his goblet. "I am off for the rest of the night. I presume you will keep yourself occupied with your pleasure in the dungeon. I shall be home by sunrise."

Soren acted as though he could care less and didn't acknowledge his brother. He waited until his brother left, and then grabbed a bottle of Midnight. He wandered back to his suite, and loaded up on a few weapons, strapping his sword to his back. It was a perfect night to visit Umbria.

Soren teleported out and circled her villa several times. There was only one light on inside her upstairs bedroom. He licked his lips, "I am coming for you Queen of Borgia, but first, an appetizer."

He landed quietly on the roof and could see Tito leaning against the side of the villa below him. The warrior was young and no match for him. Soren watched him with interest, as the young warrior walked to the door of the villa and looked in the windows. *Ah, he is waiting for Donatella to take her nightly stroll.* Soren swooped down with lightning speed, landing behind the warrior and snapped his neck in one swift move. Tito never knew what hit him. He was dead before he hit the ground. "You do not deserve to be a Borgia warrior."

Soren kicked open the front door, splintering it to pieces. He strolled inside with the bottle of Midnight in his hand. He felt her fear as it floated on the air like a fog. He grinned as he heard his voice echo off the rooms throughout the house. "Honey, I'm home! I have a gift for you."

***

Dona was upstairs in her bedroom reading when she heard the door crash open and Soren's familiar voice calling out to her. Her blood ran cold. As evil as Rodrigo could be, he was no match for Soren. She set the book aside and was wondering if she had any avenue for escape. Would Tito help her? She quickly dismissed the thought. Tito would be no match for Soren, and even if he could help her, he'd never stand in defiance of his master. Looking about the room, there was no place to hide. She decided her feminine wiles were the only thing that could save her. She slid off the bed and made her way to the top of the stairs. "Soren? Is that you?" She started down the stairs to the entry hall. "I wish I had known you were coming. I would have prepared. I fear I look a mess."

He stood with his arms open to her, his eyes on fire, his beast already loose. He'd waited a long time to put the bitch in her place. "You requested Midnight, and it has been delivered."

He walked slowly toward her, his eyes boring into her, and feeling her fear. She'd fall to this Borgia beast. With his bare hands, he pulled the cork from the bottle and held it out to her. His growl was guttural and menacing and sent a chill through Dona's spine. He handed her the bottle. "Drink, my lovely."

Her hands shook as she took the bottle, and he stepped away from her to explore the room, his eyes taking in the bare walls and sparse furnishings. "Someone has cleaned up since last I was here."

As she grasped the bottle, Dona knew Tito had betrayed her, and delivered her note to Soren. Or perhaps it was a coincidence? She'd play innocent. "Oh, I had been hoping for some Midnight, how very kind of you to bring me some." She found a glass as he walked about her almost bare parlor. "May I pour you a glass as well?

Please, have a seat. I know my room is not what you are used to, but you are always welcome here."

He lowered his head and stared at her, her soft white nightdress floated around her body as if she were a ghost, her black tresses down her back, bouncing lightly as she walked in her bare feet. She looked like a virgin prepared as an offering to the gods. "I have a thirst, but not for what you have in that bottle." As she turned to him, his eyes absorbed her and held her there. She couldn't look away. She was much too weak. "There was another request in your letter."

Dona swallowed hard, stopping mid-pour and setting the bottle back down on the counter to hide the fact her hands were shaking. "My letter?"

Walking toward her, his eyes flared red. He grabbed a fist full of hair and pulled her head back in a tender gesture. Extending his tongue, he licked from her cleavage up the center of her neck, stopping at her chin. He closed his eyes as he relished in the taste of her skin. His tongue circled her ear, leaving a trail of wetness, as he whispered menacingly. "You dare to play coy with me? I am not my brother. I have no use for games."

Dona stuttered. "No, I... I would not play games. You are much too clever for games. I have always thought it was you who should be head of the Borgia coven. You are much cleverer than your brother."

He stepped back and roared with laughter. His fangs punched through, long and white, dripping with saliva. "You cannot manipulate me so easily with your flattery, bitch. I am not a Medici, I am Borgia!" He grabbed her with speed and spun her to face the table. He pulled one weapon at a time from his jacket and laid them out on the table: a shuriken, a small dagger, a medium-sized knife, and at last, his sword from the sheath across his back. "Choose."

Dona was wide-eyed with fear as he laid the weapons before her. What did he plan to do? Was he going to kill her? If so, she wanted it to be quick. He'd only torture her with the smaller weapons, drawing out her death. "I choose the sword."

Lifting the sword from the table, he held it tight in his fist in front of her. "As you wish, my queen."

Grabbing her by the neck with his other hand, he squeezed her throat enough to impede her breathing but not suffocate her. Using the sword, he sliced through her nightdress, letting it float to the floor. She was naked now, his canvas exposed. He laid the sword back on the table and picked up the small dagger, its tip razor sharp. He spun her around, forcing her face to the wall, as he held her in place with the pressure to her neck. He began to carve an elegant B into her back, starting between her shoulder blades and ending at the curve of her ass. The blood trickled slowly down her golden skin, and he tossed the dagger to the floor as it clattered and skid across the room. His tongue snaked out as he licked the blood from her wound.

Dona winced in pain. She could tell he'd branded her with the letter B on her back. She knew it would heal, and her skin would be flawless once again, but only if she lived that long. She dared not struggle or make him angry. She'd seen Soren when he was angry, and she didn't want to be on the receiving end of that. Memories of Marie and Mario flashed through her head, and she wondered if she'd share their fate.

Soren felt her weaken, but only slightly. Picking up the sword once again, he dragged her back into the middle of the room and shoved her to the floor. He held the sword like a master warrior, swirling it above his head. He then lowered it and pointed to the fireplace "Make a fire, a large blazing fire."

Dona crawled to the fireplace and placed the logs stacked next to the hearth onto the grate, as tears started to stream down her cheeks. She remembered seeing her servant's bones stacked in the fireplace. Was that his plan for her? She placed some kindling beneath the logs and willed a fire. The flames flickered, small at first, as the smoke traveled up the chimney.

Soren bent down and dragged her backward along the floor by her hair. He sat in front of the fire, pulling her into his lap, as he held the sword across her neck, barely touching her skin. He sat with her in silence, as they watched the fire build until it was roaring, and they could both feel the heat on their faces. He stood up, removing the sword from her neck, and lifting her by the hair. He went to the logs stacked near the fire and selected a small log and held it over the fire until it was aflame. He handed the burning torch to her, and using his sword, pointed at her, and nodded to the stairs. "Move."

Dona was shaking as they climbed the stairs, and he held the sword at her neck. He barked his orders. "The bed-chamber."

She walked carefully, holding the flaming torch, and made her way to her bedroom. Her heart was beating hard and fast in her chest.

As they stepped into her room, Soren looked about. "It is time to light up the night. Light anything that will burn."

Dona was horrified when he told her to start a fire. She could no longer hold back her sobs, "Soren, please! Don't do this. Does Rodrigo know you are here?"

Watching her following his instructions as she lit her childhood estate on fire, his eyes glowed with wickedness. "I take no orders from my brother. I do as I please."

He held the sword to her heart as the flames began to quickly consume the curtains, taking hold, licking, and leaping to the old wooden beams in the ceiling. "Move now, the other rooms."

He proceeded to move her from room to room, setting each on fire before leading her back downstairs. He could already feel the heat above him as the fire quickly took hold. He pointed the sword at her chest. "I take pleasure in knowing the last face you see will be Borgia. It will remind you you are nothing but a whore to us, as you burn in hell, Alizzi."

He thrust the sword deep into her chest, avoiding her heart. He didn't want her to die too quickly, but bleed out, watching her home burn around her before she, too, was consumed by the flames. He held her upright at the end of his sword, refusing to let her fall until he could hear the creaking of the beams overhead, and the smoke became too thick for them to breathe.

Dona gasped as the sword pierced her chest, and she stared back at him wide-eyed. *So, this is it then. This is where I die.* As he held her suspended on his sword, the evil in his eyes was the last thing she saw as she slipped in and out of consciousness. His blade had punctured a lung, and she could hear the blood gurgling in her chest with every breath. She smelled the smoke and felt the heat before he finally released her, and she crumbled to the floor.

Soren removed the sword swiftly, as her body lay in a heap. The flames were creeping closer, and he needed to leave. He raced for the door and out into the night air. Quickly, he hurled Tito's body into the now burning villa, which was being fast consumed by the flames. Teleporting away from the house, he landed in a wooded area and watched as the flames roared toward the sky. He grinned as he watched it burn to the ground. He knew the warriors on both sides of the border would see the flames. "Where is your Medici savior now, Alizzi?" He teleported home, having completed one more move his brother couldn't accomplish, the death of the whore he'd mated for a patch of dirt in Umbria.

107

Lorenzo received word from the border there had been a huge fire, and that the Alizzi villa had been burned to the ground. It didn't take long before they got confirmation Dona had died in the fire. It was clear she would have to have been killed before the fire started, as she could have easily escaped the fire on her own. Lorenzo showed no emotion on the field before his warriors, but barked out his orders, sending another regiment of warriors to the border and putting everyone on high alert. He didn't know if this incident had anything to do with them or not, but they'd be on guard. As his warriors took their leave, he saw Alfie on the far side of the training field but turned instead in the direction of the camp office. He'd need to let Henry know, just as a precaution, and he'd need to call his father.

His feelings about Dona were a tangled mess. He'd been close to her once. As a young boy, first arriving here at the camp, Dona had been like a mother to him, and he'd relied heavily on her. As a young male, she'd betrayed his trust. With the passing of time, he'd been able to look at that betrayal through her eyes and see her fear of ending up alone. It didn't excuse her actions, but he at least felt as if he understood her motivations. He no longer hated her. The hate had faded years ago and left him with ambivalence. Still, with all that had passed between them, he didn't wish on her an end such as this. She didn't deserve this. He stepped into the office and poured himself a Midnight, downing it in a single gulp. Dropping into the desk chair, he fished the cigarettes from the drawer and was lighting up when Alfie entered. He tossed the pack to Alfie. "Take a load off, brother."

Alfie dropped into a chair, feeling a little numb on hearing the news. He had his own memories of Dona. Before she'd tried to seduce Lorenzo, Alfie had been lured in by her. She'd been the first female non-feeder he had sex with, and she'd always treated him like someone special, teaching him how to make love. He couldn't say he was surprised at her death nor how it played out for her.

Borgia threw away mortals and immortals like trash when their purpose had been served. "What's your next move?"

Lorenzo leaned back in the chair, inhaling deeply on the cigarette before releasing the smoke into the air. "My move? I'm not sure this had anything to do with us. I think Rodrigo used her. He wanted Umbria so he could get an advantage, placing himself on our border. Once he had that, he had no more use for Dona. It may mean they are escalating, or it may mean nothing. I'll call Henry, and my father, of course, just to be on the safe side."

Alfie nodded. "I think that's wise, brother." He knew Lorenzo's emotions were running deeper than he showed. Dona had been a lifeline for him when he first came to Castello, leaving his family in the States. "You okay?"

Lorenzo paused before he answered. "It's complicated. You know our history. I think I forgave her a long time ago, just because I didn't want to carry that crap around. Still, for all the pain she caused me, I never wished this on her."

Alfie nodded as he stood up. "She holds a lot of memories for us both, but more for you than me. No one should have to die like that. She must have been terrified if she even knew what was happening. I'm going back out on the field. Take your time. I'll keep things under control in the camp." Alfie walked back onto the field and realized that he, too, had buried the memories of Dona long ago.

Lorenzo made a quick call to Henry to give him a head's up, and then made the more difficult call to his father. Checking the time, he figured his father would be waking from his death slumber and called him on the house phone. Once again, it was Gi's face he saw on the screen, and Lorenzo asked if his father was awake yet. Gi told him to hold on, he'd inform Shade his son was on the office screen.

Gi made his way up the stairs to his master's bedroom. He'd heard them stirring earlier and knew they were both awake. He tapped on the door and heard Kate's voice respond to enter. He opened the door slightly. "Master, Lorenzo has called."

"*Grazie*, Gi, tell him we are on our way."

Taking Kate's hand, he kissed her softly. "Come with me. Let's see what is going on at Castello." He walked hand in hand with her to the office to find Lorenzo on the large screen. Shade could see the anxiety on his son's face. He took a seat in his huge leather chair and pulled Kate into his lap. "Lorenzo, is everything okay? You get two for one tonight. Talk to us."

Lorenzo looked surprised to see his mother. "Mom! I wasn't expecting you."

Kate sat forward and looked at her son. "Is everything okay? Did you need privacy?"

He shook his head. "No... I guess I'm just still processing the information, and not really sure how I even feel about it myself."

Kate looked at him with concern. "What's wrong, Lorenzo? Is it Chantal? Grace?"

He looked up, making eye contact with her through the screen. "No, nothing like that. The family is fine. We're all fine. It's about Dona."

Shade furrowed his brow. "What about Dona?"

Lorenzo looked at his father sadly. "She's dead. Her villa was burned to the ground. We're not sure if it was Soren or Rodrigo, we're getting conflicting information from the border, but she was left to burn in her own home. Donatella Alizzi is dead."

Kate held her hand over her mouth, as she watched her son rub his hands over his face. She could see his conflict.

Shade took a deep breath, his heart feeling heavy, his emotions scattered. He'd forgiven her at the ball, and he'd known then that Rodrigo would soon grow tired of her. "There was nothing we could do, Lorenzo, she was lost to Rodrigo. I tried when I heard he was snooping around her, she refused to listen. You cannot take this personally, let it go. Any changes on the border since this happened?"

"Not really. I sent another regiment in, just to be safe, and I called Henry. I don't think this really has anything to do with us, so we're just taking precautions. Apparently, whichever brother did the killing took out the warrior that was left to guard her villa. Sounds like they didn't want any witnesses to whatever went down. That's just gossip across the borders though. We don't have any details."

Shade ran his hand through his hair. "You have some of Raven's warriors now, and some from Henry that should help out. Why don't you take some time to yourself, and let Alfie deal with the camp? Go to Chantal. Let her comfort you, it will heal whatever pain you still hold for Dona. We did all we could, within our limits. Dona made her own choices, Lorenzo, no one could have changed her mind. Do you understand?"

Lorenzo looked back at him. "Not sure I do, Dad. I keep thinking I could have handled things better. Maybe if she hadn't been so isolated, she would never have fallen prey to the Borgia. I mean, I know she had a hand in her own downfall. She made bad choices and burned bridges." He shook his head. "There's a lot in my head right now I need to sort out. I can't help but feel some guilt."

Shade knew exactly how he felt. He was feeling the guilt himself, maybe even more than his son. "Have to be honest, son, I am carrying a heavy burden of guilt myself right now. We cannot wallow in our past or carry our regrets like a weapon on our backs. We can't change the past. Remember her in the good times, *sí*? Get some rest, son. Call me if there are any changes."

Lorenzo nodded his head. Kate spoke softly to her son, "We love you, Lorenzo." She saw the same shy, half-smile he had as a child and it tugged at her heart.

"I know, Mom, and it gives me strength every day."

The screen went dark, and Kate turned to Shade. "I don't understand the evil of the Borgia. They had what they wanted. They had her territory. She was no threat to them. I could see at the ball she was broken. I just don't...I can't understand this need they have to destroy everything in their path, and it scares me."

Shade nodded. "Fear and destruction are how the Borgia got where they are, *mi amore*. Rodrigo's gift as a sin-eater set his path, and Soren only uses his gift of dream-walking for evil and destruction. You have been exposed to many things since you met me, but our culture has changed dramatically through the centuries. You never saw all the coven wars and the power struggles. Power can be a very wicked thing." He lifted her gently from his lap and stood up from the chair. "I need a smoke."

He went outside on the patio. His mind was a tangle of images from long ago, random conversations and mixed emotions, all of them involving Donatella. He lit up a smoke and stood there, trying to grasp all the 'what ifs'.

Kate could tell he had more on his mind than he'd shared. Dona's father and Christofano had signed a contract when Shade was still young that the two would be mated. She was aware that even though he'd rejected that contract, he'd had a relationship with Dona at one point in time. Kate had been jealous of her at first and then had come to an uneasy acceptance, as Lorenzo seemed so attached to her. It had been a complicated relationship through the years, ending harshly when Dona betrayed Lorenzo. She followed him outside, stepping up behind him and placing her arms around his waist, her head resting on his back. "What troubles you, lover? I can feel your conflict."

He sighed heavily but her arms around him were his strength. She was small in stature, but her heart was larger than any he'd ever encountered. She knew him better than he knew himself and was always there for him. "So many things, *mi amore*. *Madre* fought with *Padre* about the mating contract. I had never heard them argue like that, before or after. But I didn't love her, and I knew, somewhere in my soul, someone was waiting for me. I see now I made a grave mistake in having the affair with her. I knew her feelings for me, and I knew I could never offer her that in return. It only gave her a false hope. I protected Umbria after her father's death, and I wouldn't change that, but perhaps I was hasty in withdrawing that protection. I never paid attention to how my actions affected her entire life. I should have fixed this. I should have never removed my protection, but my pride ruled, and I would not admit my mistake. I should have helped her with money. Hell, it is not like we don't have it. It would have put her back on her feet. She would not have run into Borgia arms. I knew better, I knew he would destroy her. I gave her warnings when I should have done what was honorable and helped her. She must have suffered in his palace, and I'm sure her death did not come easy. She didn't deserve that, nothing she ever did to anyone would make her deserve such an end, yet I stood back and let it unfold."

Kate let the silent tears fall down her cheeks as he spoke. She wondered if she'd played a role in Dona's demise as well. When she was younger, and not feeling as secure in their relationship, would she have felt resentment had he tried to help her, knowing he'd once shared her bed? "Dona certainly must own her role in her final fate, but I fear we all had a hand in how things evolved; you, me, and Lorenzo. But it was complicated. She loved you, and when she couldn't have you, she turned to Lorenzo. I don't have the answers.

In hindsight, we should have handled things differently, but we were each caught up in our own emotions of anger and jealousy. I'm sorry it has ended this way, but I'm glad she knew, in the end, we harbored no ill will. At least we have that."

He turned and crushed her to his chest, his hands tangling in her crimson locks. "I have you to thank for that, *mi amore*. You asked me to do that for you, and I was reluctant. Now, I am so grateful she knew I had forgiven her." He lifted her up as her legs wrapped around his waist, her arms around his neck and he gazed into her amber eyes. "I never loved her, *mi amore*. I don't think I knew how to love until I met you. I cannot change my past, but I will never change how much I love you."

108

Vanni teleported as fast as possible to the Borgia palace in Rome. The warriors at the new Umbria camp had tried to extinguish the fire at the Alizzi villa, but it was fully engulfed and impossible to put out without them being burned alive themselves. He found his master inside, just getting home from a night in Rome. *Why the fuck do I have to be the one to tell him this news?* Vanni was pretty sure if killing the Alizzi had been part of Rodrigo's plan, he would have been informed, which left him with one possible answer, this was Soren's doing.

Rodrigo was surprised to see his warrior and knew something had happened if Vanni thought it important enough to come tell him in person. "What news do you bring, warrior? I hope it does not spoil my mood. I have had a most enjoyable night."

Vanni had the balls of a bull but telling his master anything he didn't want to hear wasn't on his list of favorite things. Warriors had lost their lives for less. "There's been an... accident at the Alizzi villa."

Rodrigo strolled toward him. His eyes already hard. "Accident? There are no accidents. What the fuck has happened?"

Vanni took a step backward. *Damn, son of a bitch Soren is going to get me fucking killed!* "The house has been razed to the ground, nothing left. The villa was old, and it went up fast. We tried to put it out, but it was out of control. No sign of Tito. No sign of the Queen."

Rodrigo growled like an animal, rattling the palace. "No sign of them? Nothing? What the hell do you do out there, you useless vagrant of a warrior? Tito did not call for help? You saw nothing?"

Rodrigo's anger was boiling, and he growled as he walked circles around Vanni. He could smell the acrid scent of smoke and death on the warrior's clothes.

Vanni stood his ground as he answered, keeping his eyes straight ahead, "No sign of anything, master. Tito had reported for duty, and then took his post. There was no communication from him after that. Perhaps the Medici infiltrated the area. We neither saw nor heard a thing. No screams, nothing. It was a fast-burning fire. The house went up almost instantly."

Soren overheard the conversation and stood in the doorway, a wide grin on his face. His brother was angry with the news, just as he'd hoped. He listened as Vanni suggested perhaps the Medici had done the deed. He was going to stop that bullshit right here and now. No one was taking the glory from him. He leaned against the door jamb, neither his brother nor the warrior noticing him yet. "It was not a Medici. It was a Borgia."

Rodrigo spun like a top hearing Soren's confession, and his beast rushed his brother, grabbing him by the throat. "What have you done?"

Vanni quickly teleported out, no way in hell was he getting in the middle of this shit storm!

Soren gripped his brother's wrists and lifted his knee into his stomach, hurling Rodrigo across the room. Rodrigo went flying into the wall, crashing hard, as pieces of plaster crumbled to the floor of the elegant room. Rodrigo quickly crouched on all fours, eyes flaming and fangs seething to rip Soren to pieces.

Soren let his beast loose, ready to take on his brother, to make him understand one thing. If he didn't make a move on Medici soon, Soren would. "Don't ever touch me again. You have no right to control it all. This coven belongs to both of us, and you snivel and cower behind a fucking pack of warriors and gilded walls of gold. You promised me, once Umbria was ours, you would fucking attack. Let's see if the death of that bitch you called queen will prompt you to do something?"

Rodrigo lost all control and attacked Soren with speed and power, knocking him about the room and through the wall into the hallway. Soren skidded backward on his ass for the length of the hallway until he came crashing against another wall, the wind knocked from him as he slowly rose to his feet.

Rodrigo was coming at him like a steamroller, building speed and roaring the whole way. "She was mine! My queen, not yours. You insignificant second born, you had no right to take her life. That was my decision to make, my privilege. Father should have ripped your wicked stupid head from your shoulders the moment you came into this world. You useless, arrogant fool!"

Soren took off teleporting through the grand hall, with Rodrigo trailing him. Their chase creating absolute chaos inside the palace, as priceless porcelain and antiques crashed and fell to the floor, and artwork was sucked completely off the walls by the virtual tornado that was building around their chase. Soren kept the pace and finally came to the room he wanted. Swords hung on the walls and he grabbed one as he went by and landed on his feet. The air around him spun and whirled, a dark evil unleashed. He saw his brother do the same and stand opposite him with sword in hand. Soren spat out his response. "I can kill whomever I choose. She was a useless whore with nothing. What are you going to do, brother, kill me? That would solve all your problems, would it not? I will not make it easy for you, Rodrigo. I exist. I want the Medici dead!"

Rodrigo could care less about the death of Donatella, but it wasn't his brother's decision to make. He was used to Soren's insolence, but this was far beyond acceptable. He'd love to kill Soren right now, but that would only cause more chaos, and he feared he'd need his brother in the battle against the Medici. "I am firstborn and king of this coven, whether you like it or not. I decide when the Medici die, not you! You are lazy, Soren, and you refuse to think or obey. Killing you would be such a delightful pleasure at this moment."

Soren growled and went at Rodrigo full force. The tornado began again but, this time, swords were in play. Light bounced off the weapons like lightning streaks across the room, and the clashing of metal against metal sounded like thunder inside the palace, as they each drew blood.

The servants took cover. They'd seen the brothers fight before, but this was more than the ordinary sibling rivalry; this looked like a fight to the death.

Soren battled with intensity, but he could feel the cuts and slashes on his body. He cared not. They would heal. He gave as many strikes as he received, with one thought in his head. If his brother was dead, he'd be the reigning king of Borgia. He knew he couldn't openly kill his own brother for the crown. He'd lose the respect of all the other covens. Soren also knew if they battled the Medici, every warrior would be concentrated on taking out Rodrigo. If his brother fell in the battle, then Soren would rise as king. Making sure his brother fell on the battlefield was a much better option.

Rodrigo battled tirelessly, but he didn't want to kill his brother, only wound him to end this foolish fight. Soren was losing his grip on his sword as his hand became wet with blood. Soren lunged toward him, and Rodrigo was able to swipe the sword from his hand and strike his brother through the thigh. Soren fell to the floor and Rodrigo stood over him, the tip of the blade pointed at his throat. His beast filled the room with power and majestic evil. "You will, from this moment on, be locked inside your room, guarded at all times. You will not leave this palace until we are ready to battle. I will chain your insubordinate ass to the bed and stake you there if need be. I am done with your attitude, and with you!"

Rodrigo called to his warriors telepathically and felt them surround him. He turned to see Tomas and Vanni, and over twenty of his finest warriors in awe of the mess and blood, and his own brother lying on the floor with a gaping hole in his thigh. He bellowed orders like a raving madman. "Get him out of my sight! Clean him and see to his wounds. He does not leave his suite. If he does..." He looked straight at Tomas. "Kill him, or you will be next."

He threw the sword like a spear across the room and watched as it stuck in the blood-splattered wall. "This is my coven, I rule here, and I will not be disrespected."

He stomped from the room, still fuming at the hell his brother could create in his life. But Soren had gone too far this time, stripping him of his last piece of patience. He shoved two warriors out of his way as he stormed out of the room, his anger still outrageously out of control.

Walking out into the main hall of the palace, his bellowing could be heard for miles. "Where are my servants? Come out, you sniveling, little beggars. Clean this filth from my palace. I want to see nothing amiss when I awake from my slumber!" The servants crept out from hiding places, quivering in his presence. Grabbing a young servant girl, he threw her over his shoulder and headed for his private wing of the palace, her fear only feeding his beast further. He'd feed from her and heal. He was master and king of Borgia, and nothing was going to get in his way.

109

The fight with Rodrigo had left Soren with an injury to his thigh, but it was healing nicely. Besides, this gave him time to think. Rodrigo had left warriors to guard him, both inside and outside the door of his suites. He couldn't do anything without being observed. He remained calm, never speaking to the warriors as he lay about, letting the feeders come to him, and allowing his wound to heal. He played up his injury, appearing weaker than he actually felt. He'd been planning his revenge, and the time had finally come. As the electronic blinds softly whirred, shutting the room into complete darkness, he lay in his bed, letting the death slumber take him down, as the plans settled into place.

Rodrigo could lock him away, and place all the guards in camp around him, but he had no control over Soren's gift. No one, not even his brother, could stop him. He closed his eyes, sinking deeper into his slumber, and let himself escape his physical body, traveling to a house in the Blue Ridge Mountains in Virginia to dream-walk with the queen. Soren's last dream-walk with Shade was a great success, but he dared not attempt that again. He'd hoped it would spur Shade into initiating the battle, but it hadn't, and if he tried to dream-walk with Shade again, he would no doubt be prepared to take him on this time. Everyone was aware of how protective the Medici was of his queen, so perhaps if Soren made her the target, Shade would respond quite differently.

Soren was tired of waiting and wanted this battle to begin. He'd killed his brother's useless mate, the Borgia Queen, now it was time for the redhead to have a heavy dose of fear and know that Borgia intended to bring death to the Medici.

Soren hovered over her, watching her sleep with the Medici beside her, well into his own death slumber. Soren caressed her hair gently, and she didn't stir. He slipped inside her mind and quietly observed her random thoughts. He masked his identity, morphing his physical frame to look like Shade Medici. She looked up and saw him, and he smiled back at her. "Come..."

He reached out to her, and she walked toward him. Soren observed her beauty, and how her red hair flowed about her as she moved. "Come closer. Do you not have a kiss for your lover?"

Kate saw Shade appear in her dream. It had been a while since he'd come to her in a dream-walk. He held out his hand, asking her for a kiss. "For you, lover, I always have a kiss." She stepped into his embrace, as his mouth covered hers, and his tongue explored.

Soren searched her memory and could see how Shade reacted to her, and she to him. He could hear the words he spoke and could summon things from her memory long forgotten. It made it easy to impersonate his enemy. His kiss was deep, a kiss only lovers shared. His hand wandered to her beautiful plump ass and he squeezed, drawing her closer into his body. His tongue trailed down her neck, and the moan that escaped his lips sounding convincingly like Shade. "You are so beautiful, *mi amore*. I can't get enough of you, my lily-white. I need you even in our dreams."

His hands explored her body, as he grabbed the nightdress by the hem and lifted it over her head. She responded and shook out that mane of red hair.

Kate felt a slight hesitation. *Lily-white...he hasn't called me that in years.* She watched as his eyes scanned her body. There was something in his eyes, and the way he looked at her that gave her a moment's pause, something not quite Shade. Before she could process that feeling, he was pulling her back to his chest, holding her close. He buried his nose into her hair and inhaled.

Soren felt the smallest doubt creep inside her mind, but he held her strongly, she wouldn't be able to escape his dream-walk. "*Mi amore*, I need you."

Kate slid her hand up his chest and unbuttoned the buttons on his shirt. "Then we should do something about that."

She'd only opened two buttons when he hastily removed the shirt, the remaining buttons flying free. He pulled the shirt off, tossing it aside, and started to remove his belt. There was something in how he moved that wasn't right to her. She knew Shade's thoughts before he thought them, and every inch of his skin. The man standing before her looked like Shade, and his voice sounded like Shade, but there was something off and Kate couldn't figure it out. Was this her dream, or his? She'd thought he was dream-walking, but now she felt confused. He stepped out of the jeans, kicking them aside, and pulled her hard against his bare chest.

Soren's mind held her, and his body responded instantly to her soft white skin against his. She was small and delicate, like the mortals he stalked, but she was strong like an immortal. He was wary of mounting her, knowing it would awaken the Medici. Even in his death slumber, Shade would sense her distress and know she was being violated.

Soren lifted her up, as she wrapped her legs around his waist, and the feel of her was intense. She was one delicious morsel. His cock was rock hard, and his beast wanted her, even in the dream-walk. Burying his head into her chest, he suckled her nipples, nipping at them, teasing, and playing. He was walking a thin line. If she became too aroused, the Medici would feel it, and if she became fearful, he'd feel that as well, but he fought hard not to take her and fuck her until she screamed.

Kate felt his mouth at her breasts, and it felt wrong. This wasn't his touch. Shade had held her a million times, made love to her a million times, and this wasn't Shade. She felt confused and started to struggle, pushing against his shoulders, but he was strong, and he gripped her tightly. She shook her head, trying to escape the dream, but he was holding her there. Her heart started to beat faster as she tried to fight the feeling of being trapped.

Soren struggled to control her as she fought to be released. Her subconscious was sending out alarm bells, warning her he wasn't Shade. He could easily control her. His strength was much greater. He released her, and set her down on her feet, but spun her around with her back to his chest, his arm held tight under her naked breasts. He created a vision of the battle, complete with all the screams of those who lay dying. He conjured forth an image of the blood-soaked grounds of Castello, their precious Medici castle burning to the ground. Shade lay dead, his head unattached beside his body, and beside her mate was her son, his chest laid open, his heart missing. The scene was one of gruesome violence and death. Pulling back her hair, he snuggled into her neck, his voice low and wicked as he spoke into her ear in his own voice. "I have killed one queen, and now I have another. When your mate and your son lie dead, you will be my spoils of war, the Borgia Queen to its King."

She clawed at his arms, trying to free herself, to get to the bodies of Shade and Lorenzo. She knew it wasn't real. Shade had dream-walked with her many times, and created beautiful visions that felt, looked, and smelled real, but were all conjured from his gift. The voice in her ear changed, it was no longer Shade's voice, and she turned her head to see Soren. His voice was deep and evil, as he was telling her he'd keep her as his prize after he'd killed her mate and her son. Kate fought against him, as he held her tighter, and she started kicking her feet against his legs, reaching over her head to claw at his face, and she screamed, "Shade!" She heard his evil laugh in response, as he dragged her onto the battlefield.

***

Shade felt her turmoil while deep in his death slumber. It drew him closer to the surface. His subconscious mind tried to unravel what had her upset. He felt her beside him, and she was restless and tense. Something was off, and he was struggling to pull himself from his slumber when he heard her scream for him. His heart beat rapidly in his chest, and he sat straight up in the bed, calling back to her, *"Mi amore!"* He saw her lying beside him, her face contorted in a frown, her body in a cold sweat, and realized she was being attacked in her dreams. He lay down and closed his eyes, instantly inserting himself inside her dream. He found himself inside the battle for Castello, stepping over the field of death and destruction, as he called out to her, screaming her name, and following her scent through the stench of burning flesh and smoke. What he saw made him stop dead in his tracks. His beast rose at the vision of Soren, holding Kate captive, as they both stood nude and she struggled as he dragged her, kicking and screaming, through the battlefield. He teleported to where they stood, landing right in front of them. "You filthy fucking bastard, let her go! It is me you want, not her."

Soren laughed as his hold on the little redhead tightened. "Oh, did she not tell you, Medici, she is mine now? She prefers the Borgia cock over the Medici prick."

Kate had seen Shade emerge through the smoke and fire on the battlefield, clad in leathers, as he rushed toward her. She held out her arms to him, screaming his name.

Shade's breathing was ragged, and his body shook from the intense emotional trauma of seeing her in this situation. It may only be a dream-walk, but for the participants, the events were real. Soren had perfected his gift far beyond anything Shade had ever attempted in dream-walking, the realism played out in deadly clarity. Kate screamed for him, and he started to move toward her but found Soren was blocking him, weighing him down from being able to respond. "You will not take me down, Soren! Let her go. She has done nothing to you."

Shade struggled to break free, but he could barely move. *No, this can't be happening. Soren can't possibly have this much power over me!* He felt like he was mired in a tar pit, moving in slow motion.

Soren's laughter filled his ears with its wicked sound, as Kate's screams intensified.

Shade called out for Luca, Christoph, and Skelk, and pulled them into the dream-walk. There'd be no way Soren could take them all down, or at least he hoped that was the case. His heart was breaking that he couldn't get to her fast enough.

Kate could see him struggling to get to her, as if Soren was somehow keeping him at bay without even touching him. She clawed at Soren's arms, screaming louder, as he laughed at her. Through the smoke on the battlefield, she saw the others appear, Luca with sword raised, Skelk with a crossbow, loaded with an arrow, and Christoph with a gun. She heard her grandson mutter, "Fuck this!"

Shade felt them coming, felt his grandson's strength, and watched as Soren's eyes became large in his head. Soren couldn't hold them all, and the momentary distraction caused by their arrival, caused him to release his hold on Shade, freeing him suddenly to move. Shade scrambled on all fours toward her when he heard the arrow swoosh over his head, and then saw Soren shove Kate in front of him to block the arrow. He quickly disappeared in a wisp of smoke. Almost instantly, Shade heard the gunshot and he screamed, as he reached her and rolled with her away from the chaos.

Kate clung to him, sobbing. She knew this was a dream, but the sense of reality inside a dream-walk, the sense of touch, and smell, and taste, was all very real. She knew a powerful dream-walker could kill inside a manufactured dream, so the danger was very real. She heard his voice, calming her, as the vision around her faded to vapor.

Christoph, Luca and Skelk faded, and the fires disappeared as the smoke drifted away, along with the bodies of the fallen warriors on the battlefield. It was just the two of them now.

Shade crushed her to his chest, rocking her in his arms as she sobbed uncontrollably. He stayed quiet with her until everything disappeared and then pulled her to the surface, as they awoke in their bed. "Look at me, *mi amore*, we are awake now. He can't hurt you anymore. *Cazzo*, I thought I was going to lose you."

He thought he'd crush her bones he was holding her so tight. Her body was covered in sweat and she couldn't stop shaking. This was the final straw. This meant war. No one was going to do this to his mate and live to tell the tale. They'd done nothing to provoke such an act of violence on his family, and he wanted the Borgia dead now. "I will kill them all for this, no more waiting. They just pushed me past any further tolerance. No one attacks my queen without retribution."

Kate was awake now and sitting in their bed as he comforted her, but she knew the Borgia had pushed too far. Luca appeared at their door, as did Christoph, pulled back from the surreal dream-walk in time to hear Shade's proclamation that they'd no longer wait for the Borgia to make the next move. The battle they'd hoped to avoid was inevitable now.

110

Kate sobbed uncontrollably against his chest. She could still smell the smoke in her hair and on her skin. Shade was comforting her, but she felt the need to escape, to wash this stink away. Someone had turned on a lamp in the room, as the windows were still sealed against the sun. Luca and Christoph both stood ready to protect them both, just as they had in the dream-walk. It took her a second to realize they were real, and not still part of the dream. She realized Shade must have pulled them into the dream-walk, as Soren wouldn't have conjured them. She felt confused and knew it was still day outside. The adrenaline would keep Shade awake for a short period of time, but now the danger had passed, he'd be pulled back into his slumber soon. "I need a shower. I need to wash him off me."

He spoke to her in a soft tone, soothing her. He understood the experience was traumatic. A good dream-walker could create a vision of pleasure, or one of pain, and could even kill his victim inside the dream. "I will come with you and help. I will not leave you alone right now."

He turned to Christoph and Luca. "Step outside but stay close."

He watched as his warriors left the room and closed the door. He'd give orders later. There was nothing that could be done now in the light of day. His heart knew, right now, he needed to take care of Kate. He lifted her from the bed, cradling her, and walked to the shower. Stepping inside, he turned on the water and set her down on her feet. He pulled her close to him and let the water wash away the remnants of the dream-walk. "I love you, *mi amore*. Talk to me."

She felt almost numb, and let him take control, gently washing her, letting the water run through her hair, and working up a lather. "Lover, I knew it was a dream-walk, but he was able to control everything. We were on the battlefield, and you were dead, Lorenzo was dead, he said he was keeping me as the spoils of war! That I was the Borgia queen now. Please tell me that can't happen!"

He massaged her head as he washed her hair, the rose scent rising in the steam. "First of all, there is no way either of them is taking Lorenzo or me down. We are going to kick his fucking ass and every warrior with him. Secondly, you have a band of warriors yourself and without his damn gift, I dare him to tangle with your ass when you are pissed off." He picked up the soap and began to briskly scrub her skin, cleaning the stench of her dream down the drain, but it was her mental state he was worried about. The dream-walk was psychological warfare, meant to create doubt and fear.

Kate was already planning in her head. She wouldn't have her own warriors in Florence, but she could command the animals bonded to Sophia and Bianca. It would be like the Battle of Bel Rosso. She could use the animals to overwhelm the Borgia army, attacking them from all sides. She took strength from his confidence, but she knew this wouldn't be the same. The Battle of Bel Rosso was a skirmish by comparison to what they must face, and she felt a cold hand of fear grip her heart. Shade rinsed her hair clean and softly kissed her lips as the water fell around them before turning off the faucets and wrapping her in soft towels. He dried himself off, wrapping a towel around his hips and led her back to their bedroom, where Theresa had already laid out a fresh gown and was just finishing up changing the sheets, removing all traces of the smell of smoke from the room. "My lady, you can rest easy now."

Christoph and Luca both stood just outside their room. Kate knew, without asking that Christoph was waiting for further orders, and Luca would stand guard now for the rest of the day just outside their door.

Shade laid her down on the bed and pulled the fresh gown over her head as he kissed the top of her head and sat beside her. His hand softly slid along her cheek. "Remember, *mi amore*, his whole purpose is to put doubt in your mind, plant the seed. Only you can let it grow out of control. I want you to rest. I need to speak with everyone, get things in motion. We are going into battle. The time has come. Rest now, and I will be back shortly. I love you." He leaned in, kissing her softly, pulling the blankets over her shoulder. He slipped into some jeans and pulled a t-shirt over his head. "I will be inside the house, *bel*, if you need me."

He walked to the door and left it open, standing to look back at her for a moment and taking a deep breath. "Luca, stay beside this door until I return. You and Shannon need to be ready to leave at sunset. Christoph, come with me to the office, there are things we need to do."

Kate reluctantly let go of him but knew he'd set things in motion now. There would be no more waiting. She lay back down but doubted she'd fall back asleep. Every time she closed her eyes, she saw the images of the battlefield that Soren planted in her head, and understood, clearly, the power of the dream-walk.

Luca looked at her and knew she was troubled. He'd experienced a dream-walk and knew how real the experience felt. "Don't let him get to you, Kate. The dream-walk can be used as a powerful weapon, meant to break you down. It's not a vision. Soren can't predict or control the outcome of this battle."

She nodded, trying to feel reassured, but unable to erase what she'd seen. "It's hard."

Luca closed his eyes. He could only imagine the images Soren conjured for her. "It was meant to be. You need to fight back now. You need to be the warrior I trained you to be. Shade will need to know you're all right when he goes to battle."

Kate looked back at him. That was something she understood all too well. Her fear would hold him back, even put him at risk, if he were preoccupied with her during the battle. She let her anger push away the fear. "I'll be ready."

He smiled at her and winked. "Get some rest then. Master will be back soon, and I'm not going anywhere."

As they rolled into the office, Shade went to the screen and called Henry, telling him they were on Red Alert. Any warriors Henry had selected to be assigned to Castello from his troops in France and Greece that hadn't already been sent, were to report there, immediately. He then called Ottavio Farnese and relayed a similar message. He watched as Christoph paced, his agitation filling the room. "Chris, relax, everything is ready, I'm just setting things in motion."

He then called Raven and told him to get himself and the warriors ready, and to move out to Castello. When he ended the call, he fixed himself a large Midnight and handed one to Christoph. "I want Theo, Skelk, and the assigned warriors out of here as soon as the sun sets. Lorenzo will be expecting them. You'll remain here. You know my reasons. Right now, I want you to go to Aislynn, be with her, do whatever you need to do, then she needs to get to Castello as well, *si*?"

Christoph stared at him, it was hard to stay behind, but he understood his grandfather's strategy in protecting the bloodline, as well as in protecting Virginia and D.C. should it come to that. "I understand. I wish I was going with you, P-bear."

Shade shook his head. "You need to be here for us. I can't leave this responsibility to anyone else. Now, get moving. You have a lot to do." He watched as his grandson left the room, then Shade flopped down in his chair. He needed to make one last call to Lorenzo. He spoke his name and waited for the computer to connect, as he sat and stared at the screen.

***

At Castello, it was a quiet evening. Everything had almost returned to their normal routine as Chantal had fully recovered from the poisoning. Lorenzo lingered a while longer in the evening before reporting to camp, spending more time with Chantal and Grace. Antonio heard the phone ring in Lorenzo's office, and answered the call, seeing Master Shade on the large screen. "Master, how may I help you?'

"Antonio, I need Lorenzo immediately. This is urgent."

Antonio moved quickly to the private rooms on the second floor and found Lorenzo with Chantal in the infant's nursery. "I'm sorry to interrupt, master, but your father is on the phone in the office. He did say it was a matter of urgency."

Chantal gave him a worried look. "Don't fret, *cherie*. Stay here with Grace. I'll be back as soon as I speak to my father."

He kissed Grace before handing her back to her mother and followed Antonio back down the stairs. He entered the office to see his father's face on the screen, a look of concern on his face. "What's going on, Dad?"

"Son, I have escalated to Red Alert. Soren dream-walked with your *madre*. I had to step in and bring Christoph, Skelk, and Luca to help me. She is all right, resting for now, but it is time, Lorenzo. You need to put your plan in place. Raven and his warriors will be there soon. So will Theo and Skelk, along with some of my warriors from the Bel Rosso camp, and reinforcements from Henry. Aislynn will follow shortly. She needs some time with Christoph before leaving here. Farnese has been notified as well. They will send some reinforcements but keep the bulk of their warriors to approach from the rear. His warriors will be reporting to you. I will arrive with your mother, Luca, Shannon, and Theresa tonight."

Lorenzo stared back at his father. He knew this day would come, and they'd been preparing for it for some time. On one level, he almost felt relief, to finally get it over with, but he knew the cost of lives lost would be great. "So, it's finally time? I will tell Alfie. Our warriors are ready, they've been ready. The camp is already prepared to take in the extra warriors. Is Mom okay? Do you need me to do anything else?"

Shade ran his hands through his hair and looked back up at the face of the warrior who was his mirror image. "As we discussed, son, I want to keep everything normal, change nothing. Keep the same schedule on the border and do nothing that would alert the Borgia. Get the warriors fed, they will need it. Inform them, but make sure they do not instigate yet. I want nothing to happen until I get there. Let's not arouse suspicion. Be the king and warrior I taught you to be, son, that's all I ask of you."

Lorenzo smiled back at him, "I guess it's time to see if the son can live up to the legend."

Shade grinned. "I have no doubt. You are already legend in my heart and to your coven, son. We will take them down, standing side by side. Your *madre* is fine, do not worry about her. I am bone-ass weary right now, I need more slumber. I need to get moving. I have to call Natalia before I can sleep. Get Sophia and Bianca to Castello immediately. Also, send warriors to escort Henri and Amelia, we need them inside our protection as soon as possible as well. I love you, son. I will see you around midnight."

Lorenzo nodded as the screen went dark, and the smile faded from his face. It was time to get serious, deadly serious.

Shade sat for a long moment, it was time to face the hell he'd been dreading, but they were ready. He pulled out his cell phone and scrolled to Marcello's name. He knew they'd both be sleeping, but he was hoping Marcello would answer his cell. Natalia wouldn't awaken from her death slumber. He dialed and listened to it ring about four times when he heard a groggy voice answer. He let out a breath he didn't even know he was holding.

***

Marcello was pulled from his sleep when he heard the soft vibration of the phone on the table next to their bed. Natalia slept on his shoulder, her mass of thick brown hair almost covering her face. He brushed the hair back from her cheeks before reaching for the phone and seeing Shade on the caller ID. He knew immediately something was wrong. Shade wasn't a day-walker, and if he was calling at this hour, something had gone wrong. He gently slid Natalia off his shoulder and sat upright in bed. "Master? What's going on?"

"Marcello, sorry to wake you but we are on Red Alert. I have implemented our plans. Soren has dreamed-walked with Kate. She is fine, but I need you to do me a favor. I don't care what in hell you have to do to manage this, but get it done. I need you and Natalia here as soon as she wakes. We need to see her before we leave. I am heading back to my slumber and once we can move out, we will. Can you do this, Marcello?"

Marcello looked at Natalia, sleeping peacefully beside him, and knew whatever lay ahead would change their lives. "Of course, master. We'll be there as soon as she wakes."

"*Grazie*. Tell her what has happened before she gets here, I think she will be fine if she is with you, don't leave her side. Kate is fine. Please make sure she understands that. See you soon."

Shade hung up and downed the rest of his Midnight. Dragging himself to the second floor, he saw Luca standing guard. "Go to Shannon, get ready, we leave at midnight."

He stepped inside their bedroom and closed the door, stripping from his clothes and laying down beside her. In an instant, her head was on his chest, her arm and leg tossed across him. They had slept like this every single day. "Sleep, *mi amore*, I am here now. He will no longer hurt you. I will protect you always. *Ti amo*." He felt the pull almost instantly and let the slumber take him.

111

Marcello had dressed and was waiting for Natalia to emerge from her death slumber. He'd let her know as soon as she woke what had taken place, and her family would be leaving for Castello soon, and her father had requested to see her. As soon as her eyes fluttered open, he gently explained what her father had called to convey. Natalia leaped from the bed and rushed to shower and dress. Marcello had already dressed in leathers and was ready to leave when she was.

Natalia called to him as she dried off from the shower. "Do me a favor, please. Go tell Emerald I have a family emergency, and I'll be gone for a few hours."

Marcello kissed her lightly, her brow already furrowed with worry. "Of course, and don't look so concerned. All will be fine."

She looked back at him and started to speak but stopped and nodded. "Hurry please. I'll be ready when you return."

Marcello checked for any sounds in the hallway before exiting, then went off to find Emerald.

Natalia finished dressing and wished she had time to call Malachi. She felt like she had a rock in her stomach. She hadn't had any further visions of the battle, and she hadn't heard anything from Malachi.

When Marcelo returned, he strapped the sword onto his back and turned to her. She looked near tears. "Natalia, what's wrong?"

She stared back at him, wondering how much she should reveal. "There's something I want to share, but I'll tell you now, it's a burden to carry it, and you can't tell anyone."

He sat down in the room they shared and waited for her to speak. "You have my word."

She shared with him the information she'd uncovered in the Council archives in Florence years ago when she was just a young girl, and Marcello listened in silence. When she was done speaking, he was quiet for a few minutes before he spoke. "You think this is related to the battle?"

She shook her head. "I don't know. Neither does Malachi."

Marcello looked away, wondering how she'd carried such a burden for so long. "Does anyone else besides Malachi know?"

"Well, my father, of course."

Marcello's head snapped around to look at her. "Shade knows?" He couldn't bear the sadness in her eyes.

"Yes, he’s always known. He knew centuries before I found the information in the archives."

Marcello sighed heavily. "But it may have nothing to do with the battle, look at how many battles your father has fought in the centuries he has lived."

Natalia nodded. "I tell myself that, as does Malachi. There is nothing that indicates when it occurs, or even that it is related to a battle."

He kissed her hand. "Then let's cling to that, Nattie."

She wiped away a tear. "Yes, I’ll cling to that."

He stood up and placed his arms around her. "We should go. Your father wanted to leave for Florence by midnight, and we don't have a lot of time."

She was perfectly capable of teleporting herself, but he held her tight as they teleported out to Bel Rosso.

***

Shade had held Kate through what remained of their day, and his troubled death slumber. His warriors were preparing to leave for Castello, but he wouldn’t go until he could see Natalia. He dressed quickly and kissed her, telling her to get ready to travel while he wrapped up a few last details. He made his way to the study and pulled out a large box he’d been keeping just for Nattie. Leaving the box on his desk, he stepped outside onto the patio and looked across the rolling foothills that stretched to the mountain range. This was his home, and it was as much a part of him as the land of his birth. It had been nothing when he took it over, but together, he and Kate had created a paradise for the two of them, as well as for their children, and grandchildren. The memories of their life here flooded his mind with such clarity, and he took a deep breath, his emotions overwhelming. He was going to battle and fight for this place, as well as the land he inherited from the Medici’s who lived before him. As he stood in the night air, he felt the energy shift, as both Marcello and Natalia teleported in.

As Marcello landed, he set her down gently and Natalia ran to her father, arms open. He grabbed her up in a bear hug, squeezing her tight. "Daddy, I'm so scared."

He crushed his daughter to his chest, closing his eyes and inhaling her scent, storing it in his memory. "Shhh, Nattie, you need not be scared. Medici will win this war and become the greatest coven in all of Europe." He rubbed her back and let her get her emotions in check. "I need to speak with you before you go see your *madre*."

He led her back into the office, and Marcello followed at a distance, stopping at the door, unsure of whether he should intrude on their private conversation. Natalia looked back at him over her shoulder and motioned for him to follow. Turning to her father, she confided, "I told Marcello about the archives."

Shade paused a second and then nodded. He knew his warrior would forever keep the secret, and that Natalia needed someone to share the burden. Marcello entered and took a seat on the sofa, giving them some space. Natalia took a seat in her father's chair behind the desk, as Shade sat on the corner of the desk, facing her. "Daddy, we know the battle is inevitable. But you can control this. We can win this battle, and all you have to do is keep Mommy safe. That's the key to everything. Don't you see? The curse? It can't happen if she's not there!"

He perched on the desk, watching her face. She'd always been so determined. Nothing was ever going to stop her, not even an ancient curse. "Are you done giving me battle plans, Nattie?"

She smiled shyly back at him. "I guess."

He cracked a smile. "Your mother is my strength in all things. I am nothing without her, Nattie, and vice versa. As for the curse, we don't know if it will play out here, or centuries from now. I have lived with the knowledge of the curse, and I admit, I allowed it to control my decisions when I was younger. But I can't live my life around the curse, or let it hold me back. I would never have accomplished a thing."

She chuckled. "Nothing holds you back, Daddy."

He stood up from the desk and slid the box wrapped in white paper in front of her. "This is something I want you to have. It belonged to your great-grandfather. I always thought I would give it to Lorenzo, but as time passed, I knew you would have greater use for it. Open it."

Natalia accepted the box and tore away at the paper, lifting the lid to reveal an ancient leather-bound ledger. She carefully removed the heavy book from the box and opened it to parchment pages, the text written by hand in Italian. Natalia was careful with the delicate pages. "What is it, Daddy?"

He took a deep breath, just seeing the ledger again brought back memories. "That is the diary that belonged to Christofano's father, your great-grandfather. I only knew him briefly, but I remember how carefully my father guarded this ledger. It was all he had of his own father. I thought it had been destroyed in the Bonfires, but someone salvaged it and saved it from the flames. It is all that remains of him and is very precious to me. I pass it down to you now, to preserve for future generations."

Natalia touched the ink that was placed on this page by her great-grandfather's hand, a man who'd died centuries before she was born. She'd always felt a strong connection to their ancestors and found it ironic she would be the only Medici who wouldn't be allowed to bear a child to carry the Medici name forward. She was fluent in Italian, and many other languages, and she knew she'd read, and re-read this ledger until it was memorized. "Thank you, Daddy." Her heart skipped a beat, as the fear crept back in, wondering why her father felt compelled to give her this now. "I'll make sure it's kept safe, and future generations will know his story as well."

He pulled her into his arms. "I love you, my sweet Nattie. I will always love you. You must go to your mother now. We don't have much time before we must leave." He kissed her on the cheek. "Go now."

Natalia left the office, asking Marcello to wait for her, and headed up the stairs to her parent's bedroom. The door was open, and she could see her mother packing some things for the journey. Marcello had told her about the dream-walk, and her mother still looked a little shaken. She stopped in the doorway. "Mommy?"

Kate looked up to see her youngest daughter, and rushed toward her, hugging her. "Nattie! I'm so glad you came! I was afraid I wouldn't get to see you before we left."

Natalia sat on the bed as her mother continued to fold and pack clothes. "Are you okay? Daddy told Marcello about the dream-walk."

Kate paused and closed her eyes. "I'm fine, Nattie. It was unnerving, and I had no control, but your father entered the dream and pulled in Luca and others. I know it's a mind game, and I have to shake it off. Please, don't worry about me. Don't worry about either of us. Your father has pulled warriors from every camp, and the Farnese will attack the Borgia from the rear, coming up from Sicily. I have my gift, and I won't hesitate to use it. We didn't come this far to hand it all over to the Borgia. I can't believe that. Look at us, look at all of us. When the dust of the battle settles, it is the Medici who will rule."

Natalia smiled. "Well, now you sound just like Dad...and every warrior I ever met who was trained in our camps."

Kate sat next to her on the bed and caressed her face. "Your father promised me forever, and I intend to make him keep his promise."

Natalia looked back at her and answered softly. "Well, it's settled then. Daddy never breaks a promise."

***

Once Natalia had left the office, Shade turned to Marcello. "Listen to me, Marcello. I don't think the Borgia will come here, but should that happen, I don't care if this place is on fire, you keep Natalia at Council. Do not, under any circumstances, come here, or let her come here. Understood?"

Marcelo placed his hand on his master's shoulder. "She won't leave that fucking fortress, and no one will get inside. That is one worry you can put aside as you go into battle. No harm will come to Nattie."

Shade pulled him into his arms and pounded his back. "Take care of my daughter." He hugged the warrior hard and knew Nattie would be fine. "Come on, I have to get Kate moving." They headed for the second floor together.

112

The Borgia lieutenant advanced quickly to the palace to deliver the latest information to his master. He was taken immediately to Rodrigo's office, looking disheveled from the trip. The warrior ran his hands through his hair and brushed off his leathers as Rodrigo looked up. Rodrigo recognized the warrior's face but couldn't recall his name. "What is it, warrior, speak!"

The warrior proceeded to relay the information that the Medici camp at Castello was rapidly filling with warriors. Rodrigo roared with anger. Even with Soren sequestered, he had no doubts he'd had a hand in escalating the situation. Rodrigo had his approach well planned, but Soren seemed intent on taking control.

Rodrigo dismissed the lieutenant, sending him back to the border and stormed through the corridors to Soren's private wing of the palace. The warriors on guard outside of Soren's door stepped aside as Rodrigo barreled through and headed straight for Soren's throat.

Soren heard his brother coming and grinned as the door crashed open. He'd known the dream-walk with the redhead would be all it would take to push the Medici to go on the offensive. Soren was tired of waiting for his brother, and this battle to begin. He saw Rodrigo coming at him with great speed, his eyes flaring. Soren raised his arms across his face to block his brother's hands, grappling for his throat. Soren's eyes turned a flaming red, lighting the room in the fiery glow as his fangs punched, and he shouted at his older brother. "I warned you to never touch me again!"

Rodrigo stood before his brother, his body visibly shaking with anger. If he didn't need his brother for the battle, he'd be tempted to kill him. "What have you done, you fool?"

Soren rolled off the bed and lowered his arms. "I have done what you could never do and brought this situation to a head." He chuckled. "Did you think you could exile me to my suite, brother? Chain me down?" Soren waved his hands in the air, dancing like a jester before a king to illustrate he'd freed himself from his restraints. "Did you forget my gift?" He laughed then as he pointed to the two warriors standing guard over him. "Do you think these idiots could prevent me from attacking my enemy without ever leaving my bed? You are such a fool, brother. I have dream-walked with the Queen of Medici. I showed her the death and devastation we will bring to their coven, and I promised her she would be my spoils of war."

Rodrigo felt his beast rise up. "You have foiled my plans of a surprise attack. Now you give me no choice!" Rodrigo paced the room in agitation. He stood before Soren and locked eyes with him. "Prepare yourself for battle, brother. We have no option but to strike now and hope they have not had adequate time to prepare. I should rip your heart out where you stand, but once again, I will refrain from taking you out of this world."

Soren grinned. "Glad to see you still have your balls, brother. I am more than prepared to kill those bastards, once and for all."

Rodrigo stormed from the room. He had no time to play these games now. He had to prepare for battle. The time had come to take the final step in this long journey. He telepathically informed Tomas and Vanni to prepare for battle immediately, and he and Soren would meet them at the Umbria camp.

The two brothers teleported out, landing among the warriors gathered in Umbria. Rodrigo met with his lieutenants, issuing orders. "This will be a battle to the death. Leave no Medici man, woman, or child standing, and take Castello and its territory." Rodrigo broke up his warriors into regiments. He'd lead the center charge, and Soren, Vanni, and Tomas would each have their own regiments, flanking him. This wasn't the battle Rodrigo had planned, but Soren had backed him in a corner. No matter, they still outnumbered the Medici, and Rodrigo had no doubt he'd rule all of Italy at the end of the night. As Rodrigo stood ready, he could see the Medici gathering a thousand or more strong. He knew they'd come at him full force, but his legion was hungry for Medici blood to flow.

113

Shade had left Gi in charge of the Bel Rosso household and had Hyde move Cory into the main house so he could be more closely guarded. They'd said their goodbyes to Natalia and Marcello, and left Christoph in charge of the Virginia and D.C. covens. The camp remained on Red Alert in the event they called for more warriors or in the rare circumstance the war was brought to the States. When Shade and Kate arrived at Castello, they found it battle-ready. Lorenzo and Alfie had done their jobs well in preparing. Shade quickly made the rounds, checking the camp, reviewing the assignments of the numerous regiments, and inspecting the underground vault at Castello where the house staff and the females would be locked away during the battle. He'd called a meeting of his top warriors and he headed now to the study where he'd review their battle plans one last time.

He heard the rumble of their conversation as he neared the study. As he walked in, it took a few seconds for the conversation to die down. He scanned the room and saw Lorenzo, Alfie, Raven, Theo, Skelk, and Aislynn. No master could have asked to have more brave or well-trained warriors at his side. His eyes caught sight of his *padre* as he stood back in the corner, observing, and it gave Shade comfort to have him there. He felt the pride of Medici roll through him and knew his father believed in him. The room fell silent as his warriors looked back at him. "Someone pour me a fucking drink."

Lorenzo smiled to himself as he moved toward the bar and poured his father a goblet of Midnight. "Don't tell me you're getting cold feet. I've been waiting a long time for this."

Shade took the drink from his son and shook his head. "I have never had cold feet, especially when it comes to protecting our family. No one messes with my family and lives to tell about it." Shade downed the Midnight and paced around the room. "Let's go over this one last time. If you have any concerns, now is the time to speak, *si*?"

He looked around as all heads nodded in agreement. "Act from your head, not your heart. You must fight smart, think strategically. Don't allow yourself to be provoked so you respond impulsively. I know we all feel we have an ax to grind, but we must work together as one. Stick to the plan. You know we will lose many, it is a fact of war. You can't be distracted by the fallen. If a warrior has given his or her life for the cause, it is imperative you make sure that life was not in vain. Stay focused on why you are on that battlefield. We teleport to that border as a family, fighting for all we hold dear. We will come home victorious if we fight like Medici warriors."

He paced a bit and placed himself across the room, so he could see Christofano. His father nodded at him. "Each one of us will lead a regiment of warriors. I am purposely neglecting to assign Skelk to a regiment because he will have free reign to assist wherever he sees trouble. Raven will take charge of the regiment of warriors surrounding Castello. Nothing is to penetrate that line and enter Castello with all I love and treasure inside."

Raven nodded. "No one is getting inside Castello, master."

Shade lit up a smoke and continued to speak. "I will lead my regiment straight up the middle to the Umbrian border. Lorenzo will flank my left with his regiment; Alfie will flank my right. Theo and Aislynn will keep their regiments back, one to the left, one to the right. We will purposefully allow the Borgia to push us back, and when they do, you will enfold them from both sides. The Borgia will recognize me, as well as Lorenzo and Alfie. It is what Rodrigo will expect to see. He does not know Theo and Aislynn and the surprise we lead him to."

Shade took a long drag on his cigarette and exhaled the smoke. "I want this victory to take place on Castello land, in full view of our home. They took my parents' lives from me here, and I will take theirs. We will lure them into our territory where they will die, just as my parents did." He looked up at his father and he saw him nod his head in acknowledgment. "Our final nail in Rodrigo's coffin is our alliance with the Farnese. Ottavio and Amondo wait to the south, out of sight. They will come in from behind the Borgia and we will have him surrounded. If you have a gift, use it to its full capacity. Keep your mind focused. We are going to lose warriors. It is inevitable.

Fight as you have been trained to do, keep moving no matter what lies in front of you."

Shade looked around the room at each of them. He had spent his life training them, now he had to believe what he'd taught them would get them through. "Now is the time for thoughts, questions or anything else you need to say to me or anyone else in this room. We have to go out there together, as one unit, or this will never work."

Lorenzo looked around the room at the warriors that had each risen in the ranks to lead. They all had their eyes glued to Shade, except Skelk, who was nonchalantly smoking a cigarette like this was just another day. Lorenzo had never been in battle with him before. "Skelk? Any questions?"

Skelk looked up and gave him a half-smile. "Nah, just tell me who to kill, brother."

Shade laughed out loud, and it actually felt good. "Now you know why I let Skelk do his own thing."

Skelk put out his cigarette, wondering what all the damn fuss was about.

Lorenzo looked at Aislynn and saw some worry in her eyes. He was aware she'd left Christoph at home, and she'd fight this battle without her mate. "You good, Aislynn?"

Asilynn stood upright after leaning against the desk. "I'm a Medici by blood and mating now, not just as a member of this coven. I have my sister Fiamma with me tonight. So, let's take care of these psycho bastards and go the hell home. I've got a Medici warrior waiting for me."

Lorenzo chuckled. "We all have someone waiting on us... well, except Skelk."

The warriors laughed nervously as Skelk shrugged. "Maybe, maybe not."

Raven looked at the warrior he'd first met on the streets of D.C. "You holding out on us, brother?"

Skelk cast him a sideways glance and winked. "I had a mate once. She was mortal, a witch of great power. She's long gone now, but her spirit surrounds me."

They all stared back at him, as he revealed the only personal information he'd ever shared. Shade grasped immediately Skelk's penchants for remoteness, all these years, if he had outlived his mate. Raven shook his head, his locks flying. “You what? After this battle, I want details, brother.”

Skelk smiled at the bitter-sweet memory of her. “Maybe. Not something I talk about.”

Raven snorted. “No shit!”

Shade smiled at the light-hearted banter among his warriors, as he absorbed this new information from Skelk. He’d seen it many times as warriors prepared to meet their fate and recognized it as part of their preparation. He couldn’t imagine going into battle with anyone other than the people around him. "All right, warriors, we meet at camp in one hour. I have a queen to attend to and need to get my leathers on. Go to your regiments, go to your mates, take care of unfinished business, so you can stay focused on the task in front of you."

He walked to the middle of the room and extended his arm, his hand balled into a fist. The others gather around him in a circle, their one fist outstretched, touching one another. Lifting their fists into the air, the sound of their raised voices shook the old castle with a glorious sound. "*Per sempre* Medici!"

Shade watched them file out of the office, then turned to see his father now sitting in the old leather chair behind the desk. Shade took the chair opposite the desk. It was a position he was quite familiar with, sitting across from his father when he was still a young boy in the camp. "So, we have come full circle, *Padre*. You fought them once, and now I will fight them as well."

Christofano nodded. "Your battle plans are in place, son. You must fight now, for all that you have built, and for the legacy that is Medici. Perhaps you understand, now, my insistence on your mating contract with the Alizzi. None of this would have played out for you had you listened to me long ago. Mating the Alizzi would have changed your course. I knew it was only a matter of time before the Borgia would come."

Shade shook his head. "No, *Padre*. I didn’t love her, and I never would have. I knew deep in my heart she was not the one. I love Kate. No one could have loved me, as she has. I understand your motivation and insistence, but Donatella was not for me."

Christofano sat back in his chair and threw his booted feet onto the desk, crossing them at the ankles. "You were always stubborn.

You could have had both, you know. You could have mated the Alizzi to secure the territory and the safety of the coven, and still found your precious Kate."

Shade chuckled to himself. "*Si*, but I would not have been able to mate her, and it is not the same." Shade stood up and placed his hands on the desk, leaning into his father. "Finding love will always be more important to me than any territory, no matter how precious, *Padre*. Kate has taught me love conquers all."

He turned then to walk out and go find his *bel*, when he heard Christofano's boots hit the floor. "*Figlio.*"

Shade turned to look at him as his father approached and threw his arms around him. His *padre* had never been one to show affection, and Shade held him tight, knowing that, for once, they were both on the same page with each other.

"I love you, *mio figlio*. I am proud of the king you have become, and I am proud of your queen. You made the right choice, as your *madre* is quick to remind me. Had you mated the Alizzi, she may or may not have helped you avoid this battle, but I can see that for you, a life without Kate is not a life worth living. This coven is powerful and respected. You followed the right path. Fight your fight, win this battle. *Per sempre* Medici."

Shade felt his heart explode with the words he'd longed to hear since he was a young warrior. "I love you too, *Padre*. I will make you proud." He walked from the study and never looked back.

Christofano watched his son walk away, knowing whatever happened now was in the hands of fate. He knew he'd been hard on him growing up and had continued to push him even from the spirit realm, but there had never been a day when he wasn't proud of him. Shade was his only son, the only link to a future for the Medici legacy, and he'd dared not make it easy for him. Everything had rested on his shoulders, and he had more than lived up to the task.

114

Kate stood at the window looking out over the formal gardens of Castello. The castle was a flurry of activity as everyone prepared for the battle, and the tension was palpable. Shade was with his top warriors, going over last-minute plans. She'd stepped into an unoccupied bedroom to escape the chaos and calm her thoughts. She laid her forehead against the cool glass and closed her eyes, letting her thoughts wander. Castello had never officially been her home, but so much had happened inside these walls that had altered her life. Shade had brought her here the first time he'd allowed her to feed from him, sealing their blood covenant. It was in the sealed chamber beneath the castle where she was turned, and where all three of their children were born. It was here where she was crowned queen and recognized by the coven. Now, her grandchildren were born here, and all future generations to come. It was easy for her to imagine it, their legacy, reaching far into the future. She felt a soft hand on her shoulder and turned, expecting to see Sophia, and discovered Portia. "*Madre*!"

Portia smiled back at her, a soft, sad smile. "Daughter, you are lost in your memories. They are good memories, *si*? Come sit with me." Portia took her hand and led her to the bed where the two women sat side by side.

"Every key milestone in my life has taken place here. I was thinking of my children, born inside the chamber, and Lorenzo and Sophia's children, also born here. I know Shade has taken precautions to protect the bloodline, sequestering the females inside the vault, and keeping Henry and Christoph out of the country. It isn't hard for me to envision a future for the Medici. That's a good sign, don't you think? A good omen? I find it hard to believe we've come this far that we've built so much, only to have it all destroyed by the Borgia."

Portia squeezed her hand. "My son has planned well. He has made good choices, and his warriors are ready for whatever comes, but I have no view into the future. No more than you do. Natalia is the only one with the gift of sight. Did she see nothing?"

Kate shook her head. "She says no, as does Malachi."

Portia looked at the floor and closed her eyes. "Then the outcome is not ours to see. The fates have already decided, and it is time for each of you to play out your role."

Kate looked at her with alarm. "What does that mean?"

Portia lifted her hand and softly stroked Kate's cheek. "There were so many years I thought my son was lost. He worked hard, he trained hard, but he lacked focus or direction. Happiness was elusive. I worried about him, as did Christofano. He looked for love, but he made bad choices that only made his life more complicated. It is not our place to intervene in the lives of the living, and Christofano was not happy when I placed you in his path. He did not think a mortal was befitting our son, but I saw something in you that I knew would fill the void in his heart and heal what was broken. He has loved you like no other, and his love for you grows still. It is only with you he has been able to fulfill his destiny and secure the legacy of the Medici. I know you love him with the same intensity. I see it in your eyes, every time you look at him, but I must ask, do you regret your choice?"

Kate shook her head. "I regret nothing. I can't imagine my life without him."

Portia smiled again. "I feel that way about Christofano, even after all this time. I know Christofano was hard on him, and Shade did not always feel he had his father's approval, but so much was expected of him for the coven to thrive. His father knew things would be hard, and Shade was our only child. Everything depended on him; the very future of the Medici coven was in his hands. For so long, he carried that burden alone, no siblings, no mate, but look at him now. Look at the both of you."

Kate looked back at her, her brow creased. "I feel like you're telling me everything will be okay."

Portia brushed the lock of red hair back from Kate's face, and locked eyes with her. "He will try to face this alone and protect you at all cost. I am asking of you what I have always asked of you. Take care of my son. You will know what to do."

Kate started to answer her when Portia faded into the mist. "Wait! Portia! I will always take care of him. I have so many questions!" She looked around the room, waiting to see if Portia might reappear, but she only heard a soft whisper from Portia.

"You will know what to do."

Kate stood silent in the room. Would she know what to do? There were so many questions she needed to ask, and she knew they were running out of time.

115

As Portia's vision faded, Kate felt both comfort and fear. Would she know what to do? She knew the Medici's were ready, the warriors had prepared for every eventuality, but she also knew life held no guarantees. She left the empty bedroom and returned to the room she shared with Shade. The castle had been a flurry of activity ever since their arrival, as the warriors moved in and out, receiving last-minute orders from Lorenzo and Shade, and the house staff readied the castle, securing the valuable art and jewels into steel vaults, sealed beneath the castle floors. All the females and the house staff would be moved to secure vaults underground as well, and the castle would be surrounded by warriors as the last line of defense, overseen by Raven. She remembered the Battle of Bel Rosso, and how many warriors fell, and she knew this battle would take a bigger toll. They'd lost Fiamma in that battle and she closed her eyes, not wanting to feel that pain of loss again. She'd dismissed the house staff sent to help her unpack, wanting the time alone with her thoughts. She was thinking about Portia's visit when she heard his footsteps on the stairs and she smiled that she could recognize Shade simply by the sound of his boots against the floor, the distinctive sound of his determined stride.

He stopped in the doorway to their bedroom and stared at her, her hair hanging loose, the sweater baring one shoulder and the jeans hugging her hips and slender legs, her feet bare. It made his heart sing. She was as beautiful in a jewel-encrusted gown as she was in a pair of jeans. It had never made a difference to him. For him, she was the most beautiful creature he'd ever laid eyes on and always would be. He smiled back at her. He had little time now before he'd need to lead his warriors into battle. He needed her touch to prepare him for the toughest battle of his life. He took her in his arms and laid his head on top of hers. She was his greatest strength and his biggest weakness. "I need to prepare, *mi amore,* and so do you. Put on some shoes now."

She allowed herself to be enveloped by him. He was her safe place, and always had been. He'd leave her soon and go to the battlefield. "How can I help you? Tell me what you need to make sure you come back to me. I know we'll lose so many, and there will be such sadness and grief, but I can't bear the thought of losing my son, or Sophia losing Alfie. I can't bear the thought of Christoph losing Aislynn when they have just begun their journey. But most of all, I can't bear the thought of losing you. It feels selfish of me, because I know so many will fall to save this coven and save it they must. The Borgia can't prevail. I refuse to believe we have come this far only to relinquish everything to such evil."

He held her tight before reaching down and tipping up her chin, drawing those amber eyes to his own icy blue ones. "There will be losses, we cannot escape that, but you must not fret. Medici blood is strong. Our warriors can stand against the best. You must have faith we will all return. No one has ever been able to keep me from you for long, *mi amore*. I need to get into my leathers. Will you tie back my hair? Damn mess of curls needs to be out of my eyes, so I can see that bastard, to slay his ass."

Kate watched him pull on the leathers, something she'd seen him do a million times, but she knew this was no mock battle he prepared for. He wasn't training warriors tonight. He'd be fighting for his life. As he sat on the bed to lace up his boots, she crawled around behind him and pulled his hair back into a ponytail, securing it tightly with a strip of leather, even as a few shorter curls sprung loose, and hung around his face. She kissed his neck, and inhaled his scent, fighting back tears. He wouldn't want to see tears before a battle. He needed her to be strong, so she'd be strong.

Closing his eyes, he felt her fear, and the tears she fought back. He heard her inhaling him, to keep his scent in her heart as he battled. "I need you to listen to me, *bel*, listen closely."

He turned and pulled her to him, cradling her in his lap. "Lorenzo and Alfie and I will go to the Umbrian border, where we will draw the Borgia as close to Castello as we can. I will have Theo and Aislynn, with their regiments, waiting to flank them. Raven will have the castle surrounded. You need to trust Raven. He won't let anything penetrate that final barricade. Farnese warriors come in from the south behind Borgia. We will have them surrounded."

He kissed her on the forehead. "If you hear nothing else, please hear this. Under no circumstances are you to leave the vault. The vault is sealed from the inside. It can't be breached. Luca will be with you. I mean it, Kate. You are not to leave!" He stared into her eyes. "Chantal is royal, but her family is not warrior born. She has never faced a battle before. She will need your strength. She will feel what Lorenzo feels and will not understand all the emotions rushing through her. You will need to comfort Sophia and Bianca. They are Medici born and bred, and they have grown up around warriors, but they have experienced nothing to prepare them for this. But most of all, I know you will feel me, just as I will feel you. I will be letting my beast lead, and I will need to know that you are safe."

She stared back at him. She knew she'd feel him, and she'd know if he were injured, even locked deep below the castle. "I have no fear for myself. I know Raven would die for this coven. I have no doubts about the skill of the Medici to protect this castle that has stood for hundreds of years. I know Luca will never leave my side. If the Borgia should break through the castle walls, then we have lost, and the females are all prepared to take their own lives. We would never allow ourselves to be captured and killed by the Borgia. But you ask a lot of me, lover. You know my powers, and I can't stand idle if there's something I can do to change the outcome of this battle."

He growled softly. The curse ran through his brain, and he shook his head to clear it, he had no time for those thoughts. "Kate, I can't go out there if I think you are at risk. I know your powers, but this is a chance we must take. I cannot lose you, *mi amore*. I will come back to you. Please, I am begging you to not leave the safety of the vault!"

She laid her head against his chest. How could he ask this of her? She heard Portia's whisper in her head. **"You will know what to do."**

Kate spoke softly. "I'll promise you I'll stay unless I feel peril. I don't need to leave the castle walls to call forth the animals, but these aren't my warriors I command, they're Sophia's and Bianca's. They'll need to see me, hear my command. I promise you I'll stay below ground unless I feel I'm needed. If I must leave the vault, I'll go to the highest parapet. Our daughter and granddaughter won't leave the protection of the vault under any circumstances. Luca will be at my side, and Raven guards us all. I can promise you that. Don't ask of me what I cannot give. This is my coven too. I'm their queen, I'm your queen, and I'll fight in the only way I know how."

Shade laid his head against her forehead. "In my darkest days, I asked for a queen who was worthy of my coven. I know it is useless to argue with you now. You are as stubborn as I am. So, promise me at least you will only respond as a last resort and do not leave the safety of Castello." He kissed her then as if it might be their last kiss, absorbing all of her. He felt their heartbeats synchronize with each other, as their souls entwined. "I love you, *mi amore*. I have lived many centuries, and experienced things long forgotten, but my sweetest years were with you and our children. Your love made the waiting worthwhile. Please tell me you have no regrets."

She looked back at him, lost in the bluest blue of his eyes. "My only regret is you didn't find me sooner, and don't you dare say goodbye to me. You promised me forever, Shade Medici, and you promised you'd never break my heart. I expect you to keep your promises."

Smiling at her, he kissed her again over and over. "*Si*, my Queen. A promise is a promise. I have no intentions of breaking it now." He heard the light tap at the door and Luca's familiar voice.

Luca stepped inside their room. "Master, the scouts have spotted Rodrigo and Soren at the border. We've taken all the females and the house staff below ground." He looked at Kate. "You need to come with me now."

Kate nodded, and swallowed hard, blinking back tears. She kissed Shade one last time before leaving him, stopping at the door to look over her shoulder. "You promised."

He nodded at her. "*Ti amo, mi amore*."

His eyes locked with Luca. They both knew he was putting her into Luca's care, and it would be his responsibility to keep her safe. Luca nodded in acknowledgment, and he watched as Luca led her away. He felt his heart lurch and he swallowed hard. He needed to focus now on the complete annihilation of the Borgia and nothing less. He pulled his *padre's* sword from the closet and strapped it to his back next to his sword. He looked around the room one last time. He'd spent many more years at Castello than he ever had at Bel

Rosso. This was his boyhood home, where his parents lived and died, and where they resided still, where he'd turned his mate, and watched his children being born. "*Madre* and *Padre*, bring me back to her."

He walked out of the room and down the corridor to the stairs, his boots echoing against the marble floors in the grand foyer. He left the castle and headed to camp. His stride was proud and determined. He was the warrior's warrior.

***

Kate walked with Luca down the wide marble staircase and into the grand foyer. She paused and remembered the first time he brought her here, and how overwhelmed she'd been with the grandiosity. She realized the history here, and all the grandeur inside these castle walls. Others had tried to destroy it in the past, as Kate thought about the story of the bonfire. She looked at Luca. "You promise me those motherfuckers won't breach this castle!"

He almost laughed out loud at her ferocity, but smiled back at her and answered, "You have my word, my lady."

She smiled then, as he reverted to using the title she hated. "Let's go then."

They walked down the hall of ancestors, and Kate looked at the busts on pedestals, and oil paintings hanging on the wall, passing the large portrait of Shade as a young boy, standing with Portia and Christofano. The house staff was removing the last of the portraits and packing away the busts. She paused and looked at Portia standing regally beside her mate before Luca tugged at her arm. "Come on, Kate. I want to seal the vault from the inside."

She followed him through a door and down uneven stone stairs, and the memory of the sex chamber flashed through her head. She knew it had long been disassembled and had been glad to see it go, even though neither of them had ever spoken of it again. Luca took her hand as they walked down a darkened corridor until they reached a massive steel door. He pulled the door open and waited for her to enter. She walked in, and he stepped in behind her, pulling the door closed and sealing them inside. The significance of the vault wasn't lost on Kate. She was acutely aware that Shade had kept the females and his grandsons off the battlefield and safely secured. There would be no more children for her and Shade, but he was making sure the Medici bloodline prevailed in the event Lorenzo didn't survive. The room was dimly lit, as she looked around at the upturned faces of Chantal's parents, and Chantal, as they huddled together with Grace. Shannon smiled when she saw Luca enter, and he moved to give her a hug, reassuring her. Sophia sat with her arms around Bianca. Kate scanned the faces of the house staff, catching Emma's eye, and then Theresa's. She held Theresa's gaze. They had been through everything together, and Kate was comforted by her presence. She looked at all of them. "And so, it begins."

Chantal had never experienced anything like this in her life, and her fear was overwhelming. She was watching the Medici women and trying to model their behavior. Grace squealed and reached for Kate and Chantal stood up. "*Oui*, it is your bebe. Now settle down, *mon ange*."

She went to Kate and gave her a shy smile, even though she didn't feel like smiling. "I am frightened. I am trying to remain calm, for Grace's sake. She knows when I am upset."

Kate took the baby in her arms. "My son will come back to you. I refuse to accept any other outcome. He is the firstborn male in a long line of warriors, a king, a fire-thrower. How long do you think the Borgia can stand against the power of a fire-thrower? Soren is a dream-walker and that won't help him on the battlefield, and Rodrigo is a sin-eater. Lorenzo will lay waste to the Borgia, and he'll rule in this castle for centuries to come."

Bianca spoke with the confidence of youth and innocence. "Uncle Lorenzo and P-bear will take them all out, and no one is going to mess with my daddy! Amondo and his father are sitting to the south. I'd like to see them try to stop my Amondo." She turned to Kate and took Grace into her arms. "Besides that, Bebe, Mommy, and I have warriors as well. They don't stand a chance."

Kate relinquished the baby to Bianca and smiled. Bianca had never seen a battle and had never lost anyone on the field of war, but Kate wouldn't say anything to diminish her confidence in the outcome. She'd need that strength to get through. The pain would come soon enough. She took a seat next to Sophia, and Sophia took her hand, squeezing it hard. Kate could feel her daughter's fear. "He'll be fine, daughter, they'll all be fine. Natalia didn't have a vision of losing our males, or she would have told me."

Sophia bit her lip and nodded. She spoke in a whisper, so the others wouldn't hear. "Natalia doesn't see everything, you know that."

Kate was silent for a moment before turning to face her daughter. "Don't you dare give up hope. Not ever. Alfie needs your strength, as does your father and your brother. The Medici will win this battle. Get that in your head right now. You are a Medici princess, and you have a gift once thought extinct to our kind. We will prevail, do you understand me? Some will fall that we can't change, but we will rule!"

Sophia stared back at her mother and drew strength from her as she answered. "We will rule."

Kate looked hard at her. "Say it like you mean it, daughter. I'll accept nothing less. You are the children of the Medici. You bore him the next generation, and they will bear the next. The Medici legacy is secured."

Sophia nodded again and remained silent, but her mother's message was clear. No matter what happened on the field of battle, they had secured the future for the Medici, but they all may have to sacrifice something for it.

Everyone in the room had their eyes on Kate. Chantal returned to her seat, next to her parents, and sat next to her father. He put his arm around her. "You must remain strong."

She looked at the three redheads seated next to each other and saw nothing but confidence and strength, true Medici women, and she was determined to be one of them. "I am Medici and Valois, I am strong, *Papa*."

They sat in silence for some time, and Chantal was lost in her efforts to feel Lorenzo. She sat straight up and inhaled loudly. "They are moving."

Closing her eyes tight, Chantal sent a simple telepathic message, but one filled with all the love she held in her heart. **"I love you, Lorenzo."**

The room was deadly still. Everyone felt the moment the warriors moved into battle. There would be no more waiting. Their warriors were about to decide their fate.

116

Shade entered the camp and all he could see was leather-clad warriors, weapons visible. The warriors had built a small platform from the wooden crates that had been used to ship weapons from Bel Rosso to Castello. Shade climbed atop the platform and looked out at the league of warriors that had pledged their life to the Medici. The crowd fell silent as he scanned the faithful. He'd never seen so many Medici warriors gathered to battle, and he was proud of all of them. Lorenzo and Alfie were standing in front of the warriors, and Shade reached out his hand to his son and pulled him up beside him. This battle would go down as their legacy, the ultimate victory for all of Italy.

Lorenzo locked eyes with him and Shade nodded as they drew the swords from their backs and raised them high in the air. They watched as thousands of swords were raised before them, creating a large ripple in a sea of shining steel as each warrior raised his weapon, in unison, to their kings. Shade turned to his son and with swords held high, they crossed them above their heads, as they raised their voices. "*Per sempre,* Medici!"

The warriors shouted back, and the sound was deafening and awe-inspiring. Shade and Lorenzo lowered their swords and turned toward the Umbrian border. The warriors assembled behind them, finding their regiments, and preparing to march out. Shade looked at Lorenzo as he prepared to leave his side and lead his own regiment into battle. "I love you, Lorenzo. You're ready for this. Now let's go get these bastards."

Lorenzo gave him a cocky grin. "Did they really think they stood a chance?"

They took off, teleporting into the night sky, blacking out the moon, as thousands of Medici warriors followed them. Once airborne, the warriors realigned themselves with their regiments. Shade, Lorenzo, and Alfie took the lead, and Theo and Aislynn allowed their regiments to fall back.

***

Rodrigo waited at the Umbrian border. He looked at the charred ground of Donatella's home laid to waste and had every intention of doing the same to Medici. Tomas' regiment was to his left and one of his lieutenants to his right. The warriors lined the border for miles on either side of him. Soren and Vanni had their regiments directly behind Rodrigo and would move up as their warriors fell to prevent the Medici from penetrating their ranks.

Soren could easily pick out his brother in the crowd, as he was the only warrior with the Borgia crest in red on his back, and the Borgia flag staked in the ground beside him. The flag began to wave erratically from the wind stirred up by the approaching Medici, their teleporting throngs creating turbulence in the air as they moved closer. Soren looked at Vanni, and he could almost see his mouth-watering for the kill.

Vanni felt Soren staring at him and watched as Soren pulled the flamethrower from his back and strapped it to his chest. Vanni grinned from ear to ear. He couldn't wait to see the flamethrower turned on Lorenzo. Flames couldn't kill Lorenzo, but it would still be worth it to see the look of shock on his face. Vanni had been hoping for the glory of taking out that royal bastard, but Soren obviously wanted to claim that privilege for himself. Vanni looked skyward when he felt the shifting winds, and knew the Medici were close. He was startled when Soren grabbed him by the shoulder, his face a mask of evil and wicked intent.

Soren issued his orders. "When we get there, get to the castle, penetrate it, and take the two queens' hostage. Make sure you take the half-breed baby as well. Fucking kill the rest."

Vanni looked at Soren. "Those weren't my orders, master."

Soren growled. "There are two masters of this coven, and I am one of them. Do as I say, or you will die by my hand before we even get started."

Vanni had no doubt Soren meant every word. "*Si*, master, as you wish."

Soren walked away, eyeing the troops, and waiting impatiently for his time to slaughter the high and mighty Medici. He was tired of waiting. The thought had crossed his mind, more than once, that should his brother fall, he'd emerge as the only master of Borgia, and all of Italy would bow at his feet.

***

Shade led his warriors straight to the Umbrian border, where he saw the Borgia lined up and waiting for the attack. In mid-flight, he withdrew his father's sword and held it high in the air. As they approached the border, the Medici warriors hit the ground, running at full speed. Shade felt the power of the beast rise up in him. Rodrigo was easy to spot in the raging chaos, his dark, shoulder-length hair blowing in the wind, the Borgia flag announcing his presence. As Shade touched down, he fought his way through the mass of warriors to get to Rodrigo. The Borgia warriors came at them in a swarm, swords swinging. The air was already filled with the scent of sweat and blood as the Medici warriors were being pushed backward, toward Castello. Shade tried to keep his bearings through visual landmarks, without losing concentration. This was their plan, to intentionally lead the Borgia warriors back toward Castello, where Theo and Aislynn waited to flank them. It would create a false sense of winning for the Borgia and would give Farnese time to move in behind the Borgia without being detected.

Shade's concentration was as focused as a pinpoint of light in front of him. He couldn't allow himself to be distracted by the battles taking place around him but remained focused on whichever warrior he encountered, quickly dispatched them. The noise level of the battle rose, the sound of metal against metal mixed with the cries and groans of the fallen. Shade was being pushed backward, faster than he'd anticipated. He tried to hold his ground, but his feet couldn't find purchase, the blood already running like a river over this land he called home. He was fighting for his life, as was every warrior on the field, and he was already stepping over bodies.

All sense of time disappeared. After hours of battling, his body felt the blows from sword against sword, yet he pushed onward. He spun and found Tomas mid-swing in an attempt to take Shade's legs out from under him. Shade did a backflip into the air to avoid the strike and pulled another sword from the sheath on his back. It was time to get deadly serious. He felt the air around him move and knew Tomas was on his heels. Shade landed on his feet, a sword in each hand, ready to go head-to-head with Tomas.

Tomas felt confident as they pushed the Medici back into Tuscany with ease. There were more Borgia warriors than Medici, and if this was all they could muster, this battle would be a short one. He had laid waste to at least fifty of their warriors already. He saw Shade in front of him, battling several warriors at a time, and Tomas sliced a path of death to get to him. He'd finally take revenge for Max and the Aries coven. Long ago, in D.C., he'd infiltrated Alex's group of mercenaries, and had won the trust of the Medici, earning the rank of SIC in the newly formed arm of the Medici warriors in the U.S. Max had a taste for the little blonde bitch that belonged to Alec Canton, and had paid him well to spy on both Alec and Shade. Max had a plan to bring down Alec and the Medici, by going after the redhead, who was still mortal then. They'd hired Cuerpo to kill her, but she'd managed to dupe them all. Tomas had remained a mercenary, and never pledged to the Medici, so no questions were asked when he took his leave, and Shade had never known he was the one that had been the informer. Now, Tomas would get his chance to kill Shade, and his only regret was Shade would die never knowing Tomas was the one who'd betrayed him. He flipped through the air, matching his movements to Shade, and landed opposite him. As his feet hit the ground, he began a battle of swords. They were an equal match in height, strength and determination, and Tomas wouldn't back down until he drove the sword through his royal heart.

Shade could feel the sword become heavy in his arms when Tomas approached him, and they faced off. Shade got in a good striking blow to Tomas' arm, but Tomas swerved away at the last second and sustained only a minor injury which just served to piss him off. Shade was aware of Skelk moving high above the chaos, firing his crossbow with deadly aim.

Skelk was trying to keep his eyes on Lorenzo and Shade, providing cover where he could, but it was difficult to track them both in the mass of clashing warriors on the field. He swooped low and saw Shade in a struggle against Tomas. "You fucking low-life bastard." Skelk didn't want to take the kill from his master but gave him an advantage. He fired the crossbow into Tomas' injured arm that was already bleeding profusely. He reloaded the crossbow and was ready to fire again when he saw Shade get a clean strike. Tomas' head tumbled through the air and his body fell limp to the ground, spewing blood from his neck, only adding to the rapidly rising river that ran under the warriors' feet.

Shade moved quickly to the next attacker and Skelk knew he needed to keep moving. He spotted Theo coming into the fray as they approached the boundaries outside Castello. He scanned the battlefield, and it was clear the Medici were falling far more than Borgia. He hoped to fuck the Farnese got here soon.

***

Lorenzo led his own regiment on the battlefield, following their plan to allow the Borgia to push them back toward Castello. It wasn't difficult since the Borgia seemed to have the upper hand. He and his warriors had sliced their way through hundreds of Borgia, until his hand was so covered in blood it made holding his sword difficult. He could see his father and Alfie, as they both led their own regiments, and appeared to be having as much difficulty as he was. He felt the sword slip in his wet hand and needed time to regain his grip. With his free hand, he swung his arm in an arc, and laid down a trail of fire, engulfing the warriors that surrounded him. As his enemies dropped their swords, squirming from the flames that licked up their legs, Lorenzo used the time to wipe his right hand across his leathers and get a better grip on the sword. He heard the cries of the burning enemy as they writhed on the ground, creating a wide space around him, as the other Borgia warriors considered their odds in taking on the fire thrower.

Alfie caught a whiff of the smell of smoke and burning flesh and cast a glance in Lorenzo's direction to see he'd laid down a swath of fire. He smiled to himself. "About fucking time, brother."

Lorenzo scanned the faces of the Borgia warriors and watched as they communicated with each other telepathically, planning their approach. He saw them close ranks and try to attack him in mass. He tossed his sword from one hand to the other, waiting for them to move in closer. When they charged him, he again swept his arm from left to right, laying out a wide path of the fire, which quickly engulfed many of the warriors. Most screamed out in pain, dropping to the ground, but some broke through the wall of fire, and he engaged with them, one on one, with his sword. He was aware of Skelk, who'd managed to teleport above the fray and swoop in as needed when anyone got too close. Between the two of them, they managed to slay the Borgia's who had escaped the flames. The smoke filled the air and was carried by the wind back over the Borgia hoards. Lorenzo could hear them coughing and saw some of them wipe at their eyes. At least the wind was on the side of the Medici tonight.

***

Vanni was keeping a close eye on their position as they pushed the Medici back across Tuscany and were now near Castello. He could see Soren was working his way closer to Lorenzo. The fucking brat was easy to spot as he stood in the center of a ring of fire, untouched by the flames. He was throwing fire at everything that fucking moved. He knew Soren desperately wanted to take out Lorenzo personally, and Rodrigo had laid claim to Shade. It was time for Vanni to head for Castello, besides, the air on the battlefield was thick with smoke and the fire was spreading rapidly on the ground. If not for the fact it was so deadly, Vanni had to admit, it was a glorious sight.

Vanni led his regiment straight into the warriors who stood surrounding the castle and protecting those inside. He roared with laughter, knowing his face would be the last they saw before he strolled inside and captured the two queens and the baby half-breed for Soren, and killed everyone else. He'd become a hero in his master's eyes. Who else had the balls to take on those two bitches? His regiment followed him with a fury, attacking the warriors on the ground. The Medici pushed them back, killing many, but the Borgia kept coming. Vanni noticed the Medici would only move so far from the castle, remaining close to the walls of Castello. He let his regiment do the work, as he stood back observing, and kept seeing a large, black bird swooping down. *Damn fucking crows are already feeding on the bodies of the dead.*

***

Raven fought back, as did all his warriors. He wasn't having any of this fucking bullshit. The only female he'd ever loved sat inside that castle, counting on him to protect her family, and he had no intentions of letting her down. Fucking Borgia bastards fought dirty, with no honor, as he saw Medici warriors begin to fall, being stabbed in the back. He got a whiff of smoke, carrying the horrid smell of death as it blew on the wind, and he knew Lorenzo was out there laying down a path of destruction. Poe landed on his shoulder, squawking in a high-pitched rant before taking off again and Raven saw him circling one black-haired Borgia warrior who seemed to be standing back observing. Raven knew this must be Vanni, and he was here to try and take over the castle. Raven took off like a speeding bullet and attacked him head-on, Poe not far behind.

Vanni was caught off guard when he was attacked by the long-haired warrior looking like some crazed lunatic. He had speed like nothing Vanni had ever seen. He remembered Tomas saying there was a warrior named Raven, with the gift of incredible speed and agility so fast that not even a vampire could see him. He battled the warrior and found himself quickly overwhelmed, and unable to respond to the erratic and unpredictable moves from the Medici warrior. The smoke wasn't helping as it whirled on the wind, heavy and black with death on its wings. Suddenly, the black bird swooped down at his face and Vanni dropped his sword, batting at the bird that was intent on clawing out his eyes. He felt the bird's talons clawing at his face, opening large gaping wounds, and Vanni screamed, not able to fight off the bird.

Raven moved in quickly for the strike as Poe went for Vanni's face. Poe was as much a warrior and in love with his queen as Raven was. Raven plunged his sword through Vanni's heart and watched the look of surprise on Vanni's face as he clutched the blade that was embedded deep in his chest. As he started to fall, Poe plucked his eye from its socket, and Vanni's scream died in his throat as he collapsed to his death. The Borgia regiment was aware when their leader fell and continued to attack for a bit longer, but they couldn't penetrate the wall of Medici warriors, led by Raven and Poe. Raven had sworn to his queen his barrier wouldn't be breached, and he had no intentions of defaulting on that promise.

***

Inside Castello, they could hear the battle raging and Kate started to pace. She knew Shade and Lorenzo weren't injured, she'd feel that, and she knew Alfie was still standing, as Sophia hadn't reacted. Still, the sounds were growing louder, and they were well below ground, so she could only imagine the chaos outside these walls. She looked at Luca. "They're getting closer."

He nodded, sitting with his arm around Shannon. "That was the plan, Kate. You know that. Shade wants to pull them in close, and then flank them on both sides, and have the Farnese attack from the rear."

Her palms were sweating, and she wiped them dry on her jeans, before rubbing her neck. The muscles in her neck and shoulders felt hard as steel she was so tense. She bit her lips as she paced. "I need to see him, Luca."

He shook his head no. "You're not going out there."

She took a deep breath. "You don't understand. I need to be able to see him. I'll know when he's injured, but it may be too late then. I need to see the battle. I don't need to go outside. I only need to be up high. Take me to the parapet."

He shook his head. "It's too exposed. You could be taken out with an arrow. If you go down, Shade will lose the will to fight. He needs to know you're safe."

She turned on him in anger and shouted back, "And I need to know he's safe! We can stand just inside the entrance. I don't care what measures you take, but I'm going to the parapet. I'm asking that you take me, stand with me, but if it's an order you must hear from your queen, then I command it! I can't help him from here!"

Luca sighed heavily and shook his head in resignation, looking at Shannon. She answered him softly, "She's right, and you know it. Her gift is a powerful one, and it could mean the difference between win or lose."

Luca looked at the faces of the people assembled, to find them all nodding yes. Sophia spoke up, "She needs to go, Luca. I know my father ordered us all to stay, and the rest of us will be safe here, but only if we win. Use my mother's gift."

Luca looked to Henri, the only master in the room, and Henri nodded yes. "I have to agree with them, warrior. We will need every advantage to bring down the Borgia. It does no good to have such a powerful weapon at our disposal and not use it. I would go myself if I thought I had any power to influence the outcome."

Luca looked back at Kate. "He'll kill me if you're hurt, you know that."

Kate looked back at him, her face emotionless. "If I'm hurt, then it means the Borgia have breached Castello, and we've already lost this battle. It will no longer matter. Now, take me to the parapet."

Luca kissed Shannon, and she hugged him tight. "Go, we'll be fine here."

He opened the steel door to the vault, instructing Henri to lock it behind him, as he led Kate outside. He took her hand and walked with her back down the long, dark corridor and up the stone steps to the main floor of the castle. Kate could smell the smoke as they opened the door onto the main floor. "Keep going. Hurry!"

He led her up the marble staircase, and up again, past the second floor, to the parapet that overlooked the Tuscan hillside. This is where Shade had brought her after she was turned, and she was recognized by all as the queen of this coven. It was here they presented their children and grandchildren to the coven. She stared out, now, at a sea of destruction, and she gasped at what she saw. So many fallen. The sound of clanging swords was deafening, and the smoke filled the air. She saw Raven attacking a black-haired warrior from the Borgia, as Poe assisted him. She sent Poe a message, **"Good job!"** and heard the bird cry out loudly in response.

In the far distance, she could see Lorenzo. He was easiest to find, as she only had to follow the arc of flames. She peered through the smoke and singled out Shade and Alfie. The three of them were standing their ground, but it was clear the Medici were at a disadvantage and had paid a heavy price for this battle.

***

Shade knew they were being pushed into a tight circle by the Borgia. Medici ranks were falling fast and hard. Lorenzo was using his gift, and the smell of burned flesh filled his nostrils. He gave the order to have Theo and Aislynn arc their regiments to move inward towards them. He quickly scanned the battlefield as he saw his fresh regiments push forward, converging on the Borgia from both sides. His eyes were momentarily caught by a warrior in red leathers, her red hair flying free as she swung her sword in a high arc. *Fiamma?* He shook his head and looked back, but she was gone. He didn't have time to contemplate what he'd seen. The Borgia were pushing them close to the castle and he needed reinforcements to surround them. He felt someone slam into his back and knew it was Alfie. His breathing was ragged, and Shade knew whoever was attacking him was seriously pushing him to his limits. Shade tried to shout over the horrendous den of clashing swords and screamed to Alfie. "When I move, dart to your left fast and hard."

Shade flipped over Alfie's head, landing in front of him and got the attention of two of the three Borgia that were attacking Alfie. Shade held them off, pulling out a shuriken and sending it whistling as it sliced across the warrior's neck and took him down. It gave Alfie enough time to get himself situated and take out one warrior, then Shade and Alfie attacked the remaining Borgia together and laid him to waste. Shade scanned the battlefield. The more warriors he killed, a dozen more seemed to take their place. He telepathically gave Farnese the order to move out and fast, they needed to quickly bring up the rear and begin to slaughter from behind and annihilate them all. He spun around, trying to get a scope of what in hell was going on, but the smoke was disorienting. He saw a leathered warrior with a red Borgia crest on his back and his target had been spotted. As he zeroed in on Rodrigo, he felt a hand on his shoulder and turned to see Marco. Marco grinned as he spoke to him. "Did you think I would let you have all the fun you old goat? It is time to cut off the head of the snake." Before Shade could answer, his oldest friend had disappeared in the smoke.

***

Lorenzo continued to battle, trying to keep an eye on his father and Alfie. He was aware of another arc of flames and looked in the distance to see what was going on. He knew he was the only warrior with the gift of fire-throwing. He caught sight of Soren on the crest of a hill, with a military-grade flamethrower strapped to his chest. Soren was using the flamethrower against the Medici warriors in his path, and Lorenzo could hear their wails of pain as the fire washed over them. "You Borgia motherfucker. I'll make sure to have a special gift for you."

There were too many warriors between them, and Lorenzo needed to stand his ground, and keep any more of the enemy from breaking through, but he kept his eye on Soren.

***

The one opponent Shade was intent on killing lay before his eyes and he focused everything he had on this moment. He landed in front of Rodrigo, crouched with sword in hand. "Looking for me?"

Rodrigo circled the Medici and grinned, with his sword held above his head. "I thought I smelled a royal bastard."

Shade roared as his beast was finally facing a worthy opponent. "You are scum of the fucking earth, Borgia. This is Medici land, and you will die trying to take it."

Rodrigo made a taunting jab at Shade's heart. "The Borgia killed the last king and queen of the Medici, and we have waited a long time to be able to lay claim to what should be ours."

Shade's beast attacked full force with his sword, and the resistance of Rodrigo's forged steel blade reverberated up his arm and into his shoulder. They were a perfect match, their skills equal in all areas. They fought with intensity, each one jabbing and throwing arcing slices back and forth, as their breathing became labored, and the blood began to flow from the cuts and slashes they each inflicted. Shade could feel his rage building as he remembered the sight of Castello, and the burned ashes of his parents, when he returned home after the bonfires. He was inflamed with anger and pain, and he pushed through, even though his body was tiring. They had all been battling for hours, and yet, he knew if he slew Rodrigo, Soren still remained to be slaughtered.

Shade could hear others around him battling for survival, but he never took his eyes off the enemy in front of him. He watched Rodrigo's eyes to see where his next move would be. He saw Rodrigo lunge at him, and he moved to avoid the killing blow but was a millisecond too slow and the blade caught him in his side, wedged into his rib cage.

Rodrigo cried out with victory and Shade lifted his foot and kicked him hard in the crotch as Rodrigo roared in pain, stumbling backward, and pulling his sword from Shade's body. Shade could feel the blood running inside his leathers. It was a steady trickle, a wound deep enough to be fatal if he didn't get help, and one that would tire him from blood loss, making him more vulnerable. But he'd keep fighting, he had no choice.

***

As they stood in the parapet, Kate doubled over in pain, clutching her side, and knew he'd been injured.

Luca bent over her, protecting her with his own body, looking for the warrior who might have injured her when he heard her cry out. "It's Shade. He's been struck. He fights still, but the injury is serious."

Holding her hand against the side of her chest, as if she herself were bleeding, Kate made her way to the balcony wall and looked for him. Portia appeared at her side, staring out across the battlefield, tears on her cheeks. Luca moved in front of her, shielding her with his own body. She could see Shade fighting Rodrigo but could also feel his pain. She screamed loudly above the cacophony of noise from the battlefield, calling forth the animals under Sophia's command. She saw them respond, the packs of wolves darting onto the field of battle, and viciously attacking the Borgia, adding to the chaos. The ravens and falcons darkened the sky, swooping down, using their talons and their beaks to tear at the flesh of the enemy.

***

Shade crouched. He was ready, his whole body as tense as a coil, his teeth bared to kill.

Rodrigo unleashed a flurry of strikes with his sword, as Shade blocked them. Rodrigo knew he'd injured the Medici and he would tire soon enough. Rodrigo watched him closely, keeping himself just out of range of Shade's blade and its deadly intent.

Shade locked eyes with his enemy, trying to second guess his next move. He could feel the blood flowing down his leg and into his boot. He lunged for Rodrigo's heart and Rodrigo lifted his sword with both hands above his head and brought it down in an arcing sweep toward Shade's neck. Shade moved quickly to the left, but Rodrigo's blade caught the edge of his shoulder, leaving a gaping wound that took him down to his knee. His roar of pain shook the earth as he quickly rose to his feet.

Skelk was aware of the battle between the masters below him and saw when Shade went down and knew he had to create a distraction to give Shade time to recover and get back on his feet. Skelk swung low and circled above them. Aislynn was close enough to hear Shade's roar and rushed to his aide, quickly assessing the situation, and looking skyward at Skelk. Skelk dropped to the ground behind Rodrigo, and Aislynn joined him, forcing Rodrigo into close quarters with Shade.

Rodrigo realized too late they'd surrounded him and saw the Medici come at him, blade held high, his scream deafening in his ears. He moved backward to escape the blade but stumbled into Skelk just as Shade drove the blade straight through his heart with deadly accuracy. Rodrigo's eyes flared red, and his body shook in a death throe as his beast crumbled. Shade removed the blade, wincing in pain as Rodrigo fell to his knees, clutching his chest, trying to rise, attempting to raise his sword in defense. Shade screamed into the night as he swung his father's sword with force, slicing off Rodrigo's head and watching his dead body fall limp to the blood-soaked soil.

Shade dropped to his knees, covered in Rodrigo's blood, and grabbed his enemy's severed head, holding it up to the sky and roaring, "*Per semper* Medici!" The blood pulsated from Rodrigo's neck until it was just a slight ooze, when it was followed by an evil swirl of blackness rising in the air, mixing with the smoke, as all the sins the sin-eater had absorbed over his lifetime were released into the night sky. Skelk grabbed the Borgia flag that Rodrigo had kept near, hoping to plant it at Castello, and drove the spiked end of the flagpole through Rodrigo's lifeless body. "Claim that, you Borgia motherfucker." Shade shouted out to both Skelk and Aislynn, "Go! Help the others now!"

***

Kate felt the blow to his shoulder and stumbled, as Luca steadied her to keep her from falling. She cried out in pain and fear and struggled to get free, but Luca held her tight. She heard his battle cry when he finally defeated Rodrigo, but he was injured badly and needed to feed, but she knew he wouldn't leave the field, as long as a Borgia warrior was still standing. Portia remained at the balcony, staring at her only child. Both mother and mate called out to him, "Shade!"

***

Lorenzo was aware his father was fighting one on one against Rodrigo, and the fight wasn't going well. He was trying to maneuver himself into position so he could get closer when he saw both Skelk and Aislynn come to his father's aid. He breathed a sigh of relief when he saw Rodrigo fall. He heard another war cry and looked up to see the Farnese warriors crest the hill, pushing the Borgia's closer. They now had them flanked on all sides, and the Medici were finally able to get the upper hand in this battle. He focused his attention on the warriors in front of him, and laid down another swath of fire, as they jumped back, trying to avoid him. They could only back away so far, as the Farnese warriors and Kate's wolves were at their backs.

***

Soren could see his brother fighting hard against Shade and tried to clear a path of all warriors standing in his way with the flamethrower, as he tried to get to Rodrigo. He heard the wolves howling and turned to see them attacking his warriors. He stopped and turned the flamethrower in their direction, laying down a swath of flame that took down the wolves and his warriors with them. Everything around him was on fire, but he used no discretion in where he pointed the flame. Warriors were expendable, even his own, and he stood and stared as the fire consumed trees, buildings, bodies, animals... They could all burn in hell for all he cared. He forged on toward his brother and caught sight of them through the smoke as they battled with swords. He grinned to himself, thinking his brother would easily kill the Medici when he felt the painful stab into his chest and he clutched his heart, roaring in pain and anger. He saw his brother fall to his death at the hands of the enemy, and the thought flashed through his head that he was now the King of Borgia. His beast rose up in agony as he saw the Medici hold his brother's head to the sky and scream his war cry. Forgetting his target was Lorenzo, Soren was now intent on going after Shade. He moved quickly toward the Medici, the flamethrower on full blast as he swung it right and left, clearing the path in front of him. He saw the Medici rise and stumble, and knew he was injured, which sent a jolt of joy through his veins. This revenge would be his and his alone! He'd kill the father, and then kill the son, and he alone would rule over all of Italy!

He approached Shade slowly, keeping his distance from his blade, and aimed the flamethrower at his feet. His laughter was evil as he watched Shade jump back from the flames that quickly consumed his brother's body and spread across the ground, lapping up the Medici's legs.

Shade felt the heat and watched as flames consumed Rodrigo. He leaped up quickly and moved to get away from the flames. He felt the burn on his ankles and tried to brush out the flames and looked up to see a wall of fire coming at him. He felt someone at his back and glanced over his shoulder to see his father. "Stand strong, *mio figlio.* You have always made me proud."

***

Kate could see Soren advancing toward Shade and screamed again, trying to warn him. She turned to Luca and screamed, "Go to him!"

Luca saw his master was in peril, but he had his orders. "You know I can't leave you."

Portia turned to her and quietly said, "You know what to do, my daughter. It is time." Kate pushed hard against Luca, breaking free, and called out to Bianca's warriors to join the fray. Another wave of animals crested the hill, as Kate teleported to Shade. She could see the flames at his feet, as Soren closed in on him. She landed hard a few feet away from him and stumbled over the bodies of the dead. Coughing from the smoke, she crawled toward him on her hands and knees as the flames licked higher. Luca had taken off immediately behind her and was stepping over the dead to try to get to her.

***

Soren heard the squawks from the air and looked up to see the winged creatures swoop down on him. He lifted the flamethrower to the sky and laughed as birds of prey fell dead at his feet. The wolves growled and leaped at him, ready to rip him to shreds, when he scorched them as well and their high-pitched wails echoed into the night. This was almost as much fun as killing Medici warriors! He refocused his attention on Shade when he saw his queen land near him and stumble forward. She was coming for her king, and Soren laughed as he threw another blast of fire in Shade's direction. *What fun! Two for one.*

Shade felt her presence nearby and turned his head to find her when he felt the intensity from another blast from the flamethrower. *What has she done?* She couldn't come near him. He'd lose her and couldn't bear that pain. He saw her crawling on hands and knees to reach him and screamed at her above the roaring of the approaching fire. "No, *bel*! Go back to Castello!"

As the words left his mouth, he felt the fire hit his back and swirl around him, the pain consuming him and almost dropping him to his knees, but his eyes never left her face.

Kate screamed as she saw the flames engulf him and flung herself against him. The wails of the dying warriors blended with the howling wolves, and she knew her warriors had failed to save them in this battle. She wouldn't live without him. "Please, don't leave me!"

Luca scrambled across the bodies, trying desperately to reach her when he saw her leap for him. He screamed, "No!" As the tears streamed down his face, Luca saw the flames surround both of them. He locked eyes with Shade, as Luca tried in vain to break through the flames and drag Kate away from him while he still could but knew he'd failed. "Master, I've failed you!"

***

Shade watched as if in slow motion as the female that was his heart and soul leaped into his arms. He cradled her as the fire raged around them both. He saw Luca and heard his plea. **"You have not failed, warrior. You have always known this was our destiny. Do not take this guilt with you."**

Shade felt the flames swirl around them as they both began to burn. He pulled her close to his chest, wrapping his arms around her as she clung to him. "*Ti amo, mia bel rosso*."

He felt her arms tighten around him and he cradled her tightly, shielding her body with his. He'd protect her to the end.

Kate's tears fell, but not from pain, she was oblivious to the flames and the pain. She clung to him, as his arms enveloped her, providing her a safe place, even now. She looked up at him and those piercing blue eyes. His face would be the last thing she saw. "You lead, and I follow. You promised me forever."

The heat was searing, their clothes burning away, their flesh melting into one, as they were both consumed by the flames, but not before she heard him say, "And so we will be."

Luca watched in horror as they both disappeared behind the wall of flames, and he screamed at the top of his lungs, "*Per sempre*, Medici!" He heard the Medici warriors answer back, as they raged forward to avenge their fallen king and queen.

***

Lorenzo had seen Soren change course and head for his father, laying down a path of flames. He started to push his way through the throngs of fighting warriors when he saw the flames at his father's feet, and his mother landing on the battlefield. He screamed at her to go back, as he pushed forward, through the battling warriors, throwing fire to clear his path to Soren. The pain in his heart was wrenching when he saw his mother fling herself against his father, as the flames engulfed them, licking toward the sky, and he knew he'd lost them both.

He approached Soren from the rear and could hear his evil laughter. Anger rose in Lorenzo, as his beast took control, and he released a ball of blue fire that engulfed Soren and left him writhing in pain on the ground. Lorenzo stepped up close to him and watched him burn. He wouldn't behead him or stab him through the heart. He'd watch him die the same slow, painful death he'd inflicted on his parents. The battle continued to rage around him, but the Medici had the upper hand now and quickly slaughtered the remaining Borgia warriors, now leaderless.

***

Raven was fighting the thinning hordes and knew this battle was almost over, and they'd emerge the victors when Poe fell dead at his feet. He dropped to his knees, and picked up the bird, cradling him to his chest. If Poe was dead, he knew his queen had fallen too. His wail of sorrow and pain could be heard for miles.

Aislynn and Theo fought back the last of the Borgia until only the Medici warriors were left standing. They stood in silence, as the smoke cleared across the bloodied field. This battle was won, and Medici now ruled all of Italy, but they had paid a price too high to bear.

117

Christoph had been on edge all evening. He knew the battle had started, and he'd kept his senses tuned. He'd know immediately if Aislynn was injured, as he'd feel her pain. He'd also feel his father, Lorenzo, and his grandfather, but with less intensity. He'd made rounds in the camp, just to check on their readiness. He didn't expect any trouble here, and they had sent a lot of their warriors to Florence, so the camp was quiet, but on high alert. He wanted to get back to the house and stay with his family. They'd moved Cory and Jules inside Bel Rosso as they could be better protected there. He was walking back to the house when he felt a mild stabbing pain in his side. He stumbled slightly and doubled over, trying to catch his breath. It wasn't Aislynn, but he wasn't sure whether the injury was to his father or grandfather. It wasn't a lethal blow, he knew that much, but it gave him great concern. He stood upright and took a deep breath, shaking off the pain as he continued his way back home.

He was almost at the stables when he felt another blow to his shoulder that caused him to stumble backward. He caught his balance and closed his eyes. It was Shade's pain he felt. "P-Bear. Don't let the bastards take you down!"

He could hear a commotion in the stables and detoured in that direction. Angelo was struggling to keep Pavi in the stable. The massive horse was rearing up on his hind legs and kicking at the doors of the stall. Angelo shouted back at him over the loud screaming of the horse. "I'm afraid if I don't let him out, he's going to hurt himself!"

Christoph nodded. "Free him! He feels his master!"

Angelo opened the door to the stall and the horse raced out to the pasture, running in a wild panic. Angelo looked at Christoph. "I've never seen him like this before."

Christoph felt the heat on his own feet, as it slowly crawled up his legs, and knew his grandfather's life was in peril. "He feels his master's death is near."

Angelo stared back at him, his mouth open, refusing to believe what he was hearing. Christoph pushed past him, as he rushed back to the house. "I need to get back to the house!"

As he ran toward Bel Rosso, the lights on in every window, he saw his grandmother's warriors, pacing nervously: Aegis and Night-Stalker, the mountain lion named Riparo, Danica the falcon, the great white owl named Wizard. There was a small fox, and others he didn't recognize by name, but who followed Bebe 's every move. As he got closer to the house, he felt the searing heat engulf him, and he stumbled face forward, crying out as he landed on the ground. When he looked up, what he saw turned his blood cold. Her army of warriors fell dead where they stood, and Christoph screamed, "Bebe!"

He knew then he'd lost them both. He heard the loud panicked scream from Pavi, followed by Angelo's wail when the magnificent horse fell dead in the pasture. The animals were bonded to the immortal connection of their owners, kept alive all these years through that bond. Christoph rose to all fours, sobbing, when he heard the back door of Bel Rosso open, and he looked up to see the tear-stained face of his cousin, Jules.

***

Jules had been pacing inside the house. He could hear the howls of both Aegis and Night-Stalker, a warning sign that all wasn't going as planned. He first felt the pain in his side, followed by the blow to his shoulder. It wasn't his father nor Alfie, so he was certain it must be P-bear. He rushed to the window in time to see Pavi running in a panic through the pasture. Jules gripped the windowsill as he felt the pain from the searing heat.

Cory watched Jules in confusion, pushing back his long white hair as his gnarled fingers gripped the wheelchair. He tried to rise up and Hyde was beside him immediately. "No, Cory, you'll fall. Tell me what you need."

Cory struggled again to stand. "Help me to the window."

Hyde lifted him and helped him to the window next to Jules as they both watched the animals begin to drop to their death. Cory clutched his heart and cried out in pain. He had lost them all now. His birth mother had died long ago, Madison as well, and now he'd lost his father and Kate. His grief almost dropped him to the floor as

Hyde steadied him. Hyde helped Cory back into his chair, as the tears streamed down his wrinkled face. "I never thought I'd outlive him. How can this be happening?" Hyde shook his head. He had no answers.

Jules took off for the back door when he saw Christoph fall to the ground in pain. He rushed headlong to Christoph, helping him rise. They clung to each other as Jules cried out, "I can't accept they're dead. I can't. It's not worth it!"

Christoph hugged his cousin, as they both consoled each other. "Our grandfather is a warrior. It was inevitable he'd die in battle. Did you think he'd die an old man, lying in his bed? And do you think for a moment Bebe wouldn't follow him in death? Don't ever say it wasn't worth it. He died protecting all of this, so we can carry the Medici name forward. Come inside, cousin. We need to stay close to each other now and wait for the final outcome." He slung his arm over Jules' shoulder and they both returned to the house.

Gi was standing near the door, looking every bit his age. His normal rigid posture gone, as he stood stoop-shouldered under the burden of losing his king and queen. He'd once served Christofano and Portia, and he'd served Shade for almost 700 years, and now he'd transfer that allegiance to his new master. Looking up at Christoph, his voice raspy with emotion, he asked, "Is there anything I can do for you, my King?"

Christoph looked confused for a second until it dawned on him he now ruled Bel Rosso, and all who lived here, and Aislynn, if she survived, was now a queen. He looked into Gi's sad eyes. "I think we could all use some Midnight and pour some for you, then join us in the living room. We all need to stay together."

Gi nodded and shuffled off to get the Midnight. Christoph and Jules walked into the living room and couldn't help but feel their grandmother's presence. It was she who'd created the beauty and peacefulness of Bel Rosso. Cory was seated in his wheelchair and was staring blankly out the window, as Hyde stood near him, helpless to ease his pain.

***

Natalia moved mechanically through the data center. She'd been unable to focus her attention on her job, knowing her father and brother were fighting for their lives. Her visions hadn't been helpful, and Malachi knew only one coven would fall. The long-ago memory of the information she'd uncovered about the Medici curse when she was exploring the Council archives haunted her. It was a secret her father had asked her to keep, and she'd kept it. She was aware the security around the Council fortress had been increased purely as a safeguard, but Natalia had no concerns the Borgia would attack here, or at the Council in Florence. Even though the Council was always heavily guarded, to kill a Council member meant certain death for the perpetrator, and the loss of all their covens and territories.

She was finding it more difficult to concentrate, and finally excused herself, deciding to go back to her suites. Pulling the hood well over her face, she exited the data center and started down the long corridor when she encountered Marcello at the elevator.

"Are you okay?"

She nodded. "Just distracted."

As the doors to the elevator opened and she stepped inside, she felt a stabbing pain in her chest. She clutched her side, and fell against the wall of the elevator, as Marcello reached out to steady her. She cried out, "Oh, Daddy, no!"

"What is it? What's happened?"

Natalia allowed him to support her weight as the elevator moved to the second floor. She knew her father was still alive, and an injury during battle wasn't unusual. She tried to reassure herself, and him. "It's not a fatal blow. And I feel nothing from Lorenzo, so I know they haven't been overtaken."

He helped her from the elevator and walked with her to their suites when she stumbled again and gasped in pain. Her heartbeat accelerated with the surge of adrenaline through her body. Two injuries would impede his effectiveness. She knew her father was in trouble and was hoping someone could get to him in time. "Somebody help him!"

Marcello grabbed her up in his arms and carried her to the suite. Opening the door, he carried her inside and heard the door lock behind him upon closing. "You have to have faith, Natalia, please tell me he's still fighting." He held her to his chest and felt a sense of dread, knowing deep down inside, this wasn't going to end well.

She felt the heat at her feet and was, at first, confused. Then she felt them both being consumed by the flames and knew they were together. It was the promise of the Medici curse, being played out for the final time, the firstborn male and his mate of each generation would die together in flames, just as Christofano and Portia had died, and each generation that had preceded them. It was never a question of if it would happen; it was only a question of when. She knew it was a burden her father had carried and kept secret from his beloved *bel*. He'd told her years ago, when she discovered the secret of the curse, he never wanted Kate to know their violent end, and he always carried a measure of regret for loving her so much he couldn't walk away.

Natalia sobbed uncontrollably into Marcello's chest, and he felt in his own heart, his master and queen were gone.

***

Lorenzo stood among the fallen and looked about as the smoke cleared and he was joined by Alfie, Theo, Skelk, and Aislynn. No Borgia was left standing, or allowed to surrender, and the only warriors on the field strewn with the dead were Medici. The warriors were weary, but they had one last task at hand. Lorenzo issued the orders, leaving Darius in charge. "Bury our dead and leave the Borgia bodies to burn in the sun." Lorenzo turned to Aislynn as she stared in shock, feeling numb with grief. "You are a queen now, and Chris a new king. You must fill my mother's shoes."

Aislynn stared back at him, dumbfounded. "What?" The thought had never crossed her mind. How could she ever live up to the legacy that was Kate?

Darius took charge and started directing the efforts of the warriors. Turning to Aislynn, Lorenzo sent her back to the castle to get an urn. She teleported away as the three males walked to the spot where Luca stood guard, even now, watching over Shade and Kate. Raven teleported in, to pay honor to his king and queen one last time, and Skelk uncharacteristically draped his arm over Raven's shoulder. "I should have saved him."

Raven looked at the grizzled warrior, his face streaked with soot, and shook his head. "It wasn't to be, brother, even though he saved us all at one time or another."

Lorenzo stood over the spot where they had died and there was nothing left of them but ash. He picked up his father's sword, as his tears dripped onto the blade, cutting a path through the layer of ash on the scorched steel. Alfie retrieved the sword Christofano had once carried. Aislynn returned, holding a clay urn from Castello, and Lorenzo knelt and scooped their ashes into the urn. The moonlight reflected on something shiny, and he brushed away the ash to find the diamond ring his mother wore and that his grandmother had worn before her. He kissed the ring and slipped it into a pocket in his leathers. His queen would wear the ring now. He looked skyward at the full moon and the clear night sky and wondered how so much death and destruction could befall them all on such a beautiful night. He continued to scoop their ashes into the urn when he uncovered the titanium steel ring his mother had given to his father. He slid the ring on his finger. Satisfied that he'd gathered their ashes, he stood up and looked at the faces of his loyal warriors. "We need to go back to Castello. The others will know already that they're gone."

Lorenzo led them all back inside Castello, where the warriors shed themselves of bloodied leathers, dropping their weapons to the floor. Lorenzo placed the urn on a table and caught Luca's eye. "We have one more task before us."

Luca nodded, and together they made their way down the long corridor to the stairs that led underground. Lorenzo knew his sister and his niece would have felt the moment Shade and Kate fell, so he was only bringing confirmation to what everyone in the vault already knew. As they reached the massive steel door, Lorenzo called out to Henri who unlocked the vault from the inside, allowing Lorenzo to swing the massive door open. He and Luca stood silent as they looked at the faces of the family they loved so dearly, filled with grief. Sophia locked eyes with her brother and simply said, "Both of them?"

He nodded as his sister broke down.

Chantal had such mixed emotions. She felt so much relief that Lorenzo was alive, but the pain of losing Shade and Kate was overwhelming. She had watched Sophia and Bianca and knew her grief was nothing compared to theirs. She sat on the floor with Grace in her arms, her face stained with the trail of her tears. It felt like a nightmare, but the brutal reality hit home when she saw

Lorenzo's face. She'd need to put her own pain aside now, and comfort him, as she'd watched Kate do so many times. She stood up with Grace in her arms. The child had remained silent throughout the battle, as if she knew about the devastation around her. She went to Lorenzo, his hair crusted in blood, his face smeared with ash and dirt. They carried the burden of this legacy now. She shifted Grace in her arms as Lorenzo pulled them both to his chest. She whispered, "I am here for you."

Lorenzo embraced her, burying his face in her hair and inhaling, clearing his nose of the smell of burning flesh. He removed the ring from his pocket and slipped it on her hand. "My Medici Queen now, you rule all of Italy, and Bebe would want you to have it."

As he slipped the ring on her finger, she felt a sudden and powerful aura of protection and love. She looked up into his eyes, so blue and clear. He was truly his father's son. "Then let us move forward, my King, we have a family and a coven to see to."

Lorenzo smiled through his tears, as Chantal had finally come into her own, no longer in Kate's shadow. He knew she'd be a strong queen to their expanding coven.

Shannon was in tears, and rushed toward Luca, clinging hard to him as he soothed her. Through their entire lives together, she'd been prepared to lose him in service to Shade and Kate, and she knew he was carrying the weight of the fact they both lay dead, while he still lived. She felt like she was on an emotional roller-coaster, feeling such relief that Luca was alive, but she'd lost her best friend. She felt his body racked with sobs as he cried on her shoulder. "You did everything, Luca, and you know he loved you. They both loved you."

Luca, too, had always known of the curse but had vowed to Shade never to speak of it. He could protect them both from many things, but against this, he was powerless. Shade had wrestled with this knowledge from the time Luca was chosen as her protector. He'd shared with Luca his guilt over loving her, yet unable to walk away, even knowing how it would end. His master felt guilt for not telling her and giving her the choice to remain mortal, but Luca knew in his heart, Kate would have followed him anywhere.

118

It had been a year since the battle. Theresa had been working all week to get all the bedrooms ready at Bel Rosso, and Gi had brought up extra bottles of Midnight and Red Moon from the wine cellar, in preparation for a full house. Christoph was walking back from the camp. He wanted time to clean up before the rest of the family arrived. They had all agreed they'd gather annually at Bel Rosso on the anniversary of Shade and Kate's deaths.

In the days after the battle, Jules had read the will. It had been written by Shade, in a single document, and signed by Shade alone, as if he'd known all along, they'd die together. It was then Natalia shared the knowledge of the burden she'd carried for so long, the secret she'd discovered in the Council archives when she was just a young woman, the curse of death by fire to the firstborn male and his mate. She'd also shared that the curse ended with their father. Lorenzo's gift as a fire thrower protected him from the curse and broke the chain. Luca confessed he, too, had been aware of the curse and Shade's guilt over never telling Kate.

The will made sure each of them was well-established to carry the Medici legacy forward and ensure the success of the growing coven well into the future. Shade had left the North Italian territory and Castello to Lorenzo and Chantal, but since the battle with the Borgia's expanded their territory, Lorenzo now held all of Italy, except Sicily. Lorenzo's daughter, Bianca, had mated Amondo, which secured an alliance with the Farnese coven that controlled Sicily, and made the Medici the most powerful coven in Europe.

Sophia and Alfie were given money and additional land, expanding well into Northern Italy, along with the villa they occupied, and Alfie remained as Lorenzo's loyal and trusted SIC in the camp. Henry was set to inherit the Valois chateau upon the death of Henri and Amelie, as well as inheriting all the vineyards and warrior camps in France and Greece. Jules was given Max's mansion in Virginia, and it was converted from an inn back to a private home once again. Natalia wasn't allowed to own property but was left a large sum of money instead, which she'd assigned to Jules to manage for her. It would ensure the maintenance of the orphanages in perpetuity. There was money to insure for Cory's care, not that any of his siblings wouldn't have taken care of him.

Luca was given the choice to be released from servitude, and he and Shannon were also given a large sum of money. They chose to move back to Luca's ancestral home in Empoli, but would always remain part of the family, and the family business, as Shannon continued to help run the businesses with Sophia as her new business partner. Luca had assumed control of overseeing the lemon groves, and the production of limoncello under the Medici brand.

Then there was their beloved Bel Rosso, which had been given to Christoph and Aislynn, along with all the territories in the U.S. They all had their hands full, managing the camps and the businesses, as well as the expanding orphanages while adjusting to a life without Kate and Shade.

***

Christoph looked up at Bel Rosso and could see Aislynn's silhouette in the upstairs window. The smile spread across his face. She'd proven herself a valiant warrior on the battlefield and racked up many kills. After her return to Bel Rosso, they'd discovered she was pregnant. Christoph had refused to let her work in the camp during her pregnancy, and since their son had been born, she'd wanted to stay close to him until he was old enough to be sent to the camps himself. It didn't take a lot of discussion to decide on a name for him; there could only be one choice, and that was Shade.

He burst through the back door of the house and up the stairs, lifting her up and swinging her around, as she laughed and shushed him, as baby Shade lie sleeping in that old hand-carved cradle, sent over from Florence.

"Chris, stop! You'll wake the baby! Besides, don't start something you can't finish. We have the entire family arriving." She laughed as he spun her around in the room. It was an exciting time, the entire family gathering for the first time since the Battle of Castello. "I'm happy everyone can make it tonight. It just feels like we should all be together, that's what P-bear and Bebe would have wanted."

He set her down on her feet, still holding her close. "I'm looking forward to all of us being together. It will be the first time some of them have seen the baby. Are you ready to go downstairs? They should be arriving soon."

Before the words were out of his mouth, they heard the doorbell and Gi shuffling to answer it. "Come on, let's see who made it first."

Aislynn lifted the infant from the crib, and the baby grunted to show his displeasure at being disturbed. She held him over her shoulder and Christoph slid his arm around her waist and walked with her down the two flights of stairs. They'd discussed moving from the third-floor suites into Kate and Shade's old bedroom but decided against it. They wanted to leave the room just as Bebe and P-bear had left it. There were plenty of other bedrooms for any future children they might have. As they reached the main floor, Christoph saw his father, Lorenzo, holding chubby toddler Grace on his hip. Gi was gathering everyone's coat when he glanced at his mother, to see her holding an infant in her arms. Aislynn gasped and rushed toward Chantal, as Christoph exclaimed, "What's this? You didn't mention another baby!"

Chantal was overjoyed. She could hardly contain her excitement to meet her new grandson, as well as to show off the newest infant they had adopted. They'd told no one of the new half-breed baby girl. "Meet your new sister, Lily. Grace House has been overwhelmed with new arrivals. I took one look at her and the rest is history! Now let me see my grandson."

Chantal looked into Aislynn's eyes and could see the happiness reflected there. Aislynn held Shade cradled in her arms. His huge blue eyes looking back at Chantal, and she gasped. "He is the spitting image of Christoph as a baby, and definitely a fine Medici warrior!"

Grace held out her pudgy hands, opening and closing them. "Baby, baby, baby."

Chantal looked at Lorenzo. "You might as well let her down. She will want to touch the baby. Grace, be gentle for *Maman*."

Christoph shook his head and laughed. "I have a son and a new sister! Let's go into the living room, Gi made a fire and there will be plenty of Midnight."

Christoph led them into the room to find Cory in his wheelchair near the fire. They'd decided to permanently move Cory out of the house he'd shared with Madison and back into Bel Rosso as he had aged and needed more attention. Christoph raised his voice, so Cory would hear him. "Cory! Your brother is here!"

Cory looked up, his eyes clouded, and smiled. Lorenzo bent forward to hug him, feeling how frail his bones were through his skin. The crowd was getting settled, and the females were removing the blankets from around the babies when the doorbell rang again and Gi led Sophia and Alfie into the mix. Sophia squealed when she saw the two new infants and gathered around the other women as Lorenzo shrugged and laughed. "Well, I know where I stand in the pecking order."

The doorbell rang again, as Henry arrived with Giselle. Christoph greeted them as they entered the room. "Mated yet, brother? You can't keep her waiting forever."

Henry laughed. "Now you sound like Mom. In due time, brother."

Gi and Theresa were pouring wine as quickly as possible when the doorbell rang again, and Gi opened it for Jules, Natalia, and Marcello. The sound of laughter and everyone talking at once filled the house. Christoph looked about. "Is everyone here?"

Aislynn looked around at all the smiling faces. "No, Luca and Shannon aren't here yet. They did say they were coming, didn't they? And where's Bianca and Amondo?" She looked at Sophia. "Tell me they're coming!"

Sophia looked up. "Of course, they're coming! I told Bianca it was an order, not an invitation. Honeymoons don't last forever. And Shannon said they wouldn't miss it." As if on cue, the doorbell rang again, and Bianca arrived with her new mate, Amondo.

Alfie hugged his daughter. "P-Bear would be proud of your choice in a mate."

She smiled back at him. "I hope so, Daddy, I think about them both every day."

He nodded in acknowledgment. "I know. We all do." He kissed his daughter on the cheek before she disappeared into the crowd. Lorenzo was grabbing a refill on his glass when he looked up to see Luca and a very pregnant Shannon enter the room. The crowd was suddenly silent with the revelation of her pregnancy. Lorenzo looked at Luca. "You didn't tell us?"

Luca laughed. "We wanted it to be a surprise. We never thought we'd have children, with my obligations as protector, but once I was released from servitude, we decided it was time."

Aislynn stood up, holding baby Shade. Her smile covered her face, as she looked at Shannon. "Well, I think Bebe wouldn't know what to do with herself, had she been able to see all these babies!"

Chantal chimed in. "She would be in her glory, that is for sure."

Aislynn went to Shannon, giving her a one-arm hug, holding the infant in her other arm. "I'm so glad you could make it. Do you know if it's a boy or girl yet? By the way, meet the newest Medici warrior, Shade."

Shannon took the infant in her arms, as Luca wrapped his arms around her from behind. He peered over her shoulder at the boy child named after Shade. Shannon gently rocked the infant. "We're having a girl, and we were thinking of naming her Katherine."

Chantal smiled softly and looked at Lorenzo, his eyes turned to her and she mouthed to him, 'perfect'.

Jules laughed. "Well, it sounds like a match made in heaven. I can draw up a mating contract while I'm here."

Lorenzo smiled. "Nah. Dad finally learned not to hold much stock in those contracts. Whatever is meant to be will play out in due time. Let the children find their own way."

They all laughed and joked, moving about the room, and catching up on the latest family news, and passing the babies from arm to arm. The house almost glowed with the happiness inside.

Lorenzo looked at the family crowded inside Bel Rosso and wished his parents could see it. He felt such joy at having his family all in one place but was acutely aware of the gaping hole that had been left by Kate and Shade. Christoph approached him and refilled his glass at the bar. "You okay, Dad?"

Lorenzo nodded. "Yeah, just thinking about them, and how much they would have enjoyed this. Where did you bury their ashes?"

Christoph took a sip from his glass. "We put them in the baby's garden, next to that cherub statue. I thought about putting them inside the walls of the camp, and I know all the warriors would have honored them there, but this felt more private for them."

Lorenzo nodded in approval. "Good choice."

Christoph could see the sadness behind his father's eyes and knew it was time. He called out to Sophia and Natalia and asked that they join him. As the three siblings stood shoulder to shoulder, Christoph said, "Follow me."

The three looked perplexed but followed him up the stairs. Christoph took them to what was once their parent's bedroom and opened the door, inviting them in. The children of Shade and Kate entered the room where they had played as children and jumped on the bed to wake their parents. Christoph didn't follow them in, but stood in the doorway, his hand still on the doorknob. "Listen closely."

The trio stood in silence, as each of them were flooded with their own memories of this room. Sophia sat on the bed, remembering all the times as a child when she used to burst into the room and leap on the bed with her parents, with Poppy in tow. She ran her hand over the bedspread and smiled to herself. Her father would always scold her, but she could see the smile behind his eyes as he did so. Natalia stepped to the window, looking out over Bel Rosso, and remembered seeing her mother stand here; taking in this same view of this land she loved so dearly. Lorenzo walked over to his father's dresser, everything left exactly as it had been, as he picked up a knife and a few shurikens before replacing them back on the dresser. Stacked on the dresser was a small pile of red stones. Lorenzo picked one up and held it to the light. It was a ruby, cut in the shape of a heart. They had been a gift from his mother to his father, and he always carried them in his pocket. Lorenzo knew his father would have had them in the pocket of his leathers when he went into that last battle and he wondered how he'd missed them when he was gathering his parents' ashes. Chris must have retrieved them from the ashes in the urn and placed them here. Lorenzo was about to ask Chris about the stones when Natalia spoke up. "What is it?"

Lorenzo looked back at her "The ruby stones. The ones Mom gave Dad. He always carried them with him."

Natalia smiled. "I remember now."

Sophia creased her brow and tilted her head to the side when she heard the softest melody, barely audible, the sweet refrain of Van Morrison, singing "Into the Mystic".

"Do you hear that?" Her other two siblings stopped in their musings and tuned in, hearing the faint sound of the music.

Christoph smiled and closed the door behind him, leaving them to see what he knew would only be visible to them.

***

Shade and Kate had spent the night listening to the sounds of their children and grandchildren as their laughter filled the rooms of Bel Rosso again. Taking her in his arms, they both felt a joy beyond any words. Their children and grandchildren were settled in their lives, and their families continued to grow. The coven, once almost lost, then held together for centuries by Shade alone, was now strong and vibrant, its future secured by his progenies. Their song began to play softly in the bedroom they still shared. They inhabited Bel Rosso now, and always would. Just as Christofano and Portia had guided them in Castello, they would now forever watch over their own growing family. Shade danced slowly with her across the room, their eyes on each other. He felt the presence of their three children inside the room and stopped dancing. Kate and Shade slowly emerged from the mist, making themselves visible to their children. "Some things never change, *mi amore*. Still, they come into the bedroom unannounced."

Lorenzo locked eyes with his father and drew strength from him, and Sophia and Natalia wept softly, reaching for their mother's hand. Kate shook her head no. "I don't want to see your tears. We will always be here, and you can seek us out when you need us. It's your time now. We gave you the best of ourselves, and it's now up to you. Love your mates and stay loyal to this family, this next chapter is yours to write."

Natalia wiped away her tears. "I miss you so much."

Kate embraced her. "I'm here, daughter. I'll always be here. You need only look for us in your hearts. You have your own path to follow now. You above all, will do the most to change our culture and shape the history of our kind."

Shade rubbed Kate's back. She would always remain the anchor for their children. He reassured them. "We are okay, grief is a normal process, but you cannot get lost in it. We are here when you need us, but you must move forward, finish what we started. Take every day and live it to the fullest. Love your family, tell them, and show them. It is our strength as a family that guaranteed our legacy." He went to Lorenzo and hugged him. "I will always be with you in battle. I feel so much pride in what you have achieved."

Lorenzo choked on his words. "I should have gotten to you faster."

Shade shook his head. "Our end was inevitable. There was no one who could have stopped it. I knew from the start how things would play out for us, so stop feeling guilty."

Sophia looked at both of them with tears in her eyes. "Does Chris see you too?"

Shade shook his head. "No, he does not see us, but he does hear us from time to time, and he hears the music. He can sense our presence. With each generation, they will hear less, feel less. But we can see all of you. You have what you need. Medici blood runs in your veins, and we have taught you well."

Natalia looked at her mother. "Mommy, I'm so sorry."

Kate stroked her daughter's cheek. "No tears, Natalia. I understand you have carried the burden of knowing our fate since you were a child. No child should have to live with that. But your father promised me an eternity. He just never explained exactly how that eternity would play out. I would change nothing. We have each other, and we are happy here. We will spend our lives in the spirit realm at Bel Rosso, and I can't imagine another place I'd rather be. Your father can go into the sun now. He rides with me on sunny days. Angelo leaves two horses saddled and in the pasture in case we want to ride. I can't begin to explain the joy I feel at seeing him ride, the sun on his face, and the wind in his hair. So, don't grieve for us. All I want for my children and grandchildren is the same. Be happy. Live your life."

Sophia spoke up. "Then you've seen Chris and Aislynn's son? You know about Shannon's pregnancy? Do you know our future?"

Shade smiled back at her. "We see and hear everything. And we are here for you. I know the curse is broken, and no longer will the firstborn son of a Medici and his mate die by fire. Lorenzo's gift has broken the cycle that plagued our coven for millennia. Our coven knows no limits now. Nattie, you hold the key to changing our culture, for the half-breeds, as well as for the females. You will make our community stronger. Other than that, I don't know your future and even if I knew it, I would not divulge it. This is your journey. It is not good to know too much about the path ahead. Now, go. Be happy. Make me proud."

Shade returned to Kate's arms, and the children watched with tears in their eyes as their parents faded back into a mist, and they were left with the scent of roses in the air. They could no longer see them, but they heard their father's voice as he spoke to her, "Come dance with me, my walking sin", along with the soft refrain from the song they'd heard a thousand times when they were growing up, *"Smell the sea and feel the sky. Let your soul and spirit fly into the mystic."*

About the Author

Emily Bex is an international best-selling author, avid life-long reader, and a first-time writer of the epic six-book Medici Warrior Series. As she says, "Why start small?" She worked for over twenty years in marketing, developing ad campaigns, catalogs, product launches, and promotional literature. She figured if she could write creatively about products, then surely, she could write something about these characters that were rattling around inside her brain. She currently lives in Virginia but has used her extensive love of travel, both foreign and domestic, to create the backdrop for her characters to play out their story.

Other Titles from Emily Bex

The Blood Covenant: Book One of The Medici warrior Series

The Turning: Book Two of The Medici Warrior Series

The Medici Queen: Book Three of the Medici Warrior Series

Fall From Grace: Book Four of The Medici Warrior Series

Lorenzo's Rising: Book Five of The Medici Warrior Series

Look for The Bohannon Witch Series, coming soon from Emily Bex!

More From Foundations

www.FoundationsBooks.net

The Alyx Rayer Series: Book One, Vengeance Marked

by S.J. Pierce

Her Marked was more than just precious to her, he was precious in ways the world could only fathom. If she failed, she failed everyone.Alyx Rayer's existence in Atlanta, the eternally bustling capital of Georgia, is one of routine and blending in among the worker bees. But her 'normal' life is a facade for a higher calling. She's a three-hundred-year-old soul, sent from the darkness to capture her Marked when summoned by her superiors. Until then, she was to keep her distance. Except... something about him makes it hard to stay away.

While already trapped between honor and desire, a man in a black suit continually shows up when she least expects it, his presence evoking a strange response from the scar she was branded with at birth. Because her superiors never told her what this would mean, or much of anything except what to do when they summon, she can only conclude to try and keep her sanity-and her life-from completely shattering to pieces.This engaging first book of the series is a Paranormal Romance novel interlaced with twists, turns and thrilling suspense that is sure to satisfy readers of any genre.

May not be suitable for YA.

The Guardian League: Book One, Jasper

by TK Lawyer

Lauren was an assignment. He didn't expect to fall in love.

From her birth, Apollo watched Lauren mature, witnessing all her milestones with a strong sense of pride. Advising, protecting and whispering loving words to her, Lauren is strong and perfect. Unfortunately, she doesn't want to live.

A drastic decision one day sets Lauren face to face with her own Guardian Angel- a being she never knew existed. However, he won't leave her alone. He is relentless, encouraging her to better her life when he doesn't understand what it takes to survive on Earth. Despite this "flaw," she is drawn to him in ways she can't explain and Apollo soon becomes as necessary as the air she breathes. He asks for only one thing- to be his, forever.

Will she allow Apollo to love and care for her when many have failed?

Find, Follow, Stalk Emily Bex on her Social Media Sites!

Web page: www.emilybex.com

Newsletter:
https://landing.mailerlite.com/webforms/landing/d3o5g4

Instagram:
https://www.instagram.com/emilybexromance/

Twitter: https://twitter.com/emily_bex

Facebook: https://www.facebook.com/AuthorEmilyBex/

Pinterest:
https://www.pinterest.com/emilybexromance/

YouTube:
https://www.youtube.com/channel/UCrz4Nh_9zn-C_9zhU4nLmvw

Amazon Author Central:
https://www.amazon.com/Emily-Bex/e/B07NYB7WPB

Goodreads:
https://www.goodreads.com/emilybexromance

Book Bub: https://www.bookbub.com/authors/emily-bex

TikTok: @emilybexauthor

Foundations Book Publishing

10-9-8-7-6-5-4-3-2-1

Per Sempre Medici
Book Six in the Medici Warrior Series

ISBN: 978-1-64583-074-0

Made in United States
North Haven, CT
08 January 2022

14364513R00431